BIG TIME

ALSO BY MARCEL MONTECINO

THE CROSSKILLER

BIG TIME

MARCEL MONTECINO

WILLIAM MORROW AND COMPANY, INC.
NEW YORK

Recognizing the importance of preserving what has been written, it is the policy of William Morrow and Company, Inc., and its imprints and affiliates to have the books it publishes printed on acid-free paper, and we exert our best efforts to that end.

Library of Congress Cataloging-in-Publication Data

Montecino, Marcel.
Big time / Marcel Montecino.
p. cm.
ISBN 0-688-09374-4
I. Title.
PS3563.0539B54 1990
813'.54—dc20

90-5673
CIP

Printed in the United States of America

2 3 4 5 6 7 8 9 10

For Rohena
who I never met

And Eula
who I'll never forget

ACKNOWLEDGMENTS

I'd like to offer my thanks to

Dana Berns and BAR Weapons Consultants, for checking my weaponry and violence.

Tex Liuzza for going over my Noo Awlins stuff.

Joycene Deel and Lyn Arnold-Tuttle at Freighter World Cruises for all their help.

Stela Barsanti for the Portuguese, bedroom and otherwise.

The proud driver in Rio whose name I can't recall but who wondered why someone would come halfway around the world to visit his city's slums.

Paolo Salvador and Anna Romano for showing me the rest of Rio.

Dr. Tim Huston for the medical pointers.

Keyboard wizard Michael Boddicker for the information about the latest studio instruments.

Vicki Peterson of the Bangles for the sweet taste of fresh stardom.

Tonik Mizell, lady lawyer *extraordinaire*, for the last-minute scramble for lyric permissions.

Joan Marlow for the exhaustive copy editing.

Liza Dawson for her editorial support and brilliance.

And my friend and agent, Peter Livingston, from whom all good things flow.

PROLOGUE

FEBRUARY—GULFSTREAM PARK—HALLANDALE, FLORIDA

ANGEL gripped the reins tightly and hunched forward, so that he was almost leaning over the big stallion's neck. He felt the animal tensing under him, fighting the bit. *So,* Angel thought, *you're nervous, too. But* you *they won't kill. It's me they'll turn into dog food.* Comida de perro. *How you say—dead meat.*

These few seconds in the starting gate, while the other horses were being led or coaxed into their chutes, always seemed so much longer to Angel, as if time slowed down, eternity elongated. The bettors in the grandstand seemed to move in slow motion; the colors on the other jockeys' silks appeared to brighten in the strong Florida sun; the crowd sounds were muted, muffled.

The bay in the rail position was giving the assistant starters trouble. His jockey was fighting him.

Angel's mounts were always among the first ones in the gate, because Angel was a strong rider. He could control his horses. That's what the owners said, and looked each other purposefully in the eye when they did.

"That Angel Valdez, boy can *control* an animal."

"Break a fucking horse's *jaw* if he has to."

That's why he was on this big stallion, Transformer. He was expected to control the horse. That's the reason he was in the irons.

Oh, and his wife, La Belle, had a lot to do with it, too, he thought grimly.

The stallion shifted his weight under Angel, and he thought, not for the first time, how having a horse between his legs was not unlike fucking La Belle, big, pale, blond Alabama farm girl that she was. A spic's wet dream, he had heard one of the American jocks say about her, and he couldn't even get mad at the guy. And climbing upon her soft, luxurious body *was* like swaying up into a saddle, and when he fucked her, his short, swarthy, lean frame felt as if it were mashing a wonderful pliant pillow, or even resting on a billowy cloud floating around in heaven.

She hardly bothered to dress anymore, just lay in bed and freebased all day, Randy Travis blaring from the stereo, Oprah Winfrey on the tube. At first he found it exciting, knowing when he opened the apartment door that she would always be naked and stoned, ready for him. Sometimes he would drop his pants around his ankles in the living room, shamble into the bedroom, and she would be there, sprawled across the pink bedspread like a marshmallow on a tongue, and without saying a word he would wave his penis in her face, and she would giggle and take him in her mouth.

And then the two Colombians came to see him—*at least they didn't send guineas*—and they bought him lunch over in Hallandale and explained it all to him. How La Belle had been buying cocaine on tab behind his back, and now the tab was up to twenty-five thousand—*Jesus Christ, La Belle!*—and how they didn't even want the money, forget about the money, they just needed him to do some favors for them, from time to time, and the debt would be erased, forgotten.

That fucking La Belle, he had thought. Stupid bitch was going to get him killed.

He had gone back to the apartment in a dark, silent rage, and when La Belle saw him coming through the door, she knew that he knew and ran from him and hid in the closet—in the *closet!*—and he yanked the door open and stood over her and beat her with his fists as she lay there entangled with all her shoes and belts and handbags, pummeling her white, pliant flesh while she lay in a fetal position, screaming. Then he had sat in a chair drinking tequila, staring out at nothing, and he heard her rustling in the closet; then she peeked her tear-stained face around the bottom of the door, her eyes frightened and beseeching.

He wouldn't look at her.

She crawled across the carpet toward him, whimpering, begging. "La Belle's so sorry, Angel, don't beat her no more, baby, don't beat her no more."

Her soft, pale skin was already bruising.

She hugged his legs and looked up at him and said, "La Belle's so sorry, baby. Don't make La Belle leave her daddy, don't make La Belle leave."

He looked at her then, her wet, washed-out blue eyes and doughy face, and his heart melted for her and he took her up, cradled her face in his lap, and stroked her shoulders.

"La Belle's so sorry, Angel Daddy. La Belle's so sorry."

Down in the rail position the assistant starters were still having problems with the recalcitrant bay who was balking at the chute. It was a seven-horse field, all dog meat except for Transformer, Angel's mount, who was a 6-to-5 favorite, and Wilma's Boy, a 12-to-1 long shot, who had finished out-of-the-money in his last three appearances, but who Angel knew from morning exercises was much faster than his record. Transformer, a winner in all three of this year's starts, was the clear favorite, and the buzz around the paddock was that the stallion's owners were fine-tuning him with one more easy outing before moving him up to a stakes race. That was the talk in the grandstand, and that's probably what the owners thought.

But Angel knew that wasn't what was going to happen.

The starters had finally coaxed the rail position into the chute, and all the gates were closed and the warning light went on. These few moments always seemed even slower to Angel, as if the whole racetrack, the grandstand, the paddock, sucked in a deep lungful of air and held it, and the absence of oxygen caused life to slow to a stagger.

Angel gripped the reins and leaned even further forward, his nose against the stallion's hide, breathing in the strong animal musk. The crowd noise was tamped down to an angry growl, like a bumblebee trapped in a bottle. The sun was hot on his back.

It didn't matter which horse won the race, Angel thought. *He* was going to be a loser.

Oh, he was going to do his job, all right. Anything less was unthinkable. Deadly. But the way they got to him, through La

Belle, was messy. It left him in a vulnerable position. Because the Colombians would visit him again, of that he was certain. Either them or the Sicilians. Somebody would be back. Because in this type of thing, you're never paid up. They got you by the *cojones,* and you never get even with them. They just keep using you until they burn you down. *Then* they leave you alone, when you have nothing left to give them.

Because Transformer's owners, Golden Oaks Farm, expected their entry to win this race, Angel was sure of that. And when this thing was over, and the horses hadn't finished according to the *Racing Form,* Transformer's trainer was going to tell his millionairess owner that, you know, he had always *heard* that Angel Valdez could, you know, *control* an animal. But nothing to the effect that the jock would do it, you know, *free lance,* you know, maybe for someone *other* than the horse's owner, but you never know, there's always a first time.

And then the trainer, covering his own ass, would find some reason to go with another jockey on his better mounts. Maybe *all* his rides. And the word would get around that Angel Valdez was not to be trusted, that he would do a job on you. And the mounts offered to him would get shittier and shittier, until he could only get the dogs, the plodders, the also-rans. And his career would be over before it ever really began.

Maybe if he went somewhere else, he could start over. Not back to Venezuela, but maybe Aqueduct in New York, maybe L.A. Maybe if he got La Belle out of South Florida, he could get her to kick—

The gates jolted open, and the big stallion lunged out of the chute. Angel could feel the animal's awesome power surging under him. He was a helluva horse. *Mucho caballo.*

The horses bunched for a moment coming out of the gate, and then Transformer took the lead easily and slipped to the inside, the other horses strung out in a ragged line behind him. There was nothing in front of them but the empty curving track. For the stewards' cameras Angel made a big show of using his whip, but only lightly touched the stallion with the tip. And the big bastard responded even to that! Angel had never had such a horse between his legs. He felt like a champion.

When Transformer was two lengths ahead of the pack, the

crowd roaring its approval, Angel began to pull slowly back on the reins. It had to be done gradually, masterfully, perfectly—so that the horse understood but the crowd didn't. The animal must not be made to bolt, to fight the bit, and certainly not to stumble. After the race the stewards would be studying the race films closely. Angel slowly applied the commanding, demanding drag on the stallion's tender mouth. Through the reins, like messages on a telegraph wire, he could feel the horse's reluctance—the animal had a lot of fight in him. He wanted to run. He wanted to *win.*

Not this time, Angel thought grimly. *No este tiempo.*

Just as they cleared the far turn, a roar went up from the grandstand. Someone was moving out of the pack, moving up to challenge. Transformer seemed to sense the other animal closing on him, and Angel felt the urgency course through his mount's plunging body. The muscles and tendons in the jockey's arms were beginning to ache from the relentless *will* the horse was exerting on his rider. A hundred-seven-pound man can control a half-ton horse only when the beast submits to that control. Angel strained forward over the horse's withers, standing in the stirrups now, flailing at the air with his whip, giving the world a show of urging the stallion on while he pulled back, pulled back on the reins. In the corner of his eye he saw the dark shape moving up on his right. He glanced back over his shoulder. Wilma's Boy, coming on strong. *C'mon, Wilma's Boy!* Angel dug in as they passed the sixteenth pole, and tightened his grip on the reins. His mount was resisting him, fighting him at every stride. The horse wanted to win. He had a lot of heart.

For the first time Angel suddenly began to fear that he wasn't going to win this contest, he wasn't going to lose the race.

"*No!*" Angel shouted aloud, and the rushing wind ripped the words from his lips. "*No!*" he shouted, and increased the drag on the reins, on the bit in the stallion's tender mouth. Every pounding stride of the galloping stallion sent shock waves of pain up from the striking hooves all the way through his body and up to his tortured shoulders. Wilma's Boy had moved up beside him, crowding him, and the Panamanian aboard was whipping his mount mercilessly, shouting encouragement into the gelding's ear. They were head and head now, Transformer and Wilma's Boy, Wilma's Boy and Transformer, and the crowd in the grandstand was on its feet, screaming encouragement, the two men and horses head and head, neck and neck, pounding down the homestretch, all creaking leather, thundering hooves, heaving lungs, straining muscles.

BOOK I

FEBRUARY—NEW ORLEANS

"No! No! Noooooooo!"

Outside, the rain came down in cold gray polyethylene sheets and struck the water already standing on St. Charles Avenue so hard and so densely that there seemed to be a second surface six inches above the pavement. Inside the Sporting Life Bar & Lounge it was warm and dry, on the television set with the sound turned off Larry Bird silently sank a one-handed twenty-footer jumper over three defenders, and on the radio the announcer with the affected English accent and the maddeningly detached delivery lazily called the horse race five hundred miles away.

"It's Wilma's Boy in front by a nose—"

"No! Noooooo!"

"—Transformer in second place on the rail—"

"Come on, Transformer, you motherfucker!"

Outside the Sporting Life Bar & Lounge lightning cracked and flashed and the thunderous rain seemed somehow to intensify, becoming a solid moving wall of frigid liquid that sent the few pedestrians on St. Charles scurrying for cover and pounded on the bar's roof and gushed down the big front window and Larry Bird grabbed a rebound and started dribbling the ball back up-court.

"It's Wilma's Boy by a length-and-a-half—"

"You motherfucker! You—"

"—coming down the homestretch it's Wilma's Boy—"

"No!"

"—to the wire it's Wilma's Boy—"

"Transformer!"

"—Wilma's Boy—"

"Where the fuck is Transformer!"

"—Wilma's—"

"Where the fuck—"

"—and the winner is Wilma's Boy by three lengths, Transformer in the place position, Axiomatic in the show—"

Larry Bird faked once, twice, three times, then released his patented fall-away from the baseline, and the ball arced high and swooped down into the net. Bird raised his fist in triumph.

Sal wasn't listening to the radio any longer. He could hear himself breathing, like a man in a dark closet, like an animal in a trap. He glanced up at the gold Dixie beer clock behind the bar. It was 2:37. Sal looked around the empty bar as if he had never seen it before, as if he had just walked into the joint fresh off the fucking moon. Everything was strange, alien. The Clydesdales in the illuminated Budweiser sign looked like dinosaurs. The neon lights around the bar seemed to shimmer with heat. The red leatherette seats were bleeding slabs of flesh.

Outside, on St. Charles Avenue, lightning blazed again, momentarily bathing the street in a drenched glare. Then it was again deep night in the afternoon. And the rain kept coming.

Sal knew that from this moment on, his life would never be the same.

He stood behind the bar, stupidly staring up at the silent television, the radio still reporting his doom—

"—Wilma's Boy pays twenty-six-seventy to win—"

—and he knew that this was the most important moment of his life. He seemed to be seeing the world through a stranger's eyes. He felt newborn. It was as if his whole life had been a journey to this moment, this bar, this rainy Sunday afternoon. Emotions tumbled through his veins—rage, disbelief, fear, release, fulfillment—like water overflowing a crumbling levee.

He reached over to the bottle of Jack Daniel's on the back bar, poured himself a double, and downed it. His eyes watered, and his chest burned. He was pouring another drink when the phone on the bar rang and he started, spilling J.D. on the plasticized wood.

"Yeah?" he said into the receiver, and he didn't recognize his own fucking voice.

"This is Tony Z. Three hundred to win on Comeback in the fifth at Gulfstream."

Larry Bird was shooting two from the foul line. Lead-pipe cinch. Sal watched the first basketball bounce off the glass and jerk into the net.

"Hey, you get that? Tony Z., and I want three hundred to win on Comeback in the fifth, Gulfstream."

"Yeah, I got it." Sal hung up the phone and wrote the bet and the time on a scratch pad by the phone, then tore the slip of paper from the pad and took it into the small, cramped office just behind the bar. He stuck the slip of paper into one of the cubbyholes in an overflowing old-fashioned rolltop desk under the curling photograph of a languid blonde on a calendar promoting Black Label whiskey. Rain drummed against a high, grimy window.

Sal stood, staring vacantly around the messy little office, unable to figure out what to do next.

The phone on the bar rang again, and Sal went back to it automatically.

"This is Miz Rachel"—Rachel Silverstein, but no last names over the phone—"fifteen hundred on O'Reilly-at-the-Bar, the third at Santa Anita. To win."

"Got it."

Sal hung up the phone, then quickly took the handset off the cradle and laid it on the bar. He stared down at it as if it were a snake. A phone left off the hook in a bookie joint. It was sacrilege. Little Johnny would kill him if he saw it.

An idea flickered across Sal's mind: *Little Johnny was going to kill him anyway.*

The idea cleared away some of the haze that had clouded his thoughts. He remembered something his old man told him once, after Joe had pissed away the rent on the ponies, then got fucked up on cheap whiskey with his cabdriver partners at the stand in front of the Fair Grounds. Sal was pouring Joe into his bed in the shotgun house on St. Claude, and the wiry little wino said, "Don't be ticked at your old man, Sally. Us degenerate gamblers gotta *enjoy* our losses."

Sal went into the office and sat at the cluttered desk. From the breast pocket of his shirt he withdrew a small red spiral notebook, opened it carefully, and laid it before him on the dusty blotter. He stared down at the meticulously entered columns of names and numbers, and then he flipped a few pages and found the last circled entry: 79,542. That's where he had stood this morning, just hours ago. Almost eighty thousand dollars ahead. He could have stopped then, *should* have stopped then, and had more money than he'd ever had in his life. Money enough to pay off the seven thousand he still owed Little Johnny, the eighteen hundred the IRS wanted for back taxes, with money enough, for once, to record a demo album of his songs and bread enough to go to L.A. or New York and peddle it right, with some hotshot industry lawyer representing him. First class, all the way. He had lain in bed sleepless all last night, choosing the musicians he was going to use. All New Orleans dudes, of course. They were still the best in the whole damn country. And he was going to use that new 48-track over in Gentilly. Two 24-tracks patched together! Motherfucker! And they had the latest digital sampling synthesizer. Fucking instrument sounded like a symphony orchestra one minute, punch in another cassette and you had the fattest, funkiest slapping bass you ever fucking heard.

Sal had spent the whole night plotting the thing. For two weeks he had been on the roll of a lifetime, and last night he had gone home an eighty-thousand-dollar winner. Oh, he hadn't collected a single bet yet, but tomorrow he had planned to scheme a deal with Two Jacks, maybe for 10 percent off the top, maybe even 15. Two Jacks was one tight-mouthed motherfucker. Two Jacks would figure out in a New York minute that Sal had been sloughing off the legitimate bettors and making his own wagers with the squares' money, but Little Johnny would have to have somebody put a blowtorch to Two Jacks's nuts before the big hoosier gambler would give Sal up. Maybe not even then. Motherfucking Two Jacks *hated* Little Johnny.

So Two Jacks would have collected the money for him, and he would have been cool and laid back for a couple of months, and then watch out for Sal D'Amore.

That's the way he had had it planned. Only a few hours ago. Only one bet ago.

Over the red notebook Sal rested his head in his hands and massaged his temples with his fingertips. He was a small olive-skinned man of thirty-eight with thick black hair and a startlingly handsome face, and he was in deep, deep shit.

He reached over and flicked on the small desktop calculator. It whirred and clicked, and then the blue computer-lit zero appeared on the readout screen. Sal punched in today's figures and struck the * key. The numbers popped up. *One—Seven—Nine—Two—Two—Two.* One hundred, seventy-nine thousand, two hundred twenty-two. Dollars. Minus. *Minus.* One hundred, seventy-nine thousand, two hundred twenty-two dollars.

Us degenerate gamblers gotta enjoy *our losses.*

One hundred seventy-nine thousand, two hundred twenty-two dollars. In the hole.

Hole, as in grave.

This time I fucked up Big Time.

Sal felt sick to his stomach, and bile rose up in his throat and he was afraid he was going to throw up.

He got up and went back to the bar and filled a glass with ginger ale from the bar gun. He drank the ginger ale slowly, watching the silent TV. Larry Bird was gone. A cartoon dog was talking out to the phantom viewers. The rain hadn't lessened.

Sal sat back at the ancient rolltop desk. The calculator's numerals still glowed on the tiny screen—*179,222.00.*

Stupidly, fighting the reality of it all, Sal figured it all out with pencil and a slip of paper. He was making three hundred a week playing at the King Louis's piano bar. Everything he made in the afternoons tending bar and taking bets here at the Sporting Life went to pay the vigorish on what he already owed Little Johnny. Maybe he could pick up another hundred a week playing a wedding now and then, or an after-hours gig at an all-night joint. Say four-fifty a week. He could move in with his old man, eat red beans four times a week—*oh, yeah, the IRS!* Fuck the IRS. The IRS don't break your kneecaps. If he lived on a hundred, a hundred and a quarter a week, he could pay Little Johnny maybe three-fifty, that would be around eighteen thousand a year. Christ, that would take over ten fucking years, living like a total loser, eating out of cans, riding the bus everywhere he couldn't walk, never buying a new suit or spending a dime on a demo tape—wait! What the fuck was he thinking about? The vig alone on a hundred eighty thousand would be much more than fucking three-and-a-half bills a week. He would spend the rest of his life scuffling just to meet the interest, which he wouldn't be able to do, so each week he would be falling deeper and deeper into debt. For the rest of his fucking life.

And that was the *good* news.

The bad news was maybe he wouldn't have any fucking life left at all.

Sal reached for a pack of cigarettes. He'd been trying to cut down lately—his voice had been getting darker the last few years, and he'd already lost his top few notes—but today wasn't the day to worry about shit like that.

He had many other things to worry about.

A hundred eighty thousand things.

A month ago, when he came to work here at the Sporting Life, he had known that he was going to get into very deep shit. It was like letting the fox guard the chicken coop. But he had had a crazy bad streak for a couple of weeks where he couldn't win a fucking bet on the lead horse on a merry-go-round. He had doubled up to catch up—some basketball games, the NFL playoffs, the Super Bowl—and had booked all losers. When the smoke cleared, he was into several bookmakers for a cumulative nut of about seven thousand dollars. Seven thousand he didn't have. So his old man had gone to Little Johnny, Little Johnny Venezia, because Joe and Little Johnny had gone to St. Mary's Italian together back in prehistory, and then Little Johnny had gone on to better things, had paid his dues, buried his bodies, done his piece up in Angola, and now he was number-two man in the city and the surrounding parishes, the Big Man's right hand, with two joints on Bourbon Street—Little Johnny's and the Orleans House—another place out by Bayou St. John, and three bars out in Jefferson Parish, and was the biggest bookmaker in southeastern Louisiana. Little Johnny had consolidated Sal's debts (just like the Hibernia Bank), paid off the other bookies—half the seven thousand was owed to Little

Johnny himself. And when Sal admitted to Little Johnny that he was going to have trouble making the $210 weekly vig, the Little Guy had put him to work six afternoons a week here at the Sporting Life, until he could find a place in one of his joints for Sal to sing and play. He was to tend the afternoon bar, when there were patrons, of which there were few; and take the phone bets, of which there were many, and Little Johnny would knock a hundred a week off the vig. And since the regular afternoon bartender had cost him fifty dollars a day, Little Johnny was happy with the whole arrangement. The seven-thousand-dollar principal remained static, unchanged.

Little Johnny had smiled at him like a cobra. "When you make it big in the show business, you can pay me the seven thousand."

Then the little gray-haired man, almost as short as Sal, had laughed his famous cold chortle.

In the meantime Sal was his slave, working for nothing all afternoon, giving Little Johnny a third of what he was making every night at the piano bar.

A great fucking life.

Now, staring at the little blue numbers on the calculator, Sal realized how good he'd had it.

The first week he had just learned the job, not that it was difficult. All he had to do was answer the phone, draw a few beers, and write down all the bets. Any wagers over twenty-five hundred he had to clear with Pete the Pencil, Little Johnny's head accountant, who worked out in Jefferson Parish. Jefferson Parish was Little Johnny's *stronghold, Time* magazine called it, and nobody but nobody ever even *considered* fucking with Little Johnny Venezia in Jefferson Parish. Whenever a big bet came in, Sal made a call to Pete the Pencil, who would lay off part of the wager to other bookies around the country—that way no one ever got hurt too bad.

The Sporting Life Bar & Lounge was the hub of Little Johnny's carriage trade. The businessmen from the International Trade Center and the lawyers from the courthouse stopped in here on their way home to slug back a few quick ones and lay a couple of twenties on the next day's card. The wealthy uptown Jews from the Garden District liked to come here to bet with Little Johnny because they enjoyed the little extra jolt they got by knowing they were associating, however distantly, with Little Johnny Venezia, murderer, Mafia kingpin, and second-in-command to The Man. Likewise the professors from Tulane and the priests from Loyola. And Little Johnny still commanded strong loyalty from the old-line Italian and Cajun bettors from out Canal Boulevard and below the French Quarter—at least the ones who hadn't fled the city to get away from the niggers. Little Johnny was a downtown Ninth Ward boy who had made good and his people cherished him. Even a lot of the newly powerful black politicians and business leaders booked with Little John now, the same way they had white accountants and mistresses, for the inverted status, and also because Little Johnny Venezia paid off his winners promptly, something they often weren't sure of with the black book-makers.

Carefully, almost automatically, Sal copied down the six numbers in his little red spiral notebook: 179,222. He stared at them disbelievingly.

He had started slowly. When, on his third Monday on the job, Mrs. Romano called in from the office of her meat market with her daily hundred-dollar bet on a sure loser—she picked her ponies completely by their colorful names—Sal saw that Button-and-Bows, a horse *bred* to be bet on by Maria Romano, was going off at about 3 to 1. Instead of writing up the bet with Mrs. Romano's code number for Pete the Pencil to enter into the computer that night, Sal, using the code number of another of Little John's regulars, and remembering a childhood trick he used to pull on his drunken old man, had bet the C-note on a maiden who had finished in-the-money six of the last nine races. The horse was fucking *due*. The horse won it going away, and Sal's fate was sealed.

For two weeks Sal rode the greatest winning streak of his life. Oh, he didn't win every race—that was a square's fantasy—but every day at the close of business, when he added up the afternoon's numbers, the ebb and flow of winners and losers, places and shows, left Sal flusher and flusher every night. Some early mornings, after his gig at the King Louis, he stayed up till long past dawn, figuring and dreaming, adding and subtracting. Each day that he finagled people's bets, the names and numbers became more complex, more confused. Whose bets should he steal? Whose should he place? Who had won today?

Who would lose tomorrow? But he had handled it all, his heart singing the whole way, until last night when he had totaled up the two weeks' wagers, he had been almost eighty thousand ahead. *Eighty thousand!* And he had decided to quit. To cash in and get out.

And now he was a *hundred* eighty thousand behind.

All because of one bet, one fucking phone call.

Big Time. I fucked up Big Time.

"I got a big one for you," Albert Castiglia had said in his high, almost fruity voice. "Wilma's Boy in the third at Gulfstream." Then he paused a moment. "For twenty thou."

Sal's mind was already racing. *Wilma's Boy? Wilma's Boy? Who the fuck is Wilma's Boy?*

"All right?" Albert Castiglia asked.

The third at Gulfstream? Who else was in that fucking race? Sal was already reaching for his *Racing Form.*

"I got a bet?" Castiglia wanted to know.

"Uh—" Sal stammered, "if I don't call you back in five minutes, it's a bet."

"Five minutes?"

"Yeah."

"Okay."

Sal grabbed for the *Racing Form* and ripped through the pages until he found the line on the third at Gulfstream. He studied it.

Wilma's Boy, my ass, he thought. No way that piece of shit was going to win this horse race. Transformer was going to win it, Sal could see that, and even if he didn't, Wilma's Boy was not going to be the horse led into the winner's circle. No way. Any of the other six entries stood as much chance as Wilma's Boy.

Sal could *feel* his pulse rate quicken.

Wait a minute! Wait a minute! He could hear his Sicilian grandmother's evil-eye Palermo whisper. "Salvatore. Remember. It ain't what you know. And it ain't who you know. It's *what* you know about *who* you know. Remember."

Albert Castiglia wasn't this big a bettor. Why now? Why on this race? On this horse?

Sal remembered—he had heard that Albert Castiglia had gone to Miami last year to do some work for some people. He came back with a Colombian girlfriend. Then the girlfriend got pregnant, and Sal heard Albert Castiglia went and married her.

Could this mean something? And if so—what?

Does Albert Castiglia know something about this race?

Fuck it, Sal said to himself. *Leave it alone.*

He picked up the phone and punched out Pete the Pencil's number.

While the phone rang, Sal kept his eyes moving, moving—moving away from the *Racing Form* beside him on the bar.

"Yeah?" Pete the Pencil answered.

"Sal. I got one for twenty K. The third at Gulfstream."

"Yeah? On who?"

Sal couldn't speak.

"On what horse?" Pete the Pencil asked again.

What's the matter with you? What's the matter with—

"Sal?"

"Transformer," Sal heard himself say. "Twenty thousand on Transformer in the third at Gulfstream."

I did it! I did it!

"To win?"

"Yeah," Sal said. "To win." *To win it all. To win it fucking all.*

Pete the Pencil was shuffling some paper on the other end of the line.

"Okay," he said finally. "It's a book."

Lightning flashed against the window, and deep, throaty thunder rumbled across the sodden city.

And now Sal was here.

What the fuck was he going to do?

Absently his gaze went to the circled, marked-up *Racing Form* lying by his hand on the desk. Drawn automatically to the lineup for the next race, his eyes flicked over the entries. Maybe he could pick a favorite, a sure thing, just one more winner. Maybe he could con Pete the Pencil into taking a $200,000 bet—

He looked up at the clock on the wall: 3:32. An hour later in Florida. When the fuck was post time? Wait a minute. His mind cleared, and he could hear the phony Englishman calling the race on the radio in the bar. Too late to get down, and his mind turned inward again, as there was nothing so boring to

Sal D'Amore as a sporting event he didn't have a wager on. It was like watching television reports of Arabs killing each other. Who gives a fuck?

Sal looked at the fifth race, and his blood began to burn with the old familiar heat. Notsomuchasapeep was running in the fifth, in the *rail position.* Sal loved this horse, had won three grand on him not two weeks ago. Notsomuchasapeep had three wins in his last seven races, with two places and a show. What a horse! Who was the jock? Mother*fucker!* Angel Valdez. Helluva rider. Cocksucker owed him one anyway. How could he have let that Transformer horse lose? *How?* But that was then, and this is now. Sal could feel the warm, sensual tension start to flow through him. He had a shot here, a real shot. *What was the morning line on this motherfucker?* He quickly consulted the racing paper—*5 to 2.* Probably'll be 2 to 1 by post time, but what the fuck, all he needed was to double his money. He didn't want to *gamble,* for Chrissakes, he just needed a sure thing, and this horse, with Valdez in the stirrups, fuck, it was money in the bank. A lead-pipe cinch. All he had to do was figure a way to lay the bet. *Christ,* a voice inside of his head cried, *there is no way to lay a $200,000 bet.* "I have to," Sal said aloud. The horse was a for-sure. No way could he lose. *Notsomuchasapeep?* Shee-it! Fucking horse didn't know *how* to lose. Maybe he could win enough to come out of this whole thing a little ahead of the game. Maybe have enough to finance a real good professional-sounding demo tape. Four or five tunes, or possibly even a whole damn album. Get picked up by a major label and leave all this fucking shit behind.

Sal got up and went into the bar. The cartoon dog had been replaced by an old black-and-white movie. Bogart and Robinson snarled at each other from inside wide, double-breasted suits.

Sal picked up the phone from the bar and the door of the Sporting Life crashed open, and seven people hurried in from the rain.

Sal forgot about the bet.

For the first time the complete import of what he had done struck him like a slap across his face, and the fear, like a hand, reached between his legs, gripped his balls, and *squeezed.*

* * *

The seven people, dripping cold rainwater onto the floor, shucked off their coats, laughing and cursing. Even in a bar they smelled of liquor. The three women were whores. Tired-looking women in their late twenties, with good bodies, sad eyes, and the aura that all whores have that they were missing some important component of their personalities.

The four men were Little Johnny's people. Jimmy Van, a downtown burglar and pimp who had grown up with Little Johnny's sons. Junior Venezia, Little Johnny's second-to-youngest son, a brutal and volatile near-retard who was said to always carry a ball peen hammer in his pocket, to use on appropriate occasions. Dago Red La Rocca, at sixty-four the oldest man in the group, a contemporary of Little Johnny's who had years before taken a fall for one of the Little Guy's few fuck-ups. He had pulled a *nickel on the river*—a five-year sentence at the Louisiana State Penitentiary in Angola—thereby ensuring himself a permanent place in Little Johnny's organization. Dago Red considered himself to be nominally independent, running with the Venezia boys, who were half his age, burglarizing, dealing cocaine to the Italians and heroin to the blacks, gambling, shylocking, even still pimping a little on the side, a fact that amused his younger cohorts greatly. It was also common knowledge on the street that Dago Red La Rocca was Little Johnny Venezia's executioner of choice.

Sal chewed on that fact awhile and found it hard to swallow. But as dangerous as Dago Red was, it was the identity of the fourth man in the group that made Sal's hands tremble so much he hid them behind the bar.

Nicky Venezia was supposed to be, had been raised as, was legally known as Little Johnny's *nephew,* the son of his younger sister Rose. But everybody in the city was aware that Nicky was Little Johnny's illegitimate son. Everybody knew, but *nobody* said a word. Not so much as a peep. Nicky's mother had been a young, voluptuous little stripper of Mexican-Hawaiian heritage who in the early fifties had somehow found her way to New Orleans and into one of Little Johnny's Bourbon Street fleshpits. Little Johnny developed an immediate taste for her dusky but not Negro skin. When she came up pregnant, Venezia, who at the time hadn't fathered a child, legitimate or otherwise, for half a dozen years, set the girl up in an apartment on Governor

Nicholls and had her brought pots of rich Sicilian food from his ancient mother's kitchen. Baby food, he called it. Three nights after the baby's birth Little Johnny brought it to his childless sister's house and put it in her arms. That same night he had one of his people drive the baby's mother to one of his whorehouses in Baton Rouge, where for months afterward grown men paid dearly to nurse on her huge, milk-filled breasts. After that he sold her to a whorehouse in Texas, where she simply disappeared.

It was said on the street, although never to one of the Venezias, that Nicky was both Little Johnny's favorite nephew *and* his most cherished son. Even Little Johnny's four "natural" sons loved the wild little kid, and Nicky grew up with the warm knowledge that there wasn't much his family couldn't get him out of. Because of this, most people gave Nicky Venezia a very wide berth.

"This fucking rain!" Dago Red La Rocca said, in his harsh whiskey rasp, taking off his overcoat and shaking off the rain onto the black-and-white tiled floor. "This fucking rain! They gonna hafta cancel tonight's parade."

"No, Red!" one of the whores protested. She was a meaty, blowzy crayon-yellow blonde with a high Texas drawl. "I ain't never seen a Mardi Gras parade. You think they gonna cancel it?"

"Keeps raining." Dago Red's voice was the aural equivalent of No. 10 sandpaper. It was said his vocal cords were damaged when, a million years ago, someone had tried to poison him with a drink laced with Drano. Pity the poor motherfucker, was the thought that came to everyone's mind. Don't try that kind of thing with somebody like Red La Rocca and then don't do it right.

"Sal!" Jimmy Van greeted as he draped his trench coat over a barstool. "Where yat?"

"Jimmy," Sal said weakly.

"Pretty Boy Sally." Dago Red turned his attention to Sal. "Pretty little Sally. Give us a kiss, Sally baby." Dago Red laughed, and it sounded like a car grinding its gears.

The seven of them were all seated at the bar now, stretched out in a long line. Boy, girl, boy, girl.

"So, Sal," Nicky Venezia said in his soft, cold voice, "you

taking good care of Little Johnny's money?"

Sal didn't know if the question was rhetorical, or if Nicky wanted an answer. He chose not to compound his crime by lying. He chose not to reply.

"Didja get the bet?" Nicky asked.

"What?"

Nicky looked at him more closely. His mixed parentage had given him slightly almond eyes, a shade darker skin, and an all-consuming desire to be more Sicilian than his full-blooded relatives. His brown eyes were, like his voice, somehow both soft and cold.

"Didja get the bet?" he asked again, and pointed to the phone receiver still in Sal's hand.

"Yeah," Sal said, and quickly hung up the phone.

"So? You taking good care of Little Johnny's money?" His lips smiled, but his eyes were as frigid as river water in February.

Sal forced himself to smile back. "I better be."

"Yeah," Dago Red's voice barged in, laughing, "you fucking well better be, Sally Boy. Or I'll cut the balls off you sweet ass and make you my old lady. Ha! Ha! Ha!" His laughter was like stones in a can.

Nicky laughed along with his mentor, and then said to Sal, "We need some drinks. We having a party here, and it's too fucking cold to party."

"Baby, it's cold outside," Dago Red choked out.

"Drinks all around," Nicky ordered.

"Yeah, wine for my men and hay for the whores," Jimmy Van joked, and all the others broke up.

Sal quickly brought up the bottle of Crown Royal. That's what all the New Orleans wiseguys drank.

"Bourbon all around?" Sal asked, already pouring the drinks.

"Ugh, no!" said another whore, a pretty woman with dark hair, blue eyes, and freckles splattered across the bridge of her nose. "I can't stand that shit. Can you make me a rum and coke?"

"Coming right up," Sal said, and then the phone rang.

"Hey, you better take care of my daddy's money!" the brutish Junior Venezia said, speaking for the first time, and the other six laughed. Junior Venezia was short and squat and built like a barrel. His animal eyes darted back and forth under a heavy brow.

The phone rang again.

"You gonna answer that?" Nicky asked.

"Right now," Sal said, and picked up the phone.

"My horse win it," he heard Albert Castiglia say.

"Lemme take this in the office," Sal said softly into the phone, and then punched the "hold" button. He got back at the drinks, trying to give himself time to think.

"Red, you think they really gonna cancel the parade?" the yellow-haired whore whined.

"Can't have no parade in the rain, girl."

"Aw, shit."

Jimmy Van, at the other end of the bar, leaned over to talk down to them.

"They postponed this parade twice already. If the rain even slack up a little, they'll roll it."

"You think so, Jimmy?" the Texas blonde wanted to know.

"Rain gotta slack up a little, though."

Sal finished the last drink and walked back into the office, wiping his hands on a bar towel.

"I wouldn't walk across the street to see one of them fucking parades," Nicky said. "Buncha rich assholes dressed up in drag."

Junior Venezia gulped his bourbon, the way he always did, and chewed the ice cubes, the way he always did. "I saw on TV"—*crunch*—"where the navy"—*crunch*—"they got a way to make it stop raining whenever they want it to."

"No shit," said the pretty whore with the freckles.

"But I ain't *never* seen a Mardi Gras parade," the blonde complained.

"Yeah," Junior continued, "and they got a bomb"—*crack!*—"they drop right in the eye of a hurricane, stop that motherfucker dead."

"Is this a hurricane?" the blonde asked, glancing back at the rain coursing down the big window. "I ain't never seen no hurricane."

Sal, in the tiny office, picked up the phone.

"My horse win it," Albert Castiglia said immediately.

"Yeah, I know."

"When can I come get my money?"

"Look, Little Johnny said that much money he needs a little while to get it all together."

"Bullshit," Albert Castiglia said. "How much time?"

"Well, see, it's Sunday—"

"Bullshit. Tell Little Johnny I want my money today."

Sal thought for a moment. *What difference did it make anyway?*

"Come by tonight after ten."

"I'll be there. And I won't be alone." He hung up.

"You ain't never seen a hurricane in Texas?" Dago Red asked. "I *know* they got hurricanes in Texas."

"Not in Amarillo, honey. Ain't never seen one of them damn things in Amarillo."

The tiny blue numbers still glowed on the calculator's readout. Sal clicked off the machine and pocketed the little red spiral notebook. *Big Time.* He went back to the bar.

"Sal, where you playing now?" Jimmy Van asked. He was a trim, spare man of thirty-five with a receding hairline and horn-rimmed glasses. He looked like an accountant, but was a virtuoso with a set of lock-picks. And didn't sweat at all, as the thieves said about themselves. "Maybe we come see you tonight, do a little dancing. Where you playing?"

"The piano bar at the King Louis."

"You open Sundays?"

"Dark on Mondays. But I don't have a band anymore, Jimmy."

"You don't have your band no more?"

The blonde, who had tottered on spike heels over to the jukebox, shouted back at them.

"Red, make it stop raining, honey! I wanna see that Mardi Gras parade!"

"I'm telling you, Sandra, forget about that parade. They gonna cancel that motherfucker. Besides, whores ain't got time to go to fucking parades, for Chrissakes. Whores got *work* to do. Fucking hotels are *packed.*"

"Aw, Red, they all families with umpteen kids come in for the Mardi Gras, that's all." She was feeding quarters into the jukebox.

"Bullshit," Dago Red rasped. "They gonna be some hard dicks in them hotels. That's why the squares *come* to Noo Awlins."

She was punching out her selections.

"Aw, Red, I ain't been out the room for six weeks. Not since I met you." Dago Red again gave out his ground-glass chortle. "Shee-it, Red, I'm gonna miss the whole damn party. They liable to shut the whole thing down on account of the rain."

Nicky Venezia was lighting a cigarette. "Wettest fucking Carnival season I ever saw," he said, his teeth biting into his filter tip. "Raining every fucking day."

High honky-tonk piano fills rang from the jukebox in a gentle hillbilly waltz.

"Aw, Sandra," Dago Red growled, "you ain't playing that hoosier shit again." Dago Red La Rocca's upper body was so muscled he seemed to always be leaning forward, apelike, almost hunched. When he was younger and a prison guard had given him his name, his hair had been a violent strawberry, but now it was shocking white and his complexion pasty pale. "I'm so sick of that shit-kicking shit."

Kenny Rogers sang, "*In a bar in Toledo, across from the depot, on a barstool she took off her ring—*"

"See, Red, honey. Nicky says they liable to cancel the whole damn Mardi Gras, on account of the rain."

"The navy, they got a way to stop the rain," Junior Venezia grunted. "Stop it dead."

"Set us up again, Sally," Jimmy Van said to Sal, and laid a hundred on the polished bar. "And don't forget yourself."

Sal started mixing the drinks. "Thanks, Jimmy, I could use one."

"You ain't got your band no more, Sally?"

"Not for a long time, Jimmy."

"*I'm hungry for laughter, and here ever after, I'm after whatever the other life brings—*"

"Best fucking band I ever heard, when you was playing at the Casablanca on Iberville. Best fucking Noo Awlins Band I ever heard."

"*Dat's* where I know you from, you good-lookin' bastid." Her voice was hard, nasal Ninth Ward Brooklynese, but her face was thin and pale and angelic under auburn hair pulled back tight and twisted into a single thick braid that fell down her back. She was Nicky Venezia's new whore, and snuggled up close. "You're Sal D'Amore. My sister graduated from Nicholls with you."

"Nicholls!" Junior Venezia snorted, like a gorilla snuffling at a banana. "Nothing but niggers there now. They hung Cus Almerico's kid out the window by his heels. Kid pissed all over hisself."

"You remember Mildred O'Rourke?"

Sal paused a moment, bottle poised over a glass, staring at the auburn-haired whore, trying desperately to look natural.

"She was a beauty, but when she came to me, she must've thought I'd lost my mind—"

"Same nose, but she's shorter than you? Hair's a little darker?"

The whore smiled. "That's her. I'm her little sister." She loosened herself from Nicky's arm, sat up straighter, and held out her hand. "I'm Hadey O'Rourke."

"Ain't that some shit," Nicky Venezia said disdainfully, "a whore shaking hands. Ain't nobody gonna pay you to shake their fucking hand, 'ho."

"You picked a fine time to leave me, Lucille—"

Junior bolted his bourbon and crunched his ice. "Fucking kid hadn't ate his lunch all year. Fucking niggers jammed him for his lunch money the minute he hit the door."

"You hear what happen to Razoo?" Dago Red interjected.

Nicky's head whipped around. "What happen to Razoo? We was supposed to do something together next week."

"Razoo ain't gonna be doing nothing with nobody for a long fucking time. Last night he got popped inside of Judge Labourdette's house up in the Garden District with burglary tools in his pocket, socks pulled over his hands, and a forty-five under his belt."

"Stupid fuck carried a piece into a *judge's* house?"

"Man, I'm tellin' you. They set bail at a quarter-a-million."

"Jesus."

"Man, I'm tellin' you."

"I've had some bad times, lived through some sad times—"

Hadey, the auburn whore, had untangled herself from Nicky's arm and was leaning across the bar toward Sal, who was at his post mixing more drinks. Keeping busy.

"I graduated from Holy Angels in '79. Your band played our graduation dance. On the President."

Sal shrugged. "I played a lot of graduations on the President."

"Yeah, but remember, them two dudes from St. Roch jumped off the top deck into the river?"

Sal made himself smile. "Yeah, I remember."

"What a night that was," the whore Hadey laughed. "I'll never forget that night. I danced to your band till three or four in the morning."

"Yeah, that gig went double overtime."

"I'll never forget that night." She smiled at him. "I had a *thing* for you, man. You was the prettiest man I ever seen. I danced right in front of the bandstand all night. I would of fucked you right there on your organ." Her eyes widened as she caught her own joke. "On your organ!" She squealed with laughter.

"Set us up again, Sal." Jimmy Van pointed along the bar. Jimmy was known for being free with his money, and even more so when he was drunk, and they were all drunk. "And don't forget yourself, Sally."

Hey, what the fuck, Sal thought. *I* need *to be drunk. Maybe then I won't feel it when they break my kneecaps.*

Don't be an asshole, an inner voice argued. *They break your knees for twenty thousand. For the hole you dug for yourself, they cut your fucking throat.*

Nicky Venezia lit another cigarette. "Razoo figures he's gonna do time behind this one?"

Dago Red turned on his barstool to look at Nicky. "Nicky, he got caught burglarizing a *judge's* house. With a gun in his possession."

Nicky shook his head. His lips were a thin, tight line. When he angered, his face seemed to darken.

"How the *fuck* the stupid motherfucker come to be robbing a fucking judge's house?"

The older man turned back to the bar and rested his elbows on the leather cushion that edged the plasticized wood. "Judge's son set it up for him."

"No shit?"

"No shit. Fucking kid goes to Tulane, and his fraternity is one of Razoo's coke customers. It was the fucking kid's idea. He give Razoo the keys, a diagram of the house, and the fucking combination to the wall safe."

"Jesus."

"Man, I'm tellin' you."

"Sal," Jimmy Van said, pointing behind the bar at a photograph of a fisherman and a strung-up marlin. "Gimme that picture." On the bar Jimmy laid a glassine bag quarter-filled with cocaine. "Let's fucking *party!*"

"*Aw right!*" the pretty freckled whore said.

Lightning flashed across the big outside display window. Dago Red was combing his white hair, studying his reflection in the back-bar mirror. "Razoo said if he gets five-to-ten out of this one—"

"Red," the Texas whore complained loudly, "lookit that lightning. I'm gonna miss that parade!"

Nicky Venezia laid his hand on the older man's arm. "You let your whore interrupt you like that?"

Dago Red stared at Nicky Venezia a moment, and was about to turn to the yellow-haired whore when the jukebox again blasted to life:

"Take this job and shove, I ain't working here no more—"

"Aw, Sandra," Dago Red exclaimed as he turned away from Nicky, "not another one of them shit-kickers." He rolled his eyes comically. "You know I hate that shit."

"Red!" she laughed teasingly, and then Nicky Venezia swung his legs off the barstool, walked over to the jukebox, gripped the molded blue plastic with both hands, rocked the machine back, and slammed it against the wall. The needle bounced scratchily across the 45 until the record rejected. He waited, his tense back turned to the other people in the bar, who were all watching him. When the next side, also a country-and-western, settled, and the arm dropped down on it, Nicky did the same thing again. And then with the next, and the next, and the next, until the jukebox was finally silent. Nicky turned and faced the others. His face was glowing darkly. His eyes were somehow simultaneously piercing and unfocused, frigid and molten. He stepped the few feet to the end of the bar and looked at Sal.

"Gimme some quarters."

Quickly, Sal opened the cash register and scooped out a fistful of the red-fingernail-polished quarters that the house used for free plays. He handed them to Nicky without meeting his eyes. Nicky went back to the juke and dropped in all the coins slowly, one by one. Then he punched out a dozen selections. The music was rocking and rolling before the last quarter clinked down. Lee Dorsey's fifties New Orleans R&B hit:

"Sittin' in la-la waiting for my ya-ya, yeah. Sittin' in la-la waitin' for my ya-ya—"

Nicky Venezia turned to face them again. Now, he was smiling, his eyes bright and mischievous, like a disarming child's. He clapped his hands softly, coolly, to the backbeat.

"That's more like it." He grinned broadly and danced, badly but enthusiastically, across the black-and-white tiles.

"C'mon, Texas," he said to the yellow-blond whore, "let's dance."

The whore, who had retreated to the bar, smiled nervously, clearly confused and frightened. She looked to Dago Red.

"Go 'head, Sandra, dance with the man," Dago Red rasped, and softly slapped the whore on her ass.

Sandra shrugged, smiled coyly, tossed her mane of Crayola-yellow hair, then dipped and strutted over to where Nicky was dancing.

"Aw right, Country," Nicky laughed, "show us what you got," and they danced around each other.

The others at the bar watched them, a sense of relief visible in their faces; then they turned back to their drinks.

Jesus, Sal thought. *Even* these *dudes are afraid of Nicky.*

Lightning flashed in the dark skies outside, and seconds later heavy thunder lumbered across the roof.

Junior Venezia crunched his ice and stared up at the ceiling. "Fucking navy could stop this if they wanted to."

The first time Sal D'Amore ever saw Nicky Venezia, they were both twelve years old. Sal and his mother had just moved from down St. Claude Avenue to an apartment over a dry cleaner on Elysian Fields. There was an old Italian man down the block who still sold live chickens, his cages stacked on the banquette. The chickens were probed and prodded for fatness by the merciless fingers of the black, French, and Italian housewives of the neighborhood, then carried squawking into the back room, where they were decapitated, gutted, dipped in boiling water, cleaned, and plucked. Sal's mother folded two damp, crumpled dollar bills into his hand and sent him off to buy a fryer. Sal hated touching the stupid, breathing bundles of feathers, and rather than inspect them the way his mother would, he pointed at the first one his eye rested on. A few minutes later he was carrying the still-warm, wax-paper-wrapped carcass back to the apartment, humming Ray Charles's "Hit the Road, Jack," when the heavy glass door to Vicari's Barber Shop burst open before him, and a small, wiry boy only a few inches taller than Sal stalked out onto the steamy sidewalk. The boy wore loose-fitting navy jeans belted high on his waist, a tucked-in white T-shirt, and highly polished pointed-toe cordovan shoes.

"You *fuck!*" the boy screamed, and Sal thought the kid was talking to him, but then he pointed back to the barber-shop door. "You stupid fuck! Look what you done to my hair! I oughtta fucking rip your fucking head off and shit in your neck! Look what you done to me, you *stupid fuck!*"

His feet locked in place, Sal inspected the kid's haircut. It was close, but even.

"You *fuck!*" the kid screamed again, his voice rising to ever-higher levels of fury. His eyes bulged, and his arms trembled. "I oughtta fucking *kill* you!" The kid stooped and hefted the chunk of concrete Mr. Vicari kept by the door to prop it open on good days. The kid held the chunk threateningly above his head. It was too heavy for him, and his arm wavered.

"I oughtta throw this through the fucking glass," the boy menaced, dropping all his "h's" downtown New Orleans style. *I oughtta trow dis true da fuckin' glazz!* "How would you like that, you stupid old fuck!"

Sal could see Mr. Vicari, a small but not timid man of fifty, cowering—actually *cowering*—against the rear wall of the shop. There were three other people in the shop—two employee barbers and a customer with a sheet tied around his neck—and they, too, were backed into the rear of the barber shop.

"You fuck! *Look at me! Look what you done to me!*"

Sal's feet were bolted to the banquette. His mouth hung open. The still-supple cadaver of the moments-ago-alive pullet hung loosely from his hand. Sal had never seen a child speak to adults in this manner. It was a watershed experience. His heart thudded in his chest.

"You *fuck!*" the kid shrieked at the barber, and the wax-papered chicken slipped from Sal's fingers and slapped loudly on the banquette. The screaming boy turned to notice Sal for the first time. His dark eyes bored into Sal's, and Sal's knees weakened.

"What the fuck you looking at, asshole?" the kid demanded, and for a moment Sal thought Nicky was going to fling the chunk of concrete at him. "Whaddaya, waiting round to be a fucking *witness?* Get the fuck outta here!"

Sal hesitated only a second, then scooped up the fallen chicken and hurried down Elysian Fields toward his mother's house. Behind him he could hear the boy still shrieking at the barber shop.

"You *fuck!* How would you like this right through your fucking window, you stupid *fuck? Look what you done to me!*"

That was Sal D'Amore's introduction to Nicky Venezia.

And three days later Sal was playing shortstop in a pickup game at St. Roch playground, the neighborhood girls already aware of him and watching from the benches with hungry eyes, when Sal turned, shaded his eyes from the sun, and saw them—Nicky Venezia and two other kids he later learned were Nicky's cousins, Junior and Rocco—coming across the outfield toward him.

Oh, fuck! Sal thought, but didn't even consider running. What good would that do? The inner-city, low-income Ninth Ward was like a feudal village. Everybody knew everybody. He would run, maybe, if he had a plane ticket to Alaska. Maybe.

"Hey, you! Fish motherfucker!" Nicky talked like a convict even at the age of twelve. "Nosy fish motherfucker!"

Sal took off his baseball glove and stuffed it into his pants as the three Venezias came up and fanned out before him.

"You nosy, ain't you, fuck?"

Sal said nothing. Maybe there was a way out of this. Maybe.

"Listen, pussy," Nicky said, crowding him and jamming his finger into Sal's adolescent chest, "we mind our own business around here, you understand? We see something, we walk the other way. You understand?"

Sal nodded. "I ain't no snitch."

"*Oooooo,*" Nicky moaned, and the others laughed. "We got a tough guy here."

Sal said nothing, trying to stand tall and be invisible at the same time.

"What's your name, fish?"

"Sal. Sal D'Amore."

"You 'talian?"

"Yeah," Sal said, suddenly hoping there *was* a way out of this.

"Yeah, what about your mama, asshole?" Nicky Venezia sneered, and Sal's hopes came crashing down. "I hear your mama's a fucking Okie. Zat true?"

Sal clenched his fists at his sides, waiting. He knew now he was going to get his ass kicked, no way out.

"Leave him alone, Nicky," one of the girls on the bench shouted. "He ain't done nothing to you."

Now, it was worse. Now, Nicky knew he had an audience. He smiled.

"I hear Okies fuck niggers," he taunted. "Zat true, pussy?"

Sal knew he should swing on him now, but his arms wouldn't move. He could feel his legs trembling; his pulse throbbed in his temples.

"Don't your mama fuck niggers?" Nicky persisted.

Knowing he had to answer the challenge somehow, and still afraid to initiate the fight, Sal said, "No, but I heard your mama was a—"

Nicky's fist slammed against the side of his face. Not a strong blow, but vicious in its intent, and followed by a flurry of others. Sal put up his arms to protect his face and Nicky shoved him over onto the infield grass and then Sal was on his back and Nicky was sitting on his chest and pummeling his face with wild roundhouse hits. The girls on the benches were screaming, Nicky's cousins were shouting encouragement, and Sal's head buzzed and shook and Sal knew he was getting his ass kicked and all he hoped for now was that he wouldn't cry and Nicky wouldn't kill him. In fact, he'd rather Nicky kill him than everybody see him cry.

After a while it was over. Nicky's arms seemed simply to tire of the effort, and suddenly the crushing weight on Sal's chest was gone, and without another word Nicky and his cousins/brothers were stalking away across centerfield. Dominance had been established. The divine right of princes exercised.

Then the girls, drawn to Sal like cats toward warmth, were around him, crying and caring. Sal rolled over in the grass and puked, and one of the girls said, "Eeech!" Sal ran his hand across his face, and it came away bloody. His face felt somehow numb and burning. He struggled to his feet and pushed the girls aside. He was almost across the playground when the tears started streaming down his face, mixing with the blood and snot.

"Hey, Sally. Have a line," Jimmy Van offered.

Sal looked at the coke. *What the fuck.* A condemned man's last high.

He leaned over the bar, put one end of the three-inch-long stub of cocktail straw at the foot of one of the little white furrows that Jimmy Van had arranged on the glass, like Indian sand painting. He pressed one nostril closed and breathed in deeply. The line of cocaine disappeared. *Magic.*

When Sal finally, blindly, made his way up the stairs to the apartment over the dry cleaners, his mother looked at him, then wordlessly took his hand and led him into the bathroom. Without asking a question, she cleaned his wounds and painted them with Mercurochrome. Before meeting and marrying young Private D'Amore, stationed just outside Tulsa right before the Korean War, she had grown up the only white girl in an isolated corner of Oklahoma surrounded by a Cherokee reservation, so she understood the subtle necessities of intra-tribal puberty rituals.

Nicky never really bothered Sal after that initial incident. His ascendancy had been registered, and Sal wasn't about to challenge him. Whenever they passed in the school halls, or happened to meet on the playground, Nicky simply ignored him. By the next year, when Sal began attending Colton Junior High, Nicky had already been sent to Milne Boys Home after having been arrested for a series of midnight burglaries in the French Quarter. Little Johnny's underlings, led by Red La Rocca, had been plundering apartments where Nicky's wiry, lithe boyish body could squeeze down airshafts, tiptoe across the top of brick walls, even slide down narrow chimneys—which in New Orleans were all cosmetic anyway—and then unlock the doors for his adult cohorts. When Nicky was finally caught—inextricably wedged between the scrolls of a third-floor veranda's ornamental ironworks—and brought into the First District station on Rampart Street, he immediately began to build his lifelong reputation by spitting in the cops' faces when they asked who his accomplices were. They broke his nose, but he laughed at them and cursed their mothers, and finally they gave up and sent him to Juvenile Hall. (If he'd been of age, bail could've been arranged in minutes.) Amused and proud, Little Johnny and Dago Red La Rocca marveled at the stories they heard about the tough little bastard, and they speculated on how long it would take for Nicky to organize and grab power at the boys' home. And Little Johnny's legitimate sons overheard and instinctively understood that Nicky was their father's favorite, and would be expected to commit crimes and take risks that they themselves were not to be allowed. At least, not yet. Truth be known, Little John had vague aspirations for his four acknowledged sons to become lawyers and politicians—whom he considered the world's best thieves—but had absolutely no idea how to encourage his boys to get an education, or even to instill in them a sense of accomplishment. Little Johnny Venezia's success was not due to the American work ethic, but to bald courage and naked treachery. If you had the balls to steal something—and the smarts to get away with it—you stole it. Fuck work. Assholes worked. And to the Venezia boys' credit, they knew enough about themselves to realize that they were simply too stupid to be anything but criminals. And they also understood early on that Nicky was going to be their leader.

Lee Dorsey's record rejected, and a moment later another single dropped down with a plastic flap.

"I found my threeeeellll, on Blueberry Heeellll, on Blueberry Heeeeellll, where I found you—"

"Yeah!" Nicky said, strutting around Sandra, the Texas whore. "Tell 'em about it, Fat Man!" He clapped his hands and swayed his hips.

Jimmy Van sculpted a dozen parallel lines on the glass surface and pushed the fisherman's photograph down the bar in front of Junior Venezia.

Junior shook his head. "I got a cold."

"So what?"

Junior shrugged. "You might catch it."

Jimmy Van thought for a moment, then looked over Junior's head at Dago Red, who smiled back.

"Junior," Jimmy said, "how the fuck can we catch your cold?"

Junior shrugged again. "I don't know."

Dago Red leaned over the freckled whore and slapped Junior on his back. "Junior, don't chu know the coke kills all them germs?"

Junior looked at him. "No shit, Red?"

"No shit. Kills all them little bastids dead."

"Well, shit," Junior said, and leaned over the picture of the man and the fish. "You know," he said as he snorted the first line, "the fucking heat could walk right through that door."

"*No!*" Nicky feigned horror as he danced with his hands on Sandra's hips. "Not the *authorities?*"

"Don't worry about it, Junior," Jimmy Van said. "We'll kill 'em and bury 'em in the backyard."

Junior wet his fingertip, ran it around the edge of the picture frame, then massaged his gums with it. "This bar ain't got no backyard."

Dago Red La Rocca inched his empty tumbler over the bar, indicating that Sal should refill it. "I ain't never seen a lazy fucking screw would go out in weather like this." La Rocca was so much older than the other men that he actually said things like *screw.*

"Yeah," Nicky answered from the dance floor, "we oughtta be out there working ourselves. Rainy day like this is money in the bank."

"Aw, Nick, it's Sunday. Everybody's home with the family watching TV." As he said this, Dago Red turned to the bar's television. "Hey, that's Edward G.!"

"Sal!" Jimmy Van laughed as he pushed the coke-laden photograph down the bar to the pretty dark-haired, freckled whore. "How you feeling, man?"

Sal gave Jimmy the best smile he could muster. "Fucking dynamite, Jimmy."

The pretty freckled whore took the pink-and-white straw stub in her hand and examined it. "The coke really kills the germs?" she asked, and Jimmy Van and Dago Red fell out laughing.

* * *

Sal didn't see much of Nicky again until Sal was nineteen and went to work playing in the clubs on Bourbon Street. Nicky was everywhere then, working the doors of Little Johnny's strip joints, running whores to the conventioneers, selling weed and uppers to the musicians, burglarizing any building on the Street that wasn't under Venezia protection. Sal was playing down the block at the Casablanca on the corner of Bourbon and Iberville, and he was beginning to get a loyal local following. He had put together his first good band, and every night from nine till three they played a funky, churning New Orleans version of "blue-eyed soul," and on weekends the crowds spilled out on the sidewalk and there were frequent fistfights over who was next in line to get in. And the girls! They lined the edge of the stage and jammed the doorway and whistled and shouted whenever Sal sang one of his specialty numbers—"What'd I Say," Otis Redding's "Too Hot to Handle," and especially George Harrison's "Something." And when he came offstage on his breaks, they bought him drinks, patted the sweat from his brow with cocktail napkins, stroked his thick dark hair, and whispered in his ear. He fucked a different girl every night, sometimes two, taking them in the club's storeroom on a break. And Nicky Venezia noticed. He would saunter into the club, lean against the wall in the orange glow of the back bar's dim light, and watch through his hooded, hungry, whoremaster eyes as the girls clamored for Sal. And then their eyes would meet, and Sal, singing behind his big Hammond B 3, would bend a note, put a soulful little catch to the end of a phrase, *methodically* eliciting from the audience girlish shrieks, and over his keyboard Sal would stare at Nicky Venezia and think, *Do* that, *motherfucker,* and Nicky would glower back at him.

"That fucking Edward G.," Dago Red said, wiping the coke from his nostrils with his fingertips and licking them. "I love that guy."

The phone kept ringing, and Sal kept going to the back office with the bets.

"Who?" the pretty freckled whore wondered.

Hadey O'Rourke, the auburn-haired whore, shouted to Sal in the back office, "My sister Mildred used to go see you at the Casablanca when you worked there. How long you worked there?"

Sal came out of the tiny office. "What?"

"How long you worked at the Casablanca?" She had an unlit cigarette displayed prominently between her fingers. There was a gold lighter positioned on the bar right in front of her.

"The one in the pinstripe double-breasted," Dago Red rasped. "You don't know Edward G.?"

"The little ugly dude?" the pretty freckled whore wanted to know. "Who the fuck is he?"

"Jesus," Dago Red shook his head. "Did you just get off the boat or something?"

"Almost six years," Sal said. He flicked the lighter and held the flame for her. She smiled and dipped the tip of her cigarette into the fire.

"My sister Millie use'ta sneak me in sometimes. Jesus, I could'na been more than fifteen. Me and Millie use'ta stand right by the stage, and, shit, I swear, our fucking panties would get sopping wet." She smiled at him again. "You coudda had us both, you'da wanted us." She dragged on her cigarette.

I don't need this, Sal thought. *This I don't need.*

"Edward G. was the *best!* The fucking *best!* Made Humphrey Bogart look like a fucking *punk.*"

"The wind in the willows played, such sweet melodies—"

The pretty dark-haired, freckled whore did a line of coke, then looked up at the TV screen. "He looks funny to me."

"Funny?"

"Yeah, ugly. Stupid, like." She dipped her head and did another line.

"You crazy. Edward G. was the best. The motherfucking best." He turned on his barstool. "How long Edward G. been dead, Junior?"

Junior was startled. "Edward G. Robinson's dead?"

Dago Red looked at him. "Christ, Junior, Edward G.'s been dead ten or fifteen years."

Junior's eyes narrowed. "I don't think so, Red."

Dago Red was exasperated. "Junior, don't gimme that shit." He pointed at the television, where Edward G.'s grainy image filled the picture tube. "The man's been dead maybe twenty years."

Junior shrugged. "Nobody told me."

The pretty freckled whore dipped two fingers in a glass of

water, put them in her nostrils, leaned back on her barstool, and sucked in air noisily. She sat up and stared glassily at the TV. "Looks stupid to me."

Hadey O'Rourke blew a plume of smoke at the ceiling while lightning buzzed outside like a fallen power line.

"You made a record. Didn'ja make a record?"

"Couple of them. Forty-fives."

"I used to have them." She tapped her finger on the bar. "What was the name?"

He was refilling everyone's glass. "The one that did best? 'She's the Only One I Want.' "

"That's the one!" She slapped her hand down. "I *loved* that song. Didn'ja write that song? Millie said you wrote it yourself."

Sal nodded.

"Well—what happened with that song?"

Sal shrugged. "Nothing."

She waited for more.

He dropped some fresh ice cubes into her glass. "No localized distribution. No regional promotion. Secondary markets are moribund."

She stared at him. "What the fuck does that mean?"

Sal stopped and shrugged. "I read that somewhere. It means you have to get signed with a big record company. Columbia. Epic. A&M. One of them."

"Oh," she said. And then, "Well, you're still writing, ain'tcha? Still writing songs?"

"Been a little busy lately. Working here and at the King Louis nights. Haven't done any writing in a coupla months."

"You oughtta. You're great."

He smiled at her. Even today, in a cold panic, he was a sucker for anyone who praised his music. "Thanks."

She smiled back.

The Fats Domino record ended, and Nicky Venezia and Sandra came laughing back to the bar. There was a line of perspiration on Nicky's forehead.

"Fucking A, Tex," he said as Sandra hiked her impressive behind up onto a barstool. Sandra laughed.

"You looked real good out there, Sandra," Dago Red leaned over and said in a kindly effort to reassert his proprietorship. Red La Rocca was too old to be a very effective pimp.

She fanned her face with a handful of cocktail napkins. "Shit, Red, look at that rain. They gon' hafta cancel that damn parade, sure 'nough."

"Forget that parade, baby. Forget about it."

Nicky took off his coat and hung it over the back of a barstool. While the three other men dressed expensively but unimaginatively, running to pedestrian dark double-knits and heavy gold jewelry, Nicky had once pimped an uptown socialite hooker who taught him about clothes, and now he looked like an advertisement from *GQ*, attired in stylish Giorgio Armani imports.

Another record dropped onto the juke's turntable. Irma Thomas's funky "I Did My Part."

"You walked away and left me, out in the cold. After I was so good to you, you were so cold—"

"Aw *right!*" Nicky shouted, slapping his hands gleefully. *"Aw fucking right!"* The others at the bar smiled with him. Nicky Venezia was everyone's favorite.

"How ya doin', Hadey?" he said as he wrapped his arm around the auburn-haired whore's shoulders and pulled her to his narrow chest. "How the fuck you doin'?"

"Nicky." She turned to him. "You ever hear Sal's record?"

Nicky looked at Sal as if he had just noticed him. "Sal D'Amore, you degenerate musician motherfucker. You taking care of my uncle Johnny's money?" His smile was warm, but his eyes reflected cold cruelty.

"Doing the best I can, Nicky," Sal said, reaching for a glass to fill, keeping his hands going.

"Yeah, you pretty-boy motherfucker." He laughed. "Hey, Red, you think Pretty Boy Sal here would have trouble up at the Gola?"

La Rocca chuckled. It was a subject he found warming. "Oh, man, they'd tear you a new asshole. A brand-new asshole. 'Course"—he winked at Sal—"you might get to like it." The men at the bar erupted in nervous guffaws. Most of the wiseguys did their time with only their hand and a tube of KY jelly for company, but it was widely known that Red La Rocca always found a young convict to sodomize when he went up. It was one of his little foibles that were tolerated because he was so loyal and effective.

"Lemme tell you, Sal," Nicky went on, "here's what you do if you ever hafta go away. The first day you hit the cell-block, you stand up tall and holler, 'I want the biggest, baddest, meanest motherfucker in here to stand up!' And then this big seven-foot dude gets up, and he's got scars all over his face, and tattoos on his fucking eyelids, and one ear's missing, and he says"—Nicky deepened his voice—"Yeah? Whattaya want?"

Nicky held back the punch line, looking at the other men, who were already smiling.

"And then you go, '*Daddy!*' and run jump on his lap, and nobody in the penitentiary will ever bother you."

The others were all laughing, even the women. Dago Red's raspy chortle was like a heavy file dragged across a metal edge. Sal made himself chuckle along.

"Nicky's right," Dago Red cackled scratchily. "You too pretty to go to the joint."

"Too sweet, too," Hadey the whore purred, and Nicky quickly looked at her.

"Looka Edward G., Nicky," Dago Red growled, and nodded up at the screen. "That's how you wanna look, you go up to the Gola. Mean and ugly. That Edward G., he was something."

"He was a fucking Jew," Nicky said, low and hard, looking at his whore looking at Sal.

I don't need this, Sal thought. *I got to get out of here.*

"*No!*" Dago Red's white eyebrows went up. "Edward G. Robinson was a *Jew?*"

Nicky nodded. "That's right. Izzy from Kansas City."

La Rocca was truly shocked. "A fucking Jew. I don't believe it."

Junior Venezia, his elbows propped on the bar, shook his head. "And I just a minute ago heard he was dead."

Nicky ran his hand slowly over Hadey's behind. She turned to him and smiled, leaned and rubbed against him.

Nicky smiled back at her. He extracted a book of matches from his pocket, opened them, leaned across the bar, and buried a corner of the matchbook in the cocaine. Then he brought it up to his nose and snorted it. He did it again, to the other nostril.

"But I won't cry, I won't shed a tear. I did my part-art-art-art. Baby, you were here—"

"I gotta go to the john," Nicky announced. "Fucking coke always makes me have to shit. Jimmy, take a walk with me." Nicky Venezia had been institutionalized so early and so often, he didn't like to defecate alone.

"Gimme a fucking break, Nicky. I don't wanna hold a fucking conversation with you while I'm smelling your shit."

Nicky grinned. "I always thought you enjoyed it."

Everybody at the bar laughed again. Nicky, smiling, went back to the men's room.

Lightning flashed across the window's glass.

Junior crunched another ice cube. "They had a dude up in the Gola when I was there, motherfucker sometimes would fingerpaint his cell with his own shit."

"Ugh!" Sandra grimaced. "That's really disgusting."

Junior crunched. "Used to paint whatchamacallits. Landscapes. Trees and shit."

"Junior, stop it!"

"Some of 'em was real pretty."

"Junior!"

Jimmy Van poured out another mountain range of coke onto the photograph of the fisherman. He began to carve out foothills and ridges.

Hadey leaned across the bar, smiling.

"So, Sal. You don't have your band anymore?"

Sal was nervously cleaning spotless glasses, drying unwet ones, keeping his hands busy while his mind ran screaming down St. Charles Avenue.

"Not for a couple of years. Five or six."

She shook her head. "That's a shame, Sal. Your music was fucking dynamite."

Sal shrugged, glancing over Hadey's head at the Dixie beer clock: 3:27. He still had three hours left to his shift before the night man came on. He would never make it.

"But you still writing, you said?"

"What?"

"You said you was writing on something two months ago."

"Oh, yeah."

"How's it go?"

"How's it go?" He grinned sheepishly, in spite of his suppressed hysteria.

She laughed deeply, throatily. A whore's unspoken invitation. "C'mon, Sal. How's it go?"

"Gimme a break, girl."

She laughed again. "Please, Sal. Do it for me." She stretched her arm over the bar and scraped her long fingernail gently across his forearm. "Please."

He waved his hands helplessly. "I don't have a piano here. I can't sing it without accompaniment."

"Sure you can. Just a little bit. I want to hear it."

"Hey, I can't sing over the music." He nodded toward the jukebox.

"Listen. It's ending." The song faded out. The record rejected. "Quick, before the next one comes on. Sing it for me, Sal. *Please.*"

He wanted to tell her, *No, leave me alone. Don't be bothering a dead man.* But he didn't dare offend Nicky Venezia's new whore. What he really wanted to do was jump the bar, slam out the door, and run for a hundred miles. But to where? *A hundred miles?* A thousand miles wouldn't be far enough. Ten thousand miles.

"C'mon, Sal. Do it for Hadey."

Sal looked at the others at the bar. They were all watching him now. Curious. Noncommittal. The rain streamed down the window.

Sal cleared his throat.

"What's it called?" Hadey asked quickly.

"Huh?"

"What's the name of the song?"

Sal looked at her a moment, and she seemed like a creature from another planet, another galaxy, another reality. He studied the soft lines of her cheek, the dusting of peach fuzz over her nose, the bright blue of her eyes. She frightened him.

"'You Mean the World to Me.'"

"Ooooh, I like that. I like that a lot. Sing it for me."

Already afraid and panicked, Sal now felt small and stupid, like an organ grinder's monkey surrounded by tigers. He began to sing.

"You—you mean the world to me. The moon, the stars, the sea. And everything in between. You mean the world to me—"

His voice was a tight, blues-colored tenor. And the influence of early Stevie Wonder in his songwriting was obvious.

"Ooooh, that's beautiful, Sal. Really beautiful," she said, making him break meter and forget the next line.

He stood blinking at her.

"I don't remember the next verse."

"Oh, Sal!"

"It's not finished."

"Sal, *please!*"

"Oh, yeah." His brow knitted as he remembered. *"You—you are my every dream. You're the very air I breathe. Yeah, you—you mean the world to me—"*

The next record flopped down, a piano came in with some drunken jelly-roll licks, a bass laid down a loping oompah rhythm, and a moment later Dr. John whined, *"Such a night, it was such a night. Sweet confusion—under the moonlight—"*

"Sal!" Hadey squealed, that's great! That's great! I love it! That's a fucking hit, for sure."

Sal shrugged. "Who knows?"

"No, really, Sal. That's a *great* fucking song. Sing the rest of it."

"That's all I have."

"Sal!"

"I didn't write a bridge yet."

"Well, then, sing that first part again."

Nicky came out of the long hall that led back to the rest rooms. His face brightened when he heard the thundering jukebox.

"You came in—with my best friend Jim—and here I am—tryin' steal you away from him—"

"Dr. John, you motherfucker! My main man!" Nicky positioned his left hand on his hip and strutted across the floor toward the bar like a flambeau-carrier in a Carnival parade. "Red, you ever sell heroin to the Doctor's band?"

Dago Red snorted into his drink. "Man, I sold shit to every junkie musician 'tween here and Houston. Three generations of them sorry motherfuckers."

"Let's steal away—the time is right—"

"C'mon, Sal," Hadey wheedled. "Sing it again. Sing it again."

Sal waved his hand, and his voice had the smallest tinge of

exasperation. "I can't. Not over the record."

"'Cuz if I don't do it, somebody else will—"

"Fucking A," Nicky clapped his hands softly and swayed his hips to the beat. "If I don't do it, somebody else *will.*"

"Sure you can," Hadey pleaded. "Sure you can."

"I can't."

"Pleeeaasssss—"

Sal wanted to close his eyes and shut out the world. He wanted to close his eyes and pretend it was last year, last week, day before yesterday, before the little blue numbers on the little calculator turned against him, went from plus to minus, positive to negative, life to death.

"Sal!"

Nicky danced the few feet over to Hadey and laid his hand on her arm. "C'mon, woman, dance with me." He smiled.

She shook off his hand and whipped her head around. "*Shhhhh!*" she hissed. "Sal's gonna sing his song again." She turned back to Sal.

Everyone at the bar froze, as if they were all holding their breath. Then they turned to watch.

Sal looked at Nicky, who was looking at the back of Hadey's head. Sal watched Nicky's eyes lose their happy luster and harden into cold, dead stones.

I don't need this shit, Sal thought. *I* really *don't need this shit.*

Hadey gave him what was supposed to be an encouraging smile.

"Sal, c'mon, sing that first part again."

Sal, looking past Hadey, saw Nicky reach up and grip her plaited braid at the base near her skull. She didn't even seem to notice.

"Sal, please, just one more—"

Nicky yanked back, and Sal saw the comical look of horror on Hadey's face as she felt herself lose her balance and toppled backward off her barstool. She clawed at the bar, sending her drink flying, then landed with a sickening *thud* at the base of her spine. "*Nicky!*" she wailed, her eyes tearing with fear and pain. Nicky stood over her, wrapped her queue twice around his fist and dragged her, bumping on her behind—"*Nicky, Nicky, please don't—*" over the small dance floor, and yanked her up to her feet by her hair like a marionette on a string.

"Let's dance," Nicky said in a maniacally reasonable voice, and started moving to the beat.

Hadey's face was a smeared finger painting; tears streamed down her cheeks.

"Nicky, why—"

Nicky backhanded her hard across her mouth, and her head snapped back. Her knees trembled.

"*Shut up!*" Nicky screamed into her face. "Don't say one fucking word! Just stand right there, whore, and dance until I tell you to stop!"

There was blood in the corner of Hadey's mouth. Her lips trembled. She kept her eyes downcast.

"Such a night, it was such a night—"

Nicky boogied slowly around her, snapping his fingers.

"Dance, whore," he breathed at her in a low, venomous hiss.

Gasping for breath between her sobs, Hadey started to moved pathetically to the record.

"Sweet confusion—under the moonlight—"

"There you go, whore," Nicky urged. "You a music lover, right?" He shot a quick glare in Sal's direction. "Ain't that right?"

Snot ran from her nostrils and mingled with the blood and tears that wet her face.

"Ain't that right?" Nicky asked again, more sharply.

Quickly, she nodded assent, sobbing deeply and shuffling her feet back and forth over the parquet dance floor.

"I thought you were." Nicky smiled. He turned his back and bumped his hip rhythmically against hers. She jumped with each tiny impact.

"If I don't do it, somebody else will—"

Nicky laughed and clapped his hands to the backbeat.

Hadey stumbled blindly around the center of the dance floor, her head hanging.

"'Cuz if I don't do it, somebody else wheeeeel—"

"Tell 'em about it, Doctor," Nicky sang out.

"If I don't do it, somebody else wheeeeeel—"

Slowly, endlessly, the record faded out. Nicky applauded happily and sauntered back to the bar. Sal quickly poured him another drink. He pushed it away.

"Gimme the blow," he said, and Dago Red slid the fisherman's photograph before him. Hadey stood sobbing on the dance floor.

"When was that record a hit, Sal?" Nicky asked as he leaned over the cocaine and sucked up a long white line.

Sal cleared his throat. "Uh—'71, I think—'71 or '72."

Nicky siphoned up another toy ridge. He held his head back and snuffled deeply. He looked at Sal. "You like Doctor John?"

Hadey, on the dance floor, managed to whisper, "Nicky—"

"Hey," Sal said, forcing a smile, "who the fuck don't like Mac Rebennack? He's the best."

"Fucking A," Nicky said, and took a sip of his drink.

"Nicky—Nicky, can I go to the ladies' room?"

Nicky pointed a finger at Sal's chest. Like a gun. "You think you ever gonna be as good as the Doctor?"

"Nicky—"

Sal stared back at him for a moment, then looked away. "Someday. I hope."

Nicky laughed. "You *hope?* Yeah, I hope so, too. Then maybe you can pay Little Johnny back the money you owe him."

All the men at the bar laughed.

Not likely, Sal thought.

"Nicky—please," Hadey whimpered from the dance floor.

Staring hard at Sal, Nicky growled, "Go clean up your face, whore. Nobody's gonna buy a slut with snot hanging from her chin."

Hadey covered her face with her hands and ran, tottering on her high-heeled boots, down the long hall. The other two women wouldn't look at her.

There was a still, silent moment. The rain thudded in waves against the doors and windows, like an invisible giant trying to get in. Then the Meters' old instrumental "Sissy Strut" danced out of the jukebox speakers.

The music seemed to break the tense spell.

"Key-rist!" Dago Red said. "Is all that damn thing can play is shit-kicker or old nigger music? Don't it have no Sinatra or Tony Bennett?"

"Tony *who?*" Sandra asked.

Dago Red frowned and shook his head.

I gotta get out of here, Sal thought.

"Sal!" Jimmy Van shouted drunkenly. "Set us up again." He was lighting a cigar.

"Hey!" Red La Rocca exclaimed. "Watch this!" He was looking at the television set again. "This is where Edward G. throws this old lady in a wheelchair down a flight of stairs."

Junior turned to him. "That wadn't Edward G. Robinson. That was Richard Widmark threw that old lady down them stairs. In a different picture."

Dago Red scrunched his head into his shoulders and held out his palms. "What the fuck? A minute ago you didn't know the man was even dead, and now you an expert on all his movies?"

Junior Venezia pouted. "I know it was Richard Widmark threw that old lady down them stairs. 'Cuz the old lady's kid was a rat snitch."

Nicky gave out a short, ugly laugh. "Served the old bitch right."

Sal folded his bar towel and draped it from his well. He steeled his back and leaned over the bar.

"Nicky, could I speak to you? In the back?"

Nicky's eyes lasered into Sal's, searching for any kind of challenge, and found none. His glare softened a little, but only a little.

"Sure. Why not?" He picked up his drink and slipped off his stool. Sal raised the bar gate, and Nicky walked through and into the office.

"You got any extra condoms?" the pretty freckled-face whore asked of Sandra.

"Sure, honey." Sandra reached down for her purse on the barroom floor.

"Watch this!" Dago Red said. "This is where he does it, watch—aw, *fuck!* Commercial!"

Junior crunched his ice and shook his head. "Richard Widmark."

"What's your story?" Nicky turned and coldly asked. The tiny office seemed even more cramped and crowded.

"Nicky, I need a favor."

Nicky said nothing, only stared.

I gotta get outta here! Sal screamed inside himself.

His words tumbled out. "Georgie comes on at six-thirty, but there's something I gotta do. I was wondering, since y'all ain't going nowhere, at least I don't think y'all are, if you and Junior would cover for me. It's real slow with the rain and all, and I don't know why, but the phones ain't that hot and—"

"What is it, a woman?"

"—what?"

"You gotta meet a woman?" Nicky was smirking. "You banging some poor asshole's horny little wife?"

Sal told himself to smile. "Busted me, Nicky."

Nicky sat down in the old office chair, threw his arm over the backrest, and reclined to the shriek of the chair's dry, ancient springs. He inspected Sal from under his heavy, droopy eyelids.

"You know, Sal, you always amazed me." He leaned back even further and propped his shoes on the desk. Supple imported jobs with discreet little tassels. Nicky didn't dress Ninth Ward anymore. "The way women are always running after you, your whole fucking life, ever since I knew you, and you without two nickels to rub together, always scuffling around, always in the hole."

If you only fucking knew, Sal thought. And then, *You will, soon enough.*

"Man, don't you know you're a fucking gold mine? At least, you used to be. Could've been. Them little girls used to hang around you, scream whenever you sing, man, them bitches woudda done *anything* for you. *Any*thing. You coulda turned out a hundred of them little tramps. Made a million dollars. I never understood why you didn't take advantage of that opportunity."

Sal shrugged. He didn't know what to say, or how to say it so Nicky wouldn't take offense.

Finally he offered, "It's not what I *do,* Nicky. I wouldn't even know how to go about it."

Nicky looked at him awhile.

"I guess you right," he eventually said. "Pimping is like whatchamacallit. A calling. Like being a priest, or a forger, or a jockey, or, or—"

"Or a musician—"

Nicky shook his head and smiled coldly. "Nah, being a musician's a disease, like having AIDS. And being a degenerate gambler musician"—he motioned his hand toward Sal—"I can't think of anything worse."

Right about now, neither can I.

Nicky raised his imported Gemelli de Janeiro footwear from the desk and settled them on the floor.

"But I guess that's why some of us are winners"—the cold smile got even chillier—"and some of us are losers."

Now, Sal forced himself to laugh. "I guess so." *Yassuh, boss. Yeahyouright.*

Nicky put his hands on his knees and pushed himself to his feet.

"Even still, it's too bad about that other thing. About the girls. Because you'll never know, but one of the best feelings in the world is having a woman sell herself for you."

He looked at Sal.

"It ranks right up there with sticking a piece in a motherfucker's face and seeing the fear in his eyes while you're taking his fucking money."

Sal said nothing.

"Two of my favorite feelings in the world," Nicky bragged on. He started moving out of the office, Sal following; then Nicky stopped and rested his hand on Sal's shoulder. "Of course, the best feeling in the world, the very best, is killing a motherfucker you don't like." He leaned even closer, and his grip on Sal's shoulder tightened. "Nothing else like it. Nothing." He squeezed. "Nothing."

Then his dark face broke into a wide, evil grin. "Killing somebody you *like* ain't nearly as much fun."

Nicky's laughter was somehow simultaneously contagious and bone-chilling.

He's the devil, Sal thought. *This motherfucker is the devil.*

"Hey, Nicky," Dago Red called from the bar, "come see, ain't this the picture where Edward G. throws a snitch's mama down the stairs?"

Nicky was walking away from him, into the barroom.

"Get outta here, piano player," he growled over his shoulder. "You fucking worthless anyhow."

Sal already had his overcoat in his hand.

"Thanks, Nicky. Georgie'll know how to tally the bets, when he comes in."

"I hope so." Nicky stopped at the bar gate and turned. "Any big winners? Anything Little Johnny should know about up front?"

Sal could feel his head turning, right to left, right to left. "Nothing to speak of, Nicky."

"It's the rain," Nicky said, as he sat on his barstool. "People don't like to gamble on rainy days."

Sal came out of the office with his overcoat on and his collar turned up. Hadey the whore was back at her seat, both hands wrapped purposefully around a fresh drink. She wouldn't look at him.

"Hey, Sal!" Jimmy Van shouted. "Where you going, man?"

"He's got an important appointment," Nicky sneered. "Mr. Entertainment."

"Who the fuck gonna tend bar?" Junior barked.

"*You* are!" Nicky laughed, and Jimmy and Dago Red joined him.

Sal passed through the bar gate and folded it down gently. The door to outside seemed a hundred yards away.

"Thanks again, Nicky," Sal said cheerily as he buttoned his overcoat and moved toward the door.

Nicky made a throwaway gesture with his hand. "Getoutta-here, musician!"

"Watch this! Watch this!" Dago Red pointed at the television. "This is where he does it."

"That's another fucking picture," Junior persisted.

"*Watch!*"

The telephone on the bar rang. Sal froze, turned, and watched Nicky answer it. He turned back and opened the door. A gust of cold wet wind almost tore it from his hand.

"Jesus, would'ju lookit that rain," Jimmy Van said.

"Aw *shit!*" Sandra the yellow-blond whore cursed. "Red, they ain't gonna be no parade in weather like this!"

Junior Venezia popped a fresh ice cube into his mouth and mumbled around it. "The navy, they could stop this in a New York minute, they wanted to."

Sal stopped outside and closed the door behind him. The

wind off the river stabbed at his face like an ice pick, drove each raindrop like buckshot. Sal leaned into the icy wind, hunched his shoulders, and hurried away down St. Charles Avenue.

The wet got under his collar and ran down his neck. He threw his arm up at a taxi slushing by, but the cabbie already had a fare and didn't even look at him. A streetcar at the end of the block, its bell ringing sadly in the rain, was just moving away down St. Charles. By the time he got across the wide street, he was soaked. The rain squished in his shoes, and his toes were already numb from the cold. He stopped under the overhanging marquee of a burned-out movie theater and tried to light a cigarette. His hands shook as he held the match. He sucked on the cigarette and got absolutely no flavor from it, then tunneled his fists into his pockets and looked up and down the wet street.

He felt a giddy light-headedness, a sense of release, like an animal let out of a cage. He had gotten away from the Sporting Life alive. But what the fuck was he going to do now? What options did he have? What were his choices? He had until eight or nine o'clock to raise $180,000. *No big deal, huh? Piece of fucking cake. Yeah, you right.*

Shit, he couldn't even rob a fucking bank, he thought grimly. It was a fucking Sunday.

That's right, he told himself. *Keep your sense of humor. You'll find a way out of this, just don't lose your sense of humor.*

Sal sucked on the tasteless butt and watched the rain try to drown St. Charles Avenue, and he had absolutely no idea what to do next. Where does a lifelong loser go to raise 180 big ones? And what's a loser's life worth anyway? Very fucking little. It's just one more thing for him to lose. Another bad bet.

Lightning arced across the low slate-gray sky, and Sal flinched and heard himself make a frightened sound. It embarrassed him. Thunder rumbled over the cold, wet city. Sal stared at the dirty, clouded water rushing in the gutter and knew deep inside himself that he didn't have the stomach for whatever it was going to take to extricate himself from this trap he had sprung on himself. He was a lover, not a fighter, and the next few hours were going to take a helluva lot of fighting if he was ever going to see sunshine on the Mississippi again.

Another streetcar appeared like a ghost out of the distant rain. It shimmied down the tracks like something from a silent movie.

With a quick flick of his fingers Sal tossed away the hot-boxed Marlboro. It was a soggy mess before it hit the pavement. Sal buttoned the top button of his overcoat, turned up the collar, steeled himself with a resigned sigh, and ran out into the rainy street toward the streetcar tracks.

Vanda Maxwell was doing her makeup when the doorbell rang. "*Shit!*" she said aloud, and continued carefully lining her eyes with a soft violet pencil. Vanda Maxwell had started using makeup at the age of thirteen, much to her churchgoing mother's displeasure, and ever since, for her whole life, she had spent at least an hour and a half each day rouging, plucking, outlining, accentuating, highlighting, painting, lipsticking, pancaking, powdering, shadowing, brushing, glossing, and otherwise enhancing what she had been born with. If anyone had ever bothered to ask Vanda what she had actually *done* with her life, besides having had the good sense to marry and divorce Charlie Maxwell before the luxury-car market in Chicago went into the toilet, if anyone had ever wanted to know what she had learned from life, she would have to answer that she knew how to make up her face. That was the one thing she had really mastered. And the older she became, the more practice she got at it, since it took her longer and longer each year to make herself presentable.

The doorbell rang again.

"Shit! Shit! *Shit!*" She threw her eyeliner angrily onto the top of her vanity. For a ten-thousand-dollar annual condo fee the Pontchartrain Towers had a doorman who was supposed to phone ahead and announce visitors, not let them just wander up the fucking halls and knock right on the fucking door.

She started to rise from her chair, then saw something in the mirror she didn't like, reached for a wadded-up Kleenex, and began to slowly caress the area just below her left eye.

The doorbell.

"*Fuck!*" Now, she was angry. Would Picasso have suffered these kinds of interruptions? Does Joyce Carol Oates?

"All right, all right. I'm *coming!*" And so were the Carvers, the Steiners, and the Duplesses, who were bringing with them that delicious young man who was redesigning their weekend place across the lake in Covington. Jeannine had seen Vanda hungrily eyeing him last week at the Le Blancs' Sunday brunch. New Orleanians were so good that way. Backward in all too many areas, but totally tolerant of depravity.

Now, there were *knocks,* for Chrissakes. Someone was *knocking* on her door. Someone was going to pay for this.

And then Vanda froze. Maybe it was the Duplesses. Maybe Jeannine had gotten the times wrong. Maybe that beautiful young architect was right there, just on the other side of her door, and she *hadn't even finished her makeup yet.*

My God, what time was it? A little after four. Hadn't she told Jeannine to be here at five, five-fifteen? Surely—

"Vanda?" a voice said through the door. "Vanda?"

It took her a moment, and then she placed it, sighed, and answered, "Salvatore? Is that you, Salvatore?"

Once while she was still married to Charlie, she had spent a summer alone in Rome, and had taken young Italian lovers by the *handful,* as she liked to joke. The little conceit of calling Sal *Salvatore,* with what she mistakenly thought was an authentic accent, was her way of trying to relive that summer, fifteen years ago, when she had been fifteen years younger. And it made Sal seem more romantic, more exotic, more than just a third-rate Bourbon Street musician.

She still had made no move to open the door, even though her hand rested loosely on the knob.

"Salvatore?"

"For Chrissakes, Vanda, open the fucking door, would ya? I gotta talk to you."

"This is not a good time, lover."

"You don't know the half of it," Sal's voice came through the wood.

"I have guests coming, honey."

"Vanda, I gotta talk to you. Let me in."

"Salvatore."

"Vanda."

She put her eye to the peephole and squinted.

"Jesus, lover!" she breathed, and then turned the doorknob and drew open the door. He stood there, drenched, dripping onto the hall carpet. There was already a stain.

"My God, lover. You look like someone threw you in the river."

He shot her a dark stare. "And when did you become psychic?" Then he pushed by her into the apartment. She followed, horrified.

"Salvatore, you can't come in here now. Look, you're leaving fucking *puddles* on the flokati. Lover, don't you know better than to go out into the damn rain?"

He turned to face her. His dark hair was plastered to his skull. "Vanda, I'm in trouble."

She stared at him a moment, then broke into nervous titters. "Don't tell me you're pregnant, honey?"

"Vanda—"

"Come into the bedroom, lover." She was already moving away from him. "I think you left some clothes here from last time. And I have to finish my makeup." Sal followed her, stripping off his soggy coat. "But you can only stay for a minute. I haven't even done my eyes yet."

In the bedroom she watched as he finished undressing while she threw sideways glances at her face in the mirror, turning it this way and that. "Lover, you really picked a bad time for an unannounced visit. I have some friends in town for the Mardi Gras. They're going to be here in less than an hour, and you're going to have to be gone."

Sal was stepping out of his underwear. It was heavy with moisture. He gathered up his clothes and held them before him, looking around helplessly.

"Give me those," she said with an edge of irritation in her voice. "Jesus, Salvatore, they're *soaked!*"

She took them from him and carried them back to the small bathroom just behind her bed. They *plopped* when she dropped them into the tub. When she came back into the bedroom, Sal had lit a cigarette—*one of hers!*—and was sitting naked on the edge of her bed. She gave him a long, hard look, then went into her walk-in and came out with a dry towel, a pair of jeans, and a heavy flannel shirt he had left there on an earlier visit. She tossed them beside him on the bedspread.

"You're going to *have* to dress and get out of here, lover," she said as she settled down onto her vanity stool, getting back to her life's work.

He dragged deeply on the cigarette, staring out at a point in space, making no move to dress, to get out.

She watched him in her mirror, the eyeliner pencil held poised in her hand.

"Salvatore—"

"Vanda, you gotta help me. I'm in deep shit."

She sighed deeply and continued at her makeup.

"Lover, really, can't we talk about this some other time—"

"No—"

"—because I have to finish my makeup—"

"—we can't—"

"—and get dressed before my—"

"—it's gotta be—"

"—guests arrive."

"—now, Vanda."

"*Lover!* Now be reasonable. I have people coming over."

She looked at him then, in the mirror, and while she watched, he started to cry. He sat naked on the edge of her mattress and started to cry softly.

Oh, Christ, she thought. *Men are such little boys.* That's what her friend Janet in Chicago always used to say to her. Men are such little boys. Except when they're being big assholes. Janet in Chicago had made her fortune from a big asshole in furs.

I really don't have time for this. I've got to get him out of here.

Vanda got up from her vanity and walked over to the bed. She put her hands on the back of Sal's head and gently pulled him to her. He opened her Japanese robe and rested his face against her soft, ample breasts and cried.

"Lover," Vanda soothed. "What *is* the matter?"

He buried his face in her flesh and shook his head, sobbing softly. Vanda stroked his dark, damp hair and looked at the clock beside her bed.

"Lover. It can't be that bad. Tell Vanda about it." *And quickly.*

Sal looked up at her. Tears glistened in his eyes, trailed down the heavy five o'clock shadow on his cheeks.

"Vanda, I'm in a lot of trouble."

She picked up the fluffy blue towel from the bedspread and began to rub it caressingly across his shoulders, down his chest. Sal's body had always delighted her. It was his *mind* that she constantly found lacking.

"It can't be that bad, lover."

Sal took the towel away from her and held both her hands in his.

"It is."

Enough of this, she thought. *I have people coming.*

"So tell me, Salvatore."

He stared deeply into her eyes. "Vanda, I need some money."

She kept her composure; she didn't even blink. Her face was a study in concern, of well-meaning goodwill, but something inside of her died a little and began to stiffen like a corpse.

"I need a lot of money, Vanda."

She traced his face with her fingertips, smiling down at him. Then she dropped her hand to her side and walked to the curtains. She opened them with the curtain-pull and gazed out the floor-to-ceiling window at the city below her. From up here, on the twenty-seventh floor, New Orleans was an Old World city, neatly divided into sections, neighborhoods, quarters. Black and white. Old, new, rich, and poor. Canal Street, the Vieux Carré, the Garden District. The rain had almost stopped for the moment, and the end of the day was bathing the city in that cold delta gray that New Orleans lives in for most of the winter.

"Vanda—"

Janet in Chicago had a saying for any event, and this one would have been no different. Eventually, Janet used to tell her, eventually the pretty ones *always* ask for money. But knowing that it happened to everyone didn't make the hurt any easier to take. Vanda felt a strong, survivalistic urge to put on makeup.

She turned away from the window, back to Sal. Her smile was wide and warm.

"I don't have it, lover."

Sal looked at her a long time. Then he said, "Vanda, this is serious shit."

"Lover, I can't give you what I haven't—"

"Lissen, this is life and death."

"Salvatore, I *told* you I took a beating in the market last year. I'm practically penniless. You know that."

Sal sighed heavily, his hands gripping the bedspread. "Vanda, I haven't even told you how much I need."

Vanda stared at Sal, sitting naked on her quilted bedspread, dribbling ashes on her floor from one of *her* cigarettes, and she noticed for the first time how short he was. Or maybe it wasn't for the first time. Her eyes flicked over his dark, hairy body, and a gentle wave of nausea swept over her. He was out of shape, and around his waist there was the beginning of what Janet used to call an "inner tube." He was a short, uneducated, powerless little nothing of a man, and he was asking her for money because he had made love to her. She was displeased with Sal, and she was disgusted with herself. Until now she had managed to avoid one of these cheap, pathetic scenes. In fact, she had dreaded the very *idea* of one. She had thought she wouldn't have to deal with a situation like this until she was well into her fifties, and here she was, confronted with a pitiful little sobbing gigolo, and her not even forty-five. Oh, well, another girlish illusion shot to hell.

Vanda tied a quick overhand knot in the sash of her silk kimono and pulled it tightly around her waist. She looked away from Sal and shook her head.

"Lover, I just don't have it." She strode straight-backed to the vanity, sat down, and again picked up the eyeliner pencil. "You're going to *have* to leave, Salvatore. I really do have guests on the way."

"A hundred and eighty thousand," Sal said quickly, his eyes boring into hers in the mirror's reflection.

What is this? Vanda asked herself. *What's happening here? Is this some kind of shoddy shakedown?*

"Or," Sal continued, "some people are going to kill me."

Now, she was becoming more and more alarmed. What kind of dim-witted scam was Sal trying to effect? A hundred eighty thousand dollars? Why, she was surprised the little guinea could even *imagine* that sum of money. What else was growing like a fungus in that soggy cerebellum? Was he capable of violence? Oh, God, it was all so tawdry, so common, so—so—so *New Orleans.* Vanda wished she could discuss it with Janet Handley in Chicago. She would know what to do. Janet had never approved of Vanda's wintering in the Crescent City. "If you *have* to go away, Vee," she could hear Janet lecture, "go to Palm Springs, or Key West, or Half Moon Bay, even, but why New *Orleans?* Not New *Orleans.* For godsake."

"I'm not joking, Vanda. If I don't raise the money, they're gonna fucking *murder* me."

Vanda wouldn't look at him. She was outlining her left eye again and again. She could hear the clock ticking on her bedside table.

"Vanda, *please*."

"There is no way," she said almost absently as she continued to apply the eyeliner, "that I can give you that kind of money."

Sal was off the bed like a shot. "Well, how much *can* you give me?" he asked hopefully.

Vanda sighed. She carefully put down the eyeliner stick on the vanity's crowded glass surface. She swiveled on the stool and looked coldly at him.

"I mean," Sal was sputtering, "maybe I can hold them off if I can—"

"I have no intention of giving you a penny—"

"Vanda, you don't understand—"

"—not a dollar—"

"*—they're gonna fucking kill me!*" Sal screamed at her.

I've got to handle this correctly, she thought. *What would Janet do now? My God, he's* shouting *at me.*

Maintain your dignity, she told herself. *Don't let him think he's your equal. Even if on numerous occasions he did ejaculate on your tongue.*

"I think you'd better leave, Mr. D'Amore," she said evenly, in her best reprimanding-the-gardener tone.

"Vanda," Sal pleaded, "don't do this to me, please. I need your help."

My God, Vanda thought, suddenly shocked. *He's not getting dressed because he thinks his nakedness will entice me, influence me. How low have I sunk?*

"I didn't invite you here today, Mr. D'Amore. And people to whom I *have* tendered an invitation should be arriving any moment." Make sure he understands that. "So, I strongly suggest you dress and leave. *Now.*" But be compassionate. "I don't want a scene."

He was suddenly close to her, leaning over, his face inches from hers.

"It would only be a loan, Vanda. Just enough money to keep them off my back, and I know I'll be able to pay you back in a month or so. Maybe even a few weeks."

She shook her head. This was *so* pathetic. The man didn't make fourteen thousand a year. Even by depressed New Orleans standards he was a pauper.

"It's impossible."

He stared at her a moment. *Look at him,* she thought. *You can actually* see *his mind working. He has the thought processes of a child. What did I ever see in this little man? A pretty face? A hard cock? True, he was a good lover, but he couldn't even be called young anymore. I'm going to* have *to stop drinking so much. It gets me in the strangest situations.*

"Salvatore, please don't—"

"Look," Sal said excitedly, as if he had just made a momentous decision, "I'll give you half of what I'm gonna make in my life off my music."

She simply stared at him, not quite knowing what to say. He mistook it as interest.

"Yeah, look, that's what we'll do." He began to pull on his jeans. "I read where lots of songwriters did that. When they was just getting started, before they got their break. I hate doing it—I mean, my music is, well, you know how important my songs are to me, but, shit, I'm in a bad fucking spot, Vanda, and if you give me the hundred and eighty thousand, I'll sign over to you half of whatever I make for the rest of my career."

He stopped abruptly, a little breathless, and his eyes danced with expectation.

She had to suppress an urge to giggle. The whole situation was *so* laughable. A short, pathetic middle-aged high school dropout, half-drowned and half-naked, standing in her bedroom trying to sell her half of a nonexistent Brooklyn Bridge. This had to be handled carefully, carefully and correctly, and she decided that bluntness would be the best avenue.

"Sal," she said finally, no longer finding the Italianate affectation tasteful, "you don't *have* a career."

"Vanda—"

"You're a barroom piano player—"

"—listen—"

"—and not even a very good one."

"What about my songs, my singing? We sat right out there many a night—" he pointed at the open door that led back to the living room with the Steinway six-footer—"and I played my shit for you and you said it was great; you said you loved my stuff; you were gonna help me get a break, invest in me, be my manager and take me to New York—"

"Sal—"

"—or L.A. What were you—lying to me?" His voice was louder now, indignant even. This was getting out of hand, Vanda thought.

"Didn't you say you liked my songs? You said you loved my songs. What were you, *conning* me?"

How dare *you,* she fumed silently. *How fucking* dare *you.*

"You said you were gonna put up some money and produce an album of my music."

Fighting to keep her voice calm and even, she said, "I said you had talent, that's all. I said we *might* someday do something together."

Sal glared at her like a small boy denied his dessert. "So?"

She had had enough of this. Her rage rose to the surface like blood to a cut. "It was *pillow talk,* for Chrissakes. We *fucked,* and then we drank some wine and blew some grass and you played a few stupid songs in the moonlight and I told you they were pretty, oh, so lovely." She was on her feet now, towering over him in her high heels. She had endured entirely enough of this farce. The woman who had taken Charlie Maxwell to the cleaners for three quarters of his fucking fortune wasn't about to be pushed around by a stupid small-time New Orleans *piano player,* by God. "I seem to remember telling you you were a great fuck, too!" She was shouting now. "You didn't believe that, too? At best, you were barely mediocre. Much like your singing."

"You bitch," he said softly.

"You'd better believe it. And did you really think you were going to walk in here and talk me out of a single penny to bail you out of whatever trouble you're in? Did you? What is it, another gambling debt? A couple of months ago when you were whimpering around here about how you needed seven thousand dollars to get out of—what did you call it?—a *jackpot.* I told you then I couldn't help you. I told you never to ask me for money, didn't I? What makes you think that now I'm going to give you a hundred and eighty thousand?"

"I'm not asking you to *give* me the money," he shouted back at her. "We'll draw up a contract right here in this room, on a piece of paper, and I'll sign over half of what I make with my singing and songwriting for the rest of my life."

She smiled sadly and shook her head. "Sal," she said finally, "you are *so* fucking stupid."

"Vanda—" There was panic in Sal's voice now. "Vanda, I really need your help. I don't have anywhere else to go."

"Then you don't have anywhere at all to go. Except out of here." She gestured in the direction of the apartment's entrance door. "My guests will be here any minute and I—"

As if on cue the doorbell chimed.

"Shit! *Fuck!*" Her eyes flashed angrily. *"I haven't finished my makeup!"* Her tone left no question that she blamed that omission on Sal. She snatched up his shirt and shoes and threw them at him. "For Chrissakes, Sal, get out of here." She was pushing him, directing him out of the bedroom, through the hallway, and into the kitchen. The doorbell rang again. *"Fuck! Fuck! Fuck!"* she hissed, then called out in a sweet singsong, "I'll be right there." She shoved Sal through the kitchen door, and they were standing on the bold Italian tile floor. They had fucked doggie-style on this floor once, while a pizza disintegrated into a cinder in the microwave.

Sal clutched at the butcher-block chopping table and turned to face her. Vanda prodded angrily at him.

"Sal! *Sal!*" she threatened in a low, cold mutter. "Get out of my apartment!"

He took hold of both of her shoulders and pulled her close. Their faces were inches apart.

"Vanda," he explained softly, "if you don't give me something, *anything,* to pay them off, Vanda, I swear to Jesus Christ they'll kill me. They'll kill me, and they'll take their time doing it. Do you understand what I'm saying?"

"Sal," she snapped, and her eyes were ice picks, "it's not my problem."

"Vanda," a woman's voice called from the outside hall.

"I don't have anywhere else to go. I don't know anyone else with that kind of money."

"Vanda!" the woman's voice rang out cheerily. "Guess who this is, and guess who I have with me."

Vanda actually smiled when she turned her head and chimed, "Just a moment, Jeannine. I'll be right there." But when she whirled back at Sal, her face was ugly and tight. "Get out." She measured out each word and snipped it off. "Get—out—of—my—apartment."

"Vanda, for Chrissakes, it's not like I'm a fucking stranger off the street. We *meant* something to each other." He looked at her soulfully. "Vanda, I love you."

Inside, she seethed. *You bastard. You* bastard. *Do you really think I'll be swayed by that? Do you really think I'm so old and desperate that all you have to do is say those three words and I'll do anything you want?*

"Hey, in there. How long are you going to leave us out here?"

She smiled at Sal then. She raised her hand, slipped her fingers through his thick, damp hair. "I love you, too, Salvatore," she breathed. Then she pressed her open mouth against his and her tongue darted in around his teeth, under his lips, across his gums. Then she broke the kiss abruptly and guided him gently toward the back kitchen door that led to the service hall and emergency stairwell. "Here, lover," she promised as she reached for her purse on the cabinet top by the refrigerator. She dug around in the purse for a few moments, then opened the back door with her left hand and with her right pressed a wad of bills into Sal's fist. The service hall was cold and lined with garbage cans. She led Sal into it and pecked him lightly on the cheek and stepped back inside. "Take care, lover," she said, and closed the door in his face. He heard her lock it. Then, "Coming, Jeannine. *Coming!* My God, I haven't even had a chance to do my makeup!" Her voice trailed away as she left the kitchen. Sal stood in the cold hall and stared down at the wad of bills in his hand. Then he slowly peeled them apart and counted them. There were shouts and squeals of delight from inside the apartment, then a man's deep voice, then loud, happy laughter. A hundred thirty-two dollars. For no good reason, Sal counted it all again. Three twenties, five tens, four fives, and two singles. There was more faraway laughter from inside the apartment, and then another man's voice, not the first one but a younger one, saying, "How could you improve that face? You look *mah-vah-less.*" Then more laughter. And Vanda's silken purr. "Lover, why don't you fix us all a drink. I *need* one."

Sal jammed the bills into the pocket of his jeans, then picked up one of the dented garbage cans lining the wall, raised the empty metal can over his head, and rammed it down hard on the kitchen's service door. It made a loud, hollow *clang* and left a gouge in the back door's wood. Sal banged it down again, and again and again. Clang! Clang! Clang! Clang!

In the complete, stunned silence that followed, Sal could hear himself breathing. Then he screamed out, "*Cunt! Selfish old cunt!* Fucking you was like screwing my *grandmother!* You made me wanna *puke!*" Sal stopped shouting for a second and listened to the absolute lack of sound coming from behind the battered door.

What are you doing? he asked himself. *What good is this gonna do?*

They're gonna kill me, he told himself. *They're gonna kill me, and she could've helped me. She could've helped me, but she wouldn't, and now I am good as dead.*

"Dear God, Vanda," he heard a woman in the apartment softly gasp. "Who on earth—"

"*Fuck you!*" Sal bellowed as loudly as he could, then he flung the garbage can against the gouged door, turned, and ran down the short, cluttered hall, slammed through the heavy emergency door, and clattered down the concrete service stairway.

He had pounded down almost ten flights before he could make himself stop. Running, running away, running anywhere, was beginning to seem like the only option he had. It was an instinct that was growing stronger and stronger in his mind.

Leaning against the cool, moist cement wall of the service stairwell, he could feel his blood pounding in his head.

Funny, he said to himself, *I didn't think a dead man could have a pulse.*

That's good. That's the way. Keep that sense of humor. You're gonna need it.

Like that shit comic in the Sho-Bar used to say. You can get more with a kind word . . . and a gun. Well, from now on he was gonna need a keen sense of humor . . . and $180,000.

Forget that, Sal thought. *I'd be better off with the gun.*

No, forget *that.* Don't be *that* stupid.

He sat down on the stairs and covered his face with his

hands. Which, he noticed, were shaking violently. And it wasn't that cold in here. What, oh what the fuck, was he gonna do now? Sung to the tune of "Where, Oh, Where Has My Little Dog Gone?" You folks in the back join in next time the chorus comes around.

He was losing it, he realized. He was losing control the way he'd lost everything else. He was already giving in to the terror, and it was only—he glanced at his watch—six-fifteen. By ten o'clock things should be heating up pretty good.

Jesus Christ, what the fuck *was* he going to do? Couldn't anything his whole fucking life go right? How many bad hands can one bastard be dealt? Why do some guys fall in shit and come out smelling like perfume, and hard-luck cases like himself struggle all their lives and never have things go their way, never get two nickels to rub together? Christ, this morning, just a few hours ago, he had been on top of the world. Seventy-five, eighty thousand ahead. He had had a big breakfast at Montalbano's on Bourbon Street and had tipped Teresha a hundred dollars. His case hundred. "It's a fucking Sunday, T.," he had told her. "You and me, we shouldn't have to work on a fucking Sunday." A wide white grin had creased her wide black face, and she had answered, "Look like somebody been booking a coupla winners, huh, Sal?" He had smiled back up at her. "A couple? Try a whole slew of the motherfuckers, T.," and they had laughed happily together.

Now look at me, Sal thought bitterly. *One bad bet, one fucking loser, and I'm begging cold, ugly old Yankee cunts for money. One wrong pick and I'm hiding on the servants' stairs, trying to—*

On the floor below him someone opened a door and stepped into the stairwell. Sal stood up quickly and pressed tightly against the wall. It had to be house security. Vanda must've called them. And probably complained that there was some crazed prowler she had never met banging on her service door. Sal flattened his back against the damp wall and held his breath. Heavy heels scuffed tentatively against concrete, coming up a few steps. Maybe it wasn't security, the thought suddenly struck Sal. Maybe it was the Venezias. Maybe they had followed him over all the way from the Sporting Life. Sal's breath seemed to freeze in his lungs, and his pulse was *really* pounding now. Someone took another slow, careful step up the stairs—*he's hunting for me!*—and moved in front of the light source and a narrow, elongated shadow fell on the wall below. Sal stared down at it, terrified. It looked like the image of a monster from a thirties horror movie. The shadow stopped, and Sal could feel someone listening, listening, in the dim, echoey stairwell. Sal didn't move, didn't breathe. The moment seemed to last forever, flattened and stretched into an Einsteinian eternity. Then, as he watched, the shadow turned and retreated heavily down the steps. The massive fireproof emergency door slowly settled shut, and Sal waited a full half-minute before he exhaled in a rush with a sound like a bad exhaust pipe.

"Jesus *Christ,*" he whispered aloud, and then thought, *What the fuck was that? Just* what *the fuck was that?*

I'm losing it. I'm fucking falling apart. I'm coming to pieces.

Don't worry about it, he told himself. *If you don't do a very good job, the Venezias will finish it for you.*

That's it, asshole. Keep that sense of humor. You really are gonna need it. Need it bad.

He pushed himself away from the wall and started down the stairs, buttoning his shirt.

Outside, on Canal Street, the rain had stopped. The night had fallen completely, and although the wind had died down to a whisper, the air was wet and cold. The streetlights were on, and the Mardi Gras decorations twinkled and shone, purple and gold. City workers in watch caps and down jackets were stringing crowd-control cables along the sidewalks and the neutral ground, which everywhere else in the world is called a median strip. Sal buttoned the collar of his Pendleton shirt and humped his shoulders against the cold. His breath blew out before him in white plumes as he stood on the banquette and watched the workers pull and lock the cable. They were going to roll that parade tonight after all. *Sandra will be* so *happy,* Sal thought bitterly.

Remembering the Crayola-haired whore seemed to clear Sal's mind. Man, where was he gonna go next? He had to do *something*. He couldn't stand here freezing his nuts off while the little time he had left just slipped away. What fucking time *was* it? Six twenty-seven. Only about three-and-a-half more hours until Albert Castiglia and whoever he brought with him blew into the Sporting Life asking for his money. Over a quarter of a million. *What a surprise* that's *gonna be,* Sal thought. All the way around.

The idea propelled Sal into movement. He crossed Canal heading downtown, looking for a cab. Three-and-a-half more hours. To raise $180,000. Shouldn't be too hard to do for a guy who'd never had more than two pairs of shoes at the same time his whole fucking life. *A hundred and eighty thousand dollars.* He kept repeating it in his mind, the way this spaced-out chick singer from California he used to ball would chant her mantra over and over: *numm yoo ring he ko. One hundred and eighty thousand. Numm yoo ring he ko. One hundred and eighty thousand.* Maybe he could make it some kind of prayer, he thought. Like his aunt Lena kneeling by the statues and flickering candles in her dim, shuttered bedroom, making a novena, praying softly to Saint Joseph all day long, for days on end, until she would proudly show everyone her bruised, inflamed knees. Then, maybe a week later, she would smile and tell everybody that her request had been granted. *Can't tell you what it is, 'cuz that would break the novena, and that's very bad luck.* Maybe it was like that. Maybe if he kept saying *one hundred and eighty thousand, one hundred and eighty thousand* constantly, continually, for the next three-and-a-half hours, maybe somehow he'd come up with the money, maybe somehow the money would find *him.*

Man, he said to himself, *you really are losing it. You've already lost it. You're hoping for fucking* miracles *now. That's how bad it's gotten. Jesus.* Jesus.

Just then a single whip of wind lashed down the long, narrow corridor that was Dauphine Street. Sal shuddered, and his teeth clattered against each other, and he quickened his steps. He was in the Quarter now. The heart of Venezia territory. A dangerous place to be for Salvatore Christopher D'Amore. Maybe even lethal. Sal turned up the collar of his plaid flannel shirt and shivered as he moved along, surveying the two- and three-story buildings that lined both sides of the dark street. He had grown up not far from here, had played in these streets as a child, had lost his cherry in a narrow alley just like that one over there, had smoked his first joint on a third-floor veranda trellised by ornamental ironwork exactly like the verandas on every one of these buildings. These shadowy one-way streets had been his home for all of his thirty-eight years; indeed, he could count on one hand the few times he had been outside the city limits of Orleans Parish, and then never more than fifty or a hundred miles away for a one-nighter. And yet, tonight, with the cold winter wind blowing down these archaic streets designed for buggies and horse-drawn coaches, watching the few pedestrians huddling home from whatever fleshy pursuits French Quarterites practiced on Sunday, with music bleeding out into the air from every bar he passed, with a halo of dampness around each touristy street-lamp, Sal felt he was lost, an alien from another world, set down in this nineteenth-century city on this twentieth-century night. It was a little like the feeling he had had this afternoon, the moment after he and the horse Transformer had lost the un-losable race. When everything had looked so different to him, changed and threatening. The hit he was getting off the street now—he could almost feel it coming up through the soles of his shoes as he moved briskly along—the message he was receiving was that he was a stranger here, an outsider, an outcast. This place wasn't home anymore. Sal felt it as strongly as he had felt anything his whole life. This place wasn't home, and that meant that he had no home, because he didn't know anywhere else, had never even been anywhere else.

A cab was passing him then, sloshing gutter water up on the banquette, and Sal sidestepped before he realized the cab was empty and the cabbie was eyeing him hopefully. Sal's hand shot up, and the driver braked hard and angled over to the curb. He leaned over his seat and opened the back door from the inside. Sal got in and pulled the cab door closed behind him.

"Fuckin' cold," the cabbie said, with a Caribbean accent.

Sal rubbed his arms and felt the warmth of the overheated cab. "Yeah."

"You catch pneumonia goin' round with just a shirt, mon," the cabbie warned.

Sal looked at him and nodded. *Where am I?* he thought. *Where am I?*

"But at least it stopped the raining for a while," the driver said as he turned back to his wheel and put the car in gear. The cab started moving slowly down Dauphine.

"Where to, mon?" The driver's eyes flicked over him in the rearview.

Where? Where? Where am I going? Where is there left to go?

The cabbie's dark eyes probed his in the mirror.

"You got a destination, brother?"

Where to? Sal thought. *Who can help me now?*

The cabbie reached over and flipped his flag. He was still studying Sal in the rearview.

"You want me to just drive ar—"

"Esplanade and Decatur," Sal blurted out. "Drop me off at the corner of Esplanade and Decatur."

The cabbie smiled thankfully. People need order in their life. "Very good, brother. Very good."

"Sal!" Cathy Pecoraro exclaimed as she opened the door. "You didn't tell us you was gonna pass by." She stepped back away from the door, turned her head, and shouted, "Santo! Everybody! Sally's here." She turned back to Sal. "You shoudda told us, Sal. And you shouldn't be running around without no coat." She took his arm and led him into the house. Into the ground-floor apartment of one of the ancient three-stories-and-an-attic converted mansions that lined Esplanade Avenue from the river to City Park. She stopped just inside the tiny entrance hall. "You shoudda told us you was coming, but that's all right. You hungry? You want something to eat?" She turned again toward the sound of the television in the next room. "Hey! You guys! Whadid I tell you? Sal's here!" Then there was the pounding of childish heels on hardwood floors, and Sal was surrounded by three boys under the age of ten who snaked around Sal's legs and tugged at his sleeves.

"Uncle Sal, where yat?"

"How ya doin'?"

"Where yat, Uncle Sal?"

Usually Sal pretended to wrestle and box with the kids, but tonight all he could manage was a weak, "Hey, you guys, what's happenin'? You all get bigger every time I see you."

"That's 'cuz you don't see us very offen," piped up Dominic, the oldest, and Cathy gave Sal the fish-eye, as if to say, Hey, it ain't me. Listen to the kid.

Sal rolled his eyes back at her. Gimme a break, Cat.

Cathy and the boys were leading him through the front dining room. There were empty glasses and tomato-sauce-smeared plates sitting contentedly on the big ancient black table, and the apartment vibrated with the familiar, comfortable, garlicky odors of American-Sicilian cooking. "I'm gonna get you something to eat," Cathy confided, as if entrusting him with a special secret.

"Cathy, no, I—"

The boys ran ahead of them, shouting, "Daddy, Uncle Sal's here."

"So"—Cathy gave him a coquettish smile—"you didn't mention my new *do.* That means you don't like it." She gave her medium-length platinum-blond hair a girlish fluff.

"Cathy, I'm sorry. I was going to. It looks great, really great."

She shook her head with that sly, sad smile. "You don't mention, that means you don't like."

When Sal first met Cathy Becker Pecoraro, almost seventeen years ago, she was a stripper at the Fools Rush Inn on Bourbon Street. Actually she had started out as a teenaged tap dancer, but the audience for that particular art form hadn't survived the forties, much less made it into the seventies. So Cathy had given her young naked body a long, qualitative examination in her mother's big tailor's mirror, found herself not unsuitable for "exotic dancing," bought a secondhand beaded gown for three hundred dollars, and went out and got herself a gig. And to her total amazement, she discovered that taking her clothes off onstage for an audience of men who would, during those twelve or fifteen minutes that she pranced around before them under the colored lights, do almost anything for her—she found that surge of erotic, feminine power totally satisfying. She was a feminist's nightmare; she actually *enjoyed* being a sex object. But only onstage, only for showtime. When she wasn't working, she transformed into what the other girls called a Virgin Mary, meaning she wouldn't blow the wiseguys who owned the joint, wouldn't B-drink at the bar, wouldn't turn tricks with the horny tourists who sent waiters backstage with their room numbers scribbled on fifty-dollar bills. And she wouldn't eat pussy. For several years she was the only stripper on the Street who wasn't gay, or at least a switch-hitter. She was straight as an arrow, and the musicians and bartenders in all the clubs flocked around her like dogs to a scent, took her to breakfast, bought her presents. That's when she'd met Santo. Santo was still playing drums then, in the last live girlie-show band on the Street, and booking acts out of his house—this apartment—in the afternoons. He was still married to Gloria, his first wife, but everybody in town knew the bitch was crazy. Even Gloria's *mother* told Santo to leave her. That was all Santo needed to hear, because he had wanted Cat Ballou—her stage name—from the first moment he saw her. He pursued her continuously for three years—he shared his favorite records with her, hustled to get her high-paying bookings and refused to take commission, took her home to meet his family—and finally, disregarding the difference in their ages, she relented, dropped her other lovers, and moved in with Santo. By then Gloria, Santo's first wife, was in the nuthouse in Mandeville. Sometimes on Sundays Cathy packed a box lunch and they all went up to see her. Even now they were still trying to obtain an annulment from the Archdiocese, so they could repeat their vows in the Church.

"Santo, look what the cat drug in."

They were standing in a doorway, looking down into a small sunken den that glowed eerily with television-tube lighting. The boys had found their previous places on the floor in front of the set. On a tired-looking sofa against the back wall sat a large man in a bathrobe and down-at-the-heels slippers. He gave Sal exactly the same skeptical stare that his wife had moments before.

"You just missed supper." His voice was deep and matter-of-fact. "You shoudda called."

Cathy nodded self-righteously. "That's what I told him. I told him that."

"Hey. You guys. I'm not hungry."

Looking at her husband, Cathy said, "I'm gonna fix him something," as if Sal hadn't spoken at all.

Santo nodded. He was a heavy man with a wide, fleshy face that sported a spare, trim gray goatee that looked completely superfluous to anyone but those who knew him well.

"Siddown," Santo said, and pointed his bearded chin at the television. "I rented *Top Gun.* You ever see it?"

"He hates it," Cathy said, now leaning on the doorframe with her arms folded across her breasts. "He fucking hates it." She made the statement with a kind of pride.

"They ain't enough sex in it," Santo said.

Cathy shook her head and smiled. "Ain't that some shit?"

Santo crossed his bare legs and made a Romanesque gesture with his right hand. "I rent movies with lots of good straight sex in 'em. Men putting it to good-looking women. I want these little bastards here"—he indicated his sons with another point of his chin—"I want 'em to know where they supposed to put their peters with they grow up."

Cathy chuckled warmly and looked at Sal. "Sal, you believe this shit?"

"Hey," Santo said, "that's the frigging French Quarter right outside the front door. More faggots per square inch than anywhere in the country, 'cept maybe for San Francisco. I don't want these little bastards ever coming home with shit on their dicks or their assholes looking like a cauliflower 'cause their old man never showed them right from wrong."

The three little boys waved their heels in the air and grinned up at Sal, as if to say, You believe this shit?

Cathy made a *tsk-tsk* sound with her mouth, but her eyes were bright and happy. "I can't lissen to any more of this crap. I'm gonna go fix something for Sal."

"Make a plate for me, too, baby," Santo said to her.

She stared at him accusingly. "Man, you just finished eating supper."

"I know. I know. But I ain't full yet."

"Cat—" Sal tried to say.

"You *full* all right, but not with cavatoni." She turned to Sal. "Can you believe this shit?"

"Cat, you don't hafta—" Sal started to protest, but she was already gone, moving toward the kitchen in the back of the apartment.

"Siddown, Sal"—Santo patted the cushion beside him—"watch the rest of this piece of shit."

"Santo—"

"I'm telling you, fucking AIDS and everything, when each of these little bastards hits thirteen, just like the Jews give 'em a bar mitzvah, I'm gonna buy a hooker for 'em, the night of their birthday, lettum see the way things *s'pose* to be."

"Yeah, well," Dominic, the oldest boy, said from the floor, "you can get AIDS from hookers, too."

Santo shook his head at Sal. "Lissen the little bastards. They ain't even quit shitting yellow yet, they think they know everything."

"Santo, I gotta talk to you."

"*Siddown,* for Chrissakes. Wait till the end of the movie."

Sal moved over beside Santo, hovered over him. "Santo, I can't wait. I gotta talk to you now."

Santo looked up at him then, and studied his face. After a long while he said softly, "You motherfucker. You been gambling again."

"Santo—"

"And you *ain't* been winning."

"Santo, we gotta talk."

Santo stared into the television screen and sighed deeply. "Sally, Sally, Sally." He shook his head. Then he buried clenched fists into the yielding cushions of the sofa and bulldozed himself heavily to his feet. "If any sexy parts come on, I want you little bastards to watch it real close, maybe you'll learn something." The little boys smiled up at Sal. You believe this shit? Santo belted his bathrobe over his flaccid belly and put his meaty arm around Sal's shoulders. He towered over the smaller, younger man. "C'mon, we'll go into the office. Talk about this." He pointed down at his sons. "When your mama comes back in, tell her where we went."

Santo's office was a converted efficiency apartment directly across the cold, narrow, high-ceilinged entrance hall. There was a big, cluttered table that Santo used as a desk, some battered file cabinets, a few worn chairs arranged before the littered desk, and a tiny kitchen off to one side. Directly behind where Santo slumped into his big, cushiony chair was a huge, grainy, almost life-sized blowup of a young white boxer in a fighting stance. The boxer's black shoes and loose-fitting trunks dated the photograph to the thirties or early forties, and in fact the fighter was Santo's deceased father, Carlo, who, for some reason no one had ever properly explained to Sal, had fought under the name Billy O'Bannion. Carlo in 1929 had lost a split decision to a contender who had once been knocked out by Max Baer.

In sports-starved New Orleans, that exalted Carlo Pecoraro to the level of local legend. When he died in 1957, Rocky Marciano, Joe Lewis, and Jack Dempsey all sent telegrams.

Dominating the facing wall was another blown-up black-and-white, not as big as the other. This one was a posed glossy of a much-younger Santo in a white dinner jacket seated behind a sparkling set of Slingerland drums. Santo wore a show-bizzy smile and held crossed drumsticks over his ruffled chest, and his name was painted in slanted letters on his bass drumhead.

Every other available inch of wall space was covered by eight-by-tens of the various acts Santo had booked over the years. There seemed to be hundreds of them. Singers, magicians, acrobats, clowns, comics, strippers—there was a shot of Cathy smiling coyly from behind a beach ball—Dixieland bands, rock and roll bands, dance bands, lots of pictures of soul singers, male and female, from the late fifties and early sixties, when Santo's little record company had produced several national hits in a four-year span. Sal saw that, since the last time he'd visited, Santo had even put up a couple of publicity shots of DJs, now that the wedding market was going that way. And as he always did when he came into this room, Sal sought out and found the eight-by-ten of himself, just seventeen years old, pinned to the wall directly to the left of Carlo. He had had the shot taken in a fucking *Nehru* jacket, for Chrissakes, and Santo wouldn't change the picture, even though he had much newer shots somewhere in his file cabinets.

Santo was settled back into his creaking chair, lighting a big brown De Nobili and watching Sal over the flame.

"What the fuck you do now?" he finally growled.

Sal stood there. For some reason he felt he couldn't sit down. As if he didn't have the right. What time was it?

Santo eyed him. "What, you gonna make me *guess?*"

Santo Pecoraro had been Sal's first manager, when Sal was still in high school. Santo had heard Sal singing at a Saturday night dance at Sacred Heart, had come up to the bandstand and handed Sal his card. Later that night Sal had lost the card between the cushions in the backseat of his '51 Chevy while he was screwing Pup Bartola's little sister. He never knew her name, just "Pup Bartola's little sister." Sal lost the card and would have never thought about it again, except three weeks later Sal's band—the Gangsters—was playing a Sadie Hawkins dance at De La Salle, and on the second break, when the entire band had jammed into the drummer's old panel truck and was passing around a bottle of red wine and a joint of some hellacious Panamanian weed, Santo had knocked on the truck's door.

"Don't worry, I'm not a cop. I wanna talk to the singer. The little guy."

When Sal stuck his head out of the truck in a cloud of pungent smoke, Santo was leaning on the truck's fender.

"You didn't call me."

Sal climbed out of the truck. He stared at Santo and shrugged boyishly. "I forgot."

"You still got my card? My phone number?"

Sal scratched his arm absently. "I dunno. I think maybe I lost it."

Santo cocked his head and examined the boy. "You always get stoned on your breaks?"

Sal stared back; a glimmer of defiance had crept into his eyes. "Sometimes. So what?"

Santo chuckled. "Probably nothing. Maybe something. You Joe the Hack's kid, ain't you?"

Even though he fought it, Sal's face showed his embarrassment. He didn't answer.

"Look, kid," Santo continued, "my name's Santo Pecoraro. I book talent on Bourbon Street. And I have a record company. Maybe you heard of me." Santo paused for a moment, but Sal had nothing to say. "Anyway, I like your voice. You got a pretty good voice. Who you listen to, Sam Cooke?"

Sal shrugged again. "Well, sure, everybody likes Sam Cooke."

"You write songs?"

Sal was reticent. "Yeah, kinda."

"Kinda? How can you *kinda* write songs?"

"Well, I just started fooling around with it."

"Then you wrote some songs?"

"Well, yeah."

"Some you can play for me?"

Sal nodded almost imperceptibly.

"I'd like to hear them," Santo reached into his shirt and withdrew a handful of business cards. "Here." He handed them to Sal with a small smile. "Put one in each one of your pockets—in your pants, in your shirt, in your jacket—that way maybe you won't lose 'em all, and that way maybe you'll remember to give me a call tomorrow. Okay?"

The boy stared down at the little white rectangles. "You—you really think I'm good enough to make a record?"

Santo smiled down at the boy in the iridescent green tux jacket. "Give me a call tomorrow, kid—hey, what's your name?"

"Sal."

Santo frowned and scratched at his wispy goatee. He must have been *born* with that damn thing. "We gonna have to change that. Too guinea. Your last name's D'Amore, ain't it?"

Sal nodded. Santo thoughtfully furrowed his fingertips through his sparse crop of chin hairs. Then he grinned broadly. "I got an idea. Lissen, don't forget to call me tomorrow, will you?"

And then the school principal, Father Russo, came out of the back door of the cafeteria and said loudly in his faggy New York whine, "All right, boys. Break's over. Don't make me come find out whatcha doing in that truck."

And Sal's fellow band members came tumbling out of the old Plymouth, brushing ashes from their coats, tapping Sen Sen into their mouths, and eyeing Santo questioningly.

"Hey, kid," Santo called after Sal as the teenager followed the other players into the cafeteria-cum-auditorium, "don't lose my number. I got some ideas."

And he did. Have some ideas. He made Sal quit the Gangsters—not an easy thing for a teenage boy to do to his best friends; he listened to all Sal's songs and suggested how to make the best ones better; had Sal's hair styled in an ersatz Beatle pageboy; bought him some high-heeled boots and Mod clothes—including the Nehru jacket in the photograph; and changed Sal's name to Dee Amore. Sal hated the name, but Santo was adamant. And Sal acquiesced in short order; he was a seventeen-year-old boy in total awe of his newfound manager. As well he should have been: Less than a decade earlier Santo Pecoraro had discovered, financed, produced, engineered, and marketed six Top Twenty songs—one of which had gone to number two for a few weeks—and had been one of the chief architects of the "New Orleans Sound" that dominated R&B charts in the fifties. His successes were years behind him though, his money squandered by his crazy first wife's high living, and now Santo was trying to revive his flagging Bayou label by joining the "Paisley Revolution"—the hordes of young American club musicians in the late sixties who were scrambling to catch up with the invading Englishmen who had stolen their music and their thunder. Sal D'Amore was going to be Santo Pecoraro's first step on his climb back to the top of the recording industry. His first superstar in a whole stable of luminous New Orleans talent. But though neither he nor Sal knew it then, that first step would be a stumble. And there would be no second.

Under Santo's managership, Sal recorded seven singles—45 rpm's with an original song on each side. One of them, "She's the Only One I Want," the song the whore Hadey had remembered this afternoon in the Sporting Life, made it to the Top Ten in New Orleans and the surrounding parishes. And that was it. Nothing else. None of the other songs even cracked the charts. It didn't happen. It just didn't happen. Not that Santo didn't try, didn't work hard, didn't flog Dee Amore records the length and breadth of southern Louisiana. He booked Sal as the opening act for every touring Big Name Act that came to town. Vanilla Fudge, Sly and the Family Stone, the Young Rascals. Sal performed at a dozen venues every weekend—dances, shows, nightclubs—Santo personally chauffeuring him around New Orleans in his big white Eldorado, then standing in the back of the hall, nodding his head to the backbeat, judging and evaluating Sal's performance. When "She's the Only One I Want" had topped the local charts, Santo took the record and some of Sal's publicity pictures and boarded a plane for New York, telling Sal he was going to call in some of his markers from his fat years. When he came back a week later, his face was drawn, tight-lipped, and he refused to talk about it. Not long after that an open-ended booking opened up at the Casablanca on the corner of Bourbon and Iberville when the lead singer in the house band was busted for heroin sales, and Santo advised Sal to put some musicians together and take the gig. Sal, never one to question his manager, called up his old friends from the Gangsters, rehearsed for a week, and within a month the crowds were spilling out of the Casablanca's doors and obstructing traffic on Bourbon. Sal was a local star, and was having so much fun and so many women that he wasn't even aware, much less alarmed, that his recording career had stagnated like a Louisiana drainage ditch. Santo knew, of course, but didn't press the matter with Sal, didn't make him face the reality. That nightclub work was not the music business, it was the liquor business. That the only thing it got you was older. Oh, on a few blurry after-hours mornings at the King's Room, or over very early eggs at the Busy Bee after the gig, Santo would suggest to Sal that maybe he ought to try to travel some, see what was happening in New York, or out in L.A., which was becoming the nation's recording capital. Santo would urge Sal to write and demo some new tunes, take 'em out to the Coast, see what he could shake up. *You're only young once, you know. Now's the time to take a few chances, see the world, stretch those boundaries.* Sal would smile with his mouth full of grits and biscuits, nod toward that night's sweet young thing who would unfailingly be hanging on his arm, and say, "Santo! Desert my fans? Never." And then they would laugh comfortably, and Santo wouldn't bring up the subject for another six months.

It was just about then that Santo first saw Cat Ballou dance at the Fools Rush Inn, and his priorities changed drastically. His interest in Sal's career—or what was left of Sal's career—waned considerably. He had his own life to worry about now, his own future to repair. Santo Pecoraro stopped advising Sal to take his show on the road. Although he still functioned, in a very truncated sense, as Sal's agent and personal manager, he stopped advising Sal about anything. Oh, from time to time he still booked Sal on an occasional club date or industrial show, but he was no longer the visionary leader he had once been. And after he had bedded and wedded Cat, Santo Pecoraro resigned himself, more happily than not, to the very limited opportunities of a New Orleans booking agent. He laid to rest his dream of being the white Berry Gordy, and pragmatically decided to content himself with booking shit comics, stretch-marked strippers, mediocre bands. And with fathering the succession of sons Cathy eventually began dropping like clockwork.

Of course, by then the elusive, indefinable magic that—in the manner a woman arbitrarily takes her lovers—unaccountably bestows popularity on nightclubs, restaurants, television sitcoms, and third-rate singers, that fleeting, bankable black magic had moved on, and the crowds at the Casablanca were thinning, going elsewhere. In fact, Mondays through Thursdays, the audiences couldn't be called crowds at all. Stragglers would have been a better appellation. And the weekend customers were mostly tourists now, squares from places like Des Moines, Salt Lake City, Kyoto. The Grayline Tour buses dropped them off at the door, and the drivers herded them in like cattle. They had been shown one of the infamous Bourbon Street strip shows, had seen female impersonators singing and dancing in drag, had watched a bunch of seventy-year-old black men play some tired, touristy Dixieland, and now they were going to hear some good old New Orleans funk, of the blue-eyed variety. Though that didn't stop the more strong-hearted of the little assholes from shouting out requests for "The Saints" and "Way Down Yonder." Soon Sal found himself singing "Didn't He Ramble?" four or five times a night, and that's when he began to realize things weren't going quite the way they were supposed to. By that time, of course, it was *way* too late.

Just about then, just about simultaneously, Sal began reaching out to wealthy older women and 40-to-1 shots. The betting came naturally. His old man was a degenerate gambler, if a two-dollar-bettor could be called degenerate. The rich women were all Sal's idea. It was an outcome of his convoluted logic. Women liked him. A *lot.* Women sometimes had money. Sometimes a *lot.* Older women usually had more money. A *lot* more. Therefore he was going to pursue older women. Christ, he had to do something! he had rebuked himself. Here he was, twenty-six—not that young in show-business time, working in the same dump for the past four years, Santo had been his manager for a decade, and it was beginning to look like his best years were behind him. At twenty-six! That's the way he explained it to Ruth Wallachinsky, the first older woman he actively romanced. She was short, fat, and forty-six, and for some reason Sal could never fathom, loved fucking in front of full-length mirrors.

Her advice to Sal was to get another manager. This was not an easy diagnosis for Sal to confront. He knew the doctor was right; he knew the illness was terminal; but he couldn't bring himself to swallow the medicine. What would he do without Santo? Santo had been more of a father to him than his old man had ever been. *Joe the Hack, Joe the Hack,* Sal used to sing silently to himself. *Either drunk or at the track.*

"Look," Ruth Wallachinsky had suggested, and Sal acted as though the idea came as a complete surprise to him, "*I'll* be your manager. You already know how well I can handle you." They had laughed like kids at that. Seriously, she had persisted, she knew all kinds of show-business people in New York. Theater people. Record people. TV people. All those high-powered Manhattan Jews, who, if you didn't already know it, ran the industry. She could *move* among these people, negotiate, maneuver, promote. This was *made* for her. Wasn't Manhattan where she was from? Weren't they *her* people? Of course, she would have to invest a little capital in Sal up front—in the *product,* she called it—to round off his rough edges. To make him presentable to the New York crowd. Some new clothes, new pictures, some personalized arrangements. Maybe a kind of show, written around Sal, tailored to his talents. *You can't go to New York half-cocked, you know—not that you're* that, *dear,* she giggled breathlessly. *Oh, no, not that you could ever be* that. But Broadway wasn't Bourbon Street. Not by a long shot. *They eat unprepared people for* breakfast *up there, sweetie. Oh,* she smiled at him, *but doesn't that sound nice. I'm going to pull out all the stops for you, sweetie. Watch out, New York, here come Sal D'Amore and his manager, Ruth Wallachinsky. What a duo! What a pair! They're going to turn that old town upside down. Down. Down. Here, dear, put your tongue here, baby. Here, Sal, lick here. Here, dear.* Here. *Oh, dear! Move your head a little, baby, I can't see. I want to see!*

And Sal played hard to get for about a minute and a half, then embraced the whole notion wholeheartedly. Ruth announced that she was going back to New York to speak to her lawyers, have the managerial contracts drawn up, *everything by the book, sweetie, I'm not Jewish for nothing.* And while she was gone, Sal screwed up his courage and came here, to Santo's office, this very place, and did what he had to do. He explained to a very patient Santo how they had gone as far together as they could go, how times were changing, the music business was changing, how he needed someone with a fresh perspective, capital to invest in the *product, ayadida yadida.* At the end of Sal's nervous, sweaty performance Santo of course said he understood, he could see Sal's side of everything, life moves on. Inwardly Santo Pecoraro was not disappointed by the turn of events. Now, he was no longer responsible for Sal's career. Sal's failure would not be Santo's fault.

Sal had walked away from Santo's office actually *humming* as he sauntered lightheartedly down a hot, humid Esplanade Avenue. The world seemed stretched out before him like a blonde lounging naked on a waterbed. Like a 15-to-1 longshot coming down the homestretch ten lengths ahead. New York, New York. The place so great they had to name it twice. The streets were paved with gold, they used to tell the Sicilians, back in the old country. New motherfucking York. Home to all the places Sal had heard about all his life. Greenwich Village. Broadway. Fifty-second Street, where a nineteen-year-old Miles had struggled to keep up with the high-flying Bird. The Record Plant. The Peppermint Lounge, where the twist was born. Central Park. The Village Vanguard. And for once in his life he'd be doing things first class. No funky Times Square flophouse for him. No sleeping in the bus station like some New Orleans guys had told him they had done. Nuh-uh. Ruth had said she had an apartment on Fifth Avenue, overlooking the duck pond, whatever the hell that was. The whole fucking city would be at his feet, literally, and then, when those big-time motherfucking Jews heard his songs, saw him sing, they'd be lining up with recording contracts; they'd be begging him to take their bags of money, ride in their limos, fuck their women. Oh, yeah, and he would take care of that, too. Ruth would just have to understand that they had a business relationship now. He was sure she'd see it his way. Christ, the women would be fucking flinging themselves at him. Ruth was mature enough to see that a rock star had to project a certain image, and being a boyfriend to his dumpy, overweight manager would not fit in that picture. And besides, what was a fuck or two between friends? Especially when those friends were going to rewrite music-biz history. Bigger than the Beatles. That's what he was going to be. And she would be his Brian Epstein. His Colonel Tom Parker. She would open all the doors that led to the top. The Stairway to Heaven. People all over the world were going to hear his music. Dancers who couldn't understand English would lip-sync his lyrics as they moved to his rhythms. Women in fucking Russia would yearn for him. Girls he had never met, never heard of, was never *going* to hear of, would have his poster on their walls and would go to sleep fantasizing about doing sexual acts with him. His songs would be heard and loved by millions of people. *Millions.*

Sal softly hummed snatches of his latest song as he strutted down Esplanade, smiling at the women, nodding with self-contained assurance at the brothers. Life *was* good.

Of course, he never heard from Ruth Wallachinsky again. After about a week he called Manhattan Information for her number. There were about a hundred Wallachinskys, including a bunch of R. Wallachinskys—but no Ruth.

Sal waited another week. By then he was really beginning to panic. Then he called Manhattan Information again and, after a whole lot of sweet talk, persuaded the operator to give him all the *R*s. Definitely not company policy, but okay, she said in a nasal Brooklyn bleat.

None of the R. Wallachinskys were the right one. None had even *heard* of the right one, although one Roger J., who sounded very gay, *used* to have an *aunt* Ruth, but she died back in '71. Or was it '72? Anyway, her name was Silver. She had married Ozzie Silver and gone to live in *Cleveland,* my God, how can you call that *living,* but then I just told you she died, didn't I? Died in Cleveland. That's a redundancy, isn't it? By the way, what did you say *your* name was, and do you ever get up here to the City? I've heard such *scandalous* things about New Orleans.

At the beginning of the third week Sal was in a frenzy. Manhattan Information was tired of dealing with him. Go to your main library, the supervisor said. They'll have a Manhattan phone book. Every main library in the country has one.

When it was over, after almost a month, after phoning or trying to phone every Wallachinsky in New York's five boroughs, after Sal finally gave up and admitted to himself that somehow he'd been had—after it was all over, he'd run up a twelve-hundred-dollar bill on his father's phone, Southern Bell cut off service, and from then on Joe D'Amore always had to have his number listed in one of his sisters' names.

When a month had passed without a word from or a sign

of her, Sal allowed himself to understand that he had been conned, that there *was* no Ruth Wallachinsky, or if there was, she sure as hell didn't live in New York City. That all those conversations he and the woman who called herself Ruth Wallachinsky had had about fame and fortune, sex and stardom, music and money—it had all been just that, conversation. Talk. The cheapest thing in the world. Sal was stunned, of course. Disappointment clouded around his eyes like swamp gnats. He would have to put his dreams on hold. For a while. But more than that, Sal was surprised. Surprised to know that he possessed anything that would make a woman lie like that, surprised to learn that he had something that he could be conned out of. *Here, sweetie, put your tongue here.* He almost felt a kind of pride about it all. He had been stolen from. He possessed something worth taking. And he had a strong premonition that there would be more Ruth Wallachinskys. Many, many more. The game wasn't over yet.

And what had he lost, besides a little naiveté? Well, the managership of Santo Pecoraro. But Santo hadn't really done anything for his career in years. And he'd still be Sal's friend. Sal was sure of that.

Which is exactly how it went. Santo was such a good friend that he never mentioned Ruth Wallachinsky again. Or Sandy Turner, or Billie Worthington, or Alexis Constantine, or Vanda Maxwell, or any of the score of older women Sal seemed to have a penchant for. The tight-eyed, sharp-mouthed, well-dressed middle-aged women who were always going to help him achieve his tremendous potential. Sal would proudly introduce them to Santo, and Santo would smile blankly and stare through them as if they weren't there, as if they were ghosts.

And sure enough, very shortly they all seemed to disappear.

"So, Sal, whatcha want to drink?" Cat entered the office carrying two deep plates heaped with tomato-sauce-crowned cavatoni and ringed with small, smoking meatballs. Over one of the plates she had balanced a hunk of Romano on top of a flat, ancient grater. The thick odors of the fresh cheese and the piquant sauce filled the room. She set the plate with the cheese on the desk before her husband. Then she turned to Sal.

"What, you gonna eat standing up? Siddown, for Chrissakes." She nodded toward one of the weathered leather chairs. "I'll getcha something to drink. Whatcha wanna drink?"

"Cat, for Chrissakes, I ain't hungry."

"Save your shit, D'Amore." With her free hand she pushed him down into the chair. "Or maybe you don't like the way I cook? Is that it?" she asked with sparkling eyes, because Sal knew that she knew that couldn't be true. As so often happens in marriages like this one, Cathy had become the best Italian cook in the family. All the Pecoraro women reluctantly confessed to it.

"Here, D'Amore." She shoved the cavatoni in front of him and would have dropped it in his lap if he hadn't grabbed it. He was sure of it. "Now. What chu wanna drink?"

Sal looked up at her. "You got any poison? That would be nice."

Her eyes widened a little, and then she threw a quick glance at Santo behind his desk. He shrugged. She looked back at Sal and spoke in a softer voice. "You in trouble, D'Amore? How 'bout a nice shot of whiskey?" She trailed her fingers gently through his still-damp hair. Just the way Vanda had done.

Sal and Cat had fucked each other a few times, back in the old days, before she met Santo, when she was still "Cattin' around," as she liked to call it. It had meant nothing to them at the time, but as the years went by, the fading memory left them with a kind of sibling affection. Of course, neither of them had ever mentioned it to Santo.

"J.D.?"

Sal nodded. "That'd be great, Cat. Thank you."

As she left the office, both men watched her go. Cat Ballou had aged very gracefully, not the way a lot of ex-strippers did, going to fat and flab. Even her childbearing hadn't affected her natural litheness, her strong dancer's legs, her high, upright breasts.

When she had gone, Santo rested his De Nobili on the edge of a big glass ashtray and began to grate cheese over his plate. "I know a man ain't s'pose to say 'I told you so' in situations like this, but when the fuck else you got a chance to say it except in situations like this?" His eyes were hard, paternal. "I fucking told you so."

"Santo, lissen to me."

Santo shook his head as he dusted the cheese shavings from his hands over the top of his cavatoni. "Why? Why the fuck should I? You don't lissen to me. Never. Here." He held out the grater and the hunk of cheese to Sal. Sal shook his head and slid his own plate onto the desktop.

"Hey," Santo said, his fork already in his hand, "you gotta eat, right? I don't care how bad it is."

Jesus Christ, Sal thought, *what time is it?* His wristwatch said 7:08.

"What, you got a plane to catch?" Santo said, nodding at Sal's watch.

Maybe, Sal thought. *Maybe that's just what I should do. Maybe I oughtta walk right outta here, catch a cab to the airport, get on a plane and fly the fuck away from here.*

But to where? And what would he use for money? Vanda's hundred thirty-two dollars? Jesus *Christ!*

Santo's jaws were already working, happily gnashing his cavatoni. He seemed to suddenly notice that he was eating alone. "Eat, man. For Chris*sakes!*"

"Santo."

"Look," Santo said with a perturbed air. He didn't like the joy of his food diluted by unsolved problems. "Look, don't worry. We'll figure a way out. We'll cover your ass."

"Santo. You don't understand."

"What's to understand?" Santo chewed contentedly, but there was a scowl across his face. "You fucked up. Again." He pointed his fork at the younger man. "After all I done told you."

Cathy came in then, carrying a tumbler of whiskey in one hand and a Diet Pepsi can in the other. She looked at Sal's untouched plate, then put the Jack Daniel's in his empty hands. As she set the Diet Pepsi on the desk, she threw her husband a questioning glance.

"Thanks, baby," Santo said, and from the tone of his voice everyone in the room knew it was a dismissal, something that ordinarily Santo would never do to her. She stared at him for a moment, then turned on her heels and stalked from the office.

Sal put the tumbler to his lips and chugalugged the J.D. The ice cubes rattled against the glass when he set it down.

Santo stopped eating to watch him. Then he sighed and wiped the back of his hand across his lips.

"All right. How much?"

Sal stared at him, frozen. He couldn't say it. Santo wouldn't believe him. *He* didn't even believe it.

"What the fuck, you breaking in a ventriloquist act? Where's your fucking dummy?"

Sal sat there. He couldn't move, he couldn't speak. He was caught up in the unreality of it all. This morning he'd been almost eighty thousand dollars ahead, now he was a zombie. The walking dead.

"Jesus fucking Christ!" Santo growled, crouched over his food like a dog. "Tell how much you in for?"

Sal stared at the empty whiskey tumbler. He wished he had another.

"Sal—"

"Santo," Sal said quickly, "before I tell you how much I need, I wanna ask you a question."

Santo was popping a meatball between his lips. "You wanna ask me a question? Ask me a question."

Sal leaned forward over the desktop, pushing aside his cooling plate of pasta. Santo eyed it hungrily even as he chewed the meatball.

"Santo," Sal began slowly, earnestly, "do you believe in me?"

Santo's jaws stopped churning and hung slack. The food in his mouth was visible. "What kinda fucking question is that?"

"Just answer me."

"Yeah, I believe in you. I believe you couldn't pass up a five-dollar exacta if your fucking life depended on it."

If my fucking life depended on it—the thought flashed through Sal's mind.

"That ain't what I mean, Santo. I mean, do you believe in *me?* Do you believe in my *talent?*"

Santo stared at him, perplexed. "What the fuck?"

"No, I mean it. Do you believe in my talent? In my voice? In my music?"

"What the hell kinda fucking question is that? You know I always thought you was the best white singer I ever heard. You know that. I told you that years ago. Why the fuck else would I of invested all that time and money in ya? Why else?

Remember me? I'm the one that don't wanna sleep wit'cha."

It was a long speech, and Santo seemed relieved to get back to his cavatoni.

Sal leaned further over the desk. "Lissen, Santo. That's just what I'm getting at."

Santo eyed him suspiciously as he ate. "What? You wanna sleep wid me?"

"No, Santo, *listen* to me!"

"I *am* listening to you." Now, he was trying to ignore Sal's untouched plate. It was a losing battle.

"Santo, how much is my career worth?"

Santo stopped chewing a moment and stared at him. He had the face of a bloodhound, all stubble and jowls and Sicilian disdain. "Sally, what are you talking?"

"Listen to me. How much could you get for, say, half of my earnings from singing and songwriting? For the rest of my life."

Before he answered, Santo pushed his empty plate aside. Then he raised his eyebrows at Sal's untouched one, as if to say, "You gonna eat that?" and when Sal shook his head, he reached across and gathered it in. Grating the hard, crumbly cheese, he spoke.

"How much money are we talking about, Sal?"

"That's what I'm asking you."

Santo put down the grater and retrieved his fork from his first plate. "Lemme get this right." He waggled the fork in Sal's direction. "You want me to see if I can sell half of what you *might* make for the rest of your life. Like stock-market futures or something."

Sal nodded eagerly. "Yeah. How much you think you can get?"

Santo shook his head and buried the fork in the new plate of pasta. He shoveled it around, over itself. Hot steam geysered up from the bottom of the bowl. He speared several of the fat, hollow noddles, swirled them in the thick blood-red sauce, and raised them up to his lips. He stopped there, the forkful of food poised by his mouth. "Sal, I don't know how to do that kinda deal. You gotta have a lawyer, you—"

"Sure you can. We don't need no lawyer. Just get on the phone, call up some of them heavy-duty contacts of yours. That dude you know at Electra."

"Sal, that guy's been dead for ten years."

"Then somebody else, then. Call anybody who might be interested."

"I don't *know* anybody who might be interested."

"For Chrissakes, Santo!"

"Whattaya want me to do, Sally, *shit* these guys? You think I got contacts coming out my asshole? I book fucking *weddings,* man. Birthday parties. I been out of the Big Time for twenty-five years. Everybody I knew is either dead or in the hospital. And even then knowing them didn't help me none; I couldn't get shit happening with you, remember?"

"Santo, I'm in *trouble*—"

"You think I can't tell?"

"—and I'm asking for your help."

"What the fuck you want me to do?"

"I'm telling you. Fucking *listen* to me, man, for Chrissakes. I need one of them rich motherfucker speculators you know to front me a bunch of money, in advance kinda, and I'll sign over half of my future royalties to them. Records, tapes, concerts, publishing, everything. I'll sign over half of my career's earnings for a big advance *now.*"

Santo's eating had slowed. Now, he stopped entirely and rested his fork on the edge of his plate. He tented his fingers over his food and stared at Sal with gently appraising eyes. He chewed slowly, and then swallowed. Finally, after a long while, he said, "Sal—"

"Santo, man—"

"Sal, you gotta face reality."

"Don't gimme that shit, man."

"You ain't got nothing to sell, Sal."

"I'm fucking *good,* Santo!" Sal shouted, lunging up from his chair. "You fucking know it, too! I got motherfucking *talent,* man!" His voice was thick, impassioned.

Santo waved his hands deprecatingly. "Sal, Sal—"

"*I shoudda made it!*" Sal sputtered, and his eyes were hot and moist. "*I shoudda made it!* You told me so a thousand times. I got something! I'm good. My songs are fucking *good,* man!"

Santo picked his words very carefully and spoke in a strong, level tone. "You right, man, you shoudda made it. But things didn't work out the way they shoudda. Maybe it was my fault, maybe it was your fault, maybe it wadn't anybody's fault, but, fuck, man, you gotta face fucking facts. How old are you now? Thirty-eight? Thirty-nine? You think there's a burning market out there for forty-year-old rockers?"

"Aw, fuck that bullshit, man! Mick Jagger's almost forty-*five,* man. How old is Don Henley? Stevie Wonder?"

"Sal," Santo pleaded, "those guys were fucking *babies* when they got their first hits. Anything is possible when you got a coupla hits behind you. You can't make a comeback if you ain't never been nowhere to come back *to.*"

Sal looked down at Santo for a full half-minute. The anger in his face seemed to dissipate, like smoke in a nightclub.

"Santo," he said in a softer, calmer voice, "you gotta help me. You gotta figure out a way to get me some cash. And I ain't got nothing else to sell but my songs and my voice." He slumped back in his chair and looked at Santo. "You gotta help me."

Santo was eating again, big facial muscles slowly churning beneath his olive skin. His eyes lasered into Sal's as he chewed. "You little motherfucker," he began in a fatherly growl, "you got a lotta balls, come in here and holler at me like that. How many times I told you, nobody ever made it staying here in Noo Awlins? How many times I told you that? How many times I said you gotta go to L.A.? This fucking town is a dead-end street, I told you, didn't I?" He angrily shoveled cavatoni into his open maw. "This fucking town is a fucking show-business cemetery. Old acts come here to die. Didn't I tell you that? This is the Old Musicians Graveyard. But you knew better, right? You don't need fucking advice. You got the world all fucking figured out. One of them rich salt-meat cunt old tramps gonna make you a star. You too busy chasing pussy and ponies to listen to what an asshole like Santo Pecoraro has to say, ain't I right? Tell me I'm wrong. Call me a liar."

Sal said nothing, only returned Santo's electric gaze with wavering eyes.

Santo moved to fill the silence. "No, you got im*por*tant shit on *your* mind. You ain't got *time* to work on your career anymore. No, you gotta tend bar to pay off your motherfucking markers. Play fucking weddings. Go to the Fair Grounds and piss away what you made the night before. What you thought, stardom was just gonna walk in and fucking *invite* you to the motherfucking dance? Maybe you was gonna *win* it on a two-dollar ticket? You thought you could eat-pussy your way to the top?"

Sal said nothing.

Santo continued. He was warming to the sound of his own voice, and he was comfortable delivering this sermon to Sal. He had done it so many times before.

"I told you about that fucking gambling, didn't I? What I told you, betting's for losers, didn't I tell you that? How many times I told you that?"

"For Chrissakes, Santo—"

"No, goddamnit!" he barked. "You let me finish! You come in here ask me to call all over hell and gone and represent you in some cockamamy idea to raise money—you come in here and do that, you gonna listen to whatever the fuck I have to say."

Sal slumped resignedly back into his chair, stealing a quick look at his watch: 7:22. *Like sand through an hourglass . . .*

Santo had paused from eating again, but he kept the half-finished plate before him, his hands tented over it.

"Yeah, you right, you shoudda made it. You had more talent than any white singer or songwriter I ever managed. I ever met. You shoudda made it *real* big. But you fucking lazy, man. You don't wanna work on anything. You write a fucking song in the morning—it takes you maybe an hour—and that's it. You don't ever work on it again. I tell you maybe the bridge might need a little work, maybe it could be better, and you look at me like I'm a stupid old asshole don't know nothing from nothing. But *you!* You a motherfucking *genius!* You Duke Ellington. You Paul McCartney, Ray Charles, Cole Porter—all rolled into one!"

"Santo, I ain't got time—"

"Shut up! You fucking shut up! I ain't finished." Santo angrily swigged at his Diet Pepsi. "You know, I believe you *still* could fucking make it, but—talk about gambling—I wouldn't fucking bet on it. You know why? I'll tell you why. It ain't 'cuz your music ain't still viable in today's market. 'Cuz it is. Okay, everything today's synthesizers. Music by machines. All right, you couldn't find a fucking *melody* in today's Top Ten if your life depended on it. Okay, all your male stars today are fucking morphadykes. Even with all that, I think you could make it today, But you won't. You know why? Because people don't change, Sal. You been an asshole fuck-up all your life, and you gonna stay one. You pissed your talent away behind broads, and booze, and cigarettes, and weed, and coke, and poker, and long shots, and trying to get through this life the easy way, without working for anything. Without making any effort. A fucking man who looks for his salvation in racetracks and rich old ladies ain't a fucking man. A man who—hey, where you going?"

Sal, on his way to the door, whipped around furiously. His eyes were wet. "What?" he shouted. "I'm suppose to stay here while you run me down like a fucking dog? I'm suppose to just stay here and get fucking beat up on?"

Santo was genuinely surprised and alarmed by Sal's anguish. "Sally. I'm sorry." He indicated the chair. "Siddown, man, I didn't mean to—"

"You don't fucking understand, man!" Sal cried as he leaned over Santo's desk. "I'm in deep fucking water. *Deep* fucking water. And I ain't got fucking time for you to tell me what a worthless piece of dogshit I am!"

"All right. All *right.*" He held up his hands, palms out. "Okay. I'm just trying to help you. Just trying to show you how bad you fucking up."

"Believe me, Santo, I know how bad I'm fucking up. I don't need to be told."

"Okay, look." His voice had taken on a soothing, reassuring color. The obligatory scolding had been administered; now, it was time for the fatherly rescue. "Look, don't worry." He snagged some cavatoni on the tines of his fork and held them up, as though he were inspecting them. "I got a bank account Cat don't know about. I was saving up for a boat. What the fuck I need with a boat?" He emptied the fork into his mouth. "I got three thousand in there. We'll figure out a way for you to pay it back." He chewed thoughtfully. "How much you need?"

"A hundred and eighty thousand," Sal said quickly, and his heart started to race at the sound of the words.

Santo stopped chewing and stared at him. After a moment he smiled with relief. "Yeah, right." He chuckled. "Serious shit, Sally. How much do you need?"

"Serious shit? A hundred and eighty thousand."

The smile on Santo's lips slowly faded into a grim, tight line. He pushed away the bowl of cavatoni. It was the first time Sal had ever seen Santo Pecoraro leave a plate of food unfinished.

"A hundred and eighty *thousand?*" Santo slowly said.

Sal nodded.

"Dollars?"

Sal nodded again.

Santo sat there, disbelief plastered across his face like a Carnival mask, staring at Sal across the table. Then his head started to move side-to-side, as if by its own will, on his thick neck. "Don't tell me this, Sal," he breathed.

"I wish it wadn't true."

Santo was still gaping bug-eyed at him. When he finally spoke, his voice was just above a whisper. The tone of voice you hear at a wake, Sal thought.

"Sal, how the fuck did you lose a hundred and eighty thousand dollars?"

Sal shrugged. "It wadn't easy."

Santo nodded. "I can believe that." The two men sat there looking at each other. "Tell me. I'd like to know."

Sal reached into his pocket and withdrew a cigarette. He lit it with a book of matches off Santo's desk.

"I cooked Little Johnny's books," Sal said, and Santo breathed in deeply. "I finagled the incoming bets, made my own wagers. I was doing great until—"

"Wait a minute," Santo interrupted, holding up a hand. "Lemme get this right. You swindled Little Johnny Venezia outta a hundred and eighty thousand dollars—is that what you're telling me?"

"That's it."

"Jesus." Santo's voice was full of awe. "Man, you *really* fucked up this time."

"Big Time. I fucked up Big Time."

Santo picked up his dead DeNobili and stuck it in the corner of his mouth. "And when did all this transpire?"

"Just a coupla hours ago."

"Do the Venezias know yet?"

"They gonna find out at ten o'clock when Albert Castiglia

comes in the Sporting Life to collect on a quarter-million-dollar win."

Santo sat stolidly in his chair, chewing on his cigar and inspecting Sal. Sal knew he was thinking, scheming, trying to figure out a way out of this for "his boy." For the first time this afternoon Sal didn't feel he was alone in this. If anyone could pilot a way out of this mess, it was Santo Pecoraro.

Santo mangled his cigar for several minutes, his eyes boring into Sal's, his fingertips tapping on the arm of his chair. Then he propped his elbows on the desk top and leaned forward toward Sal.

"Just tell me one thing," he softly asked. "You don't make three hundred dollars a week. Did you ever stop to think, *If I lose this bet, there's no way I can cover it?*"

Sal showed Santo his palms. "Santo. There was no way I could lose."

Somehow the big man found a way to nod his head in understanding, while simultaneously shaking it negatively in displeasure. Then he lurched to his feet and went to one of the big file cabinets lining the wall. He yanked open one of the overstuffed drawers and stuck his arm in, rummaging around.

"Santo," Sal pleaded from his chair, "you gotta help me, man. I don't know what the fuck to do."

"Man, you are too fucking beautiful," Santo said with fatherly disgust as he returned to the desk with an ancient metal strongbox. Sal knew it had belonged to Santo's old man, Carlo the boxer. Santo sat down heavily behind the desk and, stretching to get around his overhanging gut, dug into his bathrobe's pocket and came up with a ring of keys. "You are un-fucking-believable. When they made you, they threw away the mold." He inserted a small black key into the lock and lifted open the strongbox lid. "Put your fucking brains in a bird, motherfucker'd fly backward."

From the metal box he withdrew a soft leather pouch, like an old change purse. He unsnapped the purse's clasp and dug out a wad of bills. He counted them quickly and laid them out on the desktop in front of Sal.

"Sixteen hundred dollars," he announced to Sal. "It's all I can get my hands on tonight."

Sal looked down at the money, then back up at Santo. "Santo, what good is this gonna do me?"

Again Santo Pecoraro shook his head in paternal exasperation. "You little asshole. I'm gonna tell you what good it's gonna do you. You take this money, you put it in your pocket, you walk out my front door, you get in a cab, you take that cab to the airport, you catch a plane for anywhere that's the furtherest you can get from New Orleans without a passport—Anchorage, Alaska, comes to mind, Fairbanks, maybe—you get off the plane, you change your name, you get plastic surgery, you marry an Eskimo, and, Sal, you never, ever, *ever,* come back here again." Santo stopped talking and stuck his cigar back between his teeth.

Sal looked at Santo for a moment, then looked more closely. "Santo," he said tentatively. "You're joking, ain'tcha?"

Santo nibbled on his DeNobili. "Only partly. Maybe. About the Eskimo. The rest of it I'm dead serious."

"Santo, I can't just run away," Sal said, and thought, *Even though that's all I've been thinking about for the last three hours.*

"That's what you *gotta* do, you wanna keep on breathing. You got no choice."

Sal leaned forward in his chair. "I was hoping maybe you could like talk to the Venezias. Maybe work out a deal."

Santo shook his head. "What kinda deal?"

"I don't know," Sal pleaded. "I thought maybe you could think of something."

"Something like what?"

"Christ, Santo, I—"

"Look," Santo broke in roughly, "lemme draw you a fucking blueprint." He jerked his cigar from his mouth and spit out a trace of soggy tobacco leaf. "You a hundred and eighty thousand dollars in the hole. You ain't gonna make a hundred and eighty thousand dollars in your whole fucking *life.* What you gonna pay the Venezias with?" Before Sal could answer, he continued, "You ain't *got* nothing to pay the Venezias with, but one thing. You know what that one thing is?" Sal knew, but didn't say. "Your fucking *blood,* Sal. And if you think a minute they ain't gonna collect, you're crazier than even *I* thought you was."

Sal nodded almost imperceptibly.

"They gonna have to make good Albert Castiglia's bet. A hundred eighty thousand is serious money, Sal. *Serious* money. Little Johnny Venezia don't eat a hundred and eighty K and smile about it." Santo pointed the wet end of his cigar at Sal's bony chest. "They catch you, they gonna kill you. No question. No questions asked. If they find out I give you the money to leave town"—he indicated the bills on the desk top—"they kill me, too. A hundred and eighty K is big money to *any*-fucking-body." He put the cigar back in his mouth. "You take this bread, you catch a plane, you find somewhere a long where from here, where they ain't too many *paisans,* maybe in a year or two you call me and we can figure out something. Right now, what chu gotta do is get outta town. Just get the fuck outta town." Santo got up quickly from his chair and moved around the desk. Under his bathrobe he wore a ratty red T-shirt that advertised BREAUX BRIDGE, LOUISIANA—CRAWFISH CAPITAL OF THE WORLD. He gathered up the sixteen hundred and held it out to Sal. "Just take the money and get outta town, man. You ain't got no time to fuck around."

Sal looked up at him. His eyes were cloudy and unfocused. "Santo, I can't leave Noo Awlins. I ain't never been nowhere else." A tear ran in a rivulet down his cheek. "Where I'm gonna go? Where? I don't know nobody—"

Santo slapped Sal hard with his open hand. *Whap!* Sal's head snapped back, and his arm flew up instinctively to protect himself. "Don't!" he cried, suddenly very frightened, as if he felt this little taste of violence was a portent of things to come.

"You listen to me, you little pussy," Santo growled, towering over him. "You listen to me, 'cause I'm trying to save your fucking life. You done fucked up real bad, don't you understand that? You act like a little kid. You act like a little boy, and your mama gonna come along and clean up after you. Well, you done fucked here so bad ain't nobody can help you now. Now, it's time you started acting like a man for once. Now, you gotta take responsibility for what you done. You take this money and you get the fuck outta town. Right now, or I swear to Jesus, by tomorrow morning the Venezias will've cut your heart out and fed it to their pit bull." He gripped Sal's upper arm and began to lift him from his chair. "You take this money and get outta here. Now!"

Sal clutched at Santo's hand, tried to pry loose the strong, thick fingers. "Santo, let me stay here with you," he begged. "Lemme hide here for a few days until we can think of something. *Please,* man. We'll think of something."

Santo's grip tightened, and he pulled Sal closer. His breath smelled of garlic, and his eyes were dark and hard.

"Sal, these are bad people you picked to fuck over. You knew that, and you went ahead and done it anyway. That's *your* problem. Don't put that burden on my back. On my family's."

"Santo—"

"The Venezias are crazy. They kill people like spics do, like niggers do. It don't matter to them. You remember when they found out Joey Zito was a snitch? They shotgunned the poor motherfucker while he was eating breakfast in his own fucking house. Blew his fucking face off, and when his mother ran in from the kitchen, they kill her, too. Woman was sixty-seven years old and legally blind. The Venezias are like that. They walk in a house, take out everybody in it. They're like fucking A-rabs. I gotta think of Cat and the kids."

"Santo—"

"If you wanna flush your life down the toilet, that's your business." He shoved the bills into Sal's slack fist and guided him toward the door. "Don't ask me to jeopardize my family behind your stupidity."

"Santo, man, I just don't know if I can—"

"You got to. You ain't got a choice." Santo had him out in the drafty, high-ceilinged hall, and was moving him in the direction of the outside door, away from the apartment. "You gotta find your balls this time, Sally. You gotta do this, man."

The door to Santo's apartment opened abruptly, and both men whipped their heads around to stare wide-eyed at Cat Ballou, standing in the doorway. She appraised the situation with one quick all-inclusive glance, knew that something was very wrong, and moved to try to help the only way she knew.

"Sal's leaving already?" she asked with arched eyebrows.

"Yeah, I gotta, Cat—" Sal began in a not-too-steady voice.

"He's gotta go somewhere, baby," Santo offered.

Cat perused both men with disbelieving eyes. "Uh-huh, right." She stared at them. "Anyway, he can't go nowhere without no coat. He's gonna catch pneumonia going around like that. I got a jacket'll fit you perfect."

"Cat—" Sal began to protest, but she was already gone.

The two men looked at each other in silence, and then she was back, holding up a shiny black leather motorcycle jacket.

"Here," she said reassuringly as she moved behind Sal and slipped it over his arms. It fit perfectly.

"Baby," Santo complained, "that jacket's brand spanking new."

"Oh, big deal!" she snorted. "He can bring it back next time he comes over."

Sal and Santo stared at each other, and then Santo quietly said, "You right, baby. He can."

Sal started to take off the jacket but Santo propelled him toward the door. "Leave it on," Santo muttered in a low hiss.

"I don't want—"

"Leave it *on,* for Chrissakes!" He yanked open the door and stared out fearfully into the night street.

"Sal!" Cathy called from the hallway.

Both men turned back to her.

"Ain'cha gonna gimme a kiss good-bye?"

Sal shook his head helplessly. "I gotta go, Cat."

"Aw," she pouted, "after I lend you my jacket. And I don't know when I'll see either of you again." She held out her arms in a classic stripper's pose. Sal felt Santo shove him back into the hallway, toward his wife.

"Give her a kiss," he growled.

Sal walked back and took her lightly into his arms. Even in flats, she was three inches taller than he was. She flattened her body against his, snaked her arms around his neck, and bit him lightly on his cheek. "See you soon, D'Amore?"

Sal nodded. "As soon as I can, Cat."

And then Santo was pulling him away, back to the door, back to the outside. Sal didn't want to go.

"Bye-bye, D'Amore," Cat called after them as Santo steered him down the front stoop steps. It had started to mist again, a delicate film of rain.

They stood on the banquette together. Santo surveyed the street both ways. A car slushed around the end of the block, and its headlights blinded them. Santo's grip on his arm tightened. Then the car whisked by them and was gone. Sal had that queer feeling again: *Where am I? Who am I?*

"You got the money?" Santo asked him.

"What?" Sal responded in a daze.

"The sixteen hundred I give you. You still got it?"

"Uh—I think so."

"Well, where is it?"

Sal stupidly began to pat at his pockets. Then he held up his hand. The money was still clenched in his fist.

"Put it in your fucking pocket. You got any more?" Santo wanted to know.

"About a hundred and thirty-two dollars." Exactly a hundred and thirty-two dollars. Minus one cab fare.

"That's enough to get you outta town, give you time to start up somewhere else." He moved in closer to Sal and spoke in a whisper, even though the street was empty. "I'd tell you to call me in a few weeks and I'd send you some money, but these people," he shook his head, "these people can get hold of anything, including a list of my incoming phone calls." He put his big hand on the back of Sal's neck and pulled to him, massaging his flesh. "Sally, I love you. You know that."

Sal felt himself start to cry. "I know that, man," he choked out.

"I gotta think of my sons, Sally. If it was the DeMarcos, or the Monteleons, or even the Scalises—but the *Venezias.* Jesus Christ, Sal, they're fucking animals."

"I know, Santo," Sal rasped between his tears. "I know."

Santo pulled him into a rough embrace and kissed him on his lips. "I'm sorry, Sal."

"It's all right. I'll be all right." *It's not,* Sal thought. *And I won't.*

Santo released him and pushed him gently down the street. "Go. Catch a cab. Get outta here. Don't stop until you can see snow on the ground." He turned and started back up into the house. Sal watched him disappear behind the big white Victorian door. Then he looked back at the wet, deserted street. The cold mist slowly drifted by the streetlights like algae Sal had seen below the surface of Lake Pontchartrain. He had the fleeting illusion of being underwater. *What now?* he asked himself. *What the fuck do I do now?*

"Sal!" Santo was back on the sidewalk, beside him. This time he was holding an umbrella. "Listen, the last Saturday of every month you call me at—at—at the bar phone at the Sazerac Bar in the Fairmont."

"The last Saturday of every month?" Sal repeated slowly.

His mind wasn't working too well today. Reality was a fairy tale he had heard a long time ago. Like this morning.

"Yeah." Santo's eyes shined. "I think that's pretty safe. People get calls from all over the world in there. No way to trace one number. So you got it? The last Saturday. In the Sazerac Bar. I'll be waiting for you to call. Got it?"

"The last Saturday of every month," Sal parroted. "In the Sazerac Bar."

"Wait a minute." Santo's brow knitted as he plotted. "Ten o'clock. You call at ten o'clock. Noo Awlins time. I'll be waiting in the Sazerac Bar, the last Saturday of every month. At ten o'clock. You need money, I'll send you some. I'll mail a letter from the main post office."

"Thanks," Sal said, and forced himself to smile. "Thanks for everything, Santo." He held out his hand. Santo looked down at it for a moment, then he handed Sal the umbrella.

"Here, take this."

"Thanks, Santo," Sal said again, from under the sheltering umbrella, but made no move to leave.

"You gotta get outta here," Santo said.

"I know. I guess my brain ain't working too good tonight."

Santo grinned reassuringly. "When the fuck *did* it?"

Sal tried to grin back, and thought, *They probably have us in their telescopic sights right now. We're gonna die with these stupid smiles on our faces.*

Santo craned his thick neck, first in one direction and then the other. "You ain't seen no taxis?"

"Not yet."

"Well, you gotta get outta here."

"I know." He hunched his shoulders and pulled the leather jacket's lapels tight around his neck. "I'll see you, man." Then he turned and started to walk away into the rain.

"Sal."

He turned back. Santo was pointing behind himself, around the corner.

"Look. I'm gonna get the Cadillac. I got it parked in Vincent Ferrara's driveway."

Sal stared at him, uncomprehendingly. "What for?"

"What *for?* To drive you to the fucking airport, what *for.*"

Sal shook his head. "No. You shouddn't do that. You gotta think of Cat and the kids."

"Don't be a fucking hero, D'Amore," the other man growled. "It don't suit you." He was hustling down the banquette in the other direction, his wet bare legs flashing above his flopping slippers.

"You can't go to the airport," Sal called after him. "You in your *bath*robe."

"What the fuck difference does *that* make?" He stopped by the high, narrow wooden gate that led back into the alley between Santo's apartment house and the next. He turned to Sal. "Get back outta the light. I'll bring the Caddy around. I don't want Ferrara to see you with me."

"Okay," Sal said, and took a step back, watching his feet on the wet pavement. When he looked up, Santo was gone. Sal stared at the alley entrance where he had disappeared. Thank God Santo was going to drive him to the airport. Maybe on the way there they could come up with some way where he wouldn't have to leave town. There had to be *some* way. And even if he did have to get on a plane and flee for his life, he needed to talk to his manager some more. He wasn't ready to just go off by himself. He need some more advice, some more pointers. Santo would think of other things like that Sazerac-Bar-the-last-Saturday-of-every-month thing. Santo always thought of shit like that. Maybe he would even think of a way out—

A wave of fear like vomitous nausea rolled over Sal, and a scream rose in his throat and died behind his teeth as he turned his head and saw two men in full-length raincoats walking quickly toward him from the other direction. They came up on him very fast, their shoulders almost touching. Sal pressed his back against the apartment-house wall and watched, horrified, as they came upon him. His knees weakened, his heart thudded against his rib cage, and he felt his bladder fight against the urge to void itself. The two men were almost abreast of him now. The streetlight glittered off their slick wet raincoats, and their strides made crackling sounds under the treated plastic. They passed without even seeing Sal, one man saying to the other in an effeminate whine, "That *bitch!* And after all the help I gave him when he first came to town. I tell you, I'll never spend another dime on him, he can *starve* for all I care." Then they were gone, moving away down Esplanade Avenue, and they had never even been aware of him. Sal gulped some damp oxygen and tried to get quiet himself. Two faggots. He'd almost had apoplexy because two fucking faggots passed him on the street. Was that the way it was gonna be now? Well, then, the Venezias wouldn't have to bother killing him, he would self-destruct in a month—a *week,* for Chrissakes. His fucking heart would explode the next time someone called his name.

"*Sal!*" a voice called out from the street, and it wasn't Santo Pecoraro's. "*Sal!*" Sal felt the nerve endings in his scalp tingle with terror. His feet felt leaden, his fingers frozen. While he had been watching the two gays walk by, a car had slipped soundlessly up to the curb. Its occupant was rolling down the window. Morbidly Sal's eyes searched frantically for the gun barrel that would be pointed at him. Were the Venezias into Uzis now, or was the sawed-off twelve-gauge still their murder weapon of preference? But he couldn't see the gun, because his old man's smiling face was in the way. What the fuck was Joe the Hack doing in Johnny Venezia's Continental?

And then Sal realized it wasn't Little Johnny Venezia's perennial long white Mark IV. It was Joe D'Amore's battered yellow cab. And Joe was squinting at him through the drifting mist.

"Sal? What the fuck you doing standing out in the rain there?" Joe D'Amore hollered. "You look like you seen a ghost."

Sal swallowed and thought, *No, I just thought I was about to become one.*

"Ain't chu got a gig at the King Louis tonight? C'mon, I give you a ride."

Sal looked up and down the street both ways. Santo Pecoraro and his black Cadillac were nowhere in sight.

"Whatcha, waiting on somebody?" Joe D'Amore shouted. "Hey, c'mon over here, so I don't hafta fucking holler."

Tentatively Sal left the shelter of the apartment building and stepped over to the dented canary Ford. "Hey, Papa Joe," he said weakly as he bent over under the umbrella and peered into the driver's window.

Joe D'Amore leaned out of the cab into the rain and took hold of his son's arm. "You look like shit, Sally. I bet chu ain't been getting enough sleep, have you?" He twisted in his seat and opened the taxi's back door. "C'mon, I drop you at the King Louis."

Sal straightened up and again canvassed the street in either direction. Where was Santo? For a panicked, shameful moment the thought raced through his mind that Santo had run out on him. Maybe to the Venezias to tell them where he was. But Sal quickly shook off that idea and silently asked for Santo's forgiveness.

"Sally! You getting my upholstery wet!"

Maybe the best thing to do would be to leave now, with Joe, before Santo came back with the Cadillac. Maybe that would be the best thing to do for Santo. Santo was scared to be seen with him, and Santo didn't frighten too easy. Maybe leaving now would be the *manly* thing to do. Maybe—

"For Chrissakes, Sal!" Joe barked good-naturedly up at his only son. "Get out of the rain and into the friggin' car."

Sal quickly closed the umbrella and slipped into the cab, shutting the door behind himself.

"You in a fog or something tonight?" Joe D'Amore asked as he yanked the car into gear and pulled away from the curb. "What time you gotta be at the King Louis?"

Sal peered back over his shoulder, just in time to spot Santo's Cadillac come slowly around the corner a block away. He watched the big car get smaller and smaller. It was the right thing to do.

"Sal*ly*."

"Huh?" He turned back to the reflection of his father's quizzical face in the big wide wraparound mirror that Joe the Hack had used for years. It stretched from one side of the car to the other. Dangling from the mirror was, incredibly, the scapular that Joe had received at his First Communion. It had to be fifty years old, and still Joe somehow kept it held together. On the dashboard, propped behind a magnetized Madonna, rested a laminated snapshot of Sal's mother, a rawboned, washed-out Oklahoma woman, dead of cancer twenty-two years now, and twined around the photograph was the cheap but cherished mother-of-pearl rosary Joe D'Amore's grandmother had brought over on the boat with her from Palermo. It was the only thing of value she had owned back then. It had been her dowry. The dashboard of Joe the Hack's cab was an altar, a portable shrine. The Church of the Four Roses.

"What time you gotta be there?" he asked again.

"Uh—" Sal fought to figure out what the fuck his old man was talking about. "Time?"

"Jesus Christ, Son," Joe laughed, "you smoking them herbs again, you stoned or something, that's why you standing out there all by yourself in the rain?"

In the wraparound the corners of Joe D'Amore's eyes crinkled with mirth, and the eyes themselves shone with an alcoholic glaze that Sal was well acquainted with.

"What time's the gig—eight? We got ten minutes. I'll take Decatur, getcha there on time." He spun the wheel with one hand and negotiated a sharp U-turn, while flicking on the windshield wipers with the other. "Whatcha doing standing out there all by yourself in the rain?" Before Sal could answer, Joe was off again. "Aw, Son, you shoudda seen it the other day. Me and Pete Lejeune and Tubby Gulotta—you know Tubby Gulotta, don'cha?—well, me and Pete and Tubby Gulotta go out to the Fair Grounds and there's this pretty little filly, I forget her name, what the fuck was her name? Well, it don't matter, I forget her name, and she's running in the sixth race and she's going off at something like sixteen-to-one, seventeen-to-one, *pretty* little filly, and Tubby Gulotta and Pete—you remember Tubby Gulotta? He used to be married to Danny O'Brien's sister Maxine?—well, him and Pete like this other horse, Front and Center, and ain't that funny I can remember the name of that horse and not the name of the one I liked? I must be getting old."

They were passing in front of St. Louis Cathedral then, and Joe D'Amore absently made a sign of the cross as they drove by the big front doors. "Anyways, Pete Lejeune and Tubby Gulotta *love* this fucking horse, Front and Center, *love* this fucking horse, but me, I got a feeling about this filly, I don't remember her name, I got a real *feeling* about her, and me and Pete and Tubby Gulotta go back and forth, back and forth, they wanna bet this Front and Center, me, I like the little filly, they wanna bet Front and Center, I wanna bet the filly, back and forth, back and forth, Front and Center, the filly, the filly, Front and Center—well, to make a long story short, they keep running their mouths at me until I change my bet and go with Front and Center and the filly win it and paid forty-two dollars and I ain't never going to the fucking track with Pete Lejeune and Tubby Gulotta again. Your aunt Lillian said she ain't seen you for over a month"—his eyes were on his son's in the wraparound—"maybe you oughtta pass by her house, she'll fix you something to eat." He had a paper-bagged pint in his right hand, and he spun off the cap with his thumb and put the bottle to his lips. Sal could hear his old man's throat working as he gulped the whiskey. Then he grimaced into the mirror, burped, and held up the bag. "You want a hit, Son?"

Joe the Hack, Joe the Hack. Always drunk or at the track.

Sal stared at his father in the wraparound, and thought, not for the first time in his life, *How the fuck did I get stuck with you? How the* fuck *did I get stuck with you? I got all your bad points, and you didn't have no good ones to give. I'm a* little *prick like you. I drink like you. I gamble like you. And I'm a loser like you. And you used to hang out with Johnny Venezia when you was kids? They must of kept you around to run errands, go for sandwiches, open their beers. A rabbit running with the wolves. A lamb for the slaughter. Yeah, just like me again.*

"Take a swig, Son," Joe said, shaking the bottle and making the whiskey gurgle. "It'll cut the cold."

He was a small, silver-haired, insignificant man in a dirty cap and cheap, nondescript clothing. A man *destined* to drive a cab with liquor on his breath. Not a good choice for a father.

Joe the Hack, Joe the Hack. Always drunk or—

"Yeah," Sal said in a thick, coarse voice, "give it here." He leaned forward and took the bottle from his father's hand. He settled back in the seat and sighed deeply.

"Go 'head, Son," Joe D'Amore said, almost eagerly, "go 'head. It'll cut right through that cold."

You bastard, Sal thought. *You little loser bastard. And I'm just like you.*

Sal tilted his head back and poured the raw, cheap bourbon into his mouth. It burned the back of his throat and made his eyes water. It raced through his nerve endings and struck his brain like a blow from a blunt object. Sal immediately had a mental vision of hanging himself with an electrical cord in his cramped, miserable Governor Nicholls Street apartment. That was an option. That was always an option. At least then you had some control over it all.

"You Aunt Lillian's worried about you," Joe was saying, "you oughtta pass by her house. You know how Lilly's always worried 'bout something or 'nother." He reached back and took the bottle from Sal's extended hand, then took a quick snort and propped the bottle upright in a well-worn groove between the seat cushions. "That Lillian," he said as he wiped the back of his hand over his lips. "She's trying to fix me up with that Frances Dupree, you know, that widow-woman lives down the block there on Music Street. Goes to mass with her at Saint Anthony's. You remember, her husband dropped dead with a heart attack while he was driving to work and ran into a whole bunch of people waiting by that bus stop in front of Sacred Heart Cemetery. It was a big mess. Killed a couple of people, and one of 'em was a pregnant girl. You remember reading about it in the *Times-Picayune*?" Sal didn't reply; he sat mesmerized by his father's mindless babble. Sal was having a hard time relating to the world tonight. "She's a pretty thing, Son. Got these big blue eyes, and keeps herself nice and trim, if you know what I mean. Guess I'm the only wop in the world likes skinny women." With that Joe plucked his dead wife's laminated picture from behind the plastic Madonna, held it to his lips, and kissed it noisily. Then he solemnly replaced it.

Sal ducked his head and peered over his father's shoulder and through the windshield. It was still misting outside, not really drizzling yet, but a constant damp haze, like liquid fog. The cab was on Canal Street now. They had circumnavigated the French Quarter and were heading away from the river.

"So whattaya think, Son?" Joe rambled on. "I told Lillian, I said, 'Lillian, I'm too old for that shit,' and you know what your aunt Lillian said?" His eyes sought out his son's in the wraparound mirror. "Your aunt Lillian said, 'Joe, you the youngest man I know.' " He smiled proudly. "So this Sunday Lillian's gonna make a big spaghetti dinner and her and Georgie and me and Frances gonna sit down, have something to eat, then we gonna drive over to Chalmette and go to a movie. I ain't been to a movie in fifteen years. I ain't been on a date for a hundred and fifteen. A fucking date! Whattaya think of them beans?" His reflection was beaming back at Sal. "Say, Son, I was wondering," Joe began offhandedly, his smile still in place. "I was wondering you had a few extra dollars you could front me for a coupla weeks. The date with Frances coming up and all, and Mrs. Cuccia been on my ass about the rent. See, I guess I dropped the rent money betting on that Front and Center horse, and that pretty little filly run the race of her fucking life, you shoudda seen it, Son. Just for a coupla weeks."

Joe angled the cab across two lanes of traffic and brought it to a stop before the big revolving doors of the King Louis Hotel. The doorman, under a gaily colored, oversized umbrella, made a move to open the cab door, then recognized Sal as a hotel employee and backed off with a frown.

Joe turned in his seat and looked full face at his son. "Just for a coupla weeks, Son. Just till I get back on my feet. That little filly fucking broke my heart."

I'm just like you, Sal thought. *I'm a loser just like you.*

"I think I got something here I don't need," Sal said, and peeled off five hundred-dollar bills from the wad Santo had given him. He folded it over and slipped it surreptitiously into his father's hand, even though there were just the two of them to witness it.

"*Hey!*" Joe exclaimed, fanning the hundreds like a hand of cards, "looka here. You musta hit a long shot, huh, Son?"

"Something like that, Papa."

The old man's eyes warmed at the use of Sal's childhood name for him. He reached over the back of the seat and gripped Sal's arm. "You're a good boy, Salvatore. You mama always used to say that, and it's the God's truth. You're a good boy." The old drunk was almost crying. "I'm gonna pay you back, Son. In just a coupla weeks I'll be back on my feet, and then I'll pay you back with interest."

Sure you will, Sal thought. *Just like I'm gonna pay Johnny Venezia the money I owe him.*

"You're such a good boy, Salvatore, just like your mama always said."

I gotta get out of here, Sal said to himself. He looked out the window at the big bright entrance to the King Louis. In the lobby behind the gigantic glass doors mobs of people were moving to and fro. *I've worked here six nights of the week for almost three months,* Sal thought, *and I feel like I never seen the place before. I feel like I just stepped out of a fucking spaceship.*

"Just until I get back on—"

I gotta get outta here!

"Look, Papa," Sal interrupted as he pushed open the cab door, "I gotta get to the gig, I'm gonna be late."

Joe glanced up at the stick-on watch he kept on his sun visor. "Whoo*wee!* You already late. You better hurry up, Son."

Sal stepped out onto the red-carpeted sidewalk and slammed the door. He hesitated a heartbeat, then knelt by the driver's side and peered in at his father. "Look, Papa. I want you to take care of yourself. I mean, if I have to leave town in a hurry or something, I want you to take care of yourself, you hear?"

Joe D'Amore's eyes danced with excitement. "Hey, you got a call to go to Vegas or some place like that?"

Sal forced himself to smile. "You never know, Papa. You never know."

Joe D'Amore radiated pride. "Aw, Salvatore, I knew you was gonna get your break someday. What I always tell you? You got too much talent for them to leave you here."

"Anyway, Papa. I want you to take care of yourself, okay?"

Joe D'Amore reached out of the cab's window and massaged the back of his son's neck with affection. "You're a good boy, Sal. I love you, Son. I really love you." He looked at his only child expectantly.

Say it! Sal thought. *Just fucking say it! Give it to him, it don't cost nothing. Just say what he wants to h—*

"I gotta go, Papa." He straightened up suddenly. "You take care of yourself."

"I love you, Salvatore," Joe D'Amore said again, with a sodden smile.

Jesus. Sal turned around and faced the hotel. *I don't wanna go in there.* He looked back at his father. The little man gave him a cheery thumbs-up. "Good-bye, Joe," Sal murmured beneath his breath, "me gotta go," then trotted up the short flight of carpeted stairs, stepped quickly to the heavy revolving doors, and pushed through.

The lobby of the King Louis was cooking. Mardi Gras season. And the inclement weather only drove the partygoers inside; it didn't postpone the festivities for a moment. Tourists were merrily crisscrossing the packed floor, shoving and shouldering themselves from one raucous bar to another. The King Louis had four on the ground level alone. In one of them a Dixieland band was playing "Way Down Yonder," and the music seemed to bleed out and make the whole building reverberate. A man and a woman were having a loud, profane argument a few feet in front of Sal, and no one even seemed to notice. On a plush leather couch in a sunken alcove another pair were about as deep in the throes of passion as two people can get with their clothes on, and nobody paid them any mind, either. *Mardi Gras,* Sal thought. *Crazy fucking Mardi Gras.*

The concierge, encircled behind his little fort of a cubicle by jostling, demanding hotel guests, still wasn't too busy to give Sal's jeans, flannel shirt, and ill-fitting jacket a disapproving ogle.

What the fuck am I doing here? Sal asked himself. *I got a plane to catch. I gotta get outta Dodge.* He looked back over his shoulder, and through the raucous, bustling crowd that had closed behind him he caught glimpses of his old man, still sitting in his cab out there in the rain beyond the big doors, still smiling that shit-eating grin and waving that motherfucking thumb around like he was gonna shove it up God's ass.

Jesus H. Christ. What am I doing here? What time is it?

Why did I get outta the old man's cab? I can't stay here. Why didn't I tell him to drive me to the airport? I gotta get the hell outta here. Shit! he thought. *It's still not too late. Yes, it is. I could go back outside, jump in Joe's cab, and be at the airport in fifteen minutes. No,* he told himself, *don't do that. Leave the old man outta this. Or as much as you can.*

I'm gonna go up, grab my tux, he decided. *With a tuxedo and a piano, I can make a living anywhere in the fucking world. Yeah? Whose name they gonna put on the marquee? Don't worry about that now. Just go up, get the tux, and when you come down, Joe'll be gone and you can get the fuck outta here.*

Sounds like a plan to me, he said to himself. *Keep that sense of humor. Don't think too much about how scared shitless Santo was about your predicament. Just take it one step at a time. Go get the tux. Just go get the fucking tux.*

Sal pushed his way through the crowd, ignoring the evil looks he got from people whose feet he walked over, elbowing those who wouldn't get out of his way. Two at a time, he took the stairs up to the mezzanine, where he knew from experience it was much easier to catch an elevator. Wedging his way to the front of a small knot of drunks loud-talking while they waited for the next car, he was able to slip on the very first time the doors roboted open. He punched *P* and kept his eyes forward, while in back of him the good ol' boys from Dallas were having the time of their lives, ribbing each other and toasting themselves with the big hurricane glasses they all carried. *Mother Mary, to be so carefree,* Sal thought. *To not be terrified of the future. To* have *a future.*

The Texans all got off on the fourteenth floor, bragging of pussy eaten and assholes beaten, and Sal rode up to the penthouse alone. *Somehow, someway, I'll get through this day,* he promised himself. *I'll get through this day, and then I'm gonna get drunk and stay drunk for a week.*

The elevator doors parted to reveal the penthouse of the King Louis, an elegant formal dining room that presented its patrons with a 360-degree view of the city. The bridge over the river glittered like a child's toy behind the misted-over glass walls. The place was dim and subdued, rich in meaningful conversations, heavy white linen, and polished gold-trimmed silverware. The only obvious thing the restaurant seemed to lack was a tinkling piano.

Sal stepped off the elevator, directly into the laser beams of displeasure glowing from the eyes of Albert Celestine, the maître d'.

"You late, boy."

Albert Celestine was a thin, fastidious man of café-au-lait complexion who had a split-level house in Pontchartrain Park, one daughter in medical school in Boston, another in California married to a white man, and a burning contempt for all Caucasians who hadn't done as well in life as Albert Celestine had.

"You late, and you look like street trash. Get your ass in the back and get dressed, boy."

"Albert—"

"I don't wanna hear it, boy, you hear me. Get in the back

and get dressed and get your ass on that piano."

"You don't understand, Albert, I can't work tonight. I just come up here for my clothes."

Albert Celestine's hard yellow eyes bored into Sal's. "What you talkin' about, boy? Don't gimme this shit."

"Albert—"

"You signed a Musicians' Union contract with this hotel," Albert hissed. "You can't quit without giving two weeks' notice. You break that contract, I'll make sure you never get another union job."

You'll never work in this town again. Somewhere inside himself Sal laughed with whatever was left of that sense of humor. *He's actually telling me I'll never work in this town again.*

"You can't quit tonight," Albert was saying. "I got Mr. Ross sitting over there." The hotel's owner, who usually spent the winter at his other hotel, the one in Honolulu. He must be in town for the Carnival. Sal peeked around a glittering glass column and spied fat Mr. Ross in a private booth snuggled up with a fluffy little blonde on either arm. Albert leaned closer and breathed in Sal's ear, "You can't quit tonight, boy. That fat Jew'll have my ass."

"Look, Albert—"

"*You* look, boy," he said in an angry, compressed whisper. "How many times I covered for your sorry ass, you come dragging in here late and loaded?" He examined Sal's tense face. "What's the matter wit'chu? You sick or something?"

"Albert, I gotta leave. I can't—"

"You owe me, you little motherfucker. How many times I saved your job for you? How many motherfucking times? How many times I fronted you your salary so them 'talian boys don't break your fucking knees? And now Mr. Ross is sitting over there asking where the motherfucking piano player is, and you wanna forget all about what I done for you?"

"You don't understand. I can't."

"Just for half an hour—"

"I *can't*—"

"—by that time that fat bastard'll be up in his suite with *both* them little bitches sitting on his face. All I need is one half an hour."

"Albert, please don't do this to—"

"Look, boy, what am I asking for—your motherfucking *life?*"

Sal stared helplessly at the tall tan man for a moment. Then he was gripped by an intense, illogical anger. *His life was shit anyway. What difference? What fucking difference?* "Yes!" he growled furiously. "Yes, you are." He pushed past Albert on his way to the dressing rooms behind the kitchen.

"Hurry up, boy!" Celestine hissed after him.

In the cramped, funky dressing room Sal furiously ripped his clothes off and yanked his tuxedo from the high hook where it always hung when it wasn't in service or getting cleaned. *This is crazy,* he fumed. *This is totally, unalterably insane. It's suicide.* He tore the shirt off the hanger and pulled it over his shoulders. It felt clean and crisp and cool. *Like a shroud,* he told himself. *I'm getting dressed for a fucking funeral. My own fucking funeral.* Unknowingly, in his unfocused rage and disabling fear, he began to sing softly as he dressed. *"I went down to St. James Infirmary. And I found my baby there. She was stretched out on a long white table. So sweet, so cold so bare."*

He looked at himself in the big floor-length mirror. His eyes were sunken back into their sockets over a scruffy two-day growth of heavy beard on his drawn cheeks. *A corpse. I look like a fucking corpse. The corpse of a bum, a down-and-outer, a loser. Loser Big Time.*

"Let her go, let her go, God bless her—" He hummed as he attached his clip-on bow tie. *"Put a twenty-dollar gold piece on my watch chain."* He ran a brush through his damp hair and stepped back from the mirror to examine himself. The thought ran through his head, *Mr. Ross is out there. Maybe he'll wanna use me in his place in Hawaii. Maybe he'll wanna invest—*

"What the fuck am I doing?" Sal said aloud to his reflection. "I gotta get out of here."

He snatched up Cat's leather jacket, hustled out of the dressing room and through the bright, busy kitchen, and stood, anxious and tense, ignored by the bustling waiters and busboys, impatiently poking his finger at the service-elevator call button.

"C'mon! *C'mon!*" he cursed at the elevator that wouldn't come.

"Where you goin', boy?" Albert Celestine suddenly had his

lanky arm around the smaller man's shoulders. "You ain't runnin' away now, now you all dressed up?"

Sal looked up at the perfectly pressed black man with a glint of irrational panic in his eyes. "Albert," he pleaded, "for the love of Christ, man, you don't understand, I gotta leave here *now*."

The maître d' was already turning his piano player around, heading him back toward the dining room, the piano. For fifty years, working in nightclubs, restaurants, and hotels, Albert Celestine had dealt with alcoholic and addicted musicians. He had long ago lost any sympathy he might once have felt for them, and simply tried to get them through whatever of the various crises they seemed to be always getting themselves into, or at least get them through it until his shift was over. Then all you could do was hope that they'd show up tomorrow night.

"Lookahere"—Albert's bony hands dug into Sal's shoulders as he led him back into the dining room—"you got a *job* to do, boy."

"I can't—"

"'Course you can." He steered Sal into the bar area and pulled him over to a waitress's station.

"Hi, Sal," one of the drink waitresses said with a smile as she breezed by with a full tray.

"Earl," Albert held up his hand to the bartender and made a wide C with his thumb and index finger, "pour my boy here a stiff one." He turned his attention back to his piano player. "What you drink, boy, Jack Daniel's? J. D., Earl."

"Albert, a drink ain't what I need," Sal complained.

"Well, I can't give you no heroin, at least not on such short notice, so why don't chu just toss back this here and go on over to the piano over there and play a few of them tunes you know Mr. Ross likes so much." He put the drink in Sal's hand—actually *placed* it in his fist and wrapped his fingers around it.

"Albert, I gotta leave town," Sal said as Albert helped him raise the glass to his lips. "You don't understand."

"No, boy," Albert continued relentlessly, "*you* don't understand. Mr. Ross over there done signed for his check, the bitch on the right been jerking him off under the table for ten minutes now, and they all just about finished their drinks. All I need from you is go over there and sing a coupla them songs he likes you to sing. Mr. Ross sees his piano player is a little late but on the job, and he's gonna shoot outta here with them two 'hoes faster than he's gonna shoot his load when he gets to the room. All I need from you is just a few minutes, a coupla tunes."

"Albert," Sal begged, "I don't think I can do it. I *really* don't—"

"Well, I *know* you can, boy. I got *complete* confidence in you." With his hand on the base of the glass he almost *poured* the drink into Sal's mouth. "There you go. That'll fix what ails you." He maintained his pressure on the bottom of the glass until Sal had downed all of the whiskey. Then he took the empty glass away from his piano player and set it down sharply on the bar. Sal stood there blinking, shaking, the triple of Jack Daniel's raging through his body like a virus. An amber trickle coursed down through the stubble on his chin.

Albert took a firm grip on his arm and led him out of the bar area, across the dance floor, and toward the piano. "Let's have a big, warm welcome," the maître d' called out in a booming voice to the crowded dining room. "Let's have a big, warm Penthouse welcome for the King Louis's Prince of the Piano, Noo Awlins' own—Sal D'Amore!" He settled his piano player into his seat behind the big baby grand piano bar and quickly raised his hands in a show of exaggerated applause. "Let's hear it for him, folks. He had to fight the storm and the rain to get here, but here he is! Let's show him how much we appreciate him." Then Albert Celestine, still applauding, moved away, across the dance floor, and was gone.

Sal sat at the keyboard, staring out across the flat, endless expanse of the polished glass piano bar. *I can't do this.* There were no customers perched on the semicircle of low barstools, so Sal could see all the diners in the room.

And they could see him.

I can't do this. There is no way I can do this.

Earl, behind the bar, flicked on the spotlight, and Sal actually jumped when the white pinpoint lasered down from the ceiling and bathed him in glare.

Someone in the audience tittered nervously. Someone else

started to say something, and his wife shushed him.

Sal stared out through the glare of the spotlight. The only face he could make out was Albert Celestine's, glaring back at him from the dark void.

This is insanity. Total insanity. I can't do this.

Sal made himself smile out at the people. See, folks, here I am. Everything's A-okay. The show must go on. He adjusted the Beyer mike on the gooseneck and stared out at the darkness with a sickly smile frozen on his lips. He cleared his throat in the mike, and the sound went out over the P.A. system. That same asshole chuckled again. Sal stared down at the piano keys. Ebony and ivory. He began to coldly shiver when he realized the keyboard was totally foreign to him. It was as if he'd never seen one before. He couldn't play the piano. Whoever had had that idea?

I gotta get outta here. Holy Jesus, I gotta get outta here.

Still sending that horrible, stomach-turning false smile out to the people, he gently laid his hands on the Yamaha grand's sparkling keyboard and with his fingers tentatively formed an extended G-minor 9 chord—*I can't do this!*—and slowly pressed down, having absolute no confidence that what he was about to hear would sound like anything he had ever heard before in his life.

The chord wafted out soft and sweet and expectant, and there was a palpable sense of release from the audience. They were not in the company of a madman.

Sal's hands slipped over the piano keys and seemingly of their own volition spelled a C9th, the logical, mathematical follow-up to the preceding chord. Sal played the change and added a bluesy high fill at the top of the keyboard. *Headline*—the thought flew errantly through his mind—*his hands lived on long after he was brain-dead and buried.* The dining room was slowly returning to its business—glasses clinked expensively, silverware scratched softly on fine china. *Look away,* Sal begged of them, *look away. Dixieland.*

Sal played an F-major 7th, and that seemed to reassure the beasts even more. There was the beginning of the hum of contented conversation.

And just then an authoritative, steel-edged whine of a voice sliced through the others—cut them off, silenced them like an unloved schoolteacher shushing a classroom of pubescent students. "Do that one I like," the voice barked, and just like *that* Sal could feel the room's attention rivet on him again, like a pack of hounds catching the scent of its quarry. Sal's left leg began to shake violently. It had never done that before in his whole life, and he gaped down at it in horror.

"Do that one I like," the nerve-shredding screech jangled again. "You know the one. That one I like."

Sal knew the voice, knew it belonged to his boss, Eddie Ross, but still he sustained his last chord with the damper pedal, shaded his eyes with his right hand, and there was Mr. Ross, nodding at him from his raised-level booth, demonstrating to his two ripe little hookers how his employees jumped when he gave orders. Power is a turn-on.

Another irrelevant idea crossed the front of his mind. *Those two whores could be from Nicky Venezia's stable. They could be Nicky's.* The thought made Sal's leg tremble even more.

"Yeah, do that one," another voice rang out. Albert Celestine publicly kissing his boss's ass. "That's the best one you do."

Sal's hands went about their business. Like veteran assembly-line workers, they knew their job, even if management was experiencing internal convulsions. They played a gentle, descending progression, modulating unnoticeably to E-flat, Sal's key for Eddie Ross's favorite song. They conspired with each other to lay down a slow, bluesy I-IV-I-V sequence, an ancient, comfortable New Orleans chain of chords. Some of the tourists, hovering vulturine over their blackened redfish, were already tapping their toes, bobbing their heads, so eager were they to soak up some of that fabled New Orleans soul.

Sal's hands played the changes over and over, setting the mood, settling the beat, creating the tension, waiting for the rest of Sal to take over. He touched his lips familiarly against the microphone's textured windscreen, like a lover teasing a clitoris, and he closed his eyes and tried to let the music take him, but his mind wouldn't leave him alone.

I can't do this. Why would anyone ever do this? Why would anyone ever want *to do this? Sweet Jesus, I gotta get outta here.*

"*Do you know what it means,*" Sal suddenly sang to the watching audience, "*to miss New Orleans, to miss it each night and day?*"

Immediately the out-of-towners were nodding knowingly to each other. Hey, this guy can really sing. Even if he looks like a drowned rat, something the cat dragged in. *"I know I'm not wrong, the feelin's gettin' stronger—the longer I stay away."* Some of the yokels were turning in their seats, craning their necks to get a better look-see at the source of this fine, soulful tenor voice. *"Miss the moss-covered vines, the tall sugar pines—"* Sal crooned, and his mind ran ahead of him like a frightened dog. *What the fuck am I doing? I can't do this. I gotta get outta here, get outta town. "The moonlight on the bayou—a Creole tune that fills the air—"* Through the restaurant's gloom he could see, glowing in his table's candlelight like a nimbus, Mr. Ross's coarse, flabby face, smiling approval. Under the table, shining in the shadows, one of the blond hookers' pale hands rubbed back and forth, back and forth, on the fabric of Ross's crotch. *I'm gonna die tonight. I'm gonna die tonight because I'm so fucking weak I can't find the balls to just get up and walk out of here. For that I deserve to die. Maybe I'm already dead, I just don't remember getting killed. Maybe this is hell. Sure the fuck* feels *like hell. My God, what time is it?* Still singing, he glanced down at his hands, as if he were concentrating on a difficult chordal passage. His cheap digital watch read out *8:28* in little red numbers. *I'm a dead man. I got an hour and a half to live. Catch my act quick, folks, the show closes tonight. No return engagement. "Do you know what it means, to miss New Orleans,"* Sal asked, *"when that's where you left your heart?"* A beaming, well-dressed couple in their eighties danced onto the floor, enraptured by the music and the opportunity to dance. *"And there's something more—I miss the one I care for—more than I miss New Orleans."*

He negotiated the turnaround, automatically playing some whorehouse Ray Charles piano fills that deposited him back at the top of the tune. And then the waiters, the busboys, the drink waitresses—even Earl behind the bar—began to softly hum the schmaltzy, melancholy melody. It was a bit he did with the house, a little piece of business everyone was in on, but *not tonight, Dear God, not tonight.*

"Guy walks into a bar in Cleveland," Sal said, and heard his voice come back at him from the monitors over the lazy chording and bittersweet humming. "Guy walks into a bar in Cleveland and asks the waiter for a table for one in front, near the bandstand." The tourists were totally focused on him now. Even the elderly pair of dancers were absently shuffling in a lazy circle as they watched him. "They band comes back from their break and starts to play. They start to play this song, 'Do You Know What It Means to Miss New Orleans?,' the one I'm playing right now, and they feature the trumpet player on it." Sal paused here, as he always did at this point, and the humming employees did a brief comic crescendo on the melody, as they always did right here, then dropped back down to a singsong whisper. One of the customers chuckled. Sal felt himself part of some foolish theatrical farce. He had become this tragicomic figure in a third-rate regional production. He was a clown in a cheap one-ring circus. "This night the trumpet player is really *on.* I mean, he really feels it. He's playing this song for all he's worth, man, he's really getting into it. Do you *know* what it means to miss New Orleans? Man, he's *blowing!* And all of a sudden he notices the guy sitting right there in front of the stage—the guy's *crying!* Tears running down his face! And the more the trumpet player blows, the more the guy cries. He's sobbing. He can't control himself. He puts his head down on the table and wails. I mean, it's *heartbreaking!*" He paused and squinted out past the spotlight. He hated not being able to see the audience. He always had. There was something out there, some enormous, starving beast that nourished itself on darkness and air-conditioned chill and breathed secondary cigarette smoke. It was out there, crouching beyond the lights and the monitors, and it watched him hungrily, secretly, waiting for a sign of weakness, of uncertainty. "After the song's over, the trumpet player goes over to the guy and says, 'Say, man, I'm so blown away the music affected you like that. Are you from New Orleans?' The guy looks up at him and says, 'No—"

Pause. The beast must be amused.

'—I'm a trumpet player.' "

For a heartbeat of a moment there was complete stillness, total silence. And then a woman over against the wall got it and broke out laughing, and then they all saw the joke and the packed house was roaring. The patrons nudged each other and applauded appreciatively while they laughed.

It was the strongest response Sal had ever gotten from the bit, and although he had basically known when and how the audience was going to react, he wasn't ready for it. It was as if he were *surprised* by their acceptance. Their laughter startled Sal. He was supposed to come in now, before the laughs died, and sing out the last eight bars of the song, that was the timing of the piece, but he found that he couldn't. It just wasn't in him. The day had been too much for him. He had been a man dangling from a precipice by his fingertips. The audience's laughter disoriented him, and he lost his grip. He fell from the mountaintop, crashing over and over again as he tumbled down.

Sal started to cry. He took his hands from the keyboard, covered his face and sobbed. Deep, lung-wrenching, sodden gasps.

The people in the audience roared their approval. This was great! This guy's incredible! We thought he was just a singing piano player, but he's also a really great comedian! What's his name? What did they say his name was?

The audience laughed and applauded, but the waiters and waitresses watched, horrified. The house knew this was *not* part of the act. Eddie Ross pushed the whore's hand away from his wilting dick. Albert Celestine was incensed. Why on his shift? Why did this have to happen on his shift?

At the piano Sal fought to wrest control of himself, but his heart was whamming around his chest like a frightened animal in a cage. His hands could feel the wetness on his face.

Is this a nervous breakdown? It can't be a nervous breakdown. People don't have nervous breakdowns anymore. At least not Italians from down around the Industrial Canal. Jews from uptown have nervous breakdowns. Wasps from the Garden District. Ninth Ward guys like me who make fifteen K a year go nuts, lose their nerves, flip their wigs, go crazy. Ninth Ward guys like me who make fifteen K a year and lose a hundred and eighty thousand of Johnny Venezia's money lose their minds all over the backseats of their cars with the help of a 9-millimeter handgun.

Sal moaned behind his hands, and the mike picked it up and bellowed it out at the crowd. Some of the customers who a moment ago were guffawing at what they assumed was Sal's comic presentation were now becoming extremely uneasy with the show. *I know what's funny, and this is* not *funny. This guy's going too far!* The laughter was dying away, like distant thunder.

The customers were picking up the tension of the employees, who stood frozen in their tracks. Gina, the waitress who had greeted Sal just minutes earlier, sniffed and wiped at her eyes with a cocktail napkin. Something was very wrong here, and the audience was rapidly becoming aware of it.

Sal suddenly sobbed loudly into the microphone and choked out a sodden, "I'm so sorry, folks. I didn't want this to happen." He fought to hold back the tears, to regain control of himself, to *act like a fucking professional, for Chrissakes!,* but by now he was a runaway horse, panicking in a burning stable. "You shouldn't hafta see this shit!" Sal sobbed. "This is the City that Care Forgot. You came to Noo Awlins to have a good time, didn't you?" The audience was emitting an angry buzz, like a disturbed wasp's nest. This had gone too far. First this horrendous New Orleans weather, and now this! The okra gumbo was congealing, the crawfish étouffée stuck in the throat like a lump of lard. *And at these prices!*

"Get that guy out of here!" shouted an angry flat midwestern voice. "Get him *out* of here!"

"That boy's not well," bellowed a big Alabaman with a napkin tucked under his chin. "Man shouldn't cry in public like that."

"The show must go on!" Sal shouted tearfully into the mike, just as a short Japanese tourist knelt on the dance floor by the shocked-motionless Arthur Murray couple and snapped a quick shot of the crazy American. "*Domo,*" the short man said, and bowed slightly before running back to his table.

I gotta get outta here! Sal thought behind his tears, and blindly shoved away the boom mike. It swung violently around and struck a speaker cabinet, and the speakers immediately began to shriek earsplitting feedback. The diners clapped their hands to their ears and shouted for someone to *stop that noise! Stop that goddamn noise!*

Eddie Ross, the King Louis's owner, trying desperately to burrow out from behind his booth's bolted-to-the-floor table, pushed one of the delicious little hookers off her seat onto her delectable little ass. "Albert!" Mr. Ross howled. "Al-*beeerrrt!*"

Sal, clambering out from behind the grand piano, spilling drinks, knocking over cocktail tables, sending fake books sailing, cried, "I can't do this, folks! I can't do this!" with the feedback screaming in everyone's ears, the audience shouting indignantly. And then Albert Celestine was beside him, had a firm grip on his arm, and was pulling him through the dining room, spitting in his ear like a venomous snake. "You fool! What the hell you done done?"

"Albert!" Eddie Ross shouted from across the room, where he was unaware that he was standing on the little hooker's hand. "Get him out of here, Al-*beeerrrt!*"

"Lissen to Mr. Ross!" Albert sputtered as he yanked Sal around the potted palmetto plants and into the foyer, out of sight of the offended eyes of the customers. "Lissen to that man, boy. You done fucked up royally. That little Jew ain't never gonna forget what you done tonight." He pulled Sal up short before the elevator doors, then fixed his angry yellow eyes on him. "And neither will I."

"Albert, I'm so sorry," Sal stammered, "but I told you I couldn't—"

"*No!*" Albert barked as he stabbed at the elevator button, "I told *you!* I told you to go in there and just give me twenty motherfucking minutes at that motherfucking piano, everything would be all right. But no, you couldn't do that! You couldn't do that after all what I done for you? You know what the trouble with you is, boy?" He moved his forefinger from the elevator call button and jabbed it into Sal's chest. "The trouble with you is you always mistake kindness for weakness." He glared at Sal self-righteously. "But you done really fucked up now. You done tore your drawers in this town, boy. I got friends in Local One-seventy-four. I'll make sure you *never* do this to another restaurateur, you can believe *that,* boy! Huh-huh! Not in this town."

But that's just it, Sal's mind screamed. *I gotta get* out *of this town!*

The elevator doors whooshed open, and Albert almost *threw* the shorter Sal into the empty elevator. Then he pointed that accusing finger and said to Sal what Albert Celestine wanted to say to just about every white man he had ever met. "If you was colored," he sneered, "you'd *starve.* Get the hell out of the King Louis, and never come back in here again."

The doors began to close. Albert stood there, chastising Sal—"Don't chu *ever* come round here again, boy!"—until the polished metal doors closed on him and Sal was blessedly alone. He slumped back against the elevator's lightly vibrating wall and wiped his eyes boyishly with the back of his hand. He was losing his grip on reality, and he knew it. Everything was chaotic. Nothing was normal. Nothing was familiar. He felt totally exhausted, drugged even. Quaaluded out. Fixed with heroin. His limbs were leaden, weighted with the day's heaviness. He had never before lived through a day like this day. He might not live through this one. *Shit!* He had forgotten Cat's leather jacket. Maybe he could call her from somewhere and tell her where to pick it up. He had to go home and pack a few things, get the fuck out of here. *What time is it? Almost nine.* He had to leave, and leave now. He couldn't afford to fuck around any longer. Time was running out, and running out fast.

The elevator stopped at the sixth floor and was invaded by a drunken pack of big, loud cowboys in western-cut suits accompanied by their pale, peroxided Dallas-cloned women. They crowded in happily, laughing and cursing. Completely ignoring Sal, they turned their backs and jammed him hard against the elevator's back wall. A basketball-tall, broad-shouldered man with a sun-browned face under a wide-brimmed hat held his pink, hourglass-shaped hurricane glass above his head so it wouldn't get smashed. "I'm tellin' you," he continued his conversation in a voice that sounded like saddle leather creaking, "when I was a kid, I spent every winter in South Dakota haulin' my grandpa's beeves out of snowdrifts up over my head, and I ain't *never* been as cold as I was today on that damn ferry. *Jesus Howdy,* but that damn wind off that big-ass river cut right through me like a goddamn razor. And that miserable-ass rain, I swear, was colder than any hail I ever seen."

"Aw, Tom," one of other cowboys teased, "you just hadn't got enough of the Bourbon Street hurricane juice in you yet. I bet *now* you could swim in that damn river and not feel a goddamn thang!"

The elevator's cargo roared with laughter, and someone reached across in front of Sal's eyes and slapped ol' Tom heartily on his back.

"Sheeet!" Ol' Tom grinned and shook his head. "I wouldn't swim in that damn river on a bet. Me and Claudette looked down from that iron rigging when we was getting on that ferry,

and I swear, there was river rats down in them rocks big enough you could put a damn brand on!"

The elevator shook with laughter.

"Damn things was so big you could *herd* them suckers!"

More laughter. Then Claudette, a floppy-breasted brunette with pale skin, piped in, "I swear, I thought they was a bunch of Brahma bulls, tryin' to ford the Mississippi!"

Everyone roared at that, then the elevator doors parted to reveal the revelers on the first floor, and Little Johnny Venezia and Dago Red La Rocca were standing there looking anything but pleased. Sal felt his intestines quiver and his scalp tingle. *It's too early! It's too early! I still have an hour left.* He peeked under ol' Tom's armpit and Little Johnny was glowering right at him, and Sal had to steel himself to keep from blacking out, the rush of terror was that strong. And then he was washed with relief when he realized that Little Johnny was glaring at big ol' Tom, not at him. He couldn't even *see* Sal. Sal glanced quickly at Dago Red, but Red had moved a little to the left, out of his line of vision. *If I can't see him, he can't see me,* Sal thought, and then scrunched even further down behind ol' Tom's wide, western-cut back.

"First floor. Everybody out," Sal heard a low, sneering downtown voice impatiently say, and he knew it was Little Johnny's. The voice was soaked with anger and menace, and Sal's balls seemed to shrivel up into his belly at the sound of it. And then came Dago Red's bastard file of a rasp. "Yeah, everybody out!"

There was a moment of complete stillness in the elevator. The lobby behind Little Johnny and Dago Red was packed now, and very drunk. The revelers were blowing little plastic horns and strutting parade-style in tight little circles. A woman somewhere laughed hysterically.

Then ol' Tom spoke in a tone straight out of an old Gary Cooper movie. "We don't *want* the first floor, hoss. We're goin' all the way down to the parking structure." Ol' Tom smiled at him. "If that's awright with you."

Sal ducked down and from around one of Claudette's pendulous breasts caught a hidden glimpse of Little Johnny glaring hatefully up at big ol' Tom. Johnny Venezia wasn't accustomed to people not jumping when he gave orders. Besides, it was common knowledge that Little Johnny Venezia loathed rednecks. It had something to do with a very unpleasant incident once in the Texas prison system, a very unpleasant place.

The elevator doors began to robot closed, and ol' Tom grinned and said down to Little Johnny, a man almost two feet smaller than himself, "Guess you'll have to wait for the next one, Short Stuff."

The doors bumped closed, shutting out the view of Little Johnny's sputtering, enraged face, and the westerners all joined in laughing and congratulating ol' Tom.

"Didju see the look that little greaseball give you, Tom? I reckon that sawed-off little runt was about to bust a gut."

"Goddamn Eye-talians," Claudette complained. "Town's crawling with 'em."

"I betcha that little fucker was a Meskin," another cowboy drawled. "Or one of them fucking Eye-ranians."

The elevator doors bumped open to the cold, cavernous parking basement, and the cowboys and their women shoved their way off, their loud voices echoing off the damp cement walls as they walked away, telling each other tired ethnic jokes. If they had even noticed Sal, they had never given any sign of it. Sal moved to the entrance of the empty elevator and pressed his finger on the "hold" button. The nasal western voices trailed off like a ghostly sound track. In a moment there was the hidden sound of a car's cold engine turning over, followed by the grinding of gears and the gentle squealing of radial tires. Then there was a kind of impure silence. Sal ventured out of the elevator very tentatively, like a rabbit leaving its warren, first his head, then his shoulders, then his upper body. The cowboys and their wives were gone. The parking structure was deserted. From somewhere out on the street came the muffled tattoo of a marching band—bass-drum heartbeats, militaristic snares, shrill, birdlike piccolos. The parade was rolling, after all.

A buzzer in the elevator went off angrily, and Sal jumped. Someone on a floor above was summoning the elevator. *It could be Little Johnny,* Sal realized with fear. *That could be Little Johnny Venezia pressing that buzzer.* Sal released the "hold" button, and the doors immediately began to glide toward each other. Sal stepped off the elevator, and they closed behind him. He could hear the winch's whine as the elevator rose up in the shaft. Sal studied the rows of parked cars. Almost every one had out-of-state plates.

I waited too long, he said to himself. *I fucked around and waited too long, and now I'm gonna die for it.*

Shut up! he thought bitterly. *Just shut up and get the fuck outta here. Get moving!*

He jammed his fists into the pockets of his tuxedo pants and began to walk resolutely down the rows of cars. His footsteps echoed theatrically through the garage. In his pocket his trembling fingers closed over the wad of hundred-dollar bills Santo had given him. He had given Joe some money—that seemed like an eternity ago—but he still had enough to buy a plane ticket out of town. All he had to do was keep his wits about him. *Don't panic. Just* don't panic.

The concrete floor sloped up to the narrow opening, almost a full story above, that exited onto Canal Street, and as Sal leaned forward and trudged up the incline toward the outlet, the sounds of the parade passing just outside grew louder and louder. The marching band was blaring a bouncy, brassy arrangement of "Funkytown." Muffled shouts of joy drifted down the incline, sounding not that much different from screams of rage.

Little John's people might be out there, Sal thought as he got closer and closer to the parade noise. *He wouldn't have come here alone. Little Johnny doesn't go anywhere alone. Al Castiglia got nervous about his money, went to the Sporting Life a coupla hours early, somebody called Little Johnny, he figured everything out, and now they probably got twenty guys all around the hotel while he goes up to the penthouse with Dago Red.*

Sal hesitated halfway up the driveway. Looking up and out into the street, from this angle he could see the tops of the Carnival floats parading by against the misty black skies. Men in damp gold lamé and waterproof makeup tossed trinkets to the crowd. He was terrified. The fear gnawed at his insides like rats at a corpse. He wanted to turn back, but to what? Dago Red and Little Johnny would be waiting for him in the lobby. Jesus, if he could only turn back, walk back in time to this morning, yesterday, last week. If only he had stopped gambling this morning when he was—

"D'Amore!" a voice shouted out behind him. "Hey, mother-*fuck*er!"

Sal felt his anus tighten and his heart rate zoom. He turned back and saw Nicky and Junior Venezia below him in the parking garage. Nicky reached under his Giorgio Armani coat and withdrew a pistol.

Sal whirled around and began to scramble up the last few yards of the inclined driveway.

"*Hey, motherfucker!*" he heard Nicky scream, and then, just as he reached the street, two sharp reports, and he felt a pebble of blasted cement strike his leg. Then he was outside in the cold air, running on the sidewalk, and the crowd was jammed around him, lined up ten deep to watch the parade, in heavy overcoats and thermal jackets, their arms flung up, grasping to catch the souvenir doubloons and *Made In Czechoslovakia* glass beads that the rich drunkards threw from the festooned floats. The party-goers shouted the traditional, "Throw me something, mister! Throw me something, mister!," clutching out at the cheap "throws," and Sal waded frantically through the people, pushing and shoving, and a tall teenager with his girl perched high on his shoulders lost his balance, and he and his girl went down into the crowd with the girl shrieking, and the mob of people surged away from Sal, and he looked behind, and a half-block back Nicky Venezia was coming out of the King Louis's parking basement. Nicky saw Sal and Sal saw Nicky, and even at this distance Sal couldn't escape the cold fury in Little Johnny's son's eyes, and Sal pushed off wildly from the crowd and ran along the side of the hotel, running against the route of the parade, and the band marching in the street was one of those crack all-black units from some inner-city high school, and the band members were high-steppin', vogueing, performing elaborate Rap Master routines with their trumpets and trombones, and the cheerleaders flung their batons high in the wet sky and did six or seven Club MTV dance steps before they reached out nonchalantly and plucked the falling sticks from the air, and Sal heard Nicky bellow behind him, "I'll get chu, motherfucker! I'll get chu!," and he looked back and Nicky was violently shunting people aside, rushing to get at him. *He's gonna kill me! He's gonna kill me!* Sal thought hysterically, and angled off, away from the building, and jostled his way into the throng's packed backs. "Hey, watch it, asshole!" someone complained, and there was "Lookout there!" and "Who the fuck you think you are?" as he bulldozed his way through the crush, and then he was at the crowd-control cable, and there were two cops in yellow police slickers standing there, faced away from the passing parade, watching the crowd with concern, trying to identify the disturbance that was rippling along the mob's edges. Riots were a common occurrence in New Orleans during the Mardi Gras season, set off usually by nothing more serious than an untimely nudge or the senseless energy of middle-class teenagers on vacation. Sal ducked under the cable, and when he straightened up on the other side one of the patrolmen's hammy hands came down on his shoulder.

"Where you think you going, Cap?" the big rubber cop shouted over the snarling, staccato snare drums of the marching band just inches away, which, along with the rest of the parade, had come to one of those inexplicable halts that plague parades the world over. *Music Man*–jacketed kids were high-stepping in place. The rubber cop's grasp held Sal like a vise, and he suspiciously eyed the rumpled little man in the tuxedo.

"I—I gotta go to work, man," Sal shouted back. The NOPD was usually disposed to favor people who worked in the tourist industry.

"Where you work?" the other cop asked. He was a dark black man with thick, wide features.

Sal glanced with alarm over his shoulder. He couldn't spot Nicky Venezia, but there was a wave cutting through the packed crowd, like the wake of a shark's dorsal fin. "Uh—at the King Louis." He turned back to the cops. "I know I shouldn't cross through the parade route"—the lie jumped to his lips—"but I'll get fired if I'm late again."

The white cop stared at him a moment, then pointed up to the building behind Sal. "*That's* the King Louis, Cap," he bellowed into Sal's face. "You sure you know where you going?" The grasp on Sal's arm tightened. Sal kept twisting his neck and looking back to the crowd at his back.

"Something bothering you, sir?" the black cop yelled, and at that moment the band stamped to a sudden, silent standstill, and the policeman's shout hung in the quieter lull that followed.

"Look," Sal said quickly, "I got confused. I gotta go back

the other way. Thanks a lot, man." He tried to duck down behind the cable, but the white cop's grip tightened, and he yanked Sal back.

"What's your name, Cap?" he wanted to know as he pulled Sal closer.

This was not good. This was not good at all. All Nicky or Junior or Little John or any of the Venezia family had to say to these guys was *jump* and they'd ask *how high?* Little Johnny had the city's police force that deep in his pocket. They'd fucking *deliver* him to Little Johnny's doorstep. The municipal government of New Orleans owed a lot to the reign of Napoleon Bonaparte.

"Hey, gimme a break." Sal made himself laugh as he threw a panicked look back into the milling crowd. *Where the fuck was Nicky Venezia?* Sal twisted back to the cop. "I'm gonna lose my job, man."

The big cop eyed him suspiciously. "You trying to be evasive, Cap?" His grasp felt like handcuffs. "I asked you for your name."

Jesus Christ! Sal's thoughts rattled. *Jesus Christ! Where is Nicky Venezia?* On the edge of hysteria, he looked back again, and Nicky Venezia was there, ten yards away, shouldering through the pack. He ice-picked Sal with the cold, murderous glare of his dark almond eyes and then viciously shoved a man and his little daughter out of his way. *Jesus Christ!* Sal turned back to the big rubber cop, stared at him for a heartbeat, then with all his strength suddenly tried to tear his arm from the cop's clutches, but the policeman's reaction was to merely gather his prisoner in closer.

"Hey, asshole!" the patrolman growled as he reached back for the nightstick dangling from his belt.

It's over. It's over. Just like that. It's over and I'm a dead man.

Sal stood there, a captive, caught between a rock and a hard place, as Nicky Venezia waded toward him through the mob of people and the cop slipped his nightstick from its holster on his belt, and Sal suddenly thought, *I wonder how they're gonna kill me my God I hope it doesn't hurt Mother Mary I don't wanna die oh my God oh my God oh my God—*

And then three things happened in very rapid succession.

First, the drum major of the marching band, a very tall

and thin kid strapped into a ridiculously elaborate cossack's hat, who had been facing his musicians with his staff held high so the whole band could fix on it, brought the long baton down with a choreographed flourish, and the seven snare drummers, strung out in formation directly behind the two cops, loudly and abruptly cracked the first beat of the next militaristic anthem with all the pubescent muscle they could muster. They were joined at the downbeat by a crash of trumpets and trombones, cymbals and bass drums.

The big yellow-slickered cop recoiled from the startling blast, ducked, and released his grip on Sal's arm as his hand instinctively jumped toward his gunbelt.

Secondly, almost simultaneously, in the crowd the angry father of the frightened, bawling little girl who had been jostled aside by Nicky Venezia just seconds before felt Junior Venezia hurriedly elbowing his way through the mob in his cousin's wake, whirled, and planted one on the side of Junior's face with all he had. Junior, driven insensate by the pitched excitement like an animal crazed by blood, and being a man who once had got off the floor and beaten to death another man after being coldcocked with a Louisville slugger, stopped, shook his head, and lunged at his attacker like a pit bull. The man screamed as Junior drove his fists into the man's groin, and his daughter, who now was pinned under her father with a badly broken leg, screamed along with him. Like floating flotsam, the crowd surged away from the disturbance. They rushed shriekingly away from a berserk Junior Venezia trying his animal best to kill a man as painfully as possible.

The cops detaining Sal in the street, still not completely clear on what had happened directly behind them when the band had exploded into action, now realized that something very undesirable was transpiring in that part of the parade-route crowd that had been assigned to them. Their interest in Sal waned rapidly as their hands unsnapped the clasps on their handgun holsters and their eyes darted here and there into the surging mass of people, trying to pinpoint exactly what was happening, and where, and what their desired response should be.

Sal, no longer in the rubber cop's grasp and totally unaware of anything except his impending demise and how to avoid it, seized the opportunity to begin moving away quickly and surreptitiously, along the outside of the stretched cable. He turned back just once, and Nicky Venezia was there, just on the other side of the cable, maniacally pushing through the frightened revelers. He shouted something at Sal that was lost in the cacophony of the marching band, and then he reached out, his fingers clutching at the sleeve of Sal's tuxedo coat. Sal screamed, and then the third thing happened.

The skies opened up like a man's belly slit by a razor, and rain poured down as if in a biblical deluge.

The rain came down so completely and unexpectedly that the thousands of parade watchers milling in that single block of Canal Street were soaked before they even knew what had happened. The cold, pelting downpour was as shocking as a glass of icewater thrown in a hysteric's face. It came down with wintry frigidity and tropical-gale force, as it can rain only in southern Louisiana.

The members of the marching band immediately abandoned any hope of continued playing. The music died quickly, like a kitten's drowned shriek, and the kids scattered in every direction, trying to protect their instruments under their uniform jackets.

The cloudburst struck the parade floats so forcefully that one in-drag member of the nearest float's Krewe was washed from his perch on the back of a gigantic papier-mâché swan and swept screeching over the side and into the panicked stampede of fleeing carousers. Just then the papier-mâché swan's thirty-foot-high gracefully arched neck, soaked sodden in just these few seconds, collapsed under its own bloated weight and toppled into the crowd, knocking over a flambeau torch carrier and sending flaming gasoline spreading over the street. That's when people started screaming and trampling over each other.

The two yellow-slickered cops, carried away by the tidal wave of humanity, freaked and began to flail about themselves with their nightsticks. Someone with an old grudge took the opportunity to stab the big white cop in the back through his rubber raincoat with a three-inch pocketknife. The wounded patrolman shouted, "Partner! Partner!" and the other policeman drew his .38 Special, only to have it knocked from his hand by a falling chunk of the ruined swan's superstructure. The revolver struck the street, fired, and the bullet shattered the kneecap of an eighteen-year-old Tulane student who had wanted to stay home that night to study for a freshman zoology quiz.

At the sound of the gun's report, the crowd's panic escalated to hysteria, and the street became a chaotic rout of crazed beasts running for their lives.

And then it began to rain *harder.*

Sal found himself being swept about by an undulating sea of humanity. He felt his feet leave the street and his ribs bruised by the crush of the crowd. He stumbled over something, and then realized it was a human being, being stomped by the mob. A woman beside him screamed in his ear, "My baby! My baby!," and somewhere a cop was blowing like a madman on a police whistle, and all the while the rain hammered down in cold, driving polyethylene sheets of near-freezing liquid. Sal was shoved this way, and carried that way, and then he was jammed chest-to-chest against a man whose drenched hair hung down heavily across his face and whose sodden silk jacket looked all too familiar to Sal. Nicky Venezia, his arms pinned to his sides by the surging mob, looked down at Sal's face only inches away, and he screamed out in rage and frustration, "You little motherfuck—" and then he was dragged away by the crowd's momentum, twisting and turning, trying to keep Sal in sight.

And then the broken-swan float, like a wounded prehistoric behemoth, somehow slipped completely off its flatbed truck platform and toppled into the crowd, spilling its terrified riders like tinseled dolls and crushing several people beneath its waterlogged bulk. There were howls of pain and rage now, along with the screams of fear. The mob rushed away from the collapsing float, and Sal's part of the stampeding throng snapped the police cable and poured into the side streets as if through a funnel. Suddenly the crowd's crush loosened, there was more room, and Sal found himself running with the others like a pack of fleeing thieves down rain-soaked Royal Street, away from the melee. Police cars, lights flashing and sirens blaring, were racing down the street from the other direction, rushing to the catastrophe. A moment later a dozen mounted policemen galloped out of the rain like a ghostly cavalry and splattered through the crowd of dodging runners. Sal splashed through the deluge for block after block. The other runners began to drop back, hang on lampposts, huddle under awnings that gushed water like garden hoses. But Sal had no thought of stopping until he reached safety, wherever that might be. And finally he was thudding down the street alone. He kept running. Mindless, total, terrified flight. Incredibly he still had his life, and he was trying to escape with it in the most basic way possible—he was going to run away with it. His clothes were completely soaked; in fact, he was so wet it was as if he were naked, his covering did him so little good. His shoes were sloshing with rainwater, and when a bolt of lightning unexpectedly cracked across the rooftops, brightening the pounding curtain of rain like a flashbulb, he stumbled, lost his balance in the ankle-deep gutters, and did a painful pratfall on his back in the street.

He gave himself up to unconsciousness for a short moment, and when he came to, he was lying on his back in the rain as the thunder roared across the French Quarter like a giant's drum. The icy rain stung his face and flooded into his mouth and nostrils, as if it, too, were trying to kill him. Sal rolled over, slowed by the hurt, and staggered to his feet. He leaned against the side of a building and looked around. He was completely disoriented, didn't know where he was, or which way he'd come to get there. The downpour had transformed Royal Street into an alien world. He staggered into the middle of the street and squinted one way through the rain, then turned and tried to see down the other. He turned back to the first direction, and another explosion of lightning klieg-lit the wet night, and a man was standing in the street a block away, and Sal saw through the whitened torrents of rain that it was Nicky Venezia, and that what Nicky Venezia was doing was aiming a gun at him, and there was the sound of glass shattering somewhere behind him and *then* the metallic *crack!* of the .45 semiautomatic pistol, and Sal was running away again, scrambling with heartbreaking comedy on the wet sidewalk as he turned a corner and a streetlight shattered right beside him. Breathing like an animal, he tore off his slippery shoes, and his cold-numbed feet threw up waist-high geysers as he splashed down the street. There was something that sounded like a shout behind him, and then two more quick gunshots. The sound muffled by the roar of the rainfall, he heard a woman scream, and then a window being slammed shut. He splattered around another corner and desperately began yanking, one after the other, at the closely packed row of wrought-iron gates and wooden doors. Trying each doorknob, each lock. Deep thunder again grumbled across the sky, like Lucassound, and Sal rattled the locked gates, screaming, "Open up! Open up!" and then he stepped back, crouched down, and flung himself up at an intricate ornamental ironwork wall. His hands couldn't get a purchase on the wet metal, and he thudded back down to the pavement. He was up instantly and again jumped up at the wall. This time he kept his grip, and with a tortured grunt dragged himself up to the top of the wall where wicked spikes stood sentinel six inches apart, waiting to rip the balls off anyone who dared to climb up here. Sal threw one leg over the spikes and felt their points, like knives, digging into his flesh. He wrapped the fingers of both hands around a spike and was carefully lifting himself over the pikes when there was another *crack!* of a gunshot, and the *whang!* of a bullet ricocheting off the ornamental ironworks, and then he felt the vibration of the bullet's jolt travel through the ironworks, enter his hands, and shoot up his arms. He tried to throw himself over the tops of the pikes, but his left leg got stabbed by the fence, and as he toppled over, there was the sickening sound of cloth and skin ripping. Sal fell face-first down into the alley beyond the filigreed gate, and only partially blocked his impact with his arms. He stumbled to his feet and was instantly lurching down the dark passage. He knew he was badly hurt, but Sal D'Amore was way beyond pain now. He was running on high-test adrenaline and world-class fear.

The alley fed back into a wet New Orleans courtyard half-covered by the overhang of the apartment building next door. Under the overhang there was shelter from the rain; it poured off the eaves and along the edges of the rooftops in a drapery of water. Sal got out of sight of the gate, leaned his back against a wall, and gulped at the moist air. He immediately began to tremble from the wet and icy cold and the heart-ripping terror. Then there were the sudden rattling sounds of kicks on the ironwork gate, and Nicky Venezia's madman shout echoing down the alleyway. "I'm gonna *kill* you, Sal, you motherfucker!" And then there was a rapid tattoo of semiautomatic gunfire, and a row of potted ferns on a makeshift wooden stand at the end of the alley exploded, and the stand seemed to disintegrate and spilled the rest of the plants to the courtyard's concrete floor. "I'm gonna kill you, *motherfucker*!"

Sal lunged away from the wall and pulled himself up a narrow staircase. His leg was already starting to throb. As he clomped up to the third-floor landing, he could hear all the dwellers in the courtyard apartments chaining their doors and slamming their shutters. Nicky kicked at the gate and screamed, "Sal, you motherfucker!"

On the third-floor landing, Sal stepped out into the rain, hiked himself up to the top of the neighboring wall, and looked out through the rain across the roof of the apartment building next door. Sal knew these French Quarter courtyards. He had smoked dope and fucked women in most of these apartments. But Nicky Venezia knew these buildings, too. He had robbed and murdered in them.

Sal stood on the narrow brick wall, tottering in the rain, and then jumped across the narrow breezeway to the next-door apartment complex's flat roof. He lurched across the roof, splashing across huge puddles, and then slipped over the complex's other gutter line to the slanted tile roof of the old haunted house directly backing it. He couldn't hear Nicky's shouts anymore, and that meant he didn't know where Nicky was anymore, but then Nicky wouldn't know which street he would come out on. That was the beauty of the Quarter's rabbit warren of Old World alleys and courtyards.

Sal scuttled down the slanted roof, wound his arm around another flowery ironworks, this one surrounding the third-floor veranda of the ancient adjacent house, and monkey-swung himself onto the long, narrow porch. There were two or three luxury apartments that opened onto this veranda, but they were usually vacant because renters always claimed they saw things during the night in those apartments. Ghosts were the *last* thing Sal was afraid of as he tugged at the knobs of the tall French doors. The doors didn't want to open. Lined up on the veranda were two big wicker chairs with a tiny metal table between them. Covered by the roar of the rain, Sal punched the table through one of the French doors' glass panes as gently and quietly as he could, then slipped his hands around the silky curtains and unlatched the lock. He stepped into the dark room, fully expecting to be shot by a terrified, handgun-wielding old lady, but in the freezing blackness he sensed the absence of furniture and thanked God. The ghosts had run off the renters again.

After a few moments, when his eyes began to adjust and empty silhouettes started to appear, Sal lurched painfully across the dark room, thudded out into the hall, and thumped down the wide entrance stairway.

The deluge had driven the rain under the tall front door, and the rug in the foyer squished under his feet. He leaned against the wall, and by the watery streetlight seeping through the stained-glass transom inspected his gashed leg. The fence pike had slit his skin like a blade. His foot was dark with blood, and the warm stain still flowed down his leg. Shivering violently, he tore off the tail of his sodden tux shirt and wound it as best he could around the wound.

He turned the old brass lock and slowly opened the massive front door. The cold rain splattered in on his face. The downpour hadn't lessened a bit. If anything, it was raining even harder. *Where was Nicky?* And then Sal heard a voice very close.

"If she's going to drink like that every time—"

"Aubrey, for Chrissakes!"

Sal leaned out into the wet. In the narrow strip of dryness beneath the overhanging veranda next door, a dark Mercedes sedan was parked on the sidewalk. In the circle of light spilling out of the opened door of the adjacent building, a young blonde in a brocade cloak over a low-cut antebellum gown was holding up another woman done up as a French apache dancer. The apache dancer was staggeringly drunk.

"Goddamnit, just leave her there!" said the Confederate general standing just out of the rain by the Mercedes's passenger door.

"Aubrey!"

"She pulls this same shit every time we go someplace. If she can't hold it, she shouldn't drink, I don't care what kind of problems she has."

"She's my sister!" the blonde shouted angrily, and then the apache dancer gulped as if in a prelude to puking, her knees buckled under her, and she went completely limp. The southern belle struggled to hold her sister up.

"Aubrey!"

"Aw, this is it! This takes the cake!" the general cursed as he moved to help.

"Just help me get her upstairs. Then you can go to hell for all I care!"

The general took the apache dancer's other arm and draped it over his shoulder. "Don't be mad at me, Marj. I'm not the one who—"

"She's my fucking sister!" Sal heard the belle bark as the trio disappeared into the haze of light that was the entrance hall of the next-door apartment. Then there was just the sound of the relentless pounding of the torrential rains. Lightning crackled, and Sal saw steam, like breath, rising from the Mercedes's exhaust pipe.

Sal slid across the supple leather of the passenger's bucket seat and settled behind the steering wheel. The car smelled of whiskey and perfume. He realized he hadn't shut the door behind him. He leaned over, reaching for the door handle, and saw the general's gray legs coming down the lighted stairs.

Sal slammed the door, jumped back behind the wheel, threw the gearshift, and stomped the accelerator. The big sedan bounced over the curb and out from under the veranda, and then the rain was sluicing down the windshield and thudding on the car's rooftop. Sal, fumbling for the wipers control, thought he heard a shout behind him, but it was drowned in the downpour. He finally twisted something that activated the wipers, and he could see the sodden street splashing by as the Mercedes hydroplaned to the traffic light at the end of the block. Sal stood on the brakes and the big car seemed to float to a stop, and then, illuminated by another flash of lightning, Nicky Venezia ran in front of the car, his gun drawn, his head craning in every direction but at the driver of the Mercedes, and then he was gone, and Sal eased the car through the intersection, praying it wouldn't stall in the over-the-hubcaps water, and pointed the hood toward the Interstate heading north.

BOOK II

NAPLES—1919

Giovanni Gemelli was born in the hilly Neapolitan suburb of Posilipo on a sweltering August afternoon in the year of Our Lord 1919. He was the first son born to a bourgeois shoemaker and his delicate wife. There were two sisters older than Giovanni, and two younger brothers quickly followed. Giovanni, being the first son and the oldest brother, was the favorite of both of his parents and his siblings. A graceful, quick-witted, beautiful little boy with clear dark skin and luminous eyes.

All during the 1920's the Gemelli clan prospered plentifully. Signor Gemelli maintained a plush shop on the Via Toledo that catered to the wealthy patrons from the Via Orazio and the Via Caracciolo. Besides the gleaming boots and supple shoes artfully arranged in his showroom window, Signor Gemelli also made and sold handbags, wallets, belts, and gloves. A leather good with the distinctive Gemelli *G* trademark was the best to be obtained anywhere in Naples. The shop was always crowded, and Signor Gemelli grew ever richer. Even in 1931, when the great American Depression found its way across the Atlantic and rolled over Europe, Gemelli did well. He pressed his fellow *Fascisti* for favors: military contracts for saddlebags, riding boots, gunbelts. The House of Gemelli held its own.

One beautiful September Sunday in 1932, young Giovanni Gemelli, showing off for the neighborhood girls, climbed up on the ledge of his bedroom window and leapt into the shaky branches of a nearby olive tree. Laughing triumphantly, he acknowledged the pubescent applause with a bow, lost his balance, and crashed headfirst through the leaves to the cobblestones below. The fall broke his back, his pelvis, both hips, and both ankles.

Signor Gemelli spared no expense in his attempt to reconstruct his favorite son's shattered skeleton. The best physicians in Naples attended the boy. Bone specialists came from as far away as Rome and Vienna. Giovanni was in a body cast for over a year. After another six months the boy could limp about without a crutch. But he never grew another inch, and he never lost the lurching, staggering gait. His body thickened and coarsened; even his facial features seemed to become squat and blunt.

The youth's accident and its aftereffects dampened much of the laughter that had rung throughout the spacious Gemelli home, but the most obvious impact was on the old man. The elder Gemelli's heart broke for his beautiful son. Signor Gemelli sat vigil at the boy's bedside every night during the long recuperation, and then, when Giovanni could drag himself limpingly about, Signor Gemelli, rather than have his Gio return to school and the cruel childish taunts of his classmates, brought the crippled boy with him to the shoe shop. There, there would only be adults, and they at least stared without remarking. Every morning, while his sisters giggled off to convent school, and his brothers—both of whom would grow up to be over six feet tall—went off to the Fascist Academy, short, crippled Giovanni accompanied his father to the House of Gemelli.

For the next decade Giovanni worked at his father's side, learning every facet of the leather trade. With his eye he learned how to pick from a herder's pack the finest, most supple skins; with his head he learned how to bargain the skinner down to the lowest possible price; with his hand he learned how to cut and mold, craft and polish that skin into the softest gloves, or the smartest jacket; again with his head, but almost with his heart, he came to know how to send away a customer of the House of Gemelli feeling as if he or she had become the purchaser of not just a coat or a pair of boots, but a fine piece of contemporary Neapolitan craftsmanship. Narcissistic Italian males, after buying a coat from Giovanni, left the shop feeling not only fashionable but luckier, superior, and held themselves taller as they sauntered away. The breasts of bourgeois matrons ached as they saw the smiling, sunny face perched on the short cripple's body—and they purchased another pair of shoes.

For ten years Giovanni bent his already twisted body over the workbenches, counters, and account books of his father's business. And during those ten years the House of Gemelli suffered more than its share of jolts. In 1935 the less than robust Signora Gemelli succumbed to viral pneumonia contracted on a wet family outing to the seashore. Caterina, the eldest daughter, did her best to take her mother's place, but she could find no words of solace to give her father when, two years later, her little sister, Angelina, ran away with Bruno Serio, a neighborhood boy who was emigrating to Brazil. Signor Gemelli found the hastily scribbled note upon arriving home from the shop and rushed to the docks, just in time to see the ship cruising out of the bay. He stood there and cried uncontrollably, while crippled Giovanni patted his shoulder and whispered consolation.

The Gemelli house now was as grim and ugly as a child's coffin, and the two younger boys, Cagliori and Antonio, quickly enlisted in the army and were sent off to fight on the Ethiopian front. Caterina, terrified that now she would be expected to spend the rest of her life cooking and cleaning for an old man and a cripple, married the first man she could fornicate into asking her—a fat little baker thirty years her senior. They moved into a house in the neighboring town of Portici, but that wasn't nearly far enough away for Caterina. She badgered her poor husband constantly until he finally sold his bakery and the couple sailed for North America, never to be heard from again.

Now, in the house it was only Giovanni and his father, and a succession of grim-faced housekeepers who all quit after a few months, saying they could *feel* the bad luck in the place. Giovanni ran the store alone now, the old man coming down only occasionally to pretend to look over the books, then flee quickly back to the familiar coldness of his empty house.

With the war came even more work for Giovanni. Military overcoats specially tailored, embossed holsters, gleaming binocular cases for the straight-backed German officers who now swaggered down Naples's twisting streets, laughing with each other as if at some colossal private joke. Giovanni scuttled about hurriedly, waiting on his customers from morning till closing, then limped back home to his father, who sat staring out a window—the very window Giovanni had fallen from years before—sat gazing vacantly out over the city, hour after hour. Every night Giovanni would cook dinner on the big ornate wood-burning stove, then bring the pot of sauce and the platter of pasta into the dining room. He and his father would eat together by candlelight at the long, empty table, while on the radio there would be opera broadcasts from Rome, or *Il Duce*'s fiery speeches, or even news of the war from London.

News of the war.

In the fall of 1943 the army sent a lieutenant to the house to tell Signor Gemelli that his two sons had been killed in North Africa. The old man simply stared at him. The lieutenant repeated the message, and seeing no glimmer of comprehension in the *signore*'s eyes, shrugged and walked away. The old man went back to his chair by the balcony window.

In 1943 Naples experienced scattered bombing. The old man and the cripple ate together every night in the big dark dining hall, and the radio brought further news of the war. The Americans had landed in Sicily. The Italian Army was being routed everywhere. *Il Duce* had been assassinated.

In the streets of Naples communists, socialists, and republicans took out their pent-up wrath on the fascists and their supporters. Shops were looted; shopkeepers beaten. The House of Gemelli was gutted and burned. When the crowds surged through the streets outside their home, Giovanni led the whimpering old man down into the cellar, braced the door with a length of lumber, and fingered a Nazi Luger he had bought from a German soldier. From above, through the floor, came the sounds of glass breaking, furniture overthrown, laughter, and the shouts of anger. After a few hours the crowd went away. Giovanni held his father tightly to his chest and they slept.

They lived in the cellar for almost three years. Even after an American colonel with the Occupation commandeered their old home above them. Giovanni went out every day, scuffling about for bread, cheese, maybe a bottle of wine to bring back to his father in the cellar. He did odd jobs in the neighborhood—mending belts, resoling shoes. The American soldiers, thinking him much younger than he was and taking pity on his handicap, gave him candy bars and cigarettes, and Giovanni scurried back to their rat's nest in the cellar and watched his vacant-eyed father dribble chocolate-laced spittle down his whiskery chin.

At the end of September 1946, a letter from Angelina and her husband in Brazil finally found them. Giovanni cried as he read to the old man his daughter's invitation to her father and brother to join her and her husband in their modest home in Rio de Janeiro. Immigration permits had been issued, tickets purchased, visas stamped. The old man and the cripple were welcome in a land across the sea, a land unravaged by war. Giovanni laughed and rocked on his haunches with glee. The old man scratched at his crotch.

They sailed out of the Gulf of Naples on a dreary, cold day in November in the bowels of a rust-streaked freighter that carried steerage passengers in tight, airless compartments like so much live cargo. The old man whimpered with fear at the engine's lurching and clung to his son, who whispered soft encouragements. Their belongings, besides the coats on their backs, were bundled in a threadbare, discarded U.S. Army blanket: two shirts and two trousers, a single fraying sweater, a heavy iron kettle, and a dented tin teapot. And around Giovanni's waist, in a supple, glossy, highest-quality House of Gemelli money belt, almost three pounds of pure gold. For years Giovanni had been secretly converting the leather shop's profits into quarter-pound gold wafers. He had kept the hoard buried under the dirt floor of his father's cellar. The calfskin money belt was the only example of Gemelli leather goods left. Even their pants were held up by twisted lengths of rope. When they had taken final refuge in the cellar, Giovanni had made their pallet bed over the smooth little bump that marked where the gold-filled money belt, tightly wrapped in oilskin and a square of canvas, was buried. For years during the war and after, while they lived in the cellar like scavenging rats, he had been afraid to touch the stash, afraid someone would grow suspicious of the helpless little cripple, follow him home, and take his savings away from him. Now, on the freighter, Giovanni slept fitfully with one arm held tightly across the gold under his shirt, and the other wound around his invalid father.

The voyage to Rio de Janeiro took almost six weeks, with dockings in Palermo, Alexandria, and Liberia. The freighter dropped anchor in Guanabara Bay on New Year's Day, 1947. The city was in the grips of a Southern Hemispheric summer heat wave, and when Giovanni led his blinking father onto the deck, the hot, steamy oxygen-heavy air clung to their skin like moist cheesecloth. The emerald hills of Rio sprawled out around them like the legs of a languorous whore. And smelled about the same: sweat and passion and bodily fluids.

Angelina and her husband met them at the foot of the gangplank, along with a priest she had brought with them for good luck. Angelina wailed and embraced her father and her only surviving brother, crossed herself, and then cried some more. Her husband, Bruno Serio, a quiet, thickset man with timid eyes, bowed his head and mopped the sweat from his brow with a wrinkled handkerchief. The priest blessed everyone and smiled benignly.

In Bruno Serio's wide, wheezing Chevrolet they drove through the steamy, colorful streets. New Year's Eve was Rio's biggest celebration, after Carnaval, and a few diehard revelers were still staggering through the afternoon streets. Angelina Serio pointed out with distaste the little makeshift *macumba* altars the Cariocas had built the night before, to bring them luck in the New Year.

Most Italian immigrants to Brazil were settling in the burgeoning nearby city of São Paulo, but the Serios had stayed where they landed and made a life for themselves in the middle-class neighborhood of Botafogo. Bruno Serio owned and operated a butcher shop on the Rua Dona Mariana, with the family living on the three narrow floors above. Three fat, healthy, and dark-eyed Serio children politely greeted their uncle and grandfather in the cool, shadowy parlor at the top of the stairs.

That night was a holiday feast, and Angelina cooked all the Neapolitan specialties that had been favorites in the Gemelli home: pizza, fusilli, fried calamari, and for dessert a sweet blood and chocolate pudding called *sanguinaccio.* Giovanni ate and drank until he began to feel sick, and even old man Gemelli seemed caught up in the gaiety of the evening. After dinner Angelina played the upright piano and sang old songs with tearful rejoicing, and the little nephews stole glances at their strange, deformed uncle, who wasn't much taller than they were.

Well after midnight, Angelina showed Giovanni to his small, hot room in the fourth-floor attic. He waited until the house was quiet, then limped carefully down the stairs and along the hall until he heard his father whimpering for him from behind a door. He held the old man's hand until he fell asleep, then Giovanni lay down on the floor beside the bed and dozed off.

Bruno Serio offered his crippled brother-in-law a job in his butcher shop, wiping down the cases and washing the blood into the street. Giovanni declined with the prescribed politeness, and Bruno Serio smiled and diverted his eyes, much as his children were in the habit of doing.

Giovanni, in a borrowed clean shirt, ventured out into the streets of Rio. The town astounded him, but he somehow felt strangely and completely at home. The crowded streets were jammed with all manner of people: blacks—more blacks surely than in all of Africa—Indians, mulattoes, Italians, Sicilians, Syrians, blond Germans, hook-nosed Lebanese. Like all displaced Europeans of his day, Giovanni Gemelli was struck by the polyethnicity of the New World. He saw a black man almost seven feet tall, a tiny brown-skinned woman with a vast bundle on her head, a massive red-haired giant walking briskly through the streets with a huge blue-green parrot perched on his shoulder.

In a jewelry and precious metals shop in the bustling downtown Centro, Giovanni dickered with a Jew from Morocco, then sold off a small amount of the gold in his money belt for a thick wad of one thousand cruzeiro notes. Then he went to a haberdashery and bought a suit and vest of fine white linen, a widebrimmed straw hat, and a simple *cocobola* rosewood walking cane. The salesman wanted to sell him a new pair of shoes to replace the tattered, newspaper-stuffed boots he had brought from Naples, but Giovanni steadfastly refused. Instead, he wandered the streets, stopping at a dozen shoe-repair shops and cobblers, until he found just the kind of place he was looking for, just off the streetcar line that ran on the Avenida Rio Branco. The shop was a one-room garage, really, long and dark and cool, with a hard-beaten dirt floor and a small area behind a nailed-up blanket with space enough for a cot and a tiny desk. Hides and skins hung from the rafters, and a gnarled, white-haired old Portuguese hammered heels bent over a stained and crowded cutting table. A lazy yellow tomcat lounged at the shoemaker's feet. Giovanni started up a conversation with the old *Portugee,* who spoke a surprising amount of Italian. They talked for two hours, using Italian, Portuguese, and Spanish, but mostly with their hands and their hearts, and at the end of the two hours Giovanni had not only purchased a new pair of shoes from the old *Portugee,* but also the shoemaker's shop. And he had hired the old man to stay on for a few months to teach him the Brazilian words for the necessities of their trade—leather, lambskin, shoes, belt—to introduce him to the tanners and skinners, the ranchers and shepherds who came to Rio from the back country, the silversmiths who fashioned the buckles and buttons, the dry-goods salesmen who peddled the required nails and tacks, the polishes and stains, the hammers and knives.

When the deal was done, Giovanni leaned on his newly purchased cane and pulled his bent frame to his feet and shook hands solemnly with the unsmiling old *Portugee.* On his way out the door he noticed in an alcove a brilliant red-and-green parrot, much like the one he had seen on the street earlier that day, and he inquired about it to the old man, who told him that he had bought the bird from an Amazonian trapper who came through selling lizard skins, and that the parrot, like the cat at his feet, came with the shop. They belong to the place, the old *Portugee* said, and not the person.

Giovanni Gemelli held out the crook of his cane, and with a flap of wings and a raucous squawk the parrot immediately stepped onto it. The big bird was heavy, and Giovanni had to support the cane with two hands. He laughed and said over his shoulder to the old *Portugee,* "*Credo che Rio mi piacerà.* I think I'm going to like Rio."

* * *

Giovanni only needed a month to settle into his new shop. He had always been a quick study with languages, and anyway Portuguese was much prettier than the German and English he'd had to learn during the war, and to his ear, more similar to Italian than Spanish. And the craftsmen and skin traders the old man introduced him to he charmed in his most obsequious House of Gemelli fashion. At the end of the fourth week the old *Portugee* packed a new cowhide valise and bid Gemelli goodbye. He was going up the coast to the northern state of Bahia, where he would buy a small house close to the beach and take in a young Negress housekeeper to cook for him and keep him company at night. He would live out the rest of his days on the monthly stipend he and Giovanni had agreed upon as the second half of their deal. They shook hands in the street, and the old man disappeared into the dark crowds. Giovanni went back into the shop and sat at the worktable. The yellow cat rubbed against his leg and settled down over his foot. The parrot cleaned its feathers. Giovanni lit a thick Cuban cigar, then looked around his shop with satisfaction for only a moment before getting to work on a pair of new boots.

That he would prosper in his new location Giovanni Gemelli never doubted. He was a young man in his late twenties, in excellent health—excluding his deformities. He was the master of a very necessary craft, also an accomplished salesman, bookkeeper, accountant. He had a fair amount of capital, an endless supply of energy, no vices, no other interests, really, except for the care of his invalid father.

At the end of his first year in the shop, Giovanni had two assistants helping him fill the growing number of orders for custom-made Gemelli footwear. At the close of his second year he moved to a much larger location on the Avenida Rio Branco. That's when Bruno Serio sold his butcher shop and came to work for his brother-in-law. After another five years the name Gemelli de Janeiro and the distinctive stylized red-parrot-perched-on-a-crook-of-wood logo signified the finest quality shoes, boots, coats, and jackets over all of Brazil. There was a new shop in Ipanema, three in the burgeoning São Paulo area, and four more scattered along the country's coast. In that year,

1953, Gemelli bought adjoining mansions in the hilly suburb of Gavea, one for the Serio family, the other for himself and his father. Though his new house had seven bedrooms and a horde of servants to clean and change those bedrooms, Giovanni and his father still slept together, their beds pushed only a foot apart.

In 1957 Gemelli de Janeiro became an international concern, as Giovanni opened new shops in Montevideo and Buenos Aires. In 1960 the company went worldwide, and started exporting luxurious, high-fashion footwear to "Gemelli"s in New York, London, Milan, Rome, Athens, and Toronto. In 1962 Gemelli de Janeiro opened ostentatious outlets on the Champs Élysées in Paris, and in Beverly Hills on Rodeo Drive, a block south of Gucci, Giovanni's biggest competitor.

In 1965, in an act of sentiment, a Gemelli de Janeiro was dedicated in Naples, on the site of the old House of Gemelli, vandalized and razed over two decades before. Giovanni's hand shook as he cut the opening-day ribbon. Life had come full circle.

In 1971 old Signor Gemelli's eighty-two-year-old body began to fail, much as his mind had during the war. His heart sputtered and lurched, his intestines clogged, his muscles atrophied. He deteriorated quickly. Giovanni, who spent every evening at home anyway, now lingered each morning at his father's bedside, reluctant to go to work at the new high-rise Gemelli de Janeiro corporate headquarters in Flamengo, overlooking Sugarloaf. Once in his office he would shuffle some papers, then rush home at lunch to murmur words of encouragement to the unhearing old invalid. Finally, at the age of eighty, the old man collapsed and vegetated. He couldn't leave his bed; he couldn't feed himself; he couldn't recognize voices or faces; he defecated on himself and lay in the mess. Giovanni banished all the servants from their bedroom. He would care for his father himself now, around the clock. He changed the shitty sheets and sponge-bathed the old man. He spooned clear broth into the slack mouth, and then caught the overflow that dribbled from the old man's lips. He sat at the bedside and read to the old man from Italian-language newspapers and magazines, sometimes even children's books, just as his father had done for him when he was a frightened, miserable little boy in a body cast. Other times Giovanni would wheel a television set into the bedroom and give the old man an excited running commentary of a football game, as if the old man were only blind, and not also unfocused, unfeeling, feeble, and senile.

During the nights the old man had nightmares—he thought the communists and Americans were coming through the ceiling to murder him—and he shouted out for his dead soldier sons to come protect him. Giovanni held the old man and cooed soft reassurances in his ear. Sometimes father and son would simply hold each other and cry together.

The funeral was a pompous, political event. Soldiers, businessmen, designers, politicians—they came from all over Brazil to pay their respect to the father of Giovanni Gemelli de Janeiro—a man none of them had ever met. The mayors of Rio and São Paulo were there. Presidente Vargas sent an emissary. The French, Italian, and American ambassadors attended. The line of black sedans stretched for blocks—all for a man who hadn't left his bedroom for two decades.

The hole gouged in Giovanni's life by the passing of his father seemed big enough to swallow him. The two had been inseparable since the younger Gemelli's fall from that olive tree almost forty years before. Giovanni felt like a widower who had lost a beloved wife of many years. He couldn't sleep. At night the bedroom was too quiet now, without the old man's moaning. Giovanni limped barefoot through the dark, empty mansion, trailing a plume of thick cigar smoke. He stood in his bathrobe and watched the deserted treelined street, bathed in moonlight, from every window in the house, like an Impressionist painter watching the light change over a pond. The servants, at first startled by Don Gemelli's midnight ramblings, soon took to smiling at themselves and shaking their heads when they heard the little man's crooked footsteps on the floor above.

His work, his company, held no interest for him anymore. He left it for Bruno Serio and his sons—now corporate executives in their late thirties—to run. He traveled the streets of Rio all day now, in buses, in cabs, by foot. He would leave the house in the late mornings, dressed in a white linen suit, and spend the whole day walking the bustling streets of Centro, being driven by the squalid *favelas* of Canto Galo, Borel, Esqueleto; taking buses through the better neighborhoods of Le Blon, Copacabana, Ipanema.

As if in search. In search of something.

When he finally saw her, it was in the servants' alley of a big house only a few blocks from his own. Actually he *heard* her first, before he ever saw her—a rich, throaty, sensual laugh that made the hairs on his shoulders vibrate as if electrified—a deep, groin-massaging sound that bespoke the knowledge of some basic, beautiful secret—a wonderful wanton sound that whispered promises of midnight ecstasies. Giovanni rested his weight on his cane and swiveled his body toward that laughter.

She was so young—what, seventeen?—maybe even sixteen. She stood in the kitchen door of a pink Gavea mansion, bantering with some workmen who were paving the alley walkway. One of the sweaty, shirtless young men said something to her, and she laughed again. She threw back her head and laughed again, and again the sound seemed to fly up and down the nerve endings of Giovanni's body.

She was dark, with long, straight deep brown hair that hung down her back almost to her waist. Her body was thin except for her hips, where it spread out and broadened, and the thin white maid's uniform was tight across her ass. Her features were sharply chiseled, and she wore an aquiline nose over her flashing white laughter. To Giovanni she seemed a microcosm of all the bloodlines of Brazil—a single human embodiment of the gene pools of Southern Europe, the Mediterranean, the New World, and even Africa.

She was beautiful.

One hand rested jauntily, provocatively even, on her hip, and she held herself with a loose, hot grace. She stood, framed in the doorway, like a queen on a throne, and held court to the sweating, lusty bricklayers who gave her their full attention.

Then someone inside the house shouted a name—*Isabel*—and the girl jumped and was gone, the screen door slamming shut behind her. The masons laughed and went back to their work. Giovanni stared at the kitchen door a long time, then moved on.

* * *

Giovanni, in his no-longer-aimless ramblings, walked past her mansion the next day, but did not see her.

Not the next. Or the one after that.

The next day was a Sunday, and he knew she wouldn't be there.

On Monday, on the sidewalk before the big pink house, he heard her laughter again. From somewhere inside on the second floor. He walked to the end of the block and then back again, and then again.

On Tuesday morning he was back at eight o'clock. There was a bus-stop kiosk across the street from the pink mansion, and he sat down on the cool stone bench and began to read the paper he had brought. The workmen must have completed their job, because they were nowhere around. Just after eleven the front door of the house opened, and she came out with two small, well-dressed children in tow. They sat on the front lawn and played. He drank in the music of her laughter. After about an hour they went back in. Giovanni caned himself to a tiny *bodega* a few blocks away and bought a *misto-quente* sandwich, a pint of orange juice, and a magazine. He ate the ham-and-white-cheese sandwich and rested on the bus-stop bench, his eyes on the windows of the big pink house, searching for a glimpse of her white uniform. He read the magazine three times, and then, at five-thirty, she came down the servants' alley carrying a large woven-straw bag. When she reached the sidewalk, she paused and stared across the street straight at him. It was the first time she had looked directly at him, and he felt his heart stop. Then she turned and walked away, toward the Rua Marques de São Vicente. When she was a half-block away, Giovanni stuck the magazine under his arm and followed. At a busy bus stop before a shopping center, she turned to look at him again. For the first time in his adult life, Giovanni felt self-conscious and tried to minimize his limp. A bus pulled to the curb then, and Isabel moved through the opening doors. A mob of people crowded in behind her. Giovanni hurried to catch up, but the doors slid shut, the bus pulled away, and just as he lumbered after it, waving his cane, he heard her rich, stirring laughter float to him through the hot, humid late afternoon air.

* * *

The next day he followed her more closely and jammed himself into the packed bus just as the doors were closing. The crowd, recognizing by his expensive suit and gold-tipped cane that he was an important man, tried to make more room for him, and as he balanced on his toes to try to catch a glimpse of her, the crowd in the bus parted for a moment, and there she was, only a few feet away. She smiled at him, and he felt himself begin to get an erection. Then the crowd closed between them, and he heard her laugh loudly, as if—as if—as if she *knew*.

She lived over the hill from Gavea in the squalid crowded *favela* called Rocinha by its squatter inhabitants. The jumble of dusty cement houses sprawled higgledy-piggledy down the mountainside like discarded garbage. The hard, narrow alleys were jammed with dirty children, small, wary dogs, laundry hung out to dry, and shirtless men who stared back with a kind of contemptuous challenge. The air gagged with the mingling odors of shit, sweat, and greasy food. At the foot of one of the long climbing alleys, Isabel paused, slipped off her thick-soled white maid's shoes, and, dangling them from her fingertips, started up the steep hill. Giovanni, lagging fifty meters back, watched the taut roundness of her buttocks tense and glide under her thin cotton uniform. She glanced back at him and giggled. He tried desperately to keep up, but after lurching and almost falling three times on one of the alley's steep stairways, he realized the hill was too much for him, and he stopped, gasping for breath, and leaned against a peeling wall. Ignoring the laughter of the *favelados,* he watched her climb almost to the top of the hill. She stopped, stared down at him for a moment, then entered one of the larger shacks.

The next afternoon, a Wednesday, at five o'clock, a long black Ford LTD bumped on to the crooked, crowded streets of Rocinha and came to rest at the foot of one of the short series of steps. A mob of boys and young men crowded around the sleek sedan, a car exactly like the one used by Presidente Vargas, and they clamored to peer through the tinted windows. A huge black man in a chauffeur's uniform got out of the LTD's driver's seat and tried to chase away the surging mob of boys.

The bedraggled, curious children, never having seen a car like this in the *favela* before, moved back a few feet, jeering and making obscene gestures at the driver. Finally an uneasy truce was established as the big black man leaned on a front fender and glowered at the street urchins.

At a little after six Isabel, her shoes in her hand, began the ascent up the steep hill. She slowed for a moment when she glimpsed the crowd around the big black sedan blocking the street, and a smile played around her lips. As she passed the car, one of the tinted back windows rolled down, and her eyes met Giovanni Gemelli's. Then she hurried up the hill.

On a signal from Giovanni the chauffeur opened the car door and the little man lurched out, followed by one of his corporate lawyers, a fat man in a tight gray suit. The lawyer's eyes danced around the street with clear terror. He had lived in Rio all his life, and had never set foot in a *favela* before. He promised himself he never would again.

Oblivious to his employee's discomfort, and unmindful of the whispering, snickering crowd, Giovanni rested a hand on the fat man's meaty shoulders and began to limp purposefully up the hill.

It took them almost half an hour to negotiate the hill, and then Giovanni had to sit on a pile of bricks and gulp for his breath for several more minutes. Directly in front of him was the bright blue ramshackle lean-to that Isabel had disappeared into. Finally he found the strength to scramble to his feet and limp to the door.

There was no answer.

Only laughter from the street tramps who had followed them up the hill.

Giovanni knocked again, and the crooked door sprang open. A fat, blowsy woman with badly dyed red hair and a thick body sausaged into a messy black dress stood in the doorway.

Giovanni cleared his throat. "My name is Giovan—"

"I know who you are, *Senhor* Gemelli," she leered, revealing yellowed and missing teeth. "And I know what you want. Come in."

"She's a *puttana!*" Angelina Serio screamed in a vulgar Neapolitan roar. "She's a little whore!"

Giovanni wouldn't look at his sister. He kept his eyes fixed on an invisible point a foot before his nose.

"A whore! A pig! Not even eighteen and she's had three, *three*"—she waved three spiked fingers in front of his unseeing eyes—"*three abortions!* She's a whore and a murderess!"

Angelina Gemelli Serio was incensed. To be granted the God-given good fortune to have a childless, sexless, crippled dwarf of a brother who had provided her rather stupid husband and sons with a vast fortune and a rich company, all to be inherited solely and entirely by her rather stupid husband and sons upon the little dwarf's death—and now *this!* This incredible affront!

It was too much!

Angelina shrieked and tore at her hair. The fat folds of flesh hanging from her arms jiggled angrily. She had become a bigot's caricature of a wealthy immigrant Italian matriach—loud and demanding and dripping with diamonds.

"You can't do this, Giovanni! You can't bring this slut into our house!"

Giovanni haltingly found his voice. "I—I'm bringing her into *my* house."

"*Gesù Cristo! Gesù Cristo!*" she wailed up at the ceiling. "Why are you doing this to me?" Then she sprawled her bulk across the polished dining room table, and in a lewd promise of a whisper hissed at her brother, "This is Rio. We can get you *anything*. If you want a whore, a young girl who will do whatever you ask, this I can understand. This I can understand. A man has to have what he needs, of course. But, please, I beg of you," she begged of him, "don't *marry* this little gutter whore!"

Giovanni turned his angry eyes on his sister. "She will be my wife."

"*Noooooooooo!*" Angelina moaned, then her face grew dark and ugly. "What? Do you think she *loves* you? This little bitch! Why do you think she has laid this trap for you? Do you think she can't keep her hands off you? She lusts for you? Like the young studs who come sniffing after—"

"*Shut up!*" Giovanni lurched to his feet.

"—do you think she gets wet for a—a—a man like *you?*"

"*Shut up!*" Giovanni slammed his cane down on the gleaming wood. *Whack!*

"She runs the street like a dog! A bitch in heat! What do you know of women? You're like a little boy. A child! You don't understand. This girl is trash, garbage! Her mother is garbage! She never knew who her father was!"

"Angelina," Giovanni said evenly, "this girl will be my wife."

Angelina sputtered. "This girl will rob you of everything you have! Your money, your name, your dignity. The whole world will laugh at you—at us—to find that Giovanni Gemelli has married a whore, a pig of the streets, a—"

"Angelina!"

"This—this—*thing* sleeps with blacks!"

"She will be my wife!"

The wedding, unfortunately, uncharitably, would be forever referred to by all Cariocas as the Gemelli Circus, and they unkindly called Giovanni the Dwarf. Angelina Serio was the Fat Lady, and Maria Mendes, Isabel's mother, with thick makeup ladled onto her debauched face, was the Clown. All the politicians, business executives, and society scions who had dutifully attended, six months before, the funeral of Giovanni's father, now phoned each other and snickeringly congratulated themselves on their wise decision to decline their invitations to the farcical wedding. Giovanni even had difficulty finding a priest who would perform the ceremony, but after a not-inconsiderable sum found its way into the archdiocese's coffers, an old drunken priest with an already aborted career was bullied into doing the deed.

The reception was held in the vast backyard of Giovanni's Gavea estate. White tables and chairs for four hundred were carefully arranged on the lush green of the lawn like icing laid on a cake. Pink bows and balloons were festooned everywhere. White doves in bamboo cages cooed while an artificial pond filled with koi gurgled under a sheltering tamarind tree.

Since the vast majority of the groom's invitees had sent their regrets, Maria Mendes packed the reception with her cronies and lovers from the *favela.* They piled into battered trucks and topless buses, and sang and drank cheap wine and beeped their horns all the way over the mountain. Forgoing the church ceremony, they drove directly to the Gemelli mansion and invaded the frosted-cake backyard like ants into an overturned sugar bowl. Within an hour they were resoundingly drunk on the Dom Perignon that the white-jacketed waiters kept pouring into a huge, bubbling punch bowl. They stood at the buffet table and ate until they were too sick to eat anymore, then stuffed more food into their pockets. When the food was gone, they jammed the silver serving trays down the front of their pants. Waiters tried to stop the *favela* women from stealing the silverware, but the loudly dressed women yanked back the knives and forks and claimed they only wanted them for souvenirs of the occasion. One caterer was punched in the face by a thick-browed, long-haired brute in an iridescent purple suit when he tried to dissuade the brute from his practice of wringing the cooing doves' necks and dropping their limp cadavers into a rice sack he had brought for that purpose. Angelina Serio, arriving from the church, walked into the yard just in time to witness a staggering drunk taking a triumphant piss in the koi pond. The drunk winked at her and shook his penis, and Angelina marched her husband, her sons, and her sons' families back across the lawn and into her own home next door. Tears of shame and outrage streaked her mascara, and her fat arms jiggled indignantly. She double-locked the door behind her, as if to protect her Serio brood from the rabble rampaging outside, and, with a throaty wail, collapsed into Bruno's arms.

Back at the backyard bacchanalia, on the parquet dance floor assembled before the bandstand, Maria Mendes was executing a lewd leg-entwining *lambada* with a swarthy, muscled young man half her age. She rammed her belly against the boy's hard thigh, bounced her ample breasts almost free of her low-cut pink monstrosity, caressed his tight ass with her open hands, and rolled her eyes leeringly. The drunken crowd circling the dance floor laughed and stamped their feet. Isabel, stunning in a heavy ecru-colored 100,000-*cruzeiro* Givenchy original, laughed the loudest, and the sound gripped the testicles of Giovanni, standing by her side. He was oblivious to everyone and everything but his beautiful bride. It had been that way all day. In the years that followed, Giovanni would struggle to remember every moment, every second of this day—his first glimpse of Isabel in her satin-and-antique-lace wedding gown; the cool, cavernous church; the ceremony perfunctorily mumbled by the old priest with whiskey on his breath; the raucous reception in his own backyard. But though there were dull images of the church, the reception, the others, there would always be only one strong memory of this unbelievable day: Isabel—olive-skinned, dark-haired Isabel. And when he was next to her on the altar, the closest he had ever been to her, he saw a shimmering glow in her light green eyes, as beautiful as a doll's plastic eyes, only hers were alive with a kind of total understanding and a blunt sexual humor. And he would remember forever his first smell of her, right there before the altar. There was a scent of her mother's whorish perfume, a whiff of face powder, and an underlying . . . *sense* . . . of musk, of wet glands and hot semen, and right there, while the old drunk intoned the mass, Giovanni got as hard as pig iron, and he hunched his already twisted frame to hide his erection from the church, and Isabel, seeing what he was doing and understanding why, threw back her head and through her fine white, even teeth gave a deep, husky laugh, and the priest stopped his incantations and stared at her and she laughed again, and Giovanni's erection stiffened even more. Then still smiling, she reached over and took his hand in hers, and he thought that he would die.

When the fiery Brazilian sun went down and the earth began to cool, the party began to heat up. A couple was discovered fornicating under a tablecloth, and the crowd upended the table and threw cold water on the lovers and laughed uproariously. A drunk tried to yank a trumpet from one of the musicians' mouth, and the trumpeter kicked the man in the head and then the two rolled on the ground, pummeling each other until the other guests pulled them apart. Maria Mendes shouted it was time for a *batucada.* The rhythm section started laying down a visceral, percussive carnival beat, and the revelers began to dance joyously, alone, then in twos and threes. Then, when the congas and timbals began to vibrate with a hungry, sexual tattoo, the crowd formed a conga line and snaked its way around the yard and through the tables. Isabel's eyes danced with excitement, and she took her husband's small hand and dragged him to their rightful place at the head of the line, and they began to lead the others around the yard. But when the new bride noticed some of her mother's cronies laughing at

Giovanni's lurching dance steps, her dark face blooded with anger, and she hiked up the hem of her wedding dress and jumped up on the tented bandstand and waded into the musicians, screaming, "*Stop! Shut up!* Stop playing or I'll see you won't be paid a single cruzeiro!" And the musicians reluctantly let their crazed samba peter out. When the dancers moaned in protest, Isabel turned back to them, her green eyes burning, and screamed, "*Get out!* All of you scum! Get out of my house!" And then Maria Mendes came forward and complained, "These are my friends. Don't speak that way to them!" And Isabel shouted, "*You* get out, too!" And Maria Mendes said, "How dare you say that to your mother, you little whore!"

"If I am a whore, it's because *you* taught me, you sow! You are a bigger whore than me!"

Maria Mendes's fleshy breasts Jell-Oed with indignation in her push-up bra. "I am *not* a bigger whore than you. I am a *better* whore than you!"

"Ahhhhh—you can't even sell it anymore, you pig. You must give it away!" Isabel shouted. "Soon you'll have to *pay* for it!"

"*Bitch!*" Maria Mendes yelled, and her studs had to hold her back. "*Ungrateful bitch!* This is how you thank your poor mother?"

"*Mother?* You were never my mother, you were my *madam!* Now get out of my house!"

"You turn your back on your own mother so quickly? You throw your own mother into the street like this?"

"Get out! All of you, get out!" Isabel snatched a bottle of champagne from a table, took firm hold of her husband's wrist, and led him around to the front door of the Gemelli mansion. Maria Mendes followed, shouting, "They always told me you would turn on me someday, but I never believed them! I said you were my little girl. I loved you!"

At the front door Isabel whirled and cried, "You never loved anything didn't have a stiff *pau duro* between its legs!"

"You foul-mouthed little slut!" Maria Mendes hissed, and quickly crossed herself. "Damn you to hell!"

"*Get out!*" Isabel shouted into her mother's face. Then, to the crowd that had followed them to the front lawn, "All of you—*get out!*"

Trying a different tack, Maria Mendes sank to her knees, pulled at her hair, and wailed at the sky. "My little baby, don't do this to your poor mother. *Minha filha!* You're all I've got in the world." Her flesh quivered. "Take me in with you and your generous husband. Please don't turn me away."

Isabel turned to Giovanni and stuck her hand down into his tuxedo trousers. She fished out a fistful of bills and then tossed them before her pleading mother. The woman belly flopped as she lunged at them. Isabel laughed down at her and sneered, "You *are* a pig!" She opened the front door, dragged Giovanni in behind her, slammed shut the door, and leaned back against it. A moment later there was pounding on the other side of the wood. "Isabel, *meu coração,* don't do this to your *pobre mãe*!"

"Go away, pig!"

"I cannot bear this, *minha filha.* I will kill myself!"

"So kill yourself!" Isabel shouted. "The world would be a better place!"

"Isa*bel!*"

"Go away!"

"Isa-*belllll!*"

"Go away, pig, or I will see that my husband never gives you another centavo!"

Silence.

Then a tentative, "I will wait to hear . . ."

"Go away!"

A longer silence. Then a faraway call. "I love you, Isabel. *Até logo, minha filha!*"

Isabel, leaning back against the door, began to giggle. Then she broke into soft laughter, then into full-throated guffaws. Giovanni, standing a few feet away, tentatively began to laugh with her, and Isabel looked at him as if seeing him for the first time, and laughed all the harder. She held her stomach and slid down the door, her wedding dress bunching under her, and settled on the floor with a *plop* that made her laugh even more. She pounded her bare heels on the floor, and tears streamed down her cheeks. Giovanni laughed nervously along with her, not at all sure what he was laughing *at.*

Isabel threw back her head, raised the Dom Perignon bottle and poured champagne down her throat. She giggled, spit some champagne onto the marble floor, and started laughing again. Then, through slitted eyes, she spotted the house servants staring down at them from the top of the long, curving stairway.

"What are you looking at?" she shouted up at them. "Get out of my house!" She lumbered to her feet, slipped on her high heels, then immediately kicked them off again and started up the gleaming staircase. The servants looked down to Giovanni, saw that he would be of no help, and retreated hastily before Isabel's oncoming glare.

"Get out! I want an empty house on my wedding night!"

The servants scattered, and moments later doors could be heard slamming in distant parts of the house as they quickly vacated the premises. Isabel went around after them, locking doors, pulling shades, closing shutters. Then she explored the whole house, room by room, turning on all the lights and leaving them on as she left every room. When she had gone through the whole lighted mansion, she came down the stairs to find Giovanni just where she had left him, staring up at her from his place by the front hall. She took his hand and led him up to a small, airless bedroom on the third floor. She set the champagne bottle on the floor, came close to him, and turned her back. "Unbutton me," she said. Giovanni's throat was dry; his fingers shook as he slid the tiny cloth-covered buttons through the button-loops. There seemed to be a thousand of them, all in a maddeningly endless row. And as the silky material parted, he could see her dark, smooth skin. His fingertips brushed against her flesh and felt *singed* by her heat. She stepped away from him and climbed out of her wedding gown, leaving it in a gossamer pool on the wood floor. She slipped out of her bra—her breasts were small, her nipples dark. She wore no panties. Only a white garter belt and the patterned white stockings below. Her flesh, next to the stark white cloth, seemed to glow like warm, dark honey. The hair between her legs looked as if it should have belonged to an angel. Giovanni felt his heart pound and his chest constrict. He truly believed that he might die. He had never felt this way before.

She sat on the edge of the bed and held out her hand. He couldn't move. She pulled him toward her. She unbuckled his belt, unhooked the catch on his trousers, and let them fall. His rigid erection stretched the white cotton of his underwear. She giggled and yanked the garment down. His penis bounced in the cool night air. Her breath caught with a hiss. She looked up at him, and then back down at his erection. It was huge. She took it in her hand, and Giovanni gasped. She gently pushed back his foreskin. His cock was white and ramrod straight and fully eleven inches long, with a bulbous, heart-shaped glans. It was perfect. Isabel, amazed, *amused* by the awful irony of it all—the ugly little man with a twisted body and a huge, perfect cock—threw back her head and laughed her deep, free, sensual laugh, and Giovanni ejaculated in her hand. He came and came in waves and waves of hot, thick semen. It roped around her arm, splattered on her belly, ribboned her fingers. She laughed and laughed and he came and came. Then, when he had finally stopped, she stroked him gently until he was metal-hard again. She leaned back on the blue bedspread, drew him to her, and wrapped her legs around his thighs. She slipped the head of his cock inside the moist lips of her vagina, clutched his arms tightly, and hungrily thrust her hips up at him, impaling herself on him.

And Giovanni Mussimo Gemelli, at the age of fifty-three, happily lost his virginity.

If he had had any experience, any experience at all, he would have known that he had married an exceptional young woman, a singular sexual event, an unbelievable, one-in-a-million first-class fuck. As it was, he intuited, in his boundless joy, that Isabel wasn't a run-of-the-mill lover. She was a volcano under him—churning, erupting, pouring hot lava over his legs. He was helpless. He didn't even have time to wonder what to do next. She fucked *him.* She was like an animal beneath him, twisting, entwining, bouncing, exploding—again and again. She rode his enormous cock from below, like a sideshow ride. She screamed and moaned and bit his arms through his tuxedo. And then, when she finally subsided, like a spent hurricane or a receding flood, she lay under him and laughed and laughed and laughed, and he felt her laughter through the tight ring of flesh around his cock.

Afterward, Isabel naked, Giovanni in only his ruffled tuxedo shirt, they sat on the polished marble floor of the mansion's vast entry hall and opened the hundreds of wedding gifts sent from all over the world. Even the many society mavens who had declined to attend the sorry affair couldn't afford to affront a powerful man like Giovanni Gemelli by ignoring his wedding or by sending a cheap gift, and Isabel squealed with delight as she tore open the wrapping on every expensive, tasteful, one-of-a-kind, crystal, silver, embossed, hand-carved, glazed, matched offering. She drank champagne from a liter bottle and ate leftover caviar hors d'oeuvres from a vast silver serving tray she had lugged in from the kitchen, squatted on her naked haunches, and tore open all the carefully wrapped packages. Giovanni watched a trickle of champagne run down her throat and across her breast. He saw the delicate bush of dark hair jutting down between her hard legs as she rocked on her heels.

When she bored of the presents, she lit a marijuana cigarette she carefully withdrew from the top of her stockings. She showed Giovanni how to smoke it, and he sucked it in and held his breath until his ears burned, and then exhaled with a sputtering sound like an outboard motor, and they choked and giggled together in a cloud of blue smoke.

She went through the house turning off all the lights. Then she took his hand and guided him to another bedroom and opened the French shutters. Framed in the window, she gleamed in the moonglow like well-oiled wood. She pushed him back on the bed and began unbuttoning his shirt. He moved to stop her, but she pushed his hand away. She tore off the last few buttons and shredded the soft linen. She kneeled over him and looked down at him, naked in the moonlight. He wanted to be dead, to be invisible. He wanted to be a space traveler in another universe. There was a deafening roar in his ears. His throat was dry, and he could feel his pulse throbbing in his upright penis. She dipped her head, lapped at his cock like a puppy, and Giovanni felt the world tilt and right itself. She snuggled her face in the coarse gray hair at the base of his cock and took one of his testicles into her mouth. Giovanni moaned. With her tongue she pressed the kernel of his testicle against the roof of her mouth, and Giovanni moaned again and clawed at the sheets. Isabel laughed, his flesh still in her mouth, and the sound vibrated through Giovanni's body and into his inner core, and he knew no man had ever loved a woman the way he loved Isabel.

She licked every part of him. Every twisted, uneven, asymmetrical part. She sucked his toes and nibbled the back of his neck and darted the tip of her tongue into his anus. Giovanni fought for his breath. Tears streamed down his cheeks, and he pounded his clenched fist on the mattress.

She squatted over his face, her hair feathering his nose, and he smelled her scent, as he had that morning at the altar, only now the smell was strong and deep and overpowering, like an ocean. He licked at her tentatively, and she held his head and guided him. His nose slipped into her, and he thought he would drown in her wet, slick odor. She *was* like the ocean—bottomless, boundless, and forever. She rubbed her cunt back and forth, back and forth, across his face until he was drenched in her. Then he rubbed her warm, wet wound across his chest, through his hair, down his bent arms and twisted legs. She scented him like a wild-bitch animal staking out territorial boundaries.

Then she settled back on his stalagmitelike cock, enveloped him in her, and rocked back and forth on him until the yellow Brazilian dawn bled in the windows.

Within two months she was pregnant.

Giovanni immediately redecorated one of the mansion's many bedrooms into a glittering nursery, with Mickey Mouse wallpaper, Winnie-the-Pooh stuffed animals, and tiny furniture decorated with pictures of the cartoon figure Emilia, the Brazilian Betty Boop.

Isabel's already wide hips thickened and swelled. In her sixth month she waddled down the halls like a child's bottom-weighted Slinky toy.

While Giovanni looked, she stripped naked and examined herself in the floor-to-ceiling mirror. She proudly caressed her newly big breasts and offered them to his eager lips. He sucked on her distended nipples, and she laughed with pleasure.

In her eighth month she was huge. Her belly was as taut

as the tight head of a conga drum. She stayed in bed all day, and the servants, who had grown to love her, smuggled in her Dom Perignon, which she had developed a taste for, and green seedless *maconha,* which she smoked in a long clay pipe whenever Giovanni went to the office. She ate constantly. Mostly local Rio dishes—the black-beans-and-pork dish called *feijoada,* and *dobradinha,* a stew made from cow's intestines, but she also craved spaghetti and meatballs and American-style hamburgers.

Two weeks before the approximated birthdate, Giovanni took two adjoining rooms at the Hospital Das Clinicas, purported to have the best doctors in Brazil. Isabel protested. She knew the nurses wouldn't bring her champagne and marijuana, and the food would be terrible. But Giovanni was adamant. He was too nervous. He felt inadequate to handle the situation, whenever it came. Here, in the hospital, his size and infirmities couldn't prevent him from controlling the environment.

He had intended to sleep in the next room, but the first night Isabel fell asleep as they watched television together—*I Spy*—and Giovanni, not wanting to move and chance awakening her—slept sitting in his chair. The next night and all nights afterward he had a cot brought into Isabel's room and slept with his hand reaching up to rest on her hip.

They were playing cards, Isabel roaring with laughter whenever she won a hand, when the contractions started. They came every few hours, then every hour, then finally almost constantly. Isabel clenched the sheets, sweat pouring from her face, and she cursed all men and their ugly little penises and all their fathers and mothers who had fornicated through time immemorial. Then, when the pain eased, she cracked dirty jokes to the nurses, who idolized like a film star the legendary *favela* girl who had married into the enormously wealthy Gemelli family.

When the contractions came again, and Isabel howled to the ceiling, Giovanni was beside himself with frustration and concern. He rushed back and forth between his wife's bed and the doctor's side—entreating, demanding, comforting, threatening—until finally the obstetrician ordered him out of the delivery room. He limped the hall miserably, crying and praying, for two hours, until a smiling black nurse came for him.

"You have a daughter," she said softly.

Led back into the delivery room, Giovanni was dimly aware of a bawling, bloody-looking little half-formed *thing* in the doctor's arms.

"She's perfect," the nurse said reassuringly, not knowing that his handicaps weren't hereditary.

But Giovanni's eyes were fastened onto Isabel. She looked pale and used up on the sweaty sheets.

"Gio!" she cried, and held her arms out to him. "You left me alone!"

He rushed to her and held her tightly. *"Bellà! Bellà!"*

"Gio," she wept, "I'm so sorry. It's a girl."

"Shhhhh," he soothed, "don't be foolish. This is only the first. We'll have many more. I can't wait to begin!"

She chuckled then through her tears, and the chuckle became a giggle, and then she threw her head back and roared, and Giovanni sheepishly laughed with her. They laughed joyfully, holding each other tightly, and then she stopped abruptly and he heard her suddenly gasp, "Gio—"

He held her at arm's length and looked at her.

"Gio, I can't breathe. It hurts." She held a clenched fist to her chest. There was fear in her eyes.

"Doctor!" he shouted.

"Gio," she said weakly, and he could feel her slipping away, slipping under.

"Doctor! Doctor! Doctor!"

"Gio."

They were around them then, swirling and working.

"She's turning blue around her lips," one of the nurses said.

"Cyanotic," another said, reflexively.

"Her heart rate is accelerating." There was compressed tension in the nurse's voice.

"Oxygen, quickly," the obstetrician ordered.

"What's happening?" Giovanni asked as they moved him out of the way.

"She's having PVCs!" the first nurse said, studying a machine with a television screen.

"Open up the IV, wide open!"

"What's happening?" Giovanni demanded.

"Look at her blood pressure!"

"What's happening?"

"Wide open, for Chrissake! Wide open!"

"*Meu Deus,*" a nurse gasped, "she's dying!"

"Shut up! Get Dr. Salvador up here. Now!"

"*What's happening?*" Giovanni shouted. "*What's happening! What's happening!*" And then a very large orderly with very strong arms almost carried him out of the delivery room and into the hall, settled him on a hard-backed wood bench, and sat beside him.

"What's happening to my Isabel?" he begged of the big man.

"It's better to stay out here," the orderly said.

Doctors rushed by and into the delivery room, then other men came running, pushing a machine.

"What's wrong?" Giovanni asked dazedly. "What's wrong with my Isabel?"

The big, swarthy man just shook his head and said, "It's better we wait out here, *senhor.*"

Giovanni prayed then. He gripped his cane tightly and rested his head on his hands and closed his eyes and prayed. He promised God all of his wealth and power, if only He would help his Isabel through whatever was happening to her. He swore he would spend the rest of his life performing good works. He had a vision of himself, a cripple, hobbling among other cripples lamer than he. He saw himself spooning food into their mouths, washing their deformities, wiping their asses—all these things he would do, if he could have his Isabel back.

He opened his eyes, and the big orderly was gone. Giovanni felt he was in a box packed with cotton. He could hear nothing, feel nothing. He had no idea how long he had been sitting here. He closed his eyes and prayed some more.

He made an Act of Contrition. Then another. Then ten more. Then ten Hail Marys. Then a hundred. Followed by a hundred Our Fathers. He wished he had a rosary. He was on his third set of Our Fathers when he felt the weight of someone settle beside him on the bench. It filled him with dread. He refused to open his eyes. Then a hand was laid over his on the cane.

"Senhor Gemelli," he heard someone say.

He opened his eyes. It was Dr. Salvador, Isabel's obstetrician. The man looked frightened.

"I'm sorry, Senhor Gemelli. She's gone."

Giovanni refused to accept it. "God forgive me," he said quickly, making a sign of the cross. "I don't care about the baby. As long as my Isabel is all right."

The doctor gently rested his other hand on Giovanni's humped back.

"The baby is fine," he breathed. "It's your wife, *senhor.*"

"My—my wife?" Giovanni stammered.

"We didn't want to give up, Senhor Gemelli. We tried everything. Long past any rational point."

"How could this happen?" Giovanni asked, as much to the heavens as to the doctor. But only the doctor answered.

"What can I say? These tragedies occur. There will have to be an autopsy, of course. A girl that young..." His voice trailed off.

Giovanni covered his face with his hands and sobbed. The doctor, watching him, was very concerned for his career. Senhor Gemelli was a very powerful man. He sought to deflect any blame the grieving widower might level at him.

"It was a one-in-a-million accident, I'm sure, *senhor.* A stroke, or possibly a blood clot. A fluke. An act of God."

Giovanni jerked his head up, and his wet eyes were hot with anger.

"Don't blame this on God!" he hissed. "This is the work of the Devil!"

He put his face back into his hands and cried. After a while Dr. Salvador got up and went away.

It was as if the whole world were an affront to him now. A car with its radio blaring Brazilian *samba* passed on the street below his bedroom window—*their* bedroom window—and he thought to himself, *How can there still be music in the world? How can anyone sing anymore?* In his sleepless nights he sat alone at the kitchen table drinking tea and whiskey and watched the cook's two white kittens frolic at his feet, and they might as well have been jaguars tearing at each other's flesh, they were that strange, otherworldly. During the first week a servant somewhere downstairs laughed at a joke, and Giovanni stood at the head of the stairs and shrieked, "*Shut up! Shut up! Shut up,*" and then the house was sepulchrally silent.

Dr. Salvador came with the autopsy report. It was a saddle embolus, he said. A blood clot formed by the heavy uterus resting on a vein called the *inferior vena cava.* A one-in-a-hundred-thousand tragedy. No way to predict it, or prevent it. A clot passed through her veins to her heart, and then blocked passage of blood into her lungs. She died from a lack of oxygen, just as if—

Giovanni pulled himself up from his chair and lurched out of the room, out of the house, and stood in his vast backyard and squinted up at the sky. How could the sun still be there, warm and sweet, in the blue Tropic of Capricorn sky? How could it rise every day over Guanabara Bay and set every night behind the outstretched arms of the *Cristo Redentor*? How could time still go on when he was a corpse? Why didn't they come to bury him?

He ceased shaving. He forgot to bathe. He pissed in the potted plants. There was always a bottle of whiskey beside his bed, and he drank from the moment his eyes opened to the offending, sacrilegious sunshine.

He never left the house. He limped the mansion's hallways, a blanket thrown around his shoulders, reeking in his soiled pajamas. The servants scuttled away before him as if he were *enfeitiçado*—a zombie, a haunted one. He constructed a makeshift altar on the back lid of a toilet—a Madonna, a cross, blessed candles Isabel had kept around the house—knelt on the bathroom floor, propped his elbows on the covered seat, and prayed for hours in the white candlelight while tears streamed down his grizzled cheeks.

Unable to take his own life, he prayed to his Savior, begged Him to call him up, to ease his pain, to stop this madness.

One day the painful blur Giovanni lived in parted to reveal his sister, Angelina Serio, seated before him on a shellacked cane chair. The chair creaked under her floppy bulk.

"And so," she was saying, archly, "everything will be taken care of. The witch has agreed to all arrangements."

Through his pain Giovanni was distrustful of his sister. She looked happy and dangerous in her smugness.

"Everything has been arranged. There will be a considerable cash settlement, and for this she has signed away all claims." She waved a document at him. Giovanni's mind bore down hard, trying to comprehend what Angelina was saying.

"I—I don't understand," he stammered.

"You don't have to," she reassured him. "Just sign this." She stuck a pen under his nose. "Everything has been arranged. Don't worry your head."

He took the pen and paper. "What is this?"

"Giovanni! Would you not worry? Just sign it. Here." She put a fat diamonded finger on the line.

He looked up at her. Through his whiskey-sodden grief he felt an intuitive necessity to understand what Angelina wanted from him. Something was wrong. Glancing around the disheveled bedroom, he saw his brother-in-law, Bruno, standing in a corner. Bruno smiled weakly at him.

"What is this?" he asked again.

"*Ahhhhh! Afanculo!*" Angelina swore, slapping her forehead with the palm of her hand. "It's only an agreement I had drawn up. I did it as a favor to you. You are in no condition to take care of your own business."

"What kind of agreement?"

"A contract between you and that pig Maria Mendes."

"Who?"

"Your former mother-in-law!" she exclaimed, and then cackled at the absurdity of it all.

An alarm went off in Giovanni's muddled mind.

"A contract?"

The fat woman sighed deeply, then bulldozed her obese bulk from the chair to the edge of Giovanni's bed. She put her hand on his arm.

"Brother," she said gently, "I have looked after your interest in your time of sorrow. I have convinced Maria Mendes that it would be best for all concerned if, for a hundred thousand cruzeiros, she were to relinquish all rights and claims to the Gemelli fortune and properties. And all the infant's rights."

"The what?"

Angelina frowned with exasperation.

"The *baby*, Giovanni!" She spoke as if explaining something to a child. "The little girl. Mendes will raise the child. There will probably have to be a monthly stipend as the old whore will probably—"

"What little girl?"

She stared at him. "Giovanni, don't you remember? You have a daughter."

It all rushed back at him then. All of it—the delivery room, the black nurse, the bloody-looking newborn thing, Isabel's fist suddenly clutching at her breast as she said, "Gio, it hurts, it hurts!" It all rushed back then and struck him like a hammer blow to his heart, and he gasped and started to sob.

"Giovanni," Angelina said softly, "Giovanni, you must stop this."

"Where is she?" he choked out.

She looked at her brother and took a long time in answering. "We buried her in Santa Teresa Cemetery, Giovanni. You were there."

He shook his head, wiping the tears from his eyes with the back of his hands.

"No," he rasped. "My daughter."

With the money her daughter had given her during her eleven-month marriage to Giovanni Gemelli, Maria Mendes had built a rambling, garish house on the edge of the teeming Rocinha *favela.* What good was coming into wealth if you couldn't flaunt it before your old cronies?

In the street in front of the bright yellow house, Giovanni heard the infant's screaming, then Maria Mendes's shout, "*Meu Deus!* Shut up! Shut up! For *five minutes*!"

She came to the screened door at his knock, holding a bottle of beer. Her housecoat hung open, giving views of sagging flesh encased in pathetic lingerie.

"*You!*" she said when she saw him. "They said you were crazy. *Luoco.*"

Giovanni opened the door and stepped inside. He was clean, freshly shaved, and dressed in a pressed suit.

"Where is the baby?"

She turned her back and flounced away, her hips swaying drunkenly.

"What do you care now? I signed the contract."

The house was cluttered and stale-smelling. Somewhere in another room the baby wailed on.

"*Shut up!*" Maria Mendes screamed. "For Chrissake, give me *one* minute of peace!"

Giovanni moved up behind her. She turned back.

"Here," he said, and handed her the contract, already torn in half. Her eyes turned cold and shrewd.

"What is this? There was an agreement. You're trying to rob me of my money."

She looked down at him, studying him closely. "What do you want?" she asked.

"I want the baby. I want my daughter."

Reacting quickly, instinctively, seeking the path of her best interests, she feigned shock, outrage.

"*Your* daughter!" she snorted. "All of a sudden you come around. All of a sudden you want to see the poor motherless child. After six months—"

"Six months!" Giovanni gasped.

"—you come here and want to take away my granddaughter. All I have left of my beautiful Isabel, who I loved so much!" she wailed in mock emotion.

Just then a tall black man wearing only silky underwear stepped out of an adjoining bedroom.

"Stop screaming, woman! And shut up that baby! This house is bedlam. A man can go crazy around here."

"*You* shut up, you stupid black bastard!" She whirled at him. "It's my house, and I'll shout if I want to!" she shouted, as if to prove her point.

"And I'll beat the shit out of you!" the black man threatened.

"I'll cut your heart out!" Maria Mendes hissed, grabbing up a filthy butter knife from the cluttered tabletop.

Giovanni pushed past her and then down a short hall toward the sound of the baby's wailing. The last room was a hot, stuffy yellow cubicle furnished with only a sheetless double bed. In the center of the naked mattress a thin, diapered baby screamed up at the ceiling. The little girl's eyes focused on him momentarily, and then the screams intensified. The infant, waving her tiny fists in frustration, seemed almost to be angrily shaking them at him.

Maria Mendes was suddenly beside him, her shoulder against his, her breath stale and beery.

"She won't stop crying," she whispered in a desperate, almost grandmotherly tone. "She sleeps for just a few hours, and then she starts to cry again. It's been that way since I brought her home. It's driving me crazy."

"Is she hungry?"

"I feed her," she said indignantly. "You think I didn't think of that? I feed her, and all the while she's eating she's screaming and spitting the food at me. She's crazy," she whispered then, "just like her mother. All the hospital nurses said the same thing when I went to get her. They said she's crazy."

"She's perfect," Giovanni said, remembering he had heard that somewhere.

Maria Mendes shook her head slowly. "There's something wrong with the child."

Giovanni didn't want to hear any more. He scooped up the baby from the dirty mattress. In his arms she screamed even louder. Giovanni turned to leave with her. Maria Mendes blocked his way.

"Where are you taking her?"

"I'm taking her home."

"You can't come in here, after six months, after I lost my poor sainted daughter, and take away my little baby. She's all I have in the world."

Giovanni's eyes bore into her.

"How much?"

Without hesitation she said, "Seven thousand *cruzeiros*."

"Done."

"A month!"

"Yes, yes," he barked angrily. "You have it!" He tried to push around her. She jammed her belly lewdly against him and breathed, "Gemelli, there is no need to grieve alone. There are others I could get for you. Isabel's cousins. Even more beautiful than she was. What do you say?"

Horrified, Gemelli shrank away from her and hurried

through the house. She followed him, shouting and flinging open her housecoat.

"What about *me,* little man? You had the copy, why not try the original? Who do you think taught Isabel all her tricks? I'll show you all the things she hadn't learned yet!" Her laugh was a vulgar clone of Isabel's, and it sent shivers up his twisted spine. "You think you're better than me, but you're not. You're just a dirty little freak of a dirty old man. And I know what you want that baby for."

Out in the hot sun the chauffeur held the sedan's door open, and Giovanni got in, cradling the squalling baby against his chest.

"Don't forget my money, Gemelli!" Maria Mendes shouted from the door, squinting in the glare and not even bothering to pull her housecoat closed.

The LTD began to move, then stopped. Giovanni's window rolled down, and he stuck out his head.

"What's her name?"

Maria Mendes laughed again. "I call her Isabel. I guess it's a habit with me."

The Ford moved again. Maria Mendes stood in the street and shouted after it.

"Gemelli! Don't forget my money!"

The baby wouldn't stop crying. Just as Maria Mendes had said, she slept fitfully for short periods, then woke wailing up at the cherub-painted ceiling. Giovanni had every female servant in the house come into the nursery and pick up the infant, hoping for a positive response. There was none. Then he hired a wet nurse, a huge ebony woman from the northern jungle coast who wore a gold stud in her nose and cooed to the little girl in a singsong patois. Isabel seemed to improve for a few moments, then her screams would soar to a higher intensity. She suckled at the big dark nipple, her muffled wails always there, just below the surface, like distant thunder beyond a mountain range.

The best doctors in Latin America examined Isabel Gemelli. A world-renowned pediatrician observed her for an hour and called her condition "irritable beyond consolability." He ordered a spinal tap on the infant, and when the fluid came back clear, the pediatrician called in an infectious-disease specialist. The specialist injected the screaming baby with antibiotics. After a week there was no discernible improvement. *Irritable beyond consolability*. Next came the neurologist, who suggested an EEG to search for brain-wave seizures, and a radiologist who did a CAT-scan. Both doctors remarked that Isabel was the youngest patient they had ever treated, and neither doctor could find a medical reason for the baby's angry sadness. They referred Giovanni to a different pediatrician, who brought in a child psychiatrist, who did a battery of motor-response tests, then said the baby's problem wasn't mental, but must be some sort of degenerative organic brain disorder that the other specialists had missed. The pediatrician disagreed heatedly, and the two physicians got into a shouting match right there in front of Giovanni.

The baby raged on. Beyond consolability.

One day Angelina Serio appeared in the nursery, inspected the bawling baby with a cross countenance, and immediately said, "She's possessed. I'll get a priest."

The priest was a Sicilian with greasy black hair and warts on his hands. He shook holy water around the room and read from his missal. Then, with the baby shrieking, he turned to Giovanni.

"Have you tried a doctor?"

"I have lost my faith in doctors," Giovanni said evenly.

Giovanni was becoming more desperate day by day. The child could be heard in every room in the big house, seemingly every hour of the day. She was getting thinner; her growth was being arrested. She was crying herself to death.

The wet nurse, whose name was Zumira, came humbly to him, offering the services of her cousin, a *macumbeiro,* a very powerful magical man from her native village, recently moved to Rio. This man, Zumira claimed, had cured many sick people whom the doctors had given up on. Some of the children had even been administered the last rites, and the *macumba* man had cured them, practically raising them from the dead. He was also famous for his love potions.

Giovanni was reluctant—this smacked of witchcraft and devil worship. *Macumba* might be the second religion of the rest of Brazil, but Giovanni had only one God, even if He had already failed him. But though it might be sacrilegious, Giovanni had no choice.

On the midnight of the next full moon Giovanni and Zumira brought the squalling baby to a *centro,* a *macumba* "church" in a small clearing high in the Tijuca Forest. Beside a running stream, an imperative for *macumba,* the *centro* was delineated by a rough square of flickering white candles. In the middle of the glow of light was a painfully thin black man dressed completely in stark white. He frowned at Giovanni and held out his hands.

"Give me the infant."

Giovanni reluctantly handed over his daughter to the fiery-eyed wraith. The baby screamed.

"Kneel," the *macumbeiro* ordered, and Giovanni dropped to his knees on the damp soil.

The *macumbeiro* closed his eyes and passed his hand over the face of the crying baby. He shivered and looked down at the baby. "The child has a *maldição* on it." His eyes pierced into Giovanni's. "An enemy of yours has put a curse on your baby. Do you know who did it?"

Giovanni was genuinely perplexed. "I—I have no enemies."

The thin, intense man placed the crying baby on the bed of leaves he had made. Giovanni wanted to snatch the baby up from the ground, but forced himself to watch his daughter scream in fear and anger.

"Did you bring the candy?"

Zumira, kneeling behind Giovanni, handed him the small bag of sweets, and he in turn passed it to the *macumbeiro,* who set it on the ground beside Isabel. A small smile creased the black man's face.

"They love the candy," he said. Then he began to softly clap his hands in a gently repetitive tattoo. Dah—dah—*dah.* Dah—dah—*dah.* "They are lazy," he whispered. "They must be summoned. Do as I do."

Giovanni watched the long black hands and clapped along with them. He could hear Zumira doing likewise. After a moment the *macumbeiro* began to gently sway on his haunches, his eyes hypnotically rolled back into his head, and Giovanni felt something fluttering by his hand.

"The chicken!" Zumira hissed. "Give it to him!"

Giovanni looked down at the small black rooster, its talons bound together, struggling in her wide lap.

"Give it to him!"

The rooster's wings beat against Giovanni's hands as he laid the bird before the *macumbeiro*. The bony ebony fingers of the man's left hand clutched the rooster's long neck, and there was flash of steel in the *macumbeiro's* right hand, and then there was thick hot, blood spurting across the black man's stark-white clothing as he held the jerking, dying chicken over the screaming infant and let the jets of blood spew across her face.

"No!" Giovanni shouted, as he struggled to his feet. "No!"

The *macumbeiro* whirled and pointed a gory, accusing finger at him. "Don't dare to disrupt—"

Giovanni's cane slashed down across the scrawny arm, and the black man shrieked with pain.

Giovanni snatched up his daughter, wiping the blood from her anguished face, and held her to his chest as he lurched away from the clearing in the forest.

"Shhhh—" he tried to soothe her. "Don't cry, *minha filha! Don't cry!*"

He decided next to try various outside stimuli that might amuse the child and distract her from whatever internal turbulence was plaguing her.

He pulled closed the nursery curtains. He dimmed the lights.

No change.

He turned off the lights.

Nothing but wails.

He clapped his hands and pulled his nose.

Still no change.

He barked like a dog.

Zip.

He flung open the curtains, and the nursery was bathed in golden yellow.

Isabel cried.

He wheeled a television set into the nursery and turned it on. The cartoons were playing.

For a moment the baby stopped sobbing, and a quizzical look crossed her face as she tried to focus on the oversized, chaotic, anthropomorphic images.

Then she started crying again.

But Giovanni was heartened. He had had a *response!* A *positive response!* He was going to reach her; now, he was sure.

He had a 15-millimeter projector delivered to the mansion, along with a screen, a sound system, and dozens of films—most of them cartoons. He set up the projector and screen, drew the shades, and flicked on the switch. Over the wall ran a mad, chaotic tableau of dancing pigs, sputtering ducks, mincing mice, frustrated coyotes. They drove cars, shot cannons, slammed into walls, got crunched by monolithic boulders. They yelped, giggled, howled, and spun around like humanoid tops. But Giovanni didn't watch the cartoons. His eyes were on his daughter. She was still crying, but from time to time she would stop for a heartbeat, as if taking a breath, as if for a brief second she had forgotten her anger, her grief. Then she would cry again. Giovanni studied the short intervals of peace. There was something about them. They seemed to come whenever a cartoon figure jumped especially high, or moved stealthily, or, or—it was the *music!* She was responding to the *music,* not to the action on the screen, but to the accompanying sound track.

He was elated. He had the projector taken out and a complete state-of-the-art sound system set up, with the speakers turned away, so as not to damage the infant's tender ears.

Trembling with hope, the baby sobbing, he began. And since he was Neapolitan, his first selection was "O Sole Mio."

Isabel shrieked.

Next he played Verdi.

She *hated* opera.

He tried some other types of classical music.

Mozart string quartets.

She seemed to quiet.

Beethoven's Ninth Symphony.

Definitely not!

Debussy's *Études* for piano.

The child actually stopped crying for a full minute. Then

she seemed to tire of the recording and bawled even more loudly than before.

Giovanni sent the servants scurrying for all the records in the house. His deceased wife had spent a fortune on music the short while they were together, and he scrambled through the lot like a child trying to solve a puzzle.

Isabel had been fond of American and English rock and roll. He found the Beatles' last album and played "Let It Be."

Absolutely not.

He laid on the turntable a record by something called Steely Dan.

Emphatically rejected.

James Brown.

Shrieks of displeasure.

He discovered some Brazilian recordings among the albums scattered over the floor.

He dropped the needle on a collection of Jobim bossa novas. What could be more sedating?

The baby was incensed. She wailed.

Giovanni began to panic. He had thought he had stumbled on the key to his daughter's troubled psyche, and now he felt the secret slipping away, like a drunk's fleeting euphoria.

He began frantically changing recordings, dropping the stylus down anywhere, then jarringly raking the arm off when Isabel didn't respond. The baby cried harder and harder.

Finally, in desperation, he stacked a dozen records on the automatic record changer and slumped exhausted into one of the tiny pink nursery chairs. He covered his face with his hands and cried softly. After a few minutes, the baby still screaming, he began to pray. He prayed to the Virgin Mary; he prayed to Saint Jude, the patron saint of the hopeless; he made a special vow to San Gennaro, the local patron of Naples.

He had been asleep. He didn't know for how long. He woke up with a start to find himself in the delicate little chair. The sun must have set, because the room was dimmer, cooler. The stereo was still playing. Some American jazz now, a slow, bluesy ballad from the forties. There was a female vocalist. Giovanni felt ill at ease. Something was wrong. Something—

The baby wasn't crying.

Giovanni's heart soared momentarily, until he realized: *She's fallen asleep.*

Well, thank God for small favors.

He lurched to his feet and limped stealthily to the crib and looked down.

Isabel's big brown eyes twinkled up at him. She was smiling.

Giovanni blinked and stared. He had never seen his daughter smile before.

On the record the vocalist stopped singing for a few bars, the sax section swelled, and a flicker of unease slipped over Isabel's face like a shadow; then the woman started singing again, and the baby giggled.

It *was* the music, and this was the *right* music.

He lumbered over to the turntable and tried to read the circular record label going round and round. Then he turned up the volume.

The nursery vibrated with the woman's strange, plaintive voice. A voice heavy with pain and experience. A voice with all the sharp corners flattened out and compressed, so that the sound was both soothing and disturbing, mournful and defiant, sexy and angry. It was equal parts a jazzman's muted trumpet, an eerie Japanese flute, an African tribal chant. It was primordial, and at the same time totally sophisticated.

The baby laughed. *Laughed!*

Giovanni leaned over, and she held up her hands to him, as if she wanted him to hold her. He offered his finger, and she gripped it and laughingly tried to suck on it.

Then she held it and smiled up at him.

The record played on. After a few minutes the child fell peacefully to sleep, still holding her father's left index finger tightly in her doll-like grasp. And still smiling.

Giovanni raised his eyes upward and with his right hand made an awkward sign of the cross, giving thanks to the Virgin Mary, Saint Jude, San Gennaro, and Billie Holiday.

BOOK III

WAUKEGAN, ILLINOIS—JUNE

"Tell the truth, babe. Don't redheads have the prettiest pussies?"

Her clitoris was like a tumor under his tongue. Thick, wide, throbbing, it seemed to have an intelligence all its own. Sometimes it eluded him, running from the tip of his tongue like a virginal maiden, and other times it rose to meet his mouth like a wanton whore.

"Just like eating cotton candy, ain't it, babe?"

Actually it was more like nibbling an oyster with a faint medicinal flavor. Kim was fond of using flavored vaginal sprays that after a few hours of use seemed to revert to their chemical base.

"Get at it, babe. Get it! Oooh, that's nice. That's it," she purred as she ran her long-nailed fingers through his thick dark hair. She giggled and said, "Eat that fish sandwich."

Kim was a thin, angular woman of forty-seven, with pinkish-orange hair and pale skin covered with uncountable freckles. On her narrow right flank was a surprisingly professional tattoo of the Pink Panther, winking. She lay back in her wide, wrinkled bed, propped up by the mound of a dozen pillows—Kim Baxter loved pillows—grinding her hips and watching Sal root at her sexual organs. Kim Baxter had never decided which she enjoyed most—having cunnilingus performed on her, or watching it being performed on her. She threw back her head, scooted her narrow ass down an inch, and widened her already spread-eagled legs.

"Oh, you do know how to do that, don'tcha, babe?"

Sal sucked Kim's distended clitoris between his teeth and chewed lightly. She closed her eyes and moaned. *Let's get this over with,* Sal thought as he burrowed his face into her slick pink flesh. He was stretched out, ass up, legs dangling over the bed, his flaccid penis flattened under him against the mattress. Not that it mattered to this bitch. Kim Baxter was interested in having her pussy licked, period. Although Kim had never formalized the thought and would blanch at being labeled a feminist, hard dicks to her were a representation of man's domination over woman. Watching a man on his knees eating her box was power of a whole other kind—hers over him.

Sal caught Kim's clit with the tip of his tongue, pressed it against his teeth, and began to rub it back and forth over his incisors. She began to whimper and tremble. Sal increased the pressure, flattening her flesh between his gums and teeth and racing it back and forth like a stick on a picket fence. Subtlety was lost on Kim Baxter's pussy.

"Oh, Jesus, baby!" she rasped. "Oh, Jesus!" And she fumbled for the sterling silver amyl-nitrate sniffer she wore on a long chain around her neck like an amulet. Kim Baxter eschewed—disapproved of, even—all other drugs, but at the moment of truth, she couldn't get along without the ecstasy induced by the heart stimulant she bought from a sleazy doctor who frequented her barroom. Kim was an orgasm junkie.

She yanked off the popper's cover, keeping her finger over the penislike hole at the tip, and clutched the amyl nitrate to her breast like a religious icon.

"Oh, yeah, baby, don't stop! Don't you stop!"

Sal was chewing on her like an ear of corn now. He knew from past experience the only thing she could possibly feel at this juncture was if he did stop. The water was already boiling. Continuation was the key.

"Oh, shit!" she yelled, and Sal knew she was at the point of no return. "Oh, shit!" She rammed the amyl sniffer up her nose and inhaled deeply. Sal sucked at her furiously, and her wet meat felt like a collapsed balloon in his mouth. Then the orgasm and the amyl nitrate began to peak simultaneously, and Kim started to babble incoherently and thrash about the bed as if she were having an epileptic seizure. Her vagina gushed liquid into Sal's mouth, and her legs closed around his head like a vise. She raised her hips from the sheet and ground herself into Sal's face. He clutched at her legs and tried to hold on. For several long moments they were like animals caught in a pitched frenzy. And then Kim's climax subsided, her tense body relaxed, and Sal became aware of a throbbing neck ache. He crawled up from between her legs, and she raised her head from the mound of pillows and licked at her moisture on his dark face.

"I ain't never dived a muff"—she grinned—"but I do love tasting my twat on a man's mouth." Sal plopped down beside her on the damp sheets and began kneading the back of his neck.

Kim lit a cigarette and stared dreamily up at the ceiling. After a few minutes she said, "I'm trying to decide if you're the best I ever had. I mean, don't be offended, you're damn good, handsome. One of the top two or three. But I'm just trying to decide if you are *the* best." She reached for the ever-present tumbler of Wild Turkey on the bedside table. Sal had clocked her one day in the bar. Her per diem was just about a full fifth. Every day. "I had me this big nigger once, boy had a tongue like a fucking anteater. Long and skinny, you know what I mean. He'd run that sucker up inside of me, felt like a damn fire hose." Sal reached over her to get one of her cigarettes, and when his arm brushed her breast, their bodies seemed to recoil from each other. "Then there was Spiro's big brother, Gus." Spiro, Sal had learned, was Kim's deceased husband, the Greek who'd had a heart attack while making change for a fifty and left her the Tall Cold One, the bar and grill Kim owned and managed, just down the stairs and across the street from this dusty little apartment. "Gus didn't have no teeth. Calcium deficiency or something, back in Greece. Old bastard would pop them false plates out, and swear to God, Sal, he would gum my ass until I thought I'd piss on myself." She giggled. "But I always kidded Gus, with all his teeth out like that, he probably coulda sucked a dick better than anything else. Gus didn't like that." She laughed out loud, which caused her to pass gas, which made her laugh all the harder. "I think you *are* the best, sugar."

Sal had never met a woman as vulgar and profane as Kim Baxter. Even the Bourbon Street strippers and hustlers he had grown up with couldn't hold a candle to this Kentucky-born wanton. She lived for dirty jokes, Wild Turkey, and a man's hungry mouth on her privates. In the six weeks Sal had been tending bar and cooking burgers at her place, he'd been continually astounded by her candor, her lack of pretense, her simplicity. The first time he'd walked in the run-down, workingman's bar, moments after he'd stepped off the Greyhound from Chicago, Kim was behind the bar, polishing glasses. It being an early afternoon, there were only a couple of old regulars at the bar, watching the Cubs lose to the Dodgers. Sal had walked in with the handwritten BARTENDER WANTED sign that had been taped to the door.

"You think you can handle my high-class clientele?" she asked, and the old drunks snorted.

"I know how to open a beer, if that's what you mean."

She had cocked her head to one side and inspected him. "You know how to broil a burger? Deep-fry frozen potatoes?"

"I've done it before."

She had smiled at him then. "You know how to eat pussy?" she asked, and the two old farts fell over themselves laughing.

Sal had kept himself from smiling and said, "I've done that before, too."

"I'll bet you have, Good Lookin'. I'll bet you have." She had thrown a set of keys on the bar. "The pay's forty dollars a night, cash. You get one day off a week. You get all the burgers and fries you want. You get a room upstairs, you need a place to sleep and don't mind the liquor crates. You also get me, at least once."

"What happens after that once?"

"After that it depends. If you're any good with that pretty mouth of yours, I might become a permanent perk of the job."

Sal had thought a moment. "Sounds like *I'm* the perk."

She had smiled at him then and walked down the length of the bar to the beer spigots. "I like a man with confidence, Good Lookin'. Lemme buy you a tall cold one."

Sal wanted a beer now. He glanced over at Kim. She was sleeping soundly, curled into a fetal knot, her leering Pink

Panthered rump stuck up in the air. Sal reached over her and snapped off the dim bedside light. She stirred, passed gas again, then settled back to sleep. Sal got up and padded, naked and barefoot, across the dark bedroom to the window. He stood back from the window and stared down at the street. He was careful now. He'd been careless the first few weeks after he'd left New Orleans, and had made a lot of mistakes. Oh, nothing had happened, no one had come for him. But Sal had developed a sixth sense, and had nurtured it into a thriving paranoia. The last five months a little alarm had gone off in his head three times. Three times he'd been overwhelmed by a portent of danger, a compulsion to run, to just *get the fuck outta here!* And all three times Sal had dropped what he was doing, gone to wherever he was sleeping, packed his one suitcase, and got the hell out. Then and there.

Sal stared down at the deserted street. There was a full moon, and it was almost like twilight out there. At the end of the next block he could make out the ball-bearing plant that provided most of the Tall Cold One's customers. The North was full of factories that made things the Japanese felt were too unprofitable to bother with.

The Tall Cold One was on the corner, directly across. There was a simple neon sculpture of a long, slender beer glass, with a droplet of foam drifting over the edge, and the name shimmering in blue gas: TALL COLD ONE. Next to the tavern was a printing shop, next to the printing shop a cleaner, then a plumbing-supply warehouse, a religious bookstore, a second-hand thrift shop, and on and on to the end of the block. A simple, scruffy working-class neighborhood in the Rust-belt Midwest. A perfect place to hide.

Sal let his eyes drift up to the row of second-story windows directly above the barroom. That was the small storeroom with bath where he lived. He had pushed the cardboard liquor crates against the wall, stacked them up, covered the top ones with bar towels, and used them as furniture. He had a lumpy cot, a black-and-white television, a ghetto blaster, a stack of Louis L'Amours, and a naked light bulb that hung down from the ceiling.

Sal stared at the windows of his room for a moment. He thought he had left the light on. If you didn't leave the light on, you broke your neck going up the rickety old stairs. Or going down, and Sal was sure he had left the light on after he'd gone upstairs to get a case of Smirnoff's. He could swear to it. Sal stared at the windows, and then a car came down Grand Avenue, its radio blaring. It was the latest hit by that pretty-boy Englishman with the great black-sounding voice. Kim played it on the bar's jukebox all the time, and Sal still couldn't get enough of it. *Man, that motherfucker could sing.*

Sal left the window and made his way in the darkness through the narrow doorway and into the kitchen. He found a cold Old Style longneck by the refrigerator's light, a long Marlboro butt in an ashtray, and sat at the rickety table, smoking and drinking, sweating in the apartment's heat.

That fucking limey could sing all right, but Sal wasn't intimidated by him. If he had that perfect production, the pick of all the best songs in the fucking world, all the A-list musicians, Sal had no doubt he could sound just as good. Or a whole lot better.

Sal took a swig of the frigid beer and leaned back in his chair. Singing was what he missed most about his old life. Actually it was the only thing he missed. *That's not true,* he thought. He missed starched ruffled shirts and freshly pressed tuxedos. He missed the tension of an audience's attention focused on him, and the warm release when they applauded. He missed the brush of a microphone screen against his lips, and the sleeping magic of a piano keyboard beneath his fingers. But mostly he missed the validating, caressing sound of his own voice coming back at him through the monitors.

Sal brought the bottle up to his lips again, and smelled a sharp odor on his fingers. Onions, from making hamburgers for the factory-worker customers of the Tall Cold One. Sal got up and went to the sink, lathered his hands with soap, rinsed them, then washed them again. Then he scrubbed Kim Baxter's juice from his face. Beside the sink hung a thick, clean towel. Sal dried his face with it, and then draped it around his neck.

Sitting at the table in the dark, Sal picked up his beer and glanced up at the glow-in-the-dark clock above the stove: 3:57. Almost dawn. Time to go back to his rathole and get some sleep. He could sleep here, in Kim's bed, but despite the Wild Turkey she was an early riser, and Sal slept till noon. Besides, the pig always woke up in an ugly mood. He tilted his chair back and swallowed some more beer.

He missed singing a lot. More than he'd've ever dreamed he would. And that's how, two weeks ago, he'd come to make his first mistake in a long time. Oh, he'd made a bunch of mistakes the first few months after he'd fled New Orleans in that driving rainstorm, but two weeks ago had been the first in a very long time. It had been one of those nights, a Saturday, that just happen, dictated by the pull of the moon, or the urges of urban man, or *something,* but it had been one of those nights when the place was packed by eight o'clock, and everyone who walked into the Tall Cold One was just fucking crazy. Assholes who usually tossed nickels around like manhole covers were buying the bar a round. Old biddies on Social Security were flashing twenties like play money. Drinks on the bar were lined up three, four, five shots deep. At one instance Sal counted eleven shots of Seagram's Seven resting in the bar's gutter, waiting for his attention, and nobody at the Tall Cold One ever popped for the bartender. By ten o'clock everyone in the bar, Kim and Sal included, was slurringly drunk. But happy drunk. Inconceivably, there wasn't a single fight the whole night. Around eleven Teddy, a big mill hand in a plaid shirt, announced to the bar that tonight was the anniversary of the birth of his beloved wife, a woman who sported a mustache and thighs like Christmas hams. Teddy strongly suggested that the house sing "Happy Birthday" to her, and was about to lead everyone in song when Sal, loaded beyond caution or caring, like a virgin on Quaaludes, shouted the house down, stumbled from behind the bar, and weaved his way across the floor to the ancient little upright in the corner, smothered under stacks of telephone books and cartons of cocktail napkins. He drunkenly pushed the debris aside until he could raise the dusty lid, then stared down at the yellowed, cigarette-burned ivories. He traced his fingers over the keyboard, and they came away dusty. Someone shoved a chair against the back of his legs, and he plopped down drunkenly. Someone else put a shot glass in his hand, and he threw back his head and poured the whiskey down his throat. Then he suspended his hands over the keys and smiled stupidly. When his fingers touched the piano, he formed a D7 chord, arpeggioed it up the inversions, then started singing and playing the "Happy Birthday" song. The crowd behind him immediately joined in, and by the time the bar had croaked out, "Happy Birthday, dear Margaret"—the little woman's monicker—there wasn't an unsmiling face in the place. Everyone applauded. Teddy gave his elephantine wife a great hug, then Sal struck a few melancholy chords. The bar instantly quieted, and Sal began singing.

"She may be weary, women do get weary, wearing the same shabby dress. So when she's weary, try a little tenderness."

When Sal reached the bridge, there wasn't a dry eye in the whole drunken place, and when he sang "but a word that's soft and gentle—makes it easier to bear," Margaret and Teddy, enwrapped in each other's arms, began to sob. Sal finished the song with a heartrending, Delta-bred, *"Just try—eh—a, a littil—a, ten—dah—nehhhhhsssss."* There was a moment of stunned silence, then the place erupted in shouts and applause, and Sal was fairly carried back to the bar, where fifty people tried to buy him a drink. Kim, leaning on the cash register, her eyes sparkling, purred, "Why didn't you tell me you could do that, lover? I got wet just listening to you." And Sal thought, *Great, now I'm gonna hafta* sing *to her pussy, too.*

The rest of the night was a total blur. Later he was told that he had been carried upstairs and poured into his cot. Then, two days later, one of the guys who came in once or twice a week, a dark little *paesano,* leaned his elbows on the bar and said, "Say, you were really great on the piano the other night. Whadju say your name was?"

"Sal Mullins." His mother's mother had been named Mullins.

"That's a weird one."

"What can I tell you?" Sal said, volunteering nothing.

"Where you from?"

"Everywhere. I moved around a lot."

"Yeah, but where mostly?"

Sal didn't like this. "San Francisco, mostly."

The guy studied him. "You got an accent. I can't place it, but I heard it before."

Sal shrugged and walked away down the bar. He spent ten minutes polishing tumblers, refilling glasses, making cigarette change, and every time he looked up, the *paesano*'s eyes were on him. Finally he came back to his end of the bar.

"With a voice like that, whatcha doin' in this dump?" the guy wanted to know.

Sal stared hard at him. "What're you, writing a book?"

The guy held up his hands. "Hey, I'm just interested, that's all. My brother-in-law's a business agent with the Musicians' Union Local. He could find you some work playing and singing."

No unions. Little Johnny was well connected with the unions.

"My brother-in-law could—"

"Don't do me no favors, buddy, okay? I *like* it here."

"Hey, all right. Sorry. Here, lemme buy you one." The *paesan'* pushed a fiver across the wet bar.

"Nah, lemme buy *you* one," Sal said, and poured a shot into the guy's glass. Then he set another shot glass on the bar and filled it for himself. He held it up and the guy clinked his drink against it.

"A tua salute."

"A tua salute."

Then Sal went to the other end of the bar and pretended to watch the tennis match on ESPN. He looked back and caught the guy studying him. The guy looked quickly away. A few minutes later Sal looked again, and he was gone.

Sal hadn't played the piano or sung a song since, even though someone asked him just about every night. It even occurred to Sal that he was making himself conspicuous just by *refusing* to sing. But what the hell should he do? Put an ad in the paper? Hang a sign outside? PIANO PLAYER IN EXILE? COME SHOOT THE SINGER? ENTERTAINMENT KILLED NIGHTLY? Sal made a point of not getting so drunk again. And he kept an eye out for the little *paesan'*, but the nosy bastard never showed again.

Sal opened the refrigerator. There were a dozen beers, a bottle of vodka, and something in a Styrofoam container that looked very old. In the freezer compartment were a half-gallon of ice cream, three trays of ice cubes, and a large box of amyl-nitrate poppers. The cold kept them strong. Sal uncapped another beer, then opened a cabinet drawer, stuck in his hand, and withdrew a plastic-sealed Slim Jim from the collection Kim always kept there. He slit the wrapping with a knife, then sat, still naked, at the table, and washed the chewy stuff down with the beer.

* * *

That had been the mistake two weeks ago. In the six months before that he must have made dozens, it seemed now.

He had driven all night, that first night, in a headlong flight from the terror he had felt in New Orleans. By early Monday afternoon, the sky the color of gunmetal, he had reached the Memphis suburbs. He bought some clothes—jeans, Nikes, a padded jacket—in a K mart, some gauze to bandage his leg, then drove across the street to a used-car dealership. The owner was a good ol' boy with Elvis Presley hair and a jiggling gut, and his first offer was two thousand.

Sal protested. "That's a sixty-thousand-dollar car!"

The dealer chewed his cigar. "Not without no pink slip, it ain't. Without no pink slip that there's nothing but a bunch of spare parts." He looked at Sal. "I'll give you twenty-five hundred, cash."

Sal thought about it. The good ol' boy propped his elbows on his desk and leaned forward. "Son, you better take what I'm offering you. Every used-car dealer in Memphis ain't as—oh—liberal-minded as I am. You go around here shopping that car, you'll be getting a free ride back to Loosiana before the sun sets on your ass."

Sal took the money, a cab to Memphis International, then a plane to St. Louis. It was the first time he'd ever flown. He stayed in St. Louis for three weeks, holed up in a Hyatt House near the airport. Checking in, he stupidly wrote his own name on the registration card, and was too nervous to ask for a new one. He paid for a week in advance, then never left the room. He had all his meals sent up from room service, then had the boy bring him cartons of cigarettes and whiskey from a nearby liquor store. He lay in bed all day, not watching the TV he never turned off, chain-smoking, seriously drinking, and tried to figure out what the fuck he was going to do with what was left of his life. When the maids came to make up the beds, he would stand in the hall just a few feet from the door, as if he were ready to jump back in at any moment. After three weeks he had spent just over two thousand dollars, and he realized he couldn't afford to stay in this room for the rest of his life. In the middle of the night, the last day of his third week in St. Louis, Sal left the Hyatt, avoiding the deskman, walked out to the highway, and started trudging. He walked for three hours beside an empty state road before he was able to flag down a bus. He rode the bus for twelve hours, at each town buying a ticket to the next, until he found himself in a cold, clear Bloomington, Indiana. It was a small college town with a picturesque downtown about four blocks square. Sal ventured out from the bus station and strolled around the main street, peering into the little post-hippie candle boutiques and food shops. The town was the most unlike New Orleans that Sal could imagine. He had already landed a gig bartending in a sawdust-floored student hangout before he decided to stay. He gave his employer his correct name and Social Security number, knowing all the while he shouldn't.

While hiding in that St. Louis Hyatt House, Sal hadn't come to any definite decision about what to do with his life, but he had had some thoughts on how to survive.

He needed a new identity, he realized that. A new name, history, life. That would cost money, but he would find it. The bigger problem was whom to approach for his new life. Even this far from New Orleans, the people who handled this kind of thing were the very people who would know that Johnny Venezia was looking for someone who would be trying to buy a new identity.

Sal understood that the Mafia wasn't the omniscient underground monolith that the government tried to make it out to be. Organized crime was very disorganized. The myth of monthly corporate-style summits was a fantasy fed by the dramatic necessities of Hollywood screenwriters. The Mafia wasn't a democracy or a nation, but a far-flung scattering of xenophobic city-states. A feudal system administered by brutal, semiliterate warlords and their underlings. It wasn't the ultimate impersonal American conglomerate; it was instead a loose confederation of independent entrepreneurs. Mom-and-pop free enterprise gone berserk.

But the system maintained an informal network of communications. Contacts were nurtured, just like in any field of endeavor. It was a people-oriented business. Someone knew someone who knew someone who had the name of someone else. A thief in Miami could get the number of a fence in Seattle. If a trustworthy someone in Detroit needed a potential witness neutralized, he could make a call to New York and have some specialized talent imported. People knew people who knew other people. Good people. That's the way the game worked, and Sal understood the game. He also knew that sooner or later, unless he became someone else, the net would catch him. And then he would be gutted and scaled.

They wouldn't be in a big hurry to find him, Sal understood that. He wasn't very important in the scheme of things; that hadn't changed just because he had done something noticeable. He wasn't dangerous. He wasn't going to kill someone. He couldn't put people in the penitentiary with his testimony. But he had stolen *money*, and that was what the whole thing was about. Not that much money, to be sure, not seven figures. But more than could be overlooked. Much more than that. More than enough to be killed for. He had betrayed the system. He had robbed the powers that be. He had shown dishonorable disregard for Little Johnny Venezia's stature, and that couldn't be tolerated. He couldn't be allowed to get away with stealing $180,000 of Venezia money. *A piano player!* That would set a dangerous precedent, send a message to very serious men who were always on the lookout for just such a weakness. Sal D'Amore would have to be found and made an example of, and the gory details carried back to New Orleans, to add to the Venezia legend.

Sal also understood that there weren't people scouring the country actively searching for him. That wasn't how the game worked. But in the course of normal intercity business calls, his name would be mentioned. Associates in commerce would be asked to keep their eyes open for a dark, Italian-looking piano player/singer, newly arrived, who seemed to have something to hide. And these people, in turn, would make additional phone calls, all informal, all lethal, until the search for Sal D'Amore was an organic, ongoing process, like water seeping slowly downhill to the Mississippi. Never the priority, but never forgotten.

Once they had located him, *then* they would send someone for him. Sal wondered how many they would send. Or would it just be Nicky Venezia?

They would, of course, seek him where they knew he eventually had to show up. He wasn't a brain surgeon, for Chrissakes. Or an insurance salesman, or a schoolteacher, or a jet pilot. He was a fucking piano player, and sooner or later he would have to walk into a bar or a nightclub or a hotel lounge and ask for a gig on the 88s. But since Sal knew that would be tantamount to committing suicide, that was the one thing he was determined not to do.

So when they hadn't found him after a few months, they would realize he was working at some other kind of job, but they would also figure that a guy who'd spent his whole life working in liquor mills wouldn't be straying far from that pattern. They knew he could tend a little bar, so they would be looking for him to do that. There was nothing Sal could do about that. He had to make a living. He had to survive until he could formulate some definitive long-range plans. They would also be looking for him to fry-cook, to janitor, to pass out circulars—anything that didn't require any training. There were far too many of those kinds of low-skill jobs for them to find him, but they would still try.

And they wouldn't be surprised to find Sal living off an older woman.

Sal decided to stick with small towns and stay away from the cities. A place like Chicago or Detroit, crawling with Sicilians and Jews, would be a deathtrap for him. He needed places that were too rural to fit into the organization's profiteering plans, yet not so tiny that Sal would stick out. Bloomington, a small town with a fluid collegiate population, was perfect.

During the two months he stayed in Bloomington Sal saw snow for the first time—a late March flurry—saved a thousand dollars, and fucked all five waitresses who worked in the bar. Then one Happy Hour, as he was making a piña colada for an eager little freshman with damp panties, he felt a shadow cross his soul and shivered as if someone had run a sharp icicle down his back. He turned and stared at the bar's door, and knew that someone from the Venezia family was in Bloomington. He left the blender and the coed humming, walked from behind the bar, across the worn wood floor, and out the back door. He jogged the six blocks to the rooming house where he lived with seventeen undergraduates, threw his few belongings into a canvas bag, and retrieved the thousand dollars from under his mattress. Ten minutes later he was pacing at an on-ramp to

Highway 37, his finger held out. An hour after that he was in the Indianapolis International Airport, standing in a ticket-counter line. He studied the big travel posters plastered all over the terminal. SAN FRANCISCO THIS SUMMER. BOSTON, B-EAUTIFUL. MIAMI IS BEACHIN'. He had a thousand dollars. He could buy a ticket for anywhere he wanted to go. Anywhere that didn't require a passport. Hawaii. Puerto Rico. American Samoa. British Columbia. He fidgeted and smoked and watched the airport entrances, and when he finally got to the ticket counter, he bought an economy class ticket to Omaha. He just couldn't bring himself to leave the Central Time Zone. It was as if he felt that if he didn't run to the ends of the earth, then maybe this situation was only temporary, that somehow a solution could be found and he could someday go home again. He knew this wasn't true, that this wouldn't happen—he understood he would never see Bourbon Street, Jackson Square, or Joe the Hack again. But by not running too far away, he felt that somehow he was leaving one last door open in his mind.

He flew to Omaha, then took a bus to Lincoln, the capital, fifty miles southwest. He rented a room with a small kitchen in a rundown motel managed by an ancient retired couple, Mr. and Mrs. Anderson. Everyone in Omaha had names like that—Johnson, Smith, Miles, Hill. Nobody but black people in New Orleans had those kinds of WASP names. He wondered if his mother's Okie kin were the same kind of heartland prairie-dwellers.

Sal got a job turning racks of ribs in a roadhouse barbecue joint owned by Big Sid, a huge ebony man with a permanent scowl. The pay was shit, but Sal watched Big Sid closely, and in a few weeks was working right beside him in the kitchen, stirring, tasting, seasoning. Sal needed to master a new trade, and besides, if an Italian from New Orleans couldn't learn how to cook, who the fuck could?

He worked at Big Sid's for seven weeks, until he woke up one night in a cold sweat, one of Big Sid's dark-skinned waitresses lightly snoring beside him. He gulped for his breath, blinked in the darkness, and strained to hear something. A car's headlights washed momentarily across the motel room's windows, and Sal decided it was time to move on down the road. He packed in the dark—it didn't take long, there wasn't much—

then slipped out of the room, the waitress still sleeping. He avoided the main thoroughfares and walked across town using treelined residential streets until, just after dawn, he hitched a ride in the cab of an independent trucker's sixteen-wheeler. The trucker, complaining nonstop about the niggers and the Democrats, carried him all the way to Osceola, south of Des Moines, where he took Amtrak to Chicago, then caught RTA, a local line, north to Waukegan.

Waukegan, where he was now.

Sal swallowed the last of the Slim Jim and drained the bottle of beer. He belched and rubbed the back of his neck, under the towel, where it still throbbed from giving Kim head for almost two hours. He needed a cigarette. He crept soundlessly into the bedroom, tapped a cigarette from Kim's pack of Marlboros, and lit it with her disposable lighter. She sighed and turned over, pulling the sheet around her tattooed rump. He stood back from the window and smoked, staring down at the street. The sky was graying in the east, where Lake Michigan was supposed to be. He hadn't seen the lake yet, even though it was less than a mile away. He stood naked in the dark apartment and watched the dawn's gray glow creep over the street. It was time to go home. He didn't want to wake up next to Kim's ugly mood.

He carried his clothes into the kitchen and stepped into his jeans. Then he slipped on his thick-soled black bartender's shoes and, carrying his shirt in the crook of his arm, tiptoed out the front door and gently set the lock after him. He went down the wide wooden stairway, through the glass double doors, and out into the street.

He stood in the middle of the street and looked both ways. There wasn't a soul stirring. The air was summer-sweet and balmy. The locals had been complaining about the humidity, and Sal found it humorous. These Yankees didn't know what humid was.

Sal crossed the street and dug the Tall Cold One's keys out of his pants. He tossed his cigarette into the gutter and unlocked the door. Inside the bar, he had thirty seconds to disarm the alarm, and he did it smoothly, mechanically, by the phantom glow of the bar's illuminated beer signs. He went behind the bar and retrieved his pack of smokes from beside the cash register, where he had forgotten them earlier, then he opened the beer cooler and lifted out two cans of Bud. He opened one and took a deep draught, wiping his hand on the cloth towel still around his neck. Then he went through the battered swinging door that led back to the restrooms and the stairway up to his storeroom boudoir. He started up the steep, narrow, uneven stairs and immediately whacked his knee against the wall. "Fuck!" he cursed aloud in the pitch-darkness, and damned himself again for not leaving his bedroom light on. He stomped up the rest of the stairway and stumbled through the worn cast-off curtain that hung across his bedroom's doorway. The room was warm and airless, and the coming dawn turned everything a dark opaque gray. Sal set the beers and the cigarettes on the top case of a stack of whiskey cartons, and then he was overwhelmed with a deep icy feeling of dread and fear, and he knew it was time to leave Waukegan. Then something flashed before his eyes and slipped over the towel around his throat, and in his ear Dago Red La Rocca whispered in that nail-file rasp, "You shouddn't of fucked with Little Johnny's money!" And then there was sharp, biting pain as the piano wire cut through the towel's rough fabric and into the soft flesh of his neck. Dago Red twisted the garrote, a thin E-string with its ends driven through a pair of wooden handles from an old outboard-motor lanyard, and pulled Sal's body back against his protuberant belly. He tightened the noose and the wire squeezed the towel and burrowed into Sal's throat, rending the skin, and a thin noose of blood began to ooze around the wire and soak the towel's cloth. Sal thrashed and flailed and clawed at the garrote.

"Don't fight it, pussy!" Red hissed, and Sal could feel Red's rising erection pressing through the back of his jeans. "Just let it happen."

"No!" Sal tried to say, but it came out a garbled croak. "Uhhhh!"

Dago Red twisted the handles, drawing up the piano wire, and through the searing throat pain Sal felt his lungs reaching for oxygen that wasn't there. He felt himself begin to suffocate.

"Uhhhhh!" he screamed, tearing at his throat. *"Uhhhhh!"* He flailed out his legs and began to struggle about desperately.

He kicked over a wall of liquor cases, and bottles went crashing to the floor.

"Here it is, Pretty Boy," Red almost cooed into his ear, and jerked Sal's body back against his, like a violent lover. "Take it!" Sal reached back and grabbed at Red's face, his white hair, and Red twisted the garrote even tighter. Sal felt his heart pounding in his chest and his lungs heaving for air, and he raised his legs, braced his feet against a metal beer keg, and drove back with all his panicked strength. Dago Red was caught off balance and toppled over a fallen liquor carton onto his back, yanking Sal down with him. The pain in Sal's throat was like a burning flame, blood soaked the towel, streamed down his neck and chest, and he screamed out in terror and agony and denial, "Uhhhhh! Uhhhhhhhhh!" *No!*

"Mother*fucker!*" Dago Red shouted as he fought to keep his hold on his contract. Sal kicked and thrashed and clutched about with both hands, fighting for his life, but the old assassin grunted and twisted the wire ever more tightly.

"You gonna *die,* motherfucker!" Red rasped at Sal between gulps at his own breath. Sal was lying on top of the older man now, kicking and thrashing. Dago Red was beneath and behind him, breathing heavily, his mouth almost kissing Sal's ear. He hung on to his prey with murderous resolve, at every opportunity twisting the lanyard handles and shutting out the air.

Sal was gagging now, a dry, hideous death rattle, like the clicking of bones, deep in his chest. His mouth hung open, gulping for life. He screamed constantly, but no sound came out anymore. Then his vision darkened and shrank, like a television tube hit with a momentary power failure.

I'm going to die! his mind screamed, and the panic gave him a desperate surge of strength. He pinwheeled his arms, and his legs began to jerk violently. A fish flopping on a pier. He kicked the little TV set, sending it flying. *He's killing me!* His fingers tore at the bloody flesh of his throat, at the sopping red towel, trying to dig out the killing wire. *I'm gonna die!* He clutched out in all directions, a drowning man looking for straws, and his hand struck the dumpy foldout cot. He fastened his fingers around a cold metal leg and pulled himself toward it. He maniacally dragged himself and Dago Red toward the cot, the two of them bumping across the dirty wood floor. Stabbing, constricting pain flamed in his chest. His heart fluttered and his lungs heaved. Sal's hand reached up and gripped the cot's mattress, and his vision flickered again and then completely darkened.

I'm dying! I'm dying! I'm—

He was suddenly awash in a great wave of sadness, a warm floodtide of deep, ineffable grief. He heard himself sobbing, recognized his own tears in a deluge of other wails. He hadn't cried like that when his mother died. Then he heard his mother's rebuke. "You wanted this cat, now you take care of it." It was his mother's voice when he was a child, a mundane piece of the past reeling back at him from over the years. Then the blackness that surrounded him was filled with a cacophonous rush of music and voices. The sounds swirled around him like a studio tape stopped and started, stopped and started, warping the voices. He heard five-year-old Terri Saint Angelo whisper excitedly in his ear, "Be my Valentine!" Then Sister Hildegard was coaching him with her cold seriousness, "And I detest all of my sins," and he heard a child's voice echo, "And I detest all of my sins"—"Because of thy just punishment"—and his answer, "because of thy just punishment." And there was the slap of a basketball on asphalt, and little boys chanted, "In the land of France where the women do a dance, and the dance they do is enough to kill a Jew, and the Jew they kill—" And then a woman's choked scream shattered the darkness, and there was a *slap* and Sal heard himself give out his first wail and a black nurse's thick, "There's anudder one!" and the shroud of sadness that encased him seemed to deepen to oceanic depths and he felt the grief flow up out of his testicles, his penis, his very being, like warm, rising semen and it exploded in an ejaculation of grief and regret and Sal was swimming in a soup-thick multicolored current of sadness and remorse and he fought his way to the surface of the sorrow and, gulping for air, for life, screamed, "*Noooooooo!*" and then he felt himself whoosh through his blood and back into his body. His vision brightened like a light behind leaded glass, and then he found himself kneeling in a pool of his own blood on the floor of the dusty little room above the Tall Cold One. He gagged and choked and tore at the piano wire embedded in the flesh of his throat and then he got a bloody fingertip through the gore-soaked towel under the wire and ripped it out of the skin of his neck. He tore off the towel and the blood spiderwebbed down from the deep open gash that slashed across his throat and circled around the back of his neck. Sal slumped over on the bloody floor, closed his eyes, and gasped for his breath, his chest heaving like a panting dog's. The air rushed into his lungs like a sweet mountain stream, and he lay on his back and let the oxygen sweep through his veins, into his heart and his brain. *He was going to live!* His throat throbbed with a searing, raw pain, he was covered with his own blood, but he was going to live. For a while, anyway.

Where was Red?

Sal pushed himself to his elbow and opened his eyes. The dull dawn bled through the windows. Dago Red La Rocca was lying on his side on the floor a few feet away. He was staring at Sal. Fear fluttered in Sal's chest, and then he saw that there was something wrong with Red. The older man's pasty complexion was even grayer; his left arm was pinned close to his body. He stared at Sal with flat, unseeing eyes, then he clutched out with his free right hand and laboriously tried to pull himself across the floor. He had inched himself about a foot when he stopped, stared at Sal again, made a pained sound, and clutched at his chest with his good hand. His body seemed to knot itself into a tortured fetal position. He drew his knees up to his chest, his arms crossed like pincers, and his face became a ghoulish death mask, his lips curled back from his wolfish teeth, his eyes bugged and horrible. Sal knew now that he was alive because his assassin had had a heart attack. Dago Red was dying right before his eyes.

A chilling moan, like cold wind through dead trees, slipped out from between La Rocca's misshapen lips as the old murderer exhaled and gave up his soul to hell. His body immediately relaxed, and his knees thumped softly on the wood floor. Dead meat. Vomit rose in Sal's battered throat, and the pain was like a blowtorch. Sal puked up blood and beer and Slim Jims, and then retched painfully over the mess. When he could stop heaving, he hung, weaving, over the fetid pool and sucked air noisily into his lungs. Then he started to cry.

It was a full half hour before Sal could pull himself shakily to his feet and stagger into the tiny bathroom. He sat on the toilet seat, threw a washcloth into the stained washbasin, and soaked it with cold water. Then he wrapped the washcloth around his throat and let the chilly water run down his body. It felt as if he had swallowed a flame. He flinched when he saw his reflection in the cracked mirror, then he carefully unwrapped the wash rag.

There was a deep bleeding gash across his throat and complete around the back of his neck. It looked as if someone had sliced him with a knife. He gently touched the edges of the red gash with his fingertips, and winced. He sat on the toilet seat, watching the sunrise bleed through the curtainless windows, and tried to comprehend what had happened to him.

They found me, Sal thought. *They found me. They sent Dago Red to kill me. And that's what he did. He killed me. I felt myself die. I know that's what it was. I died. Dago Red choked me to death. But I'm here, alive, sitting on this shit-stained commode, and Dago Red is in there. Dead. And it's because of the towel. I don't hang the fucking towel around my neck, I'm in there dead. Fucking dead, the way the Dago is now. If I don't hang the towel around my neck, if Dago don't have a heart attack. If, if, if.*

It was too much to assimilate. Sal knew he would spend the rest of his life trying to understand what had happened in this dusty liquor storeroom.

It took him only a couple of minutes to throw his few belongings into a suitcase. He was on his way down the stairs and considering stealing the three-hundred-dollar bank out of the bar's cash register, when the idea of going through Dago Red's pockets struck him and stopped him cold. He went back upstairs and approached the body slowly. Maybe the old bastard wasn't really dead. The only dead people Sal had ever seen were laid out in coffins at Lamano, Pano, Fallo Funeral Home. He didn't know how a fresh corpse was supposed to look.

Dago Red La Rocca was hunched facedown on the dusty floor. His limbs were twisted under him. He looked uncomfortable. Sal gently inserted a foot under an armpit, then rolled him over and stepped back.

Dago Red didn't look good. Though his face now looked peaceful and reposed, his sickly white skin had turned a dirty gray. His eyelids were half-raised, but no eyes were visible. His muscles had relaxed, and he had urinated on himself. Sal knelt beside him—expecting any moment that the old assassin would reach out and grab him—and placed his fingertips on the old man's wrist. Even before he felt the absence of a pulse, Sal knew Dago Red was gone. The flesh, though still supple and warm, was lifeless, unfeeling. Dead meat.

Sal released the wrist and quickly went through La Rocca's pockets. In his left rear pocket was a stained, cracked calfskin wallet. There was no money in the bill compartment, even though Sal turned it inside out. In the plastic foldout were seven credit cards—all in names other than Dago Red's—a photograph of a teenage girl in a Catholic school uniform, the back inscribed *To Uncle Red, Love, Denise,* and a tarnished Saint Cristopher medal. In Dago Red's front left pocket was a wad of bills encircled by rubber bands. Sal counted out $1,723, in fives, tens, twenties, and six hundreds. Sal wrapped the money in the rubber bands and shoved it into his pocket. He hesitated, anxious to leave, and then decided to do a thorough job. Pushing the body over on its side, he found that all Dago Red's right rear pocket contained was a short, greasy comb with a few strands of fine silver hair. The right-hand pocket was damp with dead man's piss, and Sal didn't dawdle as he fished out three sets of keys. One was obviously Dago Red's house keys. Another was a set of GM ignition and trunk keys, with a little plastic car-rental fob from O'Hare. The last key was to room 206, the Skyport Motel in Chicago.

Sal turned to inspect the storeroom just before he pulled aside the curtain to leave. The place was trashed. Broken liquor bottles in cardboard crates oozed gin and vodka. The walls were splattered with Sal's blood, and there was a corpse in the middle of the floor.

Kim wasn't going to appreciate this.

Outside the sun was already hot and bright. The neighborhood children were playing on the stoops. Sal found the Beretta with the Rent-a-Car bumper sticker parked three blocks away from the Tall Cold One. For no reason he could pinpoint, he opened the trunk. It was empty.

The ride to Chicago took about an hour, but then Sal got lost several times looping around the airport, searching for the Skyport Motel. He finally found it on a side street just off the

Kennedy Expressway. It was a nondescript, no-frills, three-story affair with two long wings off a small office. The doors to the rooms opened to the outside. Traffic hummed by on the Expressway.

Sal backed into a parking place and stared up at room 206. During the ride down from Waukegan it had occurred to him that Dago Red might not have come up alone. Not that Sal's murder should have *required* two men, but sometimes guys brought other guys with them. For lookouts, or even simply for company. On something as simple and pleasurable as Sal's strangulation, Dago Red might've planned some afterwork networking with the local talent here in Chi. Maybe even a little vacation following. *Shit, he might've brought a fucking broad with him.*

Sal watched the door to room 206 for over an hour. He sat in the hot car, blood leaking from the makeshift bandages swaddled around his throat, and watched the distracted salesmen with their blow-dried hair and their worn, bulging briefcases leave their economical, adjacent-to-the-airport motel accommodations, get into their gas-efficient rented sedans, and drive off to their working-lunch appointments, and Sal wanted to jump out of his car, grab them, and say, *I died this morning, but I'm still alive. I died this morning, but I'm still alive, and the red in your tie is so bright it makes my eyes water, and the backbeat on the song you're playing on your car radio is the funkiest thing I've ever heard, and it makes me want to dance with you right here in the parking lot. I died this morning, and I heard my mother's voice for the first time in fifteen years, and it was just like she was standing beside me, and I am so fucking scared my hands won't stop shaking. I died this morning, and there's no one for me to tell, no one, no one—*

And Sal sat in the stifling car and cried and bled and sweat all through the morning and into the early afternoon.

At twelve-thirty, housekeeping, which was two very large black women, began to clean the rooms on the second level. Sal watched as they did 201, 202, 203, talking and laughing, then for no reason Sal could discern, the taller one of the two walked all the way over to 206, unlocked it, and went in. A few minutes later she came back out for her rags and sponges. Seven minutes after that the housekeeper reappeared with an armful of soiled linen, tossed it into a pile on the concrete veranda, then took a stack of fresh sheets and towels back into the room. Ten minutes later she came through the door and locked it, then pushed her cart down to the next room. The other housekeeper was now cleaning 205. Sal waited until the taller woman unlocked and entered 207, then he got out of the Beretta, walked quickly across the hot parking lot and up the long flight of stairs. He strode purposefully along the walkway, trying to look detached and preoccupied. When he passed 205, he couldn't keep himself from glancing in, and he saw the shorter maid shaking a pillow into a pillowcase as she watched a soap opera on the room's TV. He passed without her noticing him. He slipped the key into 206's lock, turned the knob, walked in, and closed the door behind him.

The room was clean and coldly air-conditioned. There was a single queen-sized bed. The closet door was ajar, and hanging inside was a lightweight sportcoat and a two-suiter canvas carry-on. There was a small leather suitcase on the aluminum stand and a pair of tan Hush-Puppies-type shoes beside the bed. Sal knew immediately that Dago Red had checked into this room alone, but he still didn't know what he was doing here.

Sal checked the bathroom first. On the counter by the washbasin was an ancient men's leather shaving kit with a rusted zipper. The kit contained deodorant, a heavy double-edge razor, a nail clipper, an old-style shaving brush, and a round bar of soap. Beside the kit was a single toothbrush and a tube of paste.

Sal went through the canvas hang-up in the closet. There were two pairs of pants still in their wrappings from a New Orleans dry cleaner. In the bottom of the hang-up was another pair of shoes.

The little leather suitcase was locked. Sal remembered seeing a tiny silver key on the key ring he had left on Dago Red's corpse. He stared at the suitcase a moment, then carried it into the bathroom and laid it on the toilet seat. Using Dago Red's nail file, he dug at the lock for ten minutes before the mechanism finally sprang.

On top were a few dark double-knit shirts of the type that Dago Red always wore. Sal set them carefully on the edge of the shower. Then there were a pair of pastel-colored dress shirts and a jumble of ties. Beneath the ties was a squashed-flat shopping bag. Sal picked it up, and it contained something wide and solid. Sal opened the bag and withdrew a slick magazine. On the cover was a teenage boy sprawled back against a black satin pillow, stroking a raging hard-on. Sal stared at the magazine in uncomprehension. He flicked through the glossy pages. Men sucked other men, fucked other men, jacked off other men, all while other men watched. This was a facet of Dago Red La Rocca Sal didn't think the Venezias were aware of. Sal felt something else in the paper bag. He dug it out. It was a long white tube with an electrical cord trailing from one end. There was a brand name on the side of the tube. *The Rectifier—your connection to auto-anal ecstasy.* This was definitely something Dago Red hadn't gone around bragging to his Sicilian drinking buddies about. La Rocca had taken one too many trips to Angola.

Sal put the Rectifier back into the bag, then he turned to the basin and washed his hands with very hot water.

Under the paper bag was a swatch of folded blanket. He lifted the blanket and stared down at a lethal-looking blue-black automatic pistol. He picked up the weapon and was surprised at its weight. On the slide along the top of the barrel was the name *Walther,* surrounded by fine scroll. *Why didn't Dago Red bring this when he came to kill me?* Sal asked himself. *Because he didn't think he'd need it.* He carefully laid the automatic on the back of the toilet and turned back to the suitcase. There was a bulging sealed envelope in the bottom of the suitcase. Sal picked it up and held it up to the overhead light fixture. Then he ripped it open, and dozens of hundred-dollar bills spilled over his hands and scattered across the tile floor.

And Sal knew that he'd found what he hadn't known he'd been looking for.

WINDSOR, ONTARIO—JULY

The black man in the Italian-cut suit carefully laid out three blue Canadian passports on the coffee table. Then, on top of each, he methodically placed, like dealing cards, a Social Insurance Card, an Ontario Province medical card, a small cardboard birth certificate, and an Ontario driver's license. The palms of his hands were pink, and he wore a diamond-cluster pinkie on his left hand. When he'd finished, he turned to Sal.

"Got anything to drink?"

Sal nodded to the minirefrigerator under the tiny wet-bar counter. The black man in the Italian-cut suit moved languidly across the hotel room and opened the minifridge. He did everything very slowly, as if he were extremely aware of himself. When he'd mixed his drink, he stood framed in the big picture window that overlooked the Detroit River and the industrial sprawl of Motown on the other side.

"Go 'head, man. Examine the product."

Sal leafed through the first pile of documents. On the Ontario driver's license was the name Andrew McIntyre. He opened the passport and saw his picture staring back. Andrew McIntyre. Born 1952, in Halifax, Nova Scotia.

"The best, man," the black man said, taking a sip of his gin. "My people are the best. I do good work."

Sal opened the second passport. The same picture, only this time he was Marco Toledano, Toronto, 1949. He looked at the address on the driver's license.

"What's this address, 451 Elm Street, Hamilton, Ontario?" His voice was still a shock whenever he heard it, and his fingers reflexively went to his neck, where the still-painful scar was hidden beneath a six-week growth of dark, thick beard. Dago Red had ruined his voice, had died and bequeathed him his tortured rasp, only worse. Sal would never have to worry about singing again.

"It's a flophouse hotel in downtown Hamilton. You ever get asked, you tell 'em you passed through, looking for work, and got a license. Everything's covered. I told you, I do good work."

There was no reason to examine the last stack of papers, but Sal was curious about the name. It was Julio Puglia. Toronto, 1954.

"I figured I oughtta go with Italian names, you being dark and all."

Sal didn't like the way the black man had said it. It felt like a probe, and he looked up sharply.

"'Course, you can always lighten up." He gave Sal a cold smile. "*You* got that option open to you. Then there's the other identity."

Sal fingered the passport and then set it down.

"How much was it?" It sounded like fingernails on a blackboard. *I know you're burning in hell, Red, and I hope you never get out.*

The black man shrugged. "Half of six is three. Three thousand is the balance."

Sal stuck his hand into his left pocket, where the wad of hundreds was. In his right was the Walther. He counted out thirty hundred-dollar bills, and left them on the coffee table beside the documents. Then he stepped back and looked at the black man.

The black man, who was hard and muscular beneath his tailored jacket, glided over to the coffee table and scooped up the money.

"I got me a plastic surgeon," he said as he counted, "motherfucker ougtta be in Hollywood, motherfucker's so good. If you need that, too."

Sal shook his head. "If I'd wanted that, I'd done it before I got these." He nodded at the documents.

The black man finished counting the C-notes and slipped them inside his jacket. "You know, I never had a client order three of these at one time before." He looked at Sal. "Just kinda aroused my curiosity."

Sal stared hard at the black man in the Italian suit and made himself think of the Walther weighing down the right side of his pants. He pictured himself pulling the automatic from his pocket, striding across the hotel room, and shooting the black man at a point just above and between his eyes. To his profound surprise, it was not an unpleasant thought.

"You know what they say about curiosity," Sal rasped.

A slow grin spread widely across the black man's face. "Yeah, killed a *lot*ta cats." He moved toward the door. "Like I said, I do good work." He opened the door and looked back at Sal. "Good luck, man. I hope whoever it is don't catch you." Then he went out and closed the door behind him.

Sal threw his new luggage on the bed and began packing.

BOOK IV

OCTOBER—THE *ANTONEA*, THE NORTH ATLANTIC

She was a ten-year-old, 174-meters-long, 14,000-ton passenger-carrying freighter, two days out of Antwerp, bound for Rio de Janeiro, Pôrto Alegre, Montevideo, and Buenos Aires. She held Bahamian registry and carried a mostly Chilean crew, though her captain and officers were Canadian and many of her stewards were West Indian. Her almost totally containerized cargo consisted of French wine for Uruguay, German machinery parts for Brazil, and Italian fabrics being shipped to Argentina. Like all freighters, she couldn't really be called beautiful, but her lines of modern design were spare and functional. Except for her aft, where the four floors of passenger cabins and crew's quarters were stacked up like a fat woman's bustle. There were twenty-four two-room suites, all first class, with beds for forty-eight luxury passengers. The fares on her rooms were very dear, and her departure dates were only approximated estimates, but the *Antonea*'s wealthy and mostly retired passengers weren't concerned with cost or calendars. They appreciated the freighter's unhurried schedule and unregimented activities; they had no particular place to go, and a lot of time and money with which to get there. The type of people who booked passage on freighters weren't the usual kind of frenzied party animals on the "seven-days-in-the-Caribbean-then-fly-home" Love Boat cruise ships. The *Antonea* didn't serve buffets around the clock, or drinks on every deck, or have a disco with throbbing lights or a floor show with young, peppy entertainers. For amusement the *Antonea*'s passengers walked the foredeck at sunset, or read thick paperback novels, or sat in lounge chairs and gazed out to sea as they mentally composed their last wills and testaments. They wanted mostly to be left alone, and the crew of the *Antonea* did that very well. The ship didn't have shuffleboard, or skeet shooting, or deck tennis, or a swimming pool, or dance lessons and aerobic classes. What the *Antonea* had was a passable chef, a large passengers' lounge with a decent paperback library, a captain who genuinely liked meeting people.

And the *Antonea* had a piano player.

Maggie Behan Pulaskey watched her husband's rigid hard-on rise and fall, rise and fall, with his every sputtering snore.

What could *the old goat be dreaming of?* she thought as she watched him. He was stark naked, lying on his back in the middle of the freshly made bed, and his turgid penis jutted out from the gray pubic hairs that grew in the cave between his slack thighs and his bulbous, overhanging belly.

Up and down, up and down, with every thunderous breath. *Is he dreaming of fucking? Is he dreaming of fucking* me?

Maggie Behan Pulaskey put down the latest Jackie Collins on the small writing desk and reached for her Shermans.

What is he thinking of? Who? And do I care?

She lit her little brown cigarette and blew out a lungful of smoke.

He must be dreaming of sex, but sex with who? With a crowd? With little girls? Little boys?

Look at him, she thought. *He never sleeps like that at night—flat on his back like that. Only when he takes his afternoon nap. My God, listen to that racket, listen to that man snore. It sounds like a fucking lawn mower! The dagos in the next cabin will complain!*

"Milt! You're snoring!" she said sharply. "Roll over!"

Milt Pulaskey snorted in his sleep, opened his eyes for a moment, then closed them and immediately began snoring again, although not nearly as loudly as before. It would take him five or ten minutes to get back up to his top volume again.

Maggie Behan Pulaskey rose from the small writing desk and walked over to the bed. She took another drag on her

Sherman and looked down at her husband's bobbing cock, and the only thought she had was, *Milt, when the hell are you going to die?*

Look at him, she told herself. *He's seventy-one years old. He's had two heart attacks, open-heart surgery, he's got high blood pressure, and his cholesterol level is fucking* lethal, *and he's got the dick of a teenager.* She shook her head. *When he's asleep.*

When she had married Milt Pulaskey eight years ago, she'd had no idea what a prenuptial agreement was; she only knew that a sixty-three-year-old man fresh out of heart-bypass surgery who refused to even *cut down* on his three-pack-a-day habit, who never ate fish when he could have ketchup-slathered beef, who thought being fellatioed was a cardiovascular workout—this is a man who can't live for long, right? *Wrong.*

He looked younger every year, while she—well, let's not get into that. She had been thirty-nine when Milt Pulaskey, of Pulaskey Bathroom Fixtures, sat in her station in Jerry's Place on Woodside Avenue out in Queens and ordered an eggs and salami scrambled, bagel with cream cheese. A good-looking, well-preserved thirty-nine, to be sure, but still, thirty-nine is not twenty-nine, you know what I mean. Thirty-nine is the threshold of old age. Thirty-nine is the door through which lie wrinkles and laugh lines, age spots and liver splotches, face-lifts and tummy tucks. My God, but she'd been in a panic back *then,* at thirty-nine, and now she was forty-seven. *Forty-seven!* She hadn't known how good she'd had it.

She gazed down at Milt's naked, snoring body, and was amazed again that a *man* could be so hairy. His tubby olive-skinned body was covered with swirling whorls and thick patches of curly silver hair. *Polacks are supposed to be fair and hairless, for Chrissakes! Dagos were dark and hairy like this. Greeks. Not fucking Polacks.* Looking down at him, she was swept by a weak wave of nausea, and turned away from her sleeping husband. She took another drag on her cigarette, to settle her stomach, but again she felt herself want to vomit. Maybe it was seasickness.

A cruise! Milt had promised her. *We fly to Europe, drive around for a month or so, then take a* cruise *to South America. A cruise!* It was a fucking *freighter,* for Chrissakes. A glorified barge. You can't brag to the salesgirls in the mall that you sailed from

Europe to Rio in a fucking *tugboat!* Sometimes Milt could be as cheap as a fucking Jew, for Chrissakes. She made herself look at him again. His dick was standing straight up. A little soldier at the ready. *Milt, you gonna live fucking forever, for Chrissakes?* she asked his cock.

Quietly, so as not to wake him, she unpacked her soft, supple Gemelli de Janeiro leather jewelry roll and laid it open on the writing desk. Her lacquer-nailed fingertips traced over the glittering diamonds—colored stones seemed so *niggery* to Maggie—and she selected a pair of one-and-a-half-carat earrings, a simple gold necklace with a flawless one-carat bluestone pendant, and picked out for her right hand a dazzling cocktail ring, a veritable fountain of eighth- and quarter-carat diamonds cascading down an almost free-form beaten-gold setting, combining for an aggregate two-and-a-half carats. On her left hand, as always, was the wide gold wedding band studded with small, perfect stones, and snuggled next to it was her centerpiece, the rock that never failed to snap other women's heads around. The stunning three-and-a-half-carat engagement ring. That diamond never left her hand, except when she cleaned it. Maggie Behan Pulaskey felt naked without her *baby,* as she called her big ring. It gave her confidence. It made her feel special. It quieted her.

Other women, planning an assignation, might dress for seduction. Maggie *bejeweled.*

Milt sputtered and groaned in his sleep, then turned over on his stomach, burying his hard-on into the mattress.

Jesus, that must be painful! Maggie thought, then stuck the earring posts through her earlobes. She hung the necklace around her throat, then slipped the cocktail ring on the middle finger of her right hand. She examined herself in the mirror over the dresser. She twinkled like a star. Maggie Turnbull might've been born to trashy Irish in the bad part of Brooklyn, but right now, today, this minute, she had a quarter-million in jewels decorating her flesh. She leaned into her reflection and inspected that flesh more closely. *Yeah, well, no doubt about it. She was forty-seven.* She didn't even try to camouflage it, bury it under layers of makeup. That wasn't Maggie's style. She didn't try to trick her lovers, entice them. She bulldozed them. She intimidated them. She overpowered them with Milt's wealth.

Almost unerringly she could pick out the hungry, the ambitious, the aspiring, and she paraded Milt's money before them like a rock collection pinned to her person. And they came to her as children to a department-store Santa, eager and full of expectations.

Maggie took her full-length black sable from the cabin's tiny closet and laid it over the back of a chair. She had hoped that after a month of traveling around Europe, she could look forward to young, supple bodies around a cruise ship's indoor pool. She had hoped that after a month of Milt's trying to remember how to use a standard shift—*why couldn't he just hire a driver like every other fucking rich American in the world?* After a month of putting up with rude French waiters and humorless German innkeepers—all of whom, she was sure, spoke to each other in English the minute you left the room. After a month of smelling damp wool and Milt's flatulence in that coffin of a Peugeot while Milt got them lost on back roads even local yokels didn't know about—*what was he trying to prove?* After a month of driving during the worst autumn weather Western Europe had seen since the War. After all that, Milt had led her to this—this—floating railcar. No disco. No movie theater. No dance instructors. No young lifeguards. And she had had such high hopes. Milt had never taken her on a cruise before, but she had heard really *delicious* things about the young staff on those cruise ships. *It's was part of what you pay for,* a friend had told her. *You're gonna love it.*

The first night on *this goddamn garbage scow* Maggie had stayed in the cabin. She had been too sick, too depressed, too disappointed, to face the ancient fellow passengers she had seen tottering up the gangplank. Why, one little old guinea limping around the deck had a *humpback,* for godsake. Bumping around the deck with one arm around the meanest old dago *mamma mia* you ever want to see, and the other around a confidence-shaking, shatteringly beautiful little teenager. Probably his damn chippie. *Fucking boat was a circus!*

The second night out Milt had coaxed Maggie out of their stateroom by promising her a bribe of a new diamond bauble when they docked at their first South American port. It was their group's night at the captain's table, and Milt was a sucker for that kind of shit. She wore the new black low-cut she had bought in Milan, and when he walked her across the dinky little dining room she could feel Milt *glow* with pride. *Earning her stones,* she always thought of it when he paraded her around like that. Well, it wasn't saying much, but she *was* the best-looking woman on the boat. Excluding the little wop bitch, of course.

As she settled down to dinner, Maggie's worst fears were realized. First of all, the old humpback guinea, or spic, or whatever the hell he was—she never could figure it out—he and his party were in their group at the captain's table. *Lucky me,* Maggie thought. The first time she looked up, the old crone was dunking her bread in a glass of milk. Maggie didn't need this on a queasy stomach. Then she noticed the diamond rings on the old lady's gnarled fingers and hated her even more. True, the gems just made the old lady look like a rich corpse ready for burying; still, Maggie didn't like competition of any sort. And the way the waiters sucked up to the little humpback, *dear God!* Like he was some kind of very big shot, running to light his smelly old cigar, always filling his wineglass, and all the while they practically ignored her and Milt. And Milt a millionaire three times over! *Oh, well, their attitude will be reflected in their gratuity.* And then that little chippie! *Who in their right mind wants to sit at the same table with a young girl who looks like that?*

It got worse. Also at their table was an old German couple who refused to talk to anyone but each other, two spinster sisters from Ireland, and an ancient, foul-smelling Argentine who kept falling asleep in his pasta. *It was an old folks' home, for Chrissakes!* And then the captain got drunk and talked to her tits all night, couldn't bring his eyes up to save his soul, which usually amused Maggie no end, but last night just contributed to the tawdriness of the whole affair. The drunk captain kept leaning over Milt, who was trying to carry on a conversation with the *dwarf, for Chrissakes!* The dwarf's little chippie was staring intently at something behind Maggie, and the captain kept leaning over and *grinning* at Maggie's boobs, as if her eyes were in her nipples or something.

And then the captain asked Maggie's breasts how they liked the music.

"The music?" Maggie asked the captain's forehead.

"My piano player," he explained to her boobs. "He's great,

eh?" Someone *was* playing something very nice.

"He's wonderful," the little spic chippie breathed from across the table, and Maggie flashed angry eyes at her. *Children are to be seen and not heard, especially chilren who look like you!* Maggie didn't particularly want the captain's attention, but then she didn't want it diverted, either.

The captain swilled some more wine and belched lightly. "None of that hard-rock noise on my ship," he said as he smacked his lips. He was short, neat, compact, with a florid alcoholic's face, and he was definitely a tit man. "I can't stand that punk-rock crap. Don't like a thing aboot it. There's nothing like a good piano man playin' the old standards in the background to put the topper on a good meal, eh? That's why I hired that one." He pushed back from the table and got to his feet. Leering at Maggie's chest, he said, "If you'll allow me." Then he walked across the dining room to the corner where the piano was. *What is this clown up to now?* Maggie turned in her chair to watch him, and her gaze riveted like a gunsight onto the piano player. *Yummy yummy yummy. Would you look at that?* All through the meal Maggie's eyes had been darting around the dining room, looking for likely talent, but she had found no one who sparked her interest. She wasn't about to sleep with anybody older than she, so that definitely excluded her fellow passengers; the ship's officers were all fat, stolid Canadians—she didn't need another Milt in her bed; the waiters were all West Indian, and she had never slept with a nigger and wasn't about to start now. But this piano player. This was good stuff. *Look at him. Long dark hair, sexy beard, black bedroom eyes. The girls at the mall will have their hair curled when I tell them about this one.*

"Ladies and gentleman, guests and crew," the captain said in a practiced cadence. He was thundering into a microphone on a mike stand set up by the little spinet. "Are we having fun yet?"

The passengers answered as vigorously as fifty people with a median age of seventy-one can applaud.

"How about a round of applause for our orchestra, eh? Let's hear it for Marco! Marco Toledano!"

Marco, Maggie whispered to herself. *I like that. Marco.*

She heard Marco the piano player go into a quiet soft-rock

vamp as the captain said, "A little something that wasn't on the brochure. Marco and I hope you like it, eh?" Then he looked across the room to Maggie's tits and started to sing, "*Bluuuuuu—Spaneeessshhhhh—IIIIIIIs—*"

She shut out the captain's lame serenade and bored in on the piano man. *This barge ride might be interesting after all.*

That had been last night. Now, Maggie Behan Pulaskey examined herself in her stateroom mirror and fantasized about fucking Marco the piano player. She dreamed that Marco was below her, on a bed with black silk sheets, and Maggie was riding his cock with sweaty abandon. In her fantasies she was twenty-five again, and her very young flesh was naked except for her sparkling diamonds.

Sal stood as far forward as he could get, pressed against the ship's railing, and watched the bow cut through the cold, heavy sea. The day was so overcast that in all directions the horizons were lost in low gray mist. If Sal hadn't known it was early afternoon, he would have had no idea where the sun was. He tried to light a cigarette—*never have to worry about singing again*—but the sharp wind kept blowing out the match. He flipped the fag over the side and pulled the collar of his down jacket close around his throat. His thumb accidentally touched the hard ridge of scar tissue that ringed his neck under his heavy beard, and he shivered, as he always did. *But there is always something there to remind me,* he thought. The old Dionne Warwick hit. Sal's life had reduced itself to song lyrics in his mind. Rock and roll rhymes and Brill Building clichés. An oil tanker emerged out of the fog two or three miles away and passed along the milky horizon like a child's electric toy. Captain McLeish, in the tower, blew a greeting, and the tanker answered, its horn like a forlorn bleat across the cold gray seas. *Two ships that pass in the night—Stop it!* Sal berated himself. *You hate Barry Manilow.*

Snatches of song lyrics and pieces of melodies had been filling his brain for months now. Ever since he had survived his encounter with Dago Red and gone running across the eastern half of Canada. It'd been years since music filled his head like this, and in the past it had always announced the beginning of a hot period of good songwriting. Sal had lost his interest in writing when he got heavily into gambling, but now he was alive again—*alive again!*—with song scraps, little fragments of memory from a lifetime of playing and loving music. He would stare into a glass of whiskey and hear Sinatra commiserating, "*That's Life, that's what all the people say, riding high in April*—" At night he lay in his cramped dark cabin, listened to the hum of the freighter's 20,000-horsepower engine, and heard Stevie Wonder sing, "*My Cherie Amour*"—He played Sammy Cahn and Jule Styne's "The Things We Did Last Summer" during the daily five o'clock cocktail party, and while he did, in his ear Aretha sang "*Rock Steady, Baby*"—just to him. This had happened to him many times in the past. It would go on that way for a while, and then suddenly it wouldn't be other people's music going around in his mind but his own. He would sing a snatch of song he hadn't known he knew, a tune he'd never heard before, and he'd realize it was *his* song, a new one he was writing almost unconsciously, as if it were a natural process, like walking or breathing.

Sal watched the oil tanker glide away into the gray horizon, then turned back to the bow and the water rushing past along both sides of the big vessel, and he heard Luther Vandross sing "*A chair is still a chair, even if there's no one sitting there*"—and he told himself, *Ballads. You're gonna be writing ballads.*

He'd been filled with music like this ever since he'd driven away from the Skyport Motel in Dago Red's rented Beretta. Filled with music and a burgeoning sense of purpose that sprouted in his breast and each day grew larger and more demanding. As he'd got on Interstate 294 heading east toward Detroit and the Canadian border, driving away from Dago Red's room 206, the blood from his wound seeping through the damp rags wrapped around his throat, the ten thousand of the Dago's dollars in a paper bag under the car seat, he'd caught himself humming U2's "And I Still Haven't Found What I'm Looking For," and he wondered if he was going insane.

It hadn't been insanity, he knew now, but his mind's reaction to his death and rebirth. He had died, Dago Red had strangled him with a piece of piano wire, and then he had been resurrected, and now he was as filled with music as a Motown songbook, as St. Louis Basilica during Sunday mass, as Saturday night on Bourbon Street. He had died, he had been saved by

Dago Red's heart attack, by the blood-soaked terry-cloth towel, and now he was a walking fucking jukebox. *It's my defense,* Sal told himself. *It's my way to deal with what happened. I died, and now I am reborn, like fucking Jesus Christ.*

Sal had nightmares now. *Who wouldn't?* He awoke covered in cold sweat and shouting into his pillow, and then sat on the side of his narrow bed the rest of the night smoking French cigarettes and staring out into the total darkness of his cramped quarters. But it wasn't visions of Dago Red coming back from the dead to garrote him in his sleep that scared Sal awake. It wasn't even the terror of dying, although he had certainly fought hard for his life when Dago Red tried to take it from him. What caused Sal every other night to bolt upright on his sweaty mattress, his pulse pounding, his testicles shrinking up into his body cavity, was the memory of that nauseous wave of remorse that had swept over him when he had died on the floor of the liquor stockroom of the Tall Cold One in Waukegan, Illinois. He couldn't forget that overwhelming grief, that bottomless sense of loss, the sad awareness that he had wasted his life. Just pissed it away, like last night's beer. That he'd dreamed of greatness but hadn't pursued it. While other Ninth Ward guys he'd grown up with had constructed worlds of wives and children and mortgage payments, Sal had conned himself into thinking he was following a dream when all he'd been doing was killing time, chasing parleys and pussy. He'd had the talent, the desire, but he'd squandered it behind a lifetime devoted to getting high and getting laid. And that had been another cold revelation when he had knelt in a pool of his blood and puke in the stockroom over the Tall Cold One. He'd ripped the piano wire from his flesh, heard his own ragged breathing beating in his ears like a wounded animal's, and in that instant he'd known that his life was a bad joke, because if he were to die, no one would grieve for him. Oh, Joe the Hack would get drunk and sob, and Cathy and Santo would feel sad for a week or so, but no *woman* would cry because he was gone. No one who *cared.* He'd been to bed with at least a thousand women in his life, and at his death not one of them would mourn him.

Sal stared out over the cold North Atlantic, and without knowing he was doing it, sang in his gravelly whisper, "*Killing me softly with her song, with her song, with her—*"

All those women. Sal watched the sea boiling under the bow and could see them parade through his past like a perverted beauty contest. A flashing fleshy montage of bare breasts, legs pulled back to shoulders, rich dark cunts spread wide beneath him. Sal heard Luther Vandross's "Never Too Much." There were so many, so different. *Fat girls give the best head,* the guys on the street joked. *Skinny girls have the biggest orgasms; beautiful girls just lay there.* Some women whimpered when you fucked them. Some wanted you to talk dirty to them, while others liked talking to you. Some needed you to give them pain to expunge some deep-seated guilt. As they climaxed, they begged you to twist their nipples, spank their rumps, even slap their faces. Others didn't really enjoy the sex act; they fucked because that's what hip girls did, like wearing the latest clothes; they fucked Sal only because other girls wanted to fuck him.

Blondes, redheads, jealous Latinas, blacks with chocolate nipples who *challenged* you with their bodies, and soft-spoken Asians with small breasts and straight black hair. Tall girls with long, slender legs, and small girls so tight you had to grease yourself to work into them. Plain girls who laughed too quickly, and hard bodies who only wanted your tongue on their flesh. There had been young girls who had only their supple bodies to offer, and older women who knew they had to offer Sal something besides their bodies. He remembered smart cookies and dumb bunnies, cunts and cuties, bitches and chicks, sweethearts and temptresses. Alkies with ninety-proof kisses, and heads who got stoned as you labored between their legs. He had fucked them in nightclub ladies' rooms, seated astride a commode, and in the back of uncountable vehicles—*Don't come knockin' if this van is rockin'.* He had humped them in beds, balled them in chairs, screwed them slumped over sofas. He had nailed one once in a phone booth. He had fucked them while their mothers talked on the phone in the next room, while their husbands slept upstairs, while their babies cooed beside them in the bed. Hundreds and hundreds of wet, hairy vaginas, years and years of heaving sweaty breasts, decades of wondrous hands and magical mouths. Bitches, broads, chicks, babes, fish sandwiches—whatever you wanted to call them, they had come for him, literally and figuratively, all those years, and now Sal felt it had meant nothing. It had been like jerking off with an audience. It was laughable and pitiable. And profoundly depressing. He'd wasted his life behind trying to see how many women he could score. He'd squandered his only birthright—his talent—in a pathetic attempt to screw his way to success. He'd been a bigger whore than any slut in Nicky Venezia's stable. *Speak of the devil.* And just like a whore, at the end he'd been left with nothing to show for the party life but an empty heart and a scarred body.

Someone laid a hand on Sal's shoulder, and Sal flinched as he felt the fear flame up inside himself. He turned to stare into Captain McLeish's wide, friendly face.

"How are ye, Marco?" Captain McLeish's family had immigrated to the Maritimes when he was still a boy, and sometimes the remnants of a gentle Scottish burr could still be heard in his speech.

"I'm okay, Cap'n." *That tortured rasp, like Dago Red's ghost living inside him.*

McLeish rested his elbows on the guardrail and stared down at the sea being churned by the ship's bow. He smiled.

"Y'know, when I was a kid in Nova Scotia, I used to go out lobsterin', and I loved sittin' in the bow watchin' the white water, just like this. I think that's why I shipped out the first time, so I could watch the sea whenever I wanted." Because of their musical relationship, McLeish treated Sal with a kind of friendly equality.

McLeish stuck his hands into the pockets of his dapper tailored captain's overcoat and stared up at the heavy sky. "Some of the passengers are complainin' about the weather. I told 'em hell, it's the North Atlantic in October."

Sal liked Captain McLeish. He believed he understood the guy. He was a friendly, fastidious man who loved what he did—captaining a ship—and who relished the opportunity it gave him to practice his other great passions—singing before an audience and screwing women passengers. Sal had played for show-biz-struck amateurs like him before. What made McLeish interesting to Sal was that the captain was the first man of authority he had ever watched operate who wasn't a politician or a murderer.

McLeish continued to examine the grayness overhead. "Stormy weather doesn't bother me. Actually I rather enjoy it. How 'boot you, Marco?"

Sal was trying to light another cigarette in the wind. "Don't faze me, Cap'n. When I was a kid, it rained half the time."

McLeish looked at him. "Vancouver, isn't that what you said? You grew up in Vancouver?"

Sal took the unlit cigarette from his mouth. "Vancouver, Seattle, Buffalo—my old man moved around a lot."

McLeish smiled. "Ah, the gypsy life already, even as a boy." He played the role of kindly captain to the hilt. He was like something from *How Green Was My Valley.* "And what did your father do?"

Joe the Hack, Joe the Hack— "He was a salesman. Went wherever the jobs were. All over the place."

McLeish came a step closer and put his hand on Sal's shoulder, and Sal knew they were about to talk music. McLeish always manufactured this phony intimacy when he wanted to discuss his singing, as if it were the only thing that was really important to him. Maybe it was

"What did you think of the new key on "Yellow Bird?" Wasn't too high, do you think?"

Sal had heard about the gig on the *Antonea* at the Seafarers' Union in Montreal, where he was hanging around trying to get a bartender's job on a cruise ship. He wanted to be aboard anything that was leaving North America, but he didn't want to ship out as a member of a band with Musicians' Union contracts and loose-mouthed players. Even with a new name, Sal was afraid he would be instantly recognizable to other musicians as a New Orleans native, just by the way he played. So he had bribed a union representative to get a work card that made him immediately eligible for service positions, and was wondering if he could bullshit his way into a waiter's job when he heard one laughing seaman tell another that "McLeish's piano player run off with a rich widow from Edmonton." Sal bought the pair a round and found out that the single gig on a freighter cruise ship called the *Antonea* was vacant since the old drunk who'd had the job had married a lady passenger and gone off to live a life of luxury in the West. *A single gig would be perfect,* Sal thought. *Just me alone to worry about.* "The captain signs you on as a bartender or something," one of the seaman said. "You see, the shipping line don't want to pay for no piano player just so's the captain can sing to the ladies." *No Musicians' Union contract. Fucking perfect.*

When Sal came on board to audition for McLeish, the captain had dropped what he was doing—going over a bill of lading—and led him hurriedly down to the piano in the dining room. The piano was surprisingly good, and McLeish had a personalized music folder, just like a professional, which contained a rat's nest of old yellowed handwritten charts and dog-eared sheet music. The captain hadn't learned a new tune since "After the Loving," so keeping current wasn't going to be a problem. This was not a Top 40 gig.

They were only halfway through the first number—Bobby Darin's "Beyond the Sea"—when McLeish stopped singing and grinned at him.

"You're very good, Marco," he said to Sal. "This is going to be fun."

The pay was only $250 U.S. a week, a bartender's salary, but Sal quickly learned to work the passengers, find out which sentimental old standards pressed which buttons in which gray-haired couples celebrating an anniversary, and the monthlong voyage across the Atlantic to England and down the Continent had earned him an extra thousand in tips. Not enough to get rich on, but more than enough to live, since the ship provided everything but his clothes. Unlike the rest of the service crew, he had small but private quarters—a perk of the captain's accompanist—and even though the crew seemed to resent him a bit, he didn't care. He wanted to be left alone anyway. He had a lot of thinking to do.

McLeish, beside him on the windy deck, still had his hand on his shoulder. "You don't think the key was too high?" he was asking.

McLeish needed stroking, like any insecure artist. "Sounded great, Cap. Sounded fine."

McLeish beamed. Then his smile turned salacious. "Marco, my boy, did you see the ornaments on that one last night? The one in the black sheath?"

The captain loved to talk pussy with Sal and allude to being a great cocksman. Somehow he thought it was all part of the show-biz mystique.

"Couldn't miss her, Cap." Bitch had a fortune in rocks on her, and her husband looked like a total schmuck. Back in New Orleans, she was exactly the type of woman Sal would have made a beeline for.

"Wouldn't you just love to bury your face between those mountains, eh?" McLeish rolled his eyes. Sal didn't think the captain talked to anyone else the way he did with his piano players. It was part of the job.

"Sounds like fun to me, Cap."

McLeish took his hand from Sal's shoulder and playfully waggled his finger in his face.

"And don't think, Marco, my boy, I didn't notice that sweet young thing oo-gling you across the room last night."

Sal was puzzled. "Which one, Cap?"

"Which one?" McLeish laughed. "Which one? Why, only the richest little princess south of the Equator!"

"Cap, I swear to God, I don't know who you mean."

The captain leaned close and leered. "The Gemelli girl. I hear she's a terror."

"Gemelli?"

McLeish shook his head in amusement. "As in Gemelli de Janeiro, Marco, my boy. That little brown tart is the old man's only child."

There *had* been a pretty little Latin chick in the dining room last night, but Sal hadn't paid her much attention. She couldn't have been more than sixteen or seventeen, but the captain had sure scoped her action. *I must be getting old,* Sal thought.

And just then, looking over the captain's shoulder to the cold gray sea, Sal heard a scrap of a half-formed melody play across the front of his brain: "*I never thought it would be this way, I never thought, something, something, la, la, la,*" and he realized with a tiny jolt of surprise that it wasn't something he'd ever heard before. It was his. He was writing again. He wanted to get to a piano.

"I tell you," McLeish chuckled, "she looked like a real hot number."

"Uh—Cap, you think I could get into the dining room now? I wanna play a little."

McLeish took a pipe from his pocket and tapped it on the ship's railing. *A pipe!* The only person in New Orleans Sal had even known to smoke a pipe was an ancient old black woman who sold cheap jewelry on the streets.

"The dining room is always empty this time in the afternoon. Just let yourself in." He squinted over the bowl as he touched the flame to the tobacco. "Marco, you think we should check that key for 'Yellow Bird'?"

Okay, enough. "The key's perfect, Cap. You sound great." *Or as good as you're ever gonna.*

McLeish glowed under Sal's praise. He had never before worked with a piano player as good as Sal, and they both knew it.

"Tonight, when I get up to sing," he said gleefully, "let's kick it off with 'Lady Is a Tramp,' what do you think, eh?"

Sal smiled back. He knew right where McLeish was coming from. "I think she'll love it, Cap."

McLeish grinned around his pipe stem. "Quite. Quite."

The dining room was dim and cool. Deserted. All of his life Sal had loved nightclubs and lounges in the daytime, when they were like this—dark, quiet, and empty. All the joints he'd played his whole fucking life, he'd never been in one he didn't feel more comfortable in when it was closed and he was alone. *Maybe I'm in the wrong business,* he thought. *I shoudda been a janitor. Give me time.*

He got an ashtray and a book of matches and sat at the piano. He smoked for a while and drank in the solitude, something in short supply on a ship. Then he dropped his hand down on the keyboard, playing a D-major seventh chord, and softly sang the snatch of a song hook that had come to him up on deck. The piano and the voice meshed perfectly, in the same key. It always worked that way, and Sal didn't even find it special anymore.

Sal put the cigarette in the ashtray and began to work on the song, playing it over and over and gently humming the snatch of melody in his whiskey rasp.

Maggie Behan Pulaskey turned up the collar of her sable coat and stepped out onto the quarterdeck. *Jesus, this weather is fucking depressing. Why didn't we just go to the Bahamas like everyone else, for Chrissakes!* She strode purposefully on the varnished boards and took pleasure in the hot stares she got from the crewmen she passed. *That* was a plus in shipping out on this floating old folks' home. She was the best-looking broad on board, hands down. *Oh, yeah. Except for that little spic bitch. Well, maybe she'll fall overboard.*

She held that pleasurable thought for a moment, until she turned a corner and there was that disgusting little hunchback with his ugly evil-eyed old crone by his side. *You'd think they would keep them below deck or something, so the rest of us wouldn't have to deal with it. It's fucking depressing.*

Maggie stepped quickly around Giovanni Gemelli and his now-cancer-thin sister, Angelina, and was proud of herself that she didn't glance at the old hag's rings. Smiling to herself, she was wondering how she was going to locate Marco the piano player—*Should I ask another crew member? Is there a shipboard directory, compiled solely for horny female passengers?*—when she looked up just in time to see that asshole Captain McLeish strolling down the deck, looking for all the world like the stuffed-up, ridiculous old fart that he was. *I don't have time for this,* she thought, and ducked into a doorway that led to a passageway down to the next deck. She was halfway down the stairs when she heard the soft piano chords. *Ah*—she smiled—*there's my baby.* She followed the sound to the hallway before the dining room's closed door and stood there a moment, listening. *I don't know that song. And is he singing in there?* She very gently turned the knob, and it was locked. She'd raised her hand to knock on the polished door when she caught a movement from the corner of her eye. Turning, she saw that little wop minx *standing on a chair, for Chrissakes!,* staring intently through a high porthole at what could only be Maggie's meat. Mag was infuriated. *This shit won't cut it,* she thought. *This has to be nipped in the bud.*

She strode over to the teenager tottering precariously on the deck chair and tapped the girl's legs. The girl jumped with a sharp intake of breath. *The little bitch almost fell on her ass,* Maggie laughed to herself. Then the girl stepped down from her perch, and Maggie was confronted at close, well-lit range with her stunning beauty. *You little cunt. You hateful little cunt.*

"Lost something?" Maggie asked with arched eyebrows. She was used to dominating women, especially younger women, with her frigid-bitch attitude, but this cheeky little kid was *angry* at being disturbed.

"What is it?" she asked sharply, with the sexiest little spic accent Maggie had ever heard. *This one is dangerous. This one must be dealt with here and now.*

"Mind how you speak to adults, child," Maggie hissed, with as much upper-class haughtiness as she could fake. "Didn't anyone ever teach you not to spy on people?"

"Didn't anyone ever tell you to mind your own business?" The girl's dark eyes flashed angrily, and Maggie thought to herself, *She's the most beautiful girl I've ever seen,* and instantly Maggie found herself wishing she had had the life this girl was going to have. She steeled herself against the little wave of sadness and snapped back at the greaser.

"Look, Carmen Miranda, run along back to your old sugar daddy before he misses you. How would he like it if he found his little cooze letching after a *musician?*"

"He is my *father!*" the girl said furiously. "And maybe your husband want to know what *you* are doing here?"

You little cunt! You impertinent little brown wench! And then an idea struck Maggie, and she smiled serenely and said, almost secretively, "Marco and I have a date for tea," as she nodded toward the sound of the piano. "So really, little girl, run back to your cabin, why don't you."

Maggie relished the crestfallen look of uncertainty that shadowed that exquisite face. Then she began to move back toward the dining room's main door. "So really, Chiquita Banana, I think it's high time you ran along."

The teenager turned and sadly walked away. She looked back just once, when Maggie waited at the door, and Maggie raised her hand to knock and said to her, "Three's a crowd, Carmen." And then, to devastate the girl further, Maggie knocked quietly and sang out, "Marco, it's me. Maggie."

The piano stopped immediately, and the young girl turned and hurried away in embarrassment. Maggie chuckled to herself. She loved asserting superiority.

Inside the dining room Sal had heard the quiet knock, and then a woman said something he couldn't make out through the door. He had just figured out how to start the second verse lyrically, and wasn't happy about being disturbed—*sometimes you could lose these things so easily*—but it was probably one of the cleaning-crew girls wanting to vacuum the place, and Sal had always had a soft spot for the maintenance people because they worked their asses off for so little. He walked quickly to the door, humming the second verse softly, unlocked the door, and walked back to the piano without looking back. The door opened behind him, momentarily flooding the room with gray light, then it was shut. He was seated behind the spinet again before he realized it was a passenger. Sal looked up at Maggie Behan Pulaskey, standing just inside the dining-room door in her full-length black sable unbuttoned to display her body and her diamonds, a smile of proprietary expectancy playing around her heavily glossed lips, and Sal felt that he knew everything there was to know about this woman. It was as if he'd met her a thousand times before, which, in a way, he had. He knew what she was going to say, in what order and manner she was going to say it; he knew, of course, what she wanted, and he knew the game they were expected to play until she got it. He even knew how she would be to fuck. She would be aggressive and dominant, and she would not be able to climax. It was not even a healthy male curiosity. He *knew,* and he sighed wearily at the knowledge.

"That was beautiful, Marco," she said with a little breathlessness that Sal knew she thought was sexy. "Play it again."

Fucking squares, Sal said to himself. *They think you're always dying to play for them. It never occurs to them that sometimes the music is just for* you.

"It's something I'm working on," Sal said, as pleasantly businesslike as possible. "It's not ready yet."

"Ooh," Maggie said as she slinked across the dining room toward him, "you *wrote* that. It's beautiful."

"I'm *writing* it. It's not finished yet."

"Oh, please, play it again."

Sal gave her a tight smile. "It's not ready."

Maggie flashed him her most promising pout. "Oh, Marco, *please.*"

She sounds just like one of Nicky Venezia's whores, he thought. *She missed her calling. Or maybe she didn't.*

Sal folded his arms across his chest and stared up at her from behind the keyboard. After a brief moment Maggie realized she was being rebuffed, and Sal saw her mind scramble a bit before she righted herself and pressed on. *This bitch is used to getting her way.*

"You know, you really are talented," she said quickly. "You're very good. Why are you hiding yourself on this shitty freighter?"

Bingo. Give the lady a stuffed animal.

"Actually I'm running from the Mafia," Sal said.

Maggie's eyes widened, and she broke out in laughter. "Right! Right! Oh, Marco—" Her smile warmed and widened, and she leaned her body over the top of the spinet, giving Sal a good look at her breast assets. "You are something, all right. And that voice—it's so *sexy!*"

"Is it?"

"What do they call that—a whiskey voice?"

A piano-wire whisper.

"I don't really know."

"Well, it's very sexy." Maggie reached over, picked up Sal's smoking cigarette, and took in a long drag. *She saw that in an old movie,* Sal thought. *She thinks she's Lauren Bacall. And who am I supposed to be—Hoagy Carmichael? Dooley Wilson?* She exhaled the smoke and gave Sal that same stupid come-hither stare. "I know your name. Don't you want to know mine?"

Not even a little bit. Not even your initials. And then he asked himself, *What's going on here? This is the kind of pig I used to* troll *for.*

"You're Mrs.—Mrs.— What *is* your husband's name?"

She was taken aback by his attitude. This wasn't working out the way she'd wanted it to.

"I'm Maggie," she pushed on bravely, extending her hand. "Pleased to meet you, Marco."

Sal let her hand hang there a moment, then reached up and took it in his. "Nice to meet you, Maggie."

She held his hand and covered it with both of hers. "These hands," she said, looking down at them, "these hands—they're magical." She raised her eyes to his. "These hands make the most beautiful music."

Gimme a fucking break, why don'tcha.

Sal gently pulled back, but she had him now, and she was caressing his flesh with her own. The diamonds on her fingers glittered like—well, like diamonds. *I just wanna finish this fucking song!*

"These hands can be so gentle," she breathed, "so sweet, so knowledgeable—"

"And where is the mister, Maggie?"

"Sleeping," she giggled, as if the two of them were already

partners in a conspiracy. "He sleeps fourteen, fifteen hours a day." She gave him a meaningful stare. "He's a lot older than me."

Yeah, I got you, bitch. He's older than you, is what you say, but what you mean is he don't fuck you enough, he don't take care of bizness, you're the world-famous frustrated American wife. And rich to boot. Gimme my hand back.

"I'm sure he needs it," Sal said, meaning her husband's sleep, but Maggie wasn't a girl to let a line like that get away.

"We all need it, Marco. Do you need it?" She was pressing his hand, digging her nails in.

Don't do this. Please don't do this.

"Maggie, I don't want—"

She reached out suddenly and brushed his longish hair away from his cheek. He wore it down the back of his neck now to hide the scar.

"We could have some fun on this boat ride, you and me. We could have a lot of fun."

"Maggie—"

"A *lot* of fun."

Sal reached up and gently pushed her hand away. "Maggie, there's something I have to tell you."

She leered evilly. "You can tell me *anything*."

Sal pulled the cover down on the keyboard and rested his elbows on it. He tented his hands before his eyes and massaged his temples with his fingertips. "Maggie, when I told you I was on this ship to hide from the Mafia?"

She chuckled. "Yeah, right."

He waited a long time. "That wasn't true."

"No kidding!" But she was disconcerted. Something was wrong.

"Maggie, I ran away to sea because—because"—he raised his eyes to hers—"because I'm dying."

She just stared at him. Finally, "Marco, I don't understand."

He swallowed hard and said, "I found out I was HIV positive."

She was confused. "HIV positive?"

He looked at her a long time, then pronounced each syllable with deadly deliberation. "Acquired Immune Deficiency Syndrome."

She pulled her hand back and straightened up. She shook her head slowly from side to side.

Sal nodded. "Yes. AIDS."

"Oh, my God," she gasped, and was already moving back, toward the door.

"So you see, Maggie"—*Don't laugh! Don't laugh!* he told himself—"even though I find you very attractive—"

She was already halfway to the door.

"—and I'm *dying* to make love to you—"

"Oh, Jesus!" she cried as she stumbled out the door and slammed it behind her.

Sal broke out into deep guffaws. It was the first good laugh he'd had in a year. And when he stopped, he could have sworn he heard someone else laughing along.

That night, after playing for the cocktail party, the dinner hour—at which Maggie's husband appeared alone—and the nightly Captain McLeish Show, Sal lay in the utter darkness of his cabin and listened to the womblike hum of the ship's engine fifty feet below. He lay in the darkness and struggled with it, tried to figure it out, make sense of it, as he did every night.

He had lived, and Dago Red had died. Dago Red had died trying to kill him, and because Dago Red had died, now he could live. It was Catholic, almost, in its beatific simplicity. He could hear Sister Hildegard teach, "*Why did He die? He died so that you may live.*"

Sal sat up on the side of the bed, felt around in the darkness, and found a cigarette and matches. He sat there, smoking.

Dago Red died and left me his voice. He lives on in me. He is resurrected *in me.* Sal smoked his Gaulois and scratched gently at the scar under his beard and thought, *Red tried to murder me, but all he killed was my voice. And then he left me his. What the fuck does it all mean?*

When he was younger, Sal had always felt he was destined for great things in the distant future, but now his destiny was as real and close as the ship's bulkhead. And, he knew now, it could be as deadly as a heart attack. Dago Red's heart attack. *Why did Red die and I live? Does it mean anything? Am I supposed to do something?*

Sal had always been a member of the largest club in the

world—nonbelieving Roman Catholics—but now he asked himself why he had been spared. Had God had a hand in it? Sal understood that Dago Red's death occurring when it did had been like drawing a card to fill an inside straight flush. Only one way to win. Once the Dago got that piano wire around his throat, even with the towel, there had been only one way Sal was going to survive, and that was if Red died himself, and that's what had happened. *The only way to win.* It was freaky. When Sal thought about it too much, he would break out in gooseflesh and shivers.

Why me? Why have I been saved? His life was a joke, a cheap comic's vulgar rap. When he had died on that storeroom floor, kneeling among the dust babies and mouse shit, the grief had been suffocating. He had choked with the knowledge of his wasted chances. His life had been as inconsequential as a fly's. He had been born a nobody, he had died a nobody, and he had done nothing in between. It would have been better if he'd never been born. Maybe he'd cheated some other poor bastard out of his chance in the world, if you looked at it in the right way.

And now, Sal felt this churning inside, this low simmering, this *yearning*. It was as if just as now he was pregnant with songs, he was also heavy with the desire to *do something* with the rest of his life. The experience of dying and then being reborn had infused him with this urgency to accomplish something—to accomplish something besides getting his willie wet and his head fucked up. He knew now that life wasn't an endless voyage. Just because he didn't know the estimated time of arrival didn't mean there wasn't one. His ship could dock at any time, in any port, without any warning. All of his life he had been an inconsequential, pathetic little man—just like his father—and now that he had met death and escaped it, he knew he didn't want to die the same way. He wanted to *matter*.

Sal slipped to his feet and snapped on the overhead light. He blinked for a moment in the glare, and then pulled his suitcase from under the bunk and laid it on the mattress. The gun—Dago Red's gun—was under the scrap of blanket, still wrapped in the square of oilcloth. Sal peeled back the cloth and stared down at the weapon. It was called, he had learned, a Walther "P-88" 9-millimeter automatic. It was manufactured in

Düsseldorf, West Germany, and held fifteen shells in the clip and one in the chamber. Sal picked it up and felt the gun's weight. It didn't feel as heavy as it had when he first found it in Dago Red's hotel room. He handled it quite a bit, now, and had got accustomed to the weight. He raised the Walther and pointed it at the cabin's closed door. *If they came in right now to get me, could I do what I had to do? Could I stop them?* Sal imagined Nicky Venezia bursting in the door, a gun in his hand and a cruel sneer on his lips. Sal pulled the trigger, and a geyser of blood spurted from Nicky's Giorgio Armani chest. Nicky stumbled forward, a look of complete shock on his face, and clutched out at Sal. Sal shot him again and again and again, and Nicky toppled over on the floor. *Dead meat.*

Yeah, right, Sal thought as he rewrapped the Walther in the oilcloth. *Piece of motherfuckin' cake. Just kill the killer. Yeah, you right. And what about* after *Nicky? And after Junior? And Rocco and Jimmy Van, and Little Johnny? There's no way you can fight them all, even if you could find the heart, the balls. It's just fucking crazy to think that way.*

But they can *die,* he reasoned. *Dago Red proved that.*

Sal shut the suitcase and shoved it back into the compartment under his bunk. The first few months after his *thing* with the Dago, Sal had slept every night with the Walther in his hand, the safety on. Dangerous as it was, it was the only way he could get some rest. And even after he'd signed on the *Antonea,* he kept the automatic under his pillow for the whole voyage across the Atlantic. Only when they'd reached port in Liverpool did Sal feel he was out of immediate danger. Actually, he'd considered, a ship is one of the safest places to be if you're on the run. The crew was constant and practically all foreign. He could check out, in an instant, any new passenger who came on board. No one could sneak up on him; there would be no more surprises in the dark; he didn't have to continually watched his back. That was the good news. On the other hand, if somehow he made a mistake, a miscalculation about a passenger or a member of the crew, if one day in the middle of an ocean his sixth sense started to scream again—well, there was no place to run on a ship. If he ever thought there was an assassin on board, well, then, he would have to deal with it. Get out the Walther and take care of business. Or get taken care of himself.

Sal put on his down jacket and stuffed his cigarettes into a pocket. He left his cabin and went down the passageway stairs to the main deck. It was deep night, and the ship seemed deserted and unmanned. A ghost ship. He zipped up his jacket and stepped out onto the main-deck passageway. The wind had died down and the skies had cleared, but the air was as icy as an open freezer. His breath floating in the dim cold, Sal walked up to the bow and leaned on the ship's railing. This sea was much calmer than this afternoon's, and in the endless night the horizons were lost in the infinite, seamless dark. There were no other ships' lights visible anywhere out there, and Sal thought, not for the first time in the last few weeks, that there was nothing more alone, more isolated, than a ship at sea. Maybe a rocket in the sky, but who the fuck—

Sal heard a sound behind him, and the skin on the back of his neck tingled with fear. He whipped around, his pulse already pounding in his ears. "Who's there?" he rasped. "Who is it?" *Take it easy,* he told himself. *Remember? No one can sneak up on you at sea. No one can—*

Just then Sal saw a figure move across the pool of light thrown through the passageway door, and he thought, *They're here! They found me, and they're on board!* Sal's back was against the railing, and he was looking around frantically for something to use as a weapon when the teenage girl from the passenger's dining room walked out onto the deck.

Jesus! Sal breathed in relief. *Jesus Fucking Christ!*

"I'm sorry," she said. "Did I startle you?"

Oh, no, nothing like that. I just have to go change my fucking pants.

"The deck's so wet," she continued. "It's so slippery." She walked precariously over to where Sal was, and grasped the railing.

Then don't walk on it. What was this kid's name? He glanced at his watch: 3:42.

"Isn't it awful late to be running around the decks?" he asked her.

"I can't sleep. I always have trouble sleeping."

Oh, yeah. Gemelli. As in Gemelli de Janeiro. Spoiled little rich kid. The same the world over.

"This time a' night, you shouldn't be up here alone."

She smiled at him then. "I'm not alone. I'm with you."

He'd noticed her staring at him both nights since they left Antwerp. She'd be hard to miss—a teenager among all the grayheads—even if she weren't so beautiful. Standing beside him now, she was just about the same height as he was. The long brown hair that had flowed down her back at dinner last night was tied up and stuffed under a Parisian slouch cap. She wore a long black overcoat with the collar turned up against the cold. Her beauty was as natural as an athlete's grace, as luminous as great talent, and Sal figured her for sixteen or seventeen years old.

Sal turned away from her then, and rested his elbows on the railing. The ship was only ten years old, but already her paint was peeling everywhere. Tramp freighter. Sal fished out a Gaulois from his pocket and put it between his lips.

"May I have one?" the girl asked. Her English was nearly perfect, but there was a blurred, indeterminate accent. Sal took the pale blue pack from his pocket, shook a cigarette halfway out, and offered it to her. She took it from him.

"Do you like playing piano on this ship?" she asked as he lit his cigarette.

Sal pointedly didn't answer her for a long time, to let her know she was intruding where she wasn't wanted. When he had finished lighting his own smoke, he tossed the dead match overboard. She had expected him to light her smoke, and when he didn't, she took a small gold lighter from her overcoat pocket and lit it herself.

"It's okay," Sal eventually replied.

"I hate ships," she said quickly. "I hate this freighter even more."

He looked at her. *Spoiled brat.* "Then why are you on it?"

"It's my father. He won't fly."

Sal shrugged. "A lot of people like that."

She nodded. "Oh, he'll fly *sometimes.* He flew to Paris to find me and bring me home. He and my aunt Angelina."

Sal knew she was baiting him, stringing him along, but he decided to bite anyway.

"He flew to Paris to *find* you? Were you lost?"

She grinned at that. "*Porquinho.* I run away from school with a French boy." She looked at him to see if he was shocked. *Not that easy, baby.*

When he didn't say anything, she hurried on, "I was in

school in Switzerland. Convent school. And this boy came through the village on a Honda. He had a guitar on his back, and I like his jeans, so—*poof!* I jump on behind him and we leave! They can't find me for three weeks."

I think I'm supposed to be impressed. "How did they find you?"

"Well, my father call Interpol!" she said joyfully. "Can you believe that? They tracked down the French boy"—she pronounced it *track-ked*—"but by then I already ditched him." *Ditch-ched.* "He can't really play the guitar. He was a fake! I meet an older man, an African diplomat. He rented an apartment for me. I was his mistress."

Sal gave her a faint smile. *Man, would Nicky Venezia like to talk to you!*

"I don't guess your father was too pleased with that."

"He was very upset, but my aunt—*mamma mia!*—she wanted to kill me." Her exquisite woman-child face turned cold and hard as she stared at the sea. "I hate my *tia* Angelina."

Sal didn't know what to say. It was obvious the girl was trying to tempt him, but he didn't want any part of it. So he gave her a patronizing, "Parents can get very worried—"

"It's not the first time I've run away. I'm what we call in Brazil a *problemática,* a trouble child. I'm always getting in trouble."

In spite of himself, Sal found the kid interesting. "Why?"

She shrugged. "Tia Angelina says I got bad blood from my mother. My mother was very famous in Rio," she said proudly, "and my aunt hated her. She hates me, too, but I hate her more. She's dying of cancer, Tia Angelina, and I'm glad." Her eyes burned in the cold. "She says I'm killing her."

"So that's not your mother at your table with your father and you?"

She shook her head. "My mother dies when I am born. The people of Rocinha say she lives on in me."

"And your father never remarried?" *A cripple with a whole lotta money.*

She smiled mysteriously and stared out to sea. "It was the love of a lifetime. A very sad and beautiful story." And then, "My father is very sweet man. He doesn't know what to do with me." She turned back to Sal and asked brightly, "You are American?"

"Canadian."

"I went to school in famous finishing school in America. Sacred Heart in New York. I got in trouble there, too, but that's why my English is so good." She stared at him as if for confirmation.

"Your English is very good."

"And I listen all my life to American records. Jazz and rhythm and blues. You know the Billie Holliday song 'Lover Man'?"

"Davis, Sherman, and Ramirez."

"What?"

"'Lover Man' was written by those three guys."

She seemed a bit taken aback. "Oh, yes, but it was recorded by Miss Billie Holliday. That is my favorite song in the whole world." She threw a sexy little smile at him. "When I hear it, I love the way it makes me feel."

Time to take this tune home, Sal thought. *I don't need any more trouble than I already got.*

He cannoned his cigarette butt out over the ocean and stuck his hands into his thermal pockets.

"Good night, Miss Gemelli," he said as formally as possible. "Be careful on the slippery deck." Then he turned from her disappointed face and walked away, down the passageway stairs.

The next morning Sal woke up with his new song playing itself in his head. He lay on his cot, staring up at the ship's metalwork, and played the tune over and over in his mind. By the time he was dressed and on his way down to the crew's pantry to get some lunch, he'd rewritten the song three or four times. He'd decided the hook wasn't strong enough but would make a great first verse. An idea for the chorus, the hook, kept hovering on the edges of his mind, but he kept it there, waiting, while he worked at the verse. The verses he'd composed yesterday he discarded, saving only one lyric image he was particularly proud of. When the new first verse was fairly solid in his head, he allowed the anxious hook idea to rush in, and he liked it a lot. *I can't get my fill.* It was going to be a medium-tempo soul ballad, à la Anita Baker, but funkier, more rhythmic. *I can't get my fill—my fill of your love.* Humming the tune lightly, he sat in the crew's dining room over a soggy bowl of cornflakes and wrote down what lyrics he had in a small spiral notebook.

A notebook much like the one he'd kept track of his gambling winnings in back in New Orleans. A long time ago. A *lifetime* ago.

When he'd finished, he stared down at the rhyming lines with less than euphoria. As a songwriter, Sal knew instinctively what rock critics never seem to comprehend: Song lyrics are not poetry—they are *song lyrics.* They only live when given breath by music. They are meant to be sung, not read. These words before him were worthless unless he managed to wed them with the perfect melody, support them with the ideal chords. He had an idea what it would sound like, but sometimes the piano held surprises.

He left the limp cornflakes untouched, too preoccupied to eat, and walked slowly down to the passengers' dining room on the main deck, his face buried in the spiral notebook. The dining room was empty, not yet vacuumed, and Sal went right to the piano and work. As he wrote, he wished he had a drum machine, so he could program in the song's *feel* and write over it. But then he also wished he had a KORG-M1 synthesizer, with a sequencer and drum machine built in, a Tascam 8-track ministudio cassette recorder, a Lexicon LXP1 spatial-effects generator for his voice, and a whole lot of other electronic instruments. *Wish in one hand, shit in the udder,* his aunt Rosalie used to tell him, *see which one gets full first.* Then she would go make a novena, Aunt Rosalie. Well, he didn't have those things. All he had was himself and this half-assed, out-of-tune spinet. The rest of the enhancers he'd have to hear in his head, which he knew he was able to do. A good song will shine through. A good song will rise above the existing musical limitations. A good song is a good song, and Sal felt that burning inner excitement he always felt when he knew he was riding a good one. *The good ones, Soul, dey write themselves,* an old black guitar player had told him once, and though it wasn't always true, it was more often than not.

After an hour and a half Sal had two complete verses and what he thought was the best hook he'd ever written. He gave his ears a rest, walked around the empty dining room, smoked a cigarette, then went back to the piano. Between his legs he placed Captain McLeish's mike stand, and then reached over and clicked on the ship's shitty old 100-watt Shure VocalMaster.

Motherfucker was a relic, an antique, but Sal needed to hear his song come back at him through the speakers, with a little echo and reverb. *With this croak I need all the help I can get,* he thought. He snuggled his lips against the mike's dented windscreen—*God, how I miss singing*—heard his gentle breathing in the rattling old speakers. He tapped his heel on the floor, setting the tempo, then closed his eyes and imagined that he could hear the bass and the bass drum lay down a simple, unobtrusive pattern. Then the guitar came in, light and rhythmic, there was a high string-patch synth line, the drummer played a perfect tom fill, and Sal was at the top of the first verse. He played the first chord and started singing. His heart dropped as he heard his damaged rasp grate at his melody like a rake dragged over polished wood—*Dago, may you rot in hell for all eternity*—but he plodded through, and by the second time through the chorus he began to hear how the song *should* sound, *would* sound—just as he imagined the other instruments—if it were being sung by someone with a good voice. When he finished vamping on the chorus—he'd write a bridge later—he went back to the top and started the song over again. He sang through the first verse and was coming into the chorus, giving it all he had, when someone in the darkened dining room began to tentatively sing a harmony a third above him. He was startled, but too much of a songwriter to stop the process when it was going so well. He ran down the second verse, finding a place where he could add a nice soulful lick, then cruised into the hook again. The singer was there again, a shy girlish soprano, but even just backing him up like this, unamplified, barely audible across the room, Sal could hear something unique, something special, about her voice. Something brand new, yet very familiar. He repeated the hook over and over again, and by the third time his backup singer had her part down cold. Nailed. The fourth time through the hook she threw in a patented Chaka Khan fill that made Sal's musician heart leap with delight at its very soulfulness. *Yeah! Go 'head!* He smiled to himself. But there was something odd about the voice in the darkness. Something—something disturbing. He stopped singing, ritarded a few bars, then struck a major seventh on the flatted sixth, bringing everything to a screeching halt, and ended it all with a soft, gentle tonic that hung wistfully in the dining room's cold air.

Sal held the damper pedal down with his foot, sustaining the chord, while he raised his hands and reached for a cigarette. He lit it slowly, methodically, then exhaled and stared out into the darkness at the far end of the dining room.

"Okay, Unknown Backup Singer. C'mon down."

There was a moment of stillness, then a gentle rustle as a chair was pushed back, the sound of a few footsteps, and a moment later the Gemelli girl emerged from the darkness and stepped into the soft glow of the spotlight shining down over the small open area before the piano. She seemed afraid.

"I'm sorry. I disturbed you." *Disturb-bed.*

Sal laid the cigarette in the ashtray, trying to look stern. "Well, it does seem like you're always sneaking up on me from the dark. I have a definite aversion to that, it's true."

"I'm sorry," she said. "I didn't mean to bother you." She turned to go.

"Wait a minute. Wait a minute." Sal motioned her back. "Where'd you learn to sing harmony like that?"

She shrugged, but there was the smallest of glows in her eyes. "I sing in the choir when I was a little girl, and I always try to sing along with the records. All my life I always try to sing along with the records."

"But you never sang with a band? Onstage?"

"No," she said slowly. "Maybe a little with the French boy, but only in the bedroom, after we make love."

Sal took another drag on his cigarette. Somewhere on the ship some crewmen were arguing in West Indian patois. She watched him closely.

"Did you write that song?" she asked. "You write it, didn't you?"

"I'm *writing* it. Big difference."

"It's very beautiful."

Sal couldn't help feeling proud. "Thank you very much."

"When will you finish it?"

"You never know about songs. Sometimes they're done in an hour, and sometimes they take years."

"I think it's very beautiful," she repeated. She moved closer and leaned on the top of the spinet, as Maggie Pulaskey had done yesterday.

Sal stared at her a moment. "Listen. Have you ever sung

with a piano player? Just you and a piano?"

She shook her head with gentle vehemence. "I couldn't do that."

"Why not?"

She shook her head again. "I couldn't do that. Besides, I'm not good enough." It struck Sal how she spoke with such honesty and straightforwardness.

"Listen, the whole damn ship will thank you if they could hear somebody besides Captain McLeish sing a coupla songs." He chuckled, but she seemed concerned, timid. "Look," he reassured, "you never know how you look until you get your picture took, right?"

She eyed him uncomprehendingly. "*Como?*"

"Just a Noo Awlins expression."

"Ah, New Orleans," she seemed to remember, "Louie Armstrong. Sidney Bechet. Wynton Marsalis."

"Oh, you're up on your New Orleans jazzers, huh?" he teased her.

She moved around the upright until she was standing beside him, sitting on the piano bench. She shook a cigarette from his pack and picked up a book of matches. She looked at him. "Are you from New Orleans?" She pronounced it New Or*leeens,* the way everyone in the world but natives did.

Sal shook his head. "Nah, I was born in Toronto, but I moved around a lot. Like I told you last night, I'm a Canuck."

She seemed a bit disappointed. "Oh, yes, I forget. Sometimes, the way you played sometimes, it reminded me of some old New Orleans records my father brought me once."

Sal leaned back on his stool and examined her. "You like those old tunes, huh?"

She was lighting the Gaulois, trying to look older. "I like all music," she said a little too self-importantly, "but, yes, I *really* like those older—what do you call them—*stand-ups*?"

"Standards. Well, then, let's learn one of those."

"You mean, to sing?"

"Yeah, the golden-agers on this bucket will eat that shit up." He had been a little perturbed at her about being interrupted in the middle of writing a song, but now the creative aura had been broken, and then, too, the idea of playing behind someone other than McLeish was very inviting. Besides, the girl was so damn beautiful, it was nice just to be in her company, even if she did take herself a little seriously. She hadn't even smiled yet. "Look," he said, "do you *want* to sing? To be a singer?"

Her face grew even more somber. "I think that that is all I want in the world." She said it as if making a wish on a star.

"Well, then, ain't no time like the present. What was the tune you asked me about last night?"

She seemed to try to remember, but Sal had the feeling she knew all along. "Oh," she said finally, "'Lover Man'?"

"Yeah, right, 'Lover Man.' What are the changes to that tune?" he asked himself as his hands flew lightly over the keyboard in a kind of sped-up musical shorthand. He slowed and stumbled as he darted over the bridge, and then mumbled, "Oh, yeah," started again, and continued on until the end of the song. He remembered the changes now.

"Now, we have to find the key. How high is your voice?"

"I—I'm not really sure what you—"

"Well, when you were in the church chorus, where did they put you, with the first sopranos or with the mezzos?"

"The first sopranos."

"Then you're probably singing it somewhere," he said as he struck a few soft chords, "somewhere around B-flat. Do you know the lyrics?"

"It's my favorite song," she answered, as if to say, *Of course I would know the words to my favorite song. Just like any teenage girl,* Sal thought.

"Here," he said as he lifted the microphone stand from between his legs. "You ever sing into a mike before?"

She shook her head. "Never."

"Well, don't look so sad. There's a first time for everything." *And the first time is always the best. Keep your hands to yourself, Mister Marco Toledano,* Sal warned himself as he adjusted the stand to the right height. *She's sixteen.* He smiled in spite of himself. *You're getting old, man. You used to think sixteen was prime time.*

"Why are you smiling?" she asked him without a smile.

"No particular reason. Now, with a microphone," he said in a tutorial tone, "you don't have to sing very loud, you understand. The mike picks up the softest tones and *amplifies* them. Makes them bigger."

She nodded. "I understand."

"Don't get too close. Don't stand too far back. Yeah, that's it." He watched her standing stiffly behind the mike. "Just relax. It won't bite you."

She stood behind the mike stand, staring at him. Waiting for him to tell her what to do next. Sal turned back to the piano keyboard. "What key was that? Oh, yeah." He began to play a soft, bluesy vamp. G-minor seventh to C7. G-minor seventh to C7. He looked up at her. She was *shaking* behind the battered Shure.

Still playing the gentle, bittersweet changes, Sal asked her, "Are you okay?"

She swallowed and nodded. Sal played a few more bars, and she still hadn't begun to sing.

"You can come in anytime," he gently urged.

Still trembling, she glanced at him, stricken, and whispered quaveringly, "I don't—I don't know where."

Sal gave her a reassuring smile. "I'll start it off. You follow me, okay?"

She gulped. "Okay," she breathed.

Sal let the changes slip by a few more times, then began to barely speak/sing in his hoarse croak, "*I don't know why, but I'm feelin' so sad—*"

And the girl joined in tentatively, her voice under his, "*I long to try something I never had—*"

Sal's scalp tingled with excitement as he heard her singing coming through the speakers. The hairs on his arms stood on end.

"*Huggin' and a-kissin'*" she sang. As Sal let his voice fade out hers grew stronger and more self-assured. "*Oh, what I been missin'.*" She needed no more prompting now, and Sal turned to watch her as he played. His mouth actually hung open in amazement, but she didn't see it. Her eyes were closed and she was in another place as she sang, "*Lover Man, oh, where can you be?*"

She held the last note of the verse, her eyes fluttered open, and she looked at him, as if to say, *Go on?,* and Sal whispered, "Don't stop."

She touched the chrome mike stand lightly with her fingertips, as if to steady herself, and with her eyelashes coming together, sang, *"The night is cold, and I'm so all alone, I'd give my soul just to call you my own—"* and Sal watched her sing and felt a little like the way he had felt that moment in the Sporting Life Bar & Lounge when Transformer had lost that race, and he knew his life would never be the same. Now, in this clear, crystalline moment in the darkened empty dining room of this ship in the North Atlantic, just below 30° latitude, Sal knew that forever after his life would somehow be unalterably changed. *This must be the way the players on Fifty-second felt the first time Bird sat in. Or the glance the studio engineers gave each other when Dion was recording "Runaround Sue." Or how God rejoiced the first time Aretha soloed in her father's Detroit church.*

No, Sal told himself. *What it was—what it was* exactly *like—it was just what the guys on the bandstand experienced when Lady Day did her first set.*

Sal was so far away from the moment that he botched the turnaround out of the bridge and stopped playing. The girl was aghast.

"I'm so sorry!" she cried. "Was it terrible? Did I—"

Sal reached over and touched her arm. "It wasn't you," he said softly. "I screwed up." Her skin was warm and taut. As he brought his hand back, he noticed that now *he* was trembling. He sat on the piano bench, his hands curled into limp fists resting on his thighs, and tried to collect himself.

"What's—what's wrong?" she stammered.

He shook his head and looked up at her. Her beauty was luminescent, like her talent. She was backlighted by the dim overhead, and the delicate fuzz on her cheeks seemed to glow like a Madonna's aura. *Alive,* Sal thought. *"I feel so alive. I died and now am reborn."* "You Make Me Feel Brand New," the Stylistics.

"What's your name?" he heard himself ask her.

She stared at him a moment, and then a slow, shy smile moved across her lips. She had won some kind of victory within herself, but Sal wasn't sure what it was.

"Isabel," she said softly. "And you are Marco?"

No, I'm not. "Yes. Marco. Marco Toledano. Listen, Isabel, is this some kind of trick or something?"

"Trick?"

"Are you a mimic? Do you do other voices? Impersonations, like?"

Her face showed her confusion. "I don't know what you mean."

"You don't know what I mean? You don't know you sound exactly like Billie Holiday?"

She was shocked. "I do?"

"Aw, c'mon!" he scoffed.

"No, really," she said quickly as she rested her hand on his shoulder. Sal felt the weight. "Do I really sound like Billie Holiday?" she asked incredulously.

Sal shook his head. "It's freaky."

"*Meu Deus!*" she said with a pleased grin. "That's wonderful!"

"I know you said you liked the old tunes, but Jesus, this is incredible! Do you listen to a lot of Billie Holiday?—*fuck!—of course you do!* You *must!*"

"When I was very little," she explained, "just a baby, I cry a lot, and whenever I cry, they would play one of Billie's records, and they say I stop crying—*poof!*—just like that. And now, even today, when I feel blue, down, you know?—I play her record and I feel, you know, sad, but happy, too, you know, oooh, I don't know how to say it, *melancólica*—"

"Melancholy." *Come to me, my*—

"Yes, that word," Isabel said, nodding. "When I play the music of Billie Holliday, I feel like that. Bad, but good too. Sexy." She smiled at him. "Like making love when it's raining outside."

Change the subject. "But before when you were singing backup on my original, I heard you do a Chaka lick. You listen to other people, too."

"Oh, I love all music. Especially female singers." She pronounced it *fee-mal-li*. "I like to hear Chaka Khan, Whitney Houston, Annie Lennox. And of course I like Brazilian music too. Djavan. Ivan Lins." She stopped talking for a moment and stared at him. "You think, Marco, you think I could become a singer?"

Sal leaned back in his stool and considered what he was going to say. "You already *are* a singer—you just haven't *sung*." He looked at her. "Do you know what I mean?"

She shook her head. No.

Sal sighed. "Look, the music is *in* you, you just need to

work on getting it *out.*" He reached for a Gaulois. "It's like you're a brilliant musician the first time he plays his ax—piano, trumpet, guitar—whatever. You start to play and it's strange and you don't have any chops and you fumble around and fuck up—" He lit the cigarette. "But you know instantly what the instrument is about, how it *makes* the music, you know what I mean. The music is in *you,* you know what I mean, the instrument is just a means of letting it out. A musician like that is a natural." He turned to her. "And that's what you are. And that musician, the first time he plays his ax, whether he's six or sixty—I believe this—anyone in the room who hears that musician play that first time understands that that player is a *natural,* they can hear it, just like I understood it when I just heard you sing."

She was knitting her brow, straining to understand everything he was saying. "Then—then you think I could be—*good?*"

"I think you could be incredible! Incredible!" He scratched the scar under his beard and stared up at the ceiling. "But is the world ready for a teenybopper who sings just like Billie Holiday?"

"Marco—you think it's bad I sing like Billie Holiday?"

Sal rubbed absently at the ridge of dead flesh. "Could be bad, could be good. You never know." He pointed a finger at her. "You sure you're not consciously trying to imitate her?"

Her face grew solemn. "Marco, I swear on the Baby Jesus. I just sing. If it sounds like her—" She shrugged her shoulders in a manner understood by Italians the world over.

Sal studied her a while. Then stubbed out his cigarette and rested his hands on the piano keyboard. "Let's run this one again," he said as he started up the vamp again.

G-minor seventh to C7. G-minor seventh to C7.

They spent the rest of the afternoon in the empty dining room, running down all the Billie Holiday songs Isabel knew. And Isabel knew them all. Not only the ones everyone was familiar with—the familiar, overworked tunes Diana Ross had sung on the *Lady Sings the Blues* sound track—"Good Morning Heartache," "God Bless the Child," and "All of Me." Those hoary mass-market chestnuts. Isabel knew the obscure tunes from the early recordings, "Miss Brown to You," "Your Mother's Son-in-Law," when she was band-singing with Teddy Wilson and Benny Goodman. Back in the thirties, before she even had that Billie Holiday *sound* that moved people the world over. That cutting, nasal, drug-drenched, pain-laden *sound.* And Sal sat at the piano all afternoon, transfixed, devastated, watching this smooth-faced, unblemished millionaire's daughter, this child from the other side of the world, this spoiled Third World teenybopper—watching this *baby* open her mouth and emit that *sound.* That unmistakable, soul-wrenching *sound.* That incredible, heartbroken *voice.* It was freaky. It was mind-blowing. It was unbelievable. Sal sat there, comping the chords, tinkling the blues fills, all afternoon as they went through the whole Eternal Lady Day Songbook—"Ain't Nobody's Business if I Do," "You Go to My Head," "I Cover the Waterfront"—Sal sat there at the keyboard and became more and more astonished with every tune. The girl got *stronger* as the day went on. From minute to minute he could hear her improve. True, she was still very much an amateur, her intonation was iffy, she occasionally dropped half a bar, but it was obvious the music was in her, and she had that *sound,* that plaintive muted trumpet of a voice, all those idiosyncratic characteristics that would almost be weaknesses if found singly in other singers, but when brought together in one tormented soul became sublime. Billie's unexpected off-the-wall phrasing, her rapid jazz player's vibrato that seemed to dip up at the end of each phrase, that behind-the-beat, out-of-breath rush of words, as if each line of lyrics were a tortured effort. All the things that made Billie Holiday unreplicatively Billie Holiday were miraculously embodied, reborn, resurrected in this young girl, this Isabel Gemelli, this rich Brazilian brat. She opened her delicate, full-lipped mouth, and out poured the voice of a legendary light-skinned black American junkie who had died more than thirty years previous, almost twenty years before this child was born. Sal comped the chords, watched the girl sing, heard that unbelievable voice come out, heard the girl's ability to reproduce that voice grow more confident and proficient with every verse, each chorus, and he was lost in the unreality of the moment. They played and sang all that afternoon. "Willow Weep for Me," "When It's Sleepy Time Down South," "Sophisticated Lady." And then "Ill Wind," "Body and Soul," and "Please Don't Talk About Me." The cleaning crew came into the dining room, only vaguely interested, vacuumed, cleaned, then left, and still Sal played and Isabel sang. A late-afternoon storm came up on the surrounding ocean, and the sound and crackle of lightning on the water bled into the dining room, and the two of them didn't notice. It wasn't until the first couple of passengers appeared in the dining room's doorway, thirsty for their pre-dinner cocktails, that Isabel abruptly stopped singing. Sal was jolted from his total absorption in her voice, raised his eyes, and looked at her.

"Don't stop," he rasped gently, as if coming out of a stupor. As if sighing to a lover.

"Marco—" she whispered shyly, and nodded at the two curious golden-agers looking into the dining room.

For a moment Sal stared stupidly at the gray-haired couple, then his mind seemed to clear, and he stood up quickly. "Shit! I gotta get dressed for the gig." He looked at her. "Listen, you wanna sing tonight?"

She couldn't even look at him as she shook her head. "I can't, Marco. I just can't."

"You wanna be a singer, sooner or later you gonna have to sing for people."

Throwing a glance at him, she said, "I know. I know. But not yet."

Sal switched off the sound system and put his cigarettes back into his pocket. "Hey, you're right. This is just the first day. You wanna get together tomorrow, go over some more tunes?"

Her eyes riveted onto his. "Yes. Yes. I would love that."

He closed the tattered old fake book he had been using for the tunes he didn't know and stacked it with some other sheet music on the lid of the old piano. He looked past Isabel to the gray-haired couple standing expectantly in the doorway, then back at the girl. "Isabel—" He smiled. "Is that what your friends call you?"

She shrugged, and her face took on that almost comical seriousness. "Yes, that is my name."

"You don't have a nickname?"

"A what?"

"A nickname. You know—Skinny, or Kid, or something like that?"

She shook her head. "No, only Isabel."

Sal reached over and brushed a piece of lint from the shoulder of her sweater. "Well, I'm gonna call you—I'm gonna call you Izzy. How do you like that?"

She gave him a small smile. "If that's what you want to call me—then I like it."

He touched her elbow lightly and began leading her across the dining room toward the door. "Tomorrow, here, two o'clock. Okay?"

"Yes."

"You and your family are getting off in Rio, right?"

"Yes."

"Well, I want you to promise me that before we dock in Rio"—they were at the door now, and the old Argentine couple standing there scrutinized them closely as they passed out into the passageway. Sal dropped his voice to a conspiratorial whisper—"I want you to promise me before we reach Rio, you're gonna sing for the passengers." He indicated the dining room with a nod.

She grinned at him. The expression on her face was usually so serious that when she smiled, she seemed to become an entirely different person.

"I promise, Marco," she whispered, too, and Sal felt his penis stir, like a beast awakening from hibernation. *Don't do this, asshole,* he warned himself. *Don't do this. Don't start thinking with your dick.*

"Okay, Izzy." He grinned back at her, then nodded his head down the passageway. "Now, you better get back to your cabin. Your father's gonna think you fell overboard. Or somebody kidnapped you."

"Okay," she beamed up at him, then her smile faded a bit as a thought crossed her face. "I see you at dinner, okay, Marco? You play piano tonight, don't you?"

"Sure, Izzy." *Isabel* sounded so formal to him. So guinea. "But, listen, let's keep what we did this afternoon a secret." *Hey, what's the big deal? You didn't fuck her,* he thought. *Yet.* But somehow he felt that McLeish shouldn't know about her singing. "For now, let's just keep it between the two of us," he said as he gently touched her hand. *I'm working her. I thought I was past that, but here I am working her.* "Just between the two of us."

She nodded as if she understood every hidden meaning. "Okay, Marco."

"Now." He pointed down the passageway and pretended a stern visage. "Go."

She moved down the narrow hall. Sal watched her until she reached the stairs and looked back. "Marco—" she said.

"Yeah?"

"Thank you," she said, and then dashed down the passageway's stairs.

That night, as Sal played under the gentle crystal clinking and china scraping of the ship's diners, he found he couldn't keep his eyes off of Isabel. He tried. He tried repeatedly. He chorded his way through "Misty" and focused his eyes on a dim light bulb across the dining room, and a moment later he was staring into Isabel's eyes, only thirty feet away; she was sitting at the captain's table. He played the "Theme from Terms of Endearment" while studying intently as a waiter carefully separated a white fish from its skeleton and laid the flesh in a fat black woman's plate, and then he was looking at Izzy, and she was looking back at him. Sal turned quickly away. He flipped open a fake book and searched the page for something he would have to read, something that would keep his eyes busy. "Early Autumn." He'd never played that one. He focused all his concentration on the written notes. Sightreading had never been his strong suit. He'd always got by on his good ear, and by the third time through the changes he had the composition's harmonic progressions down and his attention drifted up from the sheet music, over the top of the spinet, and fastened on Isabel again. She grinned at him and winked, and Sal was so surprised by her little lecherous leer that he laughed aloud. Several diners turned to look at him. Signore Gemelli stared at him. Isabel's aunt Angelina scrutinized him with an Italian matron's disapproving glare—a body search more probing than a Mafia bodyguard's. Sal quickly looked down at the back of his hands and kept his eyes there. He could feel the hot blood rushing to his face. *Dear Sweet Jesus, I'm blushing!* he thought, and then he heard joyous, carefree, girlish laughter, and he knew Isabel was laughing at him.

Afterward, while pounding out a plodding MOR rock rhythm as McLeish bleated "Knock Three Times" across the room to Maggie Pulaskey's tits, with all the old farts clapping their liver-spotted hands along with the beat, their happy eyes behind their bifocals glued to the captain's florid, alcohol-glazed face, Sal actually *cringed* as McLeish went up for a high C on the lyric *"means you ain't gonna shoooooooow"* and missed it, flat by a mile. Playing all afternoon behind someone with talent made McLeish's sorry squalling all the more unpalatable. Sal cringed as McLeish bayed full voice at the teeth-grinding quarter-tone, and stole a quick peek at the Gemelli party. Everyone at the table was gleefully applauding the captain's clinker, and then Sal's eyes found Isabel's, and she was staring back raptly. She smiled at him then, a private, sensual promissory love note that spread slowly across her full-lipped mouth, revealed white perfect teeth, and made Sal feel as if the two of them were the only people in the room. *In the world.* Later, lying in his cot in the darkness of his cabin, he remembered her smile. He stared up at the blackness and saw her smile and asked himself, *What the fuck is wrong with me?* He sat up on the side of the bed and fumbled for his smokes. He struck a match, and the small cabin was momentarily brightened. *What the fuck am I doing?* He exhaled in the dark. *A fucking teenager smiles at me, and I'm ready to go out and buy motherfucking roses, for Chrissakes! Am I stupid, or what?* He shook his head. *I got a good thing here. This is the best place in the world to hide. Let's not forget that's why we're on this fucking tub. They tried to kill me, and I'm sure Little Johnny ain't forgot about it. I ain't slipped his mind. I could probably stay on this ship for three, four years. Every day I'm on board is one more day the whole thing gets colder. The best place in the* world *to fucking hide, and I'm trying to fuck it up by fooling around with a passenger's kid. Underage to boot. A neurotic, spoiled, oversexed rich man's daughter. Big Trouble Looking for a Place to Happen. But Jesus Christ, did you hear her sing? Is that unbelievable? How is something like that possible? Where did that talent come from? What can you do with that voice? Jesus Christ, I never heard anything like that in my life.* Isabel wasn't just a pale, slick imitation of Lady Day, the way Diana Ross sounded in that movie. Isabel *was* Billie Holiday. It was as if she had ingested her, had become her, was Lady Day resurrected, born again within this little Brazilian spitfire. *How can that be?* Yet he'd heard it himself. He'd heard Billie Holiday's singular, unmistakable voice pour from that teenager's throat. With all the pain and experience and sarcasm and cynicism and anger and passion and beauty and ugliness. All of it. Spilling out of a schoolgirl's body. *What is that? How can that be?*

Sal stood up and started dressing. *What time is it? Two-fifty.* She would be waiting for him on deck. He knew that. He knew that as well as he knew anything he had ever learned. She would be waiting for him. She would say she hadn't been able to sleep, and then she would find some reason to invite him back to her stateroom. There, he would fuck her. That was her plan. That was the way the shit was supposed to go. Sal knew.

He pulled on a heavy sweater, slipped his cigs into his jeans pocket, and left his cabin. The passageways were well-lighted and empty. The ship was asleep. Out on the main deck the skies were clear and cold. A glowing, almond-colored full moon hung over the sea, like a neon sign advertising the earth. EAT. DRINK. FORNICATE. DIE. ALL HERE. Sal leaned his elbows on the ship's rail and fished out a cigarette. He lit it and flipped the dead match out over the sea. *I'll start counting,* Sal wagered with himself, *and before I get to twenty—* He shifted his weight on the railing. *One, two, three, four—* A whale broke out of the sea over a mile away. In the moonlight it was as clear as day. *Twelve, thirteen—*The ship's radar rotated soundlessly over the wheelhouse, around and around, around and around, listening to the night. *Sixteen, seventeen, eighteen, nineteen—*

"Hi," he heard her say, and turned around. She was wearing a big, bulky black coat with a hood pulled over her hair. She was heart-stoppingly beautiful.

"Hey," he answered. "Where yat?"

She was puzzled. "What?"

He smiled. "Nothing. Just an old expression." *An old New Orleans expression.* "Means 'how are you?' "

She moved closer, resting a gloved hand on the rail. *Fine leathercraft from Gemelli de Janeiro.* "I couldn't sleep." She looked out over the sea, up at the moon. "I couldn't stop from thinking."

Here it comes. There's something in her cabin she'll want me to see. Up close.

She turned to him then. Her eyes were a deep, wet brown. She and he were exactly the same height. *Here it comes.* "Marco," she started with heavy seriousness, "do you think Captain McLeish is a good singer?"

Sal had his lungs full of smoke. He stared at her a moment,

then burst out laughing. The smoke seared his throat, and he choked into a coughing fit.

"Marco! Marco!" Isabel cried with concern, and for some reason he didn't completely understand, that was even more hilarious to Sal, and he began laughing again, then coughing, then laughing, coughing, laughing.

"Marco, should I call Dr. Mahoud?" The idea of the ship's doctor—an ancient old paregoric addict who sold pills and needles to the crew—coming to anyone's rescue struck Sal funny, too, and once again he convulsed in laughter.

"Marco!" Isabel said, but this time with stern petulance, like a little girl stamping her feet. She thought she was being ridiculed, and it was obvious she didn't like it. "Stop it, Marco!"

Sal fought to gain control of himself. His throat burned, and his eyes were watering. "I'm sorry," he apologized, properly chastised. "It's just that"—he chuckled as he wiped tears from his cheeks—"I don't know—" He grinned at her. "Izzy," he said, "Charlie McLeish is the worst singer I've ever worked with. And I've worked with some real dogs. Cap is the very worst."

She nodded thoughtfully. "I didn't think he was very good. I didn't think so."

Sal leaned back, his elbows on the railing, and examined her up and down. "You, on the other hand, are going to be a motherfucker."

Again, she was confused. "Is that good?"

Sal chuckled once more. "I'm trying to say I think you are exceptionally talented. One in a million."

Even though she allowed herself only a tiny smile, Sal knew she was delighted. "You really think so, Marco? Really?"

"Unbelievable." He nodded. "But you have to understand, talent ain't the only criterion. I been in this business for over twenty years, and I seen a lot of talented people spend their whole fucking life singing in dumps and dives." *Myself included.* "You say you wanna be a singer." He felt himself growing intense. There was an urge to protect her. "What kinda singer you wanna be?"

Now, she was really confused. "What kind—?"

"You wanna sing in dumps and dives all your life? That kinda singer? A loser? A drunk?"

She swallowed, afraid to say anything.

"Or you wanna be a recording artist?" he pressed on. "'Cuz that's what they call you if you make records. A recording *artist.* You know what they call you if you sing in a barroom?"

She quickly shook her head.

"They call you 'Hey, you,' is what they call you. You know what I'm trying to say?"

No, she didn't.

He smiled and reached into his jacket pocket for another cigarette. Since Dago Red, he'd become a chain smoker. "I'm getting kinda intense." He shook out a Gaulois. "I just don't wanna see you make any mistakes." *Like I did.*

She reached for a cigarette before he could put them away. "I think you are very nice, Marco, to be so concerned for me."

Sal struck a match and lit hers first. "This right here is a mistake, you know. No singer should smoke. Even one as young as you."

After only a moment's hesitation she took the cigarette from her mouth, stepped to the rail, and threw it over the side, then she turned back to him as if to say, *I will do whatever you tell me to.*

"Is that what happened to your voice?" she asked. "The cigarettes?"

Not quite. Even cancer ain't that lethal.

"No, not really." A wind came up then and swept across the deck like a ghost. Sal shivered.

"Whenever I can't sleep, like tonight," Isabel said, looking straight into his eyes, "sometimes I smoke a little *maconha.* I have some back in my cabin. Would you like to come back with me?"

Why do that? Why waste the time? Why don't I prop you against the wall and fuck you right here? Just open your coat, pull up your skirt, wrap your legs around me, and push your panties to the side. Just slip it right in, right here. It's what you want. We both know that.

"What about your aunt Angelina? I don't think your chaperon likes me too much."

She smiled then, a beautiful sight. Her smiles were as rare and radiant as precious stones. Her laughter was diamonds. "I tell her she has to sleep in my father's cabin. I tell her she snores too loud."

"Does she?"

She giggled. A sound like a light breeze through glass wind chimes. "Like a horse!" she blurted, and then laughed full out. Sal joined her, and they laughed together. It made their aloneness even more intimate.

Take her, Sal told himself. *You need it.* He hadn't made love to a woman since that morning over the Tall Cold One when he'd died and been reborn. Since he'd chewed on Kim's medicinal-tasting clitoris, if that could be called making love. *Take her. Look at her face. She's an open book. She wants you to have her, to take her and teach her. She wants you to introduce her to the Life, to bring her into your world. She wants to know everything there is to know about you.*

"Is very good maconha," she said finally, and Sal knew she wasn't just talking about the weed. He leaned toward her, and she came in closer, raising her face to be kissed in the cold moonlight. Just then, over her head, Sal saw a meteor streak across the cloudless sky. "Look, a shooting star!" he said as he put his hands on her shoulders and turned her around. Sal had always had a thing for shooting stars. One of the few good childhood memories he had of his father was them going out nights on Lake Maurepas in a leaky old skiff, waiting for the sun to rise so they could cast for catfish. "Look for them shooting stars, Sally," Joe the Hack would cackle as he fucked with his line and gear and took long pulls on a bottle of Red Port. "You look real good for them shooting stars, 'cuz if we see one of them shooting stars, that means real good luck, Sally, and you and me, we'll go to the Fair Grounds and make us a real good bet. Can't lose on the day you see a shooting star." Then Joe the Hack would offer his little boy a drink of wine. "Don't tell your mama, Sally. She seen too many drunken Injins when she was a kid." Then he would laugh some more. "And too many drunken guineas since she married me. Dat wine'll help you spot them shooting stars, aw right."

Isabel turned back to him, her face still full and expectant, but the opportunity was lost, the mood shattered. Seeing the meteor and thinking of Joe the Hack back in New Orleans had reminded Sal that his life wasn't completely in order. Not by any means. He didn't need to add to the mess by going around screwing teenagers who looked up to him.

"Shooting stars are supposed to be very good luck," he explained lamely.

She nodded, and watched him, waiting, until she realized that he wasn't going to make his move. Not giving up that easily, she reached down and took his bare hand in her gloved one. "It's too cold here, Marco," she said. "Come to my cabin."

Sal began to lead her down the deck, but away from the cabins. "You don't understand," he said brightly. "A shooting star, *now,* at the beginning of your career," he rasped out a mock-stentorian voice, "at the very *onset* of our musical relationship. Wow, that's heavy. That's some heavy shit, luckwise."

She understood now that nothing was going to happen tonight. She accepted it gracefully. It was going to be a three-week voyage. "Marco, you sound like *um apostador,* how do you say, a gambler."

Sal smiled bitterly. "Oh, I been known to place a bet or two. Once upon a time." He entwined his fingers with hers, and they strolled the deck hand in hand. "But, say, you gonna be some kinda player yourself, Izzy. Show business is the biggest gamble in the world. In the *world.*"

Her face showed her uncertainty. "I don't know if I want to be in the show business. I think I just love to sing."

"Well, if you gonna be a singer, you gonna hafta be in show business. It's like—it's like"—he searched the skies for the right analogy—"it's like if you gonna be a painter, you hafta get paint on your clothes, you see what I'm trying to say? You can't have one without the other." He stopped and turned to her. "Say, you still think you can't get to sleep?"

She smiled at him then, almost indulgently. A sparkling gem. "I'm too *excitada,* too excited."

"Well, lookahere. Let's go to the passengers' pantry and make ourselves some sandwiches and coffee. Sound good?"

"It sounds very good," she said as she tightened her hold on his hand. "It sounds wonderful."

"You like baloney and Swiss cheese?" he asked her as they walked along.

She didn't know what baloney was. Somehow she'd missed that American experience during her two-year stay at Sacred Heart. They discussed that as they sat together, alone, in the dimly lit passengers' pantry, which was left stocked and unlocked in case any insomniac passengers needed a late-night snack. Sal and Isabel sat there for hours, undisturbed, and discussed baloney. They talked about the blues, North America vis-à-vis South America, abstract art, and the music of Ray Charles. They nibbled sandwiches, sipped tepid coffee, and talked and talked until the oncoming dawn turned the pantry a dull gray. Then they went out on deck and watched the sun emerge from the eastern ocean. It was going to be a bright, clear day.

He worked her hard. Every afternoon for the next two weeks the two of them locked themselves in the dining room from two in the afternoon until just before dinner bell. Sal bribed the cleaning crew not to disturb them and to keep their mouths shut, and somehow Captain McLeish didn't hear about Isabel's singing. At least, he never mentioned anything to Sal. Anyway, Sal was pretty sure the old letch was having an affair with Maggie Pulaskey's tits, and they seemed to be commanding most of his attention. Sal never saw the captain except at night, when they got together and performed for the passengers. So, every afternoon following lunch, when most of the mostly elderly passengers would retire to their cabins for a nice afternoon nap, Sal and Izzy would meet in the dining room. They would lock the door and turn off the brighter lights, dial the old sound system to low, and begin. Sal could remember many sexual liaisons in his life that weren't nearly as erotic and fulfilling.

They shut themselves in the dining room, Sal at the piano, Isabel behind the microphone; Sal struck a few bittersweet chords, Isabel shut her eyes and opened her mouth, and they were transported back to an after-hours barbecue joint in Harlem back in the late thirties, or a jumping bebop club on Fifty-second Street in the forties. They left the constraints of this earthly world, left this ship, this ocean, this decade, and flew back across time and distance to another place, another space. When Isabel sang "Strange Fruit," it was as if she and Sal were there, in some funky uptown joint, as if they shared Lady Day's pain and outrage when she spit out the lyrics. That's how good Isabel was. It was *freaky*. And when they smoked some of Isabel's *maconha*—which really was very good—when they got loaded, the whole thing got really spacey. For however long a song lasted, Sal and Isabel were in another dimension, an aural time warp. When the song ended, it took them several moments to remember who and where they were. Being on a ship in the middle of an ocean—a very artificial environment to begin with—didn't add to the reality of it all. And every day, every hour, Izzy got better and better. Sal had never seen or heard, or heard *of,* a talent like hers. She *absorbed* the music. She became it. And whenever Sal gave her direction—hold that note a little longer, linger on that phrase, punch that lyric—he never had to tell her twice. She was that good. *A natural,* he thought. *She truly is a natural. Like rolling an eleven on the comeout. Like Secretariat, Citation, and Native Dancer.* And without realizing it was happening to him, Sal was becoming more contented, more fulfilled—happier—than he'd ever been in his life. Each day was like a joyous adventure. He basked in the glow of her brilliance. He observed her blossoming gift with something like a parent's pride and a teacher's joy. And the fire that was Isabel's talent first warmed, then ignited him. He awoke each morning, literally, with a song in his heart. He was exploding, he was a whole songwriting staff, a musical volcano, a churning urn of burning funk. Songs came to him everywhere now—in the shower, on the john, while he played behind McLeish's bumping ass, when he ate his meals. He lay awake in his bunk—the few hours a day he wasn't playing or composing—and his mind buzzed with snatches of melodies, pieces of songs. Everything that people said to him, everything he answered, he searched for lyric content. He carried his notebook around constantly and jotted down each and every song idea, sometimes breaking off a conversation to scribble it onto paper. Whenever he wasn't with Isabel, he became distant and distracted, lost in a world of his own creation. When they were together, his senses seemed to sharpen, to open up and drink her in. He became more attuned, more focused. More *in the moment* than he'd ever been his whole besotted, postponed life.

Each night Sal and Izzy would meet on the main deck sometime after midnight, walk the cold, deserted decks for a few hours, maybe smoke a little of Isabel's *maconha* and blow the acrid-smelling clouds over the ocean—then they would go to the passengers' pantry, make a pot of coffee, and sit and talk til the dawn emerged from the horizon and the passengers and crew began to stir. They discussed anything and everything. Sal, of course, had to be careful. He had to camouflage a lot of stories from his life, specific memories that would locate him in New Orleans, that would reveal his duplicitous identity. He had to be vague, to relate general impressions rather than precise recollections. Izzy, on the other hand, told him all. She explained, in graphic terms, how she had lost her virginity in the Carnaval of her thirteenth year to a big black man in the costume of a gold lamé eagle. He spotted her on the edge of a dancing crowd, took her hand, and led her to an alley behind a raucous *galeteria* and bar, placed her on a stained mattress that had obviously been put there for occasions just like this, ripped off the pantaloons of her belly-dancer costume, and took her right there, while two leering dishwashers leaned out the restaurant's window and shouted encouragement. Isabel told Sal of the huge mansion she had grown up in on the outskirts of Rio in the exclusive mountainside suburb of Gavea, just over the hill from the teeming *favela* called Rocinha, where her mother, also named Isabel, had been born and raised. She recounted the legend of the slum girl who had attracted the attention of the immensely wealthy Giovanni Gemelli; she laughed as she described the still-infamous wedding reception, the way the servants had told it to her; she cried, and Sal put an arm around her shoulder when she explained how her mother had died giving birth, and the guilt she had always felt about that, the ugly, unbearable responsibility of taking from her wonderful, beloved, deformed father the only love, the only happiness, he had ever known. The burden that she had never accepted, that she had rejected with all her rebellious behavior. She fumbled for the words as she tried to explain to Sal the deep anguish she felt sometimes, the all-consuming depression that came over her unexpectedly and made her lock herself in her room and sob for hours. *Irritable beyond consolability,* the doctors called it when she was still a baby, and all the specialists since had labeled it variously teenage angst, depression, melancholia. Isabel simply called it "Billie's Blues," after a Lady Day composition. With odd detachment she showed Sal the thin white scars on her wrists, and told him about the other times she had attempted suicide, once with a car and once with barbiturates. And with winning shyness she told Sal of the recurring dream she'd been having ever since she was a little girl, a dream of singing in a great auditorium before a multitude of people. The people love her. They applaud and scream and throw roses on the stage. Then a man in a circus ringmaster's tuxedo and top hat comes out from the wings and leads her offstage. Behind the curtain, waiting in the wings, is a young woman Isabel has seen only in photographs. The ringmaster says, *This is your mother, Isabel.* Isabel the daughter begins to cry, and rushes toward her mother, arms outstretched. Her mother draws a stiletto from the folds of her skirt and stabs Isabel in the breast. Isabel crumples to the floor. Looking up, she sees Isabel her mother smiling down at her. At this point in the nightmare Isabel always wakes up screaming, the bedsheets soaked with sweat and urine.

They sat in the underlighted pantry talking till dawn, and with studied rationality she revealed her madness to him.

Ten days out of Antwerp they crossed the Equator. The sun hung high in the sky, and the days were torrid and steamy. That afternoon, while they were taking a coffee break from their Billie Holiday Historical Society Workshop, as Sal had dubbed their practice sessions, Sal at the piano abstractly began to play and softly hum the melody to "I Can't Get My Fill," the original he had been working on the week before when Isabel, hiding in the darkness, had started singing backup harmony. This time, as Sal absentmindedly molded the chords, Isabel unexpectedly began to sing lightly into the mike the lead to Sal's tune, and the hair on his forearms tingled in a cold wave across his skin. He had already been amazed at the breadth of Isabel's encyclopedic memory of old standards, but he was stunned that after just one hearing she could recall his song perfectly, melody and lyrics. But way beyond that, he was electrified by the way his song *sounded* when she sang it. Her voice transcended his material, lifted it above its commonness, its mediocrity, and took Sal's work to a higher level of musicality, a level he'd despaired of ever achieving. His song soared in Isabel's mouth. It sounded the way he'd always dreamed his music would sound. The way he'd never been able to make it sound when he sang it himself, even back when he was a hot young kid. There had always been something lacking. Izzy had been that missing piece to the puzzle. All these years. How could he have known? He'd never even been an especially fervent fan of Billie Holiday. She was just one of a whole mob of jazz singers he'd listened to when he was younger, listened to and tried to absorb. But because she was a woman, and Sal had never really been especially interested in female vocalists, he'd respected her achievements but she'd passed through his attention without leaving much of an impact. But now, hearing his song sung by her voice, by Billie's voice but improved in some ways because Isabel was so young, so fluid in her technique, her voice still so fresh and unspoiled by the ravages of liquor, tobacco, and drugs, by the assaults of life—it was like hearing a teenaged Lady Day, but with all the experience and strength of character she'd communicated at the drugged twilight of her career. Even more startling, it was like hearing a young but totally developed Billie Holiday sing contemporary music, hearing that incredible talent, still new and open, sing a modern rock-era composition, but with an obvious comprehension, an understanding of rock, not like listening to one of those aging Sinatra-era crooners make a fool of himself by mangling a current hit. It was as if somehow Billie had been born again, sixteen years ago in the early 1970's, had listened to and absorbed everything there was to listen to, current and past, and was here before him now, singing one of *his* songs. Sal had never given an ounce of credence to the belief in reincarnation, but now, playing the piano while he stared at Isabel singing his tune and heard Billie Holiday's voice—he was so overwhelmed that his certitude in everything was shaken. *Shit,* he'd *died and been reborn.* After that this was simply another miracle among a whole array he'd experienced in the last year. But what a wonderful, astonishing one! What a sweet, exciting, uplifting wonder. *Listen to that girl! Listen to that song!* Hearing his song like this, Sal felt himself swell with pride and confidence. There was an aura of destiny in the air, an electric energy of predetermined *fate,* as if forces beyond his ken and influence were controlling his future, and Sal at that instant made a pact with the universe to follow those forces, to go with the flow, no matter where they might lead.

"Ladies and gentlemen! Ladies and gentlemen!" Captain McLeish called out to the celebrating dining-room crowd. "Are we having fun yet?" he brayed into the mike, and the passengers shouted back, *"You betcha! You betcha!,"* which was a shipboard catchphrase that had raged through the elderly passengers like a virus and somehow struck them all as riotously funny. *"You betcha!"* Even the non-English speakers thought it hilarious.

This was the Captain's Farewell Party. Tomorrow afternoon the *Antonea* was docking in Rio de Janeiro, her first port of call since embarking from Antwerp. The passengers had been drunk since lunch, while the crew hadn't started seriously drinking until after sunset. Now, the ship's officers, inebriated and horny after two weeks at sea, were slow-dancing with the blue-haired American matrons and rotund Brazilian grandmothers, while the women's husbands had to settle for a belly-rubbing spin or two with Maggie Pulaskey, who was literally having the time of her life, much to Captain McLeish's chagrin. The last song had just ended, and two men in their seventies were arguing over whose turn it was to dance with her, while a third held her in his arms on the dance floor and refused to relinquish her.

"Toast!" McLeish bellowed over the crowd noise, and Sal at the piano winced and covered his ears as he felt himself lose some of his high tones. "A toast!" McLeish snatched his shot glass of whiskey from the lid of the piano and gazed pointedly at Maggie, who had finally managed to extricate herself from Senhor Rodrigues's ancient grasp. "To the delicious memory of the most wonderful voyage I have ever had the pleasure of captaining."

There was a round of *Hear, hears* and *Bem*s from the audience, and then the captain turned to the crowd and raised his amber whiskey to the light. "Through the lips and over the gums—look out, liver, *here it comes!*" he shouted, then threw his head back and shootered the drink. *"Skol!"* someone hollered back, and then the others chimed in. *"Saúde!" "Banzai!" "Here's to ya, Mac!"*

McLeish licked his lips and leered at the passengers. "And now Marco and I"—he heartily slapped his pianist on the back—"we've worked up this little song to kind of say goodbye to all of you." He turned to Sal and said theatrically, "Maestro, if you will."

Sal rippled out a long Liberace-like arpeggio, and McLeish faced the passengers and began to bleat in a schmaltzy vaudevillian tenor, *"Wheeeeee'll meet agiiiiin—don't know wherrrrrre, don't know whennnnnnnnn—but I know we'll meet again some sunny daaaaaaayyyy."*

By the second verse everyone who knew the old tune—and that even seemed to include most of the foreigners—had joined in, and the dining room had become a Mitch Miller sing-along.

"Keep smilin' throouuuuugh, just like youuuuu always dooooooo—"

Sal pounded out the chords to the maudlin old tearjerker and thought, *For* this *I was saved? For* this? *I lived and Dago Red died so I could hide on this motherfucking rustbucket and play this shit for the rest of my friggin' life?* His afternoons were sublime. Musical nirvana. And then every night this shit. Tonal excrement. Vocal puke. He looked over at Isabel. She was seated at her father's table, staring back at him. Her face was ashen; she looked sick, but Sal knew she wasn't. She was just scared. Scared shitless. Beside her Tia Angelina glared around with self-righteous disapproval at the rowdy drunks, while Giovanni Gemelli, small and white-suited, sat at Izzy's other hand and stroked it solicitously. His concerned eyes flicked from his daughter to Sal and back again. All night Isabel had sat there trembling, and had shaken off every old fart's offer to dance. Her father was worried about her.

She'll be gone, Sal thought as he played. *Tomorrow we dock, and she'll be gone from my life forever.*

"Don't know wheerrrrrreee— Don't know wheeeennnnnn—"

Sal kept his eyes on Izzy while he hammered out the old potboiler. She was a buoy of youth and beauty surrounded by a sea of withered, shriveled skin. *Tomorrow she'll walk down the gangway with her rich father and disappear forever. And I know I'll never meet anyone again with her kind of talent. She's a one-in-a-generation. A once-in-a-lifetime.* Sal stared at Isabel, and Isabel wouldn't look away from him. *How can I let her go?* he asked himself. *How can I let her just walk away from me?*

"—wheeellllll meet again some sunnnneeee daaayyyyyy!"

McLeish ended the song on a high, wavering note, his eyes screwed tight with drunken emotion, his arm thrown out like Jolson, and the ancient audience erupted in teary appreciation. Above the warm thunder of applause were the explosive *pops* of champagne corks at the bar and girlish squeals of delight from the septuagenarian groupies. "That was bee-you-tee-ful,

Mac!" Maggie Pulaskey's husband, Milt, bellowed in cuckolded Brooklynese ignorance. "Fuck-king bee-you-tee-ful!"

"The best, Captain!" someone else offered up.

"Bravo!"

"Bellissimo!"

"Outstanding, old man, you should be on the telly!"

McLeish's ruddy cheeks puffed and gleamed like glazed pottery as he joyfully accepted his adoration. *Cocksucker's in heaven,* Sal thought as he remembered what the warm wash of a loving audience's applause felt like.

At just the right moment—not a moment too late or too soon—*Cocksucker's a pro!*—McLeish raised his hands to silence the crowd. Looking around the dining room with wet eyes and a practiced show-bizzy expression of appreciation on his face, he breathed into the mike with phony emotion, "Thank you. Thank you so much."

C'mon, motherfucker, don't overstay your welcome. Always leave 'em asking for more.

As if cued by Sal's thoughts, there were a few encouraging shouts of, "Do another one, Mac!" "Let's hear 'Alley Cat' again!" "Give us one more, Captain!"

McLeish grinned at his fans and shook his head. "Now you lot know we still have to draw for the prizes Aqua Lines have provided. I think I saw a beautiful set of"—staring at Maggie Pulaskey's breasts—"a beautiful set of luggage that someone's goin' to win, eh? And besides, my musical director and I have been up here for over an hour—"

Then get off! Sal was watching Isabel. He was afraid she was going to pass out.

"—so we're going to take a pause for the cause, and maybe we'll do a couple more selections a little later in the evening."

"Awwwwwww—" the golden-agers moaned.

"Thank you again for the claps," McLeish said, and there were titters of repressed sexuality accompanying the round of applause as McLeish walked away from the mike toward the captain's table. He was almost seated when he heard a voice come through the speakers on *his mike!* McLeish had never heard another voice through *his mike* before. His head snapped around, and his small, Celtic face registered his surprised displeasure.

"Ladies and gentlemen," Sal's voice rasped softly over the

P.A. "Excuse me, folks. *Um momento, por favor.*" He stood at the mike stand and looked out at the audience. "Excuse me, ladies and gentlemen."

The crowd slowly quieted down and turned its attention from Captain McLeish, who was standing at his chair scowling, and onto Sal, smiling at them from behind the mike.

"Captain McLeish," Sal's voice grated amiably, "if you don't mind, I have a little surprise for you and our passengers."

"Well, Marco," McLeish tried to regain his friendly bluster with an easy chuckle, "We *do* have the drawing and—"

"Thanks, Cap," Sal interrupted with a smile. *Back off, motherfucker. I have the mike now.* "Ladies and gentlemen, *senhores e senhoras,* friends and shipmates," Sal began to work the people, slipping into the entertainer's spotlight as if he'd never left it. "Tonight we are going to partake of a singular experience." He took the mike from the stand and walked out toward the people a few feet, something McLeish never did. Sal knew exactly how far to go before the speakers would start feeding back. "Tonight we will experience something new, something wonderful, something that no matter how good it might be in succeeding nights, it ain't ever again gonna be like it is that first night." He paused for a moment, thinking *Joel Grey in* Cabaret, and then whirled and leeringly leaned over Frau Hauptman, a buxom, jovial, Bavarian sausage of a woman. "I think you know what I'm talking about, *mein liebchen,*" he whispered into the mike down at her, and the earthy, fun-loving Munich grandmother immediately began to laugh, her great, pillowy breasts heaving with every guffaw. The rest of the audience hesitated only a moment, then a good-natured roar went up from the crowd. *Nothing works with old farts like double entendre,* Sal thought. It had taken him only half a minute to make the yokels forget about the preceeding act. McLeish slowly sank into his seat, an ugly scowl darkening his sweating face.

"Tonight," Sal continued, turning his back on the audience and flipping the mike cord leisurely as he returned to what would have been center stage if there had been a stage. "Tonight"—he faced his listeners again. Their attention was riveted on him. *So easy,* Sal thought of them. *You're so easy. But it's not my night.* His smile faded and became a mask of earnest solemnity—"Tonight we're going to witness the debut of a young, fresh"—he paused between each word—"startling, incredible new talent." He stared out at them, milking the moment, and then finally intoned softly, "Ladies and gentlemen, without further ado—Isabel."

Sal left the mike and sat behind the piano. There was an awkward heartbeat of silence during which the old people threw nervous glances at each other, and then Sal started an easy, swinging left-handed-walking-bass vamp. While the soft, comfortable chord sequence drifted over the tables, Sal could *feel* the eyes of everyone in the dining room dart around the room and finally come to rest on Isabel. The chord progression went around once and then started again. He threw a glance in her direction. She was still seated at the table, shaking and staring transfixed back at him with bulging, terrified eyes. Her father and aunt, sitting on either side, were gaping at her with curiosity and concern. Sal returned her gaze for a second, and then looked down at the back of his hands as he started going through the changes for the third time. *Come on, kid. You can do it. You can do it.*

Too afraid to take her eyes off Sal and risk seeing everyone ogling her, Isabel slowly pushed her chair back from the table and rose with detached, robotic movements. She stood there momentarily—*C'mon, kid, come on*—then, staring down at the floor, she stepped around the table—*Atta, girl, that's the way*—crossed the dining room, and stood by the piano, her back to the room.

"Mrr—Marco—" she began in a quavering whisper, "I can't—"

Without looking up, Sal growled from between clenched teeth, "Don't ever show an audience your ass, girl, before you got 'em won over."

She stared at Sal in wide-eyed terror. *"Eu não tenho—"* she started, too frightened to realize she was speaking Portuguese. *"Eu não tenho coragem."* She was trying to tell him she couldn't do it.

"Do you need the first line?" Sal interrupted, still studying the backs of his hands.

"*O que?* What?" She was startled.

He looked at her now. "Do you need your first line of lyrics?"

Very slowly but not very convincingly, she shook her head.

"Then turn around and face your public."

She nodded, just as reluctantly, then slowly pivoted and stood there, behind the Shure ball mike, staring out at sixty pairs of eyes trained on her, like muzzles in a firing squad. Sal heard her say, "Oh—" in a small, desperate voice.

"Izzy!" he hissed without moving his lips. "You are the best I ever heard. You are gonna be a big star, do you understand? Do you under*stand?*"

Facing the waiting passengers, Isabel gave him a trembling, all but imperceptible nod.

"All right," he continued, as if he were talking someone off a high-rise ledge, "then you're going to start singing right after the next turnaround—here it comes, three, six, two, five, *here it is!*"

"They're writing songs of love—" she began haltingly. *"But not for Me. A lucky star's above—But not for Me—"*

A murmur ran through the crowd of old people, like a fresh breeze rustling dead leaves.

"Listen to that!"

"Is that the Gemelli girl?"

"*Ouça!* Listen!"

"I was a fool to fall and get that way—" Isabel sang, taking a step closer to the mike. Sal watched and smiled. *Get 'em, girl.* *"Hi ho, alas and all, so lackaday—"*

"Who does she sound like, George? Who does she sound just like?"

"Dead ringer!"

"Yeah, but what's her name?"

"Ohhhhh, what's her name, what's her name?"

"Colored girl."

"Yeah, that's the one!"

"And though I can't resist—the mem'ry of his kiss—I know he's notttttt—forrrrrrr—me."

"She's very good, don't chu think?" That with a cultured English locution.

"She's wonderful!"

A well-dressed Brazilian matron leaned over and lightly touched Giovanni Gemelli's tuxedoed arm. "*Sua filha é uma cantora maravilhosa!* Your daughter is a wonderful singer! You must be very proud!"

Gemelli's head nodded in dull amazement. His mouth hung open.

And then someone asked, "Hey, Mac. Don't you think the girl's great?"

McLeish didn't speak, but he managed to twist his lips into something resembling a smile. But his eyes were as flat and cruel as a pit bull's.

"Yeah, but who the hell she sound like?" Mrs. Leiberman demanded in a nasal New York bray.

"Billie Holiday," McLeish finally croaked, and his face said it was like taking poison.

"Billie Holiday! That's the one!"

"I knew it!"

"Couldn't think of her, but that's the one all right."

Sal was playing a light, tinkling solo over the first half of the song. He looked up at Isabel, who was watching him so she wouldn't have to face the crowd. He smiled at her and winked, something he had never done before in his life, and nodded. *You got 'em, kid. They love you.* Then Izzy came in, repeating the second half, *"I was a fool to fall—"* and sang the tune out, remembering how they had rehearsed it, with the extended double-ending tag, and then her first performed song ever was over, and the audience was applauding warmly. McLeish was already on his feet and moving toward the mike stand, pounding his palms together.

"Hey, let's give Mr. Gemelli's little girl a big round of applause. Wasn't she great?" He put his hand on Isabel's waist and started to move her away from the mike. "Wasn't that great? Thank you so much for—"

Sal segued right into the vamp for the next tune, a slow, bluesy standard. McLeish turned and threw a threatening glare at him. Sal could feel a burning rash of hot anger prickle over his skin. *Don't fuck with me, old man,* his eyes lasered back. *Don't get in my way.* And in his mind's eye he saw Dago Red's Walther lying under the blanket on his cot.

"Let's have another one!" someone in the audience shouted. "She's *good!*"

McLeish turned back to the people with a wide, shit-eating grin. "Hey, what aboot the drawin' for the luggage?"

"Piss on the luggage, Mac. We've all got luggage. Let Mr. Gemelli's girl sing another!"

"*Sim, mais um!* One more!"

McLeish smiled so cheerfully, his ceramic cheeks seemed about to crack. "You know, you're right. How 'boot another one, eh, missie?" he said, turning to Isabel but shooting daggers at Sal.

Izzy looked at Sal, who nodded to the mike. She stepped back into position, and McLeish turned and strode across the floor to his table.

Sal was still playing the bluesy changes. Isabel closed her eyes, touched the mike stand with her fingertips, and started singing.

"Good Morning, Heartache, you old gloomy sight. Good Morning, Heartache, thought we said goodbye last night—"

They were with her from the second line on. She *captured* them. It was like nothing he'd ever seen. Her ability, her musical maturity, her authority, grew exponentially with every phrase.

"I tossed and turned until I thought you were gone—"

Though Sal knew her well enough to know she was hiding it somewhere, all the nervousness seemed to have evaporated. Isabel stood there, her eyes slitted closed, and delivered the song like a seasoned veteran.

"—but here you are with the dawn."

Sal scanned the audience while he accompanied her. They were transfixed, mesmerized. She had nailed them. Watching their faces in the flickering candlelight, Sal understood. They *believed* her. They believed this sweet little teenager woke up every day with a broken heart, they *believed* that some man—boy?—had done her wrong, and they suffered with her, they commiserated, they cried inside because of it. Isabel *became* the song. Like all the great ones, and only the great ones, do. The singer is the song. The medium is the message. *How can she be so good so quick?* Sal wondered. It was beyond him, far beyond him. He had once known a kid guitarist, in New Orleans back in the early seventies, who had been a marginal, run-of-the-mill player—what musicians refer to as simply *adequate,* until one day the kid disappeared, stayed out of sight for a year, then one night showed up at Sal's gig, asked if he could sit in, and proceeded to blow away everyone in the fucking joint. He had woodsheded that whole year, and had become the musician his potential had only hinted at. Now, listening to Isabel hypnotize this bunch of old farts, Sal was reminded of that guitarist. But this was much more startling. Isabel was a child, an amateur, with not even a single public performance under her belt, and here she was, sounding as if she'd been doing this for years, sounding like a pro, a veteran, an entertainer, an *artist.*

"Wish I'd forget you, but you're here to stay—"

She had the natural ability, Sal realized as he examined the rapt audience, not only to become the song, but to make the listener experience it also. She communicated the *idea* of the composition. She sang to them and made them feel it. She made these aged, cranky, diseased ancients, some of them maybe seventy years from their first love and loss, relive their youth, recall that rushing rocket of emotion and its attendant heartsickening fall. Made them remember how they'd felt, how they'd loved and how they'd ached. Somehow she tore away the scar tissue put there by decades of illness, betrayal, bitterness and boredom, and conjured up for them the unspoiled emotions of their memoryless young hearts.

She's magic, Sal thought, as Isabel ended the tune and the crowd exploded in shouts and applause. *Fucking magic.*

"That was wonderful!" a little bald-headed man yelled as he leapt to his feet. "Terrific!"

Wunderbar!"

"Bravo! Bravo!"

The passengers were whistling and clapping like teenagers at a rock concert. *Looks like you can get the old ones,* Sal reflected, *but they don't buy records. Don't worry though, we'll get the kids, too.* As if she could hear his thoughts, Isabel turned to him, wearing a wide, amazed smile.

"I told you they'd love you!" Sal shouted over the crowd, and struck the opening chords to "Just Can't Get My Fill," his new original. This was a calculated gamble. Sal had plotted Isabel's little debut like a Broadway opening. Considering who the audience was, Sal had started with two tunes everyone in the room would know—an up-tempo opener and then the signature ballad from the Billie Holiday movie—and now he was taking a chance. *Unknown originals almost always fall on their face, even with young, hip audiences. With these old fossils, who knows what the fuck's gonna happen?*

The moment Isabel began to sing, the audience quieted down. *She's got 'em by the nuts!*

"Midnight, and the heat is like fire," she sang, and Sal mouthed

his lyrics along with her. *"It's all right, it's only desire—" God, she makes my shit sound good! Listen to that!* Singing the minimalist contemporary melody, with the rhythmic vocal attack required by today's music, over his modern, minor-based harmonics, Isabel transcended the status of novelty act. She started the long journey to becoming more than just a girl who sounds like Lady Day, more than just an imitation, a secondhand copy. Listening to her, Sal was able to hear not just how she sounded now, but how she was going to sound. He heard the beginnings of Isabel's *style.* He could envision the artist she was to be, using Billie Holiday's voice as only a jumping-off place to bring that *sound,* that *feeling,* to current eighties music. Even as he played for her now, and silently sang his new song along with her, he could hear new tunes forming in his head, like fruit ripening for harvest. Ballads that would wring the tears from your eyes and raise the hope in your heart, undeniable dance cuts that wouldn't allow you to sit on your ass, that would jack you up and—

"That was marvelous!" the little bald old man was screaming in his face, and Sal suddenly realized the song was over. His vision focused, and Isabel was at the mike smiling at him, surrounded by congratulating passengers. As they rushed about her, they reached out to touch, as old people do. To finger her smooth, supple skin. To feel her warmth and youth. To brush against her talent.

"Incredible!"

"Lindo!"

"Wunderbar!"

"So touching! So touching!"

"Qué bonita!"

Izzy was turning and twisting, trying to keep him in sight, but the old folks were all around her now.

"Why didn't you tell us you could sing like that?"

"Are you a professional?"

"I'm gonna buy your record! You got a record?"

"That last song was soooooo beautiful. I never heard that one before."

Sal heard Izzy say, "Marco wrote it. Isn't it beautiful?," and he felt himself swell with pride.

"You wrote that song?" the little bald-headed man

screamed into his face. *Hunter, the little bastard's name was Hunter.*

"Yes, yes, I did," Sal rasped quietly as he watched the passengers bunch around Isabel. She thanked them and allowed them to stroke her arms and fluff her hair, all the while wearing a heart-stopping smile of total bliss. The sight of her so happy warmed Sal's insides, made him feel taller and more significant than he had in years. He couldn't recall when he'd ever *liked* a female so much. "I wrote it right here on board the *Antonea.*"

"You did?" Hunter screamed in his face. "Well, it's fucking *great!* I think it's gonna be a big hit."

"I hope you're right, Mr. Hunter. I certainly hope—"

Just then the crowd parted a bit, and Giovanni Gemelli lurched on his cane through the people. He lasered a deep, penetrating look at Sal, then stopped before a trembling Isabel. The others quickly shushed themselves quiet, and all eyes were on the father and daughter. Finally, Signor Gemelli shook his head in wonder and gifted her with a smile of absolute parental pride. He held out his arms and said, *"Minha filha, tu sê um gênio!* You're a genius!"

"Oh, *Papai*!" Isabel cried. "Did you like it?"

Giovanni beamed. "I liked it so much I cried these tears, you see? You are an *artista!*" He spread his arms even wider. "When you get famous, you won't be ashamed of your poor little *papai,* will you?"

"Oh, *Papai!*" she cried and threw her arms around the tiny man's neck. "Oh, *Papai!*" There was a chorus of *ooohs* and *ahhhs* from the crowd.

Sal watched the scene with a wide sucker's smile on his face and a mark's tender heart, and then McLeish's angry hiss buzzed in his ear.

"I'll see you in my office, Mr. Toledano! *Now!*"

The captain was livid. His face was crimson from his rage and the Canadian Club he kept swilling.

"Who the hell do you think you are, Mister? Who the hell do you think you are, eh?"

The honeymoon's over now, Sal thought. *Mister* is what McLeish used to address the regular members of the crew when he was pissed off. *No more special relationship. I'm just a common sailor now.*

"This is *my* ship, Mister, don't you know that?"

"Of course, Cap. I just thought—"

"You're not paid to *think,* are ye, Mr. Toledano?" McLeish was all up in his face now, breath reeking fumes of whiskey and Maggie Pulaskey's pussy. "What you're paid to do, eh, is play the piano. And to play the piano for *me, and me alone! Nobody sings on my ships but me!*" McLeish shouted, like an enraged child, and Sal stepped back. *Don't let this get out of hand,* he warned himself. *You need this gig, this ship.*

"Boss, why are you—"

"Whose idea was it to let that girl sing on my ship?" he demanded. "Whose?"

"Well, you know, I didn't th—I guess it was—"

"And she didn't just happen to walk up unexpectedly out of the audience," McLeish whined scornfully. "That little piece of baggage was *well rehearsed!*"

Watch your mouth, motherfucker. Sal could feel the heat rise from his balls and spread through his stomach like bad liquor.

"And she sang a song *you* wrote! I didn't even know you wrote songs!" McLeish was becoming petulant now. His professional pride had been hurt. A singer scorned. "You never asked *me* to sing one of your songs!" He prowled the cramped ship's office, sucking up his CC, and before Sal could think of anything to say, he was back, shaking his finger at Sal's nose. "You are not to use that piano again without my permission, do you understand? Or that public-address system. That's my personal property, and you are not to touch it again."

"Sure, Cap—"

"I don't care what little half-breed whore shakes her little brown arse in your face!"

Motherfucker! Alky WASP motherfucker! Don't talk about her like—

"And I will not tolerate any member of my crew looking at me like that, Mister, so wipe that snarl off your face!"

No one can talk to me that way, Sal fumed. *I died and was reborn. I can't take this kinda shit anymore.*

But instead, he said placatingly, "So she sang a coupla songs, Captain. What difference does it make?"

"What difference! What difference!" For some reason that set McLeish off again. He stepped closer and pointed at the cabin's closed door. His voice had suddenly become a pained, sullen hiss. "Mister, you made a fool of me out there! You made a fool of me in front of my own ship!" His voice rose. *"And in front of Mr. and Mrs. Solomon Lindermann!"*

Sal was puzzled. "Solly Lindermann? What the fuck—"

"Oh, you don't know everything, do you, Mr. Show Business? For your information, Sol Lindermann is a big-time talent agent in Miami, and he wants to book *me!*" McLeish stuck his thumb into his own chest. "I was going to ask you to be my pianist, but—" He shrugged with smug superiority.

The absurdity of the situation struck Sal not as funny, but demeaning. Who the fuck did this no-talent square asshole think he was? *Stupid fuck!*

Sal's voice was hard and brittle when he spoke. "Captain, Solly Lindermann came to me the night we left Antwerp, the first day he was on board. I had to listen to all his tired old war stories about how he used to book big bands back in the forties. *Big bands.* In the forties. Do you understand what I'm saying to you, Captain? I'm saying to you Solly Lindermann is an old man who lives with his sweet little old wife in a nice little condo in Fort Lauderdale, and he couldn't book a hooker at a policemen's convention, do you understand what I'm saying to you?"

McLeish just got angrier. "You don't know everything in the world, Mister. It just so happens Mr. Lindermann has some very good entertainment-industry connections in the Miami area, and he thinks—"

Something snapped then, inside of Sal, and he couldn't deal with this no-talent wannabee another second.

"Jesus, Captain," Sal cried out, "you don't really think anyone's ever gonna *pay* you to sing?"

McLeish stood there shaking, his eyes bugging out from his red face, too incensed and eviscerated to move or speak.

Sal pressed on. "I mean, here on the ship, they can't get away from you. You got a captive audience. But believe me, Jackson, ain't a motherfucker in the *world* gonna pay to hear your shit!"

McLeish could take no more. He lunged across his desk at Sal, clutching a handful of tuxedo lapel.

"Take your fucking hands off me," Sal said in a voice as cold and lethal as a reptile's hiss, "or I'll get my piece and blow your fucking brains all over this fucking cabin."

And the shocker was, as Sal said the words, he knew he meant it. He heard his own voice and thought, *Motherfucker means it. He'll kill you.* He pictured shoving the muzzle of the Walther into McLeish's stomach and pulling the trigger. Blood gushed over his hand as the 9-millimeter round tore through the captain's intestines, exploded his spleen, and then severed the man's spinal cord. McLeish collapsed like an empty sack and lay motionless, moaning on the floor. Sal pictured all this, and it didn't even upset him. In fact, the idea of it made him feel *safe*.

And that's when Sal realized he'd lost something more than blood in the upstairs stockroom of the Tall Cold One.

McLeish glowered at Sal for a long moment, then released his grip on Sal's coat and stepped back. "When this ship docks in Rio tomorrow," he said in the cold voice of authority, "I want you off *first,* before a single passenger. I don't want to ever see you again. Now get out."

It took Sal about three minutes to pack. All he had was a suitcase and a duffel bag. A few shirts, even fewer pants, the tux. Not even any shaving shit, now that he wore the beard. Just some cheap cologne, toothpaste, deodorant. The portable tape player, a few Louis L'Amours from the ship's library, and seventy-five-hundred dollars in American C-notes. And, of course, the Walther 9-millimeter semi-automatic.

He sat on the side of the bed, holding the Walther in his hand, feeling its weight, studying its design. *Ain't this wonderful,* he chastised himself. *Ain't this just fucking great. Here I had a perfect thing going, and I had to fuck it up. The perfect place to hide; the captain liked me, loved the way I played for him; I coudda stayed here on this ship forever, or at least until I had a bigger stake to start a new life. What the fuck am I gonna do now? How the fuck am I gonna get a gig in fucking Brazil, for Chrissakes. I don't know ten words in Spanish, or Portuguese, or whatever the hell they speak. I threw everything away for a crazy, horny, self-destructive teenager who has the voice of a junkie angel. Jesus, did you hear her tonight? Did you hear her? My own self, I've never heard anything like that in my life. Where does it come from? Where did she get such depth of understanding, such purity of emotion, such feeling, such empathy, such tone, such, such*—soul? *Who is she? And what am I gonna do without her? How am I gonna just get on about my life now that I've been exposed to her talent? It's like being exposed to radiation or something. I must be glowing. Just being around her has caused this levee-breaking flood of creativity in me. How can I just—*

There was a soft knock at the door. It would be Isabel, wondering why he had missed their nightly rendezvous on the main deck. Why hadn't he come up to congratulate her? To say good-bye before she disembarked in Rio. What could he tell her? *Tell her nothing. This is my problem, not hers. I should be satisfied I got a chance just to work with someone like her, if only for a few weeks. Maybe I was instrumental in starting her on what will be a brilliant career. Fuck, did you hear the way she sang my song tonight? Did you—*

There was another quiet knock, and then a man's soft voice from the hall. "Excuse me."

Maybe it was McLeish. Maybe the captain had reconsidered the situation and was coming to offer him his job back. Sal quickly slid the Walther under his cot's mattress and stepped to the door. *Don't be too much of a brownnose,* he advised himself. *But don't insult him again, either.* He fixed a repentant look on his face and opened the door.

Giovanni Gemelli stood in the brightly lit passageway, leaning on his cane. "Mr. Toledano, I would like to speak to you, if that would be all right."

Sal was completely disoriented. Signor Gemelli was the last person he'd expected to see at his door. Why was he here? The old man was so ancient, so ugly and malformed, it made Sal uncomfortable just to look at him.

"Well, uh, sure, Signor Gemelli, but we're not allowed to have passenger visits in crew's quarters." *What a stupid thing to say.*

Giovanni Gemelli smiled. "I don' think they mean old man on cane when they make-a that rule. Besides, it is so difficult all these stairs. Why don't we just go in your room, have a nice-a little talk?"

Sal quickly stepped back from the door. "Of course, Signor Gemelli." He glanced around at the tiny cabin. "There isn't much room."

Still smiling, Gemelli entered. "That'sa okay, I don't take

up much." He stood there for a moment, waiting for Sal to ask him to sit down.

"Oh," Sal said finally, realizing the situation, "I don't have a chair in here."

Giovanni nodded to the bed, making it a query.

"Of course, *signore*. Sit here." Sal hurried to close the suitcase and snatch it off the cot.

Giovanni sat down and looked up at Sal. "You sit, too. I can't talk up to you thissaway. Hurt my neck."

Sal upended the packed suitcase and perched on it. It was shaky and uncomfortable.

"You pack," Giovanni Gemelli stated simply. "The captain fire you."

"You heard that already?" Sal asked.

Giovanni shrugged with an openhanded gesture familiar to people of Italian blood all over the world. "You're rich, all time people come tell you things. Some thingsa you want to know, some no." He held out a gnarled claw of a hand. "We have never been how you say—properly introduced. I am Giovanni Gemelli. And you are Marco—?"

"Toledano. Marco Toledano." The old man's hand was bony and cold, like a severed chicken claw from Mancuso's Poultries down the block when he was a kid.

Gemelli rested his hand over the other on the crook of his cane. "You are from America?"

"Canada."

"Same-a thing. *Italiano?*"

"Sì, mio bisnonno è nato a Palérmo."

"Ah." Giovanni's eyebrows raised. *"Parla italiano?"*

Sal shook his head. "Not really. Just enough to order a meal."

"Or seduce a girl?" Giovanni said then, and Sal wondered, *What the fuck is this? What does he want?*

But as if to demonstrate that he meant nothing ill by what he had said, Giovanni smiled. Then he said, "Mr. Toledano, I come-a here to your room to say thank you to you."

"I— Thank you for what, Signor Gemelli?"

Giovanni smiled again at Sal, and sighed. Then he looked around the room. "You have nothing in here to drink—ah, whatsa that? Cognac?"

"Jack Daniel's."

"Of course. An American would drink—"

"I'm Canadian."

"Sure. Sure. Can an old man wet his mouth?"

Sal was already wiping out a couple of smudged glasses. He poured out two shots, emptying the fifth, and handed one to the little man. Sal was about to shooter back his bourbon when Giovanni said, "Let'sa make a toast." He held his liquor up to the light and said, "Isabel."

"Isabel," Sal repeated. *Why is he here? What the fuck does he want?*

Giovanni sipped his drink, then held it in his claw balanced on his cane crook. He looked at Sal and asked softly, "She's-a very good, isn't she?"

For weeks Sal had been bursting with eagerness to talk to someone about his secret discovery. Why not her father?

"She has the potential to be one of the best. One—of—the—best."

Giovanni smiled proudly. The way a father should. "I think she was good. While she singing, I think so. She made me feel things, you know. Like, how you say, goose bumps all over me, but I tell myself I am Isabel's father, I am not—not—" He struggled for the right word.

"Impartial?" Sal prompted.

"Yes. Yes. That. I mean, she is my daughter, how could I be—be—"

"Impartial."

"Yes. But when everyone else stand up and shout, 'Bravo, bravo!' Well, you see"—he tapped his temple with his finger—"then I know. She issa very good."

"She's more than very good. She's scary. She's exceptional. She's incre— Look, Mr. Gemelli. I been in show business, made my living in show business since I'm fourteen years old. I ain't never seen a talent like Isabel's before. Never. And I don't think I'll ever see another."

Giovanni shifted his weight on the cot, as if he were trying to get more comfortable. Actually, since the onset of the arthritis ten years ago, he was constantly in pain.

"Why you think, Marco—I call you Marco, okay?—why you think this talent come out just *now?* I never hear nothing before about Isabel want to sing. She never come to me ask for the lesson. Why she—how—you—say—blossom like a flower, *right now?* Why is that?"

Sal, perched once more on the upended suitcase, shrugged his shoulders. "Who knows?" He thought a moment. "Well, now, really, this seems about right. She's almost seventeen, so that seems about right. Some entertainers start earlier than that, but I think it was just Isabel's time to start singing, is all. Like an internal clock or something."

Gemelli frowned and inspected Sal closely. "Thatsa what you think?"

Sal nodded. "Yes, sir."

Gemelli shook his head grimly. "No. You are wrong."

Strange old man. One strange fucking old man.

"No. The reason, the only reason," Giovanni pontificated with his finger in the air, "my daughter find thissa—thissa—thissa wonderful *voce* inside of her heart *right now* is because she meet *you.*" He pointed the finger at Sal. "Thatsa why I come down here to thank you." He raised his glass to Sal. "Thank you, Mr. Toledano."

"Marco," Sal said, his mind already spinning. *There's gotta be some way I can use this. Maybe he can introduce me to a nightclub owner or something. Maybe he can get me Brazilian working papers.*

"Marco," Giovanni echoed. Then he leaned forward on his cane. "I look around for you after Isabel sing, but you already leave. I wanted to thank you then. I wanted to thank you for the sound of my daughter's laughter. I wanted to thank you for the smile on my daughter's face. Did you see that smile, Marco?"

The father's as buggy as the kid. "Uh—well, I guess so—"

"This smile, if you see it, you remember, *capisc'?*" Giovanni's eyes were warm and liquid as he spoke about his girl. "Issa smile that comes from my Isabel's soul, you see. I know, I know my little girl, I love my little girl and I know her, and tonight, after she sing, after the people are all around her, then, whenna she smile, I know my Isabel is truly happy, *capisc'? I never in my life see my daughter smile like-a that. I can feel how she feel, la mia figlia,* and tonight, for the first time ever, I feel my Isabel is truly happy, even for just a little while. Tonight, for the first time in her life." He picked up his cane and motioned the crook in

Sal's direction. "And that is because of you."

Sal searched inside himself for the humblest voice he could muster. "Mr. Gemelli, you give me too much credit." *This has gotta be worth something. This has gotta be worth something.* "Really, I think that—"

"No," Giovanni barked, brushing away Sal's transparent complaints with a sweep of his hand. "You are the reason my daughter has found this joy. *Tu!*" He was an ugly, crippled old man, but for the first time Sal felt Giovanni's strength of will, his intelligence, his resolve. *This dude's a multimillionaire, asshole. Don't bet him light.* "I know my little girl," Giovanni continued, "better than anyone in the world." He paused then, gazing down into the amber liquid in his glass. "My daughter," he said after a long, maudlin moment, "my daughter, she have a very difficult life."

Yeah, a rich man's kid. How fucking hard can it be?

Giovanni raised his eyes to Sal's. "My daughter is a very trouble little girl. Can you imagine, Marco," he leaned forward as he spoke, "can you imagine a little child not to have a mother?"

Actually no, I can't. Sal waited for Giovanni to speak, and when he didn't, Sal moved to fill the empty space. "Uh, why didn't you marry again, Signor Gem—"

"I cannot, even in my, how you say, nightmares, imagine not to have a mother," Giovanni went on as if speaking to himself, even though his eyes were boring into Sal's. "What desolation! What pain and loneliness!" He clutched a gnarled hand to his breast. "And my Isabel, she loses her mama on the day she is born!" Giovanni sloshed the Jack Daniel's around in his glass. "For this I blame myself," he sighed softly. *Must've been a helluva woman,* Sal thought. *Everyone's still grieving for her.* "For this I blame myself, so you see, Marco, when my Isabel smiles like that, from her heart, is very special to me."

The little, twisted man smiled with a kind of grim pride and shook his head. "How can it be, Marco, that a man like-a me has two such women in his life." Sal waited, letting Giovanni talk it out. The man obviously had something to say. "My wife—my wife was like-a—like-a—like-a sunshine on the ocean, you see, *capisci?* And my daughter is like that same-a sunshine on that same-a ocean, but sometimes the clouds they come and cover the sun, and the ocean it gets dark and stormy, you see? That is my daughter." Sal understood the old man was struggling to tell him something. "Tomorrow the sun shine again and the ocean is warm, but today—today—" Giovanni shrugged and shook his head. "You see how it is? And I am not good father, Marco. I love my daughter too much. I blame myself too much. I cannot punish her. What kinda father that is?" He threw up his hands in gentle exasperation. "What kinda father that is, he won't punish his daughter? He won't punish his daughter when she is seven years old and go to a friend's birthday party, she smashes all the presents for the little girl because they are not for *her*. What kinda father is that, he can't shoutta and get mad? And when she is"—he made a snatching motion with his hand "—when she is thirteen by the police because she go to the *favela* and buy *maconha* from the *mafia*? Or when she is, see, in the back of the car *fottendo* with the gardener when she is fifteen. What kinda father?" Giovanni shook his head again. "Or when she runna from school and winda up to shoot a diplomat from Angola?"

She didn't get around to that part.

"What kinda father? I love her too much, *capisc'*? I blame myself. I am, how you say, useless. As a father—no good. My sister Angelina, she says I must be strong, I must discipline my Isabel, but what can I do? I love her too much. She look at me with her big, sad eyes, and I remember how much I love her mama, and I can do nothing. I am a failure." He gently massaged his arthritic hands. "As a father, I am a failure."

The two men sat in the dim silence for a moment, then Giovanni looked at Sal again.

"My daughter has much sadness inside of her. Too much. Sometime she stay in her room, she lock the door, and she cry for hours and hours and hours. You can hear her all over the house. The doctors say she is thissa thing, thissa manic-depressive, thissa *irritable beyond consolability*. But all that means is she has too much sadness inside—here." He touched his breast. "This great sadness, and angry, too, Marco. A very great deal of angry. Too much." He examined the drink in his glass, then took a sip. "Who would not be sad and angry, to lose your mother that way. To never know your mama." He turned to Sal. "So you see, Marco, when I see my Isabel smile like-a that, like-a she did tonight, after she sing-a for the people, when I see such happiness on the face of my daughter, happiness like-a I never see before—then I must come to you and say *grazie*, Signor Toledano, *grazie* for what you have give to my little girl. And to me."

Okay, okay. I'm a wonderful human being. What do I win?

"Marco," Giovanni began, "I wanna you to considerate something, okay?" *Okay!* "I wanna you to be Isabel's teacher. I wanna you to teach her how to be a singer, the way that tonight she tells me you have been doing on the ship. You have no job now. The captain McLeish, he fire you, no? So now I wanna hire you, okay?"

Sounds fucking great to me. I get to stay in hiding and *work with Isabel.* "Well, I don't know, Signor Gemelli. There are lots of other places I could play, you know. I get offers from all over the world. I was just sitting here trying to decide which would be best for my career."

"Yes, yes." Giovanni nodded. "I understand you are very good, very popular, many people want you to play the piano, but you must understand, we are talking about my daughter. Is very *importante* to me. I will pay you very well."

Love them words. Sal smiled at Giovanni. "I'm sure we can come to some kind of terms."

"Yes, and you must understand, you will have a Gemelli de Janeiro company apartment for you to live, and an auto. These are all how you say—*preaks?*"

Sal's smile broadened. "Perks."

"*Si. Perks.* That is the word." He straightened his deformed body as much as it could be called straightened. "*Bene.* Issa deal, yes?" He extended his clawlike hand, and Sal shook it to seal the agreement.

"Tell me, Marco. Is very exciting. How you gonna do it? I mean, she is very good, my Isabel, no? An *artista.* What you do first? Does she need the *scalas,* like the opera? Do-re-mi-fa-sol-la-ti-do? Practice, practice, practice—this is *primo,* no?"

"Actually noooooo—" Sal drew out the word.

"No, no, of course not," Giovanni said eagerly. "I am so *stúpido.* Isabel is no fat opera cow! She is beautiful, glamorous, like a cinema star. That's what you do *primo!* You take her to nightclub, she sing the samba, eh?" His eyes danced with excitement. "All of Brazil will love her!"

Sal thoughtfully scratched Dago Red's scar under his beard.

"Well, not really, Signor Gemelli," he began slowly. "You see, Isabel may be a Brazilian citizen, but she's a very American singer."

"Ahhhh—" Giovanni said, furrowing his brow in his effort to comprehend.

"And I have never believed nightclubs are the place to pursue a singing career, you know what I mean, Signor Gemelli?" He didn't, so Sal pressed on. "You see, nightclubs, discos, lounges—that's not the music business, Signor Gemelli, that's the *liquor* business. The whole thing's geared toward selling alcohol, not music, you see what I'm saying? All an entertainer gets in a nightclub is *older.*" *Take me, for example.* "I don't want Isabel to hafta go through that sh— that garbage."

"Ahhh, *io capisco,*" Giovanni said, pretending to understand and watching Sal closely.

"Records, Signor Gemelli. The recording industry. CDs. Cassettes. Airplay. It's the only way to go. *That's* the music business. What I would love to do," Sal's eyes danced with enthusiasm, "is take Isabel into a twenty-four-track studio and make some demos—some demonstration tapes—and then go to the big international labels with them. Maybe four songs, all originals. Three dance cuts and a ballad, probably, whatever comes out the best in the mix, and then try to peddle them in one of the big music centers—"

"Yes," Giovanni agreed, trying to keep up, to contribute, "New York, Hollywood, yes."

No, not yet. Can't go back to the States just yet. "Actually, sir, I was thinking more of London."

"Ah, of course, you have business associates there."

"Well, certainly, but it's more that the English market is more open to new talent, you know what I mean. America's a hard nut to crack." *And a dangerous one.* "We get a foothold in England, *then* we invade the States."

"I see, I see." Giovanni kneaded his knobby hands together. "But tell me, Marco, I know my Isabel is very good—very good for, how you say, beginner, but she is ready for this? For to make records?"

Sal stared at Giovanni a long moment, formulating his reply. Then he said, "It's kinda a pet theory I have, sir. That certain rock and roll artists—not many, very few, one a generation or so—that certain artists should be, *have to be,* recorded, *captured,* at the very beginning of their career." He leaned forward on his suitcase, enforcing his point. "Elvis, Jackie Wilson, Otis Redding, the Beatles—they went right from the corner drugstore to the Top Ten. Because they were real special. Like they were already *ready,* waiting on that street corner. They were already formulated, kinda. And their being so young had nothing to do with being so talented. Just gettum into the studio! That's what rock and roll is all about, and I think Izzy is that kind of talent."

Giovanni cocked his head a little to the side. *"Izzy?"*

Sal smiled. "Just a nickname."

The little man studied Sal a bit longer, and then said, "Marco, is one thing we must discuss."

Aw, shit, what is it? He's gonna tell me to keep away from his daughter. That fucking Isabel is a deal-breaker.

"One thing I must ask you."

"Of course, Signor Gemelli."

Giovanni fidgeted a moment, fooling with his cane.

"Is very difficult."

C'mon, old man. Don't leave me out here twisting in the wind. "Please, Signor Gemelli. You can ask me anything."

Giovanni's eyes were dark and sorrowful, a Renaissance Christ suffering the agonies of the Cross. "Marco, tell me. Are you dying with the AIDS?"

Sal stared uncomprehendingly at Giovanni for a moment. Then he understood, and threw back his head and laughed riotously.

BOOK V

RIO DE JANEIRO—NOVEMBER

Rio was a whorehouse. A long, curving, beachfront, open-air, tropical whorehouse. Even the ocean, breaking in on the narrow sand strip of Copacabana Beach, smelled like hot, urgent semen, oozing down the dark thigh of a sweating slut. And like all brothels everywhere in the world, along with the sense of sexual hunger and the promise of fulfillment, there was a sublimated but ever-present atmosphere of danger, the possibility of violence or passion around every corner, behind every door, in everyone's eye. Ragtag armies of thin, dusty boys roamed the dirty black-and-white tiles of the Avenida Atlantica and stared openly at the wristwatches and cameras of the tourists on their way to the warm sands of the beach. At night the taxis drove right through the red traffic lights rather than take a chance on stopping at the wrong intersection and getting robbed. From the seventh-floor window of his Gemelli de Janeiro corporate apartment overlooking Copacabana, Sal could watch the hookers ducking behind cars and into doorways when the foolish-looking little yellow police cars cruised slowly by, their blue lights constantly flashing. Early on Sal had decided that the girls weren't hiding to keep from being arrested, but to escape a shakedown for a bribe or a blow job. Rio was that kind of town. The ghettos spilled down the hillsides; the middle classes lived in the flats in a kind of muted comfort, like Sal's apartment and everything else in Rio, as if no one wanted to chance antagonizing the hordes of hopeless poor.

In the hot, sultry nights Sal strolled the wide, black-and-white mosaic sidewalk along Copacabana Beach, and the whores were like roaches, they were so many and so brazen. Blond whores, black ones, and others in every possible shade and hue in between. They came up to him on the street and stroked his crotch as they offered their services. Uninvited, they sat beside him as he ate his dinner at an open-air café and suggested various combinations and pleasures, with women of all ages and perversions. Sal smiled and joked with them—he had worked in joints with hookers since he was fourteen, so he was more than comfortable with them—but these girls were so desperate and persistent that sometimes he had to give them money just to leave him alone, much as he did to the bedraggled brown children who sold warm nuts in little paper cones with a kind of threatening pitifulness to the tourists drinking at the open-air tables along the Avenida. But it was cheap enough. The cruzado was like tiny Monopoly money, it was so weak against the dollar. Sometimes when Sal paid for things—a meal, a toucan-emblazoned T-shirt, a cab ride—he would calculate in his head the cost in dollars and embarrass himself into leaving a huge tip. And the inflation rate was something like 40 percent a month, 1300 percent annually. And climbing. The country seemed to exist on the edge of anarchy, on the verge of revolt. There was anger in the air, like the rusty odor of fresh blood, yet laughter could be heard on the streets at any time of the day or night, and the Cariocas walking to the beach in their string microbikinis were the most carnal-looking women Sal had ever seen. Their naked tan buttocks gleamed, and their brown breasts bounced, and they were as casual about their sexuality as a recumbent prostitute.

Rio was a whorehouse.

They recorded in a surprisingly modern 32-track digital studio in a high-rise office building in Flamengo, just around the bay from Sugarloaf. It was well equipped with a Roland R-8 drum machine, an Akai S-1000 16-bit sampler, an Emulator III, with hard disc, and a Yamaha grand piano, and everything was MIDIed—meaning they hooked all the synthesizers into one central patch and Sal controlled it all by flipping switches and playing one master keyboard. He put down all the parts himself—drum tracks, synth bass, layers and layers of punchy synthesized horn lines, percussive guitarlike pluckings, high single-note string fills—all played and controlled by Sal from his one master keyboard. Thank God his mother had stolen enough from Joe the Hack's pockets each week to pay for those five-dollar piano lessons at Miss Thibadoux's, even if the horny old spinster couldn't keep her hands off him.

Sal cut all the parts for four songs—"I Can't Get My Fill," another ballad, and two dance grooves he'd started writing on the *Antonea* and had finished here in the studio. The dance cuts were throwaway, balls-to-the-wall, get-up-and-shake-yo-ass rhythm riffs—totally engrossing and completely forgettable—but when Isabel began to record her vocals, she lifted the material to miraculous heights. The disposable disco tracks became sizzling, raucous party anthems. Saturday night specials, crackling with sexual tension and primitive energy. Just as Sal had expected, had hoped for, Izzy came into her own in the studio. This was where she was born to be. This was what she was destined to do. And now was the time to record her. In a year, or even a few months, she would be a different singer, more poised, more accomplished, maybe, but somehow not the same. This time was magical. She was fresh and eager and glowing with raw talent. Sal taught her his songs, then sat in the control booth with the Brazilian engineer and listened to her sing them in that fluid contemporary Billie Holiday voice, and he was blown away.

"Quem é ela?" Paulo the engineer wanted to know. "Who is she? What a voice! She looks so familiar."

"Isabel Gemelli," Sal replied. "Giovanni Gemelli's daughter."

"Of course!" the engineer marveled. "The Gemelli girl! *"É incrível!"*

Fueled by strong Brazilian coffee and cheap Peruvian cocaine, they worked straight through in marathon fourteen-hour sessions, not taking a day off for almost three weeks. Rather than grow tired, Isabel's voice sounded stronger and better each day, as if it had been imprisoned all these years and had needed only an opportunity for freedom and Sal's encouragement to send it off, soaring. And encourage her he did. He sat in the control booth, watching her through the big glass partition, her hands held up lightly touching her earphones as she sang into the massive, windscreened studio microphone, and he mouthed his lyrics along with her, his voice a whispery, unheard rasp. And when her phrasing didn't suit him, when she sang a lyric line not the way Sal D'Amore would've sung it, he stopped tape, and went into the vocal booth with her and croaked the phrasing while she listened intently, her eyes big and dark and thirsty for all this, so that after the second or third take Isabel's reading of the tunes was an amalgamation of Billie Holiday, Sal D'Amore, and all the thousands of influences—Chaka, Aretha, Ella, Stevie—that had entered her ears during her lifetime and been multitrack-recorded in the extraordinary tape recorder that was her mind. And all those personalities, all those colors, all those voices, like a choir of goddesses, stirred, simmered, synthesized, into this glorious, soulful, not-to-be-believed voice. This *new sound* that was Isabel's and Isabel's alone.

After three intense weeks of recording, and before they started the mix—the equalization of all the tracks—they took a day off. It was a Saturday, and the day they had their first argument. They were sitting under an umbrella at a coconut-festooned roadside refreshment stand on Ipanema Beach, drinking Cokes. Beyond them the beach was filled with sunbathers and girl-watchers. Shouting, dusky young men played an eternal game of soccer in the sand and tide.

"No!" she said with fiery resolve. "No!"

There was a hot breeze in from the sea, and it stirred her long, sun-streaked hair. Her body in her microbikini was golden brown, lithe but still girlish, with a healthy shimmer of baby fat.

"Aw, for Chrissakes, Izzy. The whole world knows the Gemelli name. The whole fucking world! Why don'tcha wanna use it?"

"No! If I use my name like that, the whole world will say I'm no good enough to be a singer on my own. They will say I am a joke, like that Princess Stephanie, and that my father *buys* a record career for me."

Sal leaned in out of the sun.

"Iz, listen to me. You think this is an easy thing to do, get a record contract? You think they give 'em away on the fucking sidewalk? You think just 'cause we did a hot demo and you're this great new talent, you think that's a lock on being successful in the music business?" She looked away, refusing to answer. "Well, it ain't. There's a hundred things you gotta consider. Timing is important. Contacts. Playing the right tune for the right guy at just the right time. It's luck. It's a crapshoot. And you need every little edge you can wangle. Being the only heir of the founder of the Gemelli de Janeiro leather-goods empire is just that kind of gimmick. It's interesting. It's hot. It's sexy. It's—"

"No, Marco!" she said angrily, whipping off her sunglasses. "I want to be called Isabel. *Isabel,* like that. Just one name, like Madonna, like Prince." She ran her hand through her long hair. She didn't shave her armpits. "Isabel. Isabel. I love it, no?"

Christ, Sal fumed, *not even finished recording her first* demo, *and she's already the temperamental* artiste.

"Aw, Izzy, those one-name names have been done to death. That's some tired shit." He studied her for a moment. "What was your mother's name, before she got married?"

She shaded her eyes with her hand and squinted at him. "My mother? My mother's name was Mendes."

Sal thought about it for a while. "No, that's no good. Everyone in the world only knows one Brazilian, and that's Sergio Mendes. We don't want people thinking you're an update of Brazil '66."

Isabel had opened a magazine that was lying on the table and was flipping through the glossy pages.

"Everyone in the world knows who Pele is," she said absently.

Sal sipped his tepid Coke. "Who's Pele?"

She shaded her eyes again, looking to be sure he wasn't joking, and then she laughed lightly, a warm, free sound. "Ah, you Americans, you think you *are* the world."

"Canadian. I'm Canadian."

She shrugged. "Canadian, American, it's all the same. Marco, look at this." She pushed the magazine across the table. "Read this article."

Sal squinted down at the sun-drenched page. "What is this?" INTERNATIONAL MUSIC FESTIVAL the advertisement headlined. JANUARY 25–30. THE PALAIS, CANNES.

"Read it," Isabel urged.

"An Annual Convention of Producers, Writers, Artists & Music Marketeers from Around the World! Representatives from Eighty-Six Countries! Major Record Deals Every Year!" *Hey, wait a minute!* "Live Performances by Major Artists! Symposiums and Workshops!" *Skip that shit!* "New Acts Premiered in Annual Televised Competition!" *Very interesting.* Then the advertisement went on to list a dozen of the annual competition winners who had gone on to fame and fortune in the industry. *I am impressed,* thought Sal, as he recognized several of the names. Very *big* names.

"Where is this Kan-nez?" he asked her.

"Oh, Marco," she chided. "That's *Con.* Haven't you ever heard of *Con?*"

"Sure, sure." He looked at her. "That's in—in—"

"It's on the Riviera. In the south of France."

Very good. Very good. Anywhere but the States was very good. He went back to the top of the article. JANUARY 25–30.

As if she were reading his thoughts she said, "Do you think we can be ready by then?"

Sal gave her a smile. "Looks like we'll have to be."

She was excited, but apprehensive, too. "Am I good enough, Marco? Will they like me?"

Sal leaned back on his flimsy metal chair. "They gonna love you. They gonna eat you—"

Just then a soccer ball crashed on the table with a hollow bounce, sending their glasses and bottles skittering over the tabletop. Sal lost his balance, and the light metal chair began to tip backward. He pinwheeled his arms in a cartoonish effort to stay upright, but the chair collapsed under him, and he landed on his back in the sand with a soft thud.

"Oh, Marco!" Isabel shrieked with laughter. "Are you okay?"

With as much dignity as he could muster, Sal picked himself up and began to slap the sand off his trunks.

"Marco," she cried, "you should have seen yourself. You were *so* funny!"

Sal eyed her balefully and muttered, "Ha-ha-ha—" just as a well-built and graceful young man with hot-chocolate skin trotted up from the beach.

"I am so sorry. It was a bad kick and—Isabel! *Oi gatinha, tudo bem?* I didn't know you were back."

Sal saw her affect a more mature demeanor. "Claudio!" He leaned over, and they kissed each other on both cheeks. "I found Swiss schools too—too—too *Swiss,* so I broke out." She giggled haughtily. "I've been back for a month."

"Then why haven't I seen you at Jazzmania or Disco Voador?" The young man had blue-green eyes and a patina of gleaming sweat under the mat of hair across his chest.

"Oh, haven't you heard? I'm making an album. I've been in the studio."

"An album? I didn't know you could sing!"

Isabel gave him a coquettish smile—a schoolgirl's taunt. "Well, you don't know everything, do you, Claudio?"

Sal plucked the black-and-white ball out of the sand and tossed it over the table to the young man. Claudio caught it easily and looked at Sal directly for the first time.

"Claudio, this is my producer, Marco Toledano." The young man extended his hand, and Sal shook it. "Claudio is an old friend," Isabel said to him.

"How ya doin'?" Sal asked.

"*Bem,*" Claudio replied, and then turned his attention back to Isabel. He knelt beside her chair and rested his hand lightly on her shoulder. He began to speak to her in Portuguese, using a soft, intimate tone. Isabel inclined her head toward him, reached up and traced her fingers over the back of his hand.

Sal stared at them a moment, then became aware of himself. He tried to set up his collapsed chair in the sand, but the fall had twisted it beyond repair. He looked at Isabel again, and the young man, still speaking to her, had insinuated his hand under the top of her microbikini and was gently massaging her breast just above her nipple. The expression on Isabel's face was hidden behind her wide sunglasses. Sal couldn't tell if she was enjoying it. They were as natural and unselfconscious as children playing in the sun, and Sal stared at them another few seconds before raising the ruined metal chair over his head and flinging it toward a nearby fifty-gallon oil-drum trash can. The chair banged loudly with a hollow *clank* against the side of the yellow oil drum, and the young man looked up sharply at Sal. Sal grinned at him. "Missed."

The young man straightened and smiled down at Isabel in

her lounge chair. "I'll call you." Then, without another glance at Sal, he clutched the ball and began to trot back toward his fellow players, waiting on the edge of the surf. Before he had gone a few steps, he dropkicked the ball back into the playing area, and a shout went up from the young men.

Sal dragged another chair over from an empty table and plopped down angrily.

"You always let men fondle you in public like that?"

Isabel slowly pushed her Ray-Bans back over her hair. Her face registered amused surprise. "Marco, you are jealous."

"No, I'm not," Sal said resolutely. "I just don't think you should do things like that."

Her face darkened just a little. "My father doesn't tell me how to behave. Why should you?"

Sal's hands moved nervously over the table, righting fallen Coke bottles, sweeping aside melting ice cubes. "I—uh—it doesn't look good." He pointed a concerned finger at her. "If you're gonna be in show biz, you hafta understand you're always gonna be in the public eye, you know what I mean? People will be watching you all the time."

"Marco, I *grow up* on this beach."

Sal shook his head. "It don't matter. Who was that dude, anyway?"

"Just an old friend." She smiled then, ready to tease him. "An old lover."

"Christ, that guy was twenty-five years old! And you *sixteen!* When did you find time to have *old* lovers?"

She took her sunglasses from the top of her head and laid them on the table.

"Marco, please, do not tell me what to—"

"You said I could! Remember, on the ship? You said you would do anything I tell you."

She studied him. A woman's countenance over her teen-aged features. "About things professional. Not personal."

Sal's hands fidgeted with his cigarette pack. "That's what I'm trying to tell you, Izzy. In this business it's all professional, there ain't no personal. You get a reputation for being *fuckable,* and everybody's gonna want some. They'll turn you into a whore." *Case in point, Sal D'Amore.*

"I think you worry too much." Then she gave him a sly, slow smile. "And I think you are jealous."

Sal busied his hands lighting a cigarette. "I'm just concerned." He looked at her. "I mean, we're business partners, right? I gotta look after my investment, right?"

Isabel studied him awhile, then she put her sunglasses back on and languidly rose from her chair. Her body possessed the kind of intrinsic awesome beauty usually associated with natural phenomena—a jungle waterfall, a jaguar stretching in the sun, a *papoula* in bloom. "Come. I want to show to you something."

She drove a red Ford Escort XR3 convertible, which seemed to be the vehicle of choice for spoiled daughters of rich Cariocas, and she drove it fast, even by Rio standards. They zoomed along the beach at Le Blon, then around the rocky cliffside highway to São Conrado, with its big, beachfront Miami-style hotels, and then inland and uphill to a place not found on any map of Rio de Janeiro.

"That is Rocinha," Isabel indicated, nodding her head toward the sprawling mountainside ghetto they were fast approaching. "Is the biggest slum in the world. A million people live there, they say. My mother was from there." She roared the red convertible around a junk-laden truck struggling its way up the steep, curving Avenida Niemeyer, and the driver blew his horn, and the grimy workers hanging on to the truck's sides shouted a welcome. "Isabel! Isabel!"

She waved at them and tooted the convertible's horn in answer. Then she turned to Sal with a wide grin on her face. "I am famous in Rocinha, in all of Rio, but especial in Rocinha," she shouted over the convertible's backwash. "You will make me famous in all the world!"

"Is that what you want?" he shouted back.

"Yes! Yes!"

I can dig it, Sal thought. *I can certainly dig it.*

At the top of the mountain she parked the XR3 on the side of the two-lane highway, on the edge of the sprawly *favela.* Looking down the slum's narrow streets—alleys, really—was like peering down into a teeming anthill. Or a cliff-dwelling community from another millennium. The hard-packed white-dusted thoroughfares swarmed with sullen-looking men, half-naked children in a rainbow of colors, alert little feral dogs. Sal turned and looked back the way they'd come up the mountain, at the big hotels on São Conrado Beach and the ocean beyond.

"Is a million-dollar view, eh?" Isabel laughed lightly. "And they give it to the poorest people in Rio."

"Look over there." Isabel pointed, and Sal saw a police van parked on the roadside a hundred yards up. The brown-uniformed cops were talking to a pair of teenage girls. "They will not go into Rocinha," Isabel said. "The people will throw stones at them. Shoot them, even." She came over and stood closer to Sal. "Ten years ago the people of Rocinha have no electricity, no water, no sewage. The government will do nothing. So the local *mafia,* they come in and give the people lights, toilets, faucets, and now the *favelados*—the people of the *favela*—they protect the gangsters. The *mafia,* they sell *maconha,* cocaine, guns—whatever, and no one in the *favela* says nothing to the police."

Sounds just like the Ninth Ward to me, Sal thought. "Is that why we're here? To buy some weed?"

Isabel laughed, then smiled mysteriously. "Maybe, Marco. Maybe."

And then a horde of children ran toward them up the dusty gray street. "Isabel! Isabel!" they shouted, and their dirty faces wore their love for her.

"Ah, my poor little ones," she laughed. "Which do you want this time, coins or candy?"

"Candy," the littlest ones begged; "Coins," shouted others; and a few of the cheekiest demanded, "Both! Both!"

Isabel's face wore an expression of mock outrage. "Who said both?" she barked. "Who said both?" And there was an infectious outbreak of giggling, and then one of the prettier little girls said, "Miguel! Miguel wanted both!"

"And which one is Miguel?" Isabel asked, her fists cocked on her hips.

The children all looked around at each other. *No one wants to finger him,* Sal thought. *I don't think snitches last too long around here.*

Finally a tall, dirty boy in a tattered Guns n' Roses T-shirt stepped forward, his eyes downcast but wearing a smug little smile. *It's a game. They've all played this game before.*

"Are you Miguel?" Isabel demanded.

The boy nodded.

"Well, Miguel, you will someday be a rich man, because

you have the *coragem* to ask for more than they want to give you." She turned to her convertible, reached down under a seat, and came up with a bulging paper bag. She held it up before the children and shouted, "Both! Coins and candy!," and the boys and girls screamed their approval.

After she had dispensed the chocolate bars and the one-*cruzado* pieces and then left the children to guard her car, they walked down the sloped, dusty alleys into the heart of the *favela*, and she asked him, "Did you understand what we were saying?"

"I understand that they love you."

And as they went into the slum's very bowels, people all along the way greeted her with friendly deference. *"Boa tarde, Isabel." "Como vai?"* And some of the older women reached over to simply touch her, while mothers wanted to show her their babies.

"They all love you," Sal said.

She was wearing a baggy oversized T-shirt over her bikini, and open-toed sandals. "Is because of my mother. She became a legend in Rocinha because she got out, she married a rich man, even if she only lived eleven months after. So they think I am lucky. They think I will make them lucky."

I think you're gonna make me *lucky.*

"Look at them," she told Sal, and as they walked, he could see that Rocinha was no depressive welfare society. There was bustling activity everywhere. Open-air upholstery shops, tiny little grocery stores that sold everything from chewing gum to beer, automotive-repair garages with grease-blackened yards, narrow fix-it shops that would recycle anything the richer Cariocas threw away. "They are the best people in the world," Isabel said. "And none of them ever get out."

"None of them?"

"None of them." Then she stopped in the street and smiled that strange smile again. "Except my *mamãe*—my mother."

They were before an electric-blue ramshackle house tottering on the edge of a steep precipice that overlooked a garbage-strewn gorge. Isabel raised her hand and pounded loudly on the peeling blue door with the ball of her fist.

"Wake up, you old pig!" she shouted in Portuguese. "I know you're in there, drunk and nasty! Open up!"

She pounded on the door for several minutes before the

door slid back a little and a slovenly, grossly obese old lady squinted out into the torrid sunlight.

"Isabel, *minha neta?* Is that you?" The skin on the fat old lady's face was tight and sickly pale, like a sausage gone bad, and she smelled of body odor and booze. "Is that you, my beloved granddaughter?"

"It's me, old hog." Isabel stepped back and pushed Sal into the doorway. "Look who I brought for you to see, you old whore. This is my record producer and songwriter. He is going to make me a great singer, and people all over the world will buy my records."

The old lady stepped out into the harshly lit street, and she looked even worse in the brightness. She was so fat, she had to squeeze through the door, and her huge billowing housecoat was stained and dirty.

"Ah, my beloved granddaughter," the old lady wailed. "I knew you wouldn't forget your poor grandmother." She tried to move closer to Isabel. "What have you brought me?"

Isabel dug into the paper bag and brought out a wad of cruzados circled with rubber bands. "Your blood money, old witch. The money you get for selling me to the cripple." She tossed the bankroll at Maria Mendes, but the old lady was too slow and too blind to see it coming, and it struck her cheek and bounced into the dust.

"Oh," Maria Mendes said, and then began to search around her immense bulk for the money.

"Hey, old whore," Isabel chided, "what do you think of this one? This man? Do you think he's got a pretty *pinto?*"

"Oh," the old lady repeated, and then spotted the cruzados lying in the street. She looked pleadingly at Isabel. "*Por favor, minha neta.* Pick up the money for me."

"*Fuck you, fat cow.* Pick it up yourself."

The old lady stared at the roll of money, then she pointed at it and began to blubber, tears streaking down her fat, unhealthy cheeks. "*Por favor! Por favor!*" she whimpered, like a child.

Sal didn't understand all the Portuguese, but he understood Isabel was torturing the old woman. He knelt and scooped up the money. Then he looked harshly at Isabel as he handed it to Maria Mendes. Isabel stared defiantly back at him.

"Obrigado, obrigado!" Maria Mendes moaned as she clutched his hand and held it to her filthy breast. *"Muito obrigado!"*

Isabel shook her head in disgust and turned to walk away. Sal watched her go as he tried to pull his hand away from the old woman's fatty clutches. *"Muito obrigado! Muito obrigado!"*

They sat in the parked convertible on the edge of the *favela.* Two teams of ragtag boys played soccer in the street fifty yards away.

"My mother hated her, so *I* hate her."

She kept her eyes forward and a petulant pout on her lips. While she almost always seemed mature far beyond her years, now she *looked* sixteen.

"Izzy, she's just a poor, fat old lady."

Isabel turned to him, and her face was twisted with hateful anger. "She sold my mother like she was a slave, she sold her like a whore!"

Sal threw up his hands. "Hey, maybe I'm not getting the whole picture. Lemme get it right. Are we talking about your father here?"

Isabel yanked the key, and the engine roared to life. "I don't want to talk about it anymore." She jammed the gearshift into reverse and stood on the accelerator. The XR3 wheeled around, and she threw it grindingly into "drive."

"Okay," Sal shouted over the rush of wind and engine, "that's fine with me. Let's go get something to eat. I'm starving."

Her face lit up as if from within, as if someone had flipped a switch, her smile was that radiant. "Oh, Marco, it's Saturday! The day for *feijoada*!"

"What the hell is *feijoada?*"

"The national dish of Brazil. And I know where they make the best *feijoada* in Rio."

Just over the crest of the mountain, only a few minutes' drive from Rocihna, was the hilly, treelined suburb of Gavea, the best address in the city. That was where the Gemelli mansion was. It was sheltered from the street by a bougainvillea-covered wall and several tall *palmeira* trees. Riding up the short curved driveway, Sal felt less a sense of *space* than of *privacy.* And the wealth it took to buy that privacy.

This place is right over the hill from where Isabel's mother lived. No wonder the old man found her. He went riding in his limo one day and spied her, his dick got hard, and he had to have her. If she looked anything like Izzy, man, I can understand it. And I'll lay 6-to-5 she was a handful, too. Just like her daughter. Sal had never met a woman—*a woman?*—like Isabel before. He'd known a lot of head cases, a lot of ladies who were damaged goods, and a whole bunch of just plain cunts, but he'd never run across someone like Isabel before. On the ship he'd thought he had her figured. He'd thought he could push certain buttons and get the desired results. He'd thought he could control her. But Sal D'Amore had never controlled a woman in his life. Sal D'Amore was a *mark,* and women knew it usually after only a few minutes with him.

"This is Zumira," Isabel happily announced, her arm around a huge ebony woman. "She was my wet nurse when I was baby. She was like mother to me." *Rich white kids and black mammies,* Sal thought. *Same as Louisiana.* They were standing in the Gemelli mansion's big, high-ceilinged kitchen, and the pungent odors wafting from the bubbling pots on the stove made Sal's stomach growl. Isabel and Zumira spoke to each other in the soft musical cadences of Brazilian Portuguese, then the two women looked at Sal, then back at each other, and then they burst into laughter, holding each other's arms and guffawing.

Sal tried to force a smile. "Uh—what's so funny?"

Izzy shook her head as she laughed. "Zumira likes little men. She says little men make the best lovers."

Sal felt he had to defend himself. "I'm five-six. Five-six ain't that fucking little."

Still chuckling, she took his arm and began to lead him out of the kitchen. "Zumira only meant to say she thinks you are handsome." She massaged his arm through his thin shirt as she escorted him through a wide, high entrance hall and into an enormous living room. The hot late afternoon was turning to warm dusk behind the tall French-shuttered windows, and Izzy snapped on a few lights. Then she motioned for Sal to sit on the long white couch. Sal had been in a home like this only once or twice before in his lifetime, and it had always been as a working pianist, never as a guest.

"We'll eat in a few minutes," she said, moving behind a

sleek, completely stocked bar. "I will fix you a drink." She twisted her lips, and in perfect Americanese barked, "What'll be, Mac?"

"Hey, that's very good," Sal complimented her as he sank into the sofa's deep cushions. "You got a one-in-a-million ear, Iz. Any Jack Daniel's behind there?"

She stooped to examine the rows of bottles on the back bar. "My father is Giovanni Gemelli. He has everything. Ah!"

She brought his drink and settled on her knees beside him on the sofa. Her body was a dark, sinewy shadow beneath her oversized T-shirt.

"Where is Signor Gemelli?" Sal asked as he tasted the liquor.

Isabel had poured a glass of red wine for herself, and now she took a sip and ran her tongue over her full lips. "My father is away on business. São Paõlo." She smiled at him then. "And since it is Saturday, all the servants are gone but Zumira, and after dinner I will drive her to Rocinha, where she lives with her man." She leaned her catlike back on the plush cushions and studied him through hooded eyes. "So, Marco. Are you afraid for to lose your virtue?"

Sal arched his eyebrows. *Sixteen? This bitch is sixteen?* "My virtue, huh?" He smiled back at her. "I put that someplace, but I can't remember where."

"You are not afraid to be alone with me?"

Sal took a sip of J.D. "In this world there are a lot of things I'm afraid of. Being alone with a girl is not one of them." *Walk that walk and talk that talk. Wait a minute—is this what you want? Is she what you want?*

Isabel studied him a long time. Then she raised her wineglass. "To us, Marco. To us."

Sal nodded. "I'll drink to that."

Feijoada was a deep pot of black beans, cooked to a thick, almost stewlike consistency, and flavored with pieces of salt pork, links of savory sausage, and whole pork chops. It was ladled over a plate of white rice, along with a side dish of *espinafre* greens, and seasoned with *farofa,* yucca root ground into a dust and sprinkled over the top of the *feijoada.*

"This shit is killer!" Sal said as he filled his plate with a third helping from the big glazed pot on the dining-room table.

"Marco, I have never seen you eat like this."

They were alone at one end of the long formal table in the narrow dining room. Isabel had lit the tall candles in the silver candlesticks. Billie Holiday at low volume was playing on the CD player. "God Bless the Child"

"You must be very, very hungry," she said, and packed each word with sexual tension.

"It's this food," Sal mumbled around a mouthful of sausage and bread. "This shit—you change a few of the seasonings, a couple of the flavors—this stuff is just like Noo Awlins red beans and rice. Some people there, they cook a pot of beans and then right away put it in the refrigerator for a few days, so it'll get thick just like this." With quick little snaps of his wrist he measured out droplets of a hot, spicy red salsa over the steaming black sludge. "This hot stuff is just like McIlhenny Tabasco, and these greens, hell, ain't nothing more Louisiana than a mess of greens." His eyes sparkled as he shoveled in a forkful of rice and beans. "Hmmmmm-*huh!*"

She had long since finished her meal, and now she sat back, sipping her wine, and watched him eat.

"Marco, you talk about New Orleans like you know it so well. Did you live there?"

Sal looked up from his plate. "Well, yeah, I played a few gigs there. Passing through, you understand."

Isabel leaned forward, her elbows on the long polished table. "It must be a wonderful place. All the music, the nightlife, the beautiful black people."

Sal smiled. "Yeah, people in Noo Awlins say the same thing about Rio. Small world, huh?"

Just then the cook stuck her face around a doorway and said something to Isabel. Isabel answered her, and then pushed away from the table. "I take Zumira home now. Her man is *doente*—sick." She stood up. "When you finish eating"—she grinned at him—"*if* you finish eating—you may look around the house, take a shower, whatever." She was moving toward the doorway. "If you want to take a nap, is all right. Any bedroom that is open is okay, okay?"

"Okay, Izzy," Sal said with his mouth full. "Thanks a lot."

A moment later there was the sound of a door closing, and then the familiar roar of her XR3 as the headlights washed over the house. Sal sat at the long table, the candles flickering and jazz floating softly from the speakers, and finished his plate of *feijoada.* Feijoda *my ass. Beans and rice is what it is. And not as good as Noo Awlins style, either. Still and all, I could eat this shit forever.*

He wiped his plate with a final piece of bread, then leaned over the pot, inspecting the remaining *feijoada. Shit, I gotta stop before I bust.* He belched loudly, then reached over and finished Isabel's glass of wine. *What a meal.*

At the bar he poured himself another J.D. Next to his hand was what looked like a humidor. He opened it carefully. *Cuban—what else?* He extracted a cigar, and lit it with a table lighter.

He strolled the house, smoking his cigar and sipping his tumbler of Jack Daniel's. *Hell of a house. I could force myself to be happy here.* He smiled to himself at that. *Yeah, I could find a way to be happy here.*

He went through the whole house, inspecting every room with an open door. *Jesus, it's as big as a fucking museum. To think that people* live *here. To think that* Izzy *lives here.*

The door to what had to be Signor Gemelli's office was ajar. Sal peeked in, then pushed the door open and entered. All leather and oiled wood, books and mementos, a standing globe. Sal stood in the middle of the room and turned on his sandals, taking in the feel of the room. *Man, you can tell no second-rate asshole works in here. This is the office of an important man, that's for damn sure.* On one wall was a huge, impressionistic painting of a big red parrot perched on a crook of wood. Sal stared at it for a full minute, wondering about its familiarity, before he realized it was the logo for Gemelli de Janeiro leather goods. He'd seen that trademark his whole life. Maybe pretty soon he'd be able to afford it.

He found a dark, empty bedroom with a bath, stripped out of his trunks, and showered. Standing under the hot water, he asked himself, *What the fuck am I doing here? What am I about to do with this girl?* Whatever it was, he was ready for it. He wanted it.

He dried off with an oversized plush towel, then wrapped it around himself and stretched out on the big double bed. *What a fucking life. Make great music in the studio all day, then come home to a house like this.* To a girl like Izzy? He yawned and turned over on his side. His drink and cigar were where he'd put them on the bedside table, along with his watch. It was a cheap Casio he'd bought in Montreal, and in the dimly lit bedroom Sal could make out the time and date, glowing in the dark: 10:37. SAT. NOV 26. Sal closed his eyes and was instantly asleep.

He awoke with a start and sat up on the side of the bed. He'd had a dream about his mother. Something about his mother's funeral. He was sixteen, standing in the back of Lamana, Pana, Fallo's Funeral Home, where his mother was laid out. Some of her Okie relatives had come down for the funeral, and they sat together in a group against one wall, looking all uneasy, country, and Protestant. There was one cousin, she was about eighteen, maybe nineteen, and she kept looking at him, looking at him, and around 2:30 A.M. of the all-night New Orleans wake, when the rest of them were asleep in their seats, she led him downstairs into the showroom where they displayed the different coffins, and leaning against the Celestial Oak Lined Model they tried to swallow each other's tongue until he couldn't stand it anymore and he yanked up her skirt, pulled out his dick, and right there against the Deluxe Celestial Model B-34 he pushed it in her, moved back and forth a few times, and immediately ejaculated, thinking, *I'm sorry, Ma.*

And then he was awake, covered with sweat, sitting in a towel on the edge of the bed, with the shadows of the *palmeira* trees moving on the wall. He looked down at his watch: 11:43. *Where was Izzy? Where was Isabel?* He stood up and walked to the door. Looking out into the empty hallway, he could hear a shower running.

"Izzy?" There was no answer. He tried a little louder. "Isabel?" Still no answer. *Probably can't hear me.* He went back to the bed, sat down, and reached for his cigar. He opened the drawer of the bedside table, searching for a match, but it was empty. His eye fell again on his watch: 11:44. SAT. NOV 26. *What was it about that time or that date? What was bothering him? It was 11:44, Saturday. Late Saturday night. On the twenty-sixth of November. Late in the month. On the last Saturday of the mon— That was it! The last Saturday of every month—Santo Pecoraro would be waiting for him—waiting for him in the Sazarac Bar of the old Roosevelt Hotel, now called the Fairmont—back in New Orleans. Waiting for Sal to call him if he needed anything. Do you think he's still waiting, what?—ten months later? For sure. Santo would be waiting a hundred years from now, if that's what he said he'd do. Well, Sal certainly didn't need anything—not the way things looked like they were going—but wouldn't it be a kick to talk to Santo, tell him he was in motherfucking Rio de Janeiro, in fucking Giovanni Gemelli's house, with Gemelli's daughter taking a shower just down the hall. Santo would just about fucking drop dead. What time was it in New Orleans? Two hours earlier? Three?*

Sal turned his head and shouted in the direction of the doorway, "Hey, Iz, I'm gonna make a phone call, okay?" *That made it official.* When she didn't answer, Sal picked up the phone.

The whole process took about five minutes. First he had to get an operator on this end who spoke English, then an overseas operator, then Information in New Orleans. Then the Brazilian operator placed the call and it rang six or seven times and Sal was just about to hang up when someone lifted the receiver and he heard the familiar sound of a bar in the midst of a Saturday night.

"Sazarac," said a faraway man's voice with that unmistakable New Orleans accent. Sal was suddenly awash in homesickness. *Yeah, right. Look around you, asshole.*

"Yeah, hello?" the voice asked again, not nearly as politely.

"Yeah, is Santo Pecoraro there?"

"I dunno, I'll see." And then the phone was dropped with a *thunk. You think he's really there?* Sal wondered. *You think Santo's really there, waiting for me to call? After all this time, you think—*

Someone picked up the phone, and then Sal heard Santo tentatively ask, "Who—who is this?"

"Where yat, man?"

Silent indecision on the other end of the line. "I don't recognize your voice."

"That's 'cause Dago Red took a piece of piano wire and—"

"Wait a minute!" Santo cut him off. Then Sal heard Santo say to the bartender, "Phil, I want to take this in your office." Then back to him, "Wait'll I get on the other phone." There were a few minutes of bar noise, and then a click as another phone was picked up and Santo said, "Wait'll he hangs it up."

There was another minute of muffled conversation, jukebox, laughter, and then Phil hung up the phone and Santo immediately said, "Sal. Sal."

"Guess where I am."

"Sal, Jesus, man—"

"C'mon, take a guess where I am."

There was a moment of silence, and then Santo said, "Sally, I can't play this—"

"I'm in Rio fucking de Janeiro, can you believe that shit?"

"Sal—"

"Guess whose house I'm at."

"Stop it, man!" Santo bellowed into his ear. "For Chrissakes, what the fuck's the matter with you?"

Sal was taken aback. "Hey, Santo—"

"Listen here, you go and fucking murder Red La Rocca and then call up six months later and wanna play fucking twenty questions?"

"Hey, that motherfucker had a heart attack trying to murder *me!* I didn't lay a hand on him."

"It don't matter how. Dago's dead, and they blame you."

"What the fuck I'm supposed to do, let the cocksucker strangle me?"

Santo didn't answer. Sal could hear him breathing on the other end of the line. In New Orleans.

Then Sal said, "Forget about them Venezias. How's Cathy? How's the boys?"

There was a long stretch of silence before Santo said, "You don't know, do you?"

Sal began to feel uneasy, right around the edges.

"Know what, Santo? I been on the run for almost a year."

"Jesus, Sal. Jesus."

Something was wrong. Something was very wrong.

"Hey, Santo, don't leave me hanging here."

Santo's voice sounded distant and echoey, like a man whispering in a mausoleum. "Aw, Christ, Sally."

"Fucking talk to me, Santo!" Sal barked. *But I don't wanna know.*

"It's your old man, Sal. It's Joe."

Joe the Hack, Joe the Hack. Either drunk—"What about him, Santo? Is he sick? Is he in the hospital?" *Christ, if Joe was sick, he'd have to go charity ward. He don't have a dime for—*

"Joe's dead, Sal," Santo said in a rush.

"Aw, Jesus. Aw, Jesus," Sal breathed into the receiver. "Poor old bastard." Sal waited awhile, waited for Santo to say something else. When he didn't, Sal asked, "What was it, his liver? I told him that cheap booze—"

"They kill him, Sal."

The old fear rose up out of the night and swallowed Sal whole. The old fear that he'd all but forgotten these last few months grabbed Sal's spine and raked its icy talons up and down his back. His hand holding the phone began to tremble. *Oh, God. Oh, God.*

"They thought he knew where you was. After you left, they thought he knew where you was. Then, when you kill Dago Red—"

"I didn't kill him!" Sal shouted into the receiver.

"—that's when they did him. Christ, Sal, I thought maybe you heard. It was in all the headlines."

Oh, Jesus! Oh, Jesus!

"What was in the headlines?" *Please don't tell me.*

Santo waited. He didn't want to say the words. *Don't tell me.* And the longer Santo waited, the more Sal's hands shook. Somehow the hot tropical night had turned freezing cold.

Then there was a sniff on the other end of the line. Santo was crying. *Don't tell me. Don't tell me.*

"You see, Sal," Santo began, his voice quavering with emotion, "they thought he knew where you was. They tried to make him tell where you was."

Oh, Sweet Jesus. Sweet Jesus, Son of God. Which art in heaven.

Santo was crying full out now. Bawling like a baby. He could hardly get the words out. "They tortured him, Sal. Oh, my God, they went at him with a—with a—a blowtorch—"

Sal's whole body began to shake violently. His leg thumped uncontrollably against the bed frame, and he had to hold the phone with both hands. He could see it. He could see it happening. He tried not to, but there it was. Poor little Joe D'Amore, stark naked and handcuffed to a chair, so scared he'd already shit on himself, squirted his bowels dry all over the floor, his eyes bulging and his mouth working with abject terror—*Joe the Hack, Joe the Hack*—encircled by Nicky Venezia and

Junior Venezia, maybe even Little Johnny, all of them standing around enjoying it, loving every minute of it. They were the kind of men who could enjoy this thing, who could work themselves into a self-righteous rage, a frenzied, bay-at-the-moon, killing thirst for blood and revenge. Sal, without knowing it, began to moan.

"I thought maybe you'd seen the headlines somewhere," Santo was saying between sobs. "Maybe you'd got holda the *Picayune* wherever you was—"

He heard his father's screams. He heard him plead for his life. He smelled the excrement and the scorched, smoking flesh. *Oh, Jesus, Jesus, Jesus, Jesus—* The fear was with him now, never to leave again. He'd forgotten it; for a while he'd taken his life for granted and simply enjoyed it; he knew now that he would never be able to do that again.

"'Cabbie Tortured in Gruesome Blowtorch Slaying,'" Santo was saying. "I thought sure you'd see it. They made it look like the niggers done it, made it look like a robbery or something. But everybody but the newspapers knows the truth."

Sal was crying now, too. The tears flowed like guilt. "He—Joe never knew where I was."

"I don't think it mattered, man. Once you killed Dago—"

"I didn't!" Sal screamed. *"I didn't!"*

"Sal," Santo said, "lissen to me. Wherever you are, you stay there, you hear me? You can't ever come back home. You can't ever come back here. And, Sal, don't call me again. I'm not gonna be waiting here Saturday nights anymore. You take care of yourself, but I gotta think of Cathy and the boys, you understand what I'm saying?"

"Santo—"

"I told you these people were animals, didn't I? I told you not to fuck with 'em, didn't I?"

"Santo—"

"Good-bye, Sal," Santo said, and hung up. Sal sat on the edge of the bed, shivering in the warm night. He held the phone until it started to hum, making him jump. *Oh, Sweet Jesus. Oh, Sweet Jesus.* Then the sobs came. Great heaving wails, like a drowning man fighting for his breath. *Oh, Joe. Oh, Daddy, please forgive me. Please forgive me. Oh, Sweet Jesus.* A boyhood memory flickered across the front of his mind: Joe cashing in a five-dollar winning ticket at the Fair Grounds, smiling and shaking his head, cackling with glee. "Love them long shots, Sally. They better'n a hot woman." Then the picture faded, fragmented, and was replaced by another. Joe was screaming, screaming, his mouth agape like a dead fish, as a sweating Nicky Venezia adjusted the flame on the acetylene torch. *Oh, Jesus. Oh, Jesus. Please forgive me. Please forgive me, my father.*

Sal twisted his hands in the sheets and clutched onto the bed and the tears rivuleted down his face and dripped onto his bare chest. He was shaking in violent spasmodic tremors. His teeth chattered, and his legs were jerking. *Please forgive me. Please forgive me.*

"Marco? Marco? Where are you?" Isabel came through the doorway from the lighted hall then, dressed in a long white robe and drying her hair with a towel. "There you are—*meu Deus,* Marco, what's wrong?"

Sal looked at her as if from an infinite distance. He tried to speak, but all that came from between his clattering teeth was a raspy moan.

She rushed to him. "Are you sick, Marco?" She brushed his hair back and felt his brow for fever. "What's wrong?"

Attempting to answer, he held up the phone receiver.

"You speak to someone?" she asked. "Is something you heard on the phone?"

Sal, still sobbing and trembling convulsively, forced himself to whisper, "My fa—my father—"

"Yes?" she said, taking the dead phone from his quaking hand. "Yes?"

He looked at her then, beseechingly. *Please help me. Please help me.* "—he died."

She sat beside him on the bed and put her arm around his shoulders. "Marco, I am so sorry. So sorry." She gently began to massage the back of his neck. Her hand was warm and tender. Through his tears, he could smell the soap on her skin, the shampoo in her straight, wet hair. "Will you have to go home?" she asked.

He shook his head. *Never. Never.* "It was a long time ago," he moaned. "I just found out." Then he began to cry even harder. He tried to will himself to stop, but it was as useless as telling his legs to be still. Between sobs he gulped for breath, like a frightened infant.

Isabel was deeply disturbed. She was accustomed to her own spells of bottomless grief, but had no mechanism for dealing with someone else's. "Please don't cry like that," she said in a low, crooning voice. "Please, Marco, it hurts me so."

"I'm sorry," Sal groaned. "I'm so sorry." *Please forgive me. Please forgive me.*

"Is okay, Marco," she said softly, and moved closer, until her side was pressed against Sal's. She draped both arms around his neck and put her face against his. "Please don't cry," she whispered. Then she licked at a tear coursing down his cheek. Sal moaned. Her wet hair traced across his shoulders, and her odor was sweet and erotic. She sipped the teardrops glistening in his bearded chin, and nuzzled her lips down his throat and along the scar around his neck. He felt himself harden, even as his body trembled.

Gently she pushed him back onto the mattress. The bed sheets were cool and dry against his bare skin, and he lay looking up at her in the shadowy glow of the hall light.

"Don't be sad, Marco," she whispered, then she lightly raked her fingernails down his chest and across his stomach. Sal's intake of breath was a soft hiss as she tugged at the fold in his towel and pulled it open. He felt the warm night air surround his hard penis like a goddess's mouth. "Don't be sad, *meu amor,*" she repeated; then, with a feathery touch, she stroked his flesh with her fingertips. Sal felt his cock strain upward, to meet her caress. She stood up and stepped back from the bed. Sal raised his head to watch her. She smiled at him from the soft shadows, then put her hands to her waist and unsashed her robe. Her robe hung open, and Sal could see her dark skin between the white folds. She gave her shoulders a simple shrug, and the garment slipped from her like a caress. Her body seemed to shine in the half-light. Her shoulders were wide and prominent; she had small, high breasts—like her mother's, but neither of them could know that—and a smooth, hard stomach. It was still a childish body, really, a schoolgirl's, still narrow and undeveloped—but Sal wanted her more than he'd ever wanted any woman.

"Isabel," he gasped. "Isabel."

She slipped over him, mounted him like a saddle, her still-damp hair cold and ticklish on his shoulders, her hard nipples dragging through his chest hair.

"Isabel—" he breathed.

"Shhhhhh—" she hissed back, and he felt the head of his hard cock slip into her like a knife into a jar of honey. She was hot and close, and he could smell her juices begin to flow. She tightened her vagina around his glans like a tender vise, then released him and let him slip out of her. He felt the chill of abandonment. Then she moved down, and her cunt sucked him up again. Then she squeezed and let him go.

"Oh, Jesus," Sal groaned. "Oh, Jesus," and there was no one else then. No one else in the world. No Santo Pecoraro. No Nicky Venezia. No Joe D'Amore with the gap-toothed scream. No Johnny Venezia. No one and no tomorrow. There was only him and her and tonight.

Isabel moved her body again, and he slid back into her. Smiling down at him, her stiffened arms holding her above, she clutched his dickhead again, and then was about to rerelease him when Sal said, "No!" gripped her narrow hips and pushed them down while he plunged himself deep up inside her. She shrieked with pleasure and flopped down on him, and he embraced her tightly and rolled their bodies over. Now, he was above her, plunging, plunging, plunging, and their bellies slapped together in wet rhythm. As he fucked her, he pushed her legs back until her knees were touching her cheeks and he whammed, whammed, whammed into her. "I love you!" he shouted. "I love you!" And then she raked his back from his hairline to his waist as she climaxed with a madwoman's scream.

CANNES—JANUARY

All the postcards in the hotel gift shop showed the town in lush green summer, with hordes of young Europeans on the warm sand beach and the bright blue Mediterranean beyond. But now, just outside the frosted windows, it was bitter winter. There were photographs of eager young starlets with proud naked breasts gleaming in the bright Côte d'Azur sunlight, while now there were daily snow flurries and the beaches were dark and empty, with no chairs and tables set out in the sand by the grand spun-sugar hotels that lined the Croisette, the main beachfront thoroughfare. The seasonal trees were bare and black; the palms drooped with shock from the icy winds. Only a few blocks away from the beach Cannes was a gray, charmless, provincial little town. On the beach it was a shuttered resort waiting for the summer sun.

Sal sat in a little café across the street from the Palais du Festivals, eating a breakfast croissant and drinking a cup of strong French coffee. For over an hour he had watched the steadily thickening crowds gather from the narrow side streets, cross the Croisette, and stream through the big glass doors of the Palais, where the weeklong International Music Symposium was starting this morning. Sal sat, slowly stirring his coffee. *What are you waiting for?* he asked himself. *There's no time like the present. It's the early bird that gets the worm. He who hesitates is lost.* Still circling his spoon in his *café au lait,* he smiled grimly to himself.

What are you afraid of? It ain't like it's the Venezias waiting for you over there. It's just a bunch of music people. A whole fucking convention *of music people. Like Shriners.* Sal lit a Gaulois and watched a tall dude with bright orange hair wait for the light to change. It had started to drizzle. *I mean, I been dealing with music people my whole fucking life. How long now? Christ, twenty years. Yeah, and how much success have you had, motherfucker? Where are the millions of teenyboppers who were supposed to cream at the mere mention of your name?* Two whiplash-thin English rockers in carefully tattered jeans entered the café and took the table next to Sal's. They were barely out of their teens. *Yeah, but this time I got something to sell. This time I got something special. So, what are you waiting for, Jack? Christmas? It's now or never. Use it or lose it. The longest journey—* Sal dropped some francs on the table and stood up. As he pulled on his new black cashmere overcoat, he caught a glimpse of himself in the mirror over the bar. *Damn,* he thought admiringly, *I look pretty good.* Isabel had bought him a whole new wardrobe, and the dark, fashionably cut suit he was wearing was only one of half a dozen she'd had tailored for him. Likewise the deep blue shirt he had on, buttoned at the collar, no tie, rock and roll entrepreneur all the way. His thick black hair was pulled back into a ponytail, and as he turned his head a bit, he could see the half-moon of filigreed silver that dangled from his left earlobe. Sal smiled at himself in the mirror, and wished it weren't raining so he could wear his shades.

Outside, the rain was still falling, and it was shockingly cold. Sal crossed the busy street as quickly as he could, ducking and dodging the little Peugeots and Fiestas. The uniformed Frog at the entrance to the Palais looked for Sal's laminated pass, and then indicated he should pin it to his lapel.

Inside the Palais the first thought that struck Sal was, *I wish I had the black leather-jacket concession in this fucking place.* There seemed to be thousands of rock and rollers moving purposefully in all directions. Spiked hair, spandex pants, and high-heeled boots looked to be de rigueur, along with a air of hip smugness, an aura of *knowing where it's at and not telling.* The place was ass-deep in attitude. The ratio of men to women was about a billion to one, and the average age was Trying to Look Younger. French girls in red blazers, obviously selected by the Palais for their multilingual beauty, were directing the hordes of young men down a wide stairway, and Sal allowed himself to be carried along in the crush. The next level, maybe an acre in size, was a rabbit warren of narrow booth-lined aisles that radiated out from the one central corridor. Each booth had a color-coded sign—yellow for radio networks, blue for record companies—that gave the company's name and its nationality. Right away, Sal saw a sign for Hugo Records—Hungary. *Hungary?* Sal elbowed his way out of the pack and pressed himself against a particle-board wall. The place was overwhelming. Smelling of new carpet, wet leather, and fresh paint, it was a bedlam of different languages and music. A combination Carnival celebration and Arab bazaar. There were safety-pin-in-the-cheek punks and dreadlocked reggae Rastamen. Zoot-suited New York Puerto Ricans and Finnish hard-rockers. Gold-chained Harlem rappers and soft-speaking world-beaters from Zaire. Directly across from Sal was a bank of television monitors—maybe fifty in all—and each one was showing a video of a different Swedish recording artist performing a recent single—in Swedish. Sal hadn't known there *were* fifty Swedish recording artists. And they seemed to be interchangeable—all of them bleached-blond Abba clones. Next to the Swedish booth was a Dutch heavy-metal stand. Monster guitar riffs blared from the company's own mounted speakers, and the stand's primary decoration was a lurid Frank Frazetta-ish painting of an impossibly full-breasted young girl bound by skin-piercing barbed wire. Fat droplets of rich red blood streaked down her fat white titties. Two middle-aged Japanese men in conservative business suits stood in front of the poster, carefully inspecting it as if to analyze its marketing strategies. They spoke only to each other, and even took notes.

Jesus H. Christ! The place was a zoo. A thousand-ring circus. A madhouse dedicated to sound. Sal hadn't been in the Palais ten minutes, and he was already discouraged, overwhelmed. *What the fuck was he doing here? He was a piano player, for Chrissakes, not a businessman. Why had he thought he could sell anything to anybody? Everybody here probably had a Ph.D. in business or something. They studied flow charts and qualitized year-end graphs; they projected sales and anticipated volume. They all knew more than he did. More than—*

"Are you looking for new acts?" Sal heard someone say in

a flat, Kennedyesque Boston accent. He turned to look at a skinny, pimply-faced kid in green leather pants talking to an overweight girl sitting behind the counter at the next booth.

"Vat kind of acts?" the overweight girl said. She was French, and the sign over her head confirmed it.

"Thrash metal," the kid in the green leather pants answered eagerly.

The girl shook her head. "Ve are onzy interested in dance."

The kid was gone before the girl finished the sentence. She went back to what she'd obviously been doing before being interrupted—filing her nails. Sal stared at her a full minute, passing people jostling him on either side, then sucked in his gut and walked the ten feet to her counter.

"I have a great new dance act," Sal heard himself say. The words didn't excite her, but when her eyes lifted and took him in, she smiled brightly. She was done up in what could only be called international rock chic: layers of black lacy fabrics, dangling oversized silver earrings, teased atomic-bombed hair, pale skin, and vivid makeup.

"Ve are onzy interested in dan—"

"I got a great new act. Girl singer. You're gonna love her."

Her smile was constant but quizzical. "Dance?" She pronounced it *dunze*.

"Got a coupla killer dance tracks." He held the cassette tape out to her. She looked at it in his hand, then opened an appointment book that lay before her.

"Ven vould you vish an appointment?"

Sal smiled at her, trying not to look too stupid. "When?"

She consulted her appointment book. "Day after tomorrow. Eleven-thirty?"

Her ratted hair was parted in the middle, and Sal could see her white scalp. "Uh—what about right now?"

She snapped her eyes up to his. "Now?". Pronounced *noo?*

He gave her his widest, most charming, it-must-be-heaven-in-your-panties smile. "If you could do that for me, wow—"

She returned the grin and stood up. "I vill see vat I can do." She turned on her heel and strode the few steps to a makeshift door in the hastily assembled particle-board cubicle behind her. Her ass was a Gallic yard wide. Just before she turned the knob, she looked back at him in hunger. "Vat hotel are you staying?"

"The Martinez."

"Ah, the Mar-ten-*nezzzzz*." With a very French inflection. "I will see you there, in the bar. Everyone goes there after dinner." She gave him a carnal once-over, then opened the flimsy door and stepped through. Sal spent the next few seconds quickly canvassing the dozens of album jackets stapled to the booth's particle-board walls. They were all Frenchies. Not one artist he recognized. Well, the international market was a whole new ball game. Over here, they probably wouldn't know who the hell the Neville Brothers were.

The door opened, and the secretary, or receptionist—or whatever she was—came back out. She nodded at Sal with a knowing smirk. "Monsieur Lacombe will see you now." She stepped back to let him pass. "My name is Clarice," she whispered as he went by.

It was a tiny, unroofed square maybe eight-by-eight, with new white walls hastily decorated with a few eight-by-tens and more album covers like the ones outside. There was no desk, only three uncomfortable-looking plastic chairs, a low, narrow table, and a miniaturized Japanese sound system against one wall. Monsieur Lacombe was an untidy-looking middle-aged Frenchman in a white business shirt with rolled-up sleeves. He was seated on one of the uncomfortable-looking chairs, smoking a cigarette and reading an American *Billboard* magazine. He looked up expressionlessly when Sal entered and held out his hand. Sal took it to shake, and only when the fingers hung listlessly in his did Sal realize the Frenchman had been asking for the cassette tape. Quickly he fished the cassette from his pocket and gave it to Monsieur Lacombe. *Wait'll you hear this, you Frog fuck. Wait'll you hear this.*

Lacombe slipped in the tape and punched the "play" button. "Do you have any photographs of the artist?" He sounded like the actor who does the Perrier commercials.

Fuck! Sal cursed. *This guy is eight-by-ten crazy. But wait'll he hears her. Wait'll he hears Isabel.* "Uh, no, I'm sorry I don't. But she's very beautiful."

Lacombe looked at him with something resembling scornful pity. "Yes, I'm sure she is."

At that moment, over the muted cacophony of all the Palais sound systems bleeding into each other, the cubicle was filled with the gently rhythmic chords of the intro to "I Can't Get My Fill," the first tune on the cassette. *Lissen to this, you French fuck.* The Frenchman looked quizzically at Sal, then Isabel's warm, wonderful, one-in-a-million voice floated into the air. *Lissen to that! What'll you think of—*

Lacombe reached over and choked Isabel off with a single poke at the "pause" control.

"Hey!" Sal cried.

"I want only dance material. Do you have dance material?" He was staring at Sal with something like open hostility.

"Yeah, sure. Further on in the tape."

Lacombe fast-forwarded the tape. Sal could hear the gentle *whirrrrr* sound.

"You didn't give a good listen to that first song," Sal said, in what he imagined was an aggressively businesslike voice. "I represent a very unique and—"

"This company," Lacombe interrupted him unceremoniously, "is only dance-oriented. Club music. New beat. Boom—boom—boom—boom." He pounded his fist softly on his crossed leg. "Only."

Yeah, disco. You mean disco, but you call it everything but that.

The Frenchman poked his finger at the tape recorder's controls, the *whiirrrrr* sound stopped, and a second later the speakers emitted Isabel's voice caught in the middle of a phrase on the second tune on the tape. Another ballad. Lacombe didn't even hesitate before he punched "eject." The cassette popped out like a burned piece of toast.

"I use only dance material," Lacombe repeated, holding out the rejected cassette.

"Wait a minute," Sal complained. "There are four uptempo cuts on there, later on."

The Frenchman stared unblinkingly. "Perhaps. But I don't have time to search for them. Thank you very much." He waggled the cassette. Sal reached out numbly and took it.

"You're making a—" He gulped. Suddenly he was dry-mouthed. Suddenly the cubicle was very close, very warm. "She's an incredible talent."

Lacombe already had his nose back into the *Billboard.*

"Dance. Only dance." Without raising his eyes, he began to light another cigarette.

Sal turned and opened the door. Everything was so small, he was already outside before he realized it. The fat receptionist looked up from her nails with a hopeful expression, but when she saw Sal's face, she knew he had been shot down, along with any chance she'd had of sleeping with him.

But not being a quitter, she brightly piped up, "So. I vill look for you tonight at the Martinez bar." Mar-ten-*neezzzzz.* "Okay?"

Sal looked at her dumbly, uncomprehendingly. He gave her a wan, forced smile and stumbled off. One step away from the booth, and he was caught up in the black leather rock and roll crush. He heard two members of a Danish metal band arguing hotly in their inpenetrable native language. A group of Spanish music publishers beside him were laughing and telling dirty jokes. The crowd practically carried him past a German video stand where they were giving away bratwurst and pretzels to anyone who wanted some. A booth representing Castro's Cuba was blaring out hot salsa, and the one opposite was selling obscure, previously unlicensed recordings by Charlie Parker. Life-sized blowups of Bird were splashed across the front of that stand. Bird in Paris. Bird on Fifty-second Street. Bird and Diz. Bird, Bird, Bird. Sal wandered into another aisle, and it was all videos. Madonna, Springsteen, Michael Jackson—all the big American acts. An adjacent booth ran soft-porn videos by some topless girl band from Norway. Pale pink nipples flattened by candy-apple-green guitars. The next corridor was devoted to compact discs. CDs up the wazoo. CDs from every nation on earth. CD releases of artists nobody ever wanted to hear on vinyl. Sal bumped into three beautiful black girl singers from Amsterdam who spoke only Dutch, and a Polish band from Warsaw that played R&B exclusively. There were managers, agents, artists, and songwriters. Promoters, packagers, and producers. Has-beens, wannabees, the hopeful and the promising. Thieves, con men, and drug dealers. American record executives who just wanted an expense-accounted trip to the Riviera—even in January—and English carpenters who had come over the Channel to set up the booths and now were wandering the halls, looking for pussy. There were singers from Stockholm, San Juan, and Sacramento—all hoping to get discovered, and washed-up old Brill Building Jews from Manhattan, trying to ignite the fire one last time, searching for an undiscovered Carole King or Neil Sedaka. There were thousands and thousands of people, from dozens and dozens of countries, and they all seemed to know each other and what they were doing.

Except for Sal.

It took him almost an hour to get up enough nerve to try his next appointment. A sweet little man from Brussels told Sal he was very sorry, very sorry, but Isabel was too "American" for the European market. After that there was a pale German kid, barely out of his teens, who already owned his own record company and distribution network, but was looking only for heavy metal; another Frenchman, this one in a black White Snake T-shirt, smugly imparted the insider industry information that girl acts were passé, out, dead, and did Sal have any cute American boys to sell? Preferably black. Light-skinned black American boy singers were all the rage that year in Paris. There followed an intense, attractive dyke from Munich, who glared at Sal as if she were angry he was so easy on the eyes, and who only signed gay and lesbian artists; a charming silver-haired gentleman from Milan who finally admitted to Sal he hardly listened to music anymore, and was here in Cannes as a vacation from his horrid wife. A fat little burgher from Liechtenstein with bad breath kept bragging he had the biggest and best record company in his whole country. Actually, Sal learned, he had the *only* record company in Liechtenstein, and a hit record there was one that sold anything over a hundred copies.

After that all the faces and refusals seemed to blur and bleed together, like the facades of the hundreds of booths, like the noise of all the competing sound systems. Sal wandered the crowded aisles, bumping into people, haltingly making appointments, and getting rejected in a dozen different languages. *What's wrong with them? Can't they hear what's there? I can't believe what's happening here.* He staggered drunkenly for hours, smiling sickly and fumbling out his cassette for men who held power over him to listen, give him a phony smile, and then refuse him. It was an exercise in humiliation. *How can things go wrong like this?* Everything in his life had been going along so smoothly lately—Joe the Hack notwithstanding. This wasn't supposed to happen. *How can they be so blind—or deaf, at least? Can't they hear? Can't they motherfucking hear?*

There were several bars and sandwich counters situated about the main floor of the Palais. The central one, the one they opened up in summer, for the film festival, was presently covered by an opaque Plexiglas roof that let in a kind of unwashed gray light. Sal sat at one of the tables, a beer and *jambon* sandwich before him, untouched. Looking around, he saw that he was the only "festival participant" sitting alone. All around him there were buzzing, productive lunches going on. Buyers with tiny headphones over their ears and Walkmans on their belts nodded their blank-faced heads as they listened to the product being pushed by the sellers, who all sat across the tables with confident smiles on their lips and terror in their eyes. *Jesus! Why the fuck did I come here?* Everyone else in the café, in the whole Palais, seemed to have a purpose, a plan, and plenty of friends. *What the fuck am I doing here?* He picked up his beer and tasted it. *Warm! Warm and flat! Sixty francs for a bottle of warm, flat beer. Ten dollars!* And he was getting a headache. He could feel the tight pain twisting across his temples. *And God help him, he wouldn't give one of those arrogant Frog barmen the satisfaction of hearing him try to ask for a motherfucking aspirin. Aw, Jesus!* He leaned his head on his chest, closed his eyes, and pressed his fingertips into his forehead, trying to force the pain back into his brain.

He didn't know how long he leaned over his table like that. It might have been several minutes, because he spaced out. Drifted off, and the next thing he was aware of was an American voice with a Malibu accent at his elbow saying, "Hey, dude. You having a bad festival?" Sal slowly lifted his head and looked into the tanned, smiling face of the quintessential southern California surf punk. Long, loose golden-blond hair, perfect white teeth, fashionably frayed jeans, and a blue Corona T-shirt. The guy was an advertisement for sunshine and surfboards, somehow washed up on these frigid French shores. "You look *wasted,* dude, you know. *Unraveled.*"

The guy was so cheery and open, Sal had no choice but to

smile back at him. "It's been a bad day. I feel like I been in the ring with Mike Tyson."

The surfer shook his head, and his flowing yellow locks moved like ocean waves. Like the surf. "The festival can be *brutal,* dude. *Brutal.* Especially your first time." He held out his hand. There was a big silver skull ring on it, like Keith Richards's. "I'm Eric, man."

Sal shook his hand. "Marco Toledano."

Eric the surf bum was already seated at Sal's table, and now he began to eat a small pizza he'd brought with him. "This *is* your first festival, dude, right?"

Sal nodded grimly. "First and last."

Eric talked with his mouth full, washing the pizza down with a bottle of Heineken. "It's my seventh, dude, so I know my way around the thing."

"Seventh?"

Eric gave him a veteran's knowing smile. "Yeah, but it gets easier, brother. It gets easier." He folded a wedge of pizza like a paper airplane and zoomed it into his mouth. "After you learn a few rules."

He waited to be asked, and Sal obliged.

"Yeah? What rules?"

Eric wiped his mouth with a tissue and sipped his beer. "First thing you gotta understand, man—this festival doesn't work for Americans."

"I'm Canadian," Sal said quickly.

Eric held out his hands, palms up, as if to say, *What's the difference?* "See, all year long the Europeans *beg* the Americans to come to this party, and then, when the thing happens, they only get the *wrong* Americans."

Sal cocked his head to one side and studied the surfer. "What d'you mean?"

"All the Americans here are ones—like yourself—selling something. And the Europeans aren't here to buy, they're trying to move product themselves." He gave Sal a comedian's can-you-believe-it stare. "Right away, dude, you see the problem."

"Right away," Sal straight-manned back.

"That's not to say the top executives from the Big Five American companies ain't here, but they're in their hotel suites, dude, snorting coke and getting head from thousand-dollar French hookers. They come here to *party,* dude." He shoveled the last slice of pizza between his teeth. "They're not gonna buy record one, man, and you know why?"

"Why?"

"'Cause when's the last time a teenybopper in Cincinnati went into her favorite neighborhood audio outlet and asked for a side by a Polish rock band?"

Of course. Of course.

"For sure, every few years some European group has a big hit in the States—Roxette, Milli Vanilli—but for the most part the U.S. record buyer has no taste for anything Continental. You see what I mean, dude?"

"I see what you mean."

"And the big American companies ain't here to sell, because what they got the Euro market's already bought. You think Michael Jackson needs promotion over here? Paula Abdul? Madonna?"

Sal slowly nodded his comprehension.

"So, dude," Eric continued, "what Americans you got over here are lone wolves like yourself. People who're only here 'cause—no offense, dude—'cause they couldn't get a deal in the States."

Close enough. Close enough.

"And the Europeans know it, man. They see it every frazzlin' year." He was picking his teeth with a matchbook cover. "So essentially what you got is people trying to sell shit to people trying to sell *them* shit. That's why rule one. That's why this festival don't work for Americans." He gave Sal a shrug. "You want me to go on?"

Sal shrugged back. "Why not?"

"For sure." He held up two fingers. "Rule two. The Brits run this party." Sal hadn't tried any English booths. They all seemed far too busy and preoccupied.

"They do?"

Eric nodded, and his bleached golden hair shimmered. "Totally. They're the only ones here that don't have a worry. *Every*body buys their product, Americans and Europeans. Ever since the Beatles, they've been on the cutting edge of music. For years most of the innovative acts have been out of Britain."

"That's true."

"U2. Sting. UB40. Chrissie Hynde." Eric unpeeled a stick of chewing gum and stuck it in his mouth. It completed his young American airhead image. "As a result, the Brits are the most arrogant bastards here. They don't *care* what you're doing, you know, dude, 'cause what *they're* doing is gonna be on your radio next year anyway, no matter *where* you live. Talking to them is brutal." He blew a bubble. "That's rule two." The bubble collapsed. "Rule three, for a dude like you, is try the Germans."

Sal shook his head in exasperation. "I been to four German—"

"The *boches,* dude," Eric went on, "'cause they're nuts for anything American, 'cause a lot of their local releases are in English, and 'cause the market is big enough to support you, but not so big you can't break in. I work for a German company." He popped his gum and looked at Sal. "Lemme hear what you got."

"What?" Sal had been mesmerized by the guy's voice.

"Cassette, dude. Lemme hear your cassette."

"Oh." Sal rummaged in his coat pocket and brought up the tape that had already been turned down seventeen times this morning. One more rejection wouldn't matter.

Eric popped the cassette into his Walkman and slipped the earphones over his beach-bleached hair. The tiny portable tape players were part of the festival uniform, along with earrings, black leather jackets, and rock-tour T-shirts. Sal seemed to be the only participant without one. His hearing blocked out, Eric smiled at him as if from a far distance, and then Sal could see on the surf rider's face the moment the music began to play in his ears. His eyes turned unfocused and inward, lost in the sounds. Sal was determined not to look like all the other anxious idiots watching their music being listened to, so he purposefully averted his glance. At the next table over sat a very young, very black man in a white robe and a fez. He was watching a sixtyish Jewish-American businesswoman in a floor-length mink coat seated across from him nod her head and tap her spiky fingernails along with the beat she was hearing in her headphones. At the table crowded in directly behind her was a swarthy Latin type, young, handsome, virile, running his story down to a bespectacled, bald-headed Englishman in his fifties. The Latin was in George Raft pin-stripes, white tie, and black shirt, the old Brit wore baggy, rustic tweeds. He looked like something out of Arthur Conan Doyle. *This place is like Mardi Gras,* Sal thought. *Everyone's in costume. Everyone's—*

"Hey, Marco, dude, this stuff's happenin'."

Sal turned his attention back to Eric the Blond. He had both his index fingers pressing his headphones into his ears, and he was smiling broadly at Sal.

"Outasight, bro." Because he was wearing phones, he naturally was speaking too loudly. "She kinda sounds like—"

Sal nodded. "Yeah, I know."

"Any thing up-tempo on here?"

"Further on."

Eric pressed some buttons on his Sony and fast-forwarded the tape. After listening for a while, he took the headphones from his ears and hung them around his neck. He looked at Sal with new respect.

"I have to tell you, bro. I am impressed."

Sal shrugged.

"So what are you selling, dude? The songs, the publishing, the singer?" Suddenly the surfer bum was a surfer businessman.

"The artist. But the songs are unsigned. We can talk about the publishing."

"My dude's got to get the publishing. He's *crazed* about that."

Sal shrugged again. He was beginning to feel the earliest beginnings of excitement, but he didn't want to show it.

Eric started the tape and repositioned the headphones. He listened intently for another minute, then raised the phones from his ears. Sal could barely hear Isabel's voice, like a fairy caught in a bottle. "Don't tell me, man, that this chick is forty and weighs two hundred pounds."

Sal smiled at him. "I won't tell you."

Eric nodded and slipped the phones back over his ears. He listened uninterrupted for another twenty minutes, until the tape was over, then rehung the phones around his neck.

"How many tunes, nine?"

Sal nodded. "A whole album."

Eric unwrapped another stick of gum, but he didn't look like an airhead to Sal anymore.

"My guy's a heavy dude, Marco." He devoured the gum bite by bite, instead of shoving the whole stick in. "Independent label with worldwide distribution. Track record. International hits. Heavy-duty financing." The two sticks of Spearmint made a lump in his cheek. "I know my dude pretty good, Marco, and I think he's gonna like what you got."

Let's get it on. "Where is he? Let's go see him."

Eric shook his head. "He never comes into the Palais. That's for losers. Why don't you let me keep this tape and play it for him?"

Sal hesitated. "It's the only one I brought."

Eric looked at him and chuckled. "The only one? Dude, you're supposed to bring these things by the *gross.*" He popped out the cassette and gave it back.

"Yeah, I know that now."

"Look, you know the Hotel Martinez?" Mar-ten-*nezzzz* again.

"That's where I'm staying."

"Meet you there tonight, in the bar." Eric pushed back his chair and stood up.

Sal looked up at him. "Must be the spot."

"It's where everybody ends up, dude. It's the happening place. Check it out around two o'clock."

At that moment there was a muffled tom-tom of thunder, and rain began to pound down on the Plexiglas roof covering. They both looked up at the water rushing across the plastic, then Sal said, "Tell me. How did a Southern California hippie wind up working for a German record company?"

Eric smiled down at him. "Fooled ja, dude. I didn't even *leave* Stockholm until I was seventeen."

"Stockholm?" Sal was confused. "Stockholm? You mean, as in *Sweden?*"

Eric beamed. He obviously enjoyed people's reaction. "On both sides. For about fifty thousand years."

Sal was amazed. "Then how did you learn—"

"Three years in a Paris flat with a student from Redondo Beach. She was studying French and had *no* inclination for Swedish." He contentedly popped his gum. "But then who does? That's why we all speak English, dude. Or American, which is what I've been accused of." He ripped his jacket—black leather, of course—from the back of his chair and started walking away. "Later, dude. Check it out."

It was still pouring rain when Sal paid the taxi under the awning of the Hotel Mar-ten-*nezzzzz* and climbed out. Across the Croisette the sea was gray and surging. It was still early afternoon, but as dark and cold as night. Sal crossed the rock and roll crowded lobby and took an elevator up to the sixth floor.

He was barely in the room when she exploded out of the bed. She *climaxed* out of the bed.

"Marco!" she cried as she flung her body against his. She thrust her sugar-tipped tongue deep into his mouth. Her hands tore at the buttons of his shirt, pushed his coat off his shoulders.

He finally managed to twist his lips away from hers. "Baby, I—" he started to say as she ran her hands hungrily under his shirt and over his chest.

"You were away too long!" she complained as she pushed him back into an armchair. She unzipped his fly and searched for him. "I miss you all day!" She found him and clutched him gently.

"Iz, baby, don't you want to hear about my day?" Sal asked, and then had to laugh at what he'd just said. She was already kneeling before him. She slipped his rapidly hardening cock through his pants and, staring up at him, opened her mouth and devoured him. She was wearing one of the several pieces of Madonnaish lingerie they'd bought last week on the Champs Élysées. This was a slutty Frederick's of Hollywood-type bustier, all white lace and garter belts, that left her ass and crotch exposed. Slumped back into the armchair, Isabel kneeling there working on him with her mouth, Sal lifted his eyes and could see in the mirrored closet the taut, tan globes of her slim buttocks waving in air, he could make out the darkness of flesh that curved into her anus, the wondrous wedge of short-cropped hair.

"Oh, Jesus, Izzy," he moaned, and ran his fingers across her bobbing head. "Oh, Jesus."

She released him then, stood up and took both his hands

in hers, walked backward, leading him to the bed. "*Me fode,* Marco," she whispered in Portuguese as she lay back on the sheets. "Fuck me. Fuck me. *Me fode.*"

At 2:00 A.M. the bar of the Martinez Hotel, intended for maybe fifty patrons, contained five hundred. They jammed the doorways, spilled out into the lobby, perched on the marble stairs, argued in the restrooms. There were empty plastic cups crumpled and overflowing in the potted plants, along the base of the walls, all over the reception desk. Inside the lounge itself the bar was lined four deep, with men waving hundred-franc notes, trying to look cool as they desperately flailed about in an effort to catch a barman's attention so they could pay exorbitant prices for bad French beer that was stacked, warm and unrefrigerated, in cases on the floor. The crush of people was so thick and closely packed that Sal, at the doorway peering in over someone's black-jacketed shoulder, thought, *It's like Mardi Gras in there.* And just like a packed Carnival street, there was the smallest but ever-present flavor of danger in the noisy, smoke-choked air, an undertone of anarchy. This was not a place for agoraphobics. Sal elbowed his way into the room and began to twist and shoulder across the dance floor, which, of course, was jam-packed with talkers, not dancers. The sound level in the bar was a decibel or two below painful, and the air was hazy with thick cigarette smoke. Pardoning and insinuating himself through the mass of trendily dressed bodies, Sal took a minute to move ten feet, and in that time he overheard conversations in six different languages. And every face he looked into seemed to be one he'd seen before, that morning. It was as if the whole festival, all seven thousand participants, had moved en masse over to the bar of the Martinez Hotel. It was incredible.

Sal paused in the middle of the pack of people, and asked himself, *Where am I going? I'm never gonna be able to find that Eric dude in this mess. This is useless.* He stood on his toes and craned his neck, scanning the sea of darkly clothed people. Once again, everyone seemed to know what they were doing except him. *I'll buy a drink. I'll go to the bar and buy a drink. I can't go back to the room yet. Isabel will wanna fuck some more, and Christ, I can't. I just can't. I'll make it to the bar and get a drink.* He tried to slide between two turned backs, and then the crowd parted for a moment and there was Clarice, the fat French receptionist, smiling and waving warmly from a table against the wall. *Thanks, but no thanks.* Besides, she was already surrounded by a half-dozen nerdy-looking gofer types. If she couldn't get lucky in here, where it was fifty horny rock conventioneers for every overweight female, well then, God help her. Sal pretended he didn't see her and tried to squeeze between the two turned backs. They resisted him like the Saints' defensive line, and Sal stood there, stopped dead. *What the fuck am I doing here? This is impossible. And I'm* never *gonna find that Eric dude. Never.* As if his thoughts were being read, someone clutched Sal's arm and Sal twisted around to look right into the surfer's blond-crowned face. But he wasn't smiling anymore. His mouth was tight and intense.

"Hey, dude, this way." He towed Sal through the crowd, and the people seemed to just part before them. *Why can't I do that?* Sal puzzled. They had gone only a few steps before Eric turned back and thrust his face close to Sal's. His breath smelled of spearmint, beer, and marijuana.

"I gotta talk to ya, dude," he shouted over the crowd noise.

Sal looked around. "Is this private enough?"

But Eric wasn't into jokes right now. "I gotta tell you about my guy, dude. He's not the warmest guy in the world." He gave Sal a meaningful stare. "A lot of people don't like Karl, but, Marco, the dude gets results. He *delivers.*"

Sal thought of what the old Bourbon Street musicians liked to say: *Fuck these nice guys—send me a prick who can play.*

"That's all that counts, man," Sal yelled back.

"That's why I work for him, bro. I think he's the best. He's been up and down a few times. Right now it's mostly downtime." He started pushing through the crowd again, yelling back at Sal, "Marco, dude, you gotta trust me. My guy can deliver what you need, for sure."

"Whatever!" Sal shouted over the din.

Eric led him through the throng to a small round cocktail table in one of the far corners. The top of the table was crowded with empty beer bottles and plastic drink cups. There were three men and a woman seated around the table. The woman was a Clarice clone—another homely behind-the-rock-scene type.

She eyed Sal hungrily, and he ignored her. Two of the men were the male equivalents of the girl—dull-looking, pasty-faced northern Europeans. The third man, however, was striking, and Sal knew instantly that this one was Eric's man. He was slumped back in his chair with that faggy Continental slouch Sal had come to recognize, his legs crossed at the knees and a cigarette dangling between his fingers. One of the other men was speaking to him, leaning over into him, of course. Eric's man hardly seemed to take notice of his companions and surroundings, he just kept listening to the other man talking into his ear, his face blank and impassive. His eyes flicked over Eric and came to rest for a moment on Sal. He had the most limpid blue and bored eyes Sal had ever seen. His eyes stayed on Sal a heartbeat, and then slipped on, as cold and impersonal as a snake's, and Sal wasn't even sure the guy had seen him. He was a fairly large—taller than Sal—very Germanic-looking man with moussed white-blond hair brushed severely back from his brow and tied in a short, tight ponytail. His face was gaunt and clean-shaven, and he would have to be called handsome by any woman's definition. The clothes he wore were rock and roll perfect—casual and costly: a silk shirt buttoned at the collar, loose black slacks, and an intentionally weather-beaten bombardier jacket that Sal figured for about a grand, American. The guy was impressive, but Sal thought he looked like a high-rolling pimp. He had the beginnings of a bad feeling about him.

Eric pushed around the perimeter of the crowd, circling the table, then leaned over and spoke in his man's other ear, not paying any attention whatsoever to the other guy talking. Eric's man's eyes, in that reptilian way, shifted back to Sal. This time he stared pointedly, actually looking Sal up and down, like a gay inspecting rough trade, only his eyes were cold and expressionless. Sal felt uncomfortable. This dude was obviously from deep money, and rich people with attitudes always made Sal uncomfortable. He had no defense against them.

The German held up his cigarette hand in a limp gesture, and the functionary talking to him stopped, turned, and looked at Sal. The little twerp's eyes were hostile behind his round John Lennon glasses.

"Marco," Eric said, "this is Karl Diederich."

Karl examined Sal another long moment, then turned to the functionary on his right and said something in German. He spoke in a low, languid voice. A *capo*'s voice. The functionary said something back, then slowly stood up. Then the girl and the other guy, seeing him stand, also got up. There was a round of *au revoir*'s and *auf Wiedersehen*'s, and they moved away into the packed crowd. Karl looked at Sal a bit more, and then with his cigarette indicated one of the vacated seats.

"Would you like a whiskey?" he asked. His words somehow carried both a German and English accent. Sal guessed the two of them to be the same age.

Sal didn't speak until he was sitting down. "Yes, please."

Without looking in his direction, Karl said, "Eric, three whiskeys, if you don't mind."

Eric turned and plowed through the people toward the bar.

Karl stubbed out his cigarette and immediately shook another one from the pack lying on the table among the empty bottles and wadded napkins. He hung the unlit cigarette slackly between his long fingers.

"Eric is very excited about what you played for him today." Somehow, sitting down, Sal thought the crowd noise seemed muffled, as if they were below it. "Eric doesn't get excited very often." It was the strangest accent—like a German actor trying to do Shakespeare.

Sal quickly—*too quickly*—fished the cassette from his pocket and held it across the tops of the beer bottles to Karl. Karl gave him a small smile—a condescending, patrician smile—then generously *accepted* the tape from Sal's hands. He pushed aside a few glasses and gently set down the cassette next to his pack of Marlboros. Then he seemed to forget about it and reached for a book of hotel matches.

"You are—?" He opened the matches and tore one out.

"Marco. Marco Toledano."

He played with his match, his cigarette. Sal wondered if he was expected to take it from his hands and light it for him. *Fuck that shit.*

"American?"

"Canadian."

He finally struck the match and held it to the cigarette with his long, aristocratic fingers. Sal wanted a smoke, but felt too uncomfortable to go rooting for one in his pockets like a ditchdigger.

"A female artist, I was told."

Sal nodded. "A girl."

Karl exhaled in a long, graceful plume. *Naturally.*

"And what is your relationship with the product? You are the artist's manager?"

Sal felt that what he was about to say would henceforth define himself in Karl's eyes, so he thought about what he was going to answer.

"In a way. I wrote and produced the cuts."

"Ah," Karl said thoughtfully, as if he had just been illuminated. "That's very good." But there was no conviction behind it. The smoke drifted lazily upward from the dangling Marlboro.

At the next table a fat little man with barbiturated eyes in a beret and fashionably oversized suit, who had been listing precariously and arguing loudly, suddenly shouted a profanity in an inpenetrable language and swept his arm across his table, sending drinks and beers crashing. He barked something else foreign, then just stood there, swaying pugnaciously. Everyone at his table and all those around him ignored him.

"The population of the United States is two-hundred-and-fifty million," Karl Diederich was saying, and Sal wondered why. "The population of Continental Europe is well over three hundred million." He puffed on his cigarette with aristocratic disdain. "Yet I can have several number-one hits in the European market—which I have—and still be considered inconsequential in the States. Do you think that fair, Mr. Toledano?"

Sal didn't know what to say, so he said, "Uh—"

"I can sell millions and millions of records, but unless I sell them in the States, to the American industry I may as well have sold one." He looked at Sal as if for an explanation. "You Americans are so provincial."

"I'm Canadian."

Diederich uncrossed his legs and recrossed them the other way. "Is your artist American?"

"She's Brazilian—"

"Oh?" An ambiguous sound.

"—but her sound is very American."

"Ah."

What the fuck does "Ah" mean?

Sal hesitated a moment before he played his secret trump card. "She's the daughter of Giovanni Gemelli de Janeiro."

Karl's face grew thoughtful. "Ah, the shoe magnate. But then, she already has all the money in the world. Why does she want to get into this dirty business?"

"What does money have to do with it?" Sal asked honestly.

Diederich gave him a twisted smirk. "That's very true, Marco. This is something her father can't buy for her, for if it were, then all the records in the world would be sung by rich men's mistresses."

Eric came back then, carrying three tall glasses with an inch of amber liquid in the bottom of each, no ice. He distributed the drinks, then sat down in one of the vacant chairs. He looked at Sal and widened his eyes momentarily, as if to ask, *How's it goin', dude?*

Sal tasted his drink. Scotch. *Naturally.* He pressed on. "Why don't you listen to the cassette?"

Karl again gave him that condescending smile. "I will, Marco. I will." He fingered the rim of his drink. "So your artist is Gemelli de Janeiro's daughter?"

Eric was shocked. "Is that right, dude? Awesome!"

"But she doesn't want to use her name to—to"—Sal waved his hands—"you know, get ahead."

"Ah, your artist has opinions," he said, as if that were the silliest thing he'd ever heard. "How old is this opinionated person?"

"Almost seventeen."

Eric's second shock in half a minute. "With that voice? Far out!"

At that moment a woman laid her brown, false-fingernailed hand on Karl Diederich's shoulder, and Sal raised his eyes to look upon the most beautiful female he'd ever seen. Tall, serene, elegant, with high cheekbones and rich Sudanese skin, she could have been thirty or fifty. Her features were finely etched and feline, and she carried herself with a model's sense of theatricality. She wore a full-length fur coat and, underneath, a tight silver sheath cut to her waist, exposing most of a pair of bountiful brown breasts.

Looking down at Karl, who had reached up to touch her hand on his shoulder, she asked, "How long are you going to be?" in perfect German.

"*Nicht lange,*" he answered. Not long. "Wait for me in the room."

"*In Ordnung.*" Then her eyes went to Eric, and finally settled on Sal. For a heartbeat she couldn't control the heated interest that flared up in her pupils, then she quickly looked back to Karl, who had seen the flame-up in her eyes.

"Don't keep me waiting," she said; then, without looking at Sal again, turned and walked away. Sal watched her move away in the crowd. He wasn't surprised by his effect on her. He'd been getting that kind of reaction from women all his life. And she *was* a beautiful woman, but he'd known enough beautiful women to know that looks meant very little. A beautiful woman could be a bad friend, a bad person, or a bad fuck, just as soon as anybody else. Well, at least he knew that Diederich wasn't a faggot. He wouldn't have to worry about that. With these swishy Europeans you never could tell.

He looked back at Diederich, and found him staring pointedly.

He felt he had to say something, so he said, "She's a very beautiful woman."

That condescending smirk of a smile again. "Yes, exquisite." Karl took a long time sipping his whiskey. "You know, I've often considered, men spend so much time and effort trying to impress women"—he looked at Sal—"and it's all so meaningless."

After a second, Sal said, "What d'you mean?"

"Well, for example, some men chase after every woman they meet, they have to seduce her, to have another *conquest*"—Sal hadn't heard that word in decades—"and then, when they bed the woman, they try so hard to be the best, to fuck the hardest, the longest, to give that woman the best *Schupt* she's ever had." Karl sipped his drink. "But perhaps he *is* the best, what difference does it make? Who will know? Who will care? Oh, the woman would know, and she may tell a few of her close friends, but what difference could it make in the lover's life, you see what I mean?"

Sal thought of looking down at Isabel's smiling, sweaty, satiated face, just a few hours ago.

"No."

"Because the people in this world," he continued, "the people with *power,* are all men. Oh, there are a few exceptions. A minuscule few. But, no, really, the powerful people on this planet are all men, and what do they care if you are the greatest lover of all time? In fact, if they did know, they would then have a reason to fear you, and if they fear you, then they must destroy you. You see? Being a great fuck is a singularly useless accomplishment."

Sal didn't know what to say, didn't know if he was required to say something. He felt Karl was telling him something, but what? He threw a quick glance at Eric, who stared back as if to say, *I told you he was weird, dude.*

"Now, I will listen to your tape. May I have your recorder, please."

Before Eric could say a word, Sal had his newly purchased Walkman in his hands and gave it over to Karl, who settled the headphones over his moussed white-blond hair.

Karl lit a cigarette, sipped his whiskey, and punched the "play" button on his tape recorder. Listening to the music, he stared down at the cluttered tabletop.

"So, dude," Eric chimed, trying to lighten the moment, "where is this mysterious girl? When do we get to see her?"

Sal smiled back, grateful for the diversion. "As soon as she loses the two hundred pounds."

Eric laughed, then he leaned into Sal. "She's really Gemelli de Janeiro's daughter? The little guy with the cane and the parrot and the ten billion dollars?" Sal nodded. "And she's only seventeen?"

"Will be in June."

"Far out, bro. Incredible."

"She's in the room upstairs. If Karl is interested in the product, I'll take you up to meet her. If Karl is interested—"

He shot a glance at Diederich, and found him staring back from under the headphones. Karl gave him the slightest of nods, then looked away.

You're fucking right it's good, Kraut. Sal's confidence was slipping back. *Karl the Kraut. The Sour Kraut.*

Karl tapped the rim of his glass, and Eric was up and making his way back to the bar. Sal fidgeted with his watch. It was almost three. The bar had thinned out appreciably in the last half hour. At the next table the swaying downer freak had been replaced by a set of Iowa-type corn-fed twins who some asshole had persuaded to wear matching see-through blouses and silver lamé tights. The outlines of their pink nipples shimmered in the bar's dim lights. Beyond them sat a table of American blacks in suits and cowboy hats. They watched everyone closely and glowered back when looked at. And all around were the sounds of foreign languages being spoken with a hipness and insularity only the music business could manufacture.

It took Karl over an hour to listen to the tape to his satisfaction. Twice he wordlessly rewound the cassette and listened to a particular track again. Sometimes he allowed a glimmer of a smile to play around the corners of his mouth, and once Sal caught him nodding along with the beat. Finally he had heard the ninth tune and took the phones from his ears. He took a taste from the untouched second-round whiskey Eric had gofered. Then he took a long time lighting a fresh Marlboro.

C'mon, asshole. C'mon.

"It's highly unusual," Diederich eventually said. "Her voice. Of course, there is the remarkable resemblance to Billie Holiday." He exhaled another graceful plume. "Clearly this cannot be ignored." *Clearly.* "On initial listening I felt this was not an advantage, but"—small, insincere smile again—"after a bit of hearing, one realizes that she is not an imitation." *No shit, Sherlock.* "The influence is undeniable, but she—what did you say the artist's name was?"

"I didn't." Sal was feeling better by the minute. "Isabel."

"Ah, Isabel." That expression of illumination again, as Karl rolled the syllables around his tongue. "Well, while Isabel's vocal sound may be derivative, her overall musical approach is quite original." *Quite, motherfucker.* Diederich gave him that shit-eating German grin again. It was more like a grimace of pain than a sign of humor. "I don't think I've ever heard Billie sing harmony with herself, the way Isabel does. Quite interesting."

Sal threw a quick look at Eric, who was beaming. Obviously

he saw something in Karl's behavior that Sal didn't.

"The songs," Karl went on, "are more than adequate." *What the fuck does that mean?* "One or two have definite hit potential." *Okay, okay.* "But the production is completely wrong."

Karl sat there, staring at Sal with that anal Aryan grimness. It was almost like a challenge.

Finally Sal said, "Oh, really? What's wrong with the production?"

Karl tapped the ash from his cigarette. "The ballads are not so bad. But the rhythm tracks—" He shook his head. "You have smothered this magnificent voice with synthesizer disco drek. You have wrapped a diamond in toilet tissue, you see? You have dressed a queen up like a tart."

The moment Sal heard the words, he knew the man was right. It was a stunning revelation.

"We must strip the tracks down to basics, to the bare necessities. This is possible, because your songs are actually quite good. Then the uncluttered sound will allow Isabel's voice to shine through."

Sal was speechless. *The guy's right. The guy's fucking right.*

He tried to talk. "Uh—you mean—uh, kinda like, oh, say, Terence Trent D'Arby's records?"

Karl considered this for a second. "Yes—but not quite. I hear a sparser mix for Isabel. More personal. More—" he rubbed his fingertips together "—more *tactile*."

Sal didn't know what the fuck Karl was talking about, but he knew Karl did. "I think—maybe, you know, maybe you've got something there."

Karl sat back and surveyed Sal with smug superiority. *The motherfucker knows what he's talking about. I hate him, but the motherfucker knows what he's talking about.* Karl raised his whiskey glass and drained it with inborn elegance.

"Now," he said, "shall we meet your Isabel Gemelli?"

ZERMATT—SEPTEMBER

"Marco, watch!" Isabel was standing straddle over the Rhine River, taking aim on the drawbridge that led across the moat into the Saxon castle. "Watch!" she shouted up to him.

"So—howa you think it goes, Marco?" Giovanni asked as the white-jacketed waiter poured steaming milk into their deep, oversized cups.

"Marco, look!" Then she gently stroked the putter, and from the slope below there was the unmistakable *plonk* in the clear Alpine air, then the rattle of the golf ball across the tiny drawbridge as it disappeared into the Saxon castle. A moment later Izzy raised her arms in theatrical triumph.

"I made it! It went in!"

Sal laughed. Then he shouted down to her, "How do I know that? I can't see the cup from here."

Giovanni was trying to unwrap his wafer of chocolate, but the fine gold foil was too delicate for his blunt, gnarled fingers.

"You don't believe me? You don't trust me?"

"Here, Gio." Sal took the chocolate from Giovanni's hands, quickly found the seam, and peeled away the foil wrapping. As he dropped the chocolate into the steaming milk, he shouted down to Isabel, "I'm just saying, all I'm saying is, I can't see the cup from here."

Isabel turned to Eric, who was leaning on a Chinese pagoda and twirling his putter like a Fred Astaire cane.

"Eric, tell him!" she demanded prettily.

Eric shaded his eyes from the bright sun and squinted up at Sal on the hotel terrace. "She's telling the truth, bro!"

"Howa you think it goes?"

Giovanni had brought them here on a week's holiday. They had been in the studio steadily for seven weeks, sometimes going ten or eleven days without taking one off, and then Giovanni had flown into Munich from Rio, aching to see his daughter. Karl had reluctantly granted a break, and the little old cripple had offered to treat everyone to this trip. Spending money was one of the few things Giovanni could do as well as any man.

"You mean, in the studio, Gio?" Sal slowly shook his head as he gazed down across the terraced miniature golf course. The whole town was like that. Cuckoo-clock kitsch. It was like living in a gift shop. Except for the narrow graveyard down the center of town where they buried the young climbers who fell off the mountain. "I don't know, G." He watched Eric and Isabel stroll over to a slowly grinding Dutch windmill. Then he turned and looked directly at the old man. "I'm too close to it to say for sure, but I swear to Jesus if it ain't the baddest thing I ever heard in my whole life."

Giovanni studied him a moment. "Thatsa good?"

Sal nodded, "That's very good."

The old dwarf smiled then. A smile of transcendental joy. "I know it! When I see my Isabel, I see in my Isabel's face this happiness, this confidence, like nothing I ever see there before. She is good then, eh, Marco?"

Sal nodded again. "She's unbelievable, Gio. A natural. A totally natural talent. She's truly unbelievable."

Giovanni beamed.

"Marco! Watch me!"

"Whatya gonna do this time?" Sal called down to her.

"Watch me!" she cried. "A hole in one time!"

Sal laughed and looked at Giovanni, but he didn't understand.

"Izzy, it's a hole in one!"

"What?" She was farther away now, and so was her voice.

"A hole in— Never mind!"

"Watch me!" She stroked the golf ball; it bounced once, then whacked right into one of the blades of the turning windmill.

"*Merde!*" she cursed. "Shit!"

"Oh, that was pretty!" Sal mocked. "If they ever make miniature golf an Olympic event—"

"Marco!"

"—you gonna win a gold medal for sure!"

"Fuck you!" she called up good-naturedly.

Giovanni leaned against the rail around the terrace. "Isabel! You don't talk thissa way!" Then he repeated the reprimand in Portuguese. Isabel's reply was light, bell-like laughter that hung in the crisp fall air.

"She'ssa never listen to me." Giovanni smiled and gently shook his head.

Sal took a sip of his hot chocolate and scalded his tongue. Karl appeared in the big glass-paned double doors that led off the terrace and into the hotel lobby. With him was the old Swiss woman who owned the place. She was tall and straight and gray, and she and Karl were speaking German. Sal wondered what they were talking about. *Probably where to send Hitler's retirement checks.*

"Karl's very good, Gio," Sal said. The chilly air seemed to make his rasp coarser.

"Ohhhh?" the little cripple inquired with arched eyebrows, trying desperately to understand everything.

"He's the best producer I've ever worked with. I wish he'd of produced me in my prime."

Maybe he wouldn't have wanted to. I was never as good as Izzy is already. Never.

Giovanni was puzzled. "I don't understand, Marco. Produced you how?"

Sal smiled and shrugged. "Nothing, Gio. Nothing."

Then the waiter came back with a basket of scones, butter, and jelly. He set it down on the starched white linen with a practiced artificial flourish, then was gone. Karl and the old woman laughed at something and went back into the hotel lobby.

"Thissa hotel wasn't here," Giovanni said as he chewed on a dry scone.

"What?"

"Thissa hotel wasn't here." He waved his crooked arm at the cluster of picturesque inns. "None of thissa was here." He turned to Sal. "When my father brought me here. I was seven or eight, I believe. It wassa before I hurt myself."

"Before your accident?"

"*Sì.*" Giovanni tasted his cup of chocolate. "There wassa nothing here. One or two hotels, a very small village, that'ssa all. Nothing else."

"Nothing else? The mountain wasn't here yet, Gio?"

Giovanni looked at Sal, then grinned broadly. He loved it when Marco teased him. No one his whole life had ever teased him—maybe because of his infirmities—and he found that he loved it.

"Yes, Signor Toledano, the mountain was here. Only it was not as big." He held out his hand. "Justa baby mountain."

They laughed together then. Sal blew on his hot chocolate and took another cautious sip. As long as the sun was out, it was a perfect day, but when the ever-present swirls of clouds that ringed the Matterhorn shut out the light, it instantly grew gray and chill. Now, the sun was shining.

Sal took another sip and looked over to Giovanni, who was lost in revelry. *Stardust memories.*

"I can remember," Giovanni said as he looked out over the rooftops and narrow streets, "I can remember running alla over the streets. It was justa before Christmas, and I remember they hook up to the horses—whatta you call—the ice wagons—"

"Sleighs."

"Yes, that. I would run so fast, grab the—the—sleighs, and let the horse pull me alla over the village." He turned back to Sal. "I wassa the fastest boy in the village." He shook his head ruefully, as if at God's questionable sense of humor. "Is hard to believe, no?"

Sal didn't know what to say, so he said nothing.

Giovanni turned back to the rooftops and the mountains beyond. "I see the men with the skis walk down from the mountain, and they looka so tall and so strong, I tell my papa I want to be that when I am a man. I want to ski." Giovanni gazed out at nothingness. "My father, he justa laugh. He was a great man, my papa, before the war and everything, everything broke-a him. He wassa always my besta friend." The lame old man sipped again at his hot chocolate, then he looked up sharply at Sal. "Isabel say you loosa your papa lasta year."

Joe the Hack. Joe the Hack. Forgive me, father, for I have sinned.

"Yeah, I did."

"I am so sorry. I offer my condolen—"

"What are you two old men talking about!" Isabel was suddenly there, hanging over the terrace railing. She was breathless, and under her tawny skin, the cool air had brought up a rosy undercoat. "You're supposed to be watching me!" She smelled of wool and autumn and apple cider, and it was intoxicating.

"Do you need an audience for everything?" Sal asked playfully.

Isabel shot her father a quick glance—more sly than shy—and softly said, "No, not everything." Then she leaned over the rail, pulled Sal to her, and kissed him. He felt her lips suck at the tip of his tongue, clutch it and pull amazingly hard for a few heartbeats; then, just at the moment it began to be painful, she released it and laughed in his mouth. He felt his penis stir against his leg, like a sleeping dog catching the scent of blood.

"Isabella," Giovanni primly reprimanded, and that made her laugh even harder.

"Now!" she said as she released the rail and dropped the two feet to the grassy slope that led down to the miniature golf course and the town beyond. "You *watch* me! You don't take your eyes off!"

"You can bet on it!" Sal called after her, and she laughed once again as she ran down the slope.

"Her mama laugh justa like that," Giovanni whispered, then made a respectful sign of the cross. "Justa like that."

Isabel trotted down to the Moorish stronghold where Eric was lining up a shot between two waist-high, gunmetal-gray minarets. She turned and waved. "You *watch!*" Her voice carried back up to them like distant music.

"She is justa like her mama in so many ways," Giovanni continued. He glanced over at Sal, then looked at him more closely. "You love her, Marco? You two are inna love? *Amore?*"

Sal D'Amore. He was embarrassed. He and Isabel had never tried to hide their feelings from anyone, but nothing was talked about, nothing was confronted.

"Giovanni, I'm too old for—"

"When I marry her mama I was fifty-three," Giovanni mused. "She was eighteen."

Way to go, Gio, Sal thought with a little twist of pride.

Giovanni pulled out a cigar from his coat pocket and absently began to go through his elaborate lighting ritual. "Marco, I must talka to you."

Aw, shit, is this gonna be one of those man-to-man what-are-your-intentions-with-my-daughter conversations? Oh, well, there's a first time for everything.

Giovanni laid the Havana on the white linen tablecloth and grasped the small gold penknife that hung on a chain across his vest. "Do you know, Marco, Isabel's mama—I only have-a eleven months with her?" His gnarled, arthritic fingers dug at the tiny knife, but he couldn't unsheath the blade. "Lessa than one year," he said as he looked up at Sal in dismay, and Sal didn't know if it was caused by the lost love or the penknife. He reached across the table and took the penknife from Gio's crumpled hands. Then he caught the blade with his fingernail and slipped it out easily.

"Less-a than one year," Giovanni continued. "It was like-a *this*—" he attempted to snap his fingers, but the twisted digits could produce no sound. "But it wassa my whole life. *Capisc'?*"

Sal was cutting the tip from the cigar. "I think so, Gio."

Giovanni smiled and leaned his small, deformed body across the table. "Sucha woman, *mamma mia!*" His eyes shone with her memory. "Do you know, I can remember every single time we make-a love. Every time. Ah, you smile, Marco, but issa true. Every damn time we make-a love. Never was there ever sucha woman. Never. Until Isabel." Sal handed the cigar back to Giovanni, who took it and held it loosely in his claw while he talked. "Isabel, she'ssa got her mother's beauty, she'ssa got her mother's laugh, she'ssa got her mother's fire—" Sal lit a match and held it out to the old man. Giovanni stuck the end of the cigar into the flame and sucked thoughtfully. When the Havana was glowing, he spoke again. "But Isabel, she hassa something her mama never have." He peered at Sal through the wreath of smoke. "She hassa—she hassa"—he searched for the right expression—"she hassa—" At that moment the sun was absorbed by the sky, blotted out by one of the Matterhorn's drifting snatches of clouds, and a shadow of darkness swept across their table just as if God had pulled down a window shade. The hotel terrace was suddenly dark and cold.

"Thatsa it! You see?" Giovanni cried. "Justa like that!"

Sal stared across the table uncomprehendingly.

"Justa like that!" The little cripple pointed up at the sky. "One minute she'ssa so bright, so happy—then the next, everything issa sad, issa angry. *Capisci?* When she'ssa little girl one minute she'ssa play with her dolls, the next minute she'ssa take the doll and twist off the head, like-a thissa, you see"—he turned his knobby claws over each other in a demonstration—"and then when she'ssa see what she'ssa done, she cry anna cry anna cry, justa like a broken heart." Giovanni stared at Sal a moment, a little out of breath, then he jammed the cigar into the corner of his mouth.

Sal turned away and looked over the terrace rail. Karl had joined Isabel and Eric on the now-shadowy golf course, and she was telling him a funny story, laughing and gesticulating wildly.

"Gio, what are you trying to tell me?"

The little handicapped millionaire watched his daughter laughing down below.

"I'mma try to tell you that my Isabel, she'ssa a good girl, but sometimes she'ssa do things that—that hurta other people."

Not looking at the little man, Sal nodded.

"I'mma try to tell you that love, love issa the biggest joy in the world." Giovanni sighed deeply. "But atta same time-a, issa the deepest pain."

At that moment the sun came out again, and the curtain of darkness was raised. Isabel's laughter drifted up at them as she finished the story and doubled over with mirth.

LOS ANGELES—FEBRUARY

It had been raining on and off in L.A. for over a week, so the skies across the whole Los Angeles basin were washed as faded blue as an old pair of jeans when the 747 banked around Century City and started its final approach over an aboriginal-artwork configuration of Westside freeways.

"We've begun our initial descent to LAX," the captain's garbled voice came through the scratchy little speakers. "It's fifty-six degrees and cloudy down there, with a fifty percent probability of rain." There was the *click* of the P.A.'s "talk" button being released, and then depressed again. "I and the rest of the crew of Flight 365, London to L.A., would like to take this opportunity to thank one of our passengers for being so gracious in meeting our demands on her time and patience. Thank you, Isabel, for all the autographs and pictures! We love you!" There was a spontaneous outburst of cheers and applause from the passengers—especially the teens and teenyboppers—back in economy, and even in the next row directly in front of their seat in first class, a trio of towheaded little sisters jumped in their seats and clapped their hands. Isabel put her finger to her lips and gave them a stern face, but its only effect was to send the sisters into a seizure of giggles. Their smiles were as wide as the L.A. horizon, and their glistening eyes feasted on her as if she were a religious icon come to life. "Shhhh—" Isabel hissed playfully at them, and the little girls squealed and ducked their cornsilk heads below the level of the seat back. They had been acting this way for almost all of the fourteen-hour plane ride. Sal felt he knew everything there was to know about these three little girls. Their names were Jennifer, Jessica, and April. They were eleven, nine, and eight, respectively. They had just spent a month visiting their grandparents in Leicester, they were traveling with their mother and father back home to Garden Grove, California, and Madonna *used* to be their very most favorite singer, but ever since "Coming On Strong," Isabel's third number-one single off her megaplatinum debut album *Tropic of Capricorn,* their cross-their-heart, truest-bluest, *special*-favorite rock star was Isabel, who had incredibly materialized in the seat behind them on this big old plane.

The top of the girls' heads appeared slowly over the top of the seatback, accompanied by suppressed giggles, then their eyes slipped into view—two sets of blue and one of green.

Sal, sitting beside Isabel, leaned forward and asked the trio, "Tell me, girls. Which song off *Tropic of Capricorn* is your cross-your-heart very special favorite?"

The kids shot up like Pop-Tarts.

"'I Can't Get My Fill'!"

"'Coming On Strong'!"

"No, 'Just Between Us'!"

Sal settled back in his plush first-class lounge chair, a wide, wicked grin on his face. Isabel shot him a sideways look, and then gave him a stiff elbow in the ribs.

"You don't have to go, what you say, fishing for compliments, Marco. They are *all* your songs."

It was true, Sal had composed all the cuts on one of the biggest-selling debut albums of all time. *Shit, the way it was selling, one of the biggest* albums, *period.* It had taken almost a year of writing and rewriting, of dissecting and discarding, of overdubbing and remixing, before Karl had finally said it was ready. The album had been released first in Germany, and the first single made number one in three weeks. Then Karl had cut a worldwide distribution deal with Gramophone/Pacific, and England had fallen next. Six months later *Tropic of Capricorn* was released in America, to even greater success, to three chart-toppers and a fourth coming up with a bullet even as they were winging in to *the Coast.* And now they were all flying to L.A.—Isabel's first trip to the States since her stardom—to make plans for her debut American tour, but more important, to attend two nights hence the Grammy Awards. Isabel and *Tropic of Capricorn* were nominated in seven categories.

And Sal was up in one. His "The Touch of a Stranger" was one of five nominees for Song of the Year. Sal felt a little cheated that if his song won a Grammy, Marco Toledano would get the credit, not Sal D'Amore. *But all things considered,* Sal thought as he gently massaged the ridge of flesh under his beard, *it's probably for the best.* It had been three years since he'd escaped New Orleans, three years packed with change and joy and success, but still, three years was not a very long time to some people.

"Check it out, dude," Sal heard Eric say from the seat behind them. He looked out the plane's little window down upon Los Angeles's burgeoning central skyline.

"L.A. Just lak I pictured it," Eric imitated Stevie Wonder perfectly. "Skyscrapers and ever'thang."

Karl, next to Eric, leaned over the top of the seat back and spoke down to Isabel, who turned around to watch him. "There'll be three limos waiting on the tarmac when we deplane. I've arranged for a wheelchair for your father." Giovanni Gemelli was with them for this trip. If she was going to win any awards, Isabel wanted the old man there to witness it. The wheelchair was one of the symptoms of his declining health. "It'll only be a few meters to the cars, but I felt the wheelchair was necessary."

She smiled warmly back at him. "*Danke,* Karl. That is very considerate."

Seems like this is happening a whole lot lately, Sal thought. *He ignores me, talks only to her, and she thanks him warmly.*

There were ten of them in their party, including Giovanni, Karl's secretary, two photographers—one still shots, one videotape—who were to shoot everything they saw for possible later use in promos and music videos, and two young English punkers who served as gofers and Isabel's rock and roll bodyguards. There were supposed to be eleven, and in fact the ticket had been purchased, but at the last minute Karl's wife, Saba, the beautiful Ethiopian woman Sal had first met in Cannes, had been left behind. No one had explained why.

"The desired perception," Karl was counseling in soft tones, "is of a harried and beleaguered *artiste,* desperate for a few moments of solitude."

"Do I ignore the fans?" Isabel asked.

Karl shook his head and gently continued his quiet coaching. "No. You *never* ignore them. They will let us off first, by the limos, so you only have to take a few steps between the airlift and the cars. You look up, you see them, you are surprised, you are pleased, you smile and you wave. But you are a big star who has traveled halfway around the world and are very tired. You need your rest, your privacy."

"You vant to be alone." Sal's very bad Garbo impression made Eric snicker, but Karl and Izzy just stared at him darkly for a second before continuing their plotting.

"Don't forget to smile when you wave. There will be a great deal of media there."

Isabel nodded solemnly. "Yes." *For someone who didn't wanna be in show business, she sure took to it,* Sal thought to himself.

Karl consulted his Rolex. "I think you should go to the ladies' room now, and freshen your makeup."

She immediately unbuckled and started to make her way back to the john. The stewardess was going to point out to her the "Fasten Your Seat Belt" light, but instead silently acknowledged a rock star's transcendental importance and kept her mouth shut. But when the three little tow-haired sisters began to unstrap themselves to follow their idol, the stew sternly intervened and buckled them back up.

Christ, Sal thought as he watched L.A. growing larger and closer, *Izzy and Karl sound like they're writing a fucking movie when they talk like that. Times like these, the music seems almost secondary. An afterthought. A merchandising opportunity to coincide with Izzy's celebrity. Oh, well, Karl knows what he's doing. Karl always knows what he's doing.*

There were fifteen hundred screaming fans waving from the upper level of LAX's Bradley Terminal, and what seemed a like number of journalists. Isabel was one of those select few rock performers who win the approval of culturally aspirant pop critics and preliterate six-year-olds alike. The kids raced along the glass-enclosed corridor, pounding their fists on the walls, as Isabel, in a moment of inspired improvisation, pushed her father's wheelchair across the tarmac and up to the three long white limos that had been reserved for the week. The little Isabel wannabees pressed their faces against the glass and shrieked their uncontrollable excitement. They were dressed up—almost to the one—in ruffled pink petticoats worn over black tights, heavily shined Doc Martin boots, and black T-shirts advertising a French condom-maker. The T-shirts were worn backward, with the logo on their shoulder blades. It was an international fashion rage inspired by the way Isabel had dressed in one of her videos, shot in the bowels of the Paris *métro.* And almost every shrieking little fan wore an incongruous gardenia stuck in her hair. It was an omnipresent trademark Karl had instructed Isabel to usurp from Billie Holiday's memory. Florists all over the world were scrambling to keep gardenias in stock, so pervasive and powerful was Isabel's fame.

The air was cool and moist as they stepped out of the plane, but it seemed like spring compared to the London weather they had departed from. The two rude boys lifted Giovanni into one of the long white limos, then went back with Eric to get the luggage. Isabel stood there holding the car door, a damp breeze riffling her hair, her eyes hidden behind super-cool Ray-Bans, a soft smile on her lips as she looked up at the screaming kids behind the glass walls, and Sal thought, *Look at her. Just fucking look at her. She's magnificent. She looks like—like—well, like a star.*

Isabel started to get into the limo with Giovanni, and Karl, standing just behind her, said, "Not yet. Let them have a bit more." She turned a little, giving them her profile. Sal could see the television cameras trained down on them.

"I am cold," she said finally, with a regal imperative.

"Yes, of course," Karl said, and held her arm as she ducked into the limo. Then he surveyed his entourage scattered about on the tarmac, found everything to his liking, and jumped in after. Sal was about to follow when Karl reached out to close the door.

"Hey," Sal laughed as he peered in the limo's coach, "you almost forgot me."

Karl looked up at him, his hand still on the door pull. "There are two other cars. Why don't you ride with Eric?"

Sal smiled in nervous confusion. "Uh—I want to ride with Izzy, Karl."

Karl stared at him with cold, dead eyes. They almost seemed to *challenge* Sal. *What's happening here? What's happening here?*

"Come, Marco," Sal heard Isabel say. "Sit over here, Karl, so Marco can be beside me."

Karl hesitated, then wordlessly pushed up from the white leather seat beside Isabel and plopped down on the other side of the coach, next to Giovanni, facing backward. Sal climbed in, and someone closed the door behind him.

Everyone sat in silent embarrassment, avoiding each other's gaze. *What the fuck's goin' on here?* The only friendly eyes Sal could find were the driver's, smiling back at him from the rear-view mirror. She was a mutantly beautiful Hollywood starlet blonde, with glossed lips, perfect fair skin, and crystal-blue irises.

Isabel looped her arm through Sal's and suggestively stroked his bicep muscle. "Maybe we have enough time, Marco, to drive to Malibu. I always hear my whole life about Malibu." The driver's eyes, under her black chauffeur's cap, registered Isabel's lover's caresses with a knowledgeable glint. She had it figured out now: Karl was the prime minister and Sal was the royal consort. Her look in the rearview grew hot and hungrier. He was the star-fucker, and therefore eminently fuckable himself. Truth be known, the one she really wanted was Isabel.

"I think any drives anywhere are simply out of the question," Karl groused. "We have a full schedule of interviews." Pronounced *shed-you-al.* "MTV. *Rolling Stone. Interview. People.*"

"Ah, excuse me," the driver interrupted from the front seat. "I thought you might want to see these." She passed back a stack of new-smelling *Time* magazines. "They've been out about thirty-six hours."

On the cover, over a bright red background, was a trick photo of a smiling Isabel dancing on a beachball-sized globe. *Isabel,* the caption read, *Foremost Purveyor of the New World Beat.* And on the folddown: *Pop Goes International.*

"It's that interview we did last month!" Isabel cried as she tore through the glossy pages.

Sal opened his copy right to the article and scanned it quickly with a mixture of elation and trepidation. "Isabel," the story read. "The ultimate international star. A Brazilian artist with an American voice, a German producer, a Canadian composer, and a world gone mad for her." Sal turned the page. There was a sidebar devoted to Giovanni Gemelli, the star's famous progenitor, and then Sal saw the photograph of *Marco Toledano, Isabel's personal songwriter.* His chest swelled with pride, and his pulse raced from fear. He studied the trimmed full beard, the thick black hair pulled back into a long ponytail, the dark, furtive eyes. He searched Toledano's face for any traces of Salvatore D'Amore, fugitive from Ninth Ward justice. He asked himself, *Do I recognize this man? Would anyone else? Would the Venezias?* He'd been hesitant to be photographed when the *Time* crew came to London to interview Isabel and her "music machine," as they dubbed it. For almost two years he'd always managed to be somewhere else whenever the media came around with their minicams and Minoltas. He'd refused to do on-camera interviews—much to Karl and Isabel's eternal consternation—and early on declared himself too old to be in Isabel's backup band, even though at first she had been very nervous without him behind her. He'd successfully avoided cameramen and photographers ever since Isabel's star had risen over all of Western Europe, but Karl had been adamant about *Time* magazine. Too big to ignore, he'd argued. Karl had finally achieved his Stateside success, and he was going to flog it for all it was worth. A flattering paragraph in a rag with a worldwide circulation of 4.3 million was simply too big to ignore. So Sal had stood in front of a hotel mirror for an hour, trying on all kinds of different expressions in an attempt to hide himself within himself, and had finally gone down to do the interview. The photographer must have shot three rolls of film, and early on Sal knew he'd never be able to control the lens's final outcome, so he'd had fun playing with the reporter, a sweet, plain girl with pillowy tits. He'd created a whole legend for himself, from his birth in Toronto to his early childhood in Seattle, to his high school graduation from Central High in Edmonton, Alberta. *Who cares about songwriters anyway?* he'd asked himself. *Nobody but other songwriters, and they ain't gonna check the facts.*

"*Papai,*" Isabel said, "look, there is a little story about you."

Giovanni smiled, but Sal could look at the old man and see he wasn't feeling well.

"Thatsa very good, Isabella. Karl"—he lightly touched the

German's knee with a gnarled finger—"do you think sometime we can go see my store in the Beverly Hills? My managers always like it when I give-a them a little visit, and I would like to take-a Isabel."

Karl looked up from the magazine and shook his head. "I'm afraid not, Mr. Gemelli. Isabel is going to be simply *inundated* with interviews these next few days. And then there will be the rehearsals for the Grammy Awards."

"They *rehearse* those shows?" Sal joked, and Karl shot him a dark glare. Sal laid his *Time* copy on the bleached white leather seats. "Gio, if you want to go to your outlet, I'll take you. Maybe Eric—"

"The reporters will want to talk to you, too," Karl barked in his cold Prussian manner. Sal was beginning to be bothered by Karl Diederich, even with all his rock-biz know-how. There were other producer-managers in the world. Isabel was contractually bound to Karl's production company for one more album, but after that Sal was going to have a long talk with her about resigning.

"I'm not doing any more interviews," Sal growled back. "That's it. *Finito.*"

Karl's eyes flattened with anger. "You will do as many as I tell you to."

Sal gave Karl a sweet little smile. "Go fuck yourself, Himmler."

Diederich recoiled as if he'd been slapped. He was very sensitive about any anti-German remarks, even though his mother had been English. "Don't you dare to speak to me—"

"Please, please." Isabel leaned between them and held each one's hand. "Don't argue. Don't argue. It's our first day in America!" She smiled brightly at each in turn. "We must be happy!"

Sal and Karl glared at each other across the plushly appointed limo coach.

"Look! We are here!" Isabel cried joyfully as the car eased up the gently inclined driveway of their hotel.

The Beverly Hills Hotel is a garish thirties monstrosity, puke pink and Japanese gardener green, lying like a spilled bottle of calamine lotion on a pool table at the base of hills and canyons that are home to $3 million "fixer-uppers." The hotel is supposed to be constructed in classic southern California Spanish, but the place actually looks like a well-kept Miami Beach retirement home. Because it's so old, the scale of the hotel's accoutrements—lobby, banquet halls, rooms—is small and narrow and a little seedy. Florists, musicians, and party-planners have no recourse but to schlepp their bouquets and basses through the front entrance. Still, the old whore has a certain cachet, and the Polo Lounge is always listed as one of the "hot" places for a power breakfast with a studio head.

Sal stepped out of his powder-blue-and-pink "bungalow" onto the small covered patio wearing only a bathrobe. The plush burgundy one Izzy had bought at Harrod's and given him for his birthday. Well, not *his* birthday, exactly. Marco Toledano's birthday, who had probably died not long after birth, the way these identity scams are run.

The southern California sky was clean and blue, but a heavy gray-blue that warned precipitation was possible at any moment. It hadn't rained in the twenty-four hours they'd been in town, but the local TV weathermen, between their incessant lame jokes, cautioned it was only a matter of time.

Sal turned and went back into the bungalow. The better rooms at the Beverly Hills Hotel weren't rooms at all, but tiny little semidetached villas, apartments, really, with kitchenettes, patios, and twenty-four-hour room service, all connected by curving walks, palm-shaded and flower-bed-lined. All the bungalows were decorated differently. No two were alike.

From the devastated breakfast plates on the room-service cart, Sal picked up a cold wedge of good old American white toast, tasteless and greasy with hardened butter, and nibbled happily while he poured himself a cup of watered-down coffee. *It was good to be home,* he thought, as he stared unseeing at the stupid game show on the telly—*TV.* Well, almost home. The menu didn't offer grits or beignets, he'd had to ask for Tabasco for his eggs, and Beverly Hills didn't have nearly enough black people to make him completely comfortable, but when anyone spoke English, he could understand it, and when they didn't, Sal wasn't made to feel it was a conscious decision made out of a sense of moral superiority. After two-and-a-half years Sal was back in the good old U.S. of A., and damn, didn't it feel good.

He slumped back into the wide, plush bed and picked up a piece of the *L.A. Times,* scattered over the bedspread. Izzy had read the paper before going out with Karl on the daylong interviews. The front page of the Calendar section was all about tomorrow night's Grammies. The hot speculation was over how many categories Isabel would win, and would she sweep like Michael Jackson had once done, or would she just garner only a few awards, like Tracy Chapman a few years back. Isabel seemed to be nominated in every category—Best Pop Vocal Female; Best R&B Vocal Female; Album of the Year; Record of the Year; Song of the Year; Best New Artist. Her album, *Tropic of Capricorn,* was even up for Best Jacket Art. The consensus of the *Times* critics was that Isabel was going to walk away with everything, and they didn't even seem unhappy about it. The Isabel myth and mystique had truly mesmerized the whole world.

Last night, lying in this bed together, he and Isabel had argued about who would accept the Grammy, should "The Touch of a Stranger" win Best Song. The songwriter is entitled to traipse up to the dais and bask in the glow of the spotlights and the fifty million watching pairs of eyes, but Sal insisted that if he won, he wanted Isabel to accept the award in his behalf.

"That is ridiculous, Marco," she had fumed. "That is stupid!"

"No, it's not, baby. People accept for other people all the time."

"You will be sitting right beside me all the night. Everyone will know you are there!"

"Yeah, I know, but I think you're gonna sweep, like they keep saying, and I think it would be nice if you walked up to the stage every time, you know what I mean. Besides, everyone wants to see *you,* anyway."

She had turned in the bed then, and inspected him through slitted eyes. "Why are you so afraid to have your picture taken?"

"Hey, wait a minute—"

"I think you have a wife and five *bebês* somewhere you don't want to tell me about."

"Iz—"

"Maybe many wives—"

"That's not—"

"—all over America!"

"—true! No!"

Back in Canada, when Sal had first changed his identity, he'd decided then and there that the only way he was going to be able to keep up the ruse was never to divulge his secret and the circumstances of his flight to anyone. And after meeting and falling in love with Isabel, he'd realized he was too ashamed of his sordid life ever to tell her the truth. She respected him, and respect was something he'd never been a big recipient of. He could never tell her anything that might shatter that regard she held for him. Also, he loved Isabel and wanted to protect her. What she didn't know couldn't hurt her.

After a long, hot, forceful American shower Sal dressed in a dark cashmere pullover, pleated trousers, and a loose-fitting King's Row double-breasted jacket. He left their bungalow and followed the leafy path up to the hotel proper.

He had a drink at the Polo Lounge Bar, hoping to see some stars, but all he encountered were some sleazy agents and classy hookers. He left a ten-dollar tip on the bar and strolled down to the pool. Even with the sun half-hidden behind the gathering clouds, the poolside scene was hopping. The pink cabanas were filled with fat men talking into white telephones while their bought-and-paid-for women lay in lounge chairs and stared up at the sun from behind oversized sunglasses. Waiters scurried to and fro, carrying trays of champagne and glasses, and Sal finally saw a famous face. That faggot Englishman whose voice he'd envied on the jukebox back in Waukegan, Illinois. He sat at the edge of the pool, languidly splashing his feet in the heated water, while his retinue of thin young men surrounded him. He was up against Isabel in three categories: Song, Record, and Album of the Year. Sal stared at the Englishman, thinking, *I could never have sung like you. I didn't have that good a voice. But now I have a better one. The best in the world. I have Isabel's voice.*

Sal was walking back from the pool area and up the curving driveway when he heard a car screech up behind him. He turned quickly, reacting instinctively, and there was Eric sitting behind the wheel of a brand new red Jeep Wrangler.

"Hey, dude, check it out!" Eric yelled as he stood up in the roofless Jeep and leaned over the windscreen. He wore Ray-Bans, a flowery Hawaiian shirt, and baggy surfer shorts. Somehow, in some dimension, Eric had come home. "Whattaya think, dude? Bitchin', huh?"

Sal laughed. "Where'd you get the dune buggy?"

"Bought it, bro. In *cold cash.* Plunked it right down on the dealer's desk."

Sal was nonplussed. "Jesus, Eric, that musta cost—"

"Seventeen thousand U.S. dollars. Plunked it right down on the salesman's desk. Dude thought I was a coke dealer or something." Eric beamed. "I been saving up."

"Obviously."

"Jump in, dude. There's someplace I'm dying to see."

Sal climbed in and plopped down in the hard bucket seat. "What's that, Malibu? Venice Beach?"

Eric shifted and the Jeep lurched forward. "Nah, man, I already checked out those spots this morning. Too cool, dude. Too cool." There was a traffic light at the end of the hotel's driveway, and Eric sat at the red and gunned the engine. "The place we're going is the other way."

"What other way?"

"The desert, dude." He turned and grinned at Sal. "Marco, my man, my bro, we're going to *Las Vegas!*"

"Wait a minute!" Sal cried with real trepidation. "I don't like gambling. I don't like—"

The light changed, and Eric screamed the Jeep out onto Sunset Boulevard.

Sal had never been in the desert before. He didn't like it. It was as different from Louisiana as anyplace he'd ever been, and he'd been a lot of places these past few years. Paris he'd found to be one big French Quarter; Italy was Sunday dinner at his aunt Lillian's; London was always the first day of fall; but this desert, this desert was the other side of the moon.

"How long's it take to get to Vegas?" Sal screamed over the Jeep's backwash.

"I don't know, dude! Forty-five minutes! An hour, maybe!"

"Eric! We already been driving two hours!"

The Swedish meatball grinned. "Then I guess we're dogging it, dude!" he shouted as he stomped on the accelerator.

It took them four hours to get to the neon light show that is Las Vegas, Nevada. The city was like the Fourth of July on acid. It was a Christmas tree burning in the desert sunset. It was as quintessentially and vulgarly American as a New Year's Day parade, stripper telegrams, or serial killers.

"Check it *out,* dude!" Eric marveled as they walked through the casinos. The big gambling parlors sparkled like a merry-go-round and hummed with the sound of money being wagered—men shouting at little red cubes, bored-looking blackjack dealers riffling decks of cards, slot machines being masturbated, roulette wheels spinning, and wheels of fortune clickity-clacking to a decision: winners or losers. The Swede was fascinated by the sideshow variety of people: Japanese tourists and Mexican laborers, grim Chinese-Americans and laughing blacks, Arabs in thousand-dollar suits and little old ladies in plastic pants. Sal's eyes darted about and found only the wiseguys, the characters, the *boys.* "Look at *that*!" Eric nudged Sal and nodded toward a full-blown cowboy, with worn jeans, leather vest, and sweat-stained Stetson, standing at a faceup blackjack table with his arm around a blowsy, boozy blonde, all pale skin and big tits. The cowboy was playing three hands at once, four $25 chips on each spot.

"Fuck, dude!" Eric whispered, "that cowboy's betting—"

"Three hundred dollars a pop."

"Far out!" The Swede dug into the pockets of his lime-green baggies and came up with a wad of bills. "This is what I have left from my Jeep money." He quickly counted it. "One thousand, four hundred dollars." He looked at Sal. "Whattaya think, bro?"

"About what?"

"You think I should bet it all? On one hand, I mean."

Sal smiled at what he was about to say. "Only if you can afford to lose it, man."

Eric shook his head in mock disgust. "You don't have any gambling blood in you, dude."

"I used to, man, but it got choked out of me."

Eric stepped to the table and slapped the bills down on a vacant spot just as the dealer was about to deal out a fresh hand of faceup "21." The dealer fanned out the greenbacks with long, delicate fingers. "Money plays fourteen hundred!" the dealer called back to the pit boss without moving his lips. The pit boss came over, looked down at the money, gave Sal and Eric a quick once-over, then nodded to the dealer. The dealer flicked out the cards. The cowboy got a deuce and a trey, an eight and a ten, and a king and an ace—blackjack. Eric's hand was two aces. The dealer had a pair of queens.

"What the hell am I supposed to do with this shit?" Eric asked Sal, who was standing just behind him.

Sal shrugged. "Only one thing you can do."

Eric waited for the rest of the advice. It didn't come. "Okay. Great. You wanna tell me what that one thing is, bro?"

"You gotta split 'em."

"Split 'em?"

Sal took out his wallet and plucked from it fourteen new hundred-dollar bills. Spending cash Karl's road manager had advanced him. He laid the crisp bills on the red felt and moved one of the aces next to the money.

"Hey, dude! You in with me on this hand?" Eric asked cheerily.

Sal shook his head. "I told you. I don't gamble. That's a loan. I'm sure a high roller who pays cash for cars is good for a pittance like fourteen hundred."

Eric grimaced in playful exasperation again, just as the cowboy caught a five, a six, and a nine to bust out on his first hand. "Fuuuuuck," he drawled out the word into three syllables. His second hand was an eighteen, but he had to hit it because the dealer was showing twenty. That's the agony and the ecstasy of faceup. He got dealt a big black king of clubs, and turned to Eric and Sal with a baleful glare, almost as if his bad luck were their doing.

Eric pointed to the first ace, and caught a three. He looked quickly at Sal, then tapped his finger again. Another three. Seven or seventeen. Eric touched the felt again, and the dealer dealt him another ace.

"Bummer," Eric breathed softly.

"You gotta take a hit," Sal said. "He's gotcha beat."

Eric nodded, then slowly raised his fingertip and lowered it back to the table. The dealer slipped him a three of diamonds, and Eric softly said, "Far out." The dealer mechanically counted out fourteen hundred in ten green hundred-dollar chips and sixteen brown twenty-fives. Then he looked to the last hand, the other split ace.

"You play it," Eric said. "It's your money."

"No, I loaned it to you. It's yours."

"Play it for me anyway, dude."

Sal drummed his index finger by the ace and the dealer flipped him a ten of clubs. Just like that.

As they walked away from the table with the twenty-eight-hundred-dollar winnings, Eric laughed uproariously and threw his arm around Sal's shoulders. "My heart was pounding there for a minute, dude. Yours?"

Sal thought for a moment, then looked into his friend's face. "No. Not for a second."

Eric frowned and shook his head. "You're hopeless, bro. You just don't have a gambler's heart."

Sal smiled at that.

"But I," Eric puffed, "on the other hand, possess in this Scandinavian body the soul of a cutthroat Gypsy dice player." He tightened his grip on Sal's neck. "Come with me, dude."

They played every game on the casino floor, or at least Eric did. Sal stood back and calmly watched, surprised and amused by his dispassionate detachment. His pulse didn't race, his heart didn't pound, and his hands didn't sweat. In short, he didn't really care if he won or lost. Sal D'Amore would have cared deeply. Sal D'Amore would have soared or crashed with each card, each roll of the dice. Every win would have meant to Sal D'Amore confirmation that he was deserving of respect, that he was blessed by the stars, that he was *somebody*. Every busted hand or seven-out would have signified that he was worthless, a washout, a loser. But that was Sal D'Amore. That person had died in the upstairs stockroom of the Tall Cold One, had died and been reborn, been replaced by Marco Toledano—Marco Toledano, that wildly successful Canadian-born songwriter who was up for a fucking Grammy in tomorrow night's presentation. Marco Toledano could care less if he caught a face or an ace, rolled an eleven or a pair of boxcars. Marco Toledano was going to make a million dollars U.S. this year. His music was at this moment being played in every country in the world. Marco Toledano went to sleep every night with Isabel Gemelli, the world's most popular rock artist and the best fuck Sal had ever encountered. And the only woman he'd ever loved.

Eric won big at craps, won bigger at roulette, lost at baccarat and the Big Wheel, then played "21" again and won again. He even tried his hand at the indecipherable Chinese games Pai Gow and Pan Nine. Unbelievably that's where he really cleaned up. *Beginner's luck,* Sal thought, standing beside him. *Fucking beginner's luck.* But there was no rancor behind it. Sal was only an observer. Gambling held no interest for him. *The thrill is gone.*

At midnight Eric was roaring drunk from all the gratis drinks, and twenty-two thousand dollars up on the house. Sal made him cash in his chips at one of the cashier windows.

"Hey, dude," Eric slurred. "Ain't as much money as your old lady makes in a minute, but not too shabby for one night's work."

Sal maneuvered his friend toward one of the light-bulb–ringed exits. "Let's get outta here, man. Let's go back. Isabel must be wondering where I am. And that Nazi fuck Karl probably called the Gestapo out on us."

As Sal was pouring him into the new red Jeep, Eric lifted his head and asked, "Can you answer a question for me, dude?"

Sal climbed behind the wheel. "I'll try."

"Can you tell me why the Nazis invaded Norway, but not Sweden?"

Sal hadn't been aware that the Nazis invaded Norway. "No, I can't. I have no idea."

Eric shook his wobbly head. "Me either, dude. Swedish girls are *much* more bitchin'."

"Go to sleep, Eric," Sal said as he fired up the engine.

"You got it," Eric groaned. Then he plopped his head back on the seat, and within seconds was snoring loudly.

Halfway back across the desert to L.A. the rain that had been promised arrived. First there were a few fat droplets on the windshield; then, after Sal pulled to the side of I-15 and struggled to unroll the Jeep's top and sides, the dark, ominous skies opened up. He got the Jeep covered just in time, and sat behind the wheel smoking a cigarette and watched the torrential downpour soak the dry, Gila-monster desert. It rained like he hadn't seen it rain since that night in New Orleans, three years before. The night he had escaped.

Not wanting to be the first one to sully the new Jeep's virgin ashtray, Sal unsnapped a corner of the Jeep's cover and tossed out his butt. In just that short second Sal's pant leg was soaked, it was raining that hard. Then there was a jagged scar of lightning across the sky, and the desert was briefly lit up. A moment later a thunderclap shook the Wrangler like a tornado of sound.

"Let's get the fuck out of here," Sal said to himself as he pulled back on the interstate. Eric, curled up now in a fetal position on the Jeep's floorboard, stirred briefly and made a swinish snuffling sound.

Only the rain didn't slack up as he neared L.A., it got worse. He couldn't outrun it. In fact, visibility was so diminished he had to slow to twenty-five miles per hour just to keep from getting washed off the lonely road. Driving like this, alone in the night, isolated, intense, he remembered a rainy day in Munich, a few weeks after their first single, "I Can't Get My Fill," had been released. He and Isabel were sitting at a light on the Leopoldstrasse, the Mercedes's windshield wipers dutifully swishing away the raindrops like good little German soldiers. Isabel was impatiently punching through the radio stations the way she always did.

"For Chrissakes, Iz, settle on something," he'd complained. "I hate it when you do that shit."

She'd turned then and playfully poked him in the ribs. "Ah, you are too old for me, Marco," she teased.

And then they'd both spaced out a bit, watching the pedestrians in their raincoats hurrying by in front of the Mercedes. The song on the radio—an old Sting standard—faded, and the opening chords to the next record began to play. *What is that?* Sal had asked himself. *That sounds so familiar. Who is that? What's the name of that tune?* And then something in his mind clicked in, and he turned to Isabel just as she realized too. And at that moment her voice singing "I Can't Get My Fill" came out of the Mercedes's speakers. It was the first time they'd heard their song on the radio, and Isabel screamed and threw her arms around Sal's neck and began to cry. Sal started to laugh, and then they were alternately laughing and crying, crying and laughing, kissing each other there in the Mercedes waiting at the red light on the Leopoldstrasse. And then a carload of German kids in a Volkswagen Golf with big boombox amplifiers thundering "I Can't Get My Fill" pulled up right next to them. Their radio was tuned to the same station, and the kids were laughing and drumming their hands on the dashboard along with the record. Izzy shrieked again, and Sal rolled down the window, stuck his head out into the drizzle, and shouted, "Hey, that's us! *That's us!*" And one of the kids turned down the radio and shouted back, "Bus? Bus to vhere?" And Izzy and Sal fell out laughing again, then the light changed and the cars behind them began to honk their horns and they laughed all the harder.

Sal turned the Jeep onto I-10 headed west toward the Pacific and switched the wipers to high as the rain descended like a curtain before his eyes. It was so dense and thick, his headlights were reflected back at him. Every once in a while he would pass solitary cars pulled over to the side because their drivers couldn't deal with the conditions. But Sal knew how to drive on wet roads. It rained half the time back in New Orleans.

He lit a fresh cigarette with the dashboard lighter and thought again about that day on the Leopoldstrasse when they heard themselves on the radio for the first time. That reminded him of another special memory. *Tropic of Capricorn* had become a big hit in Germany and the Benelux countries, and Karl had negotiated a release in France and Switzerland. He'd booked a tour, and their first date was, of course, Paris. The budget was still tight and all of them—Isabel, Karl, Sal, Eric, the band, and the roadies—had stayed at a small hotel not far from the Luxemburg Gardens. The concert went beautifully—the French idolized their pop stars—and afterward Izzy and Sal rushed back to the little two-star hotel and made sweaty, manic love until they were too exhausted to do anything but breathe. Then they opened the big iron-shuttered windows and watched the golden dawn bleed over the Montparnasse skyline. Hanging over the balcony with a single sheet wrapped around them, they smoked cigarettes and looked down as the neighborhood around the hotel woke up. The butcher opposite rolled up his storefront and washed out his tiny shop with a garden hose. You could see the bloody water rushing in the gutters. Then the flower seller put out plastic buckets filled with flowers all in primary colors—bright reds, startling yellows, pure blues and whites. They were hungry then, empty and hollowed out from all the fucking, and went down into the streets with their arms around each other. They found a café that was just opening and ordered a full breakfast—*omelettes, croissants avec confiture, café au lait.* It was still very early, and the owner and her teen-aged son grumbled about having to serve them, but finally the omelets arrived, and Izzy and Sal fell on them like wolves. While they ate, the skinny, dirty-haired boy set up all the tables around them. He covered them with red-checkered tablecloths, laid out paper *serviettes,* forks, and knives. And as he worked, he hummed something under his breath. He neared them, and his humming got louder. Isabel snapped to it first, and reached across the table to touch Sal's hand. He looked up, and she moved her eyes in the boy's direction. Sal listened for a moment, and realized the kid was humming "The Touch of a Stranger." He was stunned motionless. His music was reaching people he'd never met. Strangers were *singing* his melody. He watched the boy closely to see if maybe he had recognized Isabel and was trying to impress them, but no, the kid's face was vacant and guileless as an infant's. He finished setting up the tables and went back behind the bar. Izzy and Sal looked at each other a long time, then they went back to their breakfasts.

It was still dark, cold, and raining cats and dogs when Sal half-dragged, half-carried Eric through the lobby of the Beverly Hills Hotel and down the long leaf-motif hallway to his room. He dropped Eric into bed, then turned up his collar, dashed outside into the downpour, and ran around the curving, serpentine walkways, searching for his and Izzy's "bungalow." The fucking apartments all looked the same from the outside, and everything was so treelined and crowded with shrubbery that by the time he figured out which bungalow was the right one, he was totally drenched. He burst through the door, and Isabel shot up in the dark bed, clutching a sheet to her naked breasts.

"Who is it? Who is it?"

"It's me, baby," Sal said as he flicked on a dim light and tore off his sopping clothes. "Who'dja think it was?"

Izzy blinked at him a moment, then turned her back and buried her head under the pillows.

Shivering and teeth chattering, Sal toweled dry in the bathroom, then flicked off the light and jumped under the covers. He snuggled his body against the length of Izzy's, and folded his arms around her.

"Hey," he whispered in her ear. "You slept on my side of the bed and got it all warm for me. Thanks, baby."

She seemed to hold her breath for a few seconds, then she asked, "What did you say, Marco?"

He buried his nose in the tickling hairs at the base of her neck. He loved the way she smelled. "I thanked you for warming up my side of the bed," he mumbled, already dropping off to sleep. "Aren't you gonna ask me where I been?"

"In the morning, Marco," he dimly heard her say, then he was out.

Morning came very early. It was Grammy Day, and Karl had room service deliver a huge breakfast, and the five of them—Karl, Isabel, Sal, Eric, and Giovanni—sat around the table while Karl lectured them on how to comport themselves at the big affair. Sal was dragging ass on only a few hours' sleep, and he kept glaring at Eric, who was far too perky and alert to suit Sal. Finally Eric, with a mouthful of eggs Benedict, brightly asked, "What's up, dude? You look bummed."

"Yeah," Sal snapped, "you'd be fucking bummed, too, if you had to drive all night in the rain with a fucking drunk snoring in your ear!"

Karl paused from his incessant note-taking to assess the rain that was still falling on the bungalow's veranda. "Regrettable, this weather. They'll have to curtail the prepresentation activities." He turned back to the table. "I thought it never rains in southern California."

Sal and Eric looked at each other, their eyes lit up, and they both started to sing, *"But, man, let me warn ya—It pours, man, it pooooouuurrrsss!"*

"Christ," said Karl, looking at Isabel and shaking his head.

It was Grammy Day; Isabel was nominated for six awards, and the *L.A. Times* had Sal *favored* in his category. Sal wasn't gonna let this tight-ass Nazi spoil the day.

"Okay, Big Time," he needled Eric. "For a hundred bucks—what's the bridge?" It wasn't really a *bet.* Eric had all this shit down cold.

Eric rolled his eyes at the ceiling, swallowed his food, and sang out, *"I'm out of work, I'm out a' my head, I'm outta self-respect, I'm out a' bread—"*

"Scheisse!" Karl cursed as he tossed his napkin onto the table.

Then Eric and Sal threw back their heads and howled, *"I wanna go hoooommmmmmm!"*

"Marco!" Isabel snapped, "this is very important what we are discussing." Her dark eyes flashed. "Is my *career!*"

Sal couldn't remember Izzy ever speaking to him like that. "Hey, baby, take it easy. Just 'cuz Colonel Klink over there"—he indicated Karl with a nod—"is too tight-assed to have a good time—"

"That's enough!" Karl barked imperiously.

"Marco, please," Isabel scolded.

Then everyone at the table was shocked silent when a huge, roaring guffaw burst out of little, quiet Giovanni. He had been trying to hold back his laughter with his gnarled fists, but he couldn't suppress it any longer. They all watched him hold his belly with one hand and pound the breakfast table with the other. They looked around to each other, trying to figure out what had struck the old man so humorous. Finally Giovanni quieted down, and Sal, who had grown to love the gentle, sick old man, asked, "What's so funny, Gio?"

The old man grinned broadly, threw back his head, and in an attempt to imitate Sal and Eric, shouted, *"I wanna go hooommmmmme!"* It was so unexpected, so out of character, so off-the wall, that the four of them had no choice but to join him in unrestrained laughter. The ugly mood was completely dispelled.

Giovanni whacked his hand on the table. *"I wanna go hooommmmmme!"*

After breakfast Karl called down to have the limos brought around to the canopy awning at the hotel's entrance. There was going to be a final Grammy run-through at the downtown Music Center, and Karl wanted everyone to be there. The two English punkers appeared at the bungalow door carrying oversized black umbrellas. Isabel got under the first umbrella with Karl and pressed up close to him, giggling with the day's excitement. Karl complimented her on her new Melrose Avenue outfit, and she seemed to glow with the praise. Sal stared at the two of them, unsure of what he was supposed to do, where he was supposed to be. He was just about to say something when Eric draped an arm around his shoulders and pulled him under the other punker's umbrella.

"Hey, dude, today's the day you become immortal. How's it feel?"

Sal looked into his friend's open, smiling face, and his uneasiness began to fade. He glanced back through the bungalow door, and little, twisted Giovanni, still chuckling in his wheelchair, gave him a reassuring wave. The day suddenly seemed much lighter.

"I guess I feel—" Sal started to say, then he smiled. "Fuck, I feel great. What can I say?"

"Bitchin', bro." The Swede gave Sal's shoulder muscles a fraternal squeeze, then he nodded to the English punker, and they left the shelter of the bungalow's doorway and began to walk along the curving walk. The raindrops drummed a wet tattoo on the umbrella's taut fabric. Sal looked around, and Karl and Isabel were following a few steps behind. They were laughing and looking at each other happily. Sal turned back quickly and tried to concentrate on the business of the day. The flagstones were wet, and watching where he walked, he saw droplets of water flying off the tips of his shoes. Looking up, he saw three men in overcoats come around the corner of another bungalow. Their collars were turned up against the rain, their shoulders hunched, and their heads bent over. He heard Isabel laugh behind him, a free, sexual, inviting ripple of sound, and for a moment he was disconcerted, he didn't know where he was. There was something about the three approaching men. Something vaguely yet unavoidably familiar. They were closing in fast now, leaning forward, with the rain beading on the shoulders of their expensive overcoats. Not California overcoats, nonfunctional fashion statements, to be worn only once or twice a year. No, these were dark, no-nonsense, cold-weather garments. The kind—the kind—the kind the wiseguys back in New Orleans were partial to. At that moment the three men were almost abreast of them. The English punker holding the umbrella over Sal and Eric moved to one side of the path, and Eric had to step onto the lawn. His Nike Airs gushed in the sodden grass, and Eric said, "Shit!" The three men were passing them then, moving fast, with their heads down. Then the man nearest Sal, the one whose form was the most familiar, raised his face, and he was smiling. A cold, entrancing serpent's hiss of a smile. He smiled, and as he passed, he said, "Where yat, Sally?," and then he was gone by. Sal walked on a few feet before he allowed himself to realize, *Nicky. That was Nicky Venezia.* He stopped and turned around. Eric and the English punker holding the umbrella walked on, and suddenly Sal was left standing in the pelting rain. He watched the three men walking away, toward Karl and Isabel, who were following, her arm in his. They were still laughing. The other English punker holding their umbrella was giving Sal a questioning look, and Sal watched the backs of the three men in overcoats hurrying away, toward them. Then, as naturally as tipping a hat, Nicky Venezia stepped in front of Isabel and flung a vial of liquid in her face. Isabel immediately clutched at her eyes and screamed. *Acid! He threw acid in her face!* The punker dropped the umbrella and lunged for Nicky, and one of the other overcoats—*Junior!*—threw a crushing stiff-armed shot to the punk's jaw, and the kid went down as if his back were broken. Karl stood there, frozen by fear and confusion. Then Isabel screamed again, a heart-wrenching shriek of pain. At the sound of it Sal started to run back toward the Venezias. Jimmy Van, the third overcoated man, turned to Sal then and pulled back his coat, revealing a machine pistol in his hand. Sal saw the clip and the muzzle pointed at him, and he slid to a stop on the rain-wet flagstones. *This is it. It all ends here.* Then the three of them, Jimmy Van and the two Venezias, turned and ran away, their overcoats flapping around their legs, back among the palm trees and the thousand-dollar-a-night bungalows. Isabel screamed again. She was bent over, kneeling in the soggy grass. Sal gripped her under her arms and tried to pull her to her feet. She raised her head, and Sal saw red blood gushing from her melted eyes. He saw her beautiful face dissolve into an acidic smear. He saw her flawless skin bubble and boil like overheated soup.

Oh, baby, what have I done to you! What have I done to you! What have I done to you!

* * *

The two detectives from the Beverly Hills PD were smooth, soft-spoken, deferential, obviously accustomed to dealing with famous and powerful people. The white cop was older, heavier. He went through the questions with a by-the-book tone of voice. Not bored, but not excited, either. Nothing in this man's future was ever going to shock him after what he'd seen in his past.

"Three men in heavy winter overcoats." He was writing everything down. "Two of them were dark, swarthy, Latin types." He looked up. "Could they'da been Brazilians, maybe?"

Karl was handling the report. The "interview," the cops called it. "I dun't zink zo," Karl answered. "I zink they vere Americuns." The trauma had broadened his accent.

The handsome Chicano cop jumped in then. He was young, he knew who the victim was, and he was *very* impressed. "Why do you say that?"

Karl shrugged. "Europeans can always identify Americans."

The white cop looked to Sal then, consulting his little notebook before he spoke. "Do you agree, Mr. Toledano?"

Sal was hunched over in one of the bungalow's armchairs, his elbows on his knees, and his face buried in his hands. The detective had to ask him again. "Agree, Mr. Toledano?"

Slowly Sal realized he was being addressed, and raised his head. He looked dazedly around the room, from one face to the next. "Huh?"

With the patience of the underpaid, the white cop repeated, "Mr. Diederich believes the perpetrators were Americans. What do you think?"

Nicky Venezia American? Wiseguys from the Ninth Ward just didn't think like that. "I—I don't know."

"But one of them spoke to you as they passed you on the path," the Chicano cop pressed just a little. "Did he sound—*foreign?*"

Sal shook his head. "I just couldn't— Nobody said anything to me."

Eric was in a stool by the bungalow's wet bar. "Sure, Marco. He said something to you, dude, when he walked by."

Sal couldn't look at him. "I didn't hear anything."

"I see, Mr. Toledano," the Chicano cop said, indicating he

didn't *see* at all. "But why did you stop walking, then turn around and watch the three men?"

Sal squinted at him, trying to comprehend what was happening. Trying to avoid any pitfalls. One of the bungalow's four telephones rang. "I'm sorry," Sal said to the Mexican-American detective, "would you repeat the question?"

Sal's eyes were on Karl, who walked across the room and answered the ringing phone. Karl listened for a moment, then held the phone out to the white detective.

"Mr. Christiansted," the Chicano cop said, meaning Eric, "stated that you turned around to watch the three perpetrators after they passed you on the path. Why did you do that?"

The beefy white detective launched himself out of his chair and waddled over to Karl and the telephone.

"I don't know," Sal said. "I—I just *felt* something."

The door to the bungalow's bedroom opened, and Isabel stepped out, her hair wrapped in a thick hotel towel, wearing a silky dressing gown. She filled the bungalow with the scent of freshly showered female, and the young Mexican detective immediately lost all pretense of interest in Sal. His black eyes gorged on Isabel as she stood in front of the mirrored fireplace, inclined her head, and began to apply the eyedrops the hotel doctor had left with her.

"Tabasco," the fat white cop said with ill-concealed triumph as he hung up the phone.

The other cop reluctantly pried his eyes from Isabel's taut curved throat. "You mean *salsa?*"

The white cop shook his head as he rolled back to his white rattan chair. "Nah, Ta*bas*co. You know, that Louisiana red-hot stuff. My wife uses it all the time when she cooks Cajun." He looked to the others. "Lab said it was McIlhenny's Tabasco and some ground-up red peppers. Burns like hell, but basically harmless."

Isabel turned from the mirror. "It burn like hell, all right." She blinked rapidly, and the eyedrops made her red-rimmed eyes glisten.

The young Mexican cop was lost forever. He hurried to try to ingratiate himself. "Miss Gemelli," he said as he moved closer to her, "I think we have to treat this incident seriously. These men were obviously not teenage pranksters. I think we have to consider this assault as a warning, possibly the precursor to an extortion attempt." He stopped for a moment, and when no one contradicted him, he raced on, "I want to place a couple of my men on twenty-four-hour duty outside your door. I'd like to—"

Karl stepped between Izzy and the detective, moving to squelch the young policeman's ardor. "That wouldn't be a good idea." A German *guut,* and a limey ide—*ahh.* "We have just arrived in this country, and we don't want any negative publicity." He gave the detective a condescending, you-couldn't-possibly-understand smile. "This kind of thing can be blown out of proportion. Besides, I have already contracted for private security. They will arrive very shortly." That shit-eating smile again. "I didn't understand how things were done here in America." He pronounced "America" as if it were Beirut. "Now, I appreciate the situation." *Everyone goes around throwing Tabasco in everyone else's face.*

The Latin cop studied Karl with the kind of moral rectitude only a policeman is entitled to. "There was an automatic weapon involved, Mr. Diederich. That fact shouldn't be taken lightly."

Karl was not one to be intimidated easily. Or by a lowly functionary. "All of us didn't see a weapon. Maybe it was a toy, or even a hysterical illusion." Karl was lighting a cigarette. "As I said, I have employed the best security force in Los Angeles." He stared at the young cop. "They will arrive very shortly. I put my faith in them."

The cop stared back with barely masked insolence. Then the phone rang again. The Chicano's head snapped around toward it. Karl was going to answer it, but the young cop held up his hand and moved quickly to pick up the receiver. With melodramatic self-importance he said, "Yes, who is it?"

Karl, who spent an average of six hours a day on the telephone and considered it an extension of his arm and his instrument of virtuosity, rolled his eyes with disgust.

The young cop listened for a moment, then set the phone on the polished table. Then he looked at Sal. "It's for you. An old friend."

It's for me. An old friend for me.

"I'll take it in the bedroom," Sal said, and walked quickly toward the connecting door.

"I wouldn't take too long." The young cop was still putting on a show for Isabel. "The extortionists may be trying to get through."

Sal shut the bedroom door and saw the little pink princess phone on the bedside table. The bedroom's curtains were parted, and the still-heavy rain was sluicing down the spotless panes. *Just like that last day back in New Orleans.*

Sal sat on the satin bedcover and stared at the phone. *An old friend for me.* Then he picked it up and put it to his ear, just as someone—the Chicano cop?—hung up the receiver in the other room. There was just silence in his ear. *Dead* silence.

Sal put his hand over the mouthpiece and cleared his throat. Then he took his hand away and said, "Hello?"

There was slow, cold, evil laughter on the other end of the line, and now Sal had no doubts about who it was.

"Nicky?"

The icy laughter died, and there was just empty silence again. Nicky was enjoying himself.

Sal waited a few seconds, then again asked, "Nicky?"

Then Nicky Venezia, on the other end, said, "Your voice sounds funny, Sally. I wonder what happened to it."

Sal's hand holding the telephone began to shake, and he steadied it with his left.

"Did you run into—oh—a piece a' piano wire or something?"

Sal couldn't talk. He felt his balls liquefy like ice cubes melting on a hot sidewalk.

"Talk to me, D'Amore, you chickenshit motherfucker."

Sal *willed* himself to speak. "He—he was trying to kill me."

Nicky gave him that laugh again. A laugh you might have heard from the guards on your way to the gas ovens. "You shoudda left him do it. I'm sure your old man woudda been happy with that."

Joe the Hack, Joe the Hack, badly beaten and burned all black. Oh, my God! Oh, my God!

"Nicky," Sal heard himself say, "I have money. I can pay Little Johnny back all I owe him. With the vig."

"Do ya?" Nicky sneered over the phone line. "Where'd you get it, from that little half-nigger tramp you're fucking?"

"Keep her out of this. I don't want her to be—"

"Hey, motherfucker." Nicky's voice lost even the *pretense* of cordiality. "Don't *ever* fucking tell *me* what to *do,* understand? I'll cut your motherfucking heart out."

Sal sat there holding the phone to his ear, hearing Nicky Venezia breathing on the other end of the line. *I'm a dead man. He's gonna kill me.*

Finally Sal forced himself to say something. "He was trying to kill me, Nicky, and he had a heart attack or something. I never laid a fucking hand on him."

Nicky remained silent. Sal could hear him listening. "You can't blame me 'cuz Red had a heart at—"

"You know a place called the Hollywood Reservoir?" Nicky coldly interrupted.

"What?" Sal was confused, off balance. "The Hollywood Reservoir? No, I never heard of it."

"Find it," Nicky said. "Bring the money. Eight o'clock tonight." He laughed that evil chortle again. "I always wanted to say this to somebody—if you try to run, you know what happens to the girl." He chuckled. "You think maybe I'll get discovered by the movies out here in Hollyweird?" Then he hung up.

"Nicky! *Nicky!*" Sal stared at the dead phone a moment, then gently placed it back on its cradle.

The rain poured down the big window as if someone were aiming a hose at it. Sal got up slowly and went back into the bungalow's sitting room.

In the living room Isabel had put on another outfit, and she and Karl were preparing to leave again. The Beverly Hills cops were gone, and now there were three enormous black men in somber business suits. Their Doberman eyes riveted onto Sal, and he could almost hear them growl until Karl called them off.

"Ve are going to the Shrine," Karl said as he helped Isabel into her coat. "I called. Zhey are still rehearsing." He gave Sal an appraising glance. "Perhaps you would want to wash your face before we leave."

"You know, Karl," Sal said as he slumped into a chair, "I really don't feel very good. Getting wet in the rain, the excitement and everything." He rested his head in his hands. "I think I'll go back to bed, try to get some rest so I'll look good for tonight."

"No!" Karl barked, and the black bodyguards glared at Sal as if he'd just flashed a weapon. "You *must* come to the rehearsal! Everything must be perfect!"

Sal looked up at him. "Gimme a break, Karl. You don't need me. Eric can stand in for me." He nodded toward the Swede.

"No! No!" And then Isabel laid her hand on the German's forearm, and a look passed between them. *What was that? What did* that *mean?*

"Very well," Karl said finally. "But if you begin to feel better, I would hope you come to meet us at the venue."

"You got it." Sal watched them file out the door—a bodyguard, Karl, another bodyguard, Isabel, the last bodyguard, and then Eric, who turned around in the doorway to look back at Sal.

"Marco. You all right, dude?"

"I'm great, Eric. Listen, where's Giovanni?" The little old man had been here in his wheelchair, earlier, before Sal had taken Nicky's call in the bedroom.

"The other Brit, the one without the broken jaw, took him over to his own bungalow. Said he was tired." Eric was clearly concerned about his Canadian friend. "You sure you don't want to come with us?"

"Positive. I'm just gonna lay down for a minute." But he made no move toward the bedroom.

Eric studied Sal's face a bit more from the doorway. "Weird thing that happened this morning, eh, dude?"

Sal nodded his head. "Strange, man. *Straaannnnge.*"

Eric waited a moment before he said, "You didn't hear the dude say something to you when he walked by?"

Sal emptied his face of subterfuge and assured, "Swear to Jesus, man. Did you? What'd he say?"

"Couldn't make it out. But the dude said *something.*"

"Strange shit, man," Sal agreed. "Very strange shit."

That seemed to satisfy the Swede. He turned and looked out at the still-falling rain. "Look at this. We left London for this?" Then he looked back at Sal and smiled. "*It never rains in southern California*— See you later, dude." He walked through the door and shut it behind him.

Sal made himself wait three minutes, then he raced out

into the downpour and across the soggy lawn to number 16 bungalow, the European drawing-room one. He knocked on the door, then tried the knob. The unlocked door swung open. Giovanni was sitting in his wheelchair, before a flock of white cranes flying across a lime-green wall. The doctors had warned him about his cigars, but there was a lit one now resting in an ashtray, filling the room with pungent smoke. Giovanni had a pair of shoes on his lap, and was shining them with a soft, stained rag. It was the old man's therapy, Isabel said. Once a cobbler, always a cobbler.

Sal stood in the doorway, dripping water and breathing hard. "Gio, I have to—"

"Come in, Marco. Close the door." The little old man gestured with the gleaming Gemelli de Janeiro cordovan loafer in his hand.

Sal sat in one of the white-crane-on-green-background-upholstered chairs that matched the wall. His hair had washed down across his forehead, and his wet shirt clung to his shoulders. He had forgotten his jacket.

"Giovanni," he began haltingly, "I have a problem."

The old man held up the loafer to the light and turned it this way and that. His gnarled, arthritic hands looked all the more horrific beside the tender, supple leather. He began to buff the shoe with a soft-bristled brush.

"How mucha do they want?" he asked finally.

Sal stared at him. "How—how—"

"They are the *camorra,* no?" He was referring to the Neapolitan mob.

"The *who?*"

Giovanni was buffing the shoe leather with quick, light strokes. "The Mafia," he said softly. He stopped brushing, and looked directly at Sal. "The Siciliani. You have the troubles with the Siciliani. How mucha do they want?"

"How—how do you know?"

Giovanni was absently fingering the shoe brush. "Marco, I am cripple, not stupid." He touched the brush to the side of his head. "You think I builda my company with rocks in my head? I see you don't tella the truth when the *polizia* asks about the men. I see you know these men. They speaka to you. I understand they throwa the pepper in my Isabel's face as a warning. To scare you." He put the polished shoe in his lap and picked up its mate. "How mucha do they want?"

Sal reached over and gripped the arm of the old man's wheelchair. "Giovanni, you understand I love your daughter?"

Giovanni nodded slowly. "Yes, I understand that."

"And I never intended she should ever be harmed."

Giovanni began to work the rag over the second loafer. "No one never hurta my Isabel. Never."

"These are very dangerous men, Gio. They are killers. They think nothing of taking someone's life. They enjoy it."

Giovanni stopped shining and looked at Sal. "Marco, how come you knowa these kinda peoples?"

Sal wearily leaned his weight back into the armchair. "It's a long story, Giovanni. I grew up with them."

Giovanni appraised him with experienced eyes. "Notta in Canada, I don't think. I never believe Canada."

Sal shook his head. "No, in Noo Awlins."

Giovanni gave the loafer a halfhearted buff. "I have a shop in New Orleans." An absentminded nonsequitur. "And you owe these men money?"

"Yes. A gambling debt."

"How mucha?"

Sal breathed before he said, "I figure with the vig and all—the interest—about half a million. Dollars." He watched Giovanni's face for any sign of shock, but there was none. "I'll sign over to you all the writer's royalties from my songs," Sal hastily offered, but Giovanni cut him short with a wave of the loafer.

"When you needa this money?"

"Tonight, Giovanni. Before close of business." He looked quickly at his watch. "Is it already too late?"

"Don'ta worry about the money, I getta the money. But my question is thissa. You give-a them the money—they leave you alone?"

Sal stared at the little cripple with new respect. "Probably not, Giovanni," he said in a very small voice. "Probably they'll kill me."

"There has been blood?"

"Yes." Sal ran his fingers through his wet hair. "They murdered my father."

"Aahhhhh—" Giovanni said, tilting his head back and nodding as if this information made everything crystal clear. "And you killa one of their *famiglia?*"

Sal nodded. "Yeah, I guess you could say that."

Giovanni slowly, thoughtfully, stroked the gleaming leather of the loafer in his hand. "When you give-a these Siciliani the money?"

"Tonight."

"What happens you don't show up? You justa disappear?"

Sal shook his head. "Out of the question. They'd hurt Isabel."

"Suppose-a someone else-a brings the money? *Then* you disappear?"

"It wouldn't make any difference. They'd take the money, kill whoever brought it, then go after Isabel. These people are animals, Giovanni. They want blood."

Giovanni considered all this for a few minutes. Then he said, "Marco, I am inna your debt. Ever since-a we meet you on the boat, my daughter's life is, how you say, turn around. She is happy; she smile-a all the time; hey, she issa bigga recording star. No more tears all night; no more talk about the suicide. In my heart I know-a *you* give-a this to my Isabel." He pointed the shoe at Sal. "I owe-a you, Marco." He carefully placed the pair of loafers on the coffee table between them. Then he said, "Marco, I am old, sick cripple, but I am also very rich. I have-a friends all over the world. Let me make a few phone calls. Just one, maybe two, and we get our own Siciliani. More dangerous than these *bastardi.* We slaughter these animals."

Listen to this old lion, Sal thought. *He's more man than the rest of us put together.*

"That's a bad idea, Gio. These are only a few of the family. The *papà,* the *capo,* is very strong, very powerful, and he would send many others. They would hurt you, Isabel, Karl, all of us."

Giovanni stared at Sal a very long time. *He knows he's looking at a dead man.* Finally he said, "Thissa is the only way?"

Sal nodded slowly. "The only one." *I'm a blood sacrifice. An offering for atonement.*

Giovanni maneuvered his wheelchair around the coffee table and over to the desk, where a supple Giovanni de Gemelli briefcase lay open on the desktop. Giovanni unsnapped a compartment, slipped his hand under some papers, and withdrew a pistol encased in an exquisitely crafted holster. He rested the weapon on his knees, turned his wheelchair back to Sal, then picked up the holstered gun and traced his twisted fingers over the perfectly cut leather.

"I make-a thissa myself. Many years ago." He wrapped his crippled hand around the gun butt and slipped the weapon out of the holster, then in and out again. "See how it fits? Like a glove. Like a Gemelli de Janeiro glove." He smiled proudly in spite of himself and the circumstances. "I buy thissa longa time ago, before the war. From a German colonel in Napoli," he said as he held up the blue-black Luger. "Very nice-a man. He had a mistress, she always want him bring her gifts. So he sella things." He offered the Luger over to Sal. "Marco, I want you to take-a."

Sal stared at the gun in the old man's hands. "I already have a gun." Dago Red's Walther, buried deep under Isabel's costumes.

Giovanni gestured with the Luger. "So. Now you have-a *two*."

Sal took the weapon from the old man. "Giovanni, how'd you get this through airport security?"

Giovanni shrugged. "I am old. I am cripple. I am rich. They know who I am, they leave me alone."

Sal slipped the Luger out of the soft leather. It *looked* like a Nazi killing machine, all screws and bolts and art-deco angles. He touched the dull barrel, and his fingers came away greasy.

"I keepa clean and oiled. Alla these-a years I keepa clean and oiled."

Sal raised the Luger and sighted down the barrel at an imaginary point across the bungalow. *Nicky Venezia's heart.* "You ever fire it, Gio?"

Giovanni shook his head. "Shoota? No, never."

Sal pressed the catch, and the clip of shiny, brassy bullets dropped out of the butt. He examined the rows of 9-millimeter shells jammed into the narrow metal frame. "These are the original shells?"

"Sì."

"Gio, they're fifty years old. You think they're still good?"

Giovanni raised his shoulders and wrinkled his chin. "Why notta?"

Sal inspected the Luger a moment more, then he slipped it back into the holster and held it loosely in his fingers.

"Is a, how you say"—Giovanni made motions under his armpit—"it wrap around here."

"A shoulder holster."

"Yes, *sì*, a shoulder holster. I make myself a longa time ago."

"Thank you, Gio."

They sat for a while, neither one saying anything. The rain still plinked against the bungalow's windows.

"I make-a phone call. The money will be here in a few hours."

"Thank you, Gio."

"You needa cash, of course."

"Of course."

"I fix."

They sat, staring at the lime-green carpet, for a long time, and Sal realized this was good-bye. The old man was saying good-bye. This was a wake.

"Gio, I don't want Isabel to know about this. This is her day, and I don't want anything to—to— I don't want her to worry."

The twisted little old man understood. "Don't worry."

"And no matter what happens tonight, everything we talked about is just between you and me."

Giovanni nodded. "Of course."

"I don't want her to be involved in this shit at all, at any level."

"Yes."

"And what she don't know can't hurt her."

The old man had to agree. "Is true."

Sal looked around the room. "We could draw up a contract, right now, on hotel stationery, and I could sign over to you all of my writer's royalties—"

"Marco." Giovanni held up his hand. "Please. The money is nothing. You have given me, you have given my Isabel, so mucha. I owe-a you forever." *He's already got me buried. He sees vultures circling over my head.*

"Gio," Sal began haltingly, "whatever happens tonight. I mean, if I don't come back—" He began to cry softly. "I want—

I want you to tell Izzy—I want you to tell her how much I love her."

Giovanni averted his eyes, because he began to cry, too. "I will tell her, Marco."

My name is Sal.

"I love her very much, Gio."

The old man nodded, tears coursing down his sunken, ancient cheeks.

"I never thought I could ever love a woman like this, but I do. I love her—I love her more than life," Sal choked out.

A tear hung off the end of the old man's nose. "I understand. I understand." He looked at Sal. "I love her mother the same-a way." His eyes turned inward. "When she die, I feel like God, He ripped the heart from my breast with His fingers, so much it hurt."

Sal was crying openly now, and the old man reached over and touched his arm. Sal took the old man's knobby, blue-veined hand in his and held it tightly. *Reaching out from the grave.*

"You are so *coraggioso,* Marco," the old man sobbed. "So brave."

Sal looked up, his face wet and distressed, and said, "My name is Sal. And I'm a coward."

Isabel was one of the first artists to perform, and when her name was announced, all the kids in the third-tier balcony—the high, cheap seats—began to scream and whistle and call her name, and they continued doing so all through her performance. Some years the Grammy Awards are remarkably dominated by a single artist—Michael Jackson in '83, Christopher Cross in '80, Stevie Wonder in '73, '74, and '76—and this was obviously going to be Isabel's year. By the time she'd begun her performance of "The Touch of a Stranger," Sal's song that was nominated for Song of the Year, she'd already won in two categories: Best Pop Vocal Performance Female and Best R&B Vocal Female, and the television voice-over announcers were already predicting an across-the-board sweep for the international superstar from Brazil via Europe. As she strutted defiantly to center stage and began to sing—that voice, that face, that presence!—an electric current ran through the nominees, producers, and record executives in the twelve-thousand-dollar blocks of seats right in front of the stage. This was Isabel's premier live performance in America, so for most of the industry powers it was their first close look at her, and they were as dazzled as the kids shrieking in the top rows. Her videos were entertaining, certainly, but to an industry audience jaded by their knowledge of how studio gimmickry can make shit shine, videos were meaningless marketing tools. Seeing her here, live before them—*hearing* that voice come at them from only a few feet away—this was a whole other thing. Her videos couldn't capture her personality, her emotion, her *talent.* Not the way this live performance was doing. She had the whole auditorium literally in the palm of her hand. The television cameras following her every move broadcast out to the 50 million viewers all over the world the image of a young, supremely gifted artist, caught at the first full blossom of her musical powers and physical beauty. The number of pop performers who had brought the Academy to its knees the way Isabel was presently doing could be counted on one hand, with a finger or two left over. It had been many years since an artist of such *substance* had been able to translate his musical mastery into the unbroken string of platinum singles and double-platinum albums Isabel had accomplished. The kids loved her, and the critics lauded her with superlatives. She had topped the industry charts and the elitist reviewers' year-end Critic's Choice lists. She was a worldwide *phenomenon,* and when the band pounded out a funky little rhythm break in the middle of the tune and Isabel and her two backup singers executed some inner-city Paula Abdul dance moves that they'd done on the video, the entire Shrine Civic Auditorium, from big-money heavyweights on the ground level to teenaged airheads in the free third-balcony seats, went nuts and leapt to their feet in adoration. The accompanying roar shook the cavernous hall.

The roar was still ringing in his ears as Sal dashed up the steps to the back of the Shrine, then down to the front entrance. The security personnel nodded and opened the door for him, and Sal stepped out into the night.

Incredibly, it was still raining—a steady, droning downpour. Although it was only a little after six, the wintry weather had brought on deep night several hours early. Across the street the stands that were annually packed with screaming fans jostling to catch a glimpse of their favorite stars were largely deserted this year except for a handful of hard-core diehards who were huddled together under umbrellas and makeshift squares of canvas. The street was lined with double-parked limos, some with their motors running and their exhausts spewing thin plumes of white smoke. Halfway down the block a tent with a table of coffee urns had been set up for the chauffeurs, and they were bunched there, out of the rain, watching the Awards on portable TVs and Watchmans. For as long as he could, Sal stayed under cover of the long red canopy that stretched out to Figueroa Street—the stars couldn't be expected to get wet, could they?—then he jogged down the wet sidewalk to the driver's tent. Walking around the perimeter of the crowd of joking, laughing drivers, Sal searched for a particular face. He found it under a black chauffeur's cap and over a cup of steaming brown coffee. Feeling his touch on her arm, the blond driver turned and, seeing Sal, gave him a warm, surprised invitation of a smile. *Whatever you want,* her silent lips said, *I am at your service. Your wish is my command.*

Sal returned the smile, giving her his most poignant eye contact. "I'm so sorry," he softly apologized. "I've forgotten your name."

"Diana," she breathed back as they slowly led each other to the edge of the dripping tent, away from the others. Her peach-glossed grin grew wider. "You don't have to tell me who you are. You're Marco Toledano."

Close, but no cigar. "Listen, Diana. I need a favor."

She stepped in closer and rested a thin, pale hand on the lapel of his tuxedo, about an inch away from the bulge that was Giovanni's shoulder-holstered German Luger. "Whatever, Mr. Toledano," Diana promised. "Whatever."

"Marco," Sal said. "Please call me Marco. I'm afraid I left something in the limo," Sal delivered the line with as much shy embarrassment as he thought convincing. "Could you give me the keys and tell me where it's parked?"

Diana's eyes shone with catlike intensity. "Why don't we go look for it together?" she purred, meaning, *You came out here* after *something, all right, but not anything you* lost.

"I don't want you to miss the show." Sal nodded back at the portable televisions.

She moved her fingertips up and down the satin lapel. "*You're* missing the show. Whatever you want in the limo must be *very* important." *Let's go,* her blue eyes pleaded. *Let's go to the limo and* do it. *While she's gathering up all her awards. That would be perfect. Let me kiss the lips that kiss the lips of the most famous woman in the world. Let's go to the limo and I'll suck the cock that fucks the biggest star in the world.*

Her fingers edged closer and closer to the bulge under his tux, and Sal took her hand in his and brought it up to his lips. He gently kissed the knuckle of each finger in turn. Then he looked longingly into her baby blues and whispered, "We're gonna be in town for a coupla weeks at least. Let's wait until we have more time." He kissed the last knuckle. "And a place more appropriate than the backseat of a limo."

She gave him a wicked leer that somehow seemed right at home on her delicate English china features. "There *is* no more appropriate place than the backseat of a limo."

Sal made himself chuckle, and she held out a finger with the dangling key ring and dropped it into his open palm. Then she leaned her head into his and brushed his mouth with her glossed lips. She smelled of makeup and strong coffee. "It's the last stretch limo at the end of the block, around the corner. You're sure you want to do this alone?" She pouted so very prettily.

No, I wish I had the fucking Seventh Cavalry.

"I'm afraid I have to." He held the keys. "Be right back."

There was a tinny combined roar from the aggregated televisions. Isabel had won another Grammy. The blond driver turned away her attention for a moment, and Sal was moving quickly away, into the rain. He turned up his tux collar and held it tightly around his throat. He thought he heard Diana shout something behind him, but he didn't look back. He skidded on the wet pavement in his patent-leather dress shoes like a drunken teenager, but he found the white stretch limo with very little problem, unlocked the door, and slid in. He was already damp, cold, and miserable, and this hellish night had only just begun. He started the engine, and jumped when the television in the coach section exploded into life behind him.

"—with her win in the Best Rock Performance Female category that makes pretty much a clean sweep for Isabel in the Female Vocal Awards. Coming up next—"

She was taking them all, just as he'd thought. Just as he'd dreamed.

He settled back against the plush white leather seat, got as comfortable as a man can get with a shoulder holster and another handgun stuck in his waistband, wheeled the limo away from the curb, and was on his way. *To what? On my way to what? Christ knows.*

Stealing the limo had been a last-minute idea. He could have taken a cab up to the Hollywood Reservoir, but he'd felt that would've looked suspicious. People don't take cabs to graveyards or reservoirs. And everyone said it was impossible to catch a taxi in L.A. Or he could've rented a car, but he hadn't had the time. And it seemed to him that people who were about to get their lives ended prematurely were foolish to hassle with car-rental agencies. That little transaction was, like signing for dinner and having suits tailored by famous designers, for people who were in control of their lives, for successes, for *winners.* And anyone who has to drive up to a padlocked lake on a rainy night to offer up his life as a blood sacrifice is a stone fucking loser. *See,* he told himself, *they already got you thinking like they want you to. They already got you on the run.* No, someone who is stupid enough to drive in the rain to the scene of his own premeditated murder should *have* to steal a vehicle to get there. Preferably a limo.

"Rap music, born in the inner-city ghettos of New York and Los Angeles," the stentorian announcer pontificated, "has become a valid and valuable musical form, well loved and well traveled all around the world!"

I'm *well traveled now,* Sal thought as he negotiated the wet, snarled rush-hour L.A. traffic. *I been all over the fucking world.* The Grammy Awards Presentation was started so early because the show had to be televised live to the East Coast during prime time. *Me, who never left the limits of Orleans Parish his whole fucking life—now I been all over Europe, all through North and South America. Everywhere. What was that thing Sonny Scalise used to say? See Naples and die. Sonny's people were Neapolitan. Like Giovanni.*

"I'm a killer, I'm a gangsta, I'm a dope bad mutha—" the rapper boasted in his manic, mean-street testosterone chant. *"I got my weapons, my colors, my home boy bruthas!"*

The stretch limousine was caught in the traffic of the Hollywood Freeway like a big white whale surrounded by a school of small, dull tuna. Sal had gotten directions from a Mexican busboy at the Shrine, but within minutes he was hopelessly lost, trying to figure out how to get off the freeway. Looking around, it was obvious southern Californians had no idea how to drive in the rain, with the cars inching forward cautiously on the slick, shiny pavement.

"I don't need readin', I don't need writin'. To live in my world you need a heart for fightin'!"

Sal sat in the long white limo, stranded in a clogged river of rain-washed automobiles, staring out at the wet world beyond his windshield wipers, and thought, *I'm a dead man.* He lit a cigarette—Diana had stocked fresh packs of several different brands—and blew a stream of smoke at the fogging glass. *It all ends here, tonight. On the night that should have been the happiest of my life. God is one sick fucking comedian. Oh, my God, I am heartily sorry You have offended me so. You dangled it all right before my eyes, You allowed me to experience it all—the clean, eternal smell of Isabel's just-showered body, the clutch of her vagina, and the ripple of her laughter. The emptied yet somehow complete feeling after I've climaxed in her; the glow in people's eyes when they finally see you after waiting all night for a glimpse; the deference in a desk clerk's demeanor when he finds out who you are, or a maître d's or a concert promoter's, anywhere in the world; the smile on people's faces when they're in your presence, as if you had bestowed on them some great gift just by being there; the sound of a forty-five-thousand seat stadium singing along with your words and music when Isabel playfully held the mike out to them.*

All these wonderful experiences, these warming memories, only to be sent to a cold grave by Nicky Venezia and his verminous clan. An old half-crazy, half-white piano player, back in New Orleans, used to get drunk and leer from the keyboard at all the pasty-faced Yankee tourists, cackling, "No matter how high the eagle fly, you kin still break a windo' wid a hamma." And Sal had never quite understood what old Booker was saying, but now he knew, now he understood. There is no safety from people like Nicky Venezia. There is no sanctuary from murderers, regardless of who you are, or who you've become. They can always get to you. Lee Harvey Oswald understood this. Sirhan Sirhan and James Earl Ray, too. There is no heaven; there's only hell.

"To live in my world—You can't be 'fraid to die! To live in my world—You gotta commit homicide! To live in my world—You can't be 'fraid to die! To live in my world—You gotta be cold as ice!"

Inconceivably Sal and the big white limo were lost for almost two hours. As completely adrift in the sea of automobiles that is Los Angeles as a life raft in the North Atlantic. With the little television behind him ticking off each of Isabel's wins with a kind of mounting inevitability—"And the year's Best New Artist is . . . *Isabel!*"—Sal at first was frantic, whipping the wheel around and trying to maneuver the big, behemoth automobile like a sports car, accompanied by a following chorus of horns and rain-muffled curses. He'd wanted to get to the reservoir *before* the Venezias. He'd wanted to get the lay of the place. To see where they'd try and corner him, where they'd most probably kill him. Prevented by the traffic from doing that, he screamed in the limo, pounded on the dashboard, shook the wheel. And then the whole thing became moot. He turned ice-cold inside. Like a dead man. Which, of course, was what he was. The rain slushed down the big Cadillac's windshield, the wipers swept back and forth like a sixty-thousand-dollar metronome, and something happened inside of Salvatore Christopher D'Amore, aka Marco Toledano. Somewhere something ruptured, and a vein of ice, like a fast-moving glacier, like a volcano of frigid lava, flowed through Sal's body. He *accepted* his death. He welcomed it like a ghoulish lover. He gave himself up to it, and it gifted him back with a calm, a quiet, a deadness. It was inevitable, as incontrovertible as Isabel's sweep of the awards.

He wedged the limo through the Hollywood Hills maze of narrow, slick streets lined with Spanish stuccos and postmodern boxes, streets with names like Glen Holly and Glen Tower, San Marco Drive and Canyon Lake Drive. Mulholland. From time to time lightning would crackle across the black sky like fireworks and light up the crowded hunchbacked hills. Then the big pale HOLLYWOOD sign would glow like neon, and he could see the dark clouds hanging over the lights of the L.A. basin like God's wrath.

Sal drove in circles, up hills and down ridges, to the end of streets with missed NO OUTLET signs. Then he would have to back the big white limo around blind curves and start again. Sometimes the rain came harder, sounding like a hail of pellets on the limo's roof, and then a minute later it would slack off and the wipers would shriek dryly as they whipped across the glass. He had just started to be convinced that there *was* no Hollywood Reservoir—before the busboy had given him the obviously bad directions, he'd talked to three locals who'd never *heard* of Hollywood Reservoir—when he realized he'd been driving around it for the past several minutes. He braked the limo to a fishtailing stop on the dark wet street. A battered street sign under a rain-haloed arc light confirmed that it was Lake Hollywood Drive. There was an eight-foot chain-link fence running around what seemed to be the ridge of the reservoir's basin, and just then the lightning sparked again, and there was the lake far below, reflecting the jagged flash back up through the wet pine trees that covered her sloping banks. Sal sat silently staring down at the lake. *There it is,* he thought. *There's where I'm gonna die.* There was a gust of wind and rain across the hood of the limo, like a walking line of automatic gunfire. *I wonder if they're gonna throw my body in the lake.* He remembered a line from an old James Cagney movie about a guy being fitted for cement shoes. *That's it,* he admonished himself. *Keep your sense of humor. You're gonna need it in hell.* Sal eased his foot off the brake and gave the limo a little gas. A hundred feet farther along there was a rusting sign wired to the chain-link fence.

HOLLYWOOD RESERVOIR
WATER SUPPLY FOR THE CITY OF LOS ANGELES
ADMINISTERED BY THE DEPARTMENT OF WATER AND POWER

Sal touched a button on the limo's door, and the driver's side window roboted down. The rain instantly whipped in and slapped his face, as if it were *seeking* him. Sal shielded his eyes with his hand and leaned out the window. Even through the steady downpour he could hear the sound of water rushing powerfully to meet some secret destination. The Mexican busboy had thought there was an old dam up here somewhere—

"Es for the joggers, ju know?"—and that must be what Sal was hearing. Water being pushed along by great pressure. Gently nudging the limo down the winding, deserted street, he looked down through the chain-link fence and kept catching glimpses of the reservoir. Then he turned the limousine into what had to be the main entrance to the lake's tarmac service road, and Sal's stomach flip-flopped when he saw that the padlocked gate had been forced. One side of the gate had been pulled back, the snipped chain dangling down, while the other side rocked back and forth with the wind and rain. The busted padlock had been dropped in the middle of the service road, as a kind of signpost: THIS WAY TO ETERNITY. *I can't believe this is happening. I can't believe this is happening.* Of course, he'd known they'd be waiting for him—*Fuck, I came to meet them*—but seeing the jimmied gate and the popped lock lying in a swirling eddy of rain on the black road made the impending violence suddenly seem very close and very real. *This ain't no dress rehearsal, motherfucker.* He stared at the side of the gate that was swinging back and forth, back and forth, a few feet this way and then a few feet back. On the television the Academy, in a pretense of culture over finance, was paying tribute to some dead Spanish composer, and a young cellist was playing one of his compositions—a solemn, sorrowful étude that drifted out of Sal's open window and echoed eerily through the glittering rain, across the pines and muddy, scrub-covered hills. *I can't believe this is happening.* Sal inched the limo forward until its bumper gently kissed the swinging gate. The gate rolled open and stuck in a clump of coarse weeds. Sal slipped the big limo through the opening and eased it down the narrow, serpentine road that circled the reservoir. *This must be the joggers' track.* There was another chain-link fence along the inner edge of the pathway, and behind it the lake down below at the bottom of the pine tree-covered slopes. On the other side of the paved road, high above, lights glinted through the rain from the big homes perched on the mountains that ringed the lake. Sal slowly squeezed the Cadillac over the slippery blacktopped path for another hundred yards, then the lightning cracked again, and the pathway was blocked by another violated gate, this one thrown open across the pathway. *I can't believe this is happening.* Sal stopped the limo and got out. His tuxedo was immediately soaked. He walked up to the open gap in the fence and looked down, toward the lake. A barely discernible hard-beaten trail, almost entirely covered by pine needles, slipped down into the darkness under the trees. *This is where I'm gonna fucking die. In the forest with fucking Hansel and Gretel and the Big Bad Wolf.* The sound of rushing water was louder here, out of the car. *What do I do? Do I walk down there, or do I drive the limo? Do I hafta go down there at all? Why can't I just turn this big white bastard around and drive it all the fucking way to Vancouver? Why? Because of Isabel, asshole. You can't run out on this one. Nicky wouldn't be a very happy camper if you rabbited on him, and he would definitely take it out on Izzy. That's what he was telling you this morning with the hot sauce. Funny, any other woman in my life I wouldda let her take her chances. I wonder how Nicky knew that Izzy was different. I wonder how he knew I wouldn't run.*

The cellist finished playing, and there was tumultuous applause from the Shrine audience. Sal got back into the car just in time to hear a screaming promo for the eleven o'clock news.

"Join Chad and Tricia for all the backstage highlights—"

He had to jockey the limo back and forth several times before he could maneuver it into a position to clear the narrow fence posts. Even so, going through he felt a backup mirror get sheared off.

"—overtime for the Lakers at Golden State. Fred'll tell you who finally won it—"

Driving down the slope was like entering a tunnel. The headlights shone an unnaturally bright path through the falling rain. The tree limbs hung low and brushed at the Cadillac's fenders, bumped hollowly over the roof. The pine-needle-strewn service road was old and badly maintained, and with the wet and mud it was all Sal could do to keep the limo from veering off and slamming into a tree trunk.

"And Fritz will tell us when this storm will end, if *ever*—"

Sal followed the service road down to the lake's edge and bounced along the water's edge for a hundred feet. The water's roar was at first deafening, and then, as he got away from the dam, the noise subsided. He was inching along the slick road when he saw a light flash among the trees above him. There was someone up there. He braked to a stop and clicked off his headlights.

"And now back to the Shrine Auditorium and the Grammy Awa—"

Sal killed the limo's engine, and the night was suddenly

silent and filled with sound. The water gushing behind him, the rain *plunking* on the roof, the white leather seats creaking beneath his ass. The windshield, deprived of its wipers, quickly became opaque and impenetrable, and Sal opened the door and got out. Immediately he felt cold mud ooze over the tops of his tuxedo shoes. Raindrops crept under his collar and plunged down his back. He took a few sucking steps away from the car, blinking up at where he thought he'd seen the flash of movement. Without the limo's headlights, the reservoir's park was a different world now, dark and dense and primeval. Hardly a place that was only ten minutes from Hollywood Boulevard.

There was another sizzle of lightning from the other side of the hills, and the reservoir was momentarily lit up, as if from a giant flashbulb, and Sal definitely saw something moving up there in the pines. He cupped his hands over his eyes to keep out the rain and peered up at the dying light on the hillside.

"Looking for something, Sal?" came from behind him, and Sal whipped around to face the sound. There was a click, and for a microsecond Sal thought, *They're gonna shoot me!,* and then he was bathed in the blinding beam of an eight-battery flashlight.

"Nicky?" Sal said tremulously, squinting at the glare through his outstretched fingers. "Nicky?"

There was a chuckle through the soft rain. "Who was you expectin', asshole? Dago Red?"

They're gonna kill me. They are gonna kill me.

The flashlight's beam seemed to come a bit closer, up from the lake's edge. There was movement just to the left of the light, but Sal couldn't make out anything definite.

"I—I brought the money."

There was no answer, and Sal thought, *That was real fucking bright. Now they can kill me at any time.*

"Could you—could you turn out the light?"

For a long time there was only the gentle music of the rain falling on the lake. And then Nicky's voice said, "Move away from the car."

Sal looked down at his mud-caked dress shoes illuminated in the flashlight's beam and stumbled a few feet away from the limo. Then he squinted back at where Nicky's voice had come from behind the flashlight's blaze.

"I can't see anything." *I won't know when you're killing me.*

There was another cold chuckle, and a shiver flashed down Sal's spine. Then the flashlight's beam moved down a few degrees, and Sal blinked rapidly at the soothing darkness. In only a few seconds he could force himself to make out the shadowy image of Nicky's sneering face. Then he looked to the left, where he had seen something before, and there was Junior Venezia standing in the darkness and holding one of those "street-sweeper" shotguns, the kind with the round canister of shells bolted to the frame. Junior held the shotgun waist high, and it was pointed at Sal.

Oh, Jesus. Oh, Jesus Christ.

Then Sal forced his heart to stop thumping in the back of his throat. He made himself think, think, *think! Wait a minute, wait a minute! Where's the other one? Where's Jimmy Van? We can't have a party until everyone gets here.*

"You brought the money? Where is it?" Nicky asked calmly, just as if it were only another drug buy.

Sal willed his voice not to quaver. "It's in the trunk."

Sal could just make out Nicky's smile beyond the glare. "It's in the trunk," Nicky softly mocked. "Where the fuck else would it be? Junior?"

"Yeah, Nicky?"

"Go get the money out the trunk."

"Yeah, Nicky."

Junior laid the shotgun over his shoulder, hunter style, and then trudged like an obedient ape up the slope toward the limo, his long overcoat dragging heavily through the tall coarse grasses. Sal, looking at Nicky, could see raindrops glint like diamonds as they fell on a slant through the flashlight's beam.

"How did you find me?" Sal asked Nicky.

Nicky didn't answer right away. Killer's prerogative. "Asshole, you wanna hide from somebody, you don't hang around with the most famous bitch in the fucking world."

"It was—it was the picture in *Time* magazine, then?"

Nicky laughed again. Not a friendly sound. "What, you figure you gonna sue them for damages after I kill you?"

There was nothing Sal could say to that.

"Lemme tell you something, you stupid musician fuck," Nicky continued in an instructive tone of voice. "We knew where you were three fucking months ago, we was just waiting for you to come back to the States."

Jesus.

"Them photographers had pictures of that tramp of yours in every magazine in the country—*People, Newsweek, Rolling Stone*—and there you was, Mr. Big Time, you fucking asshole, always next to that little slut, walking out of restaurants, leaving them big parties, taking in the sights of London, Paris, where-the-fuck-ever." There was almost a note of envy in Nicky Venezia's voice. A whoremaster's chagrin. "You think that fucking beard could fool us?"

"Hey!" Junior shouted from where he was seated in the open limo. "I can't find no button for the trunk!"

"You know how to open the trunk?" Nicky asked Sal.

"Only with the key."

"Where's the key?"

"I left it in the ignition."

Nicky started to shout, "Look in the—" and then the night was filled with the audio of the coach's television again.

"And now back to tonight's host, Mr. Billy Crystal!"

"Hey," Junior marveled loudly, "they got a switch in here turns on the TV without nothing else!"

"That's fucking wonderful!" Nicky shouted back. "Now, turn it back off!"

Nicky and Sal stared at each other over the beam of light. It was starting to rain harder again. The sparkling raindrops were increasing.

"Our next category is Record of the Year, presented each year to the best single recording released during—"

"Now, I can't find the motherfucker!" Junior bellowed back.

"For Chrissakes, Junior! Just get the key out the car and get the motherfucking money!"

Sal glanced back at the limo. Junior extricated his short, thick body from the limo and slouched down the stretch limo's endless length toward the rear end. Now, he was carrying the shotgun in the crook of his arm, pointed downward. Safety first.

"Nicky," Sal began, looking back at the face over the flashlight, "I never killed the Dago." He shook his head with exaggerated honesty, like a child actor. "I swear to Christ, man, I never touched him."

Nicky said nothing. The cold raindrops were beginning to drip off of Sal's nose.

"Nicky, man," Sal pleaded, "he was trying to fucking *strangle* me, man! What the fuck was I supposed to do, just stand there like I didn't have no feelings?"

Junior finally had the trunk open. "Hey, where is it?" he yelled from where he was illuminated by the trunk's little bulb. "In the briefcase?"

Where the fuck else? Where the fuck else? Sal's mind screamed. *In the Gemelli de Janeiro briefcase.*

"Nicky, for Chrissakes, man, I didn't lay a fucking finger on him! I'm a fucking *piano player,* man. He had a motherfucking heart attack or something. You gotta believe me, man!"

"—and the Record of the Year is—"

"Yeah," Junior shouted, "it's in the briefcase!"

"Count it!" Nicky ordered.

"Ah, for Chrissakes!" Junior complained. "It's fucking *raining,* Nick!"

"Fucking count it!"

"—*'The Touch of a Stranger'!* Isabel wins another one!"

Where's Jimmy Van? Where the fuck is Jimmy Van?

"Nicky, please, you gotta understand—"

"Red La Rocca," Nicky Venezia began with cold fury in his voice, "did five years for Little Johnny. That's the kinda guy he was. Five years in the Gola, and he never asked for nuthin'. He comes out after five years, passes by the house for dinner, he never mentions the five years again. Ever. That's what he was made of, capisc'?"

They're gonna throw my body in the reservoir, Sal suddenly realized. *That's why we're here. They're gonna kill me and throw my body in the reservoir. I'm so stupid. I am so fucking stupid.*

"Red La Rocca give me my first bicycle, my first joint, he bought me my first piece of ass." Nicky's anger was palpable. It radiated out like the beam of light. "Red La Rocca was the ballsiest motherfucker I ever knew. And you, you piece of musician slime, you fucking killed him!"

Jesus Christ, it's gonna be cold at the bottom of that lake. Fish are gonna nibble my eyes. Snakes are gonna crawl up my ass.

"I didn't, Nicky! I swear it on my mother's grave!"

"Once again, I like to thank everyone," Isabel's beautiful girlish speaking voice echoed across the lake, "but *especial* my producer, Karl Diederich. Thank you, Karl! Thank you!" Then the tumultuous applause, sounding tinny and compressed in the TV's tiny speakers.

"Nicky, you gotta lissen to me, man!"

"You know what I'd like to lissen to, motherfucker?" Nicky was working himself into a killing rage. "I'd like to lissen to you scream like your old man did—"

Joe the Hack, Joe the Hack—

"—scream like your old man did when we put the torch to his fucking asshole!"

Oh, Jesus, Oh, Jesus. Sal could see it. His father stripped naked, held facedown on a dirty cement-slab floor, Junior standing on his shoulders, Jimmy Van ahold of his legs, Nicky spreading the old man's slack buttocks and exposing the tender, brown anus-flower; and Little Johnny approaching with the sputtering blue-yellow flame.

"The old wino screamed like a girl!" Sal could hear it, could hear old Joe shrieking like a rabbit in a trap, could smell the urine and excrement spreading like blood across the cement-slab floor. "But the stupid old bastard never told us where you was!"

"He never knew," Sal heard someone say, and then realized it was himself.

"Yeah, I figured that."

"Aw, fuck!" Junior cursed from the trunk of the limo. "I lost my count, Nicky!"

"He never knew," Sal said again.

"No great loss," Nicky mocked.

"Hey, Nicky!" Junior bellowed. "It's raining fucking *hard,* man. Do I have to start again?"

"You know what else I'd like to hear?" Nicky continued. "I'd like to hear that little whore of yours sing with my dick up her asshole."

"Nicky! Whattya say, man?"

"Right after this commercial message—"

He's gonna go after Izzy anyway. The money means nothing.

"Nicky!"

"Or maybe she'd sing better if I use a blowtorch, like your old man. Maybe she'd—"

Motherfucker! Motherfucker! Mother—"

Sal snatched the Walther from under his belt, pointed it through the flashlight glare at where Nicky's heart should have been and fired. The look on Venezia's face was more of comic surprise than fear as he lost his balance on the sopping ground and began to pinwheel his arms. The searchlight went flying, and Sal was in the blessed darkness. He turned to face Junior, who was scrambling to pick up the Street Sweeper shotgun he had laid in the trunk. Sal jerked off a shot at the shimmering silhouette of the white limo, and there was a *thwack* sound as the bullet slammed into the fiberglass body. Sal fired again, there was the shattering of glass, and Junior disappeared behind the limo. Sal swung the Walther back around to where Nicky was, but Nicky wasn't there anymore. And then Sal was aware of a chattering *clack-clack-clack-clack* from somewhere above and behind, and he felt chunks of mud slapping at his wet trousers.

Jimmy Van! Jimmy Van and his machine pistol! The ground around Sal's feet was being chewed up by bullets fired from too great a range. Sal threw himself to the wet dirt and began to scramble through the mud and pine needles. The coarse California grasses tore at his face as he crawled, scooted, and wriggled toward the safety of the pine trees.

"Kill him!" Nicky screamed from somewhere down around the lake. *"Kill him!"*

Sal clambered across the wet ground on all fours like an animal, scratching and clawing his way toward the sheltering trees.

"Kill the motherfucker!"

There was another series of rapid staccato reports, and Sal saw the impacts splash through a muddy rivulet twenty feet in front of him. He buried his face in the mud and covered his head with his arms.

I don't wanna die I don't wanna die I don't wanna die!

The walking line of shells passed three feet from his face, and a thrown-up wad of damp earth struck his face like a warning kiss.

"Where is he?" Nicky bellowed into the night.

No, no, no, no, no—

Then the *clack-clack-clack-clack* stopped, and without hesitation Sal stood up and started running to the trees. His ruined patent-leather shoes slithered over the wet ground, and his tuxedo pants clung wetly to his thighs, but he pumped his knees and leaned forward toward the line of pines fifty, forty-five, forty feet away.

"*Over there!*" he heard Jimmy Van shout from somewhere up the slope.

"Where?" Nicky's voice asked.

"Over *there!*"

Thirty feet, twenty-five—

Then Nicky's flashlight was probing the dark trees to Sal's right.

Fifteen, ten—

Then the beam flickered over him and searched to his left.

Eight, six, five—

The dagger of light slashed back across the ground and stabbed Sal from behind.

Four, three—

"*There* he is! Junior! *Junior!*"

There was a roar that sounded to Sal's ears like a sonic boom, and directly in front of him the trunk of a pine seemed to explode, leaving a gaping hole of splintered, fleshlike wood.

Noooooooooooooo—

Then Sal was running among the trees, and the beam of the light flashed wildly over the wet pines as it searched for him.

"*Junior!*"

Sal pumped his legs as he scrambled up the muddy slope, flailing at low-hanging branches that tore at his face, then there was another roar from the shotgun, then another and another, like a chain reaction of explosions, and Sal felt the air around him rended by pellets and rocketing bits of wood. He slooshed through a puddle and dived into a sodden pile of muddy pine needles, burrowing his head like a rabbit and screaming silently as the endless barrage ripped through the pines above.

Then the night was silent again.

"Did I get him?" Sal heard Junior shout from down the hill. Sal lifted his head and saw Nicky's flashlight beam methodically hunting for him among the tree trunks only a few yards away.

"Did I get him?"

Sal froze and watched the circle of light as it slid over the muddy ground. Then it halted, turned, and was coming for him, and he eased down into the pine needles like an animal crouching from a predator as the flashlight slipped over his back without seeing him and moved away in the rain. *I am invisible.*

"Did I get—"

"Put another canister up his ass!" Nicky's voice rolled over the slope. Sal carefully rose from the compost pile of pine needles and quickly drifted away from their voices, slinking from the shelter of one tree to another. He had almost made it to the top of the slope when there was another flash of lightning, and Sal could see the chain-link fence fifty feet in front of him. Then there was another shotgun blast, and Sal jumped for cover and pressed his back against a pine, keeping the tree between him and the Venezias. There were several more muffled-sounding explosions—one of them sending a rain of branches and needles down on Sal's head—then another long moment of dead silence.

"Did I get him?"

Junior's voice seemed distant now, echoey through the trees and sheets of rain. Sal could feel the bark of the pine pricking his back through his soaked tux. He could hear his heart pounding in his ears. Each pulse was like a kettledrum downbeat—*whump! whump! whump!*

"Where the fuck—"

"Jimmy! Jimmy!"

Sal was looking up at the top of the chain-link fence. *What was it—ten feet?* He had to get to the crest of the hill, pull himself up the fence and over to the other side. He had to—

"Jimmy!"

As if in answer, Sal heard someone not ten yards away utter a soft curse under his breath, then he saw Jimmy Van moving stealthily through the trees, the machine pistol held at the ready across his chest. Jimmy was walking right toward him, but he was looking down the hill, searching the slope for Sal. Or his body.

"Jimmy!" Nicky shouted from down by the lake.

"Did I get him?" Junior bellowed.

Jimmy Van didn't answer them. He kept approaching, his head turned and watching the hillside below for any movement. *He doesn't know I'm here. He doesn't know—*

"Jimmy!"

Jimmy Van shifted the MAC-10's weight in his hands and tightened his hold on the pistol grip. He was only a dozen feet away now, coming slowly and surely, placing each step with silent care. *He doesn't know. He doesn't know.* Sal pressed his back against the narrow tree and looked up at the fence on the top of the ridge. *Too late now. It's too late now.* He looked back at Jimmy Van, and the thin, overcoated man moved another step closer. *Oh, Sweet Jesus. Oh, Sweet Jesus.*

Jimmy Van was only a few feet away now, and Sal could see the raindrops glistening on his balding forehead. The collar of his overcoat was turned up and buttoned, and his eyes were wary and focused as they scanned back and forth, back and forth down the hillside. *Oh, my God.*

The adrenaline was screaming through Sal's bloodstream like a police siren. He looked down at his hands. In his left was a fistful of mud and pine needles he'd clutched in his climb up the hill. In his right, incredibly, was Dago Red's Walther P-88. Sal slowly raised the 9-millimeter automatic until it was level with Jimmy Van's face.

Jimmy Van moved another step nearer—he was so close now that Sal could hear the other man's breathing—and then something in Jimmy's mind alerted him to Sal's shadowy presence and the movement of the weapon, and he turned his head to look right into the Walther's muzzle, only inches away. Then his eyes raised to find Sal's, and Sal could see the terror there, and he hated it because, of all of them, he'd always liked Jimmy Van, and then with a grunt he squeezed the trigger and Jimmy Van's brow imploded and the back of his head blew out like a cheap tire doing seventy on hot asphalt. One moment he was a man, and the next he was bloody garbage lying in a puddle of mud and brains. A long way from home.

"What the fuck was that?" Junior hollered.

"Jimmy! Jimmy!"

Sal jammed the pistol into his tux pocket as he stumbled

up the rest of the slope and threw himself with a clatter as high up the chain-link fence as he could jump. He hung there, grasping at the wet wire, his muddy dress shoes scrambling for a purchase, as the sound of the Venezias crashing up the hill reverberated through the piney woods.

"Jimmy! Jimmy!"

Sal stretched his arm up to its full extension and groped frantically at the pipe running along the top of the chain link. With a grunt he finally got a solid grip and began to pull himself up. He got one elbow over the top of the wire and hung there gasping for breath. Then there was another lightning bolt, and Sal was caught in the phosphorous flash.

"Nicky! Lookit on the fence!"

No! The lightning spark faded, and then suddenly Sal was caught in the circle of glare thrown by Nicky's flashlight. He pulled on the bar with all his strength as he kicked at the wire link. Then he realized he wasn't going to make it over and let go. Just as he dropped, there was a blast from the shotgun, and the fence was struck with a hail of number 9 buckshot that pinged and zinged as it ricocheted in all directions. Sal scrambled to his feet and was already running pell-mell along the fence, when there was another *crash* and a metallic *wank!* as a bullet whizzed by and struck one of the nearby fence uprights. *Nicky's .45! Nicky's .45!*

"You're dead, motherfucker!" Nicky screamed insanely. *"You're dead! You're fucking DEEAAAAADDDDD!"*

Sal veered off from the wire fence and ran downhill. Then there was a whole thunderous salvo of gunshots as Nicky emptied his Colt automatic after him. The bullets buzzed by Sal's ears, struck trees a millisecond after he'd run by, kicked up dirt and rainwater twenty feet before him as he ducked and twisted among the tree trunks.

"I'm gonna blow your motherfucking—"

"Jesus Christ!" Junior Venezia bellowed out like a bull in pain. *"Jesus Christ! Lookit what he done to Jimmy Van!"*

Then there was only cold silence chasing Sal through the stormy night, but somehow the quiet was worse than the shouted threats. *I didn't wanna kill Jimmy Van! I didn't wanna!* Sal raced zigzagging through the trees until he was down close to the lake, and then he followed the curve of the reservoir around, trying to put as much distance as possible between himself and the Venezias. He was out of shape and operating on stark terror, and very shortly his mouth hung open and his breath came in deep, choking sobs. The cold rain stung his tongue, the mud sucked at his shoes like quicksand, and he was sure he'd never see another day. There was still another fiery crackle of lightning with the accompanying flashbulb of luminous, rainy light, and before it died, Sal whirled around to look, and Nicky and Junior were a hundred yards behind him, following him along the lake's edge. *Leave me alone! Leave me the fuck alone!* Then the light faded, the night closed in, and under cover of the blind darkness Sal once more turned away from the lake and began to labor up the steep slope, pumping his knees, scratching, clawing, and pulling himself over the wet, oozing hillside. *I'll get around them! I'll get around them and find their car! Where the fuck did they park their car?* Sal could hear his own breath thundering in his ears, but it sounded foreign, like a winded beast hot on his heels. The terrain was different along this part of the lake. There was more underbrush, sharp, brittle bushes that ripped and gouged as Sal tore through them. It was raining harder and harder, and the muddy water raged down toward the lake in crazy gorged rivulets that splashed around Sal's shoes. Sal hadn't seen it rain like this since that last night in New Orleans. *Fuck!* he cursed as he lost his footing in the soft, slippery mud and went down heavily on one knee. *Fuck!* He clawed himself to his feet as quickly as he could, but when he took the next step and pain shot up his leg like a million sharp needle pricks, he knew he'd hurt himself. *No! No! No!* He hobbled himself through the woods, lurching from one tree to another, pulling himself along by branches, dragging his damaged leg beside him. Then he reached out for a limb, misjudged the distance, and toppled to the ground. He crawled another ten yards through the mud and water, then turned over onto his back and stared up through the pine branches above. It was raining for *real,* now. Driving slanted sheets of cold, stinging liquid. It was raining so hard that Sal couldn't see the lake, and he suddenly realized he'd lost all sense of direction. He didn't know which way was out anymore. He fought his way upright again, the pain coursing through his leg, and stood there tottering, hanging on to a tree so he wouldn't fall over. He craned his neck and swiveled his head in every direction, searching for something to tell him which way to run, but the fury of the storm had reduced visibility to gray, watery shapes, indistinct in the distance.

"Sallllleeee—"

Nicky's voice sailed in through the downpour, blurred and directionless behind the curtains of rain, but close—*much too fucking close.* Sal searched the woods frantically, twisting this way and that, but there were only the walls of water. He pulled the Walther from his pocket and held it out before him.

"You're dead, Sallleee. You're a dead motherfucker!"

Where are you? Where the fuck are you? With his free hand Sal snatched up a dead branch from the mud and using it as a crutch began to hobble rapidly through the woods.

"Salllleeeee—"

Still Sal couldn't tell where Nicky's voice was coming from. *I could be running right into him. I could be—*

"I'm gonna kill you, Salllleeeee—"

And then there was another sound, another voice from out of the night.

"Double Strength paper towels—for those really *messy* cleanup jobs."

The TV in the limo! It was dim and far away, but Sal could pinpoint a direction, and he limped toward it as fast as he could.

"Double Strength paper towels—for those double-tough jobs!"

The storm played tricks with the sound waves, and sometimes all Sal could hear were his heaving lungs and his shoes in the sucking mud, and sometimes the limo's TV was audible all around the basin, coming in and out like shortwave.

"—from the Shrine Auditorium—downtown Los Angeles—annual Grammy Awards!" the announcer shouted, and his voice echoed across Lake Hollywood.

"Where are you, motherfucker!"

"—back after this message—"

Somewhere on the dark ridge above him someone was scrambling through the trees. *Junior! I gotta get to the limo! I gotta get the fuck outta—*"

"—my dandruff shampoo leaves my hair soft and bouncy—"

"Salllleeeee!"

Lightning crackled for a brief second somewhere on the other side of the mountains, and down below, through the veil of rain, Sal could see the long white limousine ghostly gleaming where he'd parked it, on the knoll just above the lake.

"—new, improved secret formula—"

Sal plunged down toward the white limo with mad, lurching strides, bracing himself with the tree branch and grunting painfully with every nerve-crunching jolt. The rain slushed from the sky like a wide-open fire hose, and the hillside was a tumbling torrent of muddy water.

"And after I do *you,* motherfucker—"

"—take to the open road in a supercharged, hard-body—"

"—I'm gonna kill *her!*"

"No!" Sal screamed, and turned in midstride, pivoting on the dead branch, toward the echoey sound of Nicky's voice.

"—twenty-seven in the city, thirty-six on the highway—"

"Yeah, I'm gonna stick my piece up that little whore's—"

Sal fired the Walther—Dago Red's gun—in the direction of Nicky's disembodied voice. He had forgotten he was still holding it.

"—Japanese engineering, American muscle—"

"I'm gonna have *fun* killin' that little slut!"

"No!" Sal fired again. The 9-millimeter automatic cracked like a circus whip.

Nicky laughed somewhere in the darkness and rain.

Sal fired again. And again. And again.

And then it was as if someone had punched him in his ribs, only much harder, and Sal thought the thought *I've been shot!* as he tumbled down the rain-drenched slope and rolled through the trees and brush.

"—welcome back to—National Academy of Recording Arts and Sciences—"

"Junior! I got him! I got him!" Sal could hear Nicky scream. His face was resting in a pool of cold rainwater. He felt it gurgle in his ear. He reached out, clutched a low-hanging branch, and pulled himself erect. The limo shimmered pale and white through the curtain of rain, just beyond the sheltering trees.

"And now, to present the award for Song of the Year—"

Sal made himself move, try to run. Every time he raised his left leg, the pain from his side snaked through his body. Every time he put his left foot down, his knee throbbed and his legs wanted to buckle. He lurched out of the trees and into the open. The lake was all around, just below the knoll where the limo waited. The roar of rushing water was close and urgent.

"—and the nominees this year—"

The limo's back doors were open, the rain ruining the bleached leather seats. The television mounted in the cabin glowed with bright, dancing colors in the darkness. The TV's volume grew louder and louder.

Sal made it to the limo and threw open the cab door on the driver's side. He fell behind the wheel and reached for the ignition.

The key wasn't there!

Where is it? Where is it?

The English rock star's nasal whine screeched in his ear from the TV turned up to just below distortion level. "—and 'The Touch of a Stranger' from the Gramophone/Pacific album *Tropic of Capricorn*—"

Junior took the keys! Junior took the keys when he opened the trunk! Sal's brain shrieked as he searched frantically between the cushions, under the seat. *No, they gotta be here! They gotta be here somewhere!*

"—recorded by Isabel"—joyous screams from the kids in the cheap seats—"and written by—"

Where are the motherfucking keys!?

"—Marco Toledano—"

That's me, the idea dimly registered in the deepest part of Sal's terrified mind. *That's me. Where are the keys?*

He ripped open the glove box and dug desperately under the maps, licenses, and registration papers, and his hand clutched something small and metallic and he yanked it up and it was a set of silver keys.

Dear God, let them be the extra set! Let them work!

His left side was numb now, and icy cold. Shock. The rain poured down on the windshield, through the open doors, and Sal fumbled the silver key around the ignition and then it slipped in and he twisted it and the motor caught instantly and the wipers began to arc across the windshield, sluicing away the rain, and Junior Venezia was standing there in the headlights, short, wet, and apelike, a few yards beyond the limo's long white hood. Junior was raising his shotgun, aiming it at Sal, and Sal screamed and stomped on the accelerator, but the big white Cadillac bastard wouldn't move and then, simultaneously, a big hole suddenly appeared in the center of the windshield while the rest of the glass spidered into cloudy crystal, the bleached white leather seat beside Sal exploded, and Sal heard the shotgun's thunderous blast. He screamed again and tried to drive his foot through the floorboard, then remembered and dropped the gearshift into "drive" and the limo lunged forward—*I can't see!*—and there was an ugly *thunk!*—and a second later Junior's body came hurtling through the shattered safety glass. Sal released the wheel and threw his arms up to shield his face, and the limo fishtailed in the mud, sideswiped one tree, sheared off two smaller ones, then both tires on the driver's side hung out over the knoll. The limo tottered there for a moment, like a dying milky-white mastodon, and then it rolled over once, twice, three times, down the knoll, and came to rest on its flattened roof, with its bloody hood submerged in the lake.

"And the Song of the Year is," the English faggot whined, "—hmmmm, how *do* you open these envelopes?" Laughter from the audience. "Ah, here we are. The Song of the Year is—'The Touch of a Stranger'!" The crowd roared, and the Englishman had to shout his name, "By Marco Toledano!" and the orchestra in the pit was blaring out his melody.

I won, he thought, and kicked out at the dead weight of Junior Venezia's corpse lying across his legs. He and the body had been thrown into the back cabin. The overturned limo reeked of champagne and whiskey from the shattered bottles that had toppled from the limo's bar. The upside-down television screen was inches from Sal's face, the speakers thundering in his ears, and Isabel, in the trendy, slouch-shouldered jacket Sal just last week had helped her pick out in King's Road, raced up the glittering movie-set stairway and the crowd roared for her and she acknowledged them with a wave and a smile and the roar was deafening in the overturned limousine.

"Isa*bel!* Isa*bel!* Isa*bel!* Isa*bel!*" they chanted, and the announcer, in a phony intimate whisper, marveled, "Well, that makes it a full sweep. Isabel, on this night, has completely captured the music world!"

"Isa*bel!* Isa*bel!*"

"—a stunning achievement for the eighteen—year—old—"

"Isa*bel!* Isa*bel!*"

"*Junior!*" Nicky screamed from somewhere close. "*Junior!*"

"Isa*bel!* Isa*bel!*"

One of the limo's doors had been ripped off in the fall, and outside the rain pounded the ground into a muddy mire. Sal inched through the broken bottles toward the twisted opening.

"*Junior!*"

Far away, through the rain, Sal saw a pair of running feet approaching. Gemelli de Janeiro tassled loafers. Only the best for Nicky Venezia.

"*Junior!*"

"Isa*bel!* Isa*bel!* Isa*bel!*"

On the small screen she was radiantly, heart-stoppingly beautiful. Her dark shagged hair streaked with punkish flashes of pink and yellow that made her dark eyes shine and her olive skin glow.

"Isa*bel!* Isa*bel!*" the kids chanted.

She stood behind the podium and smiled out at them, generously accepting their adulation. Then she raised her hands, and they were immediately silenced. Empress of the world.

The mud-splattered shoes were much closer now. Sal struggled to pull himself through the glass and blood and liquor.

"Marco couldn't be here tonight–-" In that delightfully blurred accent that wasn't there when she sang.

Nicky kneeled to peer into the overturned Cadillac and their eyes met.

"—but if he were, tonight he would want to tell you—" Her voice as loud as feedback.

The gun was pointed at him. *A .45 can take your whole fucking arm off,* someone had once told him. Sal stared into the muzzle hole, the place from where death would come. He wondered if he would see death arriving.

"—and he would want you to know how much—"

Then Nicky Venezia screamed, "*Die, motherfucker!*" and Sal shot him with Giovanni's German Luger. For the second time that night Nicky's face bore a look of total surprise, then he clutched his chest and plopped over in the mud. His eyes never left Sal's, and he began to drag his gun back up into a shooting position.

"*Leave me alone!*" Sal shouted, but Nicky gave him one of his cold smiles and shakily raised his .45 with both hands.

"*Motherfucker!*" Sal wailed as he fired round after round into Nicky's face and upper body. He didn't stop jerking the trigger until the whole clip was spent. Now, the limo reeked of whiskey and fear and cordite. And the slaughterhouse stink of fresh blood spilled in anger.

Sal lay in the ruins of the overturned limo, pointing an empty fifty-year-old gun at Nicky Venezia's bloody corpse, motionless in the rain, and he thought, *I'm alive.* It was an incredible idea, and it took a while before the reality of it seeped through his adrenalined terror. *I'm alive. I'm alive, and they're dead. All of them.* His hand holding the Luger began to shake violently. *They sent three of them, and I killed them all. I'm alive, and Nicky Venezia's dead. I killed him.* Then the limo settled a bit into the lake, oozing a few inches forward, and Sal suddenly became frantic to get out, away from the blood and fear and Junior Venezia's corpse nestled beside him. He scrambled through the broken glass, clambered over Nicky's bullet-ridden body, and crawled away on his hands and knees. When he was far enough away from the dead men, he tried to stand up, but his legs wouldn't hold him, and it wasn't the pain from his wounds. His limbs were shivering with postponed terror. He slumped back against a tree trunk, his ass in the mud, and began to cry. The rain poured down on him, and he sobbed and sobbed. Then he raised his head to the stormy clouds and screamed, "*I did 'em, Pop! I did all them motherfuckers for you! I hope they burn in hell, the motherfuckers!*" He buried his head in his arms and wailed like a frightened child, his mouth a twisted smear, his tears mixing with the raindrops pelting his face, his shoulders hunched and shaking.

* * *

It was a long time before Sal finally began to think like a man again, not like an animal struggling for survival, and the first thought that struck his still-numb mind was, *This ain't over. I gotta get outta here. I gotta put a lot of distance between me and Isabel. Little Johnny ain't gonna be happy about this shit.*

Stupidly he walked back to the limousine. It had got him down here to the reservoir, and in Sal's impaired thought processes, he imagined it would drive him back out. But the limo was a total overturned loss, sliding inch by inch into Lake Hollywood. Sal stood and looked at it awhile, and at Nicky's body, then he whispered a farewell, *Fuck you, Nicky,* and began to lurch painfully up the path that led to the road above. He had only gone a few yards when he came upon Nicky's flashlight, stuck in the mud and shining a distorted beam of light on the ground around it. There was something just on the edge of the oval of light. Sal nudged it with his foot, and it became a muddy briefcase. *Giovanni's briefcase. Giovanni's money!* Sal slipped to his knees with a tortured grunt, and began to gather up the wet packets of hundred-dollar bills scattered all around, half submerged in the cascading rivulets of rainwater. When he had stuffed all he could find into the soggy attaché, he managed to snap it closed, then rammed it under his arm and pushed his way to his feet again. His knee throbbed, and the gunshot wound in his ribs had short-circuited the entire left side of his body, so that he had to sometimes *drag* his throbbing leg behind him, but the pain was good, the pain meant that he was *fucking alive, man, while Nicky Venezia would never feel anything ever again.*

It took Sal almost an hour to climb out of the reservoir, backtrack his way around the service road and out through the burglarized gate. The rain was coming down ever harder, stinging Sal's face with hard little pellets of liquid, flooding the streets with rushing currents that tumbled over the gutters and gushed down the sloping hillsides. The downpour was so heavy, so concentrated, it was like walking in fog, or flying in a cloudbank, visibility was that drenched and limited. Sal's tuxedo was as wet as if he were naked. His dress shirt clung transparently to his chest, the left side sticky with blood. If anyone had seen Sal lurching along—limping, bleeding, sodden, with glazed eyes in a shocked stupor, an apparition from hell—they would immediately have dialed 911, but there was no one on the residential streets of the Hollywood Hills to see him this night. The storm had driven them all inside, battened down, safe and sound against the deluge, and Sal was left alone to stumble along as best he could. Somehow his clouded mind had formed the idea that he would find the car the Venezias had driven to the reservoir, but he didn't, and long after he'd left the vicinity of the lake, he still drove himself painfully onward with the dim, fixed belief he would find the vehicle—even though he had no idea what this phantom car even looked like—and drive away to safety in it. He tried the doors of a couple of cars parked in front of darkened California split-levels, but when the car alarms began to scream, he limped away hurriedly. After a while the shock and the loss of blood drained his mind of reason and he was lost—mentally and geographically—gimping along through the rain in a total daze, breathless and befuddled. Sometimes he thought he was back in New Orleans, and Nicky was hunting him. Then he'd remember that Nicky was dead, along with Junior and Jimmy Van, Dago Red and Joe the Hack. He thought of Isabel—*Izzy, Izzy*—and he saw her as he had seen her yesterday when he thought Nicky'd thrown acid in her face. Then he shouted out involuntarily, and the shout cleared his mind for a second, and he thought, *Iz's okay, Iz's okay, they didn't hurt Izzy, I fixed that. I fixed their little red wagon,* as his mother used to say. *You pick up this mess, son, or I'll fix your little red wagon.* Then Sal, without knowing why, started to sob again as he staggered drunkenly through the rain.

With a natural but unconscious logic Sal followed the streets that led downhill, and after a timeless eternity he was in the foothills just above Hollywood. Here the water cascaded through the swollen gutters with a threatening roar, carrying along garbage cans and children's toys with a vengeful force. Los Angeles is the northern terminus of a coastal desert that stretches all the way south to the tip of Baja, and as with all deserts, fierce thunderstorms very shortly overload the drainage systems, the streets flood, hillsides crumble, homes wash away, ditches become rivers, and rivers overflow their concrete banks.

Sal found himself up to his knees in roiling, fast-moving water. He clung tightly to Giovanni's briefcase and slogged with icy pain through the rushing water. Once, the current knocked him from his shaky feet, and he shouted and slashed around in a panic until he bumped against a parked car and pulled himself erect again. From then on he splashed through the water from car to car, lamp post to lamp post, one hand gripping Giovanni's briefcase, the other always reaching out for the next life buoy. Then he waded around a corner and was confronted with bedlam. The cascading currents tumbling down one of the city's canyons had rushed together with such force and volume that when the water reached the mouth of the canyon, it had been a wall of floodwater, and had picked up and carried along a dozen automobiles, depositing them like a line of children's toys at the first open intersection. And then the overlooking weakened hillside had collapsed and $3 million-plus homes—*180-degree Vus.*—had folded back upon themselves and slid down the muddy avalanche.

Sal stood in the hip-deep water and watched as what seemed like hundreds of firemen and an equal number of cops rushed about in the torrential rain, shouting, cursing, digging in the mud and dirt for the dead and the damaged. Dozens of stalled patrol cars, their wheels covered with raging water, flashed their circling bubble tops over the hellish scene. Caltrans highway workers in fluorescent orange helmets and vests sloshed through the hip-deep water with sandbags hoisted on their shoulders as they hurried to shore up the crumbling mountain. Ambulances, fire trucks, sobbing relatives crying out for their missing, rescuers screaming out directions while they worked feverishly in the raging waters and drenching rain—it was all a proper continuation of the nightmare Sal was living this P.M. This night would never end, Sal knew that now. This night would go on for the rest of his life.

Sal stumbled unnoticed past the cops and rescue workers—just another street-dweller in a tux looking to get out of the rain—and a few blocks further on he found himself on drier ground along Sunset Boulevard, the street the hotel was on. *Which way?* Sal asked himself as he squinted against the rain. *Which way is the Beverly Hills? And what time is it?* It could be midnight or four in the morning, he had absolutely no idea. And Sunset was almost totally devoid of traffic, with only a few cars fighting the slashing storm. For a moment Sal's clouded mind suspected a trap. *The Venezias were waiting for him, and everyone had cleared the street!* It was High Noon in the midnight rain. Then he remembered he'd killed the Venezias, or at least a *bunch* of them; he picked a direction—*the hills are over there, so this must be the way*—and began to lurch along the sidewalk. His knee ached, his side was numb, and his mind kept coming in and out of focus as he limped past the shuttered hot-dog stands, the iron-grated pawn shops, the twenty-four-hour porno halls that constitute the sleazy reality of the mythical Hollywood fantasy. The rain hadn't slackened even a little bit. It had been coming down hard and steadily for twenty-four hours now, and the citizens of Los Angeles had surrendered to the storm's superior power. They had suspended life and were hiding in their homes, riding out the storm's fury like Schtett Jews cowering from the cossacks. The neon-burned, billboard-decorated Sunset Strip, L.A.'s answer to the Champs Élysées, was gray and muted behind the thick haze of rainfall before Sal's eyes. He planted one shaky step after another, moving slowly, painfully, inexorably forward. His clothes had gone beyond wetness now. The fabrics were so saturated and heavy that they had become a skintight cold compress on his body, and he was racked by seizures of shivers every few yards. Sometimes he would lose consciousness—out on his feet—and would only realize it when he came to half a block further westward. Once he was brought back to reality by the blare of an angry horn and a splash of gutter water, as he had wandered out into the middle of Sunset, and a solitary passing car had to swerve to miss him.

Gradually the boulevard changed from the ugly to the merely high-priced as the Strip curved westerly. Now, there were monster record stores, designer shops, trendy trattorias, all closed—*cerrado*—because of the weather. Sal stumbled on, hardly aware of his surroundings, trying only to stay erect and moving. He had become a victim of tunnel vision—his world had reduced itself to a small wet spot centered a few feet ahead, and he trudged wearily toward it. He leaned into the cold rain, clutched Giovanni's briefcase so tightly his hand numbed, and took another excruciating step forward. Then another. Then another. The rain ran into his eyes, dripped from the tip of his nose, coursed down the back of his neck, and Sal shook his head like a dog and went forward. Toward the hotel. Toward Isabel.

Sunset Boulevard curved again, and now he was in Beverly Hills. The sidewalks here were lined with some of the most expensive houses in the world. With American palatial the only common style, these homes were blatant, unapologetic temples to capitalist success. In-your-face, fuck-you, eat-shit-and-die capitalist success. After a certain hour it's illegal in Beverly Hills to park a car on a residential street, or to walk on the sidewalks, but tonight, with the world's richest ghetto swathed in a wrapping of wet gauze, Sal staggered unseen and unstopped through the lush, soggy manicured lawns, past the iron-gated estates, the petrodollar Taras, the yen-bought English mansions. The dense, slanting rain had driven everyone deep inside, like animals burrowing from a forest fire, and Sal was left alone to pull himself in semiconsciousness through the last few blocks of wealth immortalized in brick and adobe. Then he tripped over the rock-lined edge of a flooded flower bed, recognized the sea of drowned red snapdragons, and looked up to see the green neon sign glowing tastefully through the downpour: BEVERLY HILLS HOTEL. *I made it,* his mind slowly understood. *Didn't think I would. Never thought I'd see this place again. Never thought I'd see Isabel again.*

"Izzy," he whispered, like a magical mantra as he trudged up the long driveway toward the hotel. "Izzy." Then he thought, *Gotta stay outta the lobby. Nobody should see me like this. Questions.* He kept to the shadows, away from the hotel's entrance, where, under dry cover of the brightly lit canopy, a very bored parking valet was kibitzing with one of the tall black bodyguards Karl had hired yesterday. He shakily climbed over a low, hedge-lined railing and was on the pathway that led back to the detached bungalows. *This is where Nicky threw the shit in Izzy's face,* he thought as he passed the spot. *Motherfucker'll never do* that *again.* He lurched along the wet, smooth flagstones back toward their bungalow. *Which one is ours?* The pain clouded his vision, and he wiped his eyes with his fingers and tried to peer out through the wall of rain before him. *Which one? That one? No, that is Karl's. Or is Karl's room back there?* Then he heard Isabel's voice. He couldn't tell what she said or where she was, everything was so muffled by the storm, but he'd know her voice anywhere.

"Isabel," he called out gently, turning in the rain. "Isabel."

He heard her again. This time she seemed to be crying out, and the wet hairs on the back of Sal's neck tingled. *But I killed them. I killed them all.*

Then someone behind him said, "Marco?," and Sal spun around with the German Luger in his hand. He didn't remember holstering it, but there it had been.

"Marco?" Giovanni said from his wheelchair on the flagstones. Someone had rigged a big beach umbrella to the wheelchair's frame, and the rain gushed off the taut fabric. "Marco?"

"Gio—"

"Ah, Marco!" the little old man cried out, and held his arms up to Sal. "I think they kill you! I think you are dead!"

Sal leaned over, and Giovanni threw his gnarled hands around his shivering shoulders. "I wait for you! All night I wait for you!" His ancient eyes, shiny with tears, searched Sal's dripping face. "I think they get you, Marco!" Then his eyelids narrowed. "They come here?"

Sal shook his head. "I took care of them, Gio. They won't hurt her." He laid the ruined briefcase on the old *Neapolitano's* lap. "I brought—I brought your money back." Then, through the tattoo of raindrops, he heard Izzy's voice again, and his head snapped around. "Where is she?" He looked back at Giovanni. "I gotta leave, Gio," he said sadly. "I gotta go away and never come back. She's in danger around me."

Giovanni's twisted claw gripped the sodden fabric of Sal's tuxedo. "Then go, Marco! *Go now!*"

Sal dumbly nodded. "Yes. But I gotta say good-bye to her. I gotta explain."

"Go now! I will tell her every—"

There was another muffled shout that sounded very familiar to Sal, and he turned from Giovanni and limped in that direction.

"Marco, you are hurt!" Giovanni cried with desperation in his voice. "Go now, see a doctor! *Go now, Marco!*"

Sal hardly heard the old man's cries. *Isabel. Oh, Jesus, I never thought I'd see her again, and now I have to leave her forever.* He heard her call to him again, muffled and unintelligible, and he hurried toward her. *Isabel, I love you, baby, and I'll never let anybody hurt you.*

"Marco!" little Giovanni shouted after him. "Leave now, Marco! Please!"

This is gonna be the hardest thing I ever did. I gotta go away from her forever. Now, just when we've got everything we've ever wanted. Now, when—

There was another sound, closer than ever. *I'm all turned around. I thought that was Karl's bungalow. I thought—*

Still another cry, and Sal became alarmed. *What's the matter, baby?* Instead of going around to the bungalow's front entrance, he sloshed through a muddy flower bed and was on the little patio. There was a sliding glass door; he tried it, and it slid open on oiled Beverly Hills Hotel casters. *She shoudda locked this. I gotta tell her.* Then he swept aside the light drapes and stepped inside. *Wait a minute.* He was completely disoriented. *I'm so fucked up, I thought the bedroom was over there. Where is she?* Then she cried out again, very close, and Sal peered through the darkened room, took in the flickering candles, the wide bed with the eight Grammy Awards laid around the edges like religious icons—then he saw Isabel, naked and covered with a sheen of perspiration, squatting over Karl, sliding up and down on his big, erect Aryan penis. She was popping her hips, stuffing him into her wet vagina, over and over. Sal watched her a moment, remembering all the times they'd made love in front of a mirror because he loved so to watch her fuck. He loved the way the muscles in her ass bunched and released, bunched and released, how her hands pushed rhythmically at his chest, the way a cat does when it purrs, or the way her hair hung down her back and her tongue flicked around her lips when she leaned her head way back—*there*—just the way she was doing now. And he thought, *How could anything I thought was so beautiful seem so ugly to me now? How could anything that was mine belong so completely to someone else? How could—how could—?*

Sal stepped closer to the bed. The warm, shadowy candlelight made their coupling bodies look vividly three-dimensional, like a pornographic holograph. Karl, on his back in the damp sheets, used his pale Prussian hands to guide Isabel's lascivious hips while he grunted obscenities up to her in

German. She moaned back to him in Portuguese, and somehow the impersonal, masturbatory sense of the lovers' goading made it all the more erotic and horrible.

"*Sim, sim!*" she cried out. *"Dá pra mim!" Give it to me!*

"*Hure! Hure!*" Karl grunted. Sal stood in the shadows by the bed, watching them fuck, feeling the heat from their undulating bodies, hearing their ecstatic endearments, *smelling* the odors their glands were secreting—sweat and semen and Isabel's juices—and inside of him Sal's soul said, *Enough. I can't take anymore. Tonight, tomorrow, or forever.* Sal raised the Luger and pointed it at Karl's forehead, only a few feet away. Karl's passion-slitted eyes widened as the weapon appeared slowly out of the darkness, into the glow of candlelight, and he shouted out something in German and threw Izzy off of him. Sal stepped closer and jammed the muzzle into Diederich's temple, hard. The naked German froze, and the pupils of his eyes slid to the side in an effort to see the Luger's muzzle pressed into his skull.

"Don't shoot me!" he shouted in German, and Sal understood him perfectly.

"Get up, motherfucker," Sal growled softly. "Get up."

Slowly Karl rose from the rumpled, damp sheets and stood up on the mattress. Sal had to stretch to keep the Luger pressed to Karl's brain as with his left hand he flicked on the bedside lamp. The German blinked fearfully in the drenching bright light. His cock, still shiny with Isabel's wetness, stood at three-quarters mast, uncertain what it was supposed to do, or why its mission had been aborted. Isabel, caught in the sudden glare, was standing with her back pressed against the far wall. Her small, perfect breasts were still heaving with passion, and her eyes were hot and alive. A strange smile played on her lips.

"You like this, huh?" Sal shouted at her. "You think this is all big fun?"

She didn't answer, but her dancing eyes were fixed on Sal's.

"How long has this shit been going on?" Sal choked painfully. "How long?"

She wouldn't answer, but Sal could see the pleasure on her face. Getting caught, maybe getting killed, all on this night of triumph—Isabel was living life at its ultimate extremes, and savoring every thrill.

"Maybe you'd like to see him die?" Sal took the pistol from Karl's head and shoved it in his chest, over the Kraut's heart. "Would you like that?"

"*Bitte,*" Diederich, standing up in bed, whispered. "*Bi—bitte.*"

"I already killed three other men tonight. It gets easier." Sal looked at Karl. "One more won't matter."

"*Bitte, bitte—*" Karl was sobbing.

"You think she cares?" Sal said to him. "Look at her! She's all hot and bothered to see me blow your motherfucking heart out!"

"Puh—please, Marco, I—" Karl tried to continue, but abruptly became aware that urine was arcing onto the mattress from his now-limp penis. He began to tremble violently.

"*You cunt!*" Sal screamed at Isabel. "I loved you! I fucking *loved* you!"

Isabel watched intently from the other side of the room, her back and palms pressed against the wall, her nude body still covered with sweat, her nostrils flaring every time she took a breath.

"I *loved* you!" Sal was an apparition from hell. His muddy, soaked tuxedo clung to him, his matted hair hung down his face, there were twigs embedded in his beard, and bloodstains all over his white shirt. His fury filled the hotel room like a noxious gas. "I killed three men for you tonight, you fucking cunt! Three men, so they wouldn't hurt you!"

She still wouldn't talk to him.

"I almost died tonight!" Sal shouted. "More than one fucking time! And I come back to tell you I hafta go away, and I find you fucking this piece of shit!"

Karl, in his abject fear, moaned aloud, and Sal snapped his head around. "*Shut up, motherfucker!*" Then back to Isabel, "What, is what he's got so fucking good? I'll take care of that." He took the Luger from Karl's breast and rammed it against his testicles. Diederich shouted out and had to hold the bed's backboard to keep his knees from buckling under him. "Why don't I blow his fucking dick off? Give it to you as a good-bye present! You can keep it in a jar next to the bed here, and stick it up your pussy whenever you wanna! How's that sound, you fucking cunt!"

By way of answer she ran her tongue excitedly over her lips, her eyes riveted on Sal.

"Ma—Marco, *bitte, bitte*—" Karl whined miserably.

"I told you to *shut up*!" Sal roared, then he pointed the Luger at Karl's left kneecap and pulled the trigger. The automatic *schlicked!* on the empty chamber, shocking Sal almost as much as Diederich, who immediately fainted, eyes rolling back under his eyelids and knees crumbling beneath him. *It's unloaded,* Sal thought, as he looked down on the unconscious Diederich. He'd forgotten about firing the whole clip of shells into Nicky Venezia's corpse. Sal turned his attention to Isabel, who had thrown her head back and was looking at Sal through hot, slitted eyes. *Look at her. My God, she's the most beautiful thing I ever saw. I know that look. She wants me to fuck her. She wants me to stand her against the wall and give it to her. This whole thing, it's like one big sex kick. Murder Karl for foreplay, then fuck her over his body.* And then, for the first time, he understood completely. *She's nuts. She's stark raving nuts. But that still don't excuse her.*

With Karl unconscious, it was as if there were just the two of them there, alone, and it made the pain all the more palpable, the betrayal more intimate, the rage uncontrollable.

"Why did you do this to me?" Sal whispered, standing over Karl's slumped body. "Why? I *love* you."

She still wouldn't speak, but her face was alive with lust and fear, scorn and excitement.

"*Answer me!*" Sal shouted, then he was running across the room. He rammed the butt of the Luger into the wall only inches above her head. It left a dent in the embossed wallpaper. She gave only the slightest little flinch, then glared at him defiantly. "*Fucking answer me!*" Sal repeated, then beat the gun butt repeatedly into the wall beside her head, until there was a hole in the dry wall, and little white chunks of plaster in her wild hair. "*You want me to kill you?*" he screamed, the tears streaming down his face. "*Is that what you want?*" She stood there silently challenging him, almost a sneer playing on her parted lips, and Sal lost it. With his left hand he slapped her *hard* across the right side of her face. Her eyes finally registered fear, but she fought hard not to show it. Sal hit her again, and this time as the open palm blow slipped off her cheek, she snared his hand with her teeth and bit it viciously. Sal cried out and pushed her with all his anger. Her body slammed against the wall, and her head bounced off the wallpaper like a bobble-necked toy's. Then she clutched at Sal's wet clothes as she slipped down to the carpet. He was on her instantly, his pulse up and racing, his hunger for blood like a fire flaring inside him. He slammed a hand on her chest, pushed her back against the floor, and raised the Luger high above his head, about to hammer it down on her skull—*through* her skull—when she shrieked, "Marco! *Don't! Don't!*"

Her voice was like a slap across *his* face—it was the first thing she'd said since he'd entered the room and caught them fucking—and Sal recoiled from her, from *himself,* when he realized what he'd been about to do. The Luger hung in the air like an executioner's ax; Isabel's face was frozen with the terror she'd finally allowed herself to feel; it was a moment snatched from eternity and etched in both their souls, indelible, unspeakable, immutable, and then Sal's anger slipped away like a suicide's blood down a bathroom drain and was replaced by a powerful, all-consuming sadness. It washed over Sal like baptismal water. *No more. It's all over. It's done.* Sal slowly brought the Luger down and took his hand from Isabel's chest. She scuttled out from under him and sat back against the wall. She was crying now, sobbing like an infant—*beyond consolability*—as she brought her knees up to her breasts and wrapped her arms around her legs. She didn't look like an international rock goddess now. Now, she looked like a very disturbed little girl, crying naked on the carpet.

Sal watched her cry for a long while. She didn't even seem to know he was still there, so deep was her grief and sadness. *No worse than mine, baby,* Sal thought, with only a touch of bitterness. Then he rose stiffly from the floor—now that his anger had dissipated, his pains had returned—and limped slowly back across the room. He threw only a cursory glance at Karl, watching him, terrified, from the bed, amid the obscene display of Grammys. *One of them is mine.* Then he was at the sliding door. He stopped, not looking back, and hoped for a second that she'd call out to him—*Marco! Marco!*—but she didn't, and he pushed aside the flimsy drapes and went back out into the rain.

Giovanni was just outside the door, his wheelchair stuck in the muddy flower bed. He was crying uncontrollably under the big, florid umbrella.

"Marco," he sobbed. "Oh, Marco. I am so sorry." An ancient

little cripple crying in the rain. "I am so sorry."

Sal stared down at the old man, then he said, "I want to thank you for every—"

"No!" Giovanni interrupted. "*I* want to thank *you*." His knobby, tortured hands were twisting and turning on the wheelchair's shiny rails as he cried. "I am so sorry."

Sal held out the Luger. *The murder weapon.*

"No!" Giovanni refused. "You must keep it. And *this*." With shaking hands on quaking arms he held up the muddy briefcase. "Take this, you will need it."

Sal looked down at the briefcase dumbly.

"Take it!"

Sal lifted it from the old man with his free hand. "I have to go now, Gio."

"I know. I know." It was strange to see the old millionaire crying so uncontrollably. It made Sal's sadness all the more desolate.

"I can't ever come back."

Giovanni nodded miserably. "I understand." The tears were rivuleting down his wrinkled parchment skin. *"Buona fortuna."* He held out a trembling claw of a hand and touched Sal's arm. "Take-a the money. Run far away, Marco." He fingered the sodden sleeve. "I never forget you. Never."

Sal wanted to say something, something final, something to complete things, but all he could manage was, "I loved her."

Giovanni nodded again. "I know. I know."

The two men looked at each other for another moment, then Sal simply turned away and walked back toward the hotel's entrance. He carefully avoided the lobby, and a few minutes later he was hobbling through the towering palms and well-tended shrubbery that lined the hotel's long, curving entrance. The night was still cold and empty; the rain fell in one deep, continuous sheet, crowning the streetlights with hazy auras. There was a squealing of brakes and tires right behind him, and Sal knew it was the police. He turned with the empty gun in his hand, praying to God to get shot.

"Hey, dude, where the fuck were you? You missed the whole—" Through the little plastic rain guard Eric peered out at Sal from behind the wheel of his Jeep, and his voice faded fast as he took in the scene—Sal's bloody shirt, the Luger in his hand, the look in his eyes. "Fuck, dude. What happened to you?"

Sal lurched over to the red Jeep and rested his weight on the fender. Eric's debauched, partied-out face was framed in the small zip-open square. "Eric, you gotta help me, man."

"Sure, bro. Anything." He was already shifting into "park" and opening the door to climb out.

"Whattaya need, dude?" he asked when he was standing beside Sal under the shelter of a dripping palm.

Sal nodded toward the Jeep. "I need your car. I gotta get away from here."

Eric stared at him. "Hey, dude, you wanna tell me what's happenin'?"

"Can't do it, man," Sal said as he laid the briefcase on the wet red fender and forced the ruined springs to open. He reached in and withdrew a fistful of banded stacks of hundreds. Shoving the dirty, wet bills into Eric's hands, he said, "This should cover it. If it don't, see Giovanni." He moved shakily to the Jeep's open door and started to climb in. Then he turned back to Eric. "All right?"

Eric looked down at the money, glanced over to the briefcase Sal was carrying, then looked back at Sal. "What the fuck is goin' on, dude?"

"I can't stop to explain, man. You'll read about it in the papers." Sal yanked himself into the Wrangler and threw the briefcase on the seat beside him. The effort, on top of the night's blood loss, made the world swim before his eyes, and he clutched the steering wheel with both hands and rested his forehead on his knuckles.

Eric stepped closer and reached in to touch Sal's shoulder. His hand came away bloody. "Jesus, bro, you need a doctor!"

Sal shook off the dizziness with a twist of his neck. Then he looked out at Eric. The Swede's long blond hair had been pulled back and fastened with a black silk ribbon that matched his black-tie-and-tails. On his feet he wore customized red basketball shoes. The hightops brought a trace of a smile to Sal's lips.

"I'm gonna miss you, man," he started to say. "I never had—I mean—" He looked at Eric. "Thanks for being my friend."

Eric was very concerned now, and it showed on his boyish face. "Lemme call a doctor. Lemme—"

Sal popped the clutch and fishtailed away in a shower of oily water. "*Rock 'n' roll!*" he shouted back at Eric, then watched his friend grow smaller and smaller in the rearview until he turned out of the hotel driveway onto Sunset.

Sal had learned yesterday that the drive from L.A. to the International Border Crossing at Tijuana took about four hours. Tonight, with the storm crashing down on him all the way, it took more like six. Twice he passed out at the wheel and only came to when he felt the Jeep's tires bumping over the interstate's grassy shoulders. Then he cursed and fought the vehicle back onto the concrete. When he finally reached the border, the endless downpour was begrudgingly allowing a gray, insipid light to swim its way out of the eastern hills. The Jeep was the only car on either side of the crossing, and as Sal approached the guard in the sentry box, he felt himself weakening, drifting off. *Fuck! Fuck!* His vision kept blurring and clearing, blurring and clearing, and his wavering mind held a mental image of the Jeep shearing off the sentry box, killing the guard, and him later dying from a dirty knife wound in the Tijuana jail. But somehow he willed himself to retain consciousness as he drove up to the box, and the Mexican Border Patrol officer, a sleepy-looking man in a greasy slicker, waved him through with a bored yawn.

Fifteen minutes on the other side of the border he pulled into the first open gas station he could find. No glass-enclosed booth here. No PLEASE PAY FIRST signs. Only a few rusted pumps before a ramshackle building that was dirty beyond description. The rain had finally slackened off a little, but when Sal tried to get out to pump the gas, he found he didn't have the strength to lift his legs. So he lay on the horn until finally a teenage boy with a harelip and a clouded eye appeared by his window.

Sal fished a soggy C-note from the briefcase and held it through the Jeep's window. "Gas," he said, and his voice sounded thin and weak to his own ears. *A dead man's rattle,* he thought dimly as his mind kept shutting off and on, like a light bulb shaken too hard.

The harelipped boy stared silently at him with his one good eye, and Sal leaned out with a grunt of pain and stuck the bill in the boy's torn shirt pocket.

"Gas," Sal demanded. "Petrol." And the talking seemed to take the last of his energy, and he felt himself slip under the surface of reality like a skin diver diving underwater. When his eyes opened again, he had no idea how long he'd been unconscious, but he had a dim memory of hearing that unmistakable echoey metal-on-metal sound of a gas nozzle being shoved down a feeder tube, and when he started the motor, the gas gauge jumped to "full." Sal drove out of the station's hard-packed, oil-stained dirt yard, just as the Jeep's windshield wipers began to squawk across a dry windshield. The rain had finally stopped.

The next hour was touch-and-go for Sal. He knew he couldn't go much farther, that he had to den up and lick his wounds before he drove off a cliff into the Pacific, but he also had a primordial need to *run away,* to put a lot of Mexican kilometers between him and what he'd done last night. So he gripped the wheel tightly, violently shook off the recurring bouts of light-headedness when his vision blurred and doubled, and generally just bore down hard with all his concentration so he could drive another kilometer or two before passing out.

He managed to get through Tijuana's Third World sprawl, passed Rosarita Beach with its big hotel, then he was on the toll road with no other cars on the clean white highway. Villages along the parallel service road—groupings of shacks really, clustered around a bar or *bodega*—were just waking up and venturing out into the sunrise. The storm had left ruined roofs and flooded floors in its wake, and the short brown people were already working to fix the damages.

Stopping at the tollbooths, Sal just pressed hundred-dollar bills into the hands of the sleepy attendants and drove on. This was not the way to be inconspicuous and unmemorable, Sal knew, but he had no pesos, and anyway it took all of his strength *just to keep his head off his chest, fuck coming up with the correct change.*

He forced himself to remain conscious through Puerto Nuevo—LOBSTER DINNER! $6.95!—and La Fonda—THE MOST BEAUTIFUL VIEW ON THE COAST!—but then he began to shiver furiously, and his vision fogged up with pain and stayed that way. Now, it was the periods of clearness and lucidity that came in intermittent snatches.

The highway here was curvy and dangerous, carved into the side of treacherous cliffs hanging over the Pacific, with no roadside settlements or even places to pull over. Sal shook and sweated and blinked his eyes furiously as he gripped the wheel with both hands and tried to zero in on the fuzzy white line that kept dancing before his eyes. He saw a road sign that he thought promised ENSENADA 27 KILOMETERS, but he couldn't be sure. It could have said 2 kilometers, or 270. His quaking hands were going numb on the Jeep's leather-wrapped steering wheel. He couldn't feel them, and could hardly see them. There was a sickly wetness down his left side, and that's how he knew he was bleeding again. Finally he could fight it no longer, and simply gave up, gave in to the pain and the shock and the dizziness. And the bone-weary exhaustion brought on by the lack of sleep and the mind-numbing terror he'd experienced in the last twenty-four hours. He succumbed to unawareness like a young girl to a hungry lover, and it quickly swept over him—an ocean of peace and relief. *Is this a coma? Am I dying?* Sal's own thoughts were the last things he was conscious of, until some time later—*a minute? an hour? an eternity?*—he felt something brush lightly against his face. He opened his eyes, and he was staring into the eyes of an angel. A small, brown, running-nosed angel.

"*¿Que pasa, señor?*" the angel asked, sniffing escaping mucus back up into his nostrils. "*¿Está okay?*"

Sal looked uncomprehendingly at the angel for a moment, then slowly swiveled his head on his neck and looked in the other direction. Through the Jeep's dirty windshield he saw a trio of young boys—ten, eleven—leading an unsaddled chestnut horse down a still-damp red dirt street. The street was loosely lined by small, tidy houses—cottages, in reality—painted either white or pastel pinks and blues. There were no sidewalks, the red dirt street went right up to the doorsteps, which were invariably decorated with hardy-looking cactus planted in rusting coffee cans. The three laughing boys led the chestnut—a high-spirited gelding with an arched, flowing tail—prancing by before the Jeep, and Sal's sense of unreality was complete.

"*¿Está okay?*" the little angel wanted to know, and Sal turned back to him. "*Señor?*"

The angel's face was starting to fade, and Sal closed his eyes to help the job along. When he opened them again, he found he was lying on his back, staring up at a bright, harsh light. Sal squinted and angled his head, and around the edges of the glare a cracked and peeling ceiling became visible. Sal raised a hand and shielded his face from the light. In a moment his eyes adjusted and took in a small, whitewashed cinder-block room with metal cabinets, glass jars of cotton balls and tongue depressors, white clothes laid over every surface. Affixed to the wall was a picture of Jesus Christ in glowing, cartoonish colors, and next to it a photograph frame containing a burned scrap of cloth with Hebrew lettering on it.

Sal covered his eyes with his hand and went under again.

When Sal came back to the surface the next time, the first thing he became aware of—with his eyes still closed—was a radio playing in another room. It was tuned to an L.A. station coming in clear and strong.

"—and the little girl has been missing thirteen days now. On another note, police are continuing their investigation of Tuesday night's bizarre triple murder at the Hollywood Reservoir. On Wednesday morning, following the aftermath of Tuesday's tumultuous storm, two bodies were found in the area, and later that day a stolen limousine containing another body was pulled from the lake. For two days the police divers have been searching the lake for additional victims, but their search has been hampered by the depth of the reservoir, which reaches a hundred and thirty feet in some places. We spoke to an LAPD spokesman earlier today."

Then the roving reporter's intimate, insinuating voice: "Do you think there might be still more undiscovered fatalities connected with this investigation?"

And the cop's media-ready response: "We have no way of knowing at this time. When we've completed our investigation, we'll be better prepared to draw those kinds of conclusions."

"Is it true, Lieutenant, that the victims carried no identification, that their clothing had no labels or other distinguishing marks?"

"Uh—at this time we still don't know the identity of the three victims. We won't be able to make a complete assessment of the situation until we've received the forensics report."

Sal felt the weight of a hand laid on his shoulder, and heard a man's voice ask, "Are you awake in there?"

"Can you confirm reports, Lieutenant, that the stolen limo was being rented by rock-star Isabel?"

Sal slowly cracked his eyelids. There was no harsh light anymore, and no little brown angel. Only a large, pale man with an aquiline nose. Looking up from the table, Sal could see clumps of coarse nose hairs in the man's nostrils.

"No comment at this time," the policeman replied. With his eyes open, the radio in the next room seemed much more muffled and distant.

"What about rumors that Isabel's boyfriend, songwriter Marco Toledano, was the last person seen with the limousine?"

"We can't comment on that."

"So—" the big man said. "You *are* awake in there. How do you feel? Shitty, I would imagine."

"Can you confirm if it's true Toledano hasn't been seen since Tuesday night, at the Grammy Awards?"

"Uh—yes. We'd like very much to speak to Mr. Toledano, but as of yet we've been unable to locate him."

"Would you like to eat something?" the big man asked. He was wearing a white jacket over faded blue jeans and *huaraches.* His hair was silver-gray and long.

"Lieutenant, do you think Marco Toledano's body is at the bottom of Lake Hollywood?"

"We have no way of knowing—"

"Alicia," the big man called out. "Bring a bowl of *albóndigas.*" Then to Sal, "She makes the best *albóndigas* in Baja California. Make you well in a week. Faster than my mother's chicken soup."

Someone in the other room tuned the radio to a local station, where a lively Mexican *corrido* was playing. The big man turned his back on Sal and began to drop medical instruments into a primitive sterilizer.

Sal tried to prop himself up on his elbows, and the effort made his head swim. "Where—where am I?"

The doctor turned back sharply to look at Sal while his hands kept moving over the instruments. "Does your voice always sound like that?" When Sal didn't answer, the big man looked back to his hands. "You're at the Clinica para los Niños de Ensenada. That means the Children's Hospital of Ensenada."

"Are—are you a doctor?" Sal was struggling to sit up on the bed.

The big man put a rubber-gloved hand on Sal's shoulder. "I don't think you're ready—" But when he saw that Sal was determined to sit up, he helped him swing his legs over the edge of the hard mattress and perch shakily on the side of the bed.

"Now," the big man said, "that *can't* feel better."

Sal just sat on the edge of the bed, waiting for the stars to go away.

"Anyway," the big man continued, "*yes,* I am the doctor. The *only* doctor. And if you're thinking to yourself, Funny, he doesn't *look* Mexican, I'll explain it to you." He pulled off the big yellow gloves and laid them down on the counter. Then he picked up a nearby can of Tecate beer and took a healthy swig. "I'm Sheldon Silverman, of Brooklyn and Beverly Hills." He smiled. "My grandfather was born in the Ukraine, he was a Communist. He walked from Moscow to the sea, running from the czar's soldiers. My father was born on the Lower East Side, *he* was a Communist. He raised eleven children on what he made as a high school civics teacher. I was born in Brooklyn, I wanted the big bucks, so I became a doctor. So I'm sitting around the Hillcrest Country Club one day about ten years ago, playing cards and listening to my fellow Rodeo Drive Marcus Welbys bitching about the return on their T-bills, the taxes on their place in the desert, their shiksa mistresses, and it hits me." He looked at Sal. "It hits me that my life is shit."

A teenaged girl in a leg brace brought in a bowl of steaming meatball soup and a stack of corn tortillas. The moment Sal smelled the food, he realized that he was ravenous.

"Just like that it comes to me that my life is a piece of shit. I guess it was all that 'brotherhood of man' drek I heard around the house when I was growing up. All that 'help the downtrodden.'" Sal was shoveling *albóndigas* soup into his mouth with a big dented spoon. "So there I am, in the game room of the Hillcrest CC, holding a full house and knowing—*knowing*—Irv Radner's fucking bluffing, and it hits me. My life is a meaningless piece of shit." He pointed a finger at Sal. "I think it was my grandfather speaking to me from the grave, I do. Telling me my life's a piece of shit. So—" He shrugged. "So—I liquidated. Sold everything. The boat, the house, the condo in Waikiki, the Mercedes. I mean, both my daughters were married, and my wife had long since left me for her trainer, so what did I have to stop me, huh?" He took another swallow of Tecate. "So I sold everything, came down here, and opened this place." He smiled wickedly. "I'm gonna franchise. Lose a million bucks." He set down the red can. "In Beverly Hills I dispensed birth-control pills to rich thirteen-year-olds. Here, I treat malnutrition, cholera, polio, emphysema, dysentery, *leprosy*—you name it, these people have it. They're too poor to worry about their health. And only an hour from downtown Dago."

Sal swallowed a mouthful of spiced meatball and tortilla and looked up at the doctor. "You talk too much."

Sheldon Silverman took no offense. "You'll have to excuse me. I don't get much chance to speak English down here. Not too many Americans."

Canadian, Sal started to say, then thought better of it.

"How'd I get here?" he asked.

"You ran into the place."

"I what?"

"You ran into the place. With your Jeep. Mustn't have been going more than three or four miles per hour, the only damage was a dent to your fender. A coupla of the kids found you Wednesday morning."

The little brown angel with the snotty nose.

"You'd been shot," Sheldon Silverman said matter-of-factly, with absolutely no trace of judgment in his voice. "And you were damn lucky. Know the old line from the movies 'one inch in any direction'?" He raised his eyebrows. "It applied to you. Missed a major artery by millimeters. As it was, you took four pints of blood. Also, we had to ice your knee down. It was big as a grapefruit."

Sal suddenly stopped swilling the soup into his mouth and stared at Silverman. "What time is it?"

The doctor consulted his Casio. "Little after twelve."

"No, what *day?* How long have I been here?"

Silverman gave him a funny smile. "It's Saturday. You've been sleeping for about seventy-two hours."

Sal slowly put down the bowl and looked around incredulously. "Jesus," he said finally. "I gotta get outta here." He started to slip off the edge of the mattress.

"I wouldn't do that," Silverman said as he moved quickly to Sal's side. As Sal's feet touched the chipped tile floor, a hurtful hiss escaped from between his gritted teeth and he pulled in his left arm tight to his rib cage.

"You've got *stitches, amigo,*" Silverman said as he helped Sal keep his feet. "I think this is *poco* premature." Sal clung to the bed's metal frame until the pain and nausea passed over and out, then he opened his eyes to look at the doctor.

"I can't stay," he stated flatly, and after a long moment, Silverstein nodded slightly and moved away, letting Sal stand on his own. Sal took a tentative step, balanced, took another, grimaced, then straightened up and looked down at his body for the first time. He was nude.

"Had to throw that monkey suit out," Silverstein said. "It was a total loss. But you're small enough I think we can find some things around here'll fit you." He turned to the girl in the leg brace and said something in singsongy Mexican Spanish. The girl bumped out of the room.

Sal stood by the bed, his legs very shaky under him.

"I'm still advising you to stay in bed for another week or two. Getting shot is not something your body takes lightly."

Sal merely shook his head and clung to the bed frame. In a minute Alicia came back with a soft pair of old jeans, a fresh-smelling T-shirt, and a pair of tire-soled sandals. Silverman and the girl helped Sal dress. The T-shirt was the hardest because he couldn't raise his arm. When the clothes were on him, Sal rested against the bed, waiting for the world to stop spinning. Silverman shook his head disapprovingly. When Alicia had left the room, the big doctor turned, opened a cabinet, and lifted out Giovanni's buckled, water-stained briefcase. He laid it flat on the bed beside Sal. On top of the briefcase was the German Luger.

"These are yours, I believe," Silverman said. "They were on the seat of the Jeep."

Sal stared at the briefcase a moment, then said, "Did you look inside?"

Silverman's white eyebrows shot up again. "Why should I do that? It wasn't bleeding."

Sal allowed himself a gentle trace of a smile. Then he picked up the Luger and stuck it under the waistband of his jeans, beneath his T-shirt. He put his hands on either side of the briefcase and popped the latches, but the case was so warped he had to pry it open. The money was all there. He looked over at Silverman, but the big man's face showed him nothing. Neither surprise nor curiosity nor wonder. He might have known what was in the briefcase, and then he might not have. Either way, he didn't seem to care. Sal picked out a half-dozen of the banded packets of money and laid them out on the white sheets.

"Thanks for patching me up," Sal said to him.

The eyebrows went up. Nothing else.

"I didn't steal it."

"I never said you did," Silverman answered.

"Then take it. Take it for the kids if not for yourself."

Silverman looked down at the money awhile, threw back his head and drained the Tecate, looked at the money again, then straight at Sal.

"Kids could use it."

"Damn straight. Take it, man."

Silverman nodded. "I will."

Outside, it was bright with just a *warning* of winter in the dusty air. That intimation of cold that passes for February on either side of the southern California border. As Sal was being hoisted up into Eric's Jeep by the big doctor, he looked around and remembered he was in Mexico. Settled behind the wheel, he took in a series of deep, restorative breaths.

"Now, if you feel yourself getting dizzy, pull over and let it pass," Silverman was advising. "If you don't get back in a bed by tonight . . ." He let his voice trail away. Then he held out the Jeep's keys dangling from a long finger.

"Good luck, *amigo*."

EPILOGUE

CABO SAN LUCAS—AUGUST

The two men exited the Mexicana morning flight from Mexico City and walked into a wall of dry, baking heat. Although both men had been raised in the dusty deserts of northern Chihuahua, of late they had been spending a lot of time in the temperate highlands of the Federal District, and their blood was not ready for the blast furnace that is the tip of Baja in full summer.

"*¡Cinga!*" one of the men said as they made their way down the long air ladder. "I hate this fucking place. You sweat your balls off; the girls don't bathe; and everywhere you look it's fucking American tourists."

This man's name was Magallanes. He was dressed in lightweight slacks and sport coat, his white shirt open at the collar. Magallanes was the *other* kind of Mexican—light skin, trimmed mustache, European features. He looked more Spanish or Greek than *mestizo,* and in fact his father had been a Syrian immigrant. But his mother had been a Juárez whore, so he'd never known the Syrian.

"But that's right, I forgot," Magallanes said to the other man. "You *like* gringos. You're one yourself."

The other man was almost the same height as Magallanes, and about the same age—middle thirties—but this one, whose name was Zuniga, was pure Indian, with burnished bronze skin, hawk nose, thick black hair. He, too, was dressed plainly, in generic, nondescript clothing. They were two men whose effectiveness was measured partly by their ability *not* to be remembered.

They were on the tarmac now, and the heat came up through the soles of their shoes.

"Leave that shit alone," Zuniga said as he scanned the airport crowd with his black Indian eyes. Both men spoke only Spanish.

Magallanes smiled. "Well, it's true, right?"

Zuniga ignored his companion and searched the people's faces. Zuniga had been born in a tomato field in South Texas, where his parents had been braceros—migrant workers from across the border, and although that technically entitled him to U.S. citizenship, he'd never cared to claim it. But somehow Magallanes, who had a venomous hatred of all things gringo, had discovered the facts of Zuniga's birth and never tired of needling him with it.

"Look at all the Yanquis," Magallanes mocked. He nodded at a fat, middle-aged couple—all sunburned skin, hanging camera, floral print clothes. "Why don't you go over, throw your arms around them, and say, *¡hola!* See if they welcome their compatriot."

Zuniga had spotted their man approaching through the crowd. "You know," the Indian said softly, "you're like a kid who won't stop teasing a dog until it bites him."

Magallanes's cold smile broadened across his handsome face. "I know how to take care of dogs, my friend."

Magallanes and Zuniga had worked together before, and they respected one another's abilities, but they actively disliked each other, and had for a very long time. Neither of them was the type of man who let his displeasures simmer indefinitely, but they both were employed by the same powerful individual back in Mexico City, and that person greatly disapproved of internecine warfare. Even so, each man secretly hoped that someday he would be assigned to do the other.

Their contact was before them now. He was a large, pockmarked Mexican with salt-and-pepper hair and mustache. His clothes were western—lizard-skin boots, sharply tailored slacks with flared bottoms, high-cuffed white shirt—and because he was a vain man going to fat in his middle age, everything he wore seemed to be two sizes too small. His belly jiggled over the big silver buckle he now had to cinch *below* his paunch, and his shirt buttons were painfully strained.

"Yes?" the fat man said, and the other two simply nodded. The fat man looked down at the carry-ons in their hands. "Any other luggage?" he asked, and the other two knew they were dealing with an amateur.

"We're not here on vacation," Magallanes said flatly, but the fat man wasn't even sharp enough to hear the condescension in his voice.

"The car is outside."

The car was a maroon Seville double-parked in the middle of the area reserved for taxis, and the local cabbies glared as the fat man proudly opened the doors for his guests. Magallanes and Zuniga exchanged glances as they climbed into the back-seat. This was not to their liking. This was not unobtrusive and forgettable.

There was a woman in the passenger seat. A Latina with her hair dyed bright blond. She turned around to look at them over the seat, but when they stared back at her with unfriendly eyes, she quickly looked away.

The fat man stuffed himself behind the Cadillac's wheel with a grunt and a whoosh of air from the car seat. He twisted around awkwardly and offered his hand.

"I am Adolfo Romo," he said self-importantly, but the other two already knew who he was. He was the local *jefe* of the organization they worked for. He was the grease that kept Cabo's wheel of the machine turning, and turning out profit. He was a fixer, a drug dealer, a whoremaster, a trafficker in stolen merchandise, a murderer, but of course that's not why Zuniga and Magallanes disliked him. They disliked Romo because he was an asshole, and assholes were lethal in their line of work.

They stared down at his big, meaty proffered hand, all diamond rings and manicured fingernails, and neither man made a move to accept it. After a while Romo pulled his hand back, turned, and started the car.

"I don't know why they sent you two," Romo said finally as he pulled the Seville out onto the highway. The air conditioner was blasting full out; the highway ran along the coast, and the land was completely denuded of trees. It was like driving along an ocean on the moon. "I told him to let me handle it. I told him it was nothing."

From the backseat the two men could see the grease and sweat in Romo's carefully pomaded ducktail. They could *smell* it.

"I mean, this is *my* place. He should have let me handle it."

The two men from Mexico City glanced at each other again, but said nothing.

Romo kept trying to catch their eyes in the rearview as he drove and talked. "I mean, this little *maricón,*" he chuckled, "this little *maricón borracho—*" He shook his head. "The man should have let me take care of it for him. It wasn't necessary to send you two."

Zuniga the Indian shifted his weight and said, "Let's talk about it at the hotel."

Romo's eyes shot a question back through the mirror and then they relaxed with comprehension, and the fat man reached over and pulled the girl closer to him. "Ah, Marta. Hey, she's like my shadow. I trust her completely." He was roughly massaging the back of the girl's neck, and she grinned nervously. Romo seemed to draw confidence from the touch of her flesh. "That little gringo, I'd snap his neck with two fingers." He was boasting before the girl, and the two men in the backseat recognized that and were disgusted. "I don't know why he sent you two."

Magallanes stared sullenly out the window, and Zuniga simply repeated, "At the hotel."

The hotel was a pyramided pastel-and-plants affair, boasting a towering lobby that stretched upward for four tall stories, with all the rooms facing out on guardrailed walks. The architect—a German—had tried to capture the grandeur of Mexico's pre-Columbian past, but all he had succeeded in doing was to build a totally unserviceable place to stay.

Zuniga and Magallanes would have preferred to check into a smaller hotel, but in a way the cold, anonymous immensity of this place suited their purposes perfectly. Romo made too much of a fuss with the front desk about his "special guests," but they were through the cavernous lobby and in their suite before a great deal of damage had been done. Romo immediately picked up the phone and ordered a raft of things—coffee, brandy, sandwiches, rum, cokes—from room service. Marta lit a joint and walked out on the terrace that overlooked the Pacific. She, like Romo, was into denial when it came to her weight. She wore shiny white spandex pants that made her wide ass look like the rump of one of those prancing Lipizzaner stallions from the Vienna riding school. After a while she strolled back into the room, slumped onto a sofa, and began to leaf through a magazine. Marta had that bored, relaxed air that comes to women whose only job is to provide sex for their men.

Magallanes and Zuniga were sitting around the dining table with Romo.

"Will you require weapons?" Romo asked. "I assume you brought—"

"Wait," Magallanes interrupted. This had gone far enough. He turned to the girl and said, "We need cigarettes."

Marta stared at him uncomprehendingly for a moment, then looked to Romo for direction. She was not bright, but she knew enough to know that this was an insult to her man. Magallanes shouldn't be giving her orders like that.

The fat man tried to glare Magallanes down, but he and Zuniga looked back at him with total unconcern. They had tried to accommodate this *pendejo,* but he was a fool, and they were tired fucking with him. They were here on business for the man who employed them all, and there were certain professional procedures that had to be adhered to.

"Go get some cigarettes," Romo eventually said to the girl, and she dropped her eyes and got up. Magallanes held out a handful of thousand-peso notes to her.

"Don't hurry," he told her. "We have things to discuss."

All three men watched her shimmering ass disappear behind the hotel room's door, and then Romo immediately turned to Magallanes.

"She's completely trustworthy," he challenged. "I never hide anything from her."

"She's a whore," Magallanes said bluntly. "For the right price she would do anything. When our business is concluded and we're gone, you can do whatever the hell you want. But not while we're here."

This was a direct affront to the local *jefe*'s power and prestige, and Romo's mind was visibly chagrined behind his swinish eyes. Zuniga the Indian moved in quickly to smooth the waters. He withdrew a paper photograph from his jacket pocket and placed it on the table before Romo.

"Is this him?"

Romo picked up the photo in his thick brown fingers and held it out arm's length, squinting at it from a distance. He was also too vain to wear glasses.

"Maybe," Romo grunted after a while, and laid the picture down. The photo was actually a clipping cut from a glossy magazine. "Maybe this is him, I don't know." He looked over to Zuniga. "If it is him, then he cut off his beard."

The Indian had something else. An American driver's license. From someplace called Louisiana. He placed it on the table beside the cutout. "Look at this one. This is before he grew the beard."

Adolfo Romo studied the laminated card carefully. "Yes, this is him. *Este es el hombre.*"

Magallanes leaned closer over the tabletop. "Are you sure? The man back in the city wouldn't appreciate any mistakes in something like this."

Romo slowly nodded his head as he perused the license. "I'm sure. This is the guy." With painful concentration he read the name on the license. "Sal-va-to-re Dee-a-mo-re."

"What name is he using?" Zuniga wanted to know.

Romo chuckled. "He says his name is Eric Christiansted, but he doesn't look like any Eric Christiansted." Romo tapped the license with his knuckles. "He looks more like a Sal-va-to-re Dee-a-mo-re."

"He has papers under the Christiansted name?"

"Papers my own people made and sold to him. Except for the registration on the Jeep. Those are authentic, in that name. I went through the car one night."

"Where does he stay?" Magallanes was up and nervously pacing the suite. He always got high-strung before a job.

Romo swiveled his massive head around to follow the moving man. "He lives in a shack down on the beach with a whore who used to work for me. She was an unsatisfactory whore, always crying when the customers got a little rough. I got rid of her. Now, she works sometimes as a maid for the big hotels. For this one." He pointed to the floor.

"When did he come to Cabo?" Zuniga wanted to know.

"In March, I think. At least, that's when I noticed him. I kept seeing the red Jeep parked by those shitty little shacks on Playa Perro, and, you know"—he shrugged—"I always wanted one of those Jeeps, so I watched him. A gringo staying down on Dog Beach with an ex-whore and a brand new red Jeep"—he looked from one to the other—"this is something to watch, no? And then when the man called me last week and said, Have you seen a guy looks like this?—well, I naturally thought of this one."

"How did he pay for the forged papers?" Zuniga was back-tracking, covering all bases.

Romo smiled, his greedy eyes glinting. "With twenty hundred-dollar bills. This, too, made me think, Hey, I better watch this one. Then, when the man called me last week and said look out for—"

"He lives alone with the whore?" Magallanes had opened a beer from the minibar and was holding the sweating bottle against his temple while he questioned Romo.

"The whore has two little girls. They have blond hair, both of them. I think maybe this whore has a taste for the gringos."

Magallanes smiled for the first time. "Hey," he chided Zuniga the Indian, "then she should like you."

Zuniga stared up at Magallanes with an expression on his face like a man watching a rat eat its young. Then he turned back to Romo.

"He bought no weapons when he purchased the papers?"

Romo shook his head.

"What does he do? Every day, I mean." Zuniga was unwrapping a candy bar. "Does he have a routine?"

Romo shrugged again. It was a little like watching a bull snuffle the wind. "He drinks. He drinks, he snorts *la coca,* he sits by the beach and watches the breakers come in. He's a bum, a hippie." Romo stared at them, thinking. "Sometimes he takes the Jeep out and finds an empty beach, and he takes his clothes off and runs in the sand."

Zuniga and Magallanes exchanged quick glances.

"You mean"—Zuniga started to say, a hunk of chocolate

between his teeth—"you mean, like a *lunático?*"

"No, like the gringos always do, you know, *cómo se dice—jog.*" He said the last word in English. "Only he likes to do it without any clothes."

"When does he do this? What time of the day?"

Romo opened his hands over the tabletop. "In the late afternoon. This one likes to watch the sun set into the Pacífico."

The three men shared a moment of silence in the big, upholstered hotel suite. They looked at each other, looked away, spent some time with their thoughts, looked at each other again. Then Magallanes opened the minirefrigerator and took out another bottle of Bohemia.

"What else?" Zuniga asked of Romo.

"The only other thing this one does is sometimes he comes into the hotel—this hotel"—again the finger indicating the floor—"and he goes into the lounge, drinks until he's *borracho,* then he plays the piano."

"He plays the piano?" Magallanes asked, drinking the Bohemia and staring out through the sliding terrace doors at the beach below and the sea beyond.

"Yes." Romo nodded solemnly. "He's pretty good. I like to hear him play."

Magallanes let out a short, derisive chuckle, then turned and gave the fat *jefe* a condescending sneer.

"When does he come in?" Zuniga pushed on. "How often? Which days?"

Romo shrugged his thick shoulders up around his neck. He'd popped a button, and his shirt was straining across his bulging gut, showing an obscene oval of hair and fatty brown flesh. "No special days. Just every once in a while. But always after midnight, always late. He comes in, he drinks; when Hector, the regular piano player, takes a break, this one plays."

Zuniga leaned back in his short chair, and he and Magallanes looked at each other. After a while Romo felt uncomfortable and asked, "Is this the right one?"

Zuniga balled the empty candy wrapper and placed it carefully in an ashtray. "Possibly."

Romo grinned widely, showing a mouthful of gold teeth behind his thick lips. "The man in Méjico should be very pleased I'm so—so—*aware* of things."

The other two men pointedly ignored Romo's self-congratulatory oiliness.

"We'll need a car—" Zuniga started to say, and Romo interrupted him.

"You can use my Cadillac. It's the best car in Cabo."

Magallanes laughed again. "It's also the flashiest, asshole."

Romo looked hurt, and Zuniga quickly said, "We need something plain, ordinary. Not new, not old. Something *in between* everything else—*¿comprende?*"

"What about weapons? I can provide—"

Zuniga reached over and lightly touched the back of the fat man's bediamonded hand. "Listen to me, Adolfo Romo," he said in a soft, repetitive voice. "My business partner and I, we don't care for questions—*¿comprende?* Don't ask us any more questions. If we need something, we'll ask for it. When we ask for it, you are to provide exactly what we ask for as quickly and efficiently as possible. If you fail in this, we will of course have to report this failure back to the man in Méjico. Then, possibly, at a later date he will send two other men like us, but they won't be here looking for a gringo piano player. You see what I mean, Adolfo Romo?"

Romo quickly nodded. Yes.

"So," Zuniga continued calmly, as if talking to a child, "you are to ask no more questions; you are not ever again to speak of this thing in front of the woman; and you will find us a plain, unremarkable car and have it waiting in the hotel parking lot by tonight. This is all we require at this time. Now, my business partner and I would like to be alone, all right?"

Romo stupidly nodded affirmation, then sat there a moment before he realized what had been said and lumbered instantly to his feet.

"Uh—" he stammered, unused to being ordered around like this. "Uh—"

Zuniga glared up at the big, sloppy man with hard, penetrating Indian eyes. He should get up and see their contact to the door, that was the right way to handle it, but the man had been such a total *culo* from the minute they'd met him at the airport that Zuniga felt a need to deflate the fat balloon.

"Uh—" Romo stared stricken from one to the other. "The car will be waiting in the parking lot in an hour." Then he turned and walked quickly across the room and through the door.

"What an asshole," Magallanes said when the door closed. "I can't believe the man made him *jefe* here."

"He won't last long," Zuniga said. "The next time we come to Cabo, he'll be gone."

Magallanes stepped over to the table, and with one finger maneuvered the photographs around so he could study them. "He doesn't look like much. This should be fairly simple."

Zuniga shook his head thoughtfully. "I don't know. The man said the dagos told him this one killed four men over this business. Four *serious* men."

"Shit," Magallanes scoffed. "Four *Americans*. They're all soft and lazy." He smiled coldly at Zuniga. "Gringos are easy to kill."

Magallanes had spent the first seven years of his life in a Juárez whorehouse, where he'd witnessed his mother service a continuing parade of drunken young Texans from across the border. It had planted a bitter seed in his soul. Then his mother had run off with one of the Texans, sending her son to live with her brother in the grinding poverty of the Chihuahuan desert. This had made the bitter seed take root and bear even more bitter fruit.

Zuniga watched Magallanes study the pictures. "Kills are only easy if the necessary preparations have been made."

Magallanes gave the Indian another one of his patented cold smiles. "You worry too much, *hombre*. Or maybe you don't have the stomach to kill one of your gringo countrymen."

Zuniga slowly rose from his chair and stood erect. In the tense moment that followed, Magallanes, watching the Indian closely, stiffened his body, as if waiting for something to happen.

"I'm going to get some sleep," Zuniga said finally. "Flying always makes me tired." He began to walk toward one of the bedrooms.

"Hey," Magallanes called after him, and at the bedroom door Zuniga turned around to face him.

"I think on the beach," Magallanes said. "I think when he jogs on the beach is the best time."

The Indian shrugged, as if to say, *When else?* Then he went into the bedroom and closed the door behind him.

* * *

Zuniga woke up shivering in a cold, darkened room. He'd gone to sleep naked on top of the plush hotel bedspread, and when the sun had set, the central air-conditioning had turned his room into a meat locker. He fumbled for the bedside light, located it, and clicked it on. Blinking against the sudden glare, he found his watch beside the lamp and checked it. It was after ten o'clock. Zuniga swung his legs off the bed, snatched up his pants from where he had draped them over a chair, and pulled them on.

The outer room was dark, too, and the Indian went around turning on all the lights. Scattered over the top of the marble coffee table were the remains of all the food Adolfo Romo had ordered up from room service—untouched sandwiches, tall glasses filled with cerviche, sweating ice buckets. Zuniga poured himself a cup of lukewarm coffee from a tightly sealed container, and nibbled on the corner of a sandwich. Stacked beside the trays of food were a dozen packs of cigarettes, all different brands. Zuniga opened a pack and shook out one, lighting it with a glossy book of hotel matches. Then he took the smoke and the cup of stale coffee out on the veranda and looked down on the beach. Even in the night the heat was formidable, but it felt good after the frigid air-conditioning. Over the Pacific the western skies still glowed with a kind of red blackness, as if the boiling sun had burned away the retina of the world's eyes.

Far below—the suite was on the top floor—an old white couple were playing a fast-paced set of tennis, whacking each return with a startling viciousness. Beyond the courts there were lights on the beach, and *mariachis* strolled among the lounging, bikini-clad guests, singing sorrowful songs about lost loves, sadness, and revolution.

Zuniga finished the cigarette and sent it plummeting over the veranda's guardrail. It landed on the ground four stories below with a tiny explosion, arcing a shower of sparks like a little fireworks display. Zuniga went back inside.

A few minutes later he brought a polished wood case from his bedroom and laid it on the round dining table. He sat down and opened the case. Inside, snuggled like a scientific instrument by shock-resistant rubber lining, was a MAC-10 fully automatic machine pistol. The Indian lifted the weapon respectfully from the case and began to break it down. He removed the bolt-carrier assembly from the receiver, unscrewed the barrel, and carefully laid the pieces on the tabletop. Then he slowly worked a hard-bristled brush down the barrel and began to rotate it around the bore. That's when he heard the sounds from the other bedroom. Magallanes had a whore in there, and from the rhythm of her moans and the steady thumping of the bedboard against the wall, he had just begun to fuck her well. This didn't surprise Zuniga. He'd worked with Magallanes before, and the man always needed a whore before a job. And after, too. It was the close proximity of death that heightened the senses, made life's pleasures all the sweeter.

Zuniga paused in the cleaning of the MAC-10, the bore brush pulled halfway out of the barrel, and listened to the two lovers. The girl was making a noise like the whinny of a young foal. Magallanes's deep voice was a low, constant hum on the other side of the bedroom door. Magallanes liked to talk while he fucked. Zuniga set down the barrel of the machine pistol and reached for another cigarette. While he smoked, he listened and watched the bedroom door. Zuniga considered Magallanes an evil man, a man touched by Satan. Though he himself had probably killed just as many men, he felt that in his case it was an outcome of circumstances. Early on in his exceedingly hard life Zuniga had discovered that he could achieve the greatest results with violence or the threat of violence. Some men were capable of such violence, and some weren't. The men who had this capacity had a distinct advantage over all the others. Zuniga looked upon this capability as a God-given talent, much like an operatic voice, an affinity for numbers, or a ten-inch *veraga.* You used what you had, for what else had you? But Magallanes—ah, that was another story. Zuniga had seen Magallanes take a whole day to kill a man, when the job should have been done in a second. Just because he was enjoying himself. This, Zuniga considered sinful. And very bad luck.

Zuniga was gently stroking the weapon with a solvent-soaked rag when Magallanes finally reached his climax with a furious shout of anger and joy. Then there were several minutes of silence before the door opened and he came out, a long hotel towel cinched around his waist. He left the door ajar, and Zuniga could see the whore sitting naked on the edge of the bed. She was brushing her long blond hair, and her breasts were pendulous brown cushions that shook with every brush stroke. It was Adolfo Romo's woman.

"She came back with the cigarettes," Magallanes softly laughed as he stripped the cap from a bottle of rum. "I've had worse." There was a thick gold chain around his throat, old white scar tissue on his right shoulder, and beads of perspiration shining in his chest hairs. "I've had much worse."

Then he turned to Zuniga. "You want her? She's yours if you want her."

The Indian continued wiping down the weapon.

Magallanes poured some rum over a glass filled with ice and added some Coke. He chuckled again. "She said she finds us exciting, you and me."

Without looking up, Zuniga said, "Romo will wonder where she is."

Magallanes shook his glass, rattling the crushed ice. "Fuck Romo. He's a stupid pig." Then he laughed again. "Hey, gringo, listen to me. I fucked this whore in her *culo,* and the head of my dick came out all full of shit." Magallanes found this fact inordinately funny, and he threw back his head and roared. "Ay-yi-yi—" he said finally, breathing a sigh of contentment. "Ay-yi-yi—" Then he drained the rum and Coke and set down the glass of ice. "I'm gonna take a shower, wash that whore off." Then he strolled back to the bedroom, pleasurably stroking his flat stomach.

Zuniga began to reassemble the MAC-10. He slotted the bolt assembly into the receiver and snapped it back in. He reattached the pistol grip. Then he heard the sound of a shower and glanced back at Magallanes's bedroom. The woman Marta was dressing before the open door. She stuffed herself back into the spandex pants, perched herself on her spike heels, and was about to pull on her silky blouse when she noticed him watching her. She stared at him frankly, then hung the blouse on the doorknob and walked out of the bedroom and toward him. When she was only a few feet away, she stopped and let him look at her. Then she held out her hand. In it was a vial of white powder. Zuniga stared at the vial a moment, then reached out and took it. He unscrewed the tiny cap and tapped out a little mound of cocaine onto his thumbnail. Then he raised his thumb to his nose and sniffed. After he'd repeated the process on the other nostril, he screwed the cap back on. The woman held out her hand and Zuniga stared at it a second, then slipped the vial into the pocket of his pants.

"If Adolfo Romo comes back here looking for you and I have to kill him," Zuniga said as he slapped a twenty-cartridge clip of .45 ACPs into the machine pistol's grip and locked it firmly in place, "you should know—I'll kill you, too." He ripped back the charging handle, and the weapon was as poised for inflicting death as a vibrating rattlesnake.

The woman didn't say anything. After a while she went back to the bedroom and finished dressing. Then she left quickly, without looking back.

They were at the bar on their third round of tequila shooters chased with *cervezas* when their contract walked into the hotel lounge. Magallanes was sucking on a lime when he saw him, and he took the wedge from between his teeth and said, "There he is."

The small, dark, clean-shaven man crossed the plush, dimly lit lounge and took a seat at a small round table just to the side of the piano bar. He wore a blue *guayabera* shirt, cutoff jeans, and *huarache* sandals.

"Look at him," Magallanes said softly, so only Zuniga beside him could hear. "He's nothing. A hippie. That pig Romo was right—he *could* have done this himself."

Zuniga studied the man's face—lit up by his table's candle across the dark room—and said nothing. It had been his experience that smaller men were the most dangerous. And that careless men didn't live as long as careful ones. Zuniga didn't like surprises.

The waitress brought their man a half-full bottle of José Cuervo, showed him the mark on the label, and then left the bottle with him.

"Look at this hippie, gringo," Magallanes continued. "The bar keeps his liquor for him, like a *patrón.* This one likes to drink."

Their target poured a hefty shot of the clear, golden liquid, threw back his head, and shootered the tequila in one gulp.

Magallanes laughed. "This is going to be *too* easy."

The small gringo filled the glass again, then leaned back on his banquette and nodded along with Hector the house pianist.

Zuniga studied the man, and the more he studied him, the more convinced he became that Magallanes was right. This one was a fool, a careless, sloppy fool. If someone is bothersome enough so that someone else sends two very competent men to eliminate that first someone, then that first someone should at least be cautious enough to inspect his surroundings whenever he went out in public—but this one was oblivious to the lounge's other customers. He looked neither right nor left; he didn't seem to care who was watching him; all he was concerned with were his tequila and the *maricón* playing the piano. Zuniga shook his head unconsciously. The Indian hated sloppiness wherever he found it. Even if it suited his purposes.

"There's talk of money," Magallanes said after the bartender had brought them another round. "Did the man in Méjico say anything about there being any money?"

Of course their employer had spoken of it, but Zuniga wasn't going to tell Magallanes that. The Indian truly believed that information was power, and secrecy was the harnessing of that power.

"What money?"

Magallanes sipped his tequila, sucked his lime, then washed his mouth with a cold swallow of beer. "The man wasn't definite. He'd heard rumors that this one left Los Angeles with a great deal of money."

"How much money?"

"A couple million American, the man said." Magallanes lit a cigarette with hotel matches. "But looking at this drunk hippie, I find it hard to believe." Across the dark lounge their contract was filling his glass again. "Then again, you never know. This piece of *mierda* must've done something important enough it's going to get him killed."

The Indian stared across the room at the little man rapidly and silently getting drunk. "It makes me curious," Zuniga said finally. "What do you think a drunken piano player could do that would be bad enough to make important people want him dead?"

Magallanes was picking a shred of lime out of his teeth with the corner of a matchbook. "*¿Quién sabes?* Maybe he fucked the wrong woman. Maybe he ran his mouth to the wrong people. Maybe he stole this money he's supposed to have. It doesn't matter now—he's killed four men, and it seems like they were men with a lot of friends." Magallanes chuckled and gently touched Zuniga's arm. "Can you imagine, gringo, what the man in Méjico would do to someone who killed four of his people?" Magallanes grinned and shook his head. "Ai-yi-yi— This one is dead, gringo, and that's the truth."

Sal sat there sucking up the José Cuervo and tried to endure Hector Barrientos's piano playing. He lived 90 percent of his life now in a drug- and alcohol-induced stupor that few outside stimuli could penetrate, but this fruit's wretched piano playing was one of them. *He* plays *like a faggot,* Sal thought. *All rococo arpeggios and Liberace flourishes. As nutless and pointless as an old eunuch.* It was the musical equivalent of a spinster's overstuffed sofa, or a pink toy poodle on a rhinestoned leash. It was aural cotton candy—lightweight, sugary, and totally without nourishment. Sal grimaced and threw back another shot of Cuervo Gold. *Don't this motherfucker ever take a break?*

In the five months he'd been in Cabo, Sal's universe had reduced itself to a few necessities: He had to have his liquor; he had to have his drugs; and he had to come in here every few days to play a little piano. "*That's the story of,*" he thought bitterly as he poured another tequila, "*That's the glory of love.*" He raised the shot glass to his nose and sniffed the clear aroma of the distilled agave mash, and he remembered the sweet, oceanic fragrance of Isabel's closely trimmed pussy. *Misty watercolored mem'ries*—Sal touched the rim of the shooter to his lips and threw back his head with a quick, robotic movement. The tequila burned without warming as it went down.

Hector reached the end of his latest abortion—*Listen, you can hear the fetus scream*—with a bombastically arpeggiated tonic chord, and then he stood up and bowed with exaggerated formality. There was a smattering of polite applause, and then Hector moved the boom mike to his mouth and said in English, "Ladies and gentlemen, we have a special treat for you tonight. *Damas y caballeros—Señor Eric!*"

Through the cocaine and tequila haze that surrounded him, Sal heard a name he vaguely remembered, then an even weaker round of applause, then Hector was at his elbow, gently indicating the piano bar with an outstretched arm. Sal lumbered to his feet and staggered the short distance to the bench, while behind him Hector did his professional best to hide his disapproval with a tightly drawn mouth. Hector Barrientos was a prissy homosexual with dyed hair, a penciled-in mustache, and a rigid standard of behavior for his fellow craftsmen. Entertainers, even unemployed amateurs like Señor Eric, should never appear stoned while "onstage." It gave the whole profession a bad name.

"Thank you. Thank you," Sal mumbled gravelly into the mike as he settled clumsily behind the piano. His fingers found the keyboard, fluttering over the keys until they settled down like birds coming home to roost. He struck a few bluesy Bourbon Street chords, and the cocktail lounge's patrons immediately quieted down. *Gotcha,* his murky mind whispered, and for a moment he almost felt lighthearted. He squinted out across the dark room. Because there was no spotlight over the piano bar, Sal could just about make out all of the customers. There were three tables of couples—honeymooners, probably. A party of six—three sets of silver-haired old marrieds. One middle-aged lone wolf over by the wall. Two guys drinking at the bar. Then he began to hear the music he was making, and lost all interest in his audience. He dropped his head and cocked it to one side, on his shoulder, as he immersed himself in the blues-tinged mellow ballad he was playing. It wasn't a song per se, not a recognizable tune that dredged up bittersweet memories from his listeners' pasts, that capsulized and captured a brief moment of emotion filed away in someone's heart under a particular place and time, but rather a conglomerate of many different compositions—he used the chord structure to "Willow Weep for Me," borrowed a few notes of melody from "I Got It Bad," resurrected an old Stevie Wonder turnaround. In short, Sal wasn't playing *songs,* he was making music. Fresh, new, never-heard-before music. Compositions-while-you-wait. And the music welled up inside of him a deep, overpowering sadness, a melancholia so blue and profound that Sal could feel the grief in his arms and legs, as real and palpable as extreme weariness. The sadness glowed through his body like a chemical high, like a tab of acid or magic mushrooms. It was a warm current that ran through his mind, his balls, his heart, his being. It was Isabel, and he knew it. It was the sense of her loss, both excruciatingly painful and wickedly sweet, that he felt whenever he came in here to play. It was *why* he came in here to play. He was like a lovesick teenager, feeding quarters into a jukebox and playing *their* song over and over again. Except this wasn't a *song* Sal was playing, but a mood, a feeling, an emotion. He was giving musical form to his boundless sadness, and he didn't care if the audience liked it or not. He didn't even know they were *there*.

Sal played a seamless stream of sadness for over ten minutes, and the lounge's patrons were either repulsed or mesmerized. Two of the young couples called for their checks—they weren't spending two hundred dollars a night to be fucking *depressed, for godsake*—but the older customers were transfixed. They had lived a longer time, and they understood that eventually there aren't good or bad memories, but just *memories,* and that's what's important. That's what makes up the sum of your life, the salt and pepper, the Tabasco. They sat back and listened to Sal commune with his grief, like voyeurs at a live sex show staring blank-faced at a couple copulating. Finally Sal, his head bowed and his eyes closed, wound the ballad down to something like a close, and the audience applauded respectfully, not warmly. You don't *befriend* your analyst. Sal felt the sadness within him recede like waves rushing out with the tide as the last vibrations of the final tonic chord faded out into the air.

"That was very good," he heard a heavy male voice say close by. "I like that New Orleans style."

Sal opened his eyes slowly, not at all anxious to see who was there.

It was a tall, beefy man with silver hair and a hooked nose. The lone wolf from over by the wall. He wore a faded blue T-shirt that said, LAPD ANNUAL 4TH OF JULY PICNIC 1983 over a pair of Bermuda shorts. The guy was in his late fifties, the guy was American, the guy was drunk.

"Buy you a drink?" the guy asked.

Sal studied him as he thought, *That's a new one. He's gonna drink with me before he kills me. They sent a drunk this time.*

"Why not?" Sal answered. "Can't reach my bottle." His hands, acting on their own as if out of a detached hunger, began to play a series of gentle Delta chords.

The beefy American lifted a finger to catch the waitress's attention. He was one of those functioning alkies that other juicers can spot in a minute. Sal had pegged him at first sight.

"My name's," the big American said as he turned back to Sal, "Jack. Jack Gold." He offered his heavy hand over the piano—he was seated at the nearest piano-bar stool—and Sal shook it with his left; his right couldn't seem to stop playing. "I used to be kind of a jazz buff," Gold continued as he pulled a cigar from his T-shirt pocket and prepared it for lighting. "Back in L.A. And I really like the way you play. Piano's kind of my favorite instrument, too." He held a fat bar candle to the tip of his cigar and began to puff on it. His illuminated eyes found Sal's. "Only not the way Hector plays it."

Sal chuckled in spite of himself. *Hippest assassin I ever met.*

"You ever hear anything like that?" Gold asked. "Sounds like wood nymphs pissing over little crystal toadstools."

Sal nodded. "It's pretty bad."

"Pretty bad doesn't even *begin* to describe it." Gold puffed on his cigar. The flesh of his face was marbled by tiny red veins. Whiskey rivers.

"But I really like the way you play. That tune you just did, what was that?"

Sal shrugged. "Nothing. Just something off the top of my head."

"Didn't think I recognized it. I'm pretty good remembering old jazz charts." The waitress had arrived, and the big American asked Sal, "Tequila? A double tequila for the artist and another J.B. for myself." The waitress slinked away, her wide brown ass winking out from under her ridiculously short skirt.

Sal had already dropped his head and started playing again, conjuring up the sweet sadness.

"Listen," he heard the big American say, and he raised his head and opened his eyes. Gold was wearing a shit-eating grin. "Listen, I know how you jazzers hate requests and all that, but there's this one old tune means a helluva lot to me. I was wondering if you knew it."

Encased in his cocoon of numbness, Sal basically wished

only to be left alone and allowed to get back to his self-pity, but he felt a bond with this Gold, if only the comradeship between two winos.

"Lemme guess," Sal said with an edge of condescension in his gravelly voice. "'Tie a Yellow Ribbon'."

Gold shook his head. "Hey, man, I even bought you a taste. Don't rank me like that."

Sal smiled. "I'm sorry. What's the tune?"

The waitress returned with the drinks then, and both men stopped their lives and took off half of their doubles in matching quick swigs.

"An old Mint Julip Jackson ballad," Gold said finally, as though coming back from a long distance. "'Blue Angel'."

"I know that cut," Sal said, even as his hands automatically began to run through the changes.

"Yeah, that's it." Jack Gold smiled beatifically as he heard the first familiar chords. "That's it."

"But 'Blue Angel' is a Red Greenberg composition, I thought," Sal said as he played.

"Red wrote it when he had the piano gig in Julip's band. 'Lip got all the credit." Gold looked at Sal slyly. "You like Red?"

"Oh, yeah. Used to be one of my favorite bebop piano players. Probably the best white one."

"Yeah, I agree with you. You know, he's an old friend of mine." Gold didn't try to hide his pride.

"Really?" *I used to be somebody, too. And not that long ago.*

"Me and Red, we grew up together on Fairfax Avenue. That's in L.A."

"No shit. What's Red doing now?"

"He's got a fast-food joint on Santa Monica Pier. He's not in music anymore."

Neither am I.

Then Sal began to softly caress the gentle, painful melody to "Blue Angel," and both he and Gold drifted off into their own world, their own memories of their own lost loves. Sal played the song through twice, then gave it a stark, uncluttered end, like kissing a woman good-bye, then turning quickly and walking away.

"That was real nice," Gold said just above a whisper. "You play really nice."

Sal took his hands from the keyboard and let the silence ring. He picked up his tequila shooter and gave it a quick, merciful killing.

"Great tune," he rasped finally. He turned his head and looked at Gold full-on for the first time. "You live down here—sorry, what's your name?"

"Jack. Yeah, I got a little condo over in San José del Cabo. Had it the last few years. I used to be a cop and drink a lot. Now, I just drink a lot."

Sal gave a short bitter laugh. "Sounds like my life." *I used to be and now I drink.*

Gold was relighting his cigar. "Yeah, all I do now is drink and fish." He had the end of the cigar clamped tightly in his teeth. "Sometimes I skip the fishing altogether and get right to the drinking. It's basically a shameful way to live." He signaled the waitress to bring another round. "Same thing?" he asked Sal.

"Yeah, but this time it's on me." Sal reached into his cutoffs' pocket and withdrew a wad of hundred-dollar bills. He dealt one off the top and laid it on the polished piano top.

"Son of a bitch." Gold feigned shock. "A musician springing for a round? What'd you do, marry a rich music lover?"

Sal grinned. "Nah. I'm just a fugitive from injustice."

Gold squinted at him through a wreath of cigar smoke. "Could be. That, or a rich coke dealer."

"Do I look like a coke dealer?" Sal asked as he shook out a cigarette and lit it.

"I don't know. What does a coke dealer look like? If you're a dealer, then you look like one."

Sal shook his head. "Too Zen for me, man. Way too outside."

The waitress brought the fresh round, and they drank at them.

"You live down here, too?" Gold asked.

Sal put down his shot glass slowly. "I thought you said *retired?*"

"Nah, I said *used to be.*" Gold inspected Sal over the smoking cigar he was working between his teeth. "Lemme ask you something, son. Those two dudes at the end of the bar"—he twisted on his short swivel stool and looked back—"they're gone now."

He turned back to Sal. "Did you notice them?"

Sal's eyes probed the dimness by the end of the bar. "No—not really."

"Yeah, well they sure as hell noticed you. They were *all over* your ass, man. Seemed like they had a special interest in you."

Sal didn't say anything for a while, then he looked at Gold. "You sure?"

"Son, I was a cop for thirty-five years. I know a stakeout when I see one. Only these guys weren't cops."

Sal thought about this, then gave Gold a smile. "Probably just a coupla my fans. You know, they follow me all around the world."

Gold shrugged. "Could be. Could be."

"Or maybe they were fags."

Gold considered this and said, "Nah. They would've been more interested in Hector."

Both men laughed, and at that moment Hector came back from his break. He heard his name being laughed at and shot them a disapproving glare as he gave Sal a tepid little flutter of applause.

"*Gracias, Señor Eric,*" he lisped insincerely over the P.A. as he slid behind the keyboard, almost before Sal had extricated himself.

"I tell you what," Gold said in a low voice to the now-standing Sal. "I'm getting the hell outta here, and there's two reasons. Number one, son, you're a good piano man and a decent guy to drink with, but I got a bad feeling that you're an accident looking for a place to happen, and I don't wanna be around when the shit hits the fan." Then Gold leaned closer to Sal's ear and whispered, "The second reason is, if I listen to this cocksucker"—he nodded at Hector—"play anymore, my fucking teeth are gonna rot." He held out his hand. "See you around, son. And watch your ass."

Sal shook his hand, then Gold turned on his heel and walked across the lounge. The big drunken American almost made it out before Hector flung his hands at the keys with a flowery cascade of descending arpeggios. Like wood nymphs pissing on crystal toadstools.

* * *

Sal woke up sobbing. He began to choke on his own tears, he started coughing, and that's what woke him up. He sat up on the mattress laid in the middle of Yani's concrete-slab floor and wiped at his face with his bare hands while he snuffled for a breath. Then he realized why he was crying, and a chill ran up his spine, freezing him motionless. Yani's radio, which was hooked up to the bootleg extension cord that powered almost all of the cinder-block shacks that made up Playa Perro, was playing "The Touch of a Stranger." She always had it tuned to hard-core Mexican music, but today—probably in an attempt to please him—she'd dialed it to the big powerful station in Durango that played a lot of American Top 40. Isabel's voice, echoing hollowly off the sweating cement walls, had penetrated his sleeping thoughts and unleashed in him emotions that he'd been successfully narcotizing in his waking hours. The result being that he woke up crying on a dirty mattress in the middle of the cement-slab floor of the one-room shanty that belonged to the failed whore Yanira. He listened to Isabel sing his song while his tearful eyes slipped around the nearly empty shack, and he was once again struck by the absolute absurdity of his life. Somewhere outside, through the open front door, a woman was cursing her man in fishwife's Spanish, and here inside this detached prison cell the most famous woman in the world—the girl he'd fucked every night for over two years—was singing his lyrics and music to the biggest-selling international hit of the last two years. *I don't think we're in Kansas anymore, Toto.* Sal hardly moved until the last few bars of the long fade-out, then he did what he did first thing every morning, he reached out his hand and poured three fingers of tequila from the bottle on the floor beside him. He noticed that his fingers hardly shook as he clutched the smudged glass and lifted it to his lips. *Not serious juicer shakes. That only comes after years of diligent dedication.* Sal threw back his head and flung the liquor at the back of his throat—*Take your medicine, Salvatore, it'll make you all better*—and very shortly the world became a much nicer place. Sal poured himself another stiff one and sat back on his haunches, his knees cradled against his chest. He wore only the pair of cutoffs, and his upper body was already coated with a fine sheen of perspiration. It was early afternoon—Sal was willing himself to sleep later and later each day—and the temperature inside the twenty-by-twenty cinder-block building was 95 degrees. Outside, in the sun it was sixteen degrees hotter. Sal looked at the patina of sweat on his arms and knew that it would very soon evaporate. The heat down here was different. In Louisiana the heavy, humid air made you drink cold drinks, fan yourself, and dream of naked women with syrup-colored skin. It softened your complexion and slowed your perspective and gifted its environs with natural fecundity. Down here this dry, desert hellfire was a murderer. It shriveled your skin, cooked your brain, and bludgeoned you into submission. It made you cower stock-still in the nearest sliver of shade. It wanted you *dead, motherfucker.*

Yani came in from the sunlight, carrying a pot of coffee she'd brewed on the little fire pit outdoors. It always struck Sal funny that in Yani's house the refrigerator was inside and the stove was outside.

"You wake up," she observed as she poured a cup of coffee and held it out for him. When he didn't reach for it, she placed the cup beside him on the mattress. "*Son los* two o'clock." She said this as a statement of information, totally without reprimand, although she wished that this man wouldn't spend so much time drunk and asleep. She thought of him in that manner—"*this* man"—rather than "*my* man." He was much too distant for her to have any proprietary feelings about him.

"Change the station," he muttered as he balanced the glass of tequila on his bunched-up knees.

"*¿Como?*" she asked.

"*El estación. Yo quiero musica mejicana.* I wanna hear some Mexican shit." He spoke about as much Spanish as she did English, but somehow they made their wishes understood.

Yani twisted the knob on the battered old radio, and a slurring, out-of-tune Mexican brass section filled the room. She wished she had a new radio, maybe a Sony with a built-in tape and CD player. She wished this man would buy it for her. She knew he had the money, he always had money for his tequila and his *coca,* but she was too afraid to ask for anything. Not for a radio. Not for clothes for her nearly naked daughters. Not for a television, a better place to live, or even money for groceries. Every few weeks she would come to him and say, "There is no food," and he would give her one of the stained

American hundred-dollar bills he kept under the mattress, right beside the German *pistola* he was never without. Then he would drive her and her daughters to El Super in his bright red Jeep—Dios, *how wonderful that was!*—and she would buy food and staples for another few weeks. She always offered him the change from the hundred-dollar bill, and sometimes he would absentmindedly shove the money into his pocket, but sometimes he would not even seem to notice the change, and then she would keep it for herself. She had saved almost fifty dollars this way, stuffed in an old coffee can on the shelf over the sink, but she was always worried that one day this man would remember the change from the groceries and want all his money back. This worried her greatly, and she was afraid to buy anything for herself and her daughters. She was a shy, timid young woman who was terrified of men, and because of this overpowering fear she'd been unable to perform effectively as a whore—the last chance for impoverished girls the world over. The only men who'd enjoyed her were bullies and sadists who yanked her hair and bruised her skin, and these freaks only exacerbated her fearfulness. She was afraid, too, of this man—this strange American—but only because of herself. This one didn't beat her, or even raise his voice, and she thought that he probably wouldn't care about the fifty dollars in the Medaglia d'Oro can. She thought probably that this one didn't care about anything.

Still—he *did* keep the German *pistola* under the mattress.

"I will bring *comida*—food," she said to him before she went back out into the glare.

Sal watched her leave without noticing it. He was still remembering Isabel and "The Touch of a Stranger." He was remembering the night she'd laid down the lead vocal on that cut. It'd been at a big 32-track in Munich. It was cold and snowing, he could recall that, but he couldn't remember which month. December or January, probably. They'd tried for hours to get the right take, and Izzy kept just missing it, and Karl kept demanding another take, and then the German had rewound the song to the top, and they'd recorded her vocal piece by piece, phrase by phrase, and finally word by word, and the work had been so exact and tedious that when Karl finally said, "Let's listen," she'd ripped off her headphones, rushed into the control booth, and begun to curse Karl and him in Portuguese. Then tears had flooded her eyes, and she'd snatched up her overcoat—the big blue one with the hood, he could see it now—and rushed out into the pre-dawn streets. Sal had run after her and caught her and held her to his chest while she sobbed and sobbed and the snow drifted all around them; then, after a very long time—Izzy had a jones for crying—she'd quieted down and they'd gone back into the studio holding hands, and Karl was smiling behind the big glass, and when they went into the booth, he was playing the take back in the big mounted speakers, and as they listened to the playback, Sal realized what they were hearing was perfection, sheer musical perfection, and that was the first moment he knew that she was going to make it, that she was going to be a star.

"Breakfast," Yani said softly as she held out to him the plate of tortillas, eggs, and beans. "Breakfast."

Sal looked at her and didn't see her for a long time, then she came into focus like a photograph soaking in fixer solution. He blinked as she materialized before him. "What?" he muttered.

She placed the plate of food in his lap. "*Desayuno.* Breakfast. Eat. *Come.*"

Sal stared down at the yellow eggs and steaming beans, and his stomach did flip-flops.

"I'm not hungry," he said as he started to lift the plate, but she put her hand on his and said, "Eat. *Eat.*"

He tried to look at the food without getting nauseated, but that was impossible, so he stared at the doorway and blindly shoveled a mouthful of fried egg into his maw and chewed. It wasn't so bad that way, and he tore off a piece of tortilla and shoved it in after the egg. It felt good to chew on something resistant, and for a moment Sal was as full of well-being as he was ever going to get, then his stomach rebelled, he gulped, and the taste of vomit surged up and burned the back of his throat. Sal sat there, stricken, with a mouthful of food he didn't know what to do with, then he simply spit it out on his plate, put the plate on the floor, and gave it a hard shove. It slid a few feet away. At least now he didn't have to look at it. He started to reach for his drink, but on the way there his hand got sidetracked and dropped on a folded packet of tinfoil. He laid the packet in his lap and carefully unfolded the edges. Inside, wrapped in the tinfoil like an Easter candy, was a long mound of cocaine, the remainder of the quarter-ounce Sal had bought last week from the local dealer. He buried the tip of the broken penknife blade he used as a coke spoon and lifted it to his nose. Then he did the other side. *All better.* The coke froze the burning in the back of his throat, and his stomach immediately settled down. *Everything's all better.* But just to be sure, Sal snorted two more quick hits. *Double better.* His day was officially started now, and he lit a cigarette and leaned back against the cement-block wall, his tequila shooter cradled on his knees.

Yani was ironing one of the white smocks she had to wear when she worked in housekeeping at the hotel. She'd set up the ironing board near the door, and the iron's cord ran up to the ceiling, where the bootleg extension dangled down. Sal smoked his cigarette and watched her work. The slack muscles in her thin arms quivered and strained as she pressed all of her weight down on the iron and dragged it back and forth across the stiff material. She was a colorless, shapeless girl, already the mother of a four-year-old and a five-year-old at the age of twenty-one, and she'd failed at everything she'd ever done, including whoring. Sal knew it was only a matter of time before she fucked up and got fired at the hotel. He took another hit of coke from the foil packet, another drag off his cigarette, and watched her iron. She wanted to be his woman, he knew that, but he'd never even fucked her. Had no desire to. He just liked living here on Dog Beach, away from all the vacationing Americans, away from the *Federales,* away from the fear. He liked her taking care of all the things he didn't want to have to deal with—like *life.* And he liked to hold her thin, boyish body while he slept; her breathing comforted him. It had taken him three weeks of driving and healing, healing and driving, to negotiate the whole thirteen-hundred-kilometer length of the Baja Highway, and somehow he'd ended up here at Dog Beach, drunk and falling asleep behind the wheel of Eric's red Jeep. A girl—Yani—had stepped out of one of the cinder-block shacks—this one—and Sal had shoved some money in her hand and asked for a place to sleep. She'd taken him to her bed, and he'd never left.

He popped some more blow, took another hit of tequila. He was starting to feel a lot better now. Pretty soon he'd be fucked up enough to get out of bed. Sal drained the shot glass and felt an urgent tug at his bowels. The Mexican version of a vacation keepsake. He dragged himself to his feet, slipped on his *huaraches,* and started to walk out into the glare. Then he stopped, turned, and went back to the mattress.

La pistola, Yani thought as she watched him. *This one can't even shit without his pistola.*

When he had the Luger firmly secreted under the waistband of his cutoffs and had pulled on an oversized T-shirt that said CABO and showed a tuna fighting the line, he stepped out into the sunshine.

The heat was like a wall, a kind of temperature barrier. This was truly hell's waiting room. Sal quickly shaded his eyes with his forearm and squinted out at the white glare. Dog Beach was quiet—a deserted cluster of sixteen cinder-block cubes stuck down without design along a sweltering stretch of two-lane Highway 1. There was the prerequisite scattering of cannibalized autos, stiffening laundry hanging everywhere, and beyond the houses the beach and the sea. It was just another shitty place in the world where very poor people lived out their unbearable lives.

Sal hurried over the hard-packed ground and around the corner of the house. Across the alley three straw-hatted young *vatos* were squatting Indian style in a wedge of shadow thrown by an overhanging roof, drinking beer. They were talking and smiling, joking with each other. *These people are incredible. What the fuck they got to laugh about?* Sal quick-stepped back to the little shed that contained one of the two working toilets that serviced Playa Perro. As he closed the crooked old door, he heard a fresh outbreak of laughter. *Motherfuckers are laughing at* me. But he didn't have time for that right now. He ripped open the snap on his shorts, yanked them down, and set his ass back on the toilet seat—all in one fluid movement. His bowels fluttered and released, there was an explosion of watery excrement, and Sal immediately felt a surge of relief. He sighed, and the following intake of breath made him very aware of the filth and stench of this communal toilet. He cleaned himself with a page of the Mexican newspaper left for that purpose, pulled up his cutoffs, and was about to step back outside when a fresh wave of nausea roiled inside of him, and he gagged once and then puked all over the toilet seat. He stared down at the alcoholic-reeking sludge, wiped his mouth with the back of his hand, then yanked open the ill-fitted door. The three young *vatos* were still there, squatting in the shade, watching him. Sal touched the grip of the Luger for confidence, then walked back around the corner of Yani's little house.

Inside, she was still sweating over the ironing board. Sal had settled himself back down on the mattress and had poured himself another drink before he noticed the two little girls staring back at him from under the table in the corner of the cement-slab floor. They were two half-naked brown-skinned children, each with a mop of unruly, yellow-streaked hair, and Sal was fairly sure they hadn't been there before he'd gone to the toilet. They had a way of doing that—just reappearing from time to time, and Sal had no idea where they disappeared to when they weren't around, or why they all of a sudden turned up. And then when they were here, they constantly gaped at him with their round brown eyes, as if they were wondering where the hell *he'd* come from. Almost five months, and they still couldn't take their eyes off him, as if he'd just walked in off the street for the first time and plopped on their mattress. Drove him *fucking crazy.*

He gulped at his drink and got up, saying, "I'm gonna go for a run."

He'd found the beach one day about a month after he'd arrived in Cabo. He'd driven north from the cape for about fifteen minutes, and had pulled off the highway looking for a place to piss. There was a faint old trail that led down through the sand dunes toward the ocean, and Sal had followed it easily, bouncing along in four-wheel drive. At the end of a series of moundlike hills, about a half-mile from the highway, was a narrow white sand beach, pristine and completely hidden from the passing drivers, that ran straight for about a half-mile—he'd clocked it in the Jeep—before it curved around a promontory and continued on out of sight for another quarter-mile. Sal had worked himself up to where he could run it three times—starting here, around the promontory, to the end of the beach and back—approximately four-and-a-half miles. He still didn't know how he'd got started. He'd never done any kind of exercise before in his life, and he certainly wasn't on any kind of health kick now, but that first day he'd happened upon this beach, he'd walked around in his bare feet, kicking at the sand, and had suddenly broken into a trot. It'd felt good—the hot sun on his shoulders and the hot beach on the soles of his feet. Of course, that first day he hadn't made it to the curve around the promontory before he'd collapsed in the ocean, gasping for breath. The next day he'd returned, and it was the same story. But the third day he staggered all the way to the bluff, his side aching from the still-healing bullet wound. Now, he came here almost every afternoon. Running the beach was almost as important to him as going to the hotel at night to play the piano, and he'd found that with just the right mixture of alcohol and cocaine he could anesthetize himself enough so that when he was racing naked and barefoot down the beach, screaming out obscenities with his damaged rasp, he could forget for a second or two that he was a dead man.

Today, Sal left the Jeep where he always did, in the gully between two dunes, and walked down to where the surf kept rushing in over the wet dark sand. He took off his *huaraches* and felt the surprisingly cool waves lap at his ankles. A couple of miles out in the sea there was an outcropping of rocks where sea lions congregated, and from time to time he could hear their faint barking carried in on the wind. He went back to the Jeep and put his sandals on a fender. He took the Luger from under his cutoffs and laid it on the bucket seat, then stripped off the fighting-tuna T-shirt and dropped it over the weapon. Last he unsnapped his cutoffs and let them slip to the sand. The hot air seemed cool to his penis, and he felt his testicles stir a little. Again, Sal didn't understand *why* he liked running on the beach completely naked, he just knew he enjoyed it. Sometimes his balls bounced wrong against a thigh, and there was a moment of dull, sickish pain, but somehow he enjoyed that, too. At least then he was feeling *something*—something real, something immediate, something besides the sadness that ate away at his insides.

Sal squinted for a moment down the white ribbon of beach, then began to lope easily along the hard-packed sand. By the time he was halfway to the promontory, he was running full out. Sweat stung his eyes and rocketed off the tip of his nose with each jolting stride. His own heavy breathing always sounded huge and foreign in his ears, like the breathing of a giant following just behind. The hot sun bathed his whole naked body with warmth, as if he were encased in embryonic fluid, and then Sal remembered why he liked running on this beach without any clothes. Whenever he ran, it came back to him. He hoped the sun would burn away the pain, just scorch him front and back the way Mexicans singed green peppers over an open fire. He wanted to be gutted and blackened; he wanted to be a dry husk, with nothing inside; he wanted the pain to be burned away, like a flame held to gangrenous flesh. He wanted to be free.

"You cuuuunnnnnntttt!" he screamed out as he pounded his bare feet around the big rock promontory. *"I loved youuuuuuuu!"*

"What does he say?" Magallanes asked, wiping the sweat from his face with the palm of his hand.

"¿Quién sabe?" Zuniga answered. He held the MAC-10 down against his leg side, just in case someone happened to come strolling through the dunes.

Magallanes gave the Indian a wide, sarcastic grin. "What—you don't speak English, gringo?"

Zuniga ignored the remark. He was looking all around the low sand hills, searching for the right place. "We should have brought a rifle with a telescopic sight. If we had known about this running on the beach, we should have brought a rifle."

They were kneeling in the sand and coarse grass, about a hundred yards behind the Jeep.

"This is better," Magallanes said. "I like to see their eyes when they realize." He chuckled then, and Zuniga shivered in the hot sun. *This one is evil and will bring bad luck.*

"Look!" Magallanes hissed. "Here he comes again!"

The small, naked man was rounding the rock outcropping, his pounding feet throwing up clods of wet sand as he came pounding back the other way. He came back to the Jeep, circled it running, then raced back down the beach, shouting, *"You cuuuuunnnnt!"*

Magallanes laughed and shook his head gleefully. "*Ay-yi-yi*—What a strange one this son of a whore is. Look at him, running around without any clothes, screaming at people that aren't there. He's *loco.*"

The naked runner disappeared around the curve of beach, but they could still hear him shouting.

Zuniga rose and snapped his machine pistol off the safety. "Come on. Let's search the car." He was already trotting toward Eric's red Jeep. Magallanes hurried to catch up.

"Listen, gringo—"

"We search the car, then we hide again," the Indian said. "We wait until he's tired himself out. Then it should be easy."

They were at the Jeep.

"Gringo, listen." Magallanes was speaking rapidly. "We shouldn't kill him until we ask about the money, what do you think?"

Zuniga lifted the T-shirt, and the Luger was underneath. The two men passed a professional look between them.

"Maybe not so *loco,*" the Indian said as he picked up the gun and stuck it under his belt. Then he made a quick search of the Jeep: under the seat, behind the seat, in the door pockets.

"We don't kill him until he tells us where the money is, *correcto?*" Magallanes wanted some kind of agreement.

"Quickly. He's coming." They scurried back behind a sand dune.

"We kill him *after!*" Magallanes rasped in the Indian's ear. Then they ducked their heads and watched the small American come pounding toward them down the edge of the surf. When he was a hundred yards from the Jeep, there was a sudden clamor of raucous noise behind the two hidden men.

"*¡Qué pasa!*" Magallanes turned, and on the crest of the next dune over was a rangy old rawboned dog, as gaunt and unhealthy-looking as only a Mexican stray can be, and he was glaring at them and barking a warning to the world.

"*¡Pinchi perro!* Fucking dog!" Magallanes swore, and the dog barked all the louder.

Zuniga hadn't turned to see the dog. His eyes were still on the naked runner, who had slowed down and was looking up at the sand dunes.

"Shut up! Fucking dog!"

The runner had stopped. He was maybe seventy-five yards on the other side of the Jeep. He stood there a moment, and then he unconsciously began to backpedal.

Zuniga stood up, raised the MAC-10 to his shoulder, and squeezed off a burst at the runner.

"Don't kill him yet!" Magallanes bellowed, but he, too, took aim and fired.

"That's our *job!*" the Indian hollered back. Then he was scrambling over the sand mound, firing at the small American, who was now running pell-mell back down the beach. Zuniga and the other stood on the crest of the mound and emptied their clips at the ducking, zigzagging figure. He was just out of range.

"Fucking Yanqui bastard!" Magallanes cursed as he plunged down the sand dune, pulling the empty clip out of the machine pistol and slapping in another. *"Piece of dog shit!"*

Zuniga was twenty feet ahead, pumping low and hard through the dry, powdery sand until he got to the edge of the surf, where it was wet and resilient; then he kicked off his shoes and raced after the fleeing American.

"Kill him!" Magallanes shouted after him now, forgetting about the money. They had a commission. *"Don't let him get away!"*

The American was tired. The Indian was gaining. The naked American looked back only once, then he angled off and splashed out into the surf.

"Gringo!" Magallanes screamed from behind, and Zuniga didn't know which one of them he was screaming at.

When the American was up to his hips—which doesn't take long in the waters off Cabo—he pushed out and plunged under. The last thing they saw of him was his white ass momentarily shining in the sun's glare before it disappeared under the waves.

"Ahh!" the Indian grunted, like a boxer taking a body shot. Then he brought up the machine pistol and sprayed the waters where the American had disappeared. He walked out into the onrushing surf and fired a whole clip in one continuous four-second rattle.

"Fucking piece of gringo shit!" Magallanes splashed up beside him and began to chew at the water with rapid little bites of bullets. *"Gringo shit!"*

Zuniga was reloaded, and he discharged another full clip in only a few moments. He quickly reloaded and repeated the process. Then again and again and again, until finally he had no more clips.

"Fucking Yanqui bastard!" Magallanes was still shooting. *"He got away! He got away!"*

Zuniga slowly lowered the machine pistol and stared out at the empty, roiling sea. This had never happened to him before. He was the kind of man who treasures being depended upon, and this was *not* the way this was supposed to have gone.

"No, he didn't."

"What?" Magallanes screamed. *"Then where the fuck is he? Do you see his fucking body?"* He kicked out at the waves around his feet. *"Where?"*

Zuniga kept looking over the breaking waves.

"¡Jesus Cristo!" Magallanes bellowed as he splashed around in the surf. *"What the fuck are we going to tell the man in Mexico City?"*

Zuniga was still looking out to sea. "We tell him the truth." Then he turned to Magallanes. "We tell him we did the job."

Magallanes got up close to the Indian's face. "*I* don't know that we killed him. Do you?"

"No one could live through all those clips."

"Yeah? How the fuck can you be so sure?"

"Look out there." Zuniga pointed. "Do you see him? What's he going to do, swim to China? Do you even see him trying? No—you know why? Because he's dragging the fucking bottom with an ass full of nine-millimeter caps."

Magallanes was silent. He looked out at the sea and then back at the Indian.

"We tell the man we killed him and threw his body into the ocean," Zuniga continued, "because that's the truth, that's the way it happened." Then he looked hard at Magallanes. "And there's only the two of us."

Magallanes looked away and shook his head slowly, as if in regret. "Fucking gringo shit," he breathed softly.

Zuniga turned and began to wade back to the beach. When his back was to Magallanes, he shifted his empty MAC-10 to the crook of his left arm, and with his right hand pulled the German Luger from under his belt. He turned his head slightly and shouted back, "We say he's dead and at the bottom of the sea." He wondered by the weight of it if the Luger was loaded. *Why shouldn't it be? Why would the American carry an empty gun?* "We say he was *mucho hombre,* he put up a hell of a fight, but finally we killed him." He held the Luger up against his chest and clicked off what he assumed was the safety. "But not before he finished one of us."

"What?" Magallanes shouted from behind, and then Zuniga turned in the surf, aimed the Luger, and pulled the trigger. The left side of Magallanes's throat exploded in a gusher of black-red, and he plunged down to his knees as if someone had hacked off his lower legs with an ax. Zuniga fired again, and the top of Magallanes's skull disappeared. Already dead, he pitched forward into the surf. The sea around him instantly darkened with swirling clouds of blood.

Zuniga walked slowly back to Magallanes's corpse.

"Pinchi cabrón," he said softly. "You're fucked now, you bad-luck fucking bastard." This was the way to kill a man. This was how it's done. The way they'd botched up the American had made the Indian coldly furious, but now he felt a good deal better. "You piece of shit," he muttered, "you fucked with the wrong *hombre.*" And then he spit on Magallanes's corpse. "I'm going to tell everyone the little American *maricón* killed you, you piece of shit." He bent over and pulled the other machine pistol out from under the body. Then he plodded through the surf back to the beach. *I'll keep the Luger long enough to show the man in Mexico City,* he thought, *then he can do with it whatever he wants.* Back on the wet, hard sand he turned once to scan the horizon. There was nothing out there but the sound of the surf and the muted barking of the sea lions on the distant rock outcropping. *You better be dead, American.* Then he began to trudge back to the highway, carrying the two machine pistols.

Yani didn't start worrying until after sunset. This man, whenever he went off in the bright red Jeep, this one always returned before the sun went down. He always made it back by dark—before today. Maybe he had an accident in the bright red Jeep. Maybe he finally drank too much and passed out at the wheel. Maybe the people he always carried *la pistola* for finally caught up with him.

Just after the sun went down into the Pacific, she walked out to the highway and looked north, the way he'd disappeared. Then a car drove by from the south, and someone inside shouted something rude to her, and she walked slowly back down to Dog Beach. She made an almost involuntary plea to the Virgin. *Por favor, Mary, let this one not be dead.* She crossed herself unconsciously. *Please let this one not be gone forever. Please let him come back.* She'd been having fantasies about this one driving her and her children north to *los Estados Unidos.* Those fantasies had recently crossed the boundaries and become formal prayers. Requests to the goddess. She carried her beads in the pocket of her shapeless shift and secretly said her rosary whenever she could, all the while visualizing this one driving her and her daughters through the border checkpoint in his bright red Jeep, pretending to the Border Patrol that they were his American family. All she wanted was to get to America; she would handle it from there. Her older sister, Rosa—the only other family she had in the world—worked as a domestic for a big hotel in Denver, and Rosa had written to tell her how beautiful it was there. If this one would only drive her over the border, and if she could save enough of this one's money in the old Medaglia d'Oro coffee can, maybe she could buy a bus ticket for her and her two daughters to this place Denver, and live with Rosa and get a job in the big hotel, and then her little girls would grow up to be Americans. They had light hair—no one would ever know that they'd come from Dog Beach.

But none of this was possible if this one didn't come back. She'd begun to think that this American had been sent to her by God. Since he'd started living with them, things had got much better. They ate well now, and her girls seemed to be suddenly sprouting up. They had a few new clothes. With him around there were possibilities, there was *hope.* If he didn't come back, the hope would soon follow him.

Why did he have to drink so much, Mother Mary? Why couldn't you have sent someone who didn't drink so much and sniff la cocaina?

She kept his dinner plate out until the *frijoles* became a hard, tarlike lump, then she had to throw the food out for the chickens. She made the girls stay up until they became cranky they were so sleepy, because putting them to sleep before he came home would be a kind of recognition that something had changed, that the night was going on without him—just as she would have to.

Look, he left his cocaina. *He wouldn't go away without his* cocaina. *It was too expensive.*

She searched for anything that would lighten her heart. That would give her hope.

After she put the girls to sleep on the narrow little half-mattress under the table, she walked up to the highway again and stood in the darkness, watching the speeding cars whoosh by. It was still very hot, but she felt icy inside. She felt frozen.

She was asleep sitting up against the wall just inside the open door of her house when headlights washed over her and she heard tires crunching on the dirt driveway. Her eyes popped open, and she clambered to her feet. *He's back! He's back!* Then she heard the slam of the car door, and she knew it wasn't the bright red Jeep. Confused, she hesitated for a second, then quickly shut the rickety old door and locked and latched it. She put her ear to the wood and listened. There was nothing. There was nothing, but she felt an unsettling and overpowering fear grip her. *Mother Mary. Mother Mary. Please protect me.* She backed away from the door all the way across the cement-slab floor, until the far wall was suddenly against her back. She stared at the old, unpainted door. Her heart was booming against her rib cage. *Mother Mary.* She glanced over to her daughters sleeping on the little children's mattress under the kitchen table, then looked back at the door, and at that instant the door imploded inward on its hinges and *whammed* back against the wall.

Holy Mary, Mother of God—Holy Mary, Mother of God.

Zuniga stalked quickly across the cement-slab floor and clutched Yani by her throat. *"Silencio, puta—¿comprende?"* he whispered, and she was too terrified to even nod.

"Where is the money?"

Holy Mary, Mother of God—Holy Mary—

"Where the fuck is the money!" he shouted into her face.

"¡No comprendo, señor! ¡No comprendo!"

His broad Indian face darkened with anger.

"Tell me—where—the money is." He bit off every word as he tightened the stranglehold on her throat. *"¿Donde está el dinero?"*

"Por favor, señor," she whimpered. "Please, mister—"

"You think I'm fucking with you?" he wanted to know. He raised his other hand and pressed the German Luger against the side of her head.

Somehow the sight of the American's gun panicked her more than anything.

We're all lost, she thought. *Ave Maria, Ave Maria—*

"Where's the money? Where did he hide it?" The Indian jammed the Luger's narrow muzzle deep into her skin. "Tell me, or I'll blow your fucking brains out, you *pinchi puta.*"

"Please, sir," she gasped through her tears, "I don't have any money."

"You fucking slut! Tell me where the gringo hides his fucking money or I swear to Jesus I'll do you right here and now!"

"I don't know! I don't know!"

"I'll give you what I gave him! Tell me! Tell me!"

"I don't know what you're talking about!"

Just then her mother's eyes flicked out to find her daughters and snapped back, but Zuniga looked to see what she'd been checking on. He saw the little girls—shocked wide-eyed and scared dumb under the kitchen table—and loosened his grip on her throat.

"Now, you'll tell me, you cunt," he said as he strode back across the floor and slammed shut the door. Then he turned back and looked at the little girls.

"No!" Yani screamed, and started toward him.

"Don't fucking move!" he barked, and raised the gun. She was staring right down the ugly little barrel.

"Please, sir!" she begged from the middle of the room. "Please!" Tears were streaming down her cheeks. "I beg you."

He moved quickly to the table and reached under, grasping about, his eyes and his aim never leaving Yani. His hand fluttered over the little girls, and they started to scream. He grabbed out and closed his big brown fingers around one of the skinny legs of the elder daughter. She began to shriek even louder.

"Oh, my God, *hombre,*" Yani sobbed, her hands clasped together as if in prayer. *"Please don't hurt my babies."*

"Tell me!" he thundered as he dragged the screaming little girl from under the table. The four-year-old was still under there, cringing, her mouth a smeared wail.

"Please—" Yani shouted. Then, forgetting the gun, she

rushed the Indian. When she was close enough, he simply lashed out with a foot and kicked her hard in her stomach. She fell back with a thud and tumbled across the floor.

"Tell me!" he threatened, as with one hand he lifted the shrieking child by her ankles, with her blondish hair sweeping the floor. *"Tell me, or I'll bash her fucking head in against this wall!"*

Yani was crawling painfully across the concrete floor, still trying to save her baby.

"Please! Please!" she sobbed as she inched forward on her hands and knees. *"I don't know anything about any money. ¡Yo no sé naddddaaaaaaa!"*

"You're fucking lying!" He began to swing the screaming little girl back and forth, like an athlete warming up. *"I'm telling you, whore, I'll beat her bloody against this cement wall!"*

"Noooooo!"

"Tell me where the gringo hid the money!"

"I don't know!"

"Tell me!"

"I don't know! I swear it to the Virgin Mary, I don't know!"

"You're lying!" Zuniga swung the little girl, whose name was Consuelo, back in a wide arc in preparation of breaking her against the wall like a sack of ice.

"All right! I'll give you the money!" Yani screamed desperately. *"I'll give you the moneyyyyyyy!"*

Zuniga stopped his swing and smiled grimly. "You lying little cunt. I *knew* you knew." He let the screaming little girl down almost gently to the floor, and she scuttled away from him and huddled with her sister under the table. Both girls were bawling like puppies. Zuniga stepped over to where Yani was kneeling, sobbing into her hands, and tapped her hard on the shoulder with the muzzle of the Luger. "The money."

Yani looked up at him a moment, then got up slowly—the kick to her solar plexus—and tottered shakily on her legs.

"The money, whore."

She nodded, then turned and walked gingerly to the open cupboard where she kept the groceries. Her daughters were still sobbing under the table. Yani reached up to the top shelf and took down the bright red Medaglia d'Oro can. She opened it, then turned and handed the fistful of pesos and dollars to Zuniga.

"What the fuck is this?" the Indian demanded.

"It's—that's all the money I have."

Zuniga looked down at the crumpled bills in his hands, then with one fluid motion he flung the money to the floor and backhanded Yani across her mouth with his closed left fist. She sank to her knees, blood running from her split lip.

"You stupid cunt!" he shouted down at her, and she reached out and clutched his legs, her head bowed down as if in prayer.

"Please! Please!" she sobbed down at the floor.

He leaned over and jabbed the tip of the Luger's muzzle into the back of her neck.

"If I shoot you in this place, here," he said calmly as he poked her spinal column with the Luger, "even if you don't die, you'll never move again. *¿Comprende?*"

"Yes!" she cried. "Yes, I understand!"

"Do you want me to shoot you?" he reasoned.

"Noooooooo!" she screamed at the cement slab. *"Noooooooo!"*

"Then tell me where the fucking money is."

She lifted up her tear-soaked face to him. "I swear to the Virgin Mary, I swear it upon the lives of my children—I don't know anything about any money!" Then she dropped her head and clung to Zuniga's calves. She was stretched out prostrate before him, like a novice before the altar. "I don't know anything about any money!"

Zuniga glared down at her for a long time. The children were sobbing hysterically under the table. There was a big black bug buzzing around the naked light bulb suspended from the ceiling.

Then the Indian lifted the gun from the back of her neck.

"There never was any money, was there?" he said finally. "The gringo never had any."

Very slowly Yani lifted her eyes to his. "I swear—I swear on the Baby Jesus, I don't know."

His cold dark eyes ran through her like dirks. "And you would know if he'd had any, wouldn't you?"

It was a trick question, and she didn't know how to answer it. "I swear—"

"And if you knew"—his voice was a hissing snake—"you would have told me, wouldn't you?"

"I swear to God, I don't know anything about any money. Before God and His angels I never—"

Then she saw his eyes change and begin to travel over her prone body. She knew he was thinking of raping her. Her mind flew to her girls.

"I swear—I swear—" she stammered, and he leaned down and roughly gripped her short, limp hair. Then he yanked up hard, pulling her to her feet. Yani screamed, and the girls under the table began to wail even more loudly. He pushed her back against the cupboard with a clatter.

"Please," she begged. "Please—"

He raised her formless buttocks up onto the cupboard's narrow ledge.

"Please don't hurt me," she pleaded. "I don't know—"

He gripped the neck of her flimsy cotton shift and ripped it down the front. She tried to cover her small, flaccid breasts, but he tore away the rest of her dress from her shoulders and shoved her back against the jars of *jalapeños* and cans of *mole* sauce. Then, still doing everything with one hand because his right held the Luger, he began to unbuckle his belt.

She turned to her daughters then and shouted, *"Get out! Get out!"*

"Shut up," Zuniga growled as his trousers fell to the concrete slab.

"Run! Go see Señora Mendoza! She's got candy!" But the little girls only wailed with white-eyed fear.

"I said *shut up!*" the Indian warned as he pushed her legs apart and positioned the head of his penis in her mass of untrimmed black hair.

"Don't look!" Yani shouted to her terrified daughters. *"Don't loo—"*

And then he rammed into her, and she felt the hot pain and began to cry uncontrollably.

"Don't look," she managed to choke out as he began to plunge violently in and out. Then, almost politely, he turned his face to the side and climaxed with a grunt. It was all over that quickly.

She slipped to the floor, sobbing, and curled up in a fetal position, her soft, formless body shaking with tears.

The Indian pulled up his pants and looked down at her, "If you tell anyone that I was here"—he nudged her with the toe of his Gemelli de Janeiro loafer—"I'll come back. *¿Comprende?*"

She couldn't speak, she was crying so hard. She hugged her thin arms to her chest and closed her eyes tightly. When she opened them again, he was gone. She lay on her side on the cold concrete and stared around the room. She couldn't believe he had come and gone and she was still alive. Then her eyes found her those of her daughters, still shrieking under the table.

"Consuelo, Maria," she said in a soothing voice, already scurrying across the floor to them. "It's all right, *mis hijas.* It's all right." She ducked under the table and clutched them to her naked body. "Don't cry, babies, don't cry," but the touch of her flesh made them even more disturbed, and they howled with terror. She pressed them to her, and eventually they closed their scrawny arms around her and bawled into her sides. "Please forgive me, *mis hijas,*" she crooned to them as she settled back against the cinder-block wall and held her children as they worked their screaming mouths against her flesh almost as if they were nursing. "Please forgive me. Please forgive me. Please forgive me." She breathed it over and over. *"Favor de perdonarme. Favor de perdonarme."* Like a child's catechism chant. Like a prayer. She sat like that, huddled against the wall under the old wooden table, clasping her crying daughters to her naked body, feeling his semen ooze inside of her, for over an hour, repeating her mantra, "Please forgive me. Please forgive me. Mother of God, please forgive me," until finally their sobbing spiraled down into a breathy keening. *"Favor de perdonarme. Favor de perdonarme,"* but she couldn't get them to sleep until she gave them a mixture of orange Fanta and some of the dead American's tequila and laid them down on the mattress in the middle of the floor. When they were breathing gently, she pulled on a shirt and a pair of the dead American's jeans and sat on the floor by the locked front door with all the lights off, a butcher knife in her hand, softly repeating over and over, "Please forgive me, my children. Please forgive me, my Lady. Please forgive me, please forgive me, please forgive me," until it had been an hour since the last car whizzing by on the highway had flashed its shadowy headlights over the wall. Then she opened the door and went outside. The night was hot and salty with the ocean, and she could hear faint mariachi music from the bar a half-mile down the road. She slipped into the shadows by the wall and padded barefoot around the corner, then ducked down and felt along the foundation of the house until her fingers bumped against the board covering the entrance to the crawl space under the house. It was a cave-in, actually, a long, narrow tunnel formed by the collapse of sandy soil under the cement slab. The dead American had found it the first night he was here. *Forgive me. Forgive me. Please forgive me.* With the butcher knife she pried away the loose, dirt-covered board as quietly as she could and pushed it to one side. She lay flat on the cool dark ground and wriggled her head and shoulders through the opening. The crawl space smelled of dead air and vermin, but she shoved with her toes and pulled with her fingers until her whole body was under the concrete slab. *Favor de perdonarme. Favor de perdonarme.* Then she took the candle from her shirt pocket and lit it with a trembling match. Dimly illuminated by the candlelight along the dirt wall about six feet in front of her was a row of tiny, pink eyes, and then the flame on the candle flared and she could see six, seven rats staring sullenly back at her. She could even make out the naked pups squirming in the newspaper-scrap nest. *Please forgive me. Please forgive me.* Then something beside her caught her eye, and she slowly turned her head. Half-buried under the dirt right there at her shoulder was a warped, rat-gnawed briefcase, and Yani knew instantly that this was what she was searching for.

Mother of God, please forgive me my blasphemy. My beautiful Consuelo, please forgive me. My tiny Maria, I beg of you.

Back in the house, still afraid to use anything but candlelight, the sleeping children's soft breathing filling the shadows, Yani knelt on the floor and placed the crumbling briefcase before her. Strips of gnawed leather curled from the rotting piece of luggage.

Mother Mary, please forgive me.

From time to time, in the dark hours just before dawn, the American who was now dead would rise from the mattress in the middle of the floor and steal out of the house. The first time Yani, always a light sleeper, padded barefoot behind and saw him slip under the cement slab. The next day he took her to El Super and gave her a hundred-dollar bill for groceries. After that, whenever the dead American rose from their mattress in the early morning hours, she would lie there in the darkness and try to hear him as he bumped under the house. Usually she could.

Mother of God, please forgive me.

She traced her fingers over the top of the battered briefcase.

Blessed Virgin, I did it for them, you know that. Please forgive me, please forgive me, please forgive me.

All she hoped for was enough to get them out of Dog Beach, enough to get them to *el Norte,* to the border. If only there were one or two more of the dead American's hundred-dollar bills. Or three or four. Or nine or ten.

Please forgive me, my Lady, if I appear greedy. It's just that I have to get my babies out of here. Please forgive me.

With two or three of the hundred-dollar bills she could buy three tickets on the morning bus to Tijuana—it was sixty thousand pesos apiece for the twenty-four-hour journey—and still have enough left for food and some new clothes, maybe even enough to hire a *coyote* to take the three of them across the border.

Please forgive me.

She snapped the rusted latches—one of them was sprung and she had to press very hard to get it to open—and knelt there in the candlelit darkness, beseeching her goddess.

Don't listen to my greed, Blessed Virgin, all we need is enough to get to the border. With what that evil one threw on the floor, we would be so thankful for just one more of the hundred-dollar bills. Just one.

She crossed herself.

Or two. Two would be so generous, Blessed Virgin, Our Lady of Guadalupe. I don't ask only for myself.

Then, without realizing it, she took a deep breath, held it a moment, and pulled open the ruined case.

She stared down at the banded stacks of money, and for several seconds all she felt was intense disappointment. She had prayed so hard that when she lifted the lid she would see a few scattered bills that it was a while before she realized it was *all* money. There were many *many* hundred-dollar bills. She stared down stupidly at the jumbled packs of hundred-dollar bills, and then very, very slowly the comprehension of what she was looking at crept over Yani like a shiver, and she felt more frightened than at any time that night. She was in the presence of God, she knew that. She knew that, because what she was witnessing was a miracle. She, Yanira Reyes de Guiterrez, was party to a miracle. There had been only one or two bills in the briefcase, she understood that as well as she understood the power of prayer, and at the instant of her raising the lid those two bills had been multiplied into hundreds—*thousands*—just like when El Salvador fed the multitudes with the two baskets of fish and the five loaves of bread.

"Madre de Dios," she whispered in the circle of candlelight, "Mother of God, thank you so much."

And then, at the hearing of her own voice, the full import of the miracle she was experiencing struck her like a slap. Her hands began to shake, and her skin turned icy. *Mother of God, you have given us the world. You have set us free.* "Thank you," she choked through her labored breathing. "Thank you, so much." *You tested me tonight, my Lady. You tested me, and somehow I passed your test. Something I did brought me your favor, and I thank you, I thank you, I thank you.*

She tried to count the money, kneeling there on the floor in the candlelight, but with her pulse booming in her ears she kept losing count. Finally she realized that there were a hundred hundred-dollar bills in each banded stack—ten thousand dollars—and that all she had to do was count the stacks. Even so, she lost count again and again.

Gracias, Blessed Mother. Gracias, gracias, gracias.

Finally she just gave up, but not before she understood that there were hundreds of thousands of American dollars in the spoiled attaché.

. . . Blessed art thou among women, and blessèd is the fruit of thy womb, Jesus.

It was a miracle—she was very clear on that—but everything that had presaged it was mysterious to her. She knew that the Virgin Mary had interceded with God to change the dead American's few hundred-dollar bills into thousands. It never occurred to her that the money had been there all along, because if the dead American had had this much money, he wouldn't have stayed in Dog Beach. No one would have. No, what confused Yani was the evil man who had brutalized her and her girls, and then raped her. The more she thought about him, the more she came to understand that he hadn't been a man at all, but the Devil, *el Diablo,* masquerading as a man as he was known to do, and he'd come to cheat her out of the Blessed Virgin's generous gift. Somehow she'd done battle with the forces of hell, and somehow, with the Blessed Virgin's help, she had prevailed. And Mother Mary had rewarded her.

Blessed is the fruit of thy womb, Jesus.

Then in the dark she went down to the ocean to wash the Devil's semen from her vagina.

It was still dim and gray when she saw the yellow lights of the morning bus heading north appear a half-mile down Highway 1.

"Niñas, niñas," she said softly as she gently nudged her daughters sleeping on the big cardboard suitcase. "Wake up."

She had wrapped the packs of bills in a length of cloth and strapped the bundle to her stomach, then covered the whole thing with a coarse serape, and she hoped she looked like just another pregnant peon fresh out of the desert.

From the yawning bus driver she bought three one-way tickets to La Paz and paid for them with one of the twenties she'd kept stashed in the red Medaglia d'Oro coffee can. In the bigger town, away from here, she would dare to buy passage all the way to Tijuana with one of the miraculous hundred-dollar bills. Not before.

There was only one other passenger, an old man snoring into his chest, so she bedded down her daughters, one on either side, on the low, narrow seats that ran the whole length of the bus.

She crossed her hands over the bundle tied to her midsection and leaned her back against the jostling wall of the bus.

Blessed art thou among women, and blessed is the fruit of thy womb, Jesus. Thank you, Blessed Virgin, thank you, thank you, thank you.

Looking around shyly, she crossed herself, then settled her hands back over her stomach.

The white-jacketed steward descended the spiraling polished-oak staircase into the yacht's salon, then crossed the Persian rug to the leather couch, where three people were arrayed around a fourth, who was stretched out on the couch. The steward, a small, dark Filipino, held out the steaming mug of broth to the man lying on the couch. The tall white woman scowled at the steward and took the mug from his hands.

"Manny'll fix you right up," Harry Chang said to the man on the couch, who was Sal. Harry Chang had been born in Kapiolani Catholic Medical Center in Honolulu, and when he spoke, there was just the *impression* of a pidgin accent, like something you think you hear and keep listening for, but aren't sure is really there. "Manny used to be a corpsman for the Contras," Harry Chang offered as a kind of validation. "He tends us all when we get sick or banged up."

Manny was a short, taciturn Nicaraguan, unhappy to be awakened before his watch. He wore a disapproving frown as he worked on Sal's legs, cleaning and dressing the bloody abrasions on his knees and shins. Sal's hands were already bandaged. They had dragged him naked from the sea, his fingers and arms torn to shreds by the jagged, seal-shit-covered rocks, and now he was still naked, but wrapped in a thick satin comforter. Sal hadn't realized how cold a tropical ocean gets at night, especially after ten or twelve hours of clinging half-submerged to rocks with edges like ice picks.

"Here, honey," the white woman said softly as she placed the cup of broth into Sal's bandaged hands. "This stuff will fix you right up." She was a tall, leggy woman in her middle forties with unnaturally blond hair and a very good breast job, which she was showing off under—barely under—a bikini top worn over the towel she'd knotted around her hips. She nestled the cup of broth in his bandaged fingers and let her nails gently trace his forearm as she took her hand away.

"Soup! That's not what this boy needs!" Harry Chang complained as he pushed himself up from his chair and crossed the salon to the bar. "Christ, spending the whole night out there in the ocean hanging to a damn rock." Harry Chang shook his head as he poured three fingers of Courvoisier into an oversized tumbler. "That took heart, son. Real heart." He brought the drink over to Sal. He was in his sixties, short, beefy, with salt-and-pepper temples and a gold cross hanging over his chest. He was wearing a bathrobe because one of the crewmen had fished Sal from the ocean just after dawn.

"Here," he said as he picked up the untouched broth and replaced it with the big snifter of brandy. "Want one of the boys to heat that for you?"

Sal shook his head as he took a mouthful of the strong liquor. He held it on his tongue and tried to burn away the oily, acrid stench of the wet seal shit that had covered that tiny island of rock, two miles out in the sea. He swallowed the Courvoisier and could still smell the seal shit, just as he could still hear their cacophonous barking ringing in his ears.

"Takes a lot of heart," Harry Chang repeated. "A little man with a big heart." The unspoken, of course, was that that was exactly how Chang thought of himself. "So your little sloop sprang a leak and went down before you could get your preserver on?"

Sal took another hit from the brandy snifter and nodded.

"Must've been one of those cheap new fiberglass jobbies." He gave a little grimace as he talked. "American boat-building has gone to hell, just like everything else. We moved the whole operation to Singapore years ago." He eyed Sal over his glasses. "You ever hear of Chang PCs, Chang sound systems, Chang—"

"Give the guy a break, why don'tcha?" the tall blonde whined. "For Chrissakes, Harry."

Harry Chang smiled. "That's my wife, Janis, doing her Judy Holliday impression. Before we were married, she used to be in show biz." Sal didn't even want to look at her, but he felt her eyes boring into him.

"Yeah?" he said, finally turning to her.

She was smiling at him.

"She was a showgirl—a singer and dancer," Harry Chang said with pride. "Damn good one, too."

"Harry, for Chrissakes," Janis said to her husband as she stared at Sal. "The poor man's half-drowned, and you're telling him all this ancient history."

"Aw, he's fine, aren't you, Son?" Without waiting for an answer, he started back to the bar. He returned with the cognac bottle. "Tough little bastards like us—we're hard to kill, huh, Son?" He filled Sal's glass again. "What's your name, Son?"

Sal looked up at him and pulled the comforter tightly around his chest. "Charlie. Charlie Parker."

"Well, Charlie, you want me to radio the Mexican Coast Guard, have 'em look out for that sunken boat of yours?"

Sal shook his head. "No. I saw it break apart on the rocks. It was a total loss."

"Well, then, Charlie"—Harry Chang cheerfully slapped his knees as he sat down—"I don't know what the hell to do with you. See, we're kinda in the middle of this yearlong voyage. We started off in Seattle—that's where my operations used to be centered—then sailed down the West Coast—"

"Harry, for Chrissakes!" Janis bitched.

"Hey," he replied good-naturedly, "I want Charlie to understand." Then to Sal, "We went all the way down to Acapulco, then back up to Cabo to do some tuna fishing. Now, we're bound for the open sea, heading for Hawaii, then through the South Pacific and on to Singapore—did I tell you I just moved my whole operation there?"

"Yes, you did," Janis answered icily.

"What I'm trying to say, Charlie," Harry Chang continued, "is I could radio someone to pick you up from us, or I could turn around and bring you back into Cabo myself. That would be a major pain in the ass, and put us behind schedule, but if that's what—"

"Actually, Mr. Chang—"

"Harry."

"Actually, Harry, I'm kind of a drifter. Everything I owned—even if there wasn't much of it—went down with that boat. So if it's all right with you—"

Chang eyed him, waiting.

"—I'd just as soon ride along with you to Hawaii."

Harry Chang leaned back in his chair and studied Sal with his Chinese eyes.

"If you have space," Sal hurriedly added.

Harry Chang now inclined forward, his elbows on his knees. "Nobody waiting for you in Mexico?"

"No, sir."

"No family back in the States?"

Sal shook his head with exaggerated sadness. "They're all gone, Harry."

Harry examined Sal a moment longer, then slapped his hands on his thighs again. "Well, Charlie, my boy, nobody sails on the *Jade Queen* for nothing, you're going to have to pull your weight. What can you do?"

Manny was applying the last bandages to Sal's leg, and Sal winced from a sharp point of pain. "Well, I can cook a little."

Harry Chang shook his head. "No, I've got Taiwanese in the kitchen, and they wouldn't accept an outsider. Well, obviously you're a sailor."

Sal gave Chang a shit-eating grin. "Obviously not a very good one."

Harry stared at Sal, then threw back his head and laughed uproariously. "That's true! That's true!"

Sal waited a heartbeat before he played his trump. "Well, actually, sir, what I really do is, I'm a piano player."

"You're a piano player?" Janis said, automatically moving a step closer.

Without looking directly at her—*this has to be finessed*—Sal said, "All my life. I was just taking a little breather away from it to bum around the world." He smiled at Harry. "I guess maybe it's time to start tickling the ivories again."

"Harry, am I psychic or what?" Janis asked her husband, then turned to Sal. "You're never gonna believe this, Charlie, but before we *bon voyaged,* I went and dug out all my old charts—I had a lot of special material, you know, personalized arrangements—and I brought everything with me." She smiled in triumph at the both of them. "I just had a feeling. Am I psychic or what?"

"But—but we don't have a piano on board," Harry offered.

"We'll pick up one in Honolulu. One of those little electric guys." She smiled at Sal. "I'll bet you're good, too."

Sal still wouldn't look at her.

"Well, you know," Harry Chang said, warming to any idea that pleased his wife, who he thought had hung the moon, "it *would* be fun to watch you do your act again. She's extremely talented," he said to Sal. "Could have been a star if she hadn't married me."

"Right, *sure,*" Janis mocked, but her eyes shone with pride. "I have a great rhythmic *feel,* though. The orchestra leader at the Sands told me that once."

Manny was finished dressing the abrasions on Sal's legs, and he gathered up his medical supplies and stood up.

"Look," Harry Chang began, "why don't we talk about this after you've slept for a few days. I think we're all forgetting the ordeal you've just gone through." He reached over and gently laid his fingertips on the Nicaraguan's arm. "Manny, why don't you find a bunk for—"

Janis cleared her throat, and without looking up, Sal knew that she was giving Harry a meaningful stare. And Sal knew that at that instant he was being promoted from crewman to passenger.

"She cost me a million and a half," Harry Chang was saying as he led Sal down the long, wood-paneled passageway. "Best investment I ever made." Manny the Nicaraguan had Sal's arm around his neck and was supporting him as Sal limped along. "A hundred and forty-two feet, thirty-five-hundred-mile cruising range. Carries a crew of eight, and cabin space to sleep another twelve." He stopped at a polished oak door. "Now, we're going to have a *floor show!*" He chuckled with pleasure as he opened the door. "Here you go. This is the biggest cabin—after mine and Janis's. The *Queen*'ll be empty till we dock in Hawaii, then all hell'll break loose," he said gleefully. "We've got a lot of friends in Honolulu."

The Nicaraguan helped Sal through the door and over to the bunk, where he plopped him down on the edge. Sal sat there, weak and dazed.

"Look, Charlie." Harry Chang gently rested his hand on Sal's shoulder. "Just get yourself some sleep, Son. Just—just get yourself some sleep."

Then Harry Chang and the Nicaraguan were gone, and Sal sat there for a while, looking around the well-appointed cabin. *Crazy fucking world. Crazy motherfucking world.* He pushed himself up from the bed and walked over to the window, which was not a porthole but a big, square *window,* with a latch and metal runners. He looked out over the calm Pacific and remembered struggling under the surface, churning away from the shore while the bullets tore through the water around him like little torpedoes, leaving tiny trails of bubbles in their wake. He tasted the salt water that had poured down his nostrils whenever he fought his way up to snatch a lungful of air before he dived to the bottom again, the way he used to do when he was a kid on the brackish lakes around New Orleans and Joe the Hack would put him overboard every time the old drunk snagged his hook on the bottom, which was pretty often. He remembered the sea lions, disturbed and disgruntled, and barking at him endlessly—the continuous deep-chested barking that still rang in his ears, and the waves washing over the wet ammonia-stinking shit, the rocks gouging his knees and slashing his legs as he clung to the far side of the tiny rock island, the side away from the men on the beach, away from the men with the machine pistols.

Sal looked down and saw that his bandaged hands clutching the comforter around his chest were trembling.

He remembered the long, dark night while he clung to the rocks. The waves had kicked up and were pummeling him, trying to pluck him away. Incredibly the sea lions were still barking at him, and finally his cold, numb hands had slipped from their bloody grips, and he'd shouted out as he was washed into the sea. He'd splashed and floundered for what seemed like hours, and just as he'd felt himself begin to tire of the struggle, just as the *boudoir* at the bottom of the sea had started to become overwhelmingly appealing, just at that moment the white hull of the *Jade Queen* had loomed above him in the dark dawn. He'd screamed and screamed, and then the Chinese kid at the wheel had thrown him a flotation circle.

Sal turned from the window and limped back to the bed. Once again he sat gingerly on the edge of the mattress. He yearned for a drink and a cigarette, but his mind wasn't working well enough to begin the processes needed to acquire them.

The Chink had been right. Harry Chang had said he was a tough little bastard, and Sal was starting to believe it about himself. He *wasn't* easy to kill, he knew that now. In fact, he was damn *hard* to kill.

"If you see me comin', better step aside. A lotta men didn't and a lotta men died."

He wanted to live, he knew that now, too. The hunger for stardom had been sweated out of him like a fever. His musical ego, his quest for wealth, celebrity, respect—that all seemed childish now, a boyhood dream, like pitching for the Yankees. Like—*like eternal love with one woman.* He had tasted it all and it had proved false, a brief infatuation with a bogus religion.

All that was left inside of him now was a determination to live, to exist, to *survive.*

With great care and deliberation, Sal lay back on the bunk and pulled the satiny comforter around his still-naked body.

He hadn't given a thought to the half-million dollars he'd buried under that Mexican woman's house, but his hand itched for a touch of Giovanni's German Luger. He felt naked and unprepared without it. Half-formed. He wanted to feel its greasy weight in his grip. He wanted a *weapon.*

He closed his eyes with a sigh, and the morning was gray behind his eyelids. Then he heard the cabin door open and softly close, and he didn't even have to open his eyes to know who it was.